Mark Gimenez grew up in Galveston County, Texas. Once a partner at a major Dallas law firm, Gimenez left in order to start his own solo practice and to write. He lives in Texas with his wife and two sons.

MARK GIMENEZ OMNIBUS

The Colour of Law
The Abduction

sphere

SPHERE

This omnibus edition first published in Great Britain in 2010 by Sphere

Copyright © Mark Gimenez 2010

Previously published separately:
The Colour of Law first published in the United States in 2005 by Doubleday, a
division of Random House, Inc.
First published in Great Britain in 2006 by Time Warner Books
Paperback edition published in 2007 by Sphere
Reprinted 2007 (five times), 2008 (twice), 2009 (three times)
Copyright © Mark Gimenez 2005
The Abduction first published in Great Britain in 2007 by Sphere
Paperback edition published in 2008
Reprinted 2009 (twice)
Copyright © Mark Gimenez 2007

A CIP catalogue record for this book
is available from the British Library.

ISBN 978-0-7515-4412-1

Printed and bound in Great Britain by
Clays Ltd, St Ives plc

Sphere
An imprint of
Little, Brown Book Group
100 Victoria Embankment
London EC4Y 0DY

An Hachette UK Company
www.hachette.co.uk

www.littlebrown.co.uk

THE COLOUR
OF LAW

Scout, simply by the nature of the work, every lawyer gets at least one case in his lifetime that affects him personally. This one's mine, I guess.

—Atticus Finch in *To Kill a Mockingbird* by Harper Lee

there, except a cowboy in the pickup behind him hit his horn like a bugler sounding charge. Which startled Clark. His eyes snapped open—the light had changed. He punched the accelerator and yanked the wheel hard to make a U-turn, but he gave it too much gas and now he couldn't find the fucking brake pedal so he swung across three lanes and one tire of the Mercedes climbed up onto the curb and he almost clipped a street sign. *What the hell was it doing there?* The vehicle bounced hard coming back down.

No sooner had Clark gotten the big German sedan traveling mostly in one lane when he spotted her—a nice girl from the black neighborhoods south of downtown out for a slow stroll on a warm night with her girlfriend. She was just the kind he liked—a slim black babe in a blonde wig, a hot pink miniskirt, matching high heels, and a white tube top, swinging her little pink purse back and forth in perfect tempo with the exaggerated side-to-side movement of her round ass. Her body was fit, her legs lean, her entire essence so sensual and seductive that he knew she was the one—a black hooker from South Dallas specializing in white men from North Dallas.

She would be his date this Saturday night.

Not that Clark couldn't get a date with one of the many gorgeous single white girls seeking husbands in Dallas. He was handsome and his father was rich. In Dallas, rich was required; handsome was optional. Being both, Clark McCall had recently been named one of the city's most eligible bachelors. But he preferred prostitutes for female companionship. Hookers did what they were told and did not file police complaints afterward, and he knew up front how much the relationship would cost his father.

Clark steered the Mercedes over to the curb and slowed alongside the two South Dallas debutantes. He lowered the passenger window and yelled, "Blondie!"

They stopped, so he stopped. The black girl in the blonde wig sauntered over to the car with the kind of sassy attitude he liked in a hooker. She leaned down and stuck half her body through the window. Her skin was smooth and light, more tan than black, and her face was angular with sharp features, more white than black. Her lips and fingernails were painted a shiny red; her pushed-up breasts were round and full and looked real; and her scent was more intoxicating than anything he had ingested that night. She was beautiful, she was sexy, and he wanted her.

"How much?"

"What you want?"

"All you got, honey."

"Two hundred."

"A thousand. All night."

She smiled. "Show me the money."

Clark pulled out a wad of hundreds and waved it at her like candy to a kid. She got in and slid down the slick leather seat and her pink leather skirt crawled up so high he could see her black panties tight in her crotch, and he felt the heat come over him. He hit the accelerator and turned the sedan toward home.

But his thoughts turned to his father, as they often

did in times like this. Clark McCall was a political liability to his father and always had been—the drinking, the drugs, the girls. Oh, if the senior senator from Texas could see his only son now, drunk and high, buying a black hooker with *his* money and driving her in *his* Mercedes to *his* mansion in Highland Park! Of course, his father's first thought would be political, not paternal: What damage would be done to his campaign if the press got wind of his son's latest indiscretion?

Clark laughed loudly and the hooker looked at him like he was crazy. At least he came home to Dallas to be indiscreet. Still, if his father found out that he had flown back home again, there would be more angry threats of disinheritance; but Clark would be back in Washington before the honorable senator knew he was gone. He laughed again, but he felt the rage rising inside him, as it always did when he thought of his father, a man who wanted the White House more than he had ever wanted a son.

United States Senator Mack McCall looked over at his second wife and thought what a handsome first couple they would make.

They were sitting in the leather wing chairs, enjoying a quiet Sunday afternoon in their Georgetown town house. Across from them on the sofa sat the two men who would get them into the White House. Their political consultant and pollster were poring over the latest poll results and focus group studies and staking out

4

McCall's positions on the political issues of the day—positions carefully crafted to appease every identifiable voting bloc in America, whether based on race, religion, ethnicity, gender, geography, age, socioeconomic standing, or sexual orientation—anyone who could cast a vote for Senator Mack McCall. The senior senator from Texas held a commanding lead in the preprimary polls.

Mack McCall's lifelong ambition was finally within his grasp. He glanced down at his hands, still strong and calloused from years of working the rigs. He still had the hands of a roughneck and the determination of a wildcatter. And he was determined, as always, that nothing and no one would stand in his way. He would officially announce his candidacy on Monday.

Then he would spend $100 million or $200 million or whatever it took of his own money to win the White House. He had learned long ago that with enough money a man can buy anything and anyone he wants, be it an election or a younger woman. Mack McCall had enough money to buy both. He turned his eyes to his wife again and admired her beauty as if for the first time. He was filled with a sense of proprietorship, the same as years ago when he had gone out into the oil fields and admired his wells, knowing that he owned what other men coveted.

McCall was sixty; Jean was forty. He had been a senator for two decades now, and she had been his aide since she graduated from law school fifteen years ago. She was a savvy, articulate, and photogenic asset to his political career. They had been married ten years now, long enough for the messy divorce not to be a negative in his polls.

She had no children and wanted none. He had a son, Clark, from his first marriage—the consummate ne'er-do-well offspring of wealth, a thirty-year-old adolescent. Six months ago, thinking a steady job might bring maturity to the boy's life, and to get him out of Dallas, McCall had pulled some strings and got Clark appointed chairman of the Federal Energy Regulatory Commission. But the boy kept sneaking back home to do God knows what with God knows whom in their Dallas mansion. His son was not a political asset.

"Senator?"

Bradford, the butler, appeared in the arched entry to the living room, holding a portable phone and wearing a dazed expression.

"It's Clark, sir."

McCall waved him off. "Tell him I'm busy."

"No, sir, it's the FBI, from Dallas, calling about Clark."

"The *FBI*? Jesus Christ, what the hell did he do this time?"

"Nothing, sir. He's dead."

ONE

W HAT'S THE DIFFERENCE between a rattlesnake lying dead in the middle of a highway and a lawyer lying dead in the middle of a highway?" He paused. "There are skid marks in front of the snake."

His bar association audience responded with polite laughter and diplomatic smiles.

"Why did New Jersey get all the toxic waste dumps and California get all the lawyers?" He paused again. "Because New Jersey had first choice."

Less laughter, fewer smiles, a scattering of nervous coughs: diplomacy was failing fast.

"What do lawyers and sperm have in common?" He did not pause this time. "Both have a one-in-a-million chance of turning out human."

All efforts at diplomacy had ended. His audience had fallen deathly silent; a sea of stone faces stared back at him. The lawyers on the dais focused on their lunches, embarrassed by their guest speaker's ill-advised attempt at humor. He looked around the crowded room, as if stunned. He turned his palms up.

"Why aren't you laughing? Aren't those jokes funny? The public sure thinks those jokes are funny, damn funny. I can't go to a cocktail party or the country club without someone telling me a stupid lawyer joke. My friends, we are the butt of America's favorite jokes!"

He adjusted the microphone so his deep sigh was audible, but he maintained steady eye contact with the audience.

"I don't think those jokes are funny, either. I didn't go to law school to be the butt of cruel jokes. I went to law school to be another Atticus Finch. *To Kill a Mockingbird* was my mother's favorite book and my bedtime story. She'd read a chapter each night, and when we came to the end, she'd go back to the beginning and start over. 'Scotty,' she'd say, 'be like Atticus. Be a lawyer. Do good.'

"And that, my fellow members of the bar, is the fundamental question we must ask ourselves: Are we really doing good, or are we just doing really well? Are we noble guardians of the rule of law fighting for justice in America, or are we just greedy parasites using the law to suck every last dollar from society like leeches on a dying man? Are we making the world a better place, or are we just making ourselves filthy rich?

"We must ask ourselves these questions, my friends, because the public is asking the same questions of us. They're questioning us, they're pointing their fingers at us, they're blaming us. Well, I've asked myself these questions, and I have answers, for myself, for you, and for the public: Yes, we are doing good! Yes, we are fighting for justice! Yes, we are making the world a better place!

"And ladies and gentlemen, if you elect me the next president of the state bar of Texas, I will tell the people exactly that! I will remind them that we wrote the Declaration of Independence and the Bill of Rights, that we fought for civil rights, that we protect the poor, defend the innocent, free the oppressed. That we stand up for their inalienable rights. That we are all that stands between freedom and oppression, right and wrong, innocence and guilt, life and death. And I will tell the people that I am proud, *damn proud*, to be a lawyer . . . because lawyers—do—good!"

Now, some might blame the Texas summer heat, but the audience, lawyers all—lawyers who had never protected the poor or defended the innocent or freed the oppressed, lawyers who stood up for the rights of multinational corporations—*believed* his words, like children who were old enough to know the truth about Santa Claus but who clung desperately to the myth anyway. They rose as one from their seats in the main dining room of the Belo Mansion in downtown Dallas and, with great enthusiasm, applauded the tall thirty-six-year-old speaker, who removed his tortoise-shell glasses, pushed his thick blond hair off his tanned face, and flashed his movie-star smile. He took his seat on the dais behind a nameplate that read A. SCOTT FENNEY, ESQ., FORD STEVENS LLP.

As the applause grew louder, the corporate tax lawyer whom Scott was campaigning to succeed as the next state bar president leaned in close and whispered, "You know,

Scotty, you've got an impressive line of bullshit. Now I see why half the coeds at SMU dropped their drawers for you."

Scott squeezed the knot of his silk tie, smoothed his $2,000 suit, and whispered back through brilliant white teeth, "Henry, you don't get laid or elected telling the truth."

He then turned and again acknowledged his fellow members of the bar, all standing and applauding him.

Except for one lawyer. Sitting alone in the back of the dining room, at his usual table, was an older gentleman. His thick white hair fell onto his forehead. His bright eyes remained sharp at long distances, but he wore the black reading glasses to eat. He was not a tall man, and his slightly hunched posture made him appear almost short. Even so, he was a lawyer the other lawyers either avoided outright or approached with great caution, like vassals to their lordship, waiting patiently for him to look up from his chicken-fried steak, mashed potatoes, and pecan pie and acknowledge them with a nod or, on the best of days, a brief handshake. But never did he stand. Come hell or high water, United States District Court Judge Samuel Buford remained seated until he was through eating. Today, though, as he dwelled on the young lawyer's speech, a slight smile crossed his face.

A. Scott Fenney, Esq., had just made a tough judicial decision easy.

the hardwood floor, and on the wall, the five-foot-square framed field-level blowup of himself, number 22 on the SMU Mustangs, running for 193 yards against the Texas Longhorns the day Scott Fenney became a local football legend. Keeping all these coveted perks required only that Scott serve the firm's corporate clients with the same devotion the disciples showed Jesus Christ.

It was an hour after his bar association speech, and Scott was standing on his Persian rug and admiring Missy, a twenty-seven-year-old ex-Dallas Cowboy cheerleader who ran the firm's summer clerkship program. In the fall of each year, Ford Stevens lawyers fanned out across the country to interview the best second-year students at the best law schools in the nation. The firm hired forty of the top candidates and brought them to Dallas the following summer to work as summer clerks for $2,500 a week plus room and board, parties, alcohol, and at some firms, women. Most partners in large law firms had been frat rats in college, so most summer clerkship programs had all the markings of fraternity rush. Ford Stevens's program was no exception.

Thus the first Monday of June brought the invasion of forty summer clerks, like Bob here, each trying to catch the eye of powerful partners, the partners in turn trying to divine if these budding legal eagles were the Ford Stevens type. Bob was. From the look on the face of the law student standing next to Missy, he was dreaming of having just such an office one day. Which meant he would bill two hundred hours a month for the next eight years without complaint or contempt, at which time the firm would show him the door—the odds of a new associate making partner at Ford Stevens being one in twenty. But the ambitious students still signed on because, as Scott himself told them, "You want odds, go to Vegas. You want a chance to get filthy rich by the time you're forty, hire on with Ford Stevens."

"Mr. Fenney?"

Scott pulled his eyes off Missy and turned to his frumpy middle-aged secretary standing in the door.

"Yes, Sue?"

"Four calls are holding—your wife, Stan Taylor, George Parker, and Tom Dibrell."

Scott turned back to Missy and the student and shrugged.

"Duty calls." He shook hands with the pale, homely, top-of-his-class student and slapped him on the shoulder. "Bob—"

"Rob."

"Oh, I'm sorry. Now, Rob, my Fourth of July bash, that's mandatory attendance."

"Yes, sir, I've already heard about it."

To Missy: "You bringing some girls over this year?"

"Ten."

"*Ten?*" Scott whistled. "Ten ex-Dallas Cowboy cheerleaders." The firm paid each girl $500 to spend a few hours in bikinis acting interested in law students. "Bob—"

"Rob."

"Right. You'd better work on your tan, Rob, if you want to snare one of those cheerleaders."

Rob grinned even though he had about as much chance of getting a date with an ex-Dallas Cowboy cheerleader as a one-legged man had winning a butt-kicking contest.

"Mr. Fenney," Rob said, "your speech at the bar luncheon, it was truly inspiring."

First day on the job and the boy was already brownnosing like an experienced associate. Could he possibly be sincere?

"Thanks, Bob."

Missy winked. Scott didn't know if the wink was because she knew his speech was bullshit or if she was flirting again. Like all good-looking single girls in Dallas, Missy had made flirting an art form, always managing to catch his eye when crossing her long lean legs or brush against him in the elevator or just look at him in a way that made him feel as if they were on the brink of an affair. Of course, every male at the firm felt that way about Missy, but Scott was annually voted the best-looking male lawyer at Ford Stevens by the firm's female support staff, not that it was much of a contest. Scott had been a star football player in college; most lawyers were star chess players. Like Bob here.

"Rob."

"Right."

Missy and Bob departed, and Scott went around behind his desk and sat in his high-backed leather chair. His eyes found the phone; four lines were blinking. Without conscious thought, his trained mind instantly prioritized the calls: Tom, Stan, George, wife. Tom had paid the firm $3 million last year, Stan $150,000, George $50,000, and his wife nothing.

Scott picked up the phone and punched Tom's line.

"Mr. Fenney!"

Scott was waiting impatiently for the elevator in the lobby of the sixty-second floor, on his way to see Tom Dibrell on the sixty-ninth floor. He could not restrain a smile. He was blessed with the kind of rich client lawyers dream about: a real-estate developer addicted to the deal; a client who habitually borrowed, bought, built, leased, sold, sued, and got sued, and, most important, who possessed an uncanny knack for getting himself into one precarious legal predicament after another, extrication from which always requiring the very expensive legal services of A. Scott Fenney, Esq.

Sue arrived, her face flushed from running after him.

"Mr. Fenney, you have the partnership meeting at two."

Scott checked his watch: 1:45.

"I can't make it. Tom needs me. What's on the agenda?"

Sue handed him the partnership meeting agenda. Only one item required his vote: the termination of John Walker as a partner in the firm. Unlike Scott, John was no longer a blessed lawyer. His rich client had just been bought out by a New York company, which meant his client would no longer be paying legal fees to Ford Stevens; and which now meant John Walker would no longer be employed at Ford Stevens. His $800,000 salary had just become an unnecessary expense to the firm. John was a brilliant lawyer, and he and Scott played hoops together twice a week, but this was business: brilliant lawyers without rich clients were worthless to a large law firm.

The elevator doors opened just as Scott reached into his coat for his pen. He stepped inside and Sue followed. Attached to the agenda was a partnership ballot: TERMINATION OF JOHN WALKER. The only partner in the firm who didn't know John Walker would be fired today was John Walker. Dan Ford believed surprise was critical when firing a partner; otherwise that partner might walk out the door with a few of the firm's clients. So in fifteen minutes John Walker would walk into Dan's office, be unceremoniously fired after twelve years with the firm, and then be escorted from the building by security guards. The firm had never lost a single client to a terminated lawyer.

Sue turned and offered her back; Scott put the ballot against her back and his pen to the ballot and started to sign *A. Scott Fenney*—but he froze. He felt guilty, even though his vote was a mere formality, a nod to the illusion that the Ford Stevens law firm was a partnership of equal lawyers. In fact, Dan Ford owned the firm and every lawyer, office, desk, and book in the firm; and Dan had already decided to fire John Walker. Scott could either rubber-stamp Dan's decision or refuse and . . . *what?* . . . join John in the unemployment line? He sighed and signed the ballot in the FOR column, then

16

handed the ballot back to Sue and said, "Give that to Dan."

She stared at the ballot like it was a death warrant and then said, almost in a whisper: "His wife has breast cancer."

"Dan's?"

"No. John Walker's wife. His secretary said it's in her lymph nodes."

"You're kidding? Jesus, she's young."

Scott's mother had been young, too, only forty-three, when the same cancer had killed her. Scott had watched helplessly as she lost her breasts, her hair, and her life. He now thought of John's wife and of John, who would soon be standing on the street outside this building, coat and career in hand, cursing his partners for abandoning him and God for abandoning his wife, just as Scott had cursed God as the cancer consumed his mother's body ounce by ounce until she felt like a feather pillow when he lifted her from the bed and carried her to the bathroom.

"Damn."

He could do no more for John's wife than he could for his mother, and no more for John than all the other lawyers Dan Ford had fired without warning . . . but still. Scott stared at himself in the mirrored wall until the elevator eased to a smooth stop and the doors opened on the sixty-ninth floor. The elevator chime snapped him out of his thoughts like a referee's whistle after an injury time-out. He stepped out. The elevator doors closed behind him, and he entered the domain of Dibrell Property Company, the firm's landlord and his most important client, accounting for over ninety percent of the legal fees he generated each year, fees that had bought everything Scott Fenney owned in life, from the bed he slept in to the shoes on his feet.

Eleven years ago almost to the day, Scott, at the time a new associate at Ford Stevens, had been in one of the elevators of this building when the doors opened and in stepped Thomas J. Dibrell. Scott recognized him immediately. Everyone in Dallas knew of Tom Dibrell: an SMU alum and rabid football booster, he had been implicated in the play-for-pay scandal with the governor that resulted in the NCAA giving SMU the death penalty in 1987; he had built the lavish Dibrell Tower with $300 million borrowed from a New York pension fund during the real-estate boom of the '80s; and he had somehow survived bankruptcy in the '90s, a fate so many other developers had suffered when the Texas real-estate market went bust. In fact, how Tom Dibrell had managed to hold on to his skyscraper while all the other big developers lost theirs to foreclosure remained the second greatest mystery of Dallas, right after *Did Oswald act alone?*

But just as Scott recognized him in the elevator that day, Dibrell recognized Scott. His face got that look Scott had witnessed so many times when a grown man had a close encounter with a football hero: it's a child's face on Christmas morning. They introduced themselves, Scott told Dibrell that he was a lawyer at Ford Stevens, and Dibrell invited him to lunch upstairs at the Downtown Club. Over a steak, Dibrell explained that the Dallas

18

real-estate market was in the tank, his company was on life support, and his lawyers—the disloyal bastards he had paid millions during the boom years—had just abandoned him for the Yankee banks that had taken over the insolvent local banks, the ones holding many of his defaulted notes. After lunch, Dibrell bit down on a big cigar, leaned back in his chair, and asked Scott Fenney, local football legend, to be his new lawyer.

A. Scott Fenney, Esq., had his first client.

The rest was history. Eleven years later, the Dallas real-estate market was booming again, Dibrell Property Company was on top of the world, and Tom Dibrell was again a trophy client in Dallas, a client who endows his lawyer with instant respect and social status when the lawyer announces, "I'm Scott Fenney, Tom Dibrell's lawyer." And Scott remained his loyal lawyer to the tune of $3 million a year in fees.

Scott's heels clicked against the mahogany and marble floor until he arrived at the wide entryway. Directly under a longhorn chandelier sat a round wood table on which was perched a two-foot-tall bronze sculpture of an anatomically correct calf on its side, hog-tied and held down by two cowboys, about to lose its masculinity at the hands of a third cowboy wielding a weapon that looked like a giant two-handed toenail clipper. SPRING ROUNDUP was etched in the silver plate attached to the base.

Whenever Scott entered the expansive reception area of Dibrell Property Company, he always felt like he was walking into a western museum. Frederic Remington sculptures sat atop pedestal tables. G. Harvey paintings of cowboys on horses hung on the walls, fine art with names like *When Bankers Wore Boots*, *Rio Grande Crossing*, and *The Good Lord Willin' and the Creek Don't Rise*. The furnishings were straight out of *Giant*—diamond-tufted leather couches and matching chairs with brass studs and dark wood from floor to ceiling. On the wall above the reception desk hung the museum's masterpiece, a huge portrait of Tom Dibrell astride a big black stallion. He looked like a kid whose parents had forced him to sit on the pony at a petting zoo. It was, in fact, the only time Tom had ever been on a horse. But Tom loved all things cowboy, even though no one in Dallas or Houston or Texas for that matter was ever really a cowboy. Still, it was fun to pretend.

Scott's eyes dropped from Roy Rogers Jr. to perhaps the most beautiful young woman he had ever seen, at least since the last time he had stood here. A blonde, blue-eyed beauty was sitting behind the reception desk and painting her nails over the morning newspaper. Tom Dibrell always said he firmly believed in hiring bean-counters from Harvard Business and receptionists from Hooters. Problem was, the receptionists' career path always led from this desk to Tom's office couch, which in turn led to a substantial settlement to avoid litigation.

"God, he was handsome," she said.

She didn't mean Tom. Her blue eyes were focused on the newspaper and a black-and-white photo of a young man under the headlines, "Clark McCall Murdered" . . . "Prostitute Charged" . . . "Senator McCall 'Devastated' " . . . "Presidential Campaign Delayed."

"That's a mug shot," Scott said, "from when he was busted for dope. He was always in trouble."

She shrugged. "He was rich."

"His daddy's rich."

"That's good enough for me."

"Well, then, he should've picked you up Saturday night instead of that hooker."

"Oh, I would've cost him a lot more than her. But then, I don't carry a gun."

"Girl, from where I'm standing, you're sure packing some heat."

She gave him a coy smile then dropped her eyes back to the newspaper. She shook her head slowly as if pondering a great mystery.

"Rich and handsome. Why would he want a black prostitute when he could have any white girl in town?"

"Cheaper, like you said."

Scott always enjoyed flirting with Dibrell's girls, but he had tired of this conversation. The murder of a senator's son did not concern him this afternoon. He was here to make money. So he said, "Scott Fenney, to see Tom."

The receptionist put down her polish, blew on her nails, and picked up the phone. She held the receiver carefully with the inside pads of her fingers so as not to scuff her fresh paint job, punched a button with the eraser end of a pencil, and said, "Mr. Fenney is here." She hung up, rearranged herself in her chair so as to show off her impressive upper body, and said, "So, are you married?"

Scott held up his left hand to display his wedding ring.

"Eleven years."

"Too bad." She blew on her nails again and said, "Go right back, Mr. Fenney. And call me if that changes . . . or even if it don't."

Grammar skills notwithstanding, she was a fine example of what Texas men wanted most—a gorgeous Texas girl. Texas myths were many, but one was no myth: the most gorgeous girls in the world were found in Texas. Dallas, Texas. Girls like her, they graduate from high school or maybe junior college, and from small towns all across Texas they head straight to Dallas like moths to light. They come for the jobs, they come for the nightlife, they come for the single men making lots of money, the kind of money that buys big homes and fancy cars and fashionable clothes and glittery jewelry guaranteed to bring a smile to any Texas girl's face. Girl wants to marry a refinery worker and live in a doublewide, she moves to Houston; girl wants to marry money and live in a mansion, she moves to Dallas.

Scott walked through the reception area and down a gallery filled with more cowboy art and remembered to put on his glasses. He was slightly farsighted and needed the glasses only when reading in poor light, but he made it a practice to wear them in front of clients because clients like lawyers who look smart. He arrived at Tom's office suite, which consisted of a secretarial area, a private bathroom, a study with a fake fireplace, and Tom's inner sanctum.

Marlene, Tom's middle-aged secretary, looked up from the McCall story, smiled, and waved him in. He found Tom on the far side of the vast space, his head buried in his hands, looking small behind the massive desk under the ten-foot-high ceiling. Scott walked toward his rich client, weaving his way around more leather furniture and a fancy silver-inlaid Mexican saddle on a stand and past photographs of Tom with governors and senators and presidents, and, on the coffee table, the hard hat with DIBRELL stenciled across the front, and the rolled-up blueprints he used as props at groundbreakings, even though Tom Dibrell had never held a construction job in his life.

"We're meeting downstairs on the land deal," Scott said to the top of Tom's head. "Should have it closed soon."

Tom's head started shaking slowly back and forth.

"I didn't call you about that."

Tom was fifty-five, nearly bald so he had recently gone to a comb-over, he stood five seven in his trademark cowboy boots, and he was a pudgy bastard, but for $3 million a year, Scott described him as stocky. He had been married four times to progressively younger women; the current Mrs. Dibrell was twenty-nine. Tom raised his head and Scott instantly knew it was a female problem. He sighed. His best client couldn't keep his hands off the help.

"Who was it this time, Tom?"

"Nadine."

Scott shook his head; he didn't recall a Nadine.

"Brunette, tall, built? Jesus, Scott, she's got hips like a boy!" He paused, and his eyes glazed over, as if reliving the moment. Then: "She's threatening to sue, sexual harassment." Tom held out a letter. "She's got a fucking lawyer!"

Scott grabbed the paper; his eyes went straight to the letterhead: *Franklin Turner, Esq.*, famous plaintiffs' lawyer. Scott exhaled heavily. "Shit." Twenty thousand lawyers in Dallas and she finds Frank Turner.

Scott skimmed the letter. Frank Turner was threatening to file a lawsuit against Dibrell Property Company and Thomas J. Dibrell individually on behalf of his client, Nadine Johnson, unless a financial settlement was reached within ten days.

Tom said, "Is Turner as tough as they say?"

"Yeah, he's a real hard-ass."

Scott said it with a grave tone, much as a doctor might say, *Yes, you have cancer.* It was always best to make the client sweat a little: a worried client will pay more fees with less bitching. So he put a frown on his face and stepped over to the bay window Tom had specially designed for his office just so he could enjoy a panoramic view of Dallas, so he could stand right there and gaze out on the city and breathe it in and think, *God, what a depressing sight!* Gray and dull, like you're watching an old black-and-white TV. A concrete-and-steel landscape as far as the eye can see, all the way to the brown haze of pollution that perpetually rings the city above the loop, treeless and barren, the city's master plan obvious—to pave over every square inch of green in the whole god-damned city. Which might explain Dallas's ranking as the ugliest major city in America. Other than women,

Dallas has no natural beauty whatsoever. No ocean or lake or water of any kind except the Trinity River running west of downtown, used for decades as a natural sewage system and today as a big drainage ditch. No Central Park, no Rocky Mountains, and no Miami Beach. No wonderful weather. Nothing other great cities have. All Dallas has is a white X on Elm Street marking the exact spot where an American president was killed. But then, you don't live in Dallas for any of that; you live in Dallas to make a lot of money fast.

"Scott?"

Tom's voice sounded like a child's pleading. Scott turned to his very worried client.

"Tom, going up against Frank Turner, I'll be lucky to hold this one to twice what the last one cost."

Tom shook his head. "I don't care, Scott. Pay two million if you have to, just take care of it. And keep it quiet, I don't want to lose Babs over this. I really like her."

Babs was wife number four.

"I'll take care of it, Tom, just like I took care of the others."

Tom looked like he was going to cry.

"I'll never forget this, Scott. Never."

Scott headed to the door, saying over his shoulder, "Just don't forget it when I send you my bill."

Scott maintained his serious expression past Marlene and back through the cowboy museum—he did give the receptionist a little wink—and into the elevator lobby. But once safely aboard and alone in the elevator, he broke into a broad grin and said to his image in the mirrored wall: "How can one man get himself into so many legal cracks? The guy's fucking uncanny."

In the privacy of an elevator or his thoughts, Scott Fenney regarded his rich client as all lawyers regard the rich clients who subsidize their lives: they're creatures of lesser intelligence who, by the grace of God, have inherited, stolen, swindled, connived, cheated, or simply lucked their way into enormous wealth. So, to restore balance to the natural order, the lawyers are duty bound to relieve their clients of as much of their wealth as possible in legal fees.

A. Scott Fenney, Esq., had always done his duty with respect to Tom Dibrell.

THREE

S COTT RODE the elevator down to the Ford Stevens offices and then walked down the hall to the conference room on the sixty-second floor, past John Walker's office where John's secretary was boxing up his personal belongings and the next lawyer in line was already moving in. Scott was stepping smartly and snapping his fingers, wired on the greatest intoxicant known to man: success.

He threw open the double doors and entered the conference room, a considerable space currently occupied by a forty-foot-long cherrywood table, thirty chairs upholstered in deep brown leather, and a dozen male lawyers fighting over other people's money like lions over raw meat. Today, these ravenous young lawyers were feasting on Dibrell Property Company's $25 million purchase of fifty acres of land adjacent to the Trinity River on which Dibrell planned to build industrial warehouses. Three Ford Stevens lawyers were in the fray, fighting for Scott's client at a combined hourly rate of $850. Scott stepped to the head of the long conference table.

"Gentlemen!"

The room fell silent and all eyes, ties, and suspenders turned to him.

"You guys haven't closed this deal yet? What the hell's the holdup?"

Sid Greenberg, a fifth-year associate at the firm whom Scott had put in charge of this Dibrell matter, said, "Scott, we're still fighting over the environmental escrow."

"That's not resolved yet? It's been what, two weeks?"

Sid said, "Scott, I don't think we can resolve it."

"Sid, there's a solution to every legal problem. What's the problem?"

"The problem is this, Scott: We know—but the government doesn't—that there's contamination on the land, lead from years ago when a battery plant operated there. And there's some leaching into the river whenever it rains—a lot of leaching. So we've got to escrow part of the purchase price to cover the cleanup, in case the lead is discovered before Dibrell can pave over it. The problem is how much to escrow."

"Hell, Sid, hire an environmental consultant. He'll tell us how much to escrow."

"We would've already done that, Scott, except the court ordered us to turn over all environmental reports to those stupid eco-nuts who filed suit to stop the deal."

"Trinity River Allies in Litigation?"

"Yeah, TRAIL. They want the land used as some kind of nature park, where kids can go see a river habitat up close. All they'll see is a bunch of dead fish and raw sewage. Shit, you even stick a toe in that water, you'll get a disease. Anyway, we told the court that neither party had an environmental report. If we get one, we'll have to give it to TRAIL and they'll find out about the lead contamination and use it to stop the deal—the EPA will be all over that land the next day! But without a report, we don't know how much to escrow. We want fifty percent of the purchase price escrowed; the seller wants five percent."

Sid threw up his hands.

"We may have to tell Dibrell to call off the deal."

Scott sighed. Years back he had made the mistake of telling Tom to call off a deal because of some legal nicety. Tom listened patiently to his new lawyer, and then said, "Scott, I'm not paying you to tell me what I can't do. I'm paying you to tell me how I can do what I want to do. And if you can't, I'll find a smarter lawyer who can."

Scott had learned his lesson well. He was not about to tell Tom Dibrell to call off a $25 million deal that would pay $500,000 in legal fees to Ford Stevens, and damn sure not over lead leaching into that cesspool called the Trinity River.

"Okay, here's what we're going to do. Ford Stevens will hire the environmental consultant. He'll deliver his report only to me. Seller's counsel can come to my office to read the report, but no copies will leave my office. That report will belong to Ford Stevens, not to Dibrell or the seller. That way, the report will be protected by the attorney-client privilege, and I can swear to the court that neither party has an environmental report subject to

TRAIL's subpoena. And no one will ever know about the lead leaching into the river."

"Will that work?" Sid asked.

"It worked for the tobacco companies, Sid. They kept all that evidence about nicotine being addictive secret for forty years—because their lawyers hired the scientists who conducted the studies. So the studies were protected from subpoenas by the attorney-client privilege. No one ever knew that evidence was out there, because their lawyers hid it behind the privilege. Just like we're going to do."

Sid was beaming. "That's brilliant. We can then close the deal with the appropriate environmental escrow."

"Exactly," Scott said. "And those environmentalists can go fuck a tree."

"Frank, how the hell you been, buddy?"

Scott got Franklin Turner, Esq., famous plaintiffs' lawyer, on the phone on the first try. No doubt Frank had instructed his secretary that if Tom Dibrell's lawyer called to put him right through, aware that one phone call might net him a handsome fee.

"Two million, Scott."

Scott had the door closed and Frank on the speaker-phone so he could practice his golf swing while negotiating the settlement of a young woman's claim that Tom Dibrell had used his position as her employer to pressure her to have sex with him—which, knowing

Scott's rich client, was probably true. Scott swung the 9-iron he kept in his office; he used to swing a 6-iron, but he had punched holes in the ceiling tile on his follow-through, so he had dropped down to a 9-iron. From across his office, Scott said: "Jesus, Frank, we could at least shoot the shit for a few minutes, just out of professional courtesy."

"Scott, Dibrell's a fifty-five-year-old father of five—"

"Six," Scott said while checking his golfing address position in the window's reflection.

"Father of six, married—"

"For the fourth time." Scott checked his takeaway.

"Married and CEO of one of the biggest goddamn real-estate companies in Dallas, he's a member of the business council, the chamber of commerce, and every other important civic organization in this city, and he forces himself on a naïve twenty-two-year-old young woman—"

"*Forces himself?* Give me a break, Frank. Knowing the girls Tom hires, she probably went down faster than Monica Lewinsky."

He chuckled and checked his backswing at the halfway point.

"It's not a goddamn joke, Scott! Nadine was irreparably harmed!"

"But two million bucks would make the hurt go away, right?"

"No, but it would make her go away."

There was a soft knock on the door. Scott turned

from the window to see Sue poking her head in. She said in a low voice: "Mr. Fenney, your daughter's on the phone. She says it's an emergency."

An emergency? A jolt of fatherly fear ricocheted through Scott's central nervous system like a pinball setting off alarms. Four long strides and he was at his desk. He said to the phone: "Frank, hang on the line, okay?"

Scott didn't wait for a response. He leaned the 9-iron against the desk, picked up the receiver, and punched the blinking light on the phone, putting Frank Turner on hold and his nine-year-old daughter on the line.

"Hi, baby, what's wrong?"

A tiny voice: "Mother's gone and Consuela's crying."

"Why?"

"They arrested Esteban."

"*Who?* The INS?"

"He said '*inmigración.*'"

"You talked to him?"

"Consuela talked to him first, but she started crying so I talked to him. He said they arrested him where he was building a home, said they're sending him back to Mexico. Can you help him?"

"Honey, there's nothing I can do. Esteban's a tough kid, he'll be all right. They'll bus him down to Matamoros, he'll cross back over the next day, and he'll be back up here in a few weeks, just like the last time."

"Yeah, that's what he said."

"So why's Consuela so upset?"

"She's scared they're gonna come for her, send her

back to Mexico, too. She says she has no one in Mexico, that this is the only home she's ever had."

Consuela had come with the house. When the prior owner had filed bankruptcy and could no longer afford the mansion or his Mexican maid, the Fenney family had acquired Consuela de la Rosa like an appurtenance to the property.

"A. Scott, I told her you were fixing things so she can always live with us . . . you are, aren't you?"

"Uh, yeah, I'm working on that." He'd been meaning to hire an immigration lawyer to get Consuela's green card. "Look, tell her not to worry. INS knows better than to conduct raids in Highland Park. Heads would roll."

"Huh?"

"They'd get fired if they took Highland Park maids away."

"Oh. But she's really scared. She shut the front drapes, she won't even go outside in the backyard, and she's saying the rosary. It's just us here and . . . well, it's kind of scaring me, too. No one's gonna come to our house, are they, and bust in the door like on TV?"

"No, baby, no one's coming to our house."

"You promise?"

"I promise. Let me talk to her."

Consuela was an emotional girl, given to sudden bouts of tears over fears real or imagined, which she warded off by wearing three crucifixes, saying daily prayers to various saints, and keeping enough candles lit on the windowsill above the kitchen sink to light a

33

convenience store. But the fear that never left her was being sent back to Mexico. Esteban was her boyfriend; they had met at the Catholic church in the Little Mexico section of Dallas. Scott drove her over every Sunday morning and picked her up every Sunday afternoon, their weekly visit. Esteban worked construction in other parts of Dallas and faced the risk of INS raids, but Consuela was protected by the unwritten rule that the INS did not enter the Town of Highland Park, home to the richest and most politically powerful men in Texas—and their illegal Mexican maids. Scott's illegal Mexican maid was as sweet as she was round, and after three years of tending to the Fenney household, she was like a member of the family, albeit one who reverted to her native tongue when distraught. Consuela's sobbing voice came over the line.

"*Señor Fenney, tengo miedo de inmigración.*"

"Don't be afraid, Consuela. It's okay. *Está bien*. No one's gonna take you away. You'll always live with us."

Scott had picked up some Spanish skills from his Mexican maid, who sniffled and said, "*¿Para siempre?*"

"Yes. Forever."

"Señor Fenney, you make the, uh . . . *promesa a* Consuela?"

"*Sí*, Consuela, I promise."

A sniffle. "O-kay. *Adiós, señor.*"

His daughter came back on. "She stopped crying."

"Good."

"A. Scott, you're not gonna let them take her away, are you?"

"No, baby, that won't happen."

"Okay."

"Look, honey, I'm kind of busy, so if everything's under control there, I need to get back to work."

"We're good. See you later, alligator."

"After while, crocodile."

Scott hung up and made a mental note to call Rudy Gutierrez, an immigration lawyer he had met years ago. He'd been meaning to do that for six months now, or maybe a year, almost two come to think of it, but something had always come up and . . . the blinking light on the phone caught Scott's eye and he remembered Frank Turner holding—not that Scott minded making a plaintiffs' lawyer wait for his contingency fee. The image of his daughter huddled behind closed drapes in their Highland Park home with their Mexican maid faded from his mind and was replaced by the image of a smug-faced Frank Turner, famous plaintiffs' lawyer, leaning back in his chair in his fancy office convinced he was about to win this game and beat Scott Fenney out of two million dollars to buy off sweet Nadine. Not today, Frank. Scott grabbed the 9-iron, punched Frank's button, engaged the speakerphone, and picked up right where he had left off.

"*Two million?* That's an expensive piece of ass, Frank. What, she was a virgin?"

"Her sexual history is irrelevant."

"Yeah, like it was for Kobe." Scott pointed the 9-iron at the speakerphone. "Chances are, Frank, she's been screwing since she was fourteen, so you damn well better advise your client that if she wants to go to trial, we're gonna track down every swinging dick she's ever met up close and personal, we're gonna put their owners on the stand to tell the world about Nadine's many virtues, and by the time we're through with her sweet little ass, she'll make those hookers on Harry Hines look like a bunch of goddamn nuns!"

"Oh, yeah? Well, you'd better advise Tom Dibrell that by the time I'm through with him he'll wish to God he'd stayed faithful to wife number one!"

Scott laughed boisterously, as if that was the funniest thing he had ever heard.

"You wouldn't say that if you'd seen her." He again faced the window and checked his position at the top of his backswing. "Listen to us, Frank, a couple of good ol' SMU boys going at each other like an Aggie and a Longhorn. Look, bottom line, both our clients got some downside here. So to make this go away for both of them, Tom will pay sweet little ol' Nadine half a million bucks, and that's a hell of a lot more money than she was making at Hooters."

"Tips are pretty good there, Scott. One-point-five."

"They ain't that good, Frank. One million."

"Done."

He checked his downswing. "I'll have the release and confidentiality agreement to you first thing in the morning. You get it signed and back to me, I'll have a check waiting."

"Cashier's check, payable jointly to me and Nadine Johnson."

"Frank, you make damn sure Nadine understands

that if she talks about her little roll in the hay with Tom to anyone—even her goddamned psychiatrist!—the agreement requires that she return every penny and that you return your fee. And Tom's likely to strangle her."

Frank laughed. "She talks, I'll strangle the bitch myself—she costs me three hundred thirty thousand."

"What are you taking, a third?"

"Standard contingency fee."

"Three hundred thirty thousand bucks, not a bad day's work, Frank."

"It's a dirty job, Scott, but someone's gotta do it."

Scott shook his head. Plaintiffs' lawyers. Scott was figuring on making maybe $50 million over his career, but plaintiffs' lawyers, those bastards make that every year, taking 33 percent, 40 percent, sometimes 50 percent of their clients' damage awards, almost always settlements like this because a corporation can't afford to roll the dice with a Texas jury, not when the jurors might pull another *Pennzoil v. Texaco* and come back with an $11,120,976,110.83 judgment, the largest jury verdict in the history of the world. Which made Texas a plaintiffs' lawyers' playground. To date, Franklin Turner, Esq., had amassed over one billion dollars in verdicts and settlements, the bastard.

"Hey, Scott, what do you think about that black halfback we got from Houston? He gonna break your records?"

Frank had been in the Mustang marching band at SMU. Tuba.

"They've been trying for fourteen years now, Frank. No one's come close."

"One day, Scott, one day."

"Yeah, yeah, yeah . . . Good doing business with you, Frank."

Scott reached over with the 9-iron and hit the disconnect button on the speakerphone. A successful ten-minute negotiation, for which he felt duty bound to bill his best client $50,000. The way he figured, Tom Dibrell was prepared to pay $2 million to settle with Nadine; his lawyer had skillfully held the settlement to only $1 million; so, even with a $50,000 legal fee, he was actually *saving* Dibrell $950,000. Studying his reflection in the window, he practiced his full golf swing and held his pose like a pro. Scott Fenney had found that he possessed the necessary skills to excel at three games in life: football, golf, and lawyering.

FOUR

FIVE O'CLOCK. The end of another day of crisis, conflict, and confrontation. A lawyer's life. It isn't for everyone, or even every lawyer. Lawyering either gets into your blood, or it doesn't. If you don't wake up itching for a fight, if you shy away from personal confrontation, if you're not the competitive type, if you don't possess the intestinal fortitude to go mano a mano with a famous plaintiffs' lawyer and beat him at his own game, then the manly sport of lawyering just isn't for you. Go into social work.

Lawyering is a lot like football. In fact, Scott always figured his football career was the best pre-law curriculum the school offered; it certainly made the transition to the law an easy one for him. Whereas football is legalized violence, lawyering is violent legalities: lawyers use the law to pummel each other's clients into submission. And just as football coaches want smart, mean, and tough players, rich clients want smart, mean, and tough lawyers. And they want to win. At all costs. Lie, cheat, steal, just win the goddamned case! In football and the

39

law, winning isn't everything; it's the only thing. Winners reap the rewards; losers lose. A. Scott Fenney, Esq., leaned back in his chair, locked his hands behind his head, and surveyed his world here at the Ford Stevens law firm: he was a winner. And his reward was a perfect life. An absolutely perfect life.

He heard the phone ring at Sue's desk. In seconds, she was standing in the door, purse in hand.

"Mr. Fenney, it's the federal court."

Scott shook his head. "I'll call her back tomorrow."

"It's not the clerk. It's the judge. Judge Buford."

Scott snapped forward in his chair. "Judge Buford's on the phone?"

Sue nodded.

"What the hell does he want with me?"

Sue shrugged, and Scott's eyes fell to the single blinking light on his phone. On the other end of that line was Judge Samuel Buford, the senior judge on the federal bench for the Northern District of Texas. Appointed by Carter, he had presided over every civil rights case in Dallas for the last three decades. He was now something of an icon in conservative Dallas despite being a liberal Democrat. As a federal judge he made less than a second-year associate at Ford Stevens, but lawyers who made a million bucks a year still addressed him as "sir," even outside his courtroom—and Scott had never spoken to him outside his courtroom. Scott took a deep breath, picked up the phone, and punched the blinking button.

"Judge Buford, sir, what a surprise."

"Scott, how you doing, son?"

"Uh . . . fine, Judge. Just fine. Uh . . . how are you doing, sir?"

"Well, I'm not doing so good, Scott, that's why I called you. I've got a big problem, and I need a top-notch lawyer to solve it. I figure you're Tom Dibrell's lawyer and—"

"Does this involve Tom?"

"Oh, no, Scott. It's just that being Dibrell's lawyer, you're accustomed to high-profile work, and your appearances in my courtroom have always been excellent. But, most important, you have the right attitude. Listening to your speech at the bar luncheon today, I knew you were just the lawyer for the job. Scott, I can't tell you how it made me feel, knowing there's still someone who understands what being a lawyer is all about. So many young lawyers these days, seems all they care about is getting rich."

"Yes, sir, it's a crying shame, Judge."

"You know, Scott, seeing you up there, everyone applauding you, made me recall that game of yours against Texas—damn, son, that was the best running I've ever seen. What did you get that day, a hundred fifty yards?"

"One hundred ninety-three, Judge. Three touchdowns. We still lost."

"Hell of a game."

"I didn't know you were a big football fan, Judge."

"I'm a Texan, born and raised, Scott, that makes me a football fan. Did you know I went to SMU?"

Scott chuckled. "Of course I know, Judge. Every student at the law school knows about Samuel Buford—top grade point average in the history of the school, law review editor, clerk to Supreme Court Justice Douglas, Assistant Solicitor General under LBJ . . ."

"Whoa, son, you're making me feel old."

"Oh, sorry, sir."

"You did pretty well yourself, Scott, top of your class."

"Thank you, sir."

"So, Scott, you up for helping out an old judge?"

"Always happy to help in any way, sir."

Just then his mind's peripheral vision caught a movement, like a linebacker moving in to nail him from his blind side.

"Tough job, Scott, requires a tough lawyer, a lawyer who doesn't quit, who can handle pressure, who can take a hard hit and still get up—you proved all that on the football field. You know, Scott, pound for pound, I always figured you were the toughest player I'd ever seen, except maybe for Meredith."

Before he was the star quarterback for the Dallas Cowboys, Don Meredith had been the star quarterback at SMU from 1957 through 1959, a country boy out of Mount Vernon, one of the greatest athletes ever produced by the State of Texas, and generally regarded as the toughest quarterback ever to play the position. Meredith was still a living legend in Dallas, although he lived in Santa Fe.

"But, Scott, this job also requires a lawyer who

believes like you do, that lawyers are supposed to protect the poor and defend the innocent and fight for justice."

"Absolutely, sir."

Back in his playing days, when the game was on the line, Scott Fenney, number 22, always pulled out all the stops to take home a victory. Even though he wasn't sure what he was playing for today—perhaps Buford wanted to appoint him independent counsel to investigate a high-profile political scandal, which could make Scott Fenney a very famous lawyer—his natural desire to win took over. He pulled out all the stops.

"Protecting the poor, defending the innocent, fighting for justice—that's not just our professional duty, Judge, that's our sacred honor."

Shit, that sounded good! That's a winner for sure! Scott made a mental note to add that line to his campaign speech.

"Good to hear that, Scott. You've read about the McCall case, the senator's son murdered Saturday night?"

"Yes, sir, by the hooker."

"Yeah, black girl, twenty-four, a dozen priors for prostitution, drug possession . . . says she's innocent."

Scott chuckled. "Don't they all?"

"This case is going to be a media circus—black prostitute accused of murdering a senator's son, and not just any senator, mind you, but likely the next president."

"Yeah, I wouldn't want to be her lawyer."

"Well, Scott, that's why I called."

And what the judge wanted from Scott Fenney hit him with all the force of a linebacker on a blitz.

Blindsided by a federal judge! Sweat beads erupted from the pores on his forehead. His pulse jumped. He reached up and loosened his silk tie.

"She needs a good lawyer, Scott. She needs you."

That's what he had won? That's the victory he would take home? On the verge of panic, Scott's sharp mind began devising ways to snatch defeat from the jaws of victory.

"But, Judge, what about the public defender's office?"

"Scott, I can't put a death penalty case in the hands of a wet-behind-the-ears PD lawyer who barely got through law school. This girl needs a real lawyer."

"But I'm a corporate lawyer. Why not appoint a criminal defense attorney?"

"I was going to . . . until I heard your speech. Defense lawyers, they're just hired guns. They don't care about defending the innocent or fighting for justice. They just want to get paid. Not like you, Scott. And most of them only work state court; you've got federal court experience."

"Why's a murder case in federal court?"

"Clark McCall was the FERC chairman, courtesy of the senator. Murder of a federal official is a federal crime."

"But, Judge—"

"And besides, Scott, you can make your mother proud."

"*What?*"

"You can be another Atticus Finch."

"But—"

"She has the right to counsel, and you're it, Scott. You're hereby appointed to represent the defendant in *United States of America versus Shawanda Jones*. Meet your client tomorrow morning. Detention hearing's Wednesday, nine A.M."

Scott was walking quickly—*hell, he was damn near running*—down the carpeted corridors of the sixty-second floor to the marble-and-mahogany staircase leading to the sixty-third floor. He bounded up the stairs and hurried past tiny offices occupied by smart young lawyers churning out their monthly quota of billable hours like blue-collar workers punching a clock on a factory line. Tonight, as every night, the workers were pulling double shifts, much to the benefit of the partners. But that thought did not fill Scott's heart with the usual cheer; tonight his heart was filled with fear as he rushed into his senior partner's office.

Dan Ford was sixty years old. He and Gene Stevens had founded the firm thirty-five years ago, right out of SMU law school. Dan Ford had hired Scott eleven years ago when he had graduated from SMU, taken him under his wing, taught him the profitable practice of law, got him elected to the partnership, got him the mortgage on the house, got him into the dining, athletic, and country clubs, and got him a good deal on the Ferrari. He was Scott's mentor and father figure, and he was at his desk, his station in life, from seven A.M. to seven P.M., Monday through Friday, and from seven A.M. until noon on

45

Saturdays, fifty weeks a year. Dan Ford had billed three thousand hours a year for thirty-five straight years, a feat he compared favorably to DiMaggio's fifty-six-game hitting streak. The firm was his life.

Dan's shiny head came up and a broad smile crossed his face.

"Scotty, my boy!"

Scott fell onto the sofa.

"You don't look so good, son. Problem?"

Dan Ford had solved most of Scott's problems over the last eleven years. Scott was hoping this one would be no different.

"Judge Buford just appointed me to represent the hooker who killed Senator McCall's son."

The news took the breath out of Dan. He fell back in his chair. "You're joking."

"I wish."

"Why?"

Scott threw up his hands. "Because I gave my goddamn Atticus Finch speech at the bar luncheon! The judge was there."

"He believed it?"

"Apparently."

Dan ran his hands over his smooth skull.

"This is not good. Not good at all. We can't afford to piss off the next president, and we sure as hell can't afford to piss off Buford. Goddamn murder case, why isn't it in state court? We could work with that!"

State court judges in Texas were always amenable to a call from a powerful partner in a big law firm because state court judges are elected on campaign contributions from big law firms. The threat of moving the firm's contributions to the judge's opponent in the next election has a way of keeping judges in line. Electing state court judges is a constitutional tradition in Texas dating back to 1850 and served to keep the Texas legal system orderly and predictable if not terribly fair. Thus lawyers in big law firms do not fear state court judges just as one does not fear one's own house pet.

But federal judges were a different breed. They're not elected. They're appointed by the president under Article Three of the United States Constitution—for life. They can't be voted off the bench. They don't need campaign contributions from big law firms. They don't fear powerful lawyers. Cross a federal judge and you live with it for thirty or forty years—you'll never win another case in his court. A large law firm like Ford Stevens with an active federal court practice could not afford to offend Judge Sam Buford.

"We've got a dozen pending cases on his docket. Big-dollar cases. We become personae non gratae in Buford's court, we lose our federal practice until the bastard dies."

"Or retires."

"Buford will die on the bench, just like Gene."

Gene Stevens, the firm's cofounder, had died at his desk last year, a pen in his hand, his hand on his daily time sheet, recording his last billable hour. Within twenty-four hours, his office had been cleaned out and Scott had moved in.

"Buford said it'll be a media circus," Scott said.

"Yeah, lots of publicity for the firm—all the wrong kind." Dan's pale face was pinking up like a newborn's. "Goddamnit, this firm cannot defend that whore!"

Dan closed his eyes, placed his hand over his face, and rubbed his temples. His thinking mode. And when Dan Ford thought hard, he always emerged with the correct answer. Scott's senior partner possessed a mind engineered like the Mercedes-Benz he drove: powerful, efficient, dependable, and wholly without a moral component. So Scott sat quietly while Dan's mind worked. He turned his eyes upward and checked out the walls for new trophy kills. Dan was a big-game hunter; mounted on the walls were stuffed heads of the wild animals he had bagged over the years, all looking down on Scott. It was kind of creepy.

After a moment, Dan removed his hand. He was smiling.

"Get her to plead out."

"She says she's innocent, wants a trial."

"So? Look, Scotty, go see her, explain the real likelihood the case will be lost and that she'll be sentenced to death or best case, spend the rest of her life in prison. That by pleading out she'll be released by the time she's fifty and she can still have a life . . . You know, turn on that famous charm, pretend you care."

"And if she doesn't go for it?"

"She goddamn well better go for it! I'm not going to have this firm's revenues damaged by some two-bit hooker!"

Dan's face was now a bright red, and he was pointing a finger at Scott, a sure sign it was time to leave. Scott stood and eased toward the door.

"You tell her she's pleading out whether she likes it or not!"

Scotty nodded and slid out. He was ten paces down the hall when he heard Dan's voice again: "Cop a plea, Scotty!"

FIVE

SCOTT STEERED the red Ferrari out of the parking garage, gave Osvaldo, the attendant, his customary salute, and turned north. While most downtown workers commuted to their homes in the distant suburbs via the Dallas North Tollway or the North Central Expressway, hopelessly stuck in bumper-to-bumper traffic for hours and suppressing the road rage that left a number of drivers dead each year on Dallas highways, Scott Fenney drove leisurely up Cedar Springs Road and Turtle Creek Boulevard and Lakeside Drive and then past Robert E. Lee Park, homeward bound over the same route important men of Dallas had traveled for a hundred years. Ten minutes later, he crossed a two-lane swath of asphalt and, as if his fairy godmother had waved her magic wand, his world abruptly changed: land values quintupled, home values quadrupled, per capita income tripled, students' achievement test scores doubled, and the population turned all white.

He had entered the Town of Highland Park.

Developed in 1906 on thirteen hundred acres of high

land above downtown Dallas, Highland Park today is a sanctuary of elegant homes, landscaped lawns, and broad avenues canopied by towering oak trees. On its wide sidewalks European nannies and Mexican maids can be seen pushing the heirs of the great Texas fortunes in strollers while their fathers—billionaires and millionaires and the lawyers who tend to them—work in the downtown skyscrapers and their mothers play tennis at the country club and shop at Anne Fontaine, Luca Luca, and Bottega Veneta in the Highland Park Village shopping center, its Spanish Mediterranean architecture and quaint stucco buildings with terra-cotta roofs and decorative wrought iron harking back to a distant time and place when great wealth was reserved for people of a certain class, not just anyone who could dunk a basketball. Visitors from California say the town reminds them of Beverly Hills, and with good reason: the same architect who designed Beverly Hills designed Highland Park. Only difference is, the founders of Beverly Hills did not file deed restrictions that legally limited home ownership in their new town to white people only; the founders of Highland Park did.

Almost a hundred years later, the Town of Highland Park is a two-square-mile island entirely surrounded by the 384-square-mile City of Dallas. It's an island of white in an ocean of color: Dallas, a city of 1.2 million residents, is now only 39 percent white; while Highland Park, a town of 8,850 residents, remains 98 percent white, with not a single home owned by a black person. It's an island of wealth—on any given day over a hundred homes in

Highland Park will be listed for sale at prices exceeding $1 million. It's an island immune from the crime and social ills that afflict Dallas—Highland Park kids call their hometown "the Bubble," happy to be insulated from the outside world that beckons at the town boundary—albeit an island without a river or stream or even a moat to keep the outside world out, only the highest home prices in Texas, a well-armed police force, and a long-standing reputation that if you're black or brown and don't live there, you'd damn well better be passing through.

The Highland Park police did not stop the Ferrari: Scott Fenney was white and he lived there. Like other white men of means, he made his money in Dallas but came home to Highland Park, raised his family in Highland Park, and sent his child to Highland Park schools. He turned right onto Beverly Drive and into the driveway of his two-and-a-half-story, 7,500-square-foot, six-bedroom, six-bath, $3.5 million residence. He had bought the home three years ago for $2.8 million when the previous owner had filed bankruptcy and the bank had foreclosed. Dan Ford had called in a personal favor and persuaded the bank to sell the house to Scott with one-hundred-percent financing at prime plus five. Sitting on one acre in the heart of Highland Park, the place had been a steal at that price. Scott had jumped in with both feet, into debt up to his neck. In many towns in Texas, men who owe large sums of money are looked on with suspicion; in Dallas, such men are looked on with awe.

Scott drove up the brick-paved driveway and into the

rear motor court. He cut the engine, but he didn't get out. Usually when he arrived home each evening and again admired his residence, he was filled with a sense of pride, that through brains and hard lawyering, he had achieved the perfect home for a perfect life.

But this evening was different.

For only the second time in his life, a distinct feeling of impending doom darkened his mind, just as it had when he was ten and his mother had picked him up early from school and said his father had been hurt. He knew his father was dead.

Butch Fenney had been a construction worker. A cable snapped and a load of lumber fell, crushing him. Scott's mother did the best she could, but they had to sell their small house in East Dallas. She worked for an ortho-pedic surgeon who lived in Highland Park and owned a teardown over by SMU, a tiny sixty-year-old home that would fall over if given a good push. The house was worthless, but the 75- by 125-foot lot it sat on was worth at least $250,000. The doctor planned to hold the prop-erty until his retirement, when he would demolish the house and sell the lot for a substantial profit. The good doctor rented the home to the Fenney family, mother and son.

So Scott Fenney attended Highland Park schools with the sons and daughters of governors and senators and millionaires and billionaires, scions of the great Dallas families like the Hunts and Perots and Crows. He was the poor kid on the block, the kid who didn't wear designer jeans and $100 Nike sneakers, who didn't go to

Europe for spring break, who didn't get a $50,000 BMW for his sixteenth birthday. But Scott Fenney possessed something no snotty rich boy could ever buy with daddy's money: athletic ability. Remarkable God-given physical talent revealed with a run the town would never forget. High school football. Friday night fever. Legitimate, structured violence, organized by men, inflicted by boys, cheered by all—and a tried-and-true method for pulling oneself up by one's bootstraps in Texas. Scott was strong and he was tough and he was fast. He became the star running back for Highland Park High, the best since Doak Walker.

After high school, he went to SMU. Most Highland Park kids are deathly afraid of leaving the safety and security of the Bubble, so going off to college for them means moving out of their parents' home in Highland Park, driving the Beemer a few blocks, and moving into a sorority or fraternity house on the SMU campus in Highland Park. Scott Fenney went to SMU because the school offered him a football scholarship. He starred on the varsity for four years; his 193 yards against Texas made him a legend. He was also popular enough to be elected class president and smart enough to graduate first in his class. When the pros passed on the six foot two, 185-pound white running back with jagged scars down both knees, he enrolled in SMU law school.

Now, you don't go to Southern Methodist University School of Law if you plan on pursuing a legal career in New York or D.C. or L.A. or even Houston for that matter: it's not exactly the Harvard of the Southwest. In fact, they say it's a hell of a lot easier to get into the law school at SMU than it is one of the sororities or fraternities at SMU. You go to SMU law school if and only if you want to practice law in Dallas, Texas, because SMU lawyers have begotten SMU lawyers for so many decades now that the Dallas legal community is more incestuous than the Alabama backwoods of the fifties.

Scott graduated number one in his law school class, which earned him job offers from every big firm in Dallas. He chose Ford Stevens because they offered him $5,000 more. Eleven years later, Scott Fenney was no longer the poor kid on the block.

Scott entered the house through the back door that led into a mud room and then into the spacious kitchen, where he found Consuela cooking and the small TV tuned to a Mexican game show.

"Buenas noches, señorita. What's for dinner?"

Her brown face turned up from the stainless-steel stove, and she smiled. "Enchiladas, Señor Fenney. *Especial* for you."

He walked over, put an arm around her, and said, "Consuela, don't worry. Esteban will be back soon."

She fought back tears. "*Sí*. He will come."

Consuela de la Rosa was twenty-eight, short, and chubby. She lived in the pool cabana out back, just like countless other illegal Mexican maids throughout the Town of Highland Park, which effectively granted them political asylum from the INS. Their presence was certainly no secret; strolling the aisles of the Highland Park gourmet grocery store on a weekday when the maids did the family shopping qualified as a conversational Spanish lesson these days. The real threat to his maid was not the INS but Esteban's hormones. If her *hombre* got her pregnant, Consuela would have to leave town per the tacit agreement in Highland Park: Spanish spoken in the grocery store was acceptable; Spanish spoken in the schools was not.

"Mrs. Fenney home?"

"No. Señora, she gone all day. She hit the golf ball."

"With all the golf lessons she's taken, she ought to be on the women's pro tour by now."

In keeping with his daily routine, Scott climbed the back stairs two steps at a time to the second floor. He walked down the hall and up another set of stairs to the top floor that was his nine-year-old daughter's domain. Hers was not a kid's room; there were no posters on the wall of Britney Spears or the Olsen twins. There were books, books on the bookshelves, books on her desk, books on her night table, books on the floor. Even at nine, she was a serious child, thoughtful, smart beyond her breeding. Scott found her at her desk tucked under the dormer, barefooted and wearing overall shorts and a green Dallas Mavericks tee shirt, notwithstanding her mother's threats to disown her if she didn't start dressing in designer outfits from Neiman Marcus like the other Highland Park girls her age. But she had steadfastly refused, saying she had her own identity, to which her mother would always retort, "As what, a boy?"

"Hey, Boo."

Barbara Boo Fenney. She was named after his mother, who had died before Boo was born. Scott's mother had not lived to see her son's mansion or her granddaughter. Boo spun around in her swivel chair, her shoulder-length red hair whipping around, and she gave him a smile that shot straight to his heart. Scott loved his wife, but Boo was the love of his life.

"Hey, A. Scott."

He cupped her face, leaned down, and kissed her forehead.

"Did you have a good day, baby?"

"Oh, I read and played computer games, watched TV, cooked with Consuela, you know, the usual . . . until Esteban called. Thanks for calming Consuela down—she'd still be crying."

Scott nodded. "Your mother's been gone all day?"

She gave him a look. *"Duh."*

"It's summer, she ought to spend more time with you."

"Well, I'm not on the Cattle Barons' Ball committee." She smiled. "How was your day?"

"Okay."

"Did you do important lawyer stuff?"

"Oh, yeah."

"Like what?"

Scott recalled his day—billing twelve hours for the nine he was at the office; giving his Atticus Finch speech at the bar luncheon; flirting with Missy while reeling in a law student like a hooked fish; voting to fire John Walker; flirting with Dibrell's receptionist; hiding lead contamination behind the attorney-client privilege; threatening to destroy a young woman by revealing her sexual history at trial in order to obtain a favorable settlement—and quickly decided, as he always decided, that a lawyer's day was best left at the law office. So he said, "Oh, just the things lawyers do."

"Unh-huh." She gave him another look. "You just tell me what you want me to know, don't you?"

He gave her a smile. "Yep."

She frowned. "It's not fair."

"What's not fair?"

"I'm stuck here all day while Mother meets her lady friends for lunch and plays golf and you go to your office and do your lawyer work. Mother comes home and wants to tell me all about her day, but I want to know about your day, and you won't tell me. It's not fair."

Scott sat on the edge of Boo's bed and looked at his daughter, her cute little face contorted into a frown. He knew she wasn't really mad, but it still bothered him. So he thought through his day again and decided he could tell her one thing.

"Okay, I'll tell you something about my day. I got appointed to represent a criminal defendant, the woman who murdered Senator McCall's son."

Her face brightened and all was well again.

"You're not a criminal lawyer."

"Some people say all lawyers are criminal."

Boo smiled. "You know what I mean."

"Well, I'm hoping there won't be a trial, that she'll cop a plea."

"What's cop a plea?"

"Say she's guilty."

"Is she?"

"Probably."

"Are you gonna ask her?"

"Maybe . . . I mean, yeah, sure."

"Why do you want her to cop a plea? I thought you make more money when a case goes to trial."

"Not this trial. I'm doing it for free."

"Why?"

"Judge Buford's making me."

"He can do that?"

"Yeah. I practice in federal court, so he can do that. It's a rule."

"Support his opponent in the next election."

He had taught her well.

"Judge Buford's a federal judge, appointed for life."

"Shit."

"Boo, don't cuss."

"Mother does."

"Well, she shouldn't. And you shouldn't either. It makes you sound trashy."

"They cuss in the movies, even the PGs. And all the other kids cuss."

"That doesn't make it right. Don't be a follower, Boo. Don't do the wrong thing just because everyone else does. Do the right thing."

"I don't say the F-word."

Scott smiled. "Well, that's good."

"I don't even know what it means."

"I hope not."

"Sally down the street, she says her dad says the F-word all the time when he thinks she's not around. And sometimes even when she is. You don't say the F-word when I'm not around, do you?"

"No, of course not."

A small lie.

"So she doesn't have any money to pay you?"

"Who, the defendant? No."

"Doesn't she have a job?"

"She's a, uh . . ."

"Prostitute. I heard it on TV. And a drug addict. What's a prostitute?"

When Boo asked him questions like that, Scott was never quite sure how to answer. She always seemed to know when he wasn't telling the whole truth, but, even though she was born twenty-five years old, he was reluctant to always tell the truth. So he answered like a lawyer. He fudged the truth.

"A personal escort."

"What's that?"

"She entertains men."

"Like you entertain clients?"

A closer analogy than she knew. "Well, sort of."

"Do you have any clients like her?"

"No, Boo, I don't represent prostitutes and drug addicts."

"I mean, black clients?"

"Oh. No, I've never had a black client."

"Why not?"

"Well, because I represent corporations, not people."

"What about those people who call you all the time?"

"My clients are corporations, but my contacts are executives at the corporations."

Boo screwed her mouth up. She was thinking.

"Why?"

"Why what?"

"Why do you represent corporations instead of people?"

"Because people can't afford me. Heck, Boo, I couldn't afford to hire myself, not at three-fifty an hour."

Her eyes got big. "You charge three dollars and fifty cents *an hour*?"

Scott chuckled. "No. Three *hundred* and fifty dollars an hour."

"*For real?* Is that why you work so slowly?"

Nine years old and she was qualified to be the managing partner at the biggest law firm in the country.

She said, "So we're rich because corporations can pay you three hundred fifty dollars an hour?"

"Yes . . . well, no, we're not rich, Boo."

"We live in a big house and you drive a Ferrari."

"Yeah, but I've got to work to keep all this. Rich people don't."

"Cindy's dad got fired and they had to sell their house."

"Don't worry, baby, that'll never happen to us."

*

From the Jacuzzi tub, his wife said, "You've got to talk to her, Scott, she'll listen to you! How am I ever going to be selected chair of the Cattle Barons' Ball if my daughter dresses like a boy!"

Rebecca Fenney was thirty-three, fit, and gorgeous, still the most beautiful woman in Highland Park—the perfect wife for a perfect life. And she desperately wanted to chair the next Cattle Barons' Ball, the biggest society party put on each year in Dallas, the one night when the sophisticated men and women of Highland Park get to dress up like cowboys and cowgirls and play Texan to the hilt. The twangs become stronger, the cigars longer, the skirts shorter, and the diamonds bigger; and everyone tries to out-Texan one another, arriving in Hummer limousines, Rolls-Royces, and even helicopters at Southfork Ranch, J. R. Ewing's home on the TV show *Dallas*, or another fitting venue. They drink champagne and whiskey, eat fried alligator and fajitas, ride the mechanical bucking bull, bet on the armadillo races, and dance to the likes of the Oak Ridge Boys or Dwight Yoakam or Willie Nelson.

The men compete with money, betting at the craps table in the casino or bidding at the auction offering diamonds and Porsches. The women compete with clothes. They wear black, blue, red, pink, and white cowboy boots made of lizard, ostrich, elephant, kangaroo, and suede; they wear low-cut satin bustiers, lambskin halters, leather vests, and evening gowns; they wear matching cowboy hats. Last year Rebecca wore a powder blue fringed suede miniskirt, matching cowboy boots, a low-cut pink fringed halter top, and a pink suede cowboy hat—and she was furious because no one noticed her. Scott was always amused by it all, but the Cattle Barons' Ball was deadly serious business to the women of Highland Park, all competing to be the belle of the ball. The lucky woman who chairs the ball is forever enshrined among the society elite of Highland Park—except maybe for one former chairwoman who got nabbed for shoplifting at Neiman Marcus. Providing she kept her criminal record clean, Rebecca Fenney was the front-runner to be the chairwoman of the next Cattle Barons' Ball.

Scott and Rebecca were in the master bathroom on the second floor; she was naked in the Jacuzzi tub, he was irritated in a robe. Scott had tried to talk to his wife about his day, but she had shown no interest at all. The McCall case had him irritated; his wife had ratcheted it up a notch. All she wanted to talk about was the Cattle Barons' Ball and the latest Highland Park scandal, another extramarital affair, which wasn't exactly shocking news to Scott.

Rebecca said, "Muffy, you remember her, from the last party at the club."

Scott didn't recall Muffy and wasn't particularly interested in trying to recall her. He shook his head.

"Bleached blonde, boob job, acts snotty all the time . . ."

"Well, that narrows it down to only ninety-five per-cent of the women in Highland Park."

"She's married to Bill what's-his-name, old, bald, fat."

"Oh, yeah, I remember her. She was wearing that tight two-piece outfit, nice abs. She's about twenty years younger than Bill. So she was stepping out on him?"

"He caught her in bed with the neighbor."

"Again, not exactly shocking, Rebecca."

She gave him a sly smile, which from prior experience told Scott that she was about to deliver the punch line.

"He didn't catch her with the man who lives next door. He caught her with the woman who lives next door."

"She was in bed with another woman?"

"Yes! I called to tell you, but Sue said you were busy."

"Rebecca, don't bother me at work with gossip."

"It's not gossip if it's true, you said so yourself."

"That's defamation, Rebecca—truth is an absolute defense to slander and libel claims. There's no defense for gossip."

"Not even a lesbian affair?"

"Don't they have a girl about Boo's age?"

"They did. Muffy and her girlfriend ran off to California."

"She left her kid? Why?"

Rebecca shrugged. "Everyone knows. She can't show her face in this town again. Besides, she's a lesbian; the child's better off without her."

"Rebecca, is that all you do at your lunches, gossip?"

"No . . . just during dessert. We call it scandal soufflé."

She seemed pleased with herself, which made one of them. The thought of his wife sitting at lunch gossiping while Boo sat at home alone jacked up Scott's irritation level to a new high. He was about to say something guaranteed to grate on her, but seeing her slick wet body as she climbed out of the tub, her red hair stuck to her face, her full breasts pink from the hot water, her abdomen flat from hours on her Ab Master, and her firm bottom that hadn't dropped an inch since their wedding day eleven years ago, desire drove the McCall case, the Cattle Barons' Ball, scandal soufflé, and all lingering irritation from his mind. He let his robe slip off his shoulders and looked down: he had a full erection. He went over to her, wrapped his arms around her from behind, pressed himself against her, and reached around and cupped her genitals, an act which not that long ago would have produced a soft moan leading to sex on the marble vanity. Tonight it produced only an exasperated sigh.

"Not tonight, Scott. I'm tired."

She had been tired a lot the last six months. He released her and walked into the bedroom and over to the sitting area against the bank of windows. He sat and listened to the *tak tak tak* of June bugs banging against the outside glass, seeking the light like reformed sinners. He used the remote to turn on the television and then he looked down: his erection had melted away like a Popsicle on a hot summer day.

It hadn't always been this way. They had met in his third year of law school, at a party at his old frat house after a football game. She was a senior cheerleader and the reigning Miss SMU. Scott Fenney was a football legend and a campus celebrity, so approaching the most beautiful coed at SMU was easy. They had sex in an upstairs bathroom that night. And at every other imaginable venue in the months that followed: in her car; in his car; at her sorority house; at his apartment; in a stairwell at the law school; in the park in broad daylight; on the eighteenth green at the country club late at night after jumping the fence—to this day he could not putt out on that green without thinking of that night. They were so hot, they couldn't get enough of each other.

But somewhere along the way—when, he wasn't sure—the heat had faded. And now they slept back to back, separated by two feet of king-sized mattress like a demilitarized zone. They weren't mad at each other—they seldom had words—but they seldom had sex. She had just drifted away.

He sat slumped and limp as all the irritating thoughts—the McCall case, his wife's lack of interest in his day, being denied sex again, scandal soufflé, and his daughter home alone all day—came rushing back. He yelled to his wife in the bathroom: "Why don't you spend more time with Boo? Maybe she'll listen to you then."

Rebecca appeared in the bathroom door, still naked, her hands on her hips.

"She's never listened to me. I've got these hideous stretch marks because of her, but she's your child. By the time I was her age, I had won two beauty pageants. She wears overalls. And, besides, I'm busy this summer. Why don't you spend more time with her?"

"I'm working."

"Oh, I see. What I do isn't important."

"Sounds like all you do is gossip."

"Only during dessert. During lunch we plan the ball."

"A big society party."

"Which raises money for charity."

"Which you don't give a damn about. It's just another step up the Highland Park social ladder for you. You're social climbing and Boo's being raised by Consuela!"

She glared at him, whirled, and disappeared into the bathroom. Scott was about to yell after her, *You need to spend as much time with your daughter as you do gossiping with those old society broads*, but then she'd say, *Well, you need to spend as many billable hours with me as you do with your clients*, and then he'd say, *Those clients pay for this house and those cars and your dresses and . . .*

"McCall . . ."

The reporter's voice pulled Scott out of his thoughts and focused his attention on the television.

"His son's murder," the reporter was saying, "has given the senator a sympathy boost in the polls, thus solidifying his position as the clear front-runner for the White House."

SIX

THE NOVEMBER 22, 1963, edition of the *Dallas Morning News* included a full-page black-bordered advertisement titled "Welcome Mr. Kennedy to Dallas." It was not a welcome. It was an indictment of President Kennedy that had been paid for by several right-wing Dallas oilmen, "America-thinking citizens" they called themselves. They accused Kennedy of being soft on Communism, despite the president's successful standoff with the Russians over the Cuban missile crisis. On Air Force One's flight to Dallas, an aide showed the ad to the president. Kennedy read it and remarked, "We're heading into nut country today." The ad identified the mayor of Dallas as a Kennedy sympathizer.

Earle Cabell was the mayor. He met President Kennedy at Love Field that morning and rode in the presidential motorcade, three cars behind the president's blue limousine. As his car turned onto Elm Street, Cabell heard three gunshots ring out from the Texas School Book Depository. He arrived at Parkland Memorial Hospital just as the president was being removed from his limousine. Cabell remained at the hospital until the president's body was taken away. He had hoped to show the president that Dallas was no longer the "Southwest hate capital of Dixie." He had failed. But they still named the federal building in downtown Dallas after him—Cabell, not the president.

Of course, when A. Scott Fenney, Esq., arrived at the Earle Cabell Federal Building on Commerce Street shortly after nine the next morning, he didn't know who Earle Cabell was or why they had named this dull-as-dirt twenty-one-story structure after him. All he knew was that he didn't want to be in Earle's building that day and all he cared about was getting his client to cop a plea and then getting himself the hell out of there. He exited the elevator on the fifth floor, the federal detention center. After passing through the metal detector and having his briefcase searched, he was met by a black guard.

"Scott Fenney to see Shawanda Jones."

"You her lawyer?"

Scott wanted desperately to scream, *Hell, no, I'm not her lawyer!* Instead, he nodded. The guard led him down a narrow hallway to a small room, bare except for a metal table and two metal chairs. Scott entered and stared at the bare walls until the door opened and a black woman entered, bringing with her a foul body odor that filled the room like thick smoke. She looked him up and down, covered her mouth with both hands, and sneezed violently several times. Then she said, "You the lawyer?"

"Yes, I am."

Shawanda Jones was twenty-four but she appeared

much older. She was a small woman, rising only to Scott's shoulders. Her hair was neither kinky nor slicked straight; it was brown, hung just over her ears, and appeared soft, although obviously it had gone untouched by a brush for days. Her eyes were creamy ovals with big brown centers, but they seemed hollowed out and vacant. The area below her eyes was a darker brown than the rest of her face, which was tan and smooth and glistening with a light coating of sweat. Her nose was narrow and her lips thin. Her body seemed slim but shapely under the baggy white jail uniform. Her face was angular with prominent cheekbones. She was attractive, but at one time in her life, she must have been beautiful. She reminded Scott of Halle Berry on a bad day. A very bad day.

Scott was not wearing his glasses that morning; he didn't care whether this client thought he looked smart or not. And he did not extend a hand to her even though he always shook hands with a new client: Dan Ford had explained to Scott early in his legal career that a lawyer had only one opportunity to make a good first impression on a new client, so he should always look the client directly in the eye and give him a firm handshake, which, Dan said, would project a sense of forthrightness and honesty, thus making the client less likely to question his legal bills. Instead, fearing that her hand—one of the hands into which she had just sneezed like she had pneumonia—might transmit a communicable disease, Scott gestured for his new client to sit down. But she did not sit. She paced.

She walked from one side of the room to the other and back again. Back and forth she went, again and again, rubbing her arms as if the room were cold instead of warm and kneading her fingers like Consuela saying the rosary. Her eyes darted about the room. Her legs seemed out of sync, and they twitched uncontrollably. Halfway back, she suddenly doubled over and groaned.

"You okay?"

She grunted. "Cramps."

Like most men when a woman speaks of her period, Scott didn't know how to respond. So he said, "My wife has bad cramps each month."

Between groans, she said, "Not from this she don't."

After a moment the cramps apparently subsided, and she resumed her pacing. Scott sat, removed his business card from his pocket, and pushed it to her side of the table. On her next pass by the table, she abruptly pulled out the chair, sat, and flopped her arms on the table. Scott noticed dark spots on the insides of both of her forearms, like someone was going to play connect the dots but had never connected them. Then he remembered: she's a heroin addict. She picked up his business card with her thumb and forefinger and held it before her face.

"What the *A* stand for?" she asked.

"Nothing."

"Your first name be a letter?"

Scott didn't want to discuss his name. He wanted to get this over with and get back to his office on the sixty-second floor of Dibrell Tower where he belonged.

"Ms. Jones, I'm Scott Fenney. The court appointed me to represent you. You've been charged with murder, a federal offense because the victim was a federal official. If found guilty, you could be sentenced to death or life in prison. Which is why I want to talk to you about pleading out to a lesser offense. You could be out in thirty years."

Her hands abruptly shot out and grabbed Scott's wrists. He instinctively recoiled from the woman with the wild eyes, but she was strong for her size and she had a firm grip. She said, "Get me a fix, please? I ain't sleep in two days!"

"A fix?"

"Some H! I need it bad!"

"You mean *dope*? No, I can't do that!"

"Thought you my lawyer!"

"You've had lawyers give you dope?"

"For sex. C'mon, I suck you right here!"

"No!"

She jumped up and resumed her pacing. Scott had to take a minute to gather himself. He'd had corporate clients offer him bribes (also known as legal fees) to destroy incriminating documents, suborn perjury, conceal fraudulent activities, and falsify filings with the SEC, but they were always well-dressed and well-educated white men—and none of them had ever offered him oral sex!

After he recovered, Scott said, "Now, as I was saying, you can plead out and—"

"Say I did it?"

"Yes, but not with the specific intent to murder."

She stopped and stared at him with her hands on her hips and an incredulous expression on her face.

"You telling me, say I killed him? Don't you wanna know if I did?"

"Uh, yeah, sure." He leaned back. "Tell me what happened."

She waved a hand at the bare table.

"You ain't writing nothin' down?"

Scott reached down to his briefcase and removed a yellow legal pad and black pen.

"Go ahead."

Shawanda Jones, prostitute, proceeded to pace the room and tell her lawyer the facts (according to her) of the night of Saturday, June 5.

"We was working Harry Hines—"

Harry Hines Boulevard, named after a Dallas oilman, begins just north of downtown and continues out to the loop, a north–south corridor that is culturally diverse, as they say. On this single stretch of pavement, you can obtain the finest medical care in the country at no fewer than four hospitals, earn a degree at the University of Texas medical school, purchase high fashion and fine furnishings at the Market Center or shop more economically at the Army-Navy store, play golf at the exclusive Brook Hollow Golf Club, eat a wide variety of ethnic food, buy cheap used cars, illegal drugs, fake IDs, and counterfeit designer purses, enjoy topless strip clubs and all-nude salons, lodge overnight at the Salvation Army homeless shelter, get an abortion, or pick up a prostitute.

"Who's we?"

"Me and Kiki."

"What's Kiki's last name?"

"How would I know? That ain't even her first name."

"What time?"

"Maybe, ten."

"P.M.?"

"Shawanda don't work no morning shift."

"What—"

"You want me to tell this here story or not?"

Scott held his hands up in surrender. Shawanda Jones continued her story, extremely agitated and animated, her arms flying about.

"Anyways, we was feeling good and looking good, me wearing my blonde wig, Kiki red. We was strolling, men driving by, whistling, yelling, 'Yo, mama, suck this!' Black dudes, Mexicans, they just window shoppers, can't afford no class girls like us. We wait for them white boys in nice cars. They like us 'cause we ain't dark and we in shape—me and Kiki, we do them exercise tapes most every day, got us a new one, *The Firm*? Use dumbbells. Check this out."

She pushed up the short sleeve of the jail uniform and curled her right arm and flexed her biceps, displaying an impressive bulge for a girl. Great, a heroin addict who worked out.

"So, maybe ten-thirty, white boy driving a Mercedes, one of them long black jobs got them blacked-out windows, he pull up alongside us and roll down the window and look us over. We know one of us is fixing to get

74

picked up. He say, 'Blondie, get in.' Well, Shawanda don't just get in when some trick say get in, so I saunter on over, lean in the window, car smell like a whiskey factory. He say he pay a thousand dollars for all night. I say, 'Show me the money.' I got that from that movie? He pull out a roll of bills could choke a horse, so I get in, almost slide down to the floor, my leather skirt on that leather seat. He reach over, grab my tit, say, 'Them real?' I say, 'Honey, all a Shawanda real.' "

She abruptly groaned, grabbed at her midsection, and doubled over again.

"Shit!"

She remained in that position for a long moment. Scott had often suffered leg cramps back when he played ball, and man, they could really hurt. So he had some amount of empathy for her. Still, he checked his watch and thought of billable hours going unbilled and wished she would get on with it. Finally the cramps abated, and she straightened and started talking nonstop again.

"Anyways, we drive off. I figure we goin' to a motel? 'Stead we go to Highland Park, street sign say. I ain't never been in no Highland Park—black girl know better'n to go there. Pretty soon we drive up to the biggest damn house I ever seen, through big gates, behind a big wall, go round back. Get out, I follows him inside, place is fine. He ask me I want something to drink, I say okay. I'm thinking, white boy got money and place like this and good-looking to boot—what he want with Shawanda?

"We get upstairs, in bed, I find out. He climb on top

and start working hard, he say, 'You like it?' Course, I say, 'Oh, yeah, baby, you so big.' Tricks, they like to hear that shit. Then he say, 'Tell me again, nigger, you like my white dick?' Now I don't much like nobody calling me nigger, but for a thousand bucks I don't say nothing but, 'Oh, yeah, baby.' Then he slap me, hard, say he always give it rough to his women. Well, nobody slap Shawanda. I punch that white boy in his mouth, knock him outta me and flat off the bed, jump up and say, 'Ain't gonna get rough with Shawanda, honky!'

"He come at me again, all mean now, so I scratch his face, then I pop him a good one, BAM!" She made a roundhouse swing with her left fist. "Right in the eye. We fall over the bed and he hits me again, with his fist this time, right here." She was pointing to the left side of her face, where a bruise was evident. "But I got my knee right in his balls, he fall off and start cussing me: 'You nigger bitch!' I grab my clothes, my thousand dollars, his car keys, drive back to Kiki and leave the car."

"And that's the last time you saw Clark McCall?"

"That his name?"

"Yeah. He was the son of Senator Mack McCall."

A blank face. She didn't know Mack McCall from Mickey Mouse.

"Last I seen him, Mr. Fenney, he was rolling on the floor, holding his privates and cussing me something fierce."

"He was murdered that night. Police found him Sunday, naked on the bedroom floor, shot once in the head, point-blank, .22-caliber gun next to him, with your fingerprints on it."

"Must of dropped outta my purse."

"So it was your gun?"

"Girl work the streets in Dallas, she gotta carry."

"But you didn't shoot him?"

"No, sir, Mr. Fenney."

"You're innocent?"

"Yes, sir, Mr. Fenney. And I ain't coppin' no plea."

"But, Ms. Jones—"

"Miz Jones my mama. You call me Shawanda. And I ain't pleading out. And what about bail? When I get outta here? I'm in bad need of some—"

"Dope?"

"Mr. Fenney, you looking at me like I ain't nothing but worthless dirt, but you ain't never been where I been."

Scott sighed. This wasn't going as planned.

"I'll check on the bail hearing, but don't count on getting out on a murder charge. And if the court grants bail, it'll be high. Do you have any assets?"

She slapped her butt. "This here Shawanda's only asset."

"A nice ass won't get you out of jail."

"It will in some counties." He thought she was joking, but she didn't smile. "So I be locked up till the trial? Mr. Fenney, I gotta see my baby!"

"You have a child?"

"Name Pajamae, she nine."

Scott put the pen to the pad. "How do you spell that?"

"P-a—j-a—m-a-e. *Pa—shu—may*. It's French."

"Where is she?"

"Our place down in the projects. We been through this before, but only couple days. I tell her, 'Don't even open that door, girl.' "

"Does this Kiki take care of her?"

"No, sir, Mr. Fenney. Kiki, she live with a man. I don't let no man in my place might hurt my Pajamae. Louis, he watch out for her, take her groceries, make sure she okay. He like her uncle but he ain't."

Scott pushed the pad and pen across the table.

"Write down your address . . . and Louis's phone number."

Shawanda stopped her pacing, sat, took the pen in her left hand, and began writing, but her hand was shaking like an old person with tremors. Scott realized the awkwardness of the moment.

"My daughter's left-handed, too."

She stopped and stared at her hand. After a moment, she stopped writing, put the pen down, and looked back up at Scott with wet eyes.

"Mr. Fenney, the smack, it just own me."

Then she doubled over and vomited.

Dan Ford was on the phone when Scott arrived at his senior partner's office and dropped his body onto the sofa like a load of cement.

Dan was saying into the phone: "Of course we support your reelection, Governor. Your fine leadership gave the business community everything we asked for from the legislature—no new taxes, tort reform . . . Yes . . . Yes . . . All right, I'll see you tomorrow."

Dan hung up the phone and shook his head in amazement.

"That boy couldn't find oil at an Exxon station." A long sigh. "But he is the governor." Finally, he focused his attention on Scott. "Did she go for it?"

"No. She won't cop a plea."

A knowing nod. "Figured she might not."

Scott had braced himself for one of Dan Ford's profanity-laced tirades, but his senior partner didn't seem all that upset.

"What should I do?"

"Hire her out," Dan said.

"Hire her out?"

"Yeah, hire a criminal defense attorney to take your place. It's a simple mathematical calculation, Scotty."

"Dan, what the hell are you talking about?"

Dan stood and stepped over to the grease board mounted on the wall under the head of an elk, opened the wood doors, and picked up a marker. Writing as he spoke, he said, "Say the case takes a thousand lawyer-hours, worst-case scenario. We pay a defense lawyer—now I'm not talking a summa cum laude graduate; I'm talking anyone with a license—fifty dollars an hour—"

"*Fifty an hour?* We charge a hundred an hour for our summer clerks' time."

"They're top of their class. I'm talking a bottom-of-the-class lawyer, Scott, someone who needs fifty bucks an hour. So a thousand hours at fifty an hour, that's a fifty-thousand-dollar expense to the firm."

Scott knew his senior partner had thought this through because Dan Ford didn't part with fifty cents easily much less fifty grand. He was a lawyer who calculated the profit the firm generated on each copy machine—forty cents per page—and made damn sure the copiers ran around the clock, spitting out paper and adding almost a million dollars to the firm's annual bottom line. Ford Stevens marked up the cost of everything in its offices, animate and inanimate, turning a profit on every associate, paralegal, secretary, typist, courier, copy, fax, and phone call. And Dan Ford kept tabs on everyone and everything.

He was saying, "But that frees up those thousand lawyer-hours for you to work for our paying clients at three-fifty an hour. That's three hundred fifty thousand dollars in revenues for the firm. Deduct the fifty thousand we pay the defense lawyer, and the firm still nets three hundred thousand, versus losing the entire three hundred fifty thousand if you have to work the case."

Scott's spirits started to lift. "Will Buford go for that?"

"Sure. Before the federal court had a public defender's office, we got appointed all the time. Hiring them out was standard operating procedure for the big firms." Dan shrugged. "And besides, it's a win-win situation: she gets a lawyer who knows more about criminal defense than you do, and you get rid of her."

Dan closed the doors to the grease board and said, "You know a cheap criminal defense attorney?"

RO ERT HERR N, ATT NEY-AT-L W, the sign out front read because the landlord was too damn cheap to replace the letters that had been shot off. Didn't matter, it was the only sign printed in English, and most people in this part of town couldn't read it anyway. This attorney's office was not in the best part of town; it was in a piece-of-shit strip center in East Dallas. He was a street lawyer; hence his office was at street level. He would often arrive to find someone sleeping on the stoop. He never kicked them awake as the other business owners in the strip did: hell, the guy might be his next best client. And he never called the police, which would be a monumental waste of a phone call; the police only kept the peace in the parts of town that mattered. He simply stepped over them and entered the law offices of Robert Herrin, Esq.

His professional address was a thirty- by twenty-foot space, one room and a tiny john, lodged between a Mexican bar and a Korean donut shop; he ate donuts for breakfast and drank beer for dinner. The roof leaked, the ceiling tiles were discolored, and the scent of mold permeated the place. The linoleum on the floor was cracked and curling at the corners like elves' shoes. His desk was metal, as was his chair, but it swiveled and had a nice seat cushion. Fortunately, he was a pretty fair typist because he couldn't afford a secretary. And here Robert Herrin, Attorney-at-Law, had eked out a legal living for the last eleven years, representing those members of society who wouldn't get past the security guards at a downtown law firm.

He was a fixture in this East Dallas neighborhood— he was *the lawyer*—same as the bar and donut shop were fixtures. The thin walls of his office afforded him the opportunity to pick up several foreign languages, although his Spanish skills far exceeded his Korean, probably because when he wasn't here he was usually next door in the bar shooting pool. As a general rule, Anglos were not welcome in a Mexican beer joint. But *Señor Herrin, el abogado*, was always welcome because the owner, the bartender, the waitresses, and most of the bar's customers were his clients. Which had the added benefit of keeping his plate-glass window free of bullet holes. He was the go-to lawyer when spouses, offspring, or siblings were busted, either because he showed them respect or because he offered a convenient payment plan. Often he would open the door (after stepping over the aforementioned drunk sleeping it off) and find fives and tens and every now and then a twenty on the floor with a note clipped to each so he could credit the correct client.

It was not the life he had dreamed of in law school.

The phone rang. If experience was any indication, Bobby Herrin would soon be driving over to the county jail to bail out one of his regulars. He reached for the phone.

SEVEN

BOBBY HERRIN felt like a lawyer in an out-of-town courtroom.

He was standing in the lobby of the Downtown Club, located on the top floor of Dibrell Tower and hands-down the swankiest eating place in downtown, and watching the richest men in Dallas arrive for lunch, trailed by their lawyers like a rapper's entourage. These were lawyers who owned the biggest law firms in town, who billed three, four, maybe five hundred dollars an hour—Bobby made $500 on a good *week*—and who wore wool suits, starched shirts, silk ties, and shoes shined by the black shoe guy downstairs. Everything Bobby was wearing had been purchased years ago off the sale racks and was made of polyester, except his shoes, which hadn't been shined in months. He rubbed his right shoe against the back of his left trouser leg and repeated the attempt to bring something resembling a shine with the other shoe.

"Bobby!"

He turned and was greeted by the brightest smile on

the most handsome face imaginable, the face of the friend he had once cheered and admired and envied and followed like a rock star's groupie—and loved like a brother. Scotty Fenney. Bobby hadn't seen Scotty in eleven years, and now he had to resist the urge to embrace his former best friend. They shook hands.

"Glad you could make it," Scotty said. "You haven't been waiting long, have you, buddy?"

Bobby shook his head. But, in fact, he had. He'd arrived fifteen minutes ago, parked in the underground garage, and rode the express elevator right to the top. Which reminded him. He pulled his parking ticket from his shirt pocket.

"They validate?"

If not, the ten-dollar parking fee would damn near bankrupt Bobby that day. But Scotty didn't answer; he was looking Bobby up and down as if trying to come up with a compliment for his wardrobe. He finally gave up and slapped Bobby on the shoulder.

"C'mon, let's eat."

Scotty led the way to the maître d's station, down a short corridor. One wall was a gallery of framed portraits of the club's founders and board of directors, past and present, a regular Who's Who of Dallas.

"Ah, Mr. Fenney, a pleasure to see you today," a middle-aged Hispanic man said with a practiced smile, as if seeing Scotty was the highlight of his day. He was trim, his hair was parted neatly and slicked over, and his face was smooth and brown, clean-shaven with a pencil mustache. The scent of aftershave hovered over him. He was dressed in a dark suit, dark tie, and white shirt. He could be the local Latino undertaker. He tucked two menus bound in leather under his arm. "Two for lunch, sir?"

"Yes, Roberto."

Bobby followed Roberto and Scotty through the entryway and into a dining room illuminated by fancy chandeliers and floor-to-ceiling windows and filled with dark wood paneling, dark wood columns, and dark wood tables covered with white tablecloths. Young brown men in white waistcoats and black bow ties served old white men. Roberto snapped his fingers at his underlings and gestured at glasses that needed to be filled and plates removed. The alluring aroma of grilled steaks, fresh fried shrimp, and charbroiled fish and the symphony of silver utensils against crystal and china joined together to remind Bobby of what might have been had his life taken a different turn here or there. He usually had lunch at the barbecue joint down the block where you ate at picnic tables on paper plates with plastic utensils.

While Bobby felt like Ralph Nader at a chamber of commerce meeting, Scotty strode through the dining room like the star halfback onto a football field, greeting and shaking hands with everyone he passed—that familiar Scotty Fenney entrance Bobby had witnessed so many times in the old days and from the same vantage point: behind Scotty Fenney. Bobby recognized the faces of the men Scotty was greeting from the business section of the newspaper. These men owned Dallas—the land, the buildings, the businesses, and everything else worth owning in the city. Scotty's attention was suddenly drawn across the room. He said to Bobby, "I'll be right there," and went over to a table of four men.

Bobby followed Roberto to a table by the window through which Bobby could gaze out upon the city where he had lived his entire life. Born poor in East Dallas, he had moved with his parents to a rental duplex near SMU the summer before ninth grade. They wanted a better life for their son, but they couldn't afford private school on his father's truck driver's pay. Instead their son would be educated in the Highland Park public school system just like the sons of the richest men in Dallas.

Bobby had met Scotty Fenney that first year, two renters seeking similarly situated companions—renters occupied a social status in Highland Park only a step above the Mexican household help. Bobby became Scotty's faithful follower, like Robin to Batman; and as Scotty's status rose with each football game, Bobby was pulled along in his friend's considerable wake, welcomed anywhere in Highland Park, as long as he was with Scotty Fenney.

After high school, Bobby had followed Scotty to SMU. Scotty got a football scholarship; Bobby got student loans. Four years later, he followed Scotty to law school. But a law degree had not led to a better life for him. The money is in the big law firms, and the big firms take only the best of the best, the top ten percent—the Scotty Fenneys, not the Bobby Herrins. All through law school, they had talked about practicing law together, but the big firms came calling and Scotty answered; and suddenly, like a Texas summer storm that dumps two inches of rain and then abruptly disappears, Scotty was gone. For the first time since he was fourteen, Bobby did not have Scotty Fenney to follow.

For eleven years now, Bobby had wandered through life like Moses in the Sinai Desert, trying to find his way without Scotty. He had caught glimpses of his old friend in the society section—Mr. and Mrs. A. Scott Fenney at such-and-such society ball—and sometimes in the business section—another courtroom victory or major deal engineered by A. Scott Fenney, Esq. Each time he read something about his old friend the memories would return and he would feel so completely alone again.

Still, through no real intent, Bobby had fashioned a life of sorts. Not much of a life—his exact thought that morning as he arrived at the office and stepped over a drunk on the doorstep, the start of another day of bailing out dopers at the jail, fighting evictions in J.P. court, eating Korean donuts, and drinking Mexican beer and playing pool in the bar next door. But then the phone rang and the caller identified herself as Scott Fenney's secretary. When she invited him to lunch with Scotty at the Downtown Club, Bobby thought he'd have to call 911 and have them hook him up to a defibrillator. He accepted, hung up the phone, took one look at his clothes, and immediately regretted his decision. He paced the office for an hour, deciding a dozen times to call back and cancel and a dozen times not to. When he finally pulled the old Impala into the parking garage under Dibrell Tower and the attendant looked it over and chuckled, he knew he was in over his head.

Bobby Herrin didn't belong at the Downtown Club.

He realized his finger was tapping the table like he was sending an urgent Morse code message. He craved a cigarette, but the Dallas city council had banned smoking in all public places. He desperately wanted to get up and walk out, to go back to East Dallas where he belonged. *Goddamnit, why had he accepted this lunch invitation?* Only because Scotty's secretary's call had caught him by surprise, he told himself, but he knew the truth: he wanted to see Scotty again.

He missed Scotty more than he missed his two ex-wives.

Bobby looked for Scotty and saw him several tables away, leaning over and whispering in the ear of a man whose face Bobby also recognized. Whatever Scotty said had made the man very happy. He stood and shook Scotty's hand, slapped him on the back, and damn near hugged him. Scotty walked over to Bobby with a big smile on his face and sat down across the table.

"You know Tom Dibrell?" Bobby asked.

"I'm his lawyer. Got him out of a crack yesterday. Literally." Scotty leaned over and whispered, "Tom's got a problem keeping his prick out of the payroll."

"Scotty, he's the guy who paid SMU players, got the football team the death penalty! You hated assholes like him back then. Now you're working for him? *Why?*"

Scotty smiled. "Three million bucks a year in legal fees, Bobby, that's why."

The number took Bobby's breath away: *three million*

bucks. Bobby's best year ever, he'd grossed $27,500. Only a few minutes together after eleven years apart, and he was already envying Scotty's life again. Sure, Bobby had loyal clients—one brought him homemade tamales each week, another had named her illegitimate son after him—and his money was no good at either the donut shop or the bar—free donuts and beer were the only perks his particular position offered—but his best client had paid him $500 last year; Scotty's best client paid him $3 million. In all English-speaking parts of Dallas, money was the only recognized measure of a lawyer's success; consequently, only among the Spanish-speaking population of East Dallas was Robert Herrin, Esq., not considered a total loser.

His mind was prying open the door to depression again, the point in each day when he would walk next door and down a few Tecates, when Roberto appeared with two glasses of iced tea and placed them on the table and then spread napkins in their laps, which made Bobby flinch—where he ate, someone leans in that close they're going for your wallet. After Roberto left, Bobby emptied two sweeteners in his tea, drank half the glass, and said, "Kind of surprised to get your call this morning, Scotty. Your secretary's call, anyway. But you know me, never could pass up a free lunch."

"So, how you been, Bobby?"

Bobby studied Scotty sitting there in his expensive suit and starched shirt and designer tie and looking like the Prince of Dallas and wondered if his old friend really gave a damn how Bobby Herrin had been. Used to be that when Bobby ran into an old law school classmate who had done better—which is to say, any law school classmate—they would both realize the awkwardness of the encounter and manufacture a quick escape. But there was no escaping here.

So Bobby said, "Scotty, when you get up in the morning, do you think good things are gonna happen to you that day?"

Scotty frowned a moment, then shrugged and said, "Yeah, I guess so."

"Why?"

Scotty shrugged again. "Good things have always happened to me."

"The best football player, best student, best looking, marries the most beautiful cheerleader, becomes a rich lawyer, and lives happily ever after?"

Scotty flashed that big smile again. "Something like that."

"Exactly like that."

"Yeah."

"Well, see, Scotty, it ain't like that for everybody. I don't wake up thinking good things are gonna happen that day. I wake up wondering what's the next bad thing that's gonna happen to me."

Scotty was staring at his water goblet with the same expression Bobby had seen on the faces of those other classmates he'd run into over the years, a look of abject embarrassment. But he was too far in to stop now.

"You graduated first in our class, Scotty. I graduated. Remember that old law school joke? What do they call the doctor who graduated last in his med school class? Doctor. What do they call the lawyer who graduated last in his law school class? Infrequently." Bobby lowered his eyes to the silver fork he was fiddling with. "Well, it's no joke."

Scotty did not respond immediately, so Bobby raised his eyes, expecting to see a haughty smirk; instead, he saw a hint of real concern on his old friend's face. Scotty and Bobby had been inseparable in college and law school: they had lived together, studied together, got drunk together, chased girls together (Bobby got Scotty's hand-me-downs), and played hoops and golf together. They were like brothers, right up until the day Scotty hired on with Ford Stevens at a starting salary of $100,000. They had not spoken since.

"Things haven't gone well?" Scotty asked.

"Clients you get from ads in the TV guide don't pay so well." Bobby shrugged and tried to smile. "Hey, life just didn't work out."

Scotty straightened in his chair. "Well, Bobby, let's have lunch and talk about that."

Scotty stuck a finger in the air and a waiter appeared instantly. Bobby was scanning a menu with entrées that cost more than his suit when he heard a thick Latino accent: "Mr. Herrin?"

He looked up at the waiter, a young Hispanic man, well groomed with erect posture. His face seemed vaguely familiar.

"Mr. Herrin, it's Carlos. Carlos Hernandez? Remember me, last year? You was my lawyer? Possession with intent to distribute?"

So many of Bobby's clients looked so much alike—young males, brown or black—and were charged with the same crimes—possession of a controlled substance, possession with intent to distribute, conspiracy to distribute; they were just two-bit users caught in the cross fire of the war against drugs. Sometimes he could remember a particular client by his tattoos—he vividly recalled a client named Hector (conspiracy to distribute) because his entire upper body was one big tattoo, a mural in honor of the Virgin Mary—but since Carlos here was clothed from his neck to his toes, Bobby could not remember Carlos from Jorge or Ricardo or Lupe. Still, he said, "Oh, yeah, Carlos. How you doing, man? You staying clean?"

A big grin from Carlos and a bigger lie, "Oh, yes, sir, Mr. Herrin."

They never stay clean. "Good man."

Scotty ordered salmon, Bobby a T-bone. As Carlos walked off, Bobby gestured after him. "My best client."

"You do a lot of criminal defense work?"

Bobby nodded. "I represent the petty criminal class. Guys like Carlos, they don't need estate plans."

"Federal court?"

"Yeah, since they federalized all the drug crimes."

Carlos soon returned with their food, and they ate and talked and laughed about the old days, old friends, good times, and their families. Scotty didn't know Bobby had been married and divorced twice; Bobby didn't know Scotty's mother had died or that he had a daughter. And for a brief moment it was eleven years ago and they were still best friends. But Bobby knew he was just Cinderella at the ball with the Prince of Dallas, and the fancy lunch at the fancy club would soon be over and he'd be back in his crappy office in East Dallas living his shitty life again representing clients like Carlos.

So when he finished his steak, he pushed his plate aside and said: "Scotty, I appreciate the lunch, man. It's been fun, catching up and all. But I know you didn't invite me up here just to catch up, not after all these years. What's up?"

Scotty glanced around, leaned in, and in a lowered voice said, "Buford appointed me to represent the hooker who murdered Clark McCall."

Bobby almost spit out his iced tea. "You're shittin' me."

"Nope."

Bobby Herrin might not be the brightest bulb in the box, but it didn't take him long to figure out this game: Scotty Fenney was giving him another hand-me-down.

"You want to hire her out?"

Scotty nodded. "Here's the deal. I met with the defendant this morning, Shawanda Jones, black girl, hooker, heroin addict—Christ, she damn near puked on my suit! Says she didn't kill him, but that's bullshit—her gun was the murder weapon. Says McCall picked her up on Harry Hines, offered her a thousand bucks for the night, took her home, started slapping her around, cursing her and"—his voice was a whisper now—"using the N-word." Back to his normal voice. "Anyway, they fought, she kicked him in the balls, took the money he owed her and his car keys, drove herself back to Harry Hines, and left the car. Police got her prints off the gun—she's got prior prostitution charges—and arrested her the next day. She refuses to plead out, wants a trial. Bobby, Ford Stevens can't represent a hooker!"

Bobby nodded. "Okay."

"Okay what?"

"I'll take her. What's the pay?"

"Fifty an hour?"

"Plus expenses."

"Like what?"

"Investigator, forensic experts, DNA tests . . ."

"Okay, but don't go overboard."

"Yeah, what the hell, she's just a nigger."

"I didn't say that, Bobby."

"Sorry. Cheap shot. You got a detention hearing?"

"Tomorrow morning, nine."

"I'll be there."

They stood. Bobby pulled out his parking ticket. "They validate?"

The athletic club was located on the top floor of the building adjacent to Dibrell Tower, connected by an air-conditioned skywalk so Scott Fenney didn't have to sweat on the way to his daily workout. Most of the office buildings in downtown Dallas were connected by skywalks or underground tunnels, air-conditioned passageways so the lawyers and bankers and businessmen didn't have to venture out into the heat or among the vagrants and panhandlers who called the downtown streets home; it was a prudent practice, particularly after a homeless man jumped a cop a few years back, grabbed his gun, and shot him point-blank in the face, right across the street from the downtown McDonald's.

Scott had just traversed one such skywalk. It was now half-past five and he was looking down on Dallas while running at 7.5 miles per hour up a ten-degree incline on a commercial treadmill and feeling pretty damn special. Which was not a new feeling for him. Scott Fenney had been special all his life. His father, Butch, had told him so when he was only eight, when he first put on pads and discovered his talent in peewee football. "You've got a gift, Scotty," Butch had said. Later his mother said the same thing: "You've got a gift, but I don't mean football," she said. He never understood what she meant, and then she died.

But the notion took hold and grew inside him, nurtured by eight years of high school and college football heroics; the fans, students, cheerleaders, boosters, coaches, and reporters all assured him daily that Scott Fenney was indeed special. It became a part of him, like the blue of his eyes. And it had never left him; it had only grown stronger, through three years at SMU law school and eleven years at Ford Stevens. But now, instead of athletic ability, it was money that made Scott Fenney special. Money enough to buy a mansion, a Ferrari, a perfect life—and even an old friend.

For the first time in the twenty-four hours since the judge's call, Scott's mind was clear, his spirits high, and his eyes locked on the backside of the girl running on the treadmill in front of him, her amazing buns barely shimmying as they pumped up and down like pistons. Scott pulled his eyes off her firm butt and glanced at the mirror to his right; he caught the girl on the treadmill behind him checking out his firm butt. Their eyes met and she winked, and that intoxicating feeling of male virility formed in his brain, coursed through his nerves and veins like a narcotic, and energized his muscles. He increased the speed to ten miles per hour. He loved being special.

When Scott walked into her bedroom that night, Boo was already in her pajamas and in bed, propped up on pillows against the headboard. Her hands were folded in her lap, her hair brushed smooth, and her face scrubbed pink. She smelled like fresh strawberries. She had positioned a chair next to the bed, as she did each night before bedtime, with the current book Scott was reading to her in the seat. Scott picked up the book and sat down, rubbed his eyes, and replaced his glasses.

"Where were we?" he asked.

"Number six," Boo said.

Scott opened the book and turned to the Sixth Amendment to the Constitution. Boo's teacher had mentioned the Bill of Rights in class one day, so naturally Boo wanted to know everything about these special rights she never knew she had.

So he read: " 'In all criminal prosecutions, the

accused shall enjoy the right to a speedy and public trial.' " He looked up. "What do you think that means?"

"The cops can't lock you up and throw away the key."

"That's right. And your trial can't be held in secret."

"So if your prostitute doesn't cop a plea, anyone can go to her trial."

"Yes. And she won't."

"Won't what?"

"Cop a plea."

Boo leaned forward, her eyes wide. "You talked to her?"

"This morning, at the jail."

"What's she like?"

Scott shrugged. "Young, not very well educated, strung out, says she's innocent."

"Do you think she is?"

Scott shook his head. "No. Her gun was the murder weapon and her fingerprints were on the gun."

"She had a gun?"

"Yeah."

"*Shit* . . . I mean, *wow*."

She leaned back, thinking, so he read again: " 'By an impartial jury.' You know what 'impartial' means?"

She shook her head. "Uh-uh."

"It means jurors who are fair, not prejudiced against the defendant. 'Prejudiced' means hating people just because they're different."

She nodded. "We talked about that at school last year during Kwanzaa. So if someone hates black people, they can't be on your prostitute's jury."

97

"That's right."

"How do you make sure?"

"You get to ask potential jurors questions before they become jurors."

"Like what?"

"Well, in the prostitute's case, you'd ask whether they're prejudiced against black people or prostitutes or drug addicts."

"But they'll just say no."

"Well, you don't ask it straight out; you ask subtle questions, like, uh, have they ever been to a black person's home? And you watch their body language, say a white guy is sitting next to a black guy, does he lean away."

"Have you?"

"Have I what?"

"Ever been to a black person's home?"

"Uh, no."

"But you're not prejudiced, are you?"

"No, Boo, of course not. I used to have black friends, guys I played ball with at SMU."

"Like who?"

"Well, like Rasheed . . . and Leroy . . . and Big Charlie—"

She smiled. "Who's Big Charlie?"

Now Scott was smiling. "Charles Jackson. He was my right offensive guard. He blocked for me. He saved me many times on the field . . . and a few times off the field."

"Y'all were good friends?"

Scott nodded. "Yeah. He was a great guy."

"Is he dead?"

"No . . . I don't think so."

"Why aren't y'all friends anymore?"

Scott shrugged. "He went off to play pro ball. I went to law school. We lost touch."

She nodded. "So the only reason you don't have black clients is because you don't represent people, only corporations."

"Exactly."

She pointed at the book. "What's next?"

Scott read again: " 'To be informed of the nature and cause of the accusation,' which means to be told the crime you're charged with."

"Murder, that's the crime your prostitute is charged with."

"Yes." Reading again: " 'To be confronted with the witnesses against him.' That means the prosecution must put the witnesses on the stand in court to testify against the defendant. 'To have compulsory process for obtaining witnesses in his favor.' That means you can call witnesses to help you."

"Your prostitute can get people to say she didn't do it."

"Right. If she can find anyone. And 'to have the assistance of counsel for his defense.' "

"What's counsel?"

"A lawyer."

"Your prostitute has a right to a lawyer?"

"Yes, she does."

"Even if she can't pay you?"

"Yes."

"Why?"

"Why what?"

"Why does she get you for free when everyone else has to pay you three hundred and fifty dollars an hour?"

"Well, George Washington and the other Founding Fathers . . . you know about them?" She nodded. "Well, they didn't think it would be fair for the government to charge someone with a crime but not give him a lawyer to defend him."

"Because he might be innocent and if he didn't have a lawyer to prove he's innocent, he might still go to jail."

"Exactly . . . well, the lawyer doesn't have to prove him innocent, the government's got to prove him guilty. And that's the lawyer's job, Boo, to make the government prove the defendant's guilt beyond any reasonable doubt."

"So the government proved your prostitute is guilty?"

"Not yet. And she's not *my* prostitute, Boo. She's my client."

"But you wanted her to cop a plea, say she's guilty."

"Yes, to confess that she did it."

"So the government wouldn't have to prove she's guilty."

"Right."

"Then why does she need you?"

Scott chuckled. "Well, I'm supposed to, uh . . . I mean, the court appoints a lawyer so she, uh . . . Well, the Bill of Rights says she has a right to a lawyer even if she's guilty and decides to confess. To make sure the rules are followed."

"And the judge appointed you to make sure the rules are followed for her?"

"Yes, but she doesn't want to confess. She wants to go to trial, so I hired her out."

She frowned. "Explain."

"I hired an old law school buddy to take her case to trial."

"Why?"

"Because I'm too busy."

"You're too busy to make the government prove she's guilty?"

"Yes. So I'm paying a friend to do it for me."

"Like if I hired a friend to do my homework?"

"Exactly . . . well, no, not exactly. You've got to do your own homework, Boo."

"Why?"

"Because that would be cheating."

"But it's not cheating if you're a lawyer?"

"Yes . . . well, no. I mean . . . it's complicated, Boo."

She pointed at the book. "Does that Sixth Amendment have one of those things, what did you call it, a pro . . . prov . . ."

"Proviso?"

"Yeah, a proviso."

"What do you mean?"

"A proviso that if the lawyer's real busy, you don't have a right to a lawyer?"

"No. But you don't have the right to a particular lawyer, just a lawyer."

"Any lawyer?"

"Yeah."

"Even a bad lawyer?"

Scott shrugged. "Yeah."

"Is your friend a good lawyer or a bad lawyer?"

"Well . . . I don't really know."

"Is he as good as you?"

Scott smiled. "No."

"So the judge appointed you as her lawyer and you're a great lawyer, but now she's going to get stuck with your friend, who's not so great?"

"Well, yeah. Not everyone can have me as their lawyer."

"Only corporations that can pay you three hundred and fifty dollars an hour."

"Exactly."

She sighed. "That doesn't seem like such a great deal."

"What?"

"That right to a lousy lawyer."

EIGHT

The next morning, Scott was back at the federal building at a quarter till nine, anxious to punt Shawanda Jones to Bobby Herrin and get back to his perfect life. Outside, he was mobbed by TV cameras and reporters sticking microphones in his face and shouting questions. He pushed his way through with several "No comments" and entered the courthouse. He rode the elevator to the fifteenth floor where he found Bobby standing outside Judge Buford's courtroom, wearing the same awful suit and smelling of cigarette smoke. They entered through tall double doors and took a seat in the church pews with the other lawyers awaiting their clients' hearings, arraignments, and sentencings.

For the last three decades, Judge Samuel Buford had presided over this courtroom. And looking at the waiting defendants, the drug dealers up on federal charges, black and brown and nervous, and the white-collar criminals, white and well-groomed and indignant that tax dollars were being wasted prosecuting them for securities and tax fraud—all wondering if they would be going home on probation or to the federal penitentiary for five to ten—Scott couldn't help but consider all the lives that had been changed in this one courtroom by this one judge. For raw power, it was hard to beat the law.

The bailiff called the first case on the docket: "*United States of America versus Shawanda Jones.*"

Scott put on his glasses—he always wore his glasses to court—and he and Bobby stood and stepped past the bar and to the defendant's table. A preppy lawyer, midthirties, walked over to them.

"Bobby, what, you moving up to the big leagues?" the lawyer said. His smirk indicated that it was a smartass comment, not a compliment. "I didn't know you were on this case."

"Just trying to help an innocent citizen being railroaded by an overzealous government prosecutor, Ray," Bobby said in a deadpan voice.

Ray chuckled and said, "Yeah, right," then extended his hand to Scott. "Ray Burns, Assistant U.S. Attorney."

Scott shook hands with Burns and said, "Scott Fenney, Ford Stevens."

"I heard Buford tapped private counsel for this case," Burns said. He turned his palms up and glanced from Scott to Bobby and back. "So, what, you bailing on the defendant?"

"No, I'm not bailing. I'm trying to do the right thing, hiring her a real criminal defense attorney."

"*The right thing?*" Burns said with the same smirk, clearly his trademark expression. "Looks an awful lot like bailing to me."

Ray Burns, Assistant U.S. Asshole, returned to the prosecution table, his right shoulder riding low under the weight of the king-sized chip he was carrying around. Government lawyers always have chips on their shoulders when dealing with big-firm lawyers like Scott because the big firms didn't hire them out of law school: if you can, you do; if you can't, you teach; if you can't teach, you hire on with Uncle Sam.

Bobby leaned in and whispered, "Burns is a dick. Trying to build a conviction record so he can move up to D.C. Asshole's put a couple of my clients away for life, for possession. Course he called it 'intent to distribute.' "

A side door opened and a strange black woman appeared in a white jail uniform. Scott stared at the woman for several seconds before realizing that she was Shawanda. She had looked awful yesterday; today she looked like she was dying. The same black guard escorted her into the courtroom, his arm under hers, almost carrying her over to Scott. By the time she arrived, her face was a brown frown.

"Morning, Shawanda."

Her entire body was trembling, shaking, twitching. Scott almost reached out and embraced her, to warm her like he did Boo when she got a chill after getting out of the pool, but at the last second the thought of his client throwing up on his expensive suit dissuaded him. He eased a step away from her.

"Who's him, Mr. Fenney?" she said in a weak voice, gesturing at Bobby.

"Bobby Herrin, your lawyer."

"Thought you my lawyer?"

"Shawanda, I represent corporations, not criminals . . . I mean, people charged with crimes. I hired you a real criminal defense attorney."

"All rise!"

The bailiff's voice boomed out and everyone in the courtroom stood as Judge Samuel Buford entered from a door behind the bench. He was the very image of a federal judge: the white hair, the patrician face, the black reading glasses, and the black robe. He sat behind the bench, which was elevated, as if to emphasize the supreme power of the law. To look him in the eye Scott had to angle his head up about twenty degrees.

"Be seated," the judge said. He shuffled through papers on his desk and glanced up over his glasses, first at Ray Burns, then at Scott and Shawanda and Bobby. Finally he said, "*United States of America versus Shawanda Jones.* Detention hearing."

He looked at Shawanda again.

"Ms. Jones, are you okay?"

He was a father asking his young daughter if she was hurt after falling off her bicycle. Shawanda nodded and the judge then turned to the lawyers.

"Gentlemen, please make your appearances."

Burns said, "Ray Burns, Assistant U.S. Attorney, for the government."

Then Scott said, "A. Scott Fenney, Ford Stevens, for the defendant. If I may, Your Honor, my firm has retained Robert Herrin, Esquire, to assume representation of the defendant. Mr. Herrin is a well-respected criminal defense attorney in Dallas. He possesses much more experience than I in criminal matters and will be able to provide the defendant a more competent defense. With the court's permission, I ask to withdraw from representation of the defendant and for Mr. Herrin to be substituted in my place."

The judge was eyeing Scott over his reading glasses; a wry smile crossed his face.

"Didn't really want to be another Atticus Finch after all, huh, Mr. Fenney?"

Scott knew better than to respond. The judge's smile dissolved into a look of disappointment that, for some odd reason, bothered Scott. The judge sighed and dropped his eyes. He started writing on what Scott knew was the case docket, officially substituting Robert Herrin, Esq., as counsel for the defendant in place of A. Scott Fenney, Esq. Scott felt like a kid about to get out of detention hall.

The judge said, "Well, since it's okay with Ms. Jones . . ."

Shawanda Jones rubbed her face but her skin felt numb. She hadn't slept in forty-eight hours; the cravings kept her awake all day and all night. She had never been without heroin for this long since she had gotten hooked, and it was killing her. Her mind was fuzzy and she couldn't get her thoughts straight. She had a blinding headache that wouldn't quit. She ached all over. Every muscle and bone in her body was throbbing with pain, and her skin was covered with goose bumps from the chills that swept over her regularly.

Her eyes were dry and gritty as she raised them to the white man standing to her right, this Robert Herrin Esquire. He was short, had a belly on him, and must have had bad acne as a boy because his face was pockmarked. His brown hair clearly hadn't been washed that morning. He was wearing the cheapest suit she had ever seen on a white lawyer—the damn thing *shined* under the fluorescent lights! His white shirt had yellowed a shade and its button-down collar was missing one of its buttons. His tie screamed *Sale at JCPenney!* No doubt, she made more money hooking than he did lawyering.

She turned to the white man to her left, Mr. Fenney. Tall and blond and handsome, wearing a dark pinstriped suit that hung like a silk dress over his broad shoulders, a crisp white shirt with French cuffs, a maroon silk tie, and the overall appearance of a white-boy version of the baddest pimp in the projects, he had a look that said, *I'm a stud.*

A stud or a dud?

Shawanda was twenty-four-years old. She had dropped out of school at age fifteen when she got pregnant. She had only nine years of formal education. But she wasn't stupid. And her prior experiences with the American legal system had taught her an important lesson, one she wasn't ever going to forget: rich lawyer means good lawyer; poor lawyer means bad lawyer. She looked up at the judge and said, "It ain't okay!"

Scott's heart froze as the words from the black woman standing next to him hit his brain. The judge's head shot up. His eyes locked on Shawanda Jones. Scott turned and stared down at her, stifling the urge to strangle this client who refused to go away quietly.

"What?" the judge asked.

"It ain't okay with me," Shawanda said. She pointed a trembling black finger at Scott. "Judge, I'm innocent and I want Mr. Fenney be my lawyer."

The judge yanked his reading glasses off his face and cocked his head at Scott.

"Mr. Fenney, did you not discuss this with your client prior to asking this court to substitute counsel?"

Scott cleared his throat. "Uh, no, sir."

"Well, maybe you should have." The judge returned to Shawanda. "Why?"

"Why what?"

"Why do you want Mr. Fenney as your lawyer?"

"Judge, I believe in him. I feel confidence in him. I know he can prove me innocent."

The judge again turned to Scott.

"Mr. Fenney, it's the defendant's right to counsel, so it's her decision."

"Your Honor, may I have a moment with Ms. Jones?"

The judge gave him a brief wave of the hand.

Scott stepped between Shawanda and the judge, leaned down to her, and whispered through clenched teeth: "Look, goddamnit, my firm is hiring a lawyer for you. I've got better things to do than take you to trial. I'm not gonna be your lawyer. Now you tell the judge it's okay for Bobby to represent you."

Scott straightened up and faced the judge. The judge held his hands up.

"Well, Ms. Jones?"

Shawanda again turned to Robert Herrin—*Dud!*—then to A. Scott Fenney—*Stud!* She pointed at Mr. Fenney and said, "I want him."

"Jesus H. Christ!" Dan Ford was upset now. "A goddamn hooker holding this firm hostage!"

Scott had just come from the courthouse with the bad news. "Can we appeal the appointment?" Scott asked.

"Hell, no! Even if we could, we wouldn't. That'd piss off Buford big-time. We would never be able to set foot in his court again."

"What am I supposed to do?"

Dan stared at his protégé, the finest young lawyer he'd come across in thirty-five years. The boy was a natural: smart, shrewd, articulate, and possessed of the intestinal fortitude to bill a client until he cried uncle. He looked upon Scott as his son.

"Keep Herrin on the case, let him do all the heavy lifting, write all briefs and motions, make all pretrial appearances—that'll keep the firm's name out of the papers and off TV. And no goddamn interviews, make sure Herrin knows that! You"—a finger pointed at Scott—"you work for our paying clients."

Dan checked his watch and walked over to the coat-rack. "Keep me posted. I don't want any surprises, Scott."

Scott departed, and Dan slipped into his coat; he was wearing a black suit today. He had to go to a funeral.

NINE

MOST RESIDENTS of Highland Park who knew Clark McCall always assumed he would die young. He was wild and reckless, to the degree only a child of enormous wealth could afford to be. A son of the middle class could not afford to squander his chances at admission to a top college and then law or medical school. But for Clark McCall, those considerations were of no concern: his father possessed a net worth in excess of $800 million.

Dan Ford was sitting in the sanctuary of the Highland Park United Methodist Church situated at the southern end of the SMU campus, waiting for Clark McCall's funeral service to begin. He had known Clark all the boy's life because he had known Clark's father for forty-two years. Dan had met Mack their freshman year at SMU when they had pledged the same fraternity.

With America at war in Vietnam and Uncle Sam drafting more young men to die, Dan Ford had decided to fight the war at a private college and then a private law school. He did not pursue a legal career out of any particular love of the law, only because of a particular fear of dying in some rice paddy ten thousand miles away. He wasn't alone in that fear: enrollment at America's law schools doubled during the war.

But once his future career was fixed, Dan Ford plotted a path to success. He knew lawyers got rich by representing rich clients. So, while most freshmen busied themselves with drinking and screwing, free of mommy and daddy for the first time, young Dan Ford began cultivating future clients.

Mack McCall was at the top of his list. As soon as you met him, you knew Mack was going places. He had that look about him. Born in Odessa, son of a roughneck and one himself, Mack was engaged to his high school sweetheart, the only daughter of an oil company vice president. His future father-in-law paid Mack's way through SMU.

Summers, Dan clerked in Dallas law firms, learning the ways of lawyers. Mack worked on West Texas oil rigs. Back then, oil was going for two bucks a barrel; Mack predicted ten dollars a barrel. Even he didn't dream of oil at fifty dollars a barrel.

By graduation day, Mack knew how to drill wells and, more important, he knew where to drill. Over the four years of college, he had mapped every producing well and dry hole in the Permian Basin. He hit his first wildcat well the summer after graduation. By the time Dan had graduated law school, Mack McCall was worth $20 million. Like H. L. Hunt and other Texas wildcatters before him, Mack McCall soon bored of what he could buy in an oil town, so he moved to Dallas. And Dan Ford, Esq., had his first rich client.

Dan now watched as the senior senator from Texas worked the church crowd as if his son's funeral was just another campaign stop, although he was wearing his version of a grief-stricken face. He was a handsome man, with a full head of starched gray hair, immaculately dressed as always, the kind of man teenagers go "yuk" at, but women of AARP find irresistibly attractive.

Organ music was playing softly in the background, voices were subdued, and Dan was sitting in a pew in the middle of the church, a good vantage point from which to see who came and who did not. Martha McCall, Mack's first wife and Clark's mother, arrived early and sat in the front pew with the other family members. She looked so old next to Jean McCall, but then, who wouldn't? Martha was the family station wagon parked next to a sleek sports car.

Dan's station wagon was parked next to him; she was almost his age and looked it. They had married right out of law school and immediately had a child, added insurance that Dan Ford would not be touring Indonesia courtesy of Uncle Sam. Over the years, Dan had had three brief affairs, if you called making it with a drunk secretary on the sofa in his office after the firm Christmas party an affair, but he had never considered divorcing his wife for another woman. First, there hadn't been another woman who had expressed any interest in becoming his next wife; and second, his true love was and had always been his law firm.

Political animals of every breed were making an

appearance at Clark McCall's funeral. They came not out of grief for the deceased, but because it was good for business: CEOs who needed McCall's vote to extend their special tax break or exemption from some onerous environmental regulation; members of Congress who dared not cross the most powerful man in the Senate; the vice president because network news cameras were present; cabinet members who hoped to be in a McCall administration; and judges—district court judges who wanted to be appeals court judges and appeals court judges who wanted to be Supreme Court justices, promotions requiring Senate confirmation. Clark McCall's funeral had brought together a collection of national figures from politics and business the likes of which Dallas had seldom seen. When you're the leading bet to be the next president, people come to your son's funeral.

And the stalwarts of funerals, the old ladies of Highland Park, had come, recalling how handsome Clark had been as a boy. The funeral guests were friends of the family, not friends of Clark. A few young men about Clark's age had come, themselves sons of great wealth who would forever be burdens to their parents. But no young women had come. Clark did not seem to have any female friends who mourned his passing.

Just as Dan's own son would have no female friends at his funeral; he had recently confessed to being gay. God knows, Clark's heterosexuality had never been in question. How many times had the senator called Dan in the middle of the night to bail Clark out of the Highland Park jail? Once a month, it seemed, during Clark's college career at

His only son was dead and buried.

They had never bonded, Mack McCall and his son. Clark had bonded with his mother; Mack had bonded with money. He reached into his inside coat pocket and removed and opened his billfold: not a single photograph of his son or either of his wives, but thick with the faces of Benjamin Franklin and Ulysses S. Grant. Money and power had been Mack McCall's lifelong companions, not a wife and son. Now he would use his money to buy the presidency of the United States of America.

He had spent $25 million to purchase a Senate seat, only to discover that the sole power senators wielded was the power to deliver pork to their home states, not unlike a mailman delivering Social Security checks. It was power that served only to ensure their incumbency.

But Mack McCall wanted to leave his footprints on this earth; he wanted history to know he had been here. Before the divorce, Martha had suggested he establish a private foundation, use his wealth to help the world's poor: AIDS victims in Africa, uneducated children in Mexico, homeless people in America. But even $800 million was a drop in the bucket when it came to the world's social problems. And besides, he had never concerned himself with the plight of poor people; it just wasn't his thing. So he divorced Martha and married Jean, and now he would spend as much of his fortune as necessary to buy the power he so coveted, the power to dispatch the United States Army. Wipe out a few Middle Eastern dictators, and history damn sure knows you were here.

Mack was standing in the bedroom of his Highland Park mansion where his son had been murdered. His mind began playing out the last moments of Clark's life according to the police report, moments filled with alcohol and cocaine and lust and rage and fear and a hooker—a nigger, for God's sake! His son had screwed her and fought her and then died right there on the floor where the carpet had been cut out and removed by the FBI. He saw Clark lying dead and felt the emotions welling up inside him and he thought, as he always thought when Clark came to mind:

What a major-league fuckup his son had been.

Anyone else's son and Mack would say the boy deserved it, living a reckless life, bringing a hooker home to Highland Park. But it was his son and that made it different: no one else in Highland Park was running for president. For the last twenty years, Mack McCall's every act, speech, public appearance, Senate vote—*every breath he took*—had been judged against one overriding concern: How would it affect his presidential ambitions? So now no conscious effort was required for his mind to judge his son's murder and all the publicity the hooker's trial would bring against the same concern.

Mack didn't like the conclusions his mind arrived at.

He had threatened to cut Clark out of his will on more than one occasion, an attempt to curb his son's reckless ways by threatening his future. But now it was the son who was threatening his father's future: the circumstances of Clark's death and his many indiscretions posed an imminent threat to Mack's White House dreams. And Mack McCall was not one to wait passively for a threat to become reality.

Two hours later, Mack was standing at the open double doors of the foyer, saying good-bye to those who had come to pay their respects. Dan Ford was the last to leave. Mack watched Dan walk down the long walkway to the circle drive where the valet held open the door to Dan's waiting Mercedes-Benz. Dan Ford would cooperate: a lawyer's loyalty could always be purchased for a reasonable fee.

"This Fenney boy," Mack said, "he played ball at SMU, pretty damn good as I recall."

Mack shut the front doors and turned to Delroy Lund, a big, bald, no-necked slab of beef. Delroy was not the brightest former DEA agent in the country, and he was plenty rough around the edges—subtlety wasn't Delroy's strong point—but he had proved himself a loyal bodyguard and capable private investigator, adept at uncovering dirty little secrets about senators who opposed Mack on various pork barrel bills and his ex-wife during their divorce proceedings.

"Find everything there is to find on Fenney, and I mean everything. I want his transcripts, bank records, debts, tax returns. I want to know his clients, his friends, his enemies, whether he's fucking around on his wife or she's fucking around on him." A pointed finger at his trusted manservant. "Delroy, I want to know how much he craps each morning. Understood?"

Delroy nodded.

"And no rough stuff this time, Delroy. I just want to control him."

Delroy shrugged and said, "You're the boss."

"Get me every newspaper article on the McCall murder case," Scott said to Sue. He gestured at Bobby sitting on the sofa. "Sue, this is Bobby Herrin. He's working with me on the case. Give her your card, Bobby, so she has your numbers."

Bobby dug around in his pockets, pulled out a crumpled card, and handed it to Sue, who was holding out a stack of pink message slips to Scott.

"Reporters and TV producers. They want you to appear on the morning news shows, *Dateline*, *20/20*, and—"

"Trash 'em. And call security: tell them to keep those reporters outside on the street."

"Frank Turner's still waiting."

"Show him in." To Bobby: "I always make plaintiffs' lawyers wait."

Scott slumped in his chair behind the mahogany desk. Last time he felt like this was after the knee injury his freshman season.

"Just when you think you got the world by the balls," Scott said, "you find out the world's got you by the balls."

"Welcome to my world," Bobby said.

Sue escorted Frank Turner into Scott's office. Frank

appeared every inch the rich plaintiffs' lawyer, expensively dressed, his hair perfect, looking tanned and rested from another jaunt to Cancún aboard his personal Lear jet, the bastard. Frank had lucked into one major toxic tort verdict a decade ago, and he had never had to take a case to a jury again. His reputation forced every corporate defendant to settle for a substantial sum, one-third of which went into Frank's pocket. So while Scott Fenney had a Ferrari, Frank Turner had a Lear.

Scott did not stand. "Frank, I didn't expect you to come over personally."

Frank grinned and said, "I always show up to collect funds."

"Ah, the personal touch." Scott gestured over at Bobby on the sofa. "Frank, Bobby Herrin. Bobby, Frank Turner, famous plaintiffs' lawyer."

They shook hands, then Frank gestured at the big blowup of Scott Fenney, number 22, on the far wall above the sofa.

"That the day you got a hundred and ninety-three yards against Texas?"

"Yep, that was the day."

Frank's eyes lingered on the blowup, and in Frank's eyes Scott saw the envy of a tuba player. But Frank Turner was now a plaintiffs' lawyer and he was here for money, so he finally turned to Scott and said, "You got the check?"

"You got the release?" Scott asked.

Frank held out a document, which Scott took and scanned to make sure the bastard hadn't changed anything.

Satisfied, he turned to the signature page and saw that sweet Nadine and sleazy Frank had both signed in triplicate. He then handed a cashier's check to Frank Turner.

"One million dollars, Frank."

Frank stared at the check a moment and then broke into a birthday-boy smile.

Scott said, "So is this what you do every day, Frank, walk from office to office picking up big settlement checks?"

Frank's face took on an expression of thoughtfulness, then he smiled again. "Yeah, Scott, now that you mention it, that is pretty much what I do."

The smile still on his face and a million-dollar check in his hand, he headed to the door, but stopped abruptly and turned back. He held the check up to Scott.

"Oh, just so you know, Scott, Nadine would've taken half a million."

Frank was turning away again when Scott said, "Well, since we're confessing, Frank, just so you know, Tom would've paid two million."

Frank's smile evaporated like a raindrop on the sidewalk outside and his shoulders slumped: the only thing that makes a plaintiffs' lawyer lose sleep is leaving money on the table. He turned and slithered away, not thinking that he had just *made* $333,333.33, but that he had just *lost* the same amount. Which left Scott with something of a moral victory, at least.

"Asshole," Scott said.

"Who, me?"

Sid Greenberg's head was in the door. Scott motioned him in.

"Sid, meet Bobby Herrin."

Sid stepped over and shook hands with Bobby. "How'd it go this morning? You taking over the hooker?"

"Not exactly," Scott said.

"The judge wouldn't let you out?"

"No. Looks like I'm stuck with her. Bobby's going to carry the heavy end of the log, write the briefs and motions, make all pretrial appearances—"

Sid smiled at Bobby. "Do all the work, like I do for Scott on Dibrell matters."

Sid's smile disappeared when he turned to Scott and saw that Scott wasn't smiling.

"Yeah, Sid, only difference is, I need Bobby. You can be replaced."

Sid squirmed and forced a sheepish grin. Scott never let on with associates whether he was serious when he made remarks like that, which kept them on their toes and billing hours.

"Why are you standing on my Persian rug, Sid?"

"Oh, we signed up the environmental consultant on Dibrell's land deal. He now works for Ford Stevens. That was a brilliant idea, Scott."

Sid was in damage control mode.

"That it?"

"Well, no. One more thing, Scott." He glanced at Bobby, then back at Scott. "Confidential."

Scott said, "Close your ears, Bobby."

He nodded to Sid to go on.

"Our discovery, production of documents, is due on that Dibrell lawsuit, the one where all the residents in his apartment complex are claiming they were harmed by mold in their apartments and he didn't do anything about it?"

"Yeah, so?"

"So in going through Dibrell's records, we found one letter that might prove troublesome. It mentions some of the symptoms of mold poisoning. But we've taken the position that Dibrell didn't have any knowledge of the dangers of mold."

Scott, to Bobby: "A goddamn lawsuit over mold. One jury in Austin comes back with a thirty-two-million-dollar verdict, next thing you know everyone's dying of mold poisoning."

Back to Sid: "How many pages of production are we giving the plaintiffs' lawyer?"

"Twenty-seven thousand."

"Okay, here's what you do. Double copy everything, so we give them fifty-four thousand pages. And put everything out of order, a real mess. Then make one really bad copy of that letter, you know, like our secretaries do without meaning to, where you can hardly read it. And stick it right in the middle of those fifty-four thousand pages, see if they can find it."

Sid was grinning. "That's brilliant!"

"Aggressive and creative lawyering, Sid."

Among lawyers, employing clever litigation tactics like hiding one damaging document in fifty-four thousand pages of discovery—not to mention just shredding the damn thing—is known as "aggressive and creative lawyering," and it is a skill highly praised by members of the bar. Aggressive and creative lawyering is how successful lawyers become successful, that and not getting caught. A big part of being successful, Scott had learned, was not getting caught.

Sid scurried away, and Scott gestured after him.

"First in his class at Harvard. Might make a lawyer out of him yet."

Bobby was giving him a look.

Scott held his hands up. *"What?"*

"That's what you high-rent lawyers do, play hide the ball?"

"It's just like football, Bobby—if you don't get caught holding, you didn't hold. When you're playing this game against sleazy plaintiffs' lawyers like Frank Turner, you play by the same rules they play by. You do whatever it takes to win—because rich clients don't want ethical lawyers who lose, Bobby. They want lawyers who win."

Bobby seemed unconvinced, so Scott pointed his finger at the open door.

"Bobby, that bastard Frank's got a jet!"

Scott's thoughts returned to Shawanda Jones, like one's thoughts did to a recurring nightmare.

"Oh, and no interviews, Bobby. We want to keep the firm's name out of the press."

Bobby nodded. "I'll get the police report, see what evidence Burns has got, hire a PI. He'll interview witnesses, track down leads, do background checks on Clark and anyone connected to Clark. Name is Carl, he's an ex-cop."

"Dan's gonna crap, paying for a private investigator."

"Scotty, we gotta have a PI. It's a death penalty case."

Scott sighed. "Okay, but hide his fees in your bills to the firm. So Dan doesn't see them."

"Yeah, okay. Uh, Scotty, this case is gonna eat up a lot of my time. I'll have to incur some expenses and . . . well . . . you think I could get an advance on my fees?"

"Sure." To his secretary: "Sue!" She popped in within seconds. "Sue, get Bobby a firm check for twenty-five hundred."

When she left, Bobby said, "Thanks."

Scott waved him off. Twenty-five hundred was pocket change at Ford Stevens.

"Kind of funny, ain't it, Scotty?"

"What?"

"Back in school, we used to talk about working together. After all this time, we are." He shrugged. "Kind of funny."

Scott stared at his former best friend.

"Yeah, Bobby, this is fucking hilarious."

Boo screamed with delight. "A. Scott, you're on TV!"

Her father and mother walked over to the kitchen TV and saw what she saw: on the evening news, A. Scott looking like a reluctant movie star, pushing through a crowd of TV cameras and microphones as reporters shouted questions.

"Did your client murder Clark McCall?"

"How will she plead?"

"What's your defense?"

"This morning," her father said. "The mob at the courthouse."

"You couldn't get out of the case?" Boo asked.

"No."

"You're going to trial?"

"Yeah."

"When?"

"August."

"Well, there goes Vail," her mother said with an exasperated sigh. "We'll be the only family in Highland Park suffering here in August. That'll be embarrassing."

"Can I go?" Boo asked.

"Yeah, you and Mom can still go to Vail," her father said.

"No. To the trial."

"You want to come to the trial?"

"I'll still be out of school."

"No, you may not, young lady," her mother said. "A murder trial is no place for a nine-year-old girl."

"But it'll be like, history in the making."

Her mother gave her another exasperated sigh. "Murder trials happen every day."

"No, I mean A. Scott representing a human being."

Her father looked at her and she at him; they both laughed.

*

Rebecca was not laughing.

"This won't affect your position in the firm?"

Upon retiring to the master suite, that was Rebecca's first and only question, her way of asking, *Will this affect your income?*

"No, of course not. I'm still Tom Dibrell's lawyer."

Her expression said she wasn't buying it.

"Rebecca, look, I've got Bobby working the case. He'll get me through it, she'll get convicted, and things will go back to normal. Don't worry."

But Scott was worried. That feeling of impending doom had grown stronger. He plopped down in his chair in the sitting area off the master bedroom and used the remote to turn on the TV. The late news. A story about Clark McCall's funeral this afternoon, video of people in dark suits and dark dresses entering Highland Park First United Methodist Church, wealthy people, white people, important people, the vice president, members of Congress, the governor, the mayor, and Scott's senior partner.

TEN

THE REST OF JUNE passed quietly. The temperature climbed steadily as summer set in so that by the end of the month the mercury was pushing one hundred degrees Fahrenheit. Rain became an infrequent occurrence and the sun beat down on the landscape with a vengeance. Native oak trees burrowed their roots deeper into the earth to suck the last drop of moisture from the parched Texas soil, and all God's creatures hunkered down for another merciless summer, except those wealthy Dallas families who could afford to flee to the cool air of Colorado or California. The less fortunate remained behind and relied on air-conditioning and backyard pools to survive the heat.

Rebecca Fenney continued her relentless climb up the Highland Park social ladder; Boo Fenney occupied herself at home with her computer and her books; Consuela de la Rosa was reunited with Esteban Garcia, just back from the border; Scott Fenney billed two hundred hours at $350 an hour for Ford Stevens's paying clients; Bobby Herrin billed one hundred hours at $50 an hour for the firm's only nonpaying client; and the federal grand jury formally indicted Shawanda Jones for the murder of Clark McCall. The federal magistrate set her bail at $1 million, which meant she would remain in custody until the verdict was read, at which time she would be either set free or shipped off to a federal prison to serve her sentence or await execution. She called her lawyer daily, sometimes several times a day, always crying hysterically from the combined effect of craving both her daughter and heroin. Having no idea where he might acquire heroin for her, her lawyer did the only thing he knew to get her to shut the fuck up: he agreed to bring her daughter down to the detention center to see her. Or at least to have Bobby bring her daughter to her.

But Bobby copped a plea: fear. "Shit, Scotty, East Dallas is scary enough for me," he said. "Fat white dude like myself, I wouldn't last five minutes in South Dallas. Sorry, man, but no way I'm risking my life for fifty bucks an hour!"

So it was that on the second day of July and the first hundred-degree day of the summer, A. Scott Fenney, Esq., $750,000-a-year corporate partner at Ford Stevens LLP, found himself driving a shiny red Ferrari 360 Modena slowly through a grim public housing project in South Dallas, past the rhythmic pounding of loud rap music and the glares of tough-looking young black men, and feeling as if he were driving a flashing neon sign that screamed *CARJACK ME!* Scott had played football with black teammates at SMU fourteen years ago, but he didn't figure that would count for much with these guys.

Without conscious thought, Scott slid down the leather seat until he could barely see over the steering wheel.

Thirty-six years Scott Fenney had lived in Dallas and not once had he driven into South Dallas. White people drove south of downtown three times each year and only for events held within the gated Fair Park grounds—the State Fair, the Oklahoma-Texas football game, and the Cotton Bowl game—being careful to stay on the interstate, to take the Fair Park exit, and to drive directly through the park gates without detour or delay. White people never drove *into* South Dallas, into the neighborhoods and mean streets of South Dallas, into the other Dallas of crime and crack cocaine, prostitution and poverty, drive-by shootings and gangbangers, into black Dallas, where a white boy from Highland Park driving a $200,000 Italian sports car was considered neither welcome nor very smart.

But here Scott was, parking in front of a concrete block building euphemistically called a "garden apartment" by the housing authority, although not a blade of grass much less a garden was evident to Scott's eye. He cut the engine and was working up the courage to get out—the Ferrari had attracted a crowd—when the sun was suddenly blocked out by a Dallas Cowboys jersey on the biggest black man he'd ever seen on or off a football field. Black knuckles rapped against the blacked-out window. Scott lowered the window an inch.

The jersey moved down until Scott saw wide shoulders, a thick neck, and finally a broad black face. The man lowered his sunglasses and peered in.

"You the lawyer?"

"What?"

"You Shawanda's lawyer?"

"Yeah."

"You here for Pajamae?"

"Yeah, how—"

"Shawanda call me. She figured you might need a, uh . . . chaperone, if you know what I mean."

Scott knew what he meant. He looked out both sides of the car at the crowd looking in, black women— girls really—with babies on their hips and toddlers clutching their thick legs and muscular black males, and he thought of Fight Night, the last time he had been in such close proximity to strong young black males. Started during the depths of the great Texas real-estate bust when the Dallas real-estate community desperately needed a distraction, Fight Night had become an annual tuxedo tradition: a boxing ring was set up in the swanky Anatole Hotel and black boxers were brought in to beat themselves senseless for the entertainment of rich white men smoking big cigars, eating thick steaks, drinking hard liquor, and playing patty-cake with beautiful young models hired for the night. Scott remembered thinking that the black boxers might be has-beens in the professional ranks, but they could KO every white guy in the joint with one punch—and probably wanted to.

Scott put on his glasses, not to appear smart, but in the hope that these black guys wouldn't beat up a white guy wearing glasses. He took a deep breath, opened the door, climbed out, and stood pressed against the Ferrari. He felt his face flush and heard the big man's voice boom out:

"Y'all back off, give the man some room! He's the lawyer!"

The crowd eased back several steps. Scott exhaled with relief, then inhaled the air, which felt even hotter down here, not a whiff of breeze or a tree in sight to offer shade from the sun, its full force seemingly directed down on him. Beads of sweat popped out of the pores on his forehead like popcorn and his starched shirt stuck to his skin. He glanced around at the gray bunkerlike buildings, the gray dirt yards, the gray concrete landscape, and the black residents, a strange world in the shadows of the downtown skyscrapers. If Scott's office faced south, his view would be of these projects, hence, the preferred northerly view, toward white Highland Park. Only five miles of pavement separated these projects from Highland Park, but the black kids plastering their faces against the Ferrari's windows to catch a glimpse of the plush leather interior might as well have been living in China.

"That a fine ride, mister," one black boy said with a wide grin.

The big man said, "I'm Louis." He gestured at the crowd. "Don't mind all them. We don't get many lawyers down here."

Louis stood maybe six six and weighed well over three hundred pounds. His huge hands dwarfed Scott's. So Scott didn't offer to shake hands; instead he said,

"Scott Fenney," and handed his card to Louis, who examined it intently.

"What the *A* stand for?"

"Nothing." Scott pointed a thumb at the Ferrari. "Maybe I should wait in the car."

Louis said sternly to the boys: "Touch that car, you answering to me." Then he smiled at Scott and said, "Car be okay, Mr. Fenney." Louis turned and the crowd parted. Scott followed Louis a few paces up the sidewalk, but Louis abruptly stopped and turned back. "Still, you might wanna lock it."

"Oh, yeah."

Scott dug the keys out of his pocket and beeped the Ferrari locked and one of the boys said, "Aw, man!" Scott turned and followed Louis through a gauntlet of shirtless young black men bouncing basketballs so hard against the concrete it sounded like high-powered weapons discharging—*boom boom boom*. Their torsos were knotty with muscles and glistening with sweat, their sinewy arms etched with barbed-wire tattoos, their expressions sullen. They were wearing long shorts hung low on their hips and those $100 Nikes Scott couldn't afford as a boy and looking on Scott Fenney as prey, which no doubt he would have been but for the presence of Louis. Scott avoided direct eye contact with them like they say to do with wild animals for fear of inciting them. He wanted to cut and run back to the car and drive full throttle out of here. But he'd never make it to the Ferrari: the image of a pack of wolves pouncing on a fat little rabbit flashed through his mind. So he closed the gap with Louis and followed in the black man's shadow. And he had to admit to himself, he who had never felt fear on a football field felt it now. Scott Fenney was terrified. By the time they arrived at apartment 110, Scott's heart was beating against his chest wall like a jackhammer and he had broken a full-body sweat. Louis knocked on the door.

"Pajamae, it's Louis."

No answer. Louis knocked again. Still no answer. The front window was covered with thick drapes inside and black burglar bars outside. No light was visible from within the apartment.

"Maybe she's not home," Scott said.

Louis's body shook with a chuckle. "She home all right. She afraid to come outside. Don't even open the windows even though ain't no air-condition in there. She ain't come outside since Shawanda arrested." He leaned down and lowered his voice and said, "It's a good thing you doing, Mr. Fenney, taking Pajamae to see her mama."

Scott's mind was busy considering his chances of making it back through the gauntlet alive so the words, "Why didn't you?" were out of his mouth before he realized what he was saying. But Louis didn't react angrily. Instead, his big round face folded into a gold-toothed smile.

"Well, Mr. Fenney, me and the Feds, we got some, uh, outstanding issues, if you know what I mean."

Scott knew what Louis meant. He noticed the peephole in the door turn dark. And he heard a tiny voice: "That the lawyer?"

"Yeah," Louis said.

The peephole went light again and Scott heard the sound of a heavy object being pushed away from the door, then the releasing of five deadbolts. The door opened a crack and a small brown face with big brown eyes gazed up at Scott.

"You gonna save my mama?" she asked.

"Pajamae. That's a, uh, different sort of name."

Her face glued to the Ferrari's air-conditioning vent, the little black girl said, "Mama says it's French, but it's really just black. We don't do names like Susie and Patty and Mandy down here. We do names like Shantay and Beyoncé and Pajamae."

"My daughter's name is Boo."

She smiled. "That's different."

Scott smiled back. "She's different. You'd like her."

Scott had relaxed considerably once they had left the projects and turned onto Martin Luther King Boulevard, the main thoroughfare through South Dallas. His heartbeat was near normal and his body wasn't sweating like a sprinkler hose. He wasn't even slouched in his seat. He was sitting upright, looking around at this strange environment like a Japanese tourist at a rodeo. On one side of the street was the tall black wrought-iron fence that guarded the Fair Park grounds; inside were the Cotton Bowl stadium where the Cowboys had played until they struck out for the suburbs, and the historic Art Deco buildings dating back to the Texas Centennial Exposition of 1936 that now sat abandoned and decaying like an old movie set. On the other side of the street were overgrown vacant lots that apparently served as the neighborhood's unofficial dumps, and boarded-up structures with broken-out windows and black men loitering outside.

"Crack houses," Pajamae said.

Run-down strip centers offered pawn shops and liquor stores. Ramshackle frame houses slanted at twenty-degree angles, their paint peeling like skin from a badly sunburned body. Sofas sat on droopy porches, old cars were jacked up on cement blocks in the yards, garbage was backed up at the streets, and black burglar bars guarded every door and window of every house and storefront as if each structure were its owner's personal prison. The entire landscape was dull and colorless, except for the graffiti adorning every wall and fence and the thick-bodied black women strolling by in colorful skirts and shorts and heels.

"Working girls," Pajamae said. "Mama says they work down here because they're too fat to get white tricks on Harry Hines."

Scott was imagining living in this neighborhood, walking these streets with Boo, or worse, Boo walking alone, when his peripheral vision caught a commotion at the side of the road, and he slowed . . . a little.

"What's going on?"

On the sidewalk outside a dilapidated apartment complex was a massive pile of belongings, everything from a microwave to clothes, a basketball to dolls, as if someone had backed up a truck and dumped the stuff there. Sitting on the curb were two black kids, their elbows on their knees, their chins cradled in their palms, looking like their world had just come to an end. An obese black woman in red stretch shorts and a white tee shirt was yelling and gesturing wildly at a skinny black man wearing a short-sleeve shirt and a tie. Pajamae strained her neck to see, then slumped back down.

"Eviction day," she said matter-of-factly.

"They got evicted from their apartment?"

"Yeah. Happens first of every month."

As a young lawyer, Scott had appeared in J.P. court numerous times on behalf of landlords to evict deadbeat tenants. But he had never witnessed firsthand the law in action—a family's personal property removed from their apartment and dumped on the sidewalk out front, exactly as the eviction statute mandated. He glanced back at the scene and then accelerated away. When the Ferrari's expensive racing tires hit the interstate heading north to downtown Dallas, he breathed a sigh of relief.

"My daddy, he was white," Pajamae said.

He glanced over at the girl in the passenger's seat. She was a cute kid with facial features that were more white than black. Her hair was done in neat rows braided lengthwise and snug to her scalp with long braids hanging to her narrow shoulders; she was wearing a pink tee shirt, jean shorts, pink socks folded down, and white Nike sneakers. Other than her light brown skin, she was no different from all the little girls Scott had seen in Highland Park—except for the cornrows.

"Where is he?"

"Dead."

"Oh. I'm sorry."

"I'm not. He hurt my mama."

"How did he die?"

"Po-lice shot him. He was dealing."

She ran her finger lightly over the dash, as if checking for dust, and then she turned to Scott.

"Mr. Fenney, did my mama kill that white man?"

"No, baby, I ain't killed no one," Shawanda said through the glass partition, her right palm plastered to her side of the window and matched by Pajamae's left palm on the other side. Both mother and daughter were crying and aching to hold each other. When Shawanda had said she had a child, Scott had naturally assumed she was a lousy mother—she was a prostitute, for God's sake. But seeing them together now, it occurred to him that this woman loved her daughter as much as he loved his. He turned to the black guard.

"Can't they be together?"

The guard's eyes dropped; he scratched his chin. When his eyes came back up, he said, "You here to discuss her defense?"

Scott caught on quickly. "Yes."

The guard gestured at Pajamae. "She a material witness?"

"Yes."

"Okay."

The guard led them to the small room where Scott

and Shawanda always met. He patted Scott down, but he only patted the top of Pajamae's head. When he brought Shawanda in, she dropped to her knees and embraced Pajamae for the longest time. The guard said he'd wait outside. Shawanda finally released Pajamae, then cupped her daughter's face and just stared at her, as if examining every inch of her smooth face. Then she held Pajamae at arm's length and looked her up and down.

"You dress yourself real nice," Shawanda said. "Louis bringing you groceries, watching out for you?"

Pajamae nodded. "Yes, Mama."

"You staying inside?"

Another nod. "Yes, Mama."

Shawanda appeared in much better health than the last time Scott had seen her, more alert, making Scott less worried she might puke on his suit.

"You sleeping now?" Scott asked.

"Yes, sir, Mr. Fenney. I'm over the worst part, except the headaches."

"I brought your medicine, Mama," Pajamae said.

"Good girl."

"I always take Tylenol for headaches," Scott said.

"I need something stronger."

"Ibuprofen?"

"Yeah, Ibu . . . that."

"When are you getting out, Mama?"

"I ain't, not till after the trial. If Mr. Fenney here prove me innocent."

Scott said, "No, Shawanda, I don't have to prove you're innocent. The government's got to prove you're guilty."

Shawanda looked at him like an adult at a naïve child.

"Mr. Fenney, you got a lot to learn."

"When's the trial?" Pajamae asked.

"End of August," Scott said.

Pajamae made a face. "But that's two months from now! What am I supposed to do for that long? Mama, I'm scared to be alone in the projects!"

And the fear Scott Fenney had experienced less than an hour earlier returned with a vengeance. Sweat broke out on his forehead again. His heart beat faster again. His mind played out his odds of survival again, a fat little rabbit chased by a pack of wolves. He did not want to go back into South Dallas, not today, not ever. He did not want to take this little black girl back to her apartment in the projects and get out of the Ferrari and walk her to the door through a gauntlet of strong young black males looking upon him as prey. What if Louis weren't there to chaperone? But he couldn't very well put a little girl on a public bus or in a taxi alone. What the hell could he do with her? While mother and daughter embraced and shared tears, Scott's agile mind worked through all the available options until it arrived at an answer: Consuela de la Rosa.

He figured, Consuela's raising one little girl this summer, why not two? It was a perfect solution: Boo would have a playmate, this little girl wouldn't be scared and alone in the projects, and he wouldn't have to drive back into South Dallas. So in the emotion of the moment, Scott Fenney said words his wife would soon regret: "Pajamae, why don't you stay at my house until after the trial?"

"What the hell am I supposed to do with her?"

Rebecca's face was as red as her hair, her fists were embedded in her narrow hips, and she was glaring at him like he was a Neiman Marcus salesclerk who had brought her the wrong size dress to try on.

Scott had driven home directly from the courthouse. But as luck would have it, he had picked the one day his wife was not out social climbing to bring this little black girl home to Highland Park. Boo had said, "I love your hair," and then had taken Pajamae upstairs. Consuela had retreated to the kitchen, and Scott found himself facing Rebecca's wrath alone. Of course, Scott wasn't about to tell his wife the whole truth, that he had brought this little black girl home mostly because he was scared to death to take her back to her own home. So he responded like a lawyer. He told her only part of the truth, the part that supported his position.

"She's living alone down in the projects, she's nine years old, she doesn't have anyone else—she doesn't even have air-conditioning! Hell, Rebecca, you go to Junior League and sit around with other Highland Park ladies dreaming up ways to help the less fortunate. This should win you the goddamn grand prize!"

"We help those people, Scott, but we don't invite them home. You said yourself her mother's going to be convicted. What are you going to do with her then,

142

adopt her? Raise her as your daughter? Send her to Highland Park schools? Scott, there's not another black kid at Boo's school!"

Sometimes, as now, the intensity of his wife's anger unnerved Scott, much as when his college coach would grab his face mask and pull him close and chew him out over a blown play. Back then Scott Fenney would stand mute before his coach, and now he stood mute before this beautiful angry woman. Only difference was, little bits of chewing tobacco were not spewing out of her mouth with each angry word and sticking to Scott's face. Still, he would gladly swap this angry woman for wet tobacco in a heartbeat.

"And there's sure as hell not another girl named Pajamae!"

ELEVEN

$\mathcal{S}$COTTY, WITH THIS EVIDENCE, we just might save her life." Scott had escaped his wife's wrath and found sanctuary in the friendly confines of Dibrell Tower; he and Bobby were having a late lunch upstairs at the Downtown Club. He had filled Bobby in on his visit to the projects and the Fenney family's new houseguest and Rebecca's reaction. Now Bobby was bringing Scott up to date on Shawanda's legal case.

"My man Carl, the PI, he finds this Kiki, she backs up Shawanda's story. No surprise there. But then he talks to some Highland Park cops he's buddies with." Bobby leaned across the table, close enough for Scott to smell his last cigarette on his breath; his voice dropped to a whisper. "Get this: turns out Clark McCall was accused of rape and assault a year ago. SMU sorority girl. She filed a complaint, but it disappeared when daddy— as in Senator Mack McCall—paid her off. Carl talked to the desk sergeant on duty that night, cop that took the complaint. He said the girl was slapped around pretty good."

"How are we going to find her without the complaint?"

"Desk sergeant, he ain't stupid. Figures the senator knows he knows, so he also figures it might come in handy one day: he kept a copy of the complaint."

"Did he give it to Carl?"

"No way. He said it's locked away in a safe-deposit box. Said if he gave it to Carl, they'd know it came from him, he'd get fired, and he's only two years away from a pension. Said he'll deny having it if we call him to testify. But he gave Carl the woman's name, Hannah Steele. She lives in Galveston now."

"Will she testify?"

"Carl's flying down there today to find out."

Scott turned his palms up. "So . . . ?"

"So our defense is twofold. First, she didn't pull the trigger, which is gonna be tough with her fingerprints on her gun and one of her bullets in his brain. And if she didn't, who did? Clark? He suddenly realizes his evil ways and decides to make the world a better place and off himself? I don't think so. Our backup is self-defense. He called her racial slurs, he attacked her, so she shot him in self-defense. But she's black, a hooker, and a drug addict—who's gonna believe her, right? That's where Hannah Steele comes in, corroborating testimony. Nice white girl testifies Clark beat and raped her a year ago, jury figures maybe Shawanda's telling the truth. And the jury's got to include some blacks. We show them that Clark McCall was a racist and a rapist, we might just save her life."

"An acquittal?"

Bobby gave him a look. "No, not an acquittal, Scotty. Life in prison, maybe parole in thirty with good time. You don't get acquitted when your gun is the murder weapon and your fingerprints are on the gun and the gun was fired point-blank into the victim's brain while he was lying on the floor. With that kind of evidence, life in prison is a win for her."

"Goddamnit, Dan, you tell him to drop it and drop it now!"

The senator's voice was so loud in Dan Ford's ear that he pulled the phone away a few inches. Dan had just gotten a status report from Scott on the Shawanda Jones case and, per his agreement with the senator, he had immediately placed a call to Washington. Mack McCall, the senior senator from Texas, didn't like what he heard.

"Bad enough, Dan, a hooker taking the stand and saying Clark beat her and called her nigger. But your boy starts parading white girls up there saying Clark beat and raped them, too, I'm fucking finished! I thought that girl was taken care of! And what if they dredge up that crap from college, Clark and his fraternity?"

Clark McCall had organized a "Minority Night" fraternity party where everyone dressed up as their favorite minority; Clark had gone in blackface as a pimp. Mack had bought off the newspaper to keep the story quiet. Dan Ford had been the bagman.

"The public will think he learned that at home!

From me! Press gets hold of that, I'll be branded another Strom fucking Thurmond! I'll never see the inside of the White House!" A pause. "And, Dan, you will never be the president's lawyer."

"George W. Bush?"

"Yes," Scott said.

Sid Greenberg seemed stunned. "The president used eminent domain to take people's land for a baseball stadium?"

"He wasn't the president back then, Sid. He wasn't even the governor yet. While you were at Harvard being taught by left-wing professors, George Bush was running the Texas Rangers. They were playing in a crappy old stadium, so he got the city to condemn land to build a new stadium."

"How is that a public use?"

"It's not."

"Then how could the city condemn the land?"

"Because the law allows it . . . or at least the courts haven't stopped it. They did it for the Rangers stadium, they did it for the NASCAR motor speedway, they're doing it for the new Cowboys stadium . . . Hell, Sid, they're doing it all across the country and not just for roads and parks, but for stadiums and shopping malls and big box stores . . ."

"And now we're going to do it for Dibrell's hotel."

Scott shrugged. "That's the deal Tom made with the city."

"We're going to take poor people's homes so rich people can stay in a five-star luxury hotel?" Sid looked indignant. "Why don't they ever take rich people's homes?"

"Because rich people can afford to hire lawyers and fight it in court. Poor people can't."

"So the city's gonna buy them out cheap—with Dibrell's money, bulldoze their homes, and give the land to Dibrell so he can build his hotel? What's in it for the city?"

"Millions more in property taxes. The hotel will be worth a hundred million, minimum. Those little homes are worth a million, max."

"Dibrell gets his hotel, the city gets more taxes, and poor people get screwed. And it's all perfectly legal."

"Sid, we do what the law allows . . . and sometimes what it doesn't."

"You know, Scott, screwing the government and plaintiffs' lawyers, that's fun, it's just a game. But poor people? My parents were poor. I grew up in a house like those."

"Look, Sid, I don't like it either, but that's our job. At least we're only taking thirty homes. They took a hundred twenty homes for that mall out in Hurst, and they're taking ninety homes for the Cowboys stadium."

"Well, that makes me feel better." Sid shook his head. "This is what I went to Harvard Law School for?"

Scott turned his palms up. "Sid, what do you want me to do? Tell Dibrell we won't do it? If I say no to Dibrell, he'll find another lawyer who'll say yes. This deal is gonna get done, those homes are gonna get condemned, and that hotel is gonna get built. The only question is which lawyers are going to get paid half a million dollars for doing it. If Dibrell takes this deal to another firm, Sid, that means I've got to fire one of my associates. Are you willing to give up your job—and your two-hundred-thousand-dollar salary—so you don't have to condemn those people? So you don't get your hands dirty?"

Sid stared at his shoes. Finally, he shook his head slowly and said, "No."

"Sid, when I was a young lawyer, Dan Ford told me, 'Scotty, check your conscience at the door each morning or you won't last long in the law.' "

Sid looked up. "The law sucks."

"It's just business, Sid."

"They don't tell you that in law school, do they, that the law is just a business, a game we play, with other people's lives and money? No, they need someone to pay tuition, kids who don't have a clue what being a lawyer's all about, kids who think . . ."

Scott sat silently, nodding like a therapist as his patient vented. Every lawyer goes through the same metamorphosis that Sid was now going through, like a caterpillar changing into a butterfly, only in reverse: from a beautiful human being to a slimy lawyer. Scott recalled Dan Ford nodding as a young patient named Scott Fenney vented.

Sid was saying, "Last time I went back home, my parents had all their friends in the old neighborhood over so they could show me off, their son the big-time lawyer. How am I supposed to tell them what we really do, Scott?"

"You're not. You can't. You *don't*. You walk out that door each night, you leave it here, Sid, your lawyer life. You don't take it home with you. Look, Sid, you've only been at this for five years. It takes a while to learn that you only talk about these things with other lawyers. Regular people just don't understand what we do."

"That's the thing, Scott, I think they do."

"Sid, wait till you get married, have children, you'll see. You'll go home and your wife and kids are gonna say, 'Daddy, what did you do today?' What are you going to tell them, the truth? Hell, no. You're gonna lie. We all lie."

Sid took a moment to consider Scott's words, then slowly stood and walked to the door, but turned back.

"Oh, Scott, we closed Dibrell's land deal. We got the environmental report, escrowed $10 million of the purchase price. We'll start paving over the lead soon. TRAIL will never know about the report, and the EPA will never know about the lead."

"Aggressive and creative lawyering, Sid."

Sid nodded and turned away, but Scott could hear him say, "I should've gone to med school."

After Sid left Scott turned to his computer. He was logging in one billable hour to Dibrell's account for the thirty-minute "office conference" with Sid when he felt a presence. He turned and saw Dan Ford standing in his doorway, about as ordinary an occurrence as going to Sunday morning Mass and seeing the Pope standing at the altar.

"Dan, come in."

Dan entered, his face creased with worry. He started shaking his head slowly and sighed like a man with the weight of the world on his shoulders.

"I knew this case would bring no good."

"What do you mean?"

"I just got off the phone with McCall."

"*The senator?* You mentioned him before, but I didn't realize you knew him personally."

Dan nodded. "Mack and I were fraternity brothers at SMU. I'm the executor of his will, I handle a few personal matters for him from time to time. Haven't done much work for him since he sold the company and went to Washington twenty years ago. But if he's elected and Ford Stevens is recognized as the president's personal law firm . . . Scotty, it'd be a gold mine."

"Great."

"Yes, that would be great, Scotty. We could add fifty lawyers, maybe more, on the new business we'd get, corporate clients who'd beat a path to my door and pay any fee I demanded because I could pick up the phone and get the president to answer. You got any idea what that's worth to a lawyer? I'm a big fish in a small pond here in Dallas, Scotty, but as the president's lawyer, I'd be a big fish in a big pond. I'd be playing on a national stage . . . We could open a Washington office. Think what that could do for me. For this firm. For you. Scotty, you could make a million dollars the first year he's in office, two the year after that, three by the time you're forty. You'd be filthy rich, just like you tell our summer clerks."

Dan paused and caught his breath. "But Mack made it clear that if his son's good name is dragged through the mud at this trial, Ford Stevens will not be his personal law firm."

Scott leaned back in his chair. "He wants me to hide Clark's past."

"Yes, he does."

"But, Dan, Clark McCall was a rapist and a racist. And now with Hannah Steele's testimony, we might save Shawanda's life."

"Yes, you might at that. But you would also destroy Mack's chances to be president. Scotty, if the press can put 'racist' and 'rapist' and 'McCall' in the same sentence—even if it's about his son—his chances of winning the nomination are about as good as me getting laid by Miss America."

"Dan, why didn't you tell me you did work for McCall? I could've told Buford we had a conflict of interest, gotten out of the case."

Dan nodded. "I talked to Mack about that option, but he said it would be better to have some, uh, influence with the hooker's lawyer."

"In case her lawyer learned about Clark's past."

Dan shrugged. "Mack McCall didn't make eight hundred million dollars by not thinking out all the angles."

"Clark McCall was a loser, Dan. Rich boy who liked

to beat up girls ends up dead because he beat up the wrong girl. Why should we give a damn about his reputation?"

"We don't. But this isn't about Clark McCall, Scott, it's about Mack McCall. And we do give a damn about his reputation because it's in this firm's best interest for him to be the next president. Scotty, we hold his presidency in our hands! Think about it. He'd owe me big-time!"

His eyes got a faraway look and his mouth formed a half smile, which meant inside Dan Ford was turning somersaults. After a moment, he returned to the present and said, "So what do you say, Scotty, my boy?"

Scott said nothing. The two lawyers, separated by twenty-five feet of hardwood floor and almost as many years of lawyering, stared at each other as if they were two kids trying to see who would blink first. Scott knew what his senior partner wanted him to say, that he would follow McCall's orders because what was good for McCall was good for Ford Stevens. But—and Scott couldn't put into thought why—he couldn't bring himself to say those words. Whether born of the mulelike stubbornness he had inherited from Butch or his long-standing general disdain for rich boys like Clark McCall or perhaps something deeper, something inside him wouldn't allow it. Finally, Dan broke eye contact, exhaled loudly, and turned to the door. On his way out, he said, "Scott, I need an answer for McCall. Soon."

*

Boo sat up in the lounge chair by the pool in the backyard. She was wearing a white bathing suit and sunglasses and drinking pink punch Consuela had made. Pajamae was lying facedown in the adjacent lounge chair, wearing one of Boo's many bathing suits. They were taking turns rubbing sunscreen onto each other's back. It was Boo's turn. She lifted Pajamae's long braids and squirted a line of sunscreen onto her back.

A normal summer afternoon for Boo was spent home alone, reading a book. A. Scott was downtown, Mother was at the country club, and most of the kids her age were at their summer homes or at camp or in Europe. Not that Barbara Boo Fenney had many friends here in the Bubble. Most girls her age wanted to brag about their things. She didn't. She was different. She thought different thoughts and she wore different clothes and she wanted different things. The other girls said she was weird and called her a lesbo because she didn't dress like a girl. So she usually played by herself or swam under Consuela's watchful eye. But today she had a new friend. Who was different, too.

"I love your hair," Boo said. She began rubbing the white lotion into Pajamae's brown skin. "Do black people need sunscreen?"

After a moment, Pajamae said, "I don't know. But Mama always makes me put it on."

"When will she get out of jail?"

"End of summer, if Mr. Fenney gets her out."

"If she didn't do it, she'll get out."

"Don't work that way for us."

that he could simply dictate to A. Scott Fenney, Esq., the terms of his representation of a client. The legal code of ethics to which all lawyers swear allegiance (at least long enough to obtain a license to practice law) clearly states (in theory) that a lawyer shall not be influenced by any outside interests in the zealous representation of his client. Of course, in practice the code of ethics is viewed by most lawyers in the same way career criminals view the penal code: more in the nature of suggestions than actual rules governing one's professional conduct.

On the other hand, Scott was also wondering why he hadn't readily agreed to McCall's demands as requested by his senior partner. Scott had never gone against Dan Ford's wishes—that would be like going against his own father. He had rubber-stamped all of Dan's decisions for the firm, whether firing a partner or dumping a client or making campaign contributions to friendly judges up for reelection, because Dan was always acting in the best interests of Ford Stevens and thus in Scott's best interests. Why had he hesitated this time? For the first time?

Back to the first hand: the fact that United States Senator Mack McCall just *assumed* Scott Fenney would drop his client's best defense to a murder charge simply because McCall told him to, that should have brought Scott's blood to a boil. *Who the hell does he think he is?* Back in college, if someone had even dared suggest that Scott Fenney, star halfback, might throw a game, he would have gotten pissed off and punched the son of a bitch in the mouth! Just for thinking he possessed so little integrity as to even entertain the idea of throwing a football game! So why wasn't A. Scott Fenney, Esq., similarly pissed off when asked to throw a trial? Why was he even entertaining the idea? Had he engaged in so much aggressive and creative lawyering that he no longer recognized the difference between making a deal and compromising his integrity? Had he become such a good lawyer that he had no integrity left to compromise?

He was wrestling with these thoughts as he drove past the walled estates along Preston Road that backed up to Turtle Creek, the grand residences of real-estate tycoon Trammell Crow ($13.3 million appraised value), and Dallas Cowboys owner Jerry Jones ($14.1 million), and Tom Dibrell ($18 million), and Mack McCall ($25 million)—and he realized that it had never before registered with him that McCall and his best client owned adjoining estates. He slowed as he passed the entrance to the McCall estate and was thinking back to the night of the murder, Clark and Shawanda driving in through those gates, only minutes remaining in Clark McCall's life, when his cell phone rang. He answered.

"Scott Fenney."

"Mr. Fenney, this is Louis."

"Louis . . ."

"From the projects."

"Oh, yeah, sure, Louis."

"Well, Mr. Fenney, Pajamae, she ain't come back yet, and I be getting kinda worried . . . She still with you?"

"Oh, Louis, I'm sorry, I should've had my secretary call you. Pajamae's going to stay with us until the trial's over."

"Us who?"

"Me. My family."

"You taking Pajamae in?"

"Well, yeah, you know, until this is over. We were down at the courthouse with Shawanda this morning and I didn't want to drive—" Scott decided not to mention that he didn't want to return to Louis's part of town—"and, well, I've got a daughter her age, and we've got four bedrooms sitting empty, and I just thought it might be better that way. Shawanda thought so, too."

"What about her stuff, clothes and all?"

"Oh, she can wear my daughter's clothes. They're about the same size and, hell, my daughter never wears half the clothes my wife buys her anyway."

"You want, I can bring her stuff to you."

"To Highland Park?"

The phone was silent. Scott thought again he might have angered Louis. But he was wrong again.

"Louis?"

"Projects ain't no place for a little girl living alone, Mr. Fenney. Tell her I said hey. And if you need any help down my way, you let me know."

"Okay, thanks, Louis."

"Oh, and Mr. Fenney . . ."

"Yeah?"

"I guess I wouldn't expect something like that from a white man. You a good man, Mr. Fenney."

Scott disconnected and wondered if Louis was right.

*

Boo bounced down the stairs to the kitchen and over to the table, followed by Pajamae. Mother took one look at Boo, put her hands on her hips, and said, "Young lady, what have you done to your hair?"

Boo's long red hair was now braided tight to her scalp with long braids hanging to her shoulders.

"Cornrows. Pajamae did it. Pretty cool, huh?"

Mother turned to A. Scott and said, "Well, Scott?"

He shrugged and said, "She looks like Bo Derek."

"Bo Derek?"

"Yeah, from that movie."

Mother threw her hands up. "Barbara Boo Fenney, Highland Park debutantes don't wear their hair in corn-rows!"

"Then it's not a problem, Mother, because I'm not gonna be a deb."

Mother sighed heavily, restraining her anger, and said, "Pajamae, I hope you don't have any tattoos."

Pajamae laughed, but she didn't know Mother wasn't being funny. Consuela held up the salt and pepper shakers and said from the stove, "Is twins, like these." She pointed at Boo—"Is salt"—and then at Pajamae—"is pepper." Consuela chuckled and her body shook like Jell-O. "Salt and pepper."

Mother was shaking her head and her lips were a tight line across her face, normally not a good sign.

"Finish the enchiladas, Consuela."

"Y'all expecting company?" Pajamae asked.

Boo turned to Pajamae, who was standing at the table.

"What?"

"All this food, are you having a party?"

The table was crowded with tacos and enchiladas and guacamole and refried beans and flour tortillas and hot sauce. Mexican food night.

"No."

"This is all just for us?"

Boo shrugged. "Yeah."

Pajamae smiled and said, "Where-*as*."

Butch and Barbara Fenney had always discussed family matters at the dinner table, in front of their young son: good things and bad things, successes and failures, possibilities and problems. They figured he would learn by listening. Scott recalled one such conversation, not too long before his father died, when Butch said a contractor wanted him to cut some corners on a job to reduce costs and increase the contractor's profits. The owner would never know. Butch was faced with either complying with the contractor's demands or losing the job. He asked his wife for advice. Scott's mother responded without a second thought: tell him no.

So after retiring to the master suite, while Rebecca stood naked before the bathroom mirror and removed her makeup and checked her body for early signs of aging, Scott told her about Dan's visit to his office and Mack McCall's demands and he asked his wife for advice. She, too, responded without a second thought: "Do it! If Dan says drop it, you damn well better drop it. Are you going

160

to give up everything we have for a goddamn—"

"What, Rebecca? A goddamn what?"

She whirled around, incredibly naked, and said, "A goddamn black whore, that's what!"

A. Scott Fenney, Esq., had zealously defended his rich clients against all comers—business competitors, the government, famous plaintiffs' lawyers, and young women claiming sexual harassment. But never against his wife. Of course, he had never had a black whore for a client. Still, his natural lawyerly instinct was to defend his client. So, perhaps because McCall's demands were still weighing on his mind or because he had never thrown a game in his life or because rich boys like Clark McCall had always graveled his butt or because he knew Louis was not right about Scott Fenney or because of the love Shawanda showed for Pajamae that very morning or because of two little girls with their hair in cornrows on the floor above . . . or maybe just because this beautiful woman standing naked before him had denied him sex for over seven months . . . and his heat for her now turned into anger at her—Scott Fenney lashed out at his wife, defending Shawanda Jones with a passion normally reserved for only the richest of clients: "What, she deserves to die just because she's black and a prostitute? What if you had been born black, Rebecca? Would you still have been Miss SMU and chairwoman of the Cattle Barons' Ball? Or would you have ended up a hooker on Harry Hines, too?" He pointed to the floor above. "But for the grace of God, Rebecca, Boo could be that little black girl!"

His naked wife laughed without smiling.

"Don't you get self-righteous with me, Scott Fenney. You wanted money and all the things money can buy as much as I did—this house, that Ferrari . . . How much did you pay for that suit? I married you because you had ambition, you wanted to be a rich lawyer. You didn't go to work at the legal aid so you could help poor black people in South Dallas. You went to a big law firm so you could make lots of money working for rich clients living in Highland Park. And now you're suddenly growing a conscience? I don't think so."

She pointed a finger at Scott. "You do this, you ruin my life over a whore—who you know goddamn well is guilty as sin—and I swear to God, we're through!" She now pointed upward. "And that little girl will be better off without her mother."

Upstairs on the third floor, Boo and Pajamae were getting ready for bed. A. Scott had read to them, which Pajamae enjoyed. It was fun to have a friend. Boo had insisted they share her room so they could talk. Pajamae agreed. But now Boo was kneeling up in bed and wondering what the heck Pajamae was doing, spreading out a comforter on the floor with a pillow.

"What in the Sam Hill are you doing?"

"Whose hill?"

"It's just an expression."

"Oh. Fixing my bed."

"On the floor?"

162

Pajamae looked at her bed on the floor, then at Boo in the tall bed. "You sleep in the bed?"

Boo laughed. "Of course I do. Where do you sleep?"

"On the floor."

"Oh, you don't have a real bed?"

"No, I've got a bed."

"Do you have a bad back? Sometimes A. Scott sleeps on the floor when his back acts up, from when he played football."

"No, I don't have a bad back."

"Then why?"

"It's safer."

"From what?"

"Gunfire."

After some discussion, Boo convinced Pajamae that it was safe to sleep in a bed in Highland Park, and they were sleeping side by side an hour later when Scott climbed the stairs, as he did each night before going to bed, to check on his daughter and to kiss her on the forehead. The two girls were lying so close together that when he leaned over and kissed Boo, he had only to lean over just a little more to kiss Pajamae on the forehead as well. When he did, she stirred and whispered in her sleep, "Daddy?"

TWELVE

THE COMPETITION from other Dallas law firms for the top law graduates each year was fierce. Ford Stevens offered the same starting salary, required the same billable hours, and promised the same personal chemistry between partners and associates. Money and hours were easy sells; personal chemistry, though, took all of the partners' lawyering skills, pretending to care about these students' lives when in fact they cared more about their own shoes. But then, lying to law students was just part of the game.

And that game was being played in earnest today at 4000 Beverly Drive. Scott Fenney was hosting Ford Stevens's annual Fourth of July party for the firm's summer clerks at his Highland Park home. He was standing on the patio under the awning and shaking his head: forty out-of-shape law students in bathing suits, their pale white bodies frolicking in and around his fabulous pool and professionally landscaped backyard, was not a pretty sight. Thank God they had the good sense not to wear Speedos. If not for Missy and the other cheerleaders in bikinis, the view from the patio would have been downright dismal.

"Got some good news, Scotty."

He hadn't noticed Bobby there. "What's that?"

"Talked to Hannah Steele. She'll testify. Told me the whole story about Clark, said he was the nicest guy in the world until he got loaded, then he turned into an animal. His idea of foreplay was smacking her across the face." Bobby took a swig of beer. "Shawanda did the world a favor, blowing his brains out."

"So she's it then, our only defense?"

"Yep. But she wants her name kept quiet until the trial. She's scared shitless of McCall."

"Don't we have to put her on our witness list?"

Bobby shrugged. "We're supposed to. But Buford, he'll cut us some slack, seeing how he hates the death penalty and Burns won't give it up. Did you read my brief on that, why the death penalty doesn't apply to this case under the statute?"

Scott shook his head.

"Have you read any of my briefs or motions?"

"I haven't had time."

Bobby grunted and went in search of the barbecue, leaving Scott to his thoughts, which were of Dan Ford: *Scott, I need an answer for McCall. Soon.*

"Well, if it isn't Johnnie Cochran."

Bernie Cohen had arrived with a beer in his hand.

"What's your whore's defense, Scott?" His next words came out in his version of rap rhythm. "If the condom don't fit, you must acquit?"

Bernie thought he was hilarious. He was a partner in the securities section of Ford Stevens and looked like he was fifty years old even though he was only a year older than Scott. No muscular definition was noticeable anywhere on his body; Bernard Cohen was what in junior high they called a "fat-butted boy." Bernie pointed his beer at Boo and Pajamae sitting on the edge of the far side of the pool.

"That her daughter?"

"Yeah."

"She's living with you?"

"Yeah."

"Saw your client's photo in the paper. She's a good-looking black babe." Bernie nudged Scott's arm and grinned. "She paying you in kind?"

"Shut up, Bernie."

Bernie recoiled, snorted, and walked away, leaving Scott to wonder why at one time he had sort of liked the pudgy prick. And why he wasn't enjoying the party the way he had last year when he had taken great pride in showing off his residence to the impressionable students: the one-acre estate in the heart of Highland Park; the four-car garage occupied by the Ferrari, Rebecca's Mercedes-Benz coupe, and the Land Rover they used for family road trips; and the expansive covered patio overlooking the pool and cabana, beyond which was a vast expanse of grass kept lush and green by the underground sprinkler system. Scott had set up a volleyball net out there and some of the students were now playing. He shook his head—not an athlete in the bunch.

This year he just couldn't get into the spirit of the day. The students were happy, the cheerleaders were friendly, the beer was flowing, and the barbecue was cooking . . . but Scott's thoughts were on Shawanda Jones and the little black girl sitting on the far side of the pool and his wife's threat and Dan Ford's demand. *Scott, I need an answer for McCall. Soon.* The trial was only seven weeks away, and Scott had a big decision to make, a decision he didn't want to make, a decision that had darkened his mind. That feeling of impending doom had become his constant companion.

Sitting on the edge of the pool, Pajamae said, "I haven't been around this many white people since last year when Mama took me to the State Fair. Only time we see white people."

"You haven't missed much," Boo said.

Pajamae waved her hand around. "Who are they?"

"Lawyer wannabes."

"Whatabes?"

"Students A. Scott's law firm is trying to hire."

"Those are some homely white boys. But the girls are real pretty. Are they their women?"

"The cheerleaders?"

"They're cheerleaders?"

"They used to be. A. Scott pays them to come to the party and act interested in the students, so they'll hire on. He calls it bait and switch."

"Bait and what?"

"Bait and switch, like when an ad in the paper says certain Rollerblades are on sale, but when you get to the store they say they're sold out so you should buy another brand that costs more."

"Oh, like when a trick tries to get Mama to lower her price after she gets in his car."

"Someone tricked your mother into his car?"

"No, the trick—that's the john."

"The toilet?"

"No, a man who wants to buy Mama."

"Your mother's for sale?"

Pajamae nodded. "By the hour."

"A. Scott sells himself by the hour, too. He calls them billable hours. He charges three hundred fifty dollars an hour."

"Mama makes almost that much and she didn't go to school."

"Awesome. Anyway, these students think if they hire on with A. Scott's law firm they'll get dates with beautiful girls like these, but they really won't."

"If they pay enough, they will. Mama says it's just a question of pricing."

On brutally hot days like today, Bobby would often grab a beer, go out back of his two-bedroom, one-bath lean-to in East Dallas, and sit in a six-inch-deep inflatable pool—his version of a pool party. This pool party was a lot better. For one thing, the pool was bigger. And for another, his eyes weren't closed and he wasn't dreaming of a backyard full of beautiful girls in bikinis; his eyes were wide open and the girls were real. He was really happy Scotty had invited him.

Bobby was standing alone at one corner of the pool, a beer in one hand and a long pork rib in the other, dripping barbecue sauce on his bare belly and trying not to appear too obvious as he ogled the girls. He was wearing only swim trunks. His pale body was not lean and tanned and muscular like Scotty's. Still, compared to the law students, he was feeling like a regular goddamned Adonis when an incredible looking girl in a white bikini sidled up to him, close enough that he could feel the warmth emanating from her skin. Without thinking, Bobby sucked in his gut—a little.

"Noticed you're not wearing a wedding ring," she said.

"That's because I'm not married."

"What a coincidence," she said, turning her big eyes up to him. "Neither am I."

Bobby had already downed several beers, so his courage was operating at its maximum level.

"So what's a gorgeous single girl like yourself doing at a party like this?"

"Looking for a rich lawyer like you."

You can't fault honesty, Bobby thought, as she leaned into him and her breasts pushed together and rose as one until he thought they might pop out of her bikini top. The mere touch of her skin against his raised a distinct feeling in Bobby's trunks.

"Well, just so you know, I don't have a home like

this, I'm not a rich lawyer, and chances are pretty good I'm never gonna be a rich lawyer. But, hey, we can still slip inside, find a quiet place, and screw ourselves silly."

She pulled back as if she had suddenly discovered poison ivy all over his body. She gave him a thin smile and said, "I don't think so."

And she was gone. Bobby closed his eyes and inhaled her scent one last time. But it was soon gone, too, as was the rise in his swim trunks. He walked over to the only two girls who weren't looking for a rich lawyer that day. Boo and Pajamae were sitting on the edge of the pool, dangling their feet into the water.

"Hey, Bobby," Boo said.

"Girls."

Pajamae said, "Whereas, Mr. Herrin."

Scotty had introduced Bobby to the girls earlier. Bobby now joined them, dropping his feet into the cool water.

"Where's your mother?" he asked Boo. "Haven't seen her since I first got here."

"Back inside," Boo said. "She hates these parties."

"What about you?"

"Oh, I love them. I try to guess what these people's lives are like when they're not sucking up to A. Scott for a job."

Bobby laughed. "Scotty said you're nine going on twenty-nine." He pointed the pork rib at one of the male students. "Okay, tell me about his life, the skinny one with the black glasses."

Boo studied the student for a moment and said,

"He's incredibly smart. He went to law school only because his dad is a lawyer, but he wants to do computer stuff. He'll graduate top of his class, hire on with A. Scott's firm, and quit after one year. He's never had a date, he's terribly shy, and he's wishing right now he was back home at his computer, where he's happiest. He's always going to be alone."

Bobby stared down at the child in amazement. "That's pretty good. Okay, Pajamae, your turn. What about her, the blonde over there with the, uh . . ."

"Store-bought boobs?"

"Uh, yeah, that one. What's her story?"

"She's way dumb, but she doesn't know it. She'll marry a rich lawyer and live happily ever after."

Bobby found himself nodding in agreement.

"You girls are good. Okay, Boo, what about this guy?"

Boo moved her eyes about, scanning the pool crowd. "Which guy?"

Bobby was now pointing the pork rib at himself. "Me."

Boo considered him for a moment, then dropped her eyes to the water and shook her head.

"Hey, come on, tell me."

Boo looked back up; her eyes seemed sad.

"No, Bobby."

Bobby laughed and said, "What? I'm a big boy, I can handle it," figuring she was going to say he was a pathetic loser and always would be. Hell, no surprise there. He told himself the same thing every morning in the mirror.

But Boo was quiet. Then, without looking at him, she said: "You secretly loved my mother, but she married A. Scott. You've never gotten over it. You've always wondered what your life would've been like if she had married you instead."

Bobby hadn't figured on that. He had to take a deep breath. He pushed himself up but looked down at her.

"How?"

"I saw how you looked at her when you got here. Your eyes went all over the crowd, kind of frantic like, until you saw her. Then you just looked at her for a long time. Like, forever."

Bobby walked directly to the beer cooler.

From the windows of the master suite on the second floor Rebecca Fenney was looking down on the backyard scene at two of the three men who loved her: Scott, surrounded by law students and cheerleaders and one buxom blonde in a black string bikini giving him the come-on; and Bobby, alone by the beer cooler. Poor Bobby. She had known he loved her back when he and Scott were in law school, but he had kept it to himself, never one to challenge for any of Scott's possessions. Not that he could have won her; everyone knew Bobby Herrin wasn't going places, just as everyone knew Scott Fenney was. So Rebecca Garrett had signed on for the Scott Fenney ride. And it had been quite a ride: eleven years ago she had been living in a sorority house, driving a used Toyota, and leading cheers for the SMU Mustangs; today she was living in a mansion, driving a Mercedes, and vying to be chairwoman of the Cattle Barons' Ball. But now she found herself feeling anxious and afraid and wondering: *Is the ride coming to an end?*

Rebecca Garrett had grown up in a working-class suburb of Dallas. She hated having less; she wanted more. So for her college education she looked no further than SMU. For poor Dallas kids, SMU was their entrée to a better life. It was a way in to Highland Park.

Rebecca was a smart student, in and out of class. In fact, when she drove her old car up and down the streets of Highland Park and fancied herself the woman of the house at one of the fabulous mansions, she was smart enough to acknowledge a fact of life: she would never have a Highland Park home on her own, by using her brain, by pursuing a career. No woman would.

Her future lay in her looks, as it always had. From the time she was ten, other children's mothers would stop and say, "My, what a remarkably beautiful child"; and when she was sixteen and her body had become a woman's, her friends' fathers would stare; and when she was twenty-one and the most beautiful girl at SMU and she interviewed for jobs, men's eyes lit up when they saw her beauty—they wanted it and they would pay for it.

But she would not sell her beauty by the hour or by the night or even by the job. Rebecca Garrett would sell her beauty for community property, for half of everything her husband would acquire over the course of their marriage. As every Texas girl knows by the time she graduates high school, in Texas wives don't have to beg for alimony; in Texas wives are entitled to half of everything—by law.

So she needed a husband. As she saw it, her beauty afforded her three matrimonial options: an older man who had already made his fortune (but such a man always comes with baggage, usually a couple of ex-wives and twice as many kids on the dole); the son of such an older rich man (but an inherited fortune is not community property); or a man with the ambition to make his own fortune, a fortune made during marriage, a fortune of community property. Scott Fenney, a Highland Park and SMU football legend, was just that kind of man. There is no better place in the world to be a football legend than Dallas, Texas. It's as close to an iron-clad guarantee of success as life offers.

So Rebecca Garrett bet her beauty on Scott Fenney.

She loved him back then, but she would not have married him if he had wanted to coach high school football and live in a small house in the suburbs. She could not separate her love from his ambition. She loved him because he wanted what she wanted, because his desire to have all this equaled her own. They were two of a kind. So they married and settled in a small $500,000 home in Highland Park; Scott became Tom Dibrell's lawyer and she became the most beautiful woman in Highland Park.

The early years of the Scott Fenney ride were exactly what she had expected: they bought, they acquired, they went out, they moved up. Scott fought for the family fortune at Ford Stevens; she joined the society clubs and paid her social dues. Success followed success, his and hers. They soon made the Highland Park A-list, the up-and-coming couple, young and beautiful, smart and successful, the SMU legend and Miss SMU. They were the envy of all: men wanted her and women wanted him. But they expended their sexual energies only with each other—success excited her and she excited him. Her husband wanted her with a passion that always burned hot; he needed her more than life itself, a need that never waned or wandered. Success and sex: Rebecca Fenney's life was perfect and getting better by the day.

Until the day she became pregnant.

Which came as a complete shock—motherhood had never been part of her plans—and a recurring one as she watched helplessly as her belly expanded and her body bloated up until she looked like a beached whale. She had always loved to look at herself when she passed a mirror; now she averted her eyes. Rebecca Fenney was not a squat soccer mom in a minivan! She was a sleek white woman in a black Mercedes coupe! Which she drove over to Harry Hines on more than one occasion trying to work up the courage to enter one of the clinics and have an abortion. Of course, she would have blamed the loss of the child on a miscarriage; there are no abortions in politically conservative Highland Park.

But Scott wanted the child.

He alerted all the world that a Fenney child was on the way. Men looked ahead fifteen years to when Scotty Junior would make his football debut at Highland Park High; women showered Rebecca with baby gifts to ease her descent into motherhood. With such attention focused on her pregnancy, a "miscarriage" would have been viewed as a personal failure on the part of Rebecca Fenney, and failure is not socially acceptable in Highland Park. So she resigned herself to the inevitable and became the perfect mother-to-be, eating only organic, no caffeine, no alcohol, exercising daily in the pool, acting oh so happy to be oh so fat.

But Scotty Junior was a girl named Boo. A collective sigh of disappointment went up in Highland Park, from everyone except Scott. He didn't care. When he gazed on his new daughter in the hospital nursery, it was love at first sight. And Rebecca saw that her place in his heart had been stolen.

Sex was never the same.

Rebecca Fenney needed a man who needed her more than life itself; Scott Fenney was no longer that man. But she also needed a man who could give her the life she needed; that man was still Scott Fenney. He had given her this Highland Park mansion, the home she had dreamed about since she was a little girl, the home that told the world Rebecca Fenney belonged in Highland Park. A woman living in a $500,000 house can join the society clubs; a woman living in a $3.5 million mansion can chair the society balls. This home made Rebecca Fenney's life. Her life was perfect and could get no better.

It could only get worse.

Which had become a constant worry for her over the last few weeks: Was her life about to take a turn for the worse? Was the ride slowing down . . . or coming to an end? She had thought and hoped and prayed that the

Scott Fenney ride would last a lifetime. But you never know with men. Men can always find a way to fuck up a good thing.

Would Scott Fenney?

Other Highland Park men certainly had, leaving their wives—older women Rebecca knew—for younger women. But those discarded wives were in their fifties and sixties, the family fortunes made and their community halves secure. Rebecca was thirty-three, and the family fortune was still in the making, still owed to the bank that held the mortgage on their home and her life. If Scott left her now, she would have nothing, just as her mother had nothing when her father left them. The Scott Fenney ride had to last until the mortgage was paid off.

She had bet her beauty on Scott Fenney. What if she lost that bet?

When she first became Mrs. A. Scott Fenney and went to the homes of the older lawyers' wives, she would admire their possessions, and she wanted what they had, all the things money could buy. Only recently had she realized that while she was coveting what they possessed, they were coveting what she possessed: youth and beauty—what they needed to compete for their lawyers. But their money could not buy youth and beauty, try though they did with liposuction, tummy tucks, breast implants, and face-lifts; the good doctor could help, but he could not make a fifty-year-old woman look twenty-five again. So they lost their lawyers to younger women.

And now Rebecca, thirty-three, old by Highland

Park standards, understood their fear as she observed the blonde by the pool—*what was she, twenty-two, twenty-three?*—giving her husband a come-hither look, competing for her lawyer, more than willing to use her beauty to claim what Rebecca possessed. There was always a younger, prettier, skinnier woman ready to take your place in the mansion. Rebecca Fenney was still remarkably beautiful, still the most beautiful woman in Highland Park, still able to compete with a twenty-two-year-old for her lawyer. But the day would come for her, she knew; and with each passing day, Rebecca Fenney was a day older and a day less beautiful.

If she lost Scott to the girl by the pool—and every Fourth of July there would be a girl by the pool—before the family fortune was made and her community half secure, she would have only one option for a new husband: a man fifty, fifty-five, maybe sixty years old. The thought of a sixty-year-old man climbing on top of her made her shudder. With enough money, a man could always drop down two decades, even three, for a new wife. But a woman? She would have no chance at a man her own age. Men in their thirties or forties were looking at twenty-somethings like the blonde.

Yes, in every woman's life, there's always another woman. But it was different for Rebecca Fenney: the other woman in her life, the woman competing for her lawyer, the woman who was threatening to take everything she had in life—her home, her position, her possessions—was not a twenty-two-year-old blonde with big tits and a tight ass, but a black prostitute accused of murdering a senator's son.

"I'm gonna be a hooker when I grow up."

Consuela let out a shriek from the kitchen, Scott almost choked on a mouthful of barbecued brisket left over from the party, and Rebecca glared at him from across the dining table. He turned to Boo, who had just announced her career plan to her family at the dinner table.

"Excuse me?"

"Yeah," she said, chewing on a barbecued rib, "men pay Pajamae's mother two hundred dollars an hour just to be with her, and if the trick wants her all night, then it's a thousand."

Scott looked at Pajamae, who was nodding matter-of-factly.

"Well, Scott," Rebecca said, "your little social experiment is already making our daughter a more worldly person."

"Rebecca, she doesn't understand what she's saying." To Boo: "And what does Pajamae's mom do with her tricks?"

Boo shoveled potato salad into her mouth and said, "Well, mostly they watch TV and eat popcorn, but sometimes the trick wants to fornicate."

Rebecca dropped her silverware. "Oh, this is just great!"

Calmly: "And what about that?"

Boo said, "Well, that's okay as long as he wears his rubbers, although if it's not raining, why the heck would he need rubbers?"

She turned to Pajamae for an answer, but Pajamae only shrugged, shook her head, and bit into a rib.

"Unh-huh. So that's what your mother told you, Pajamae?"

Pajamae was busy with her food, but she said, "Yeah, that's what she said. And she said if a president can make ten million dollars for writing a book about getting blow jobs in the White House, she ought to be able to make a hundred dollars for giving one on Harry Hines." She now looked up from her plate. "Mama talks a lot when she's sick and takes her medicine . . . until she falls asleep."

Boo turned to Pajamae: "What's a blow job?"

Shawanda sucked the bone dry, then licked her lips. She turned her big brown eyes up to Bobby, smiled, and said, "This here some good cooking."

Bobby handed her another barbecued rib from Scotty's party. He had walked out with a dozen ribs, two pints of coleslaw, one pint of baked beans, and two cold beers. He knew he couldn't get the beers into the federal detention center, so he drank them on the way over. Of course, before Shawanda would eat, he had to tell her all about the pool party and Pajamae, how pretty she looked.

She said, "Mr. Herrin, over last month you bring me food what, five, six time?"

"Seven, but who's counting. And don't tell Scotty, okay?"

"Why you come? You sweet on Shawanda?"

Bobby shrugged. "You're my client . . . sort of."

She looked at him like a psychic trying to read his future in his face, then nodded knowingly and said, "You ain't got no one to eat with, do you?"

Bobby stared down at his paper plate. "No."

"Well, you awful nice, bring good food for me . . . 'cept that pizza with them little fishes—"

"Anchovies."

"Yeah, them." She swallowed some coleslaw, then said, "Mr. Herrin, I'm real sorry."

"For what?"

"For thinking you ain't nothin' but a dud . . . lawyer."

Bobby laughed. "That's okay. I feel that way about myself most of the time."

"You just poor 'cause you care. You all soft inside for people like me, workin' for nothin', that's why you ain't a rich lawyer. Can't make no money givin' everyone free-bies—where I be, I do that? Nope, Mr. Herrin, that just bad business. Mr. Fenney, he rich 'cause he know to only work for rich people."

"He used to care."

"So you ain't mad, me telling the judge I want Mr. Fenney be my lawyer?"

"No. You need him, Shawanda. He's a lot better lawyer than me."

"Maybe you make him care again . . . maybe about me."

They looked at each other, and Bobby saw the hope in her eyes.

"Maybe."

The clubhouse at the Highland Park Country Club wasn't the most expensive building in Dallas or even in Highland Park for that matter, but it was the hardest to get into. To say it was an exclusive club is like saying Michael Jordan was a pretty good basketball player. You don't buy your way into this club; you're born into it, you marry into it, or you kiss so many important asses in town to get in that the American Medical Association board could certify you as a proctologist. Scott Fenney had taken the latter route to membership, a privilege available only because he was a local football legend and Tom Dibrell's lawyer.

Scott stopped the Range Rover under the porte cochere. Before he had cut the engine, the valet had their doors open. Scott gave the boy a twenty, and then walked his family into the club. Boo and Pajamae skipped ahead, giggling like the little girls they were. Scott smiled at the sight. Rebecca did not.

Even when not in the best of moods, as now, Rebecca Fenney was still the most beautiful woman in Highland Park. And Scott felt proud to squire his spouse into the clubhouse at the country club, the tall handsome ex-SMU-football-star-turned-successful-lawyer escorting the gorgeous ex-SMU cheerleader wearing a pale green sundress that showed off her fabulous figure, and to see each man discretely glance at her, wishing that she and not their wrinkled dinosaur wife was going home with them tonight. Rebecca was a big part of Scott Fenney's perfect life, albeit a severely pissed-off part tonight.

"This is a big fucking mistake," she said through her teeth.

"Oh, you worry too much. We're here for the fireworks. No one's going to pay attention to a little black girl."

"Yeah, right. The women here notice if your breasts are half an inch bigger or your butt's half an inch smaller. How am I going to explain her to them? She's sure as hell not a member's kid!"

The country club opened its doors to the members' children twice a year, for the annual Christmas Party featuring Santa Claus and for the fireworks on the Fourth of July. Otherwise, children were banned from the premises. Not that kids would find the place inviting. The average age of the members was seventy-four; Scott and Rebecca were two of the young members, "young" meaning under sixty. The decor was contemporary—for 1952; the members saw no reason to update the club, the only concession to the last fifty years being a big-screen TV in the men's grill. There was simply no sense in trying to convince a seventy-four-year-old member that change could be good; to a man that age, change could only be bad. No change could make him young again.

So, other than those two annual events, there were no kids at the country club. Or blacks, except for the caddies and the help. Or Hispanics, or anyone else who could qualify for affirmative action. Or Jews. Even though the Bible-beating Baptist members got their medical care at Zale Lipshy Hospital and their wives shopped at Neiman Marcus, they wouldn't let a Jew join their club. Go figure. Not that there was a written policy to that effect—you don't write stuff like that down. You just know how it is, like you know not to give a cop the finger: there's no law against it, but it will get you a ticket for reckless driving just the same.

The Fenneys continued into the clubhouse and down the main corridor, detained briefly by several wrinkled dinosaurs who congratulated Rebecca on her certain selection as the next chairwoman of the Cattle Barons' Ball—"She's a Junior League project!" Rebecca blurted out when the women noticed Pajamae—and then out the back doors and to the elevated grassy area behind the eighteenth green where the club had set up lawn chairs so the members could enjoy the club's fireworks show.

They found four empty chairs next to a group of geriatrics who boasted a combined net worth in excess of a billion dollars. They didn't blink an eye at Pajamae's presence; but then, they probably couldn't see her in the darkness. The two girls sat in front, with Scott and Rebecca behind. Scott leaned into Rebecca.

"See, nobody cares."

They sat quietly, enjoying the summer evening and the spectacular view of the lights of downtown Dallas. The girls were huddled together and whispering when the first fireworks suddenly exploded, a giant Roman candle—*boom!*—and Pajamae dove out of her chair and hit the deck like a soldier under incoming attack. Scott jumped to her.

"Pajamae! What's wrong?"

"Get down, Mr. Fenney! Get down! It's a drive-by!"

Some nearby kids started laughing, dredging up some bad childhood memories for Scotty Fenney, the poor kid on the block—"Scotty, where'd your mommy buy your clothes, at *Sears?*"—and jacking up his blood pressure to pregame level. Highland Park kids enjoyed taunting their poorer peers, the most recent occasion being last year's playoff game at Texas Stadium against a team from a working-class suburb: the Highland Park kids had chanted, "Cold cash versus white trash!" and tossed dollar bills down on their opponents from their daddies' skyboxes. Scott glared at the snotty brats, fighting an overwhelming urge to slap the bunch of them into the ninth fairway. But smacking the heirs of the richest men in Dallas wouldn't be good for his law business, so instead he helped Pajamae up.

"Honey, it's okay, we don't have drive-by shootings in Highland Park. It's just the fireworks."

Pajamae sat up, looked around, and said, "Oh." Scott helped her back into her chair and sat down behind her. The geriatrics were now staring intently at Pajamae.

Rebecca sighed and said, "Well, that should make the club's newsletter."

THIRTEEN

CARLOS HERNANDEZ, Bobby's favorite waiter at the Downtown Club, got busted on the Fourth of July. He went to a party in East Dallas, figuring on firing off a few fireworks. It's illegal to even possess fireworks in the City of Dallas, but since Carlos was also in possession of cocaine and marijuana, he wasn't thinking about the city's fireworks ordinance—or much else, for that matter—as he stood drunk and stoned out of his mind in the middle of Grand Avenue blowing off bottle rockets at passing vehicles. When a Dallas police cruiser happened by, Carlos put a bottle rocket right in the cop's lap. Carlos was busted for possessing two dozen bottle rockets, five strands of firecrackers, fifty Roman candles, ten grams of cocaine, and two Baggies of weed. Due to his prior experience in the federal system, he was turned over to the Feds. They charged him with possession with intent to distribute—the dope, not the fireworks. With his five priors, Carlos was looking at ten to life in a federal prison.

Which is what brought Bobby downtown four days

later. Carlos's mother had hired him to represent her son for the total sum of $500, $100 down and $100 a month until paid in full. Bobby parked six blocks down from the federal building to avoid a parking fee and to smoke another cigarette. By the time he arrived at the U.S. Attorney's office on the third floor, he reeked of sweat and cigarette smoke. After stating his name and purpose to the receptionist, Bobby took a seat in the waiting room. He had come to negotiate a plea bargain with the Assistant U.S. Attorney handling Carlos's prosecution. He tried not to look surprised when Ray Burns walked through the door.

"Bobby!" A big smile from Burns, as if he were happier to see Bobby Herrin this morning than any other person on the planet. "Good to see you, man."

"Ray."

Ray sniffed the air, then gave Bobby a funny look.

"You run over a skunk?"

"You're the AUSA on Carlos's case?"

"Yeah. Some coincidence, huh?" A slap on his newest best friend's shoulder. "Come on back, Bobby, let's talk about your main man Carlos."

Ray's genial disposition got Bobby's mind to churning. It occurred to him that it was a pretty goddamn big coincidence that Ray Burns was the Assistant U.S. Attorney on this case, too. He followed Ray down a corridor and into his office. It was standard government issue, but compared to Bobby's office, it was lavish: a leather chair, a wood desk, two guest chairs, and Sheetrock walls thick enough so you didn't hear Jin-Jin cussing Joo-Chan for messing up a batch of Korean donuts. On the walls were Ray's diplomas, licenses, and photos of important politicians. Ray gestured Bobby to a chair, then he sat behind his desk, leaned back, and said, "What would you think about two years for Carlos?"

"*Two years?* You're reducing the charge to simple possession? No intent to distribute?"

A shrug between friends. "Sure, why not?"

"Why?"

The two lawyers stared at each other across the wide wood desk; a thin smile crossed Ray's face. And Bobby knew his instincts were on the mark.

"What do you want, Ray?"

No pretense now. "I want the bitch's guilty plea. You get Shawanda to plead to second-degree murder, we'll agree to forty years."

"*Forty years?* She'll be eligible for Medicare by the time she gets out."

"Thirty. And that's as low as we're going."

Bobby studied Ray Burns. "Why the change of heart, Ray? You were gung-ho for the death penalty."

"I still am—a death sentence would round out my résumé nicely. But we're political appointees, at least the U.S. Attorney is, and he doesn't want to spend the rest of his career in this hellhole, a hundred and ten in the god-damn shade. He's thinking maybe California. This case might be his ticket west."

Bobby Herrin was not a lawyer whose clients were beneficiaries of political power. So it took a moment for the motive behind Ray's generosity to dawn on him.

"You know about Clark's past?" he said.

"Yep."

"And Senator McCall wants to keep it quiet?"

"Yep again."

"So he calls up the United States Attorney General and asks for a small favor. And the Attorney General calls up the U.S. Attorney in Dallas and asks for a small favor. Which the U.S. Attorney will grant, for a small favor in return. And, just like that, a person's life is suddenly changed."

Ray smiled and turned his palms up.

"What, you complaining? Two of your clients are getting good deals because of McCall's power."

"Ten years, Ray. Ten years for Shawanda, or you can tell the good senator to forget the White House and your boss to forget California. And I want Carlos's charges dismissed."

Ray grinned. He was such an asshole that he actually liked the game, two lawyers negotiating over other people's lives. Liking the game is an annoying character trait in a lawyer; liking the power is a dangerous one.

"Twenty, and that's a great deal, Bobby, and you know it. But if she rejects this deal, I won't back off the death penalty, understand? And if that information about Clark becomes public, the offer is withdrawn. So get the bitch to agree, fast."

Bobby stood and walked to the door, but he turned back.

"Ray, one more thing: if you call my client a bitch

again, I swear to God I'm gonna punch you in your fucking mouth."

Scott, I need an answer for McCall. Soon.

"You called, Scott?"

Karen Douglas was standing in front of his desk.

"What? Oh, yeah, sit down, Karen."

Scott pushed Dan's voice out of his mind. Karen sat in one of the chairs on the other side of his desk and tucked her legs under so as not to reveal any thigh. She was twenty-six, pretty enough to be noticed on the street, and the youngest of the four associates working under Scott. She had graduated first in her class at Rice with a degree in literature and first in her law class at Texas. Book smart, but she was having a difficult time adjusting to the practice of law. As a supervising partner, Scott felt a responsibility to teach his new associates the necessary practice skills they weren't taught in law school. If Dan Ford hadn't taught Scott those same practice skills, he wouldn't be the lawyer he was today.

"Karen, I know you've been with us only a few months, but it seems like you're having some problems. Am I right?"

She nodded and Scott worried she might cry.

"Okay, let's see if I can get you back on track. First thing, your billable hours. You haven't met your monthly quota once. Karen, my associates *exceed* their quotas."

"But, Scott, two hundred hours a month? Ten bill-able hours a day? That's impossible, if I'm honest."

"Karen, this is a law firm, not a seminary."

He smiled; she didn't.

"Look, here's how billable hours work. First, you always round up. Twenty minutes becomes half an hour, forty minutes becomes an hour, an hour and a half becomes two. Second, every phone call you make and every letter you read is a minimum quarter-hour. You read ten letters, a quarter-hour each, that's two and a half billable hours. Heck, I usually bill four or five hours just reading my mail each morning. And travel—didn't you fly to San Francisco with Sid last month?"

She nodded.

"Did you bill your flight time?"

"Two hours. I worked on another matter."

"How long was the flight?"

"Four hours."

"Then you should bill eight, four hours to the client you're flying to San Francisco for, and another four to the client whose work you're doing during the flight. See? That's six hours you didn't bill last month. If every lawyer here dropped six hours each month, Karen, that's twelve hundred hours that wouldn't get billed. That's three hundred grand we wouldn't collect. *Each month.* Twelve months, that's three-point-six million. See how it adds up? See why every hour counts? Billable hours are a law firm's inventory, Karen, so when you don't bill your quota, it's like you're working at McDonald's and giving away hamburgers."

Karen was looking at Scott like a freshman coed watching her first porn flick at a frat party.

"Scott, you're telling me to pad my hours. Isn't that cheating?"

"Every place except a law firm."

Bobby entered the Ford Stevens lobby and was waved through by the smiling receptionist. Each time he walked into the Ford Stevens offices, he smelled something in the air. Like a funeral home, a downtown law office has its own unique smell; but instead of formaldehyde, this place smelled of money.

Bobby walked down the carpeted corridor to Scotty's corner office. Scotty was sitting behind his desk and addressing a young woman. He noticed Bobby and waved him in.

Bobby stepped into the office. The young woman stood and when she turned to face Bobby, he was struck by her appearance: she was very attractive and from her sharp suit, a lawyer.

"Bobby, this is Karen Douglas. Karen, Bobby Herrin."

Her eyes widened. "You're working the Shawanda Jones case with Scott. That must be very exciting. When I was in school, I always thought I'd work in the public defender's office."

"But we pay better," Scotty said. He pointed at the sofa. "Sit, Bobby, I'll be right with you." He picked up a thick document and turned back to Karen. "Now, Karen, you're clear on billable hours?"

Karen sighed heavily and nodded. "I guess so."

"Okay, the other thing I wanted to talk to you about is your memo. I've read it and it's great. You researched the law perfectly, you applied the facts, you did everything exactly right . . . except—"

"Except what, Scott?"

"Except you didn't answer my question."

"But you asked whether Dibrell could sue that little town over its denial of his rezoning request. The answer is no."

Scotty was shaking his head. "Karen, I didn't ask you *whether* Dibrell could sue the town, I asked you *how* Dibrell could sue. We're going to sue; we've already decided that. It's part of our strategy to get the town to give us the rezoning we want. And believe me, after their lawyer tells them how much the litigation will cost in fees and expenses even if they win, the town will crater. What I wanted from you is a legal position we can take to justify our lawsuit. You answered whether. I asked how."

Karen's face expressed that dismay unique to a new lawyer learning the ways of lawyers.

"I . . . I didn't understand, Scott. I'll try again."

"Good girl."

Karen departed and Scotty said, "Nice body, but she'll never make it as a lawyer. What's up?"

Ten minutes later, they were driving to the federal building.

"Scotty," Bobby said, "twenty years is a good deal. I've had two-bit dealers go down for life."

But Scott wasn't thinking about what was good for his client; he was thinking about what was good for himself. Which was Shawanda's pleading out, for twenty or thirty or forty years, he didn't give a damn. Because if she pleaded out, he wouldn't have to make a big decision. *Scott, I need an answer for McCall. Soon.*

"Twenty years? Mr. Fenney, Pajamae, she be twenty-nine by then, I won't even know her. She all I got."

Shawanda was pacing the small room, around and around, circling Scott and Bobby in their chairs.

"I understand, Shawanda, but if you're convicted of first-degree murder, you might get the death penalty."

"Twenty years in prison, I die anyway. Mr. Fenney, why don't you believe me? I didn't do it! I didn't kill nobody!"

In civil litigation, judges routinely order the parties to mediate their disputes before going to trial. Mediation allows the lawyers to hammer their clients into settlements they don't like, force them to pay amounts they don't want to pay, and make them end lawsuits they don't want to end. But there is no court-ordered mediation in criminal cases. So all Scott could do to try to convince his client to take the plea deal was stand and shout: "Shawanda, please think about this!"

She stopped short.

"I don't gotta think no more about it, Mr. Fenney. I told you before, I ain't coppin' no plea!"

Ray Burns was not happy when Scott and Bobby informed him of their client's decision to reject the plea offer.

"That bi—" Ray's eyes met Bobby's. "That woman is making a big mistake. And her lawyers are making an even bigger mistake if they go public with Clark's past."

"What about ten years?" Scott asked.

"No way. We don't give ten-year deals to people who stick a gun to a guy's head and blow his fucking brains out!"

Scott was back in his office, sitting behind his desk, his elbows on the top, his head in his hands, his eyes closed, and his mind a jumble of thoughts and images: Scotty Fenney, number 22, racing down the field, scoring the winning touchdown, the campus hero . . . two little girls, one white, one black, sleeping side by side in the big bed, their faces smooth, their hair in cornrows . . . Rebecca, beautiful and naked and angry . . . Shawanda, alone in her cell, crying for her daughter and heroin . . . and Dan Ford, who had replaced the father who had died when Scott was just a boy. What son wouldn't do what his father asked? *Scott, I need an answer for McCall. Soon.* But the boy had a mother, too, and just as the image of a mother reading to her son flashed across his mind's eye, Scott opened his eyes to find Dan Ford standing over him. And he knew what his senior partner had come for.

"She turned down the deal?"

Scott leaned back in his chair. "Word travels fast."

"The U.S. Attorney called Mack, Mack called me."

"And now you're calling on me? What's that saying, shit rolls downhill?"

"Something like that."

Dan strolled around the office and stopped at the huge framed photograph of Scott Fenney, number 22 for the SMU Mustangs, running the ball against Texas. "One hundred ninety-three yards . . . unbelievable," he said. After a moment, he broke away and sat on the sofa. Finally, he turned to Scott.

"Scott, I need an answer for McCall. Now."

"I don't know, Dan."

"What's there to know? We know what Mack wants."

"And I know what my client wants."

Dan chuckled. "Your *client*? Clients pay us fees, Scott. Ms. Jones isn't paying us anything. She's costing us. She's an expense to this firm. And she's expendable."

"Dan, I'm her lawyer!"

Dan stood. "Scott, do you really believe she's innocent? Do you really believe she didn't kill Clark?"

Scott shook his head. "No."

"Then what's the problem?"

"The problem is, Dan, if I don't introduce that evidence about Clark's past, she's gonna die!"

A look of absolute puzzlement came over Dan's face. He said, "And how does that affect your life?"

And that had been the guiding principle of A. Scott Fenney's professional life since the day he joined Ford Stevens: How would it affect his life? Or, more to the point, his income. Any event—a lawyer fired, a client dumped, a case won or lost, a law enacted or repealed, a natural disaster, a stock market crash, a war, a presidential election—that affected his life and income was, by definition, important. Any event that did not affect his life or income was unimportant, irrelevant, as inconsequential to him as another gang murder in South Dallas. Now, driving home to his $3.5 million mansion in a $200,000 automobile, Scott found himself wondering: How would Shawanda Jones being sentenced to death affect his life and income?

The answer was obvious: not at all. The day after her conviction, he would be back at his desk, working to make rich clients richer and bringing home $750,000 a year. As he would the day after her execution. She would quickly become part of his past. A year from now he wouldn't even remember her name.

Scott had always followed Dan Ford's advice, and he knew he should follow Dan's advice now. He should chalk up Shawanda's pathetic heroin-addicted life as unimportant and irrelevant and inconsequential to his life. He should lose her case and move on, as he had with other clients whose cases he had lost. Even Scott Fenney couldn't win every case. Those few times he had lost, he had moped around, cursing the judge and jury for a few days, but once the client paid his final bill and the check cleared, he had gotten over it and moved on.

But there was a difference.

Scott Fenney had never thrown a case. Or a contest. Or a game. He had always played to win. Every game he had ever played—football, golf, lawyering—had been a test of his manhood, so he had played every game to win. All-out, no-holds-barred, win at all costs—that's what made him a winner. Every cell in his body was infused with the desire to win, a desire that had taken him from being the poor kid on the block to owning a mansion on Beverly Drive in the heart of Highland Park. But Dan Ford was now telling him to play to lose. Could Scott Fenney play to lose and still be a winner?

That thought bothered him all the way home. But as he pulled into the motor court behind his mansion, a new more bothersome thought had invaded his mind: How would Shawanda's death affect Pajamae's life?

Scott had said bedtime prayers with the girls, tucked them in snugly, and was standing to leave, but he needed to ask Pajamae a question.

"Pajamae, do you think your mother could hurt anyone?"

"No, sir, Mr. Fenney. Mama, she's got a good heart. She cares about people. Her problem is, she doesn't care enough about herself. She's always telling me to love myself, but she doesn't love herself. My daddy made her like that, hitting her, making her sick. So don't blame her, Mr. Fenney, it's not her fault."

Then she turned her big brown eyes up at Scott and asked him a question.

"Mr. Fenney, are the po-lice gonna kill my mama, too?"

FOURTEEN

*E*XECUTION OF THE DEFENDANT *would violate her civil rights under the Eighth Amendment to the Constitution of the United States . . .*

The defendant. Her mother. Execution. Damn.

Pajamae was playing in the pool with Boo; they were standing in opposite shallow ends and tossing a Frisbee back and forth across the deep middle part of the pool. Scott was sitting on the patio reading Bobby's brief that argued Pajamae's mother should not be put to death if found guilty of murdering Clark McCall.

It was another blazingly hot Sunday afternoon in Highland Park. The girls were cool in the pool. Scott was sweating in the shade of the patio awning. Rebecca was down in the exercise room climbing the Stairmaster to nowhere in air-conditioned comfort. Consuela was in Little Mexico being courted by Esteban Garcia. Scott had driven her down that morning to the Cathedral Santuario de Guadalupe Catholic Church located at the northern boundary of downtown Dallas, which was also the southern boundary of Little Mexico. Esteban was waiting at the curb, dressed in black boots, black trousers, and a long-sleeve white shirt starched crisp; he was clean shaven and his hair was slicked back. He looked like a Mexican matador. He greeted Consuela de la Rosa like a princess, taking her hand to help her up and out of the low-slung Ferrari. She turned and waved good-bye to Scott, then walked to the entrance of the church like a teenager in love. She was brown and beaming.

Scott was white and worried.

Scott, I need an answer for McCall. Now.

What if he said no to McCall? What could Mack McCall do to *Scott Fenney, Tom Dibrell's lawyer*? McCall might be the senior senator from Texas and Dan Ford's former fraternity brother, but he paid no legal fees to Ford Stevens. So saying no to McCall would not harm the firm; of course, it wouldn't help the firm either. But still, no harm, no foul. Sure, McCall could block A. Scott Fenney's future nomination to the federal bench, but that did not concern Scott; he had no intention of taking a pay cut to only $162,000 a year. Saying no to McCall would result only in a pissed-off U.S. senator; Scott could live with that.

But could he live with a pissed-off senior partner?

How would Dan Ford take no for an answer? Saying no to Dan would be breaking new ground for Scott; he had never said no to Dan, never even considered saying no. Now Dan wanted to be the president's lawyer, which required that Mack McCall be elected president, which required that Scott Fenney hide Clark McCall's past, which required that Scott say yes.

Dan would not be happy if Scott said no.

But Scott brought in over $3 million in fees for the firm each year, and that always had a way of brightening Dan's mood. And if Scott promised to increase his billings to Dibrell to $4 million this year—*which would require some seriously creative accounting*—surely Dan would forgive Scott (who was like a son to him) this one act of rebellion. Surely.

Still, Scott Fenney had never said no to a coach, a client, or his senior partner. If the coach called an end sweep on third and 20, he ran it. If a client wanted him to coerce a sexual harassment settlement by threatening to bring up the woman's sexual history, he threatened it. If a senior partner wanted him to rubber-stamp a decision to fire a fellow partner, he did it. But now a U.S. senator and his senior partner wanted him to hide critical evidence and watch his client be executed. Could he do it?

What if he did? What if Scott Fenney said yes to Mack McCall and Dan Ford? Both men would be very happy. McCall would be elected president, Ford Stevens would be the president's law firm, and Dan Ford would be the president's lawyer. The firm would open a Washington office, new corporate clients would pay millions in legal fees to the firm, and the partners would double their income. Scott Fenney would be filthy rich. All of which sounded good until he heard Pajamae's little voice: "Catch it, Boo!"

Mr. Fenney, are the po-lice gonna kill my mama, too?

Scott heard the French doors behind him swing open

and felt the rush of cool air against his warm neck. Rebecca stood beside him and he smelled her sweaty scent. She was wearing a tube top and short running tights that clung to every surface of her lean body. Scott felt the urge to pull his wife onto his lap and hold her close; but like a dog who had gotten smacked the last hundred times he had gone after a bone, Scott did not make a move in that direction. They watched the girls play.

"It's good she has a friend now," he said.

"She has friends," Rebecca said, "girls from the best families in Highland Park. She just refuses to do anything with them."

"Then they're not her friends, Rebecca."

They watched in silence again. After a moment, Rebecca said, "A black girl for her best friend. That'll be such a positive on her debutante application."

She abruptly pivoted and went back inside. Scott shook his head. *Her debutante application.* Barbara Boo Fenney would never be a Highland Park deb; she just wasn't the right type. Neither would Pajamae Jones; she just wasn't the right color. She had been born on the wrong side of life, just as Scott had been, but she could not run with a football to the right side of life as he had. Maybe that was why Scott felt a bond with this little black girl, because they were both from the poor side of the tracks; or maybe because Scott had always taken up for the weak kids, like Bobby. Back in high school, Bobby would've been beaten up daily if he hadn't been under Scott's protection.

Pajamae Jones was now under Scott Fenney's protection.

She threw the Frisbee over Boo's head. Boo retrieved it and flung it from far across the yard. The Frisbee landed in the middle of the pool, in the deep section. Pajamae climbed out of the shallow end and walked around to the far side where the Frisbee floated on the water. She knelt down and reached out for it, just out of her grasp. She leaned farther over the pool and before she fell in and sunk below the surface of the blue water, Scott had already dropped the brief and was running toward the pool.

Boo screamed, "She can't swim!"

"Stay there, Boo!"

Scott dove into the pool, not even thinking that he was still wearing sneakers and shorts. He went straight to the bottom and grabbed Pajamae around her waist. He pushed hard with his legs; they broke the surface with a splash. Pajamae was coughing up water. Scott lifted her out of the pool and onto the deck, then climbed out and knelt beside her. She rolled over and heaved more water. She slowly sat up.

"Are you okay, baby?"

Pajamae looked up at Scott. "I thought I was gonna die, Mr. Fenney."

"Not on my watch."

She wiped her nose and leaned into Scott. She buried her face in his wet shirt and wrapped her arms around him. He patted her back.

"Girl, you're getting swimming lessons."

FIFTEEN

SCOTT FENNEY led a double life: at the law firm, he was a successful lawyer practicing law like he played football—winning at all costs, working the margins, gaming the system, bending the rules, mastering the art of aggressive and creative lawyering, and making lots of money. At home, he was a good man, a faithful husband to Rebecca and a loving father to Boo, in whom each night at bedtime he tried to instill the virtues of living a good and decent life. Rebecca didn't want to know what he did each day at the office and Boo didn't need to know. The only part of his lawyer life he brought home each night was the money.

All lawyers lead such a Jekyll-and-Hyde life, diligently maintaining a strict separation between their dual lives, lying to their wives and children, and hiding their lawyer lives like a drug addict hides his illegal habit. Scott always told everyone he was a lawyer, but he never told anyone what he did as a lawyer. A lawyer learns that such matters are best left at the law firm. You walk into the office each morning and become a successful lawyer;

you leave each night and become a good man again. But with each night, the transformation back—from Hyde to Jekyll—becomes harder. The lawyer in you doesn't want to let go. But you beat it back because you cannot allow the boundary between your two lives to be breached. Scott Fenney had never brought his lawyer life home—*never!*—until the day he brought home a nine-year-old black girl.

Pajamae Jones was now part of his life—both lives. She was part of his home life, her mother part of his lawyer life. She loved her mother, and he was her mother's lawyer. His decisions as her mother's lawyer would determine if she had a mother much longer: if he said yes to Dan Ford, he was sending Pajamae's mother to death row. The boundary between his dual lives had been breached, and now, like the last two teams standing at the end of a long season set to play for the championship, his two lives—Dan Ford versus Pajamae Jones—were locked in a life-and-death struggle for Scott Fenney's soul.

I need an answer for McCall. Now.

Are the po-lice gonna kill my mama, too?

Would he be the lawyer Dan Ford wanted him to be? Or the man Pajamae needed him to be? He could no longer be both. He had to choose between his two lives. He had to face it head-on, like all those times when the blocking broke down and number 22 found himself alone on a football field facing five defenders. Then, as now, he had a choice to make: step out of bounds before getting hit or charge forward and take the hits and make the extra yards. Football coaches call those moments "gut checks," because it is in those moments when you find out what you're made of.

Scott Fenney was facing a gut check.

The trial date was one week closer, and Scott was sitting at the small table in the small room at the federal detention center next to Bobby and across from Shawanda. She was happy, upbeat, and full of energy. Bobby was showing her photos from Carl's background checks.

"This is Clark in his better days. He ever try to pick you up before that night?"

She shook her head. "No, sir. Course, drunk white boys all look the same on Saturday night."

Bobby held up another photo. "The honorable senator."

Shawanda stared at the image of Mack McCall and said, "He make my skin crawl."

"Yeah." Bobby pointed to a big bald man standing in the background of the same photo. "You ever see this guy?"

"No, sir . . . and I wouldn't forget that face."

Scott said, "Who's he?"

"Delroy Lund, McCall's bodyguard. His goon, according to Carl. Ex-DEA. Carl says he can smell a dirty cop a mile away."

"So what's he got to do with the case?"

Bobby shook his head. "Nothing."

"So Carl came up empty?"

"Yeah, but he never quits looking."

With that news, Scott decided to make one last attempt to convince his client to accept the plea offer. "Shawanda, all we have is this Hannah Steele woman. Clark raped her a year ago." Scott turned to Bobby. "Did Carl get a photo of Hannah?"

"No, she's real shy, wouldn't let him. Carl said she's like a piece of china, a real fragile girl. Said he wouldn't bet a six-pack on her holding up under a tough cross. And Ray Burns is gonna be damn tough, he'll try to make her look like a . . ." Bobby's eyes cut to Shawanda. "He'll explore her sexual history."

"Yeah." Scott turned back to his client. "Shawanda, if you made a deal, at least you wouldn't be facing a death penalty."

"Mr. Fenney," she said, "if I can't be with Pajamae, I just as soon die."

Scott sighed and nodded at Bobby.

"Okay, Shawanda," Bobby said, "we'll go to trial. But you've got to understand, the evidence against you is substantial, more than enough to put you on death row. Our only hope is Hannah. We'll put you on first, then we'll put her on. She'll corroborate . . . back up your testimony, which gives the jury more reason to believe you."

"Why can't I take one of them lie detector tests, prove I ain't lying? I seen them on that TV show—they make the boy wanna marry the daughter take a lie detector test, ask him if he was cheating." She laughed. "Them white boys lie every time."

Bobby was shaking his head. "That's not a good idea,

Shawanda." He turned to Scott. "Scotty, I was thinking about those reporters calling you, asking for TV interviews with Shawanda? Maybe we should do that, let her tell the world what happened. That'll condition the jury pool. And after she's told her story, you can ask that any other woman who was beaten or raped by Clark McCall come forward so Shawanda doesn't go to jail for a crime she didn't commit."

"That sound good to me, Mr. Fenney," Shawanda said.

Scott dropped his eyes and said, "I don't know, Shawanda, that might not be the best strategy."

Scott's eyes were still down when Bobby said, "Shawanda, Scotty and I need to talk outside."

Bobby stood and knocked on the door. The guard opened the door, and Scott pushed himself up out of the chair and followed Bobby into the hall. They had walked ten steps down the corridor when Bobby stopped and leaned against the wall.

"She's doing a lot better," Scott said.

"She's high."

"What?"

"She's feeling the rush."

"You mean heroin?"

Bobby nodded.

"How do you know?"

"Scotty, my best clients are dopers. You can see it in their eyes when they're on it. It's like they own the world."

"How'd she get it in here?"

Bobby shrugged. "Guard, janitor, who knows."

"She looked good the last time. I figured she was over it."

Bobby shook his head. "A junkie's never over heroin. The cravings are always there. I get them probation conditioned on treatment, they get the methadone, stay straight a couple weeks, a couple months, then go right back to it like an old lover."

"Her life's on the line and she can't stop shooting up? My wife's pissed off at me, Dan's pissed off at me, I'm taking all this grief so she can get high? All this for a goddamned junkie?"

"Scotty, if you lived her life, you'd probably shoot up, too. You got the best of life, she got the worst. But she can still be happy when she's high. And now the stuff on the street is so cheap, she can spend every waking minute high—until she dies." Bobby sighed. "And she'll die from the stuff one day."

"We're trying to save her from the death penalty so she can kill herself with heroin?"

"Yep, that's exactly what we're doing. I can see it in her eyes, Scotty, she's a junkie for life. And hers will be a short life." He stared at his shoes a long moment, then stood straight. "But not as short as Ray Burns wants it to be. So, you catching some heat over this?"

Scott nodded. "Big-time. Why not a polygraph?"

"My junkie clients always think they can beat the machine. Course, when they're high, they think they're fucking Einsteins. But they always fail. She takes it and fails, she's history."

"Polygraphs aren't admissible. Burns can't use it against her."

"Not in court. But Ray'll leak it to the press, it'll be front-page news. Every juror will know she failed."

"Maybe she'll plead out if she fails."

"Look, Scotty, I know this is a tough decision for you and I know you don't want to make it, but hey, man, that's why you make the big bucks. What do you want to do?"

"McCall's pressuring Dan Ford to get me to drop this defense, not to drag his dead son through the mud."

"Clark lived in the mud, Scotty. He was a bad boy." Bobby checked his shoes again. "So Dan told you to drop it?"

"He advised me to. He wants to be the president's lawyer. Good for business."

"But bad for Shawanda. Is your job on the line?"

"*My job?* No! Dan wouldn't fire me. I'm like his son."

Bobby nodded. "Three, four years ago, I represented a father who killed his son over a football game." He chuckled softly. "Look, Scotty, I'm not a big-time lawyer like you, I don't represent important people, I don't make much money, . . . but I've never screwed a client. I've always done my best for every client, even if my best isn't much. Clark beating her up, raping Hannah Steele, maybe more women—Scotty, that evidence might be the difference between life and death for her."

Bobby ran his hands over his head of thin hair.

"All my clients are just like her, poor, black or

brown, living in an alternate world where daddies are dealing and mamas are hooking. Difference is, all my clients are guilty, no bones about it. But she may really be innocent—or at least have acted in self-defense. We drop Clark's past, we're sentencing her to death by lethal injection—you and me, Scotty, not a jury. We'll be responsible, same as if we push that needle into her arm." He shook his head. "Scotty, I need the money you're paying me for working this case, but I can't live with that."

"What do you mean?"

"I mean, you drop this evidence, I'm out."

"Bobby—"

"Scotty, I followed you every step of the way—high school, college, law school. Back then, I would've followed you anywhere. I was weak and you were strong and you protected me. But you ain't Batman no more, and I ain't Robin. I can't follow you on this. It just ain't right. She may not be a white society girl . . . she may be a junkie hooker, living in the projects, but her life means something, too. Maybe not to you, maybe not even to herself . . . but to me. And to her little girl. She needs someone strong to protect her . . . someone like you used to be." He paused. "When your secretary called that day, said you wanted to have lunch, man, I about cried. All those years, I really missed you." His eyes were watering. "And being around you again now, it's been great . . . just to breathe your air again." He breathed in and out. "But, Scotty, you do this to that girl, I don't want to see you no more."

212

"Come on, Bobby."

"Scotty, the court appointed you. You're her right to counsel. You do what you think is right."

Scott turned away, wishing this gut check could be answered by simply running into five frothing-at-the-mouth testosterone-charged linebackers.

Scott got into the Ferrari, but he couldn't go back to the office. Downtown suddenly felt claustrophobic. So he drove onto the Dallas North Tollway and hit the accelerator hard. He felt the power of the machine beneath him as he took the engine through the gears. The 360 Modena topped out at 180 miles per hour, but Scott eased off the accelerator at eighty, the customary highway speed in Dallas. No one drove the speed limit in Texas, not even women putting on their makeup. Northbound traffic was light at this time of the morning, so he drove unimpeded in the left lane. He often drove aimlessly about the 4,000 miles of roads in Dallas when he needed to think. For some reason, he thought better in a Ferrari.

Without thinking, Scott suddenly veered across three lanes of traffic and exited at Mockingbird Lane, cut over to Hillcrest, and drove north. He turned left, stopped three doors down on the right, and stared at the new two-story monster house, arched entry, dormers, vaulted roof. But in its place he saw the small one-story cottage that had once occupied this lot, the home he and his mother had rented from the good doctor. Living room, kitchen, two bedrooms, two bathrooms, less than one thousand square feet including the porch where they often sat after dinner and waved at neighbors taking their evening walks. He remembered crawling into bed, lying back on the pillow, and waiting for his mother to come in, sit down, open the book, and read a chapter. And when she finished, she'd close the book and say, "Scotty, be like Atticus. Be a lawyer. Do good."

It's hard to do good when your clients are bad.

Lawyers never believe their clients because clients lie. They lie to the IRS and the SEC and the FBI. They lie about their taxes, they lie about their financial statements, and they lie about their lies. Most of the time, they don't get caught. When they do get caught, usually for lying about their lies to the FBI—a felony called obstruction of justice—their lawyers stand outside the courthouse and proclaim their client's innocence right up to the moment the client plea-bargains, pays a fine, and lives to lie again.

A lawyer always assumes his client is lying.

So Scott naturally assumed his heroin-addicted hooker-client was lying. But maybe he would believe a nice white sorority girl. He had gotten Hannah Steele's unlisted phone number in Galveston from Bobby. Now he sat in the Ferrari and listened to the call ring through. A soft voice answered.

"Hello."

"Hannah Steele?"

"Who's calling?"

"Scott Fenney. I'm Shawanda Jones's lawyer. My cocounsel, Bobby Herrin, spoke with you."

"Yes, Mr. Fenney."

"Hannah, I need to hear your story. I need to hear you tell me what Clark McCall did to you."

A long sigh. "I've told Carl and Bobby, I don't—"

"I know this isn't easy, Hannah, but Senator McCall is pressuring me not to bring up Clark's past at the trial, not to call you as a witness. For me to make a decision, I need to hear for myself what happened."

"All right."

Hannah Steele told Scott of her encounter with Clark McCall. She had met him on the SMU campus after a football game. He asked her out for the next night. He picked her up at her sorority house. They had dinner at a Mexican restaurant in the Uptown section of Dallas, the nightlife area between downtown and Highland Park. They had a few drinks and they went to the McCall mansion, where Clark attacked her, beat her, and raped her. Afterward, he acted as if nothing out of the ordinary had happened. He gave her a ride back to the sorority house and even smiled at her when she got out of his car. She got in her car and drove straight to the police station and filed a complaint. She was taken to Parkland Hospital for a rape analysis and then returned to the sorority house. The next morning, a man came calling for her, saying he was Senator McCall's lawyer. He handed her a document and a pen, said it was a release and confidentiality agreement, and he gave her a cashier's check for $500,000 to settle all claims against Clark and cover her relocation costs.

"Relocation costs?"

"He said I had to leave town. He said my life would be better that way. He said I didn't really have a choice, that if I pressed charges against Clark, his father would destroy me. He said they would bring out my prior sex life at trial, make me look like a whore."

"What was his name, this lawyer?"

"I don't think he told me."

"What did he look like?"

"Like a lawyer. Old. Bald. Creepy. The way he looked at me and talked to me—my God, I'd been raped! He acted like it was just business."

Scott ended the call and he knew. Lots of old lawyers he knew were bald and most were creepy. But he knew one such lawyer who would view paying off a rape victim as just business.

"You knew about Hannah Steele?"

"Of course."

Scott had driven directly back to the office, parked in the underground garage, taken the elevator straight to the sixty-third floor, and hurried down the hall to Dan Ford's office. He was now staring in disbelief at his senior partner, who was looking at Scott with a bemused expression.

"Scotty, you think this is the first time something like this has happened—college girl claiming a rich boy raped her? Maybe he did, maybe he didn't, but she wanted money, she got money, everyone's happy."

"She didn't seem so happy when I talked to her."

Dan shrugged. "Seller's remorse."

"And you just bribed her to drop her complaint? Threatened to destroy her by bringing out her sexual history at trial?"

"*Bribed her? Threatened?*" Dan laughed. "How many girls have you paid off for Tom Dibrell? How many times have you threatened to bring up their sexual histories at trial if they didn't settle? Do you still use my 'every swinging dick' line?"

When Dan had first taught him that tactic, it had seemed so clever, so goddamn lawyerly clever. As it had when Scott used it on Frank Turner, famous plaintiffs' lawyer, negotiating a settlement with Tom's last girl— what was her name, Nadine? Now, after talking to Hannah Steele, it didn't seem so clever.

Scott sat down on the sofa and said weakly, "Tom's girls didn't claim rape. They claimed sexual harassment."

Dan dismissed Scott's comment with a wave of his hand.

"Semantics. Sexual harassment, rape—bottom line, someone got screwed. Scotty, my boy, you did exactly what a lawyer's supposed to do, exactly what I taught you to do: you settled a legal dispute for your client. Just as I did."

Even more weakly: "Doesn't make it fair."

Dan laughed again. "*Fair?* Fair ain't got nothing to do with the law, son. Fair is where you go to see farm animals and ride the rides."

"Why didn't you tell me about Hannah?"

"You didn't need to know, Scotty. Why didn't you tell me you hired a PI to go digging into Clark's past?"

"Dan, I really believe Clark beat and raped Hannah."

"Well, if it makes you feel any better, so do I. Of course, I believed all the others, too."

"The *others*? There were more?"

"Seven, counting Hannah." Dan shook his head. "That little fuckup cost his dad almost three million, just buying off girls. Plus, of course, my fee: twenty-five thousand dollars."

"Twenty-five thousand dollars to buy off a rape victim?"

Another bemused look from his senior partner. "As I recall, you charged Dibrell fifty thousand to buy off his last girl."

Scott's face felt hot. "I thought it was just business."

"It is, Scotty. It's just business. Clark's girls were just business, Dibrell's girls were just business, and this is just business."

"Not to Shawanda. It's her life." Scott met Dan's gaze. "I can't drop it, Dan."

"Sure you can . . . because I'm asking you to. Scotty, are you going to say no to Mack McCall—to *me*—for a goddamn heroin junkie? For a prostitute?"

"No . . . for her daughter."

"Her *daughter*?"

"Yeah. She needs her mother and her mother needs me. And I might be able to save her life."

"Don't start believing your own bullshit, Scott."

"What are you talking about?"

218

"Your campaign speech. You're not Atticus Finch. No one is. Hell, who would want to be? He lived in a middle-class home, drove a middle-class car—what was it, a Buick?"

"Chevrolet."

"You drive a Ferrari." That amused Dan. "Scotty, that movie did more damage to the legal profession than Watergate. Lawyers of my generation, we went to law school to dodge the draft. But the generations that followed us didn't have a war to worry about, so they went to law school to be some kind of goddamn hero. But that's not what being a lawyer's all about. And truth is, they don't want to be another Atticus Finch any more than I do, any more than you do. He had nothing. But they—and you—and me, we want it all—the money, the house, the cars, all the things a successful lawyer can have today. And how does a lawyer become successful? By doing his job, which is making rich people richer. And we get paid very well indeed for doing our job, and not in chickens and nuts like Atticus. Our clients pay us in cash. Which is a very good thing, Scotty, 'cause you can't buy a Ferrari with chickens and nuts."

Dan walked over to the window and gazed out.

"When I graduated from law school, Scotty, a wise older lawyer gave me some good advice. He said, 'Dan, every new lawyer must make a fundamental choice from which every other decision in his professional life will follow. And that choice is simple: Do you want to do good or do well? Do you want to make money or make the world a better place? Do you want to drive a Cadillac or a Chevrolet? Do you want to send your kids to private schools or public schools? Do you want to be a rich lawyer or a poor lawyer?' He said, 'Dan, if you want to do good, go work for legal aid and help the little people fighting their landlords and the utility companies and the police and feel good about it. But don't have regrets twenty years later when your classmates are living in nice homes and driving new cars and taking vacations in Europe. And you have to tell your kids they can't go to an Ivy League school because you did good.' "

Dan turned from the window.

"My son went to Princeton and my daughter went to Smith."

Dan sat on the edge of his desk and folded his arms.

"That's the choice every lawyer makes, Scotty, and you made your choice eleven years ago when you hired on with us. You chose to do well. You stood right there, said you were tired of being the poor kid on the block, said you wanted to be a rich lawyer. Now you want to be a good guy? I don't think so.

"Scotty, this law firm exists for one reason and only one reason: to make as much goddamn money for the partners as humanly possible. And how does this firm do that? By representing clients who can pay three and four and five hundred dollars an hour for our services. By doing what our clients want, when they want it. By never saying no to our clients. Because we know they can always take their legal fees to a law firm across the street or across the state or across the country. Because there's always another law firm ready to take our place at the trough."

"Dan, she's got a little girl. I've got to do right by her."

"You've got a little girl, too. You want to do right by her?"

He rose and came over to Scott, sat beside him, and put his hand on Scott's shoulder. His voice was now fatherly.

"Scotty, you've always followed my advice, and you've done okay by my advice, haven't you?"

Scott nodded. "Sure, Dan, but—"

"Then follow my advice now. C'mon, son, don't do this. Not to yourself, not to this firm . . . not to me. I need an answer for McCall, Scott. Now."

Scott buried his hot face in his hands as the battle within raged on, Dan Ford versus Pajamae Jones fighting for his soul:

I need an answer for McCall. Now.

Are the po-lice gonna kill my mama, too?

And he heard Bobby's voice: *She needs someone strong to protect her . . . someone like you used to be.* Gut-check time for Scott Fenney.

"No, baby, they're not gonna kill your mama. I'm not gonna let them."

"What?"

Scott removed his hands from his face and turned to Dan, who was looking at him oddly. Scott realized that when his gut had answered the call, it had done so out loud. He said, "Tell McCall no."

Dan removed his hand. "That's not the right answer, Scott. Try again."

"My answer is no."

Dan stood, walked across the room, and sat behind his desk. He folded his hands on the mahogany top.

"Scotty, Mack McCall's a U.S. senator now. He dresses nice and talks nice on those Sunday morning political shows . . . but underneath that politician's demeanor, he's still just a Texas roughneck. He grew up poor in the West Texas oil fields, started working the rigs when he was fifteen. It's a hard life, it makes a man hard—it makes some men mean. Mack's one of those men."

Dan picked up a pen and studied it a moment; then he said, "Back in college, we were at a party at Martha's sorority house. She was Mack's fiancée then, a pretty girl and wealthy. She was Mack's ticket, and he wasn't about to let someone else punch it. Well, a football player got drunk and made the mistake of flirting with Martha. Mack told him to leave, but he said no. So Mack told him to step outside. Now, that boy outweighed Mack by fifty pounds, but he didn't stand a chance. Mack beat him with brass knuckles, might've killed that boy if I hadn't pulled him off. I said, 'Mack, why the hell did you do that?' All he said was, 'No one takes something that belongs to me.' "

Dan shook his head in apparent disbelief at the memory.

"Scott, I learned three things about Mack McCall that night: he doesn't take no for an answer; he doesn't fight fair; and he's the meanest son of a bitch I've ever met."

Scott let out a nervous chuckle. "So what's he gonna do, beat me up?"

Dan sighed. "I don't know what he's going to do, Scotty. Forty-two years, I've never said no to him." He paused, then said, "But I do know one thing, Scott: Mack McCall thinks the White House belongs to him."

SIXTEEN

*¡U*STED ME LO PROMETIO, *Señor Fenney! ¡Usted me lo prometio!"*

Consuela's brown face was wet with tears and contorted with fear as she cried out—*You promised, Señor Fenney! You promised!* Her eyes were begging for help, her round body was shaking uncontrollably, and her arms were held behind her colorful Mexican peasant dress by handcuffs. INS policy, the agents had said.

Two agents from the Immigration and Naturalization Service had arrived at the Fenney residence at exactly 6:30 A.M. that Monday morning. Consuela had collapsed into Scott's arms when they flashed their INS badges. The fear that had haunted her always now possessed her. All her protections had failed her: the crucifixes, the prayers, the candles, the Town of Highland Park . . . and Señor Fenney.

Ten minutes later, the agents were departing with Consuela de la Rosa in federal custody. Scott stood by helplessly as the agents escorted her to their waiting car. He shouted, "INS doesn't come into Highland Park, that's the deal! This is gonna cost you your jobs!"

One agent smiled and said, "I don't think so, sir."

"Half the homes in Highland Park employ Mexican maids! Why'd you come to my house?"

"Anonymous tip, sir," the same agent said over his shoulder.

Scott gave the agent the best glare he could work up in his boxer shorts.

"Anonymous tip, my ass!"

Boo pushed past Scott and ran barefooted in her nightie down the walkway shouting, "Consuela! Consuela!"

Consuela turned back just as Boo threw her arms around the older woman's wide waist and clutched her tightly. Consuela bent over and said, "Oh, *niña*." Boo reached up and wiped tears from Consuela's face. After a moment, one agent tugged at Consuela's arm, so she kissed Boo and motioned for her to return to the house. Boo ran straight into Scott's arms, her face frantic.

"You promised they wouldn't come to our house! You promised! Where are they taking her? What's gonna happen to her?"

Pajamae was now standing next to them. "That's how they do it," she said. "They just come and take you away."

Finally Rebecca appeared. She punched her fists into her hips, sighed, and said, "That's just great. Who's gonna cook now, *me*?"

One agent put Consuela in the backseat of the dark sedan while two morning joggers stopped and gawked. Down the street, less noticeable than a soft breeze on this warm summer morning, a truckload of brown men, young and middle-aged and old, arrived for work, just as a hundred other truckloads of brown men were arriving at grand residences on quiet streets throughout the Town of Highland Park: the yardmen. Mexican men just up from Matamoros or Nuevo Laredo or Juárez, willing to toil under the cruel summer sun for the chance at a better life.

The second agent was standing at his open door, but turned back when Scott yelled at him: "You want to bust illegals?" He pointed down the street at the yardmen. "Go arrest them! You can drive all over Highland Park this morning and arrest a hundred more Mexican nationals! But they mow the lawns of the richest men in Dallas, so you're not going to their homes, are you? I know why you came to my house! I know the asshole giving you orders!"

"It's McCall."

An hour later, Scott was standing in front of Dan Ford's desk, his adrenaline still pumping hard.

Dan sighed and said, "Perhaps. Perhaps you should reconsider your decision."

"What, this is a warning from McCall, that he can hurt me? He didn't hurt me, he hurt a poor Mexican girl! Who didn't do a goddamned thing to him!"

Scott headed to the door, but stopped and turned back. "Oh, Dan, when you call the senator, tell him I said to go fuck himself."

*

Scott stormed past Sue and into his office where he found Bobby stretched out on the sofa.

"Mr. Fenney?" Sue was at the door, pink phone slips in hand. "Reporters. They won't stop calling."

"No reporters." Sue disappeared. Scott wiped sweat from his forehead, looked over at Bobby, and said, "They took Consuela."

Bobby sat up. "Who?"

"INS. They showed up this morning, anonymous tip."

"From McCall."

Scott slumped. "Jesus, Bobby, her face. She was so scared."

His anger rose again, and he desperately needed to hit something, so he kicked the trash basket across the room.

"That son of a bitch doesn't know who he's messing with!" He pointed a finger at the blowup of himself on the wall. "I got a hundred and ninety-three yards against Texas!"

"Football's got rules, Scotty. Game McCall plays, ain't no rules."

"We'll see about that."

Bobby climbed up from the sofa and said, "I'll be in the library if you need me—briefs for Shawanda. Lunch?"

Scott nodded. Bobby turned to leave but stopped dead in his tracks when Karen Douglas appeared in the door. They looked at each other like two preteens, then Karen broke eye contact and entered the office. Bobby left and Karen said to Scott, "He's cute."

"Yeah, that's what I always tell him."

Scott sat down hard in his chair and tried to get his breathing under control.

"You okay?" Karen asked.

"No." After several deep breaths: "What's up?"

"We're ready to file the Dibrell zoning lawsuit." Sid walked in as Karen continued: "But Richard down in litigation says Dallas County state court isn't a favorable venue for this type of action. He says the judges are all Republicans and aren't inclined to overrule a city's zoning decisions."

Sid winked at Scott and said, "Karen, what's the single most important fact a lawyer needs to know before going into court, the one fact that will determine whether you win or lose?"

Karen seemed confused. Finally, she shrugged and said, "Which party was in the right and which was in the wrong?"

Sid chuckled. "Not exactly. This wasn't on the bar exam, Karen, but the single most important fact to know is whether the other lawyer contributed more money to the judge's last campaign than we did. Right, Scott?"

Scott nodded at Sid, but his thoughts were on Consuela . . . and the look on her face . . . as if Señor Fenney had betrayed her.

Sid said, "Only problem is, Scott, cases are assigned randomly. How can we be sure of getting one of our judges?"

Scott's mind, though clouded with Consuela, remained ever aggressive and creative.

"Karen, tell Richard to file the lawsuit six times back to back. The six suits will be assigned to six different judges. We'll pick the judge we gave the most money to, proceed with that suit, and nonsuit the others."

Sid was duly impressed. Karen had that same freshman-coed-watching-her-first-porn-flick expression. Scott thought of his maid . . . he had betrayed her. He yelled out to his secretary:

"Sue, get me Rudy Gutierrez's number! He's an immigration lawyer!"

Karen asked, "Scott, is that ethical? Filing the same suit six times?"

"It's a code of legal ethics, Karen, not the Bible."

"Where's the goddamn coffee?"

In the commercial-style kitchen at 4000 Beverly Drive in Highland Park, Rebecca Fenney was opening and slamming cabinet doors, trying to find the coffee beans and the grinder so she could make her own coffee for the first time in three years, angry and agitated because her anxiety and fear had increased exponentially. Had her husband fucked up a good thing? Was losing Consuela just the beginning—the beginning of the end? The arrest of the Fenney maid would be the main topic at every luncheon of Highland Park ladies this Monday. What would they think of Rebecca Fenney now? How would it affect her chances to chair the Cattle Barons' Ball?

"What's gonna happen to Consuela, Mother?"

Sitting at the table were the two little girls.

"I don't know, Boo. Eat some breakfast."

Pajamae jumped up. "I can cook, Mrs. Fenney. I cook for Mama all the time, eggs, bacon, biscuits, grits—"

"Skip the grits." Rebecca tried another cabinet. "Where's the coffee?"

Pajamae was now pulling out frying pans and utensils and dragging a chair to the range. She climbed up.

"Where-as. This is a cool stove."

Rebecca gave up on coffee. "I'll be downstairs on the Stairmaster. You girls try not to start a fire. We've got to get another maid. Soon."

"INS came to your home in Highland Park? Jesus, Scott, who'd you piss off?"

Scott had called Rudy Gutierrez, the immigration lawyer.

"Her name is Consuela de la Rosa. Get her out today."

"No way, Scott. INS won't let go of her."

"Why not? She's just a maid."

"Scott, since 9/11 every Mexican here illegally is an international terrorist as far as INS is concerned. They play hardball. They were pricks before—now they're goddamned pricks."

"I'll pay whatever it takes, Rudy, just get her out."

"Scott, it'd be cheaper not to fight deportation. Let INS bus her across the border, then she can cross back over and work her way back up here."

"Consuela can't handle that."

"Okay, but it ain't gonna be cheap."

"How much?"

"Twenty-five . . . thousand."

"I'll send you a check today. You find her today, Rudy, tell her everything is gonna be okay, that we're her family and she'll be back with us . . . and Rudy, tell her I'm sorry."

Bobby had returned from the library shortly before noon. They were now taking the elevator upstairs to the Downtown Club. Scott was still aching to punch something. Or someone. He straightened his tie in the mirrored wall and said, "Bobby, we're gonna show the world what kind of boy Clark McCall was."

"For Shawanda or because McCall got your maid arrested?"

Scott stared at himself in the mirror a moment.

"I don't know."

"Let me know when you do."

The elevator doors opened and Scott led the way down the corridor to the maître d's station.

"Two, Roberto."

Roberto stood frozen, his brown eyes wide, as if the Virgin Mary herself stood before him. Scott expected him to make the sign of the cross.

"Roberto?"

"Uh, Mr. Fenney, I, uh, I, uh . . ."

"What, Roberto? We want lunch."

"Mr. Fenney, I no can do."

Roberto was suddenly no longer the suave maître d' of the Downtown Club; he was a *no habla inglés* immigrant just up from the border.

"You no can do *what*?"

"Give you seat."

"Why not?"

Roberto's forehead shone with a layer of sweat.

"You no member."

"What the hell you mean I'm not a member?"

"Mr. Fenney, is no more."

"You're telling me I'm not a member anymore?"

Roberto nodded. *"Sí."*

"Get Stewart."

Roberto hurried off in search of the club's manager. Scott turned and nodded at the three men waiting behind him to be seated. In less than a minute, Stewart appeared, trailed by Roberto—and the club's security guard.

"What the hell's going on, Stewart?"

Stewart regarded Scott with the same disdain he would a homeless person seeking a handout at the swanky Downtown Club.

"Mr. Fenney, your membership has been revoked by action of the board of directors, effective immediately. I must ask you to leave the premises." He gestured at the members in line behind Scott. "Roberto, seat these gentlemen."

The three men followed Roberto into the dining room, but not before giving Scott a curious glance and whispering among themselves, "That's Scott Fenney, Tom Dibrell's lawyer."

"You're joking?"

"No, Mr. Fenney."

Stewart held out an envelope. Scott snatched it, opened it, and removed a letter from the board of directors of the Downtown Club informing A. Scott Fenney, Esq., that his membership had been terminated. Scott's blood pressure ratcheted up until the veins in his forehead felt like they would blow any second.

"Please leave, Mr. Fenney. Or Darrell will escort you out."

Darrell, the security guard, took a step toward Scott. Darrell was young, early twenties, maybe two hundred pounds, wearing a clip-on tie and a brown polyester sports coat the sleeves of which were straining against his thick arms. Sporting a flattop, he had a square jaw and the protruding brow of a weight lifter fashioned from steroids. Scott had played football with what God gave him; he hadn't bought it in a goddamned drugstore. But he had played against many such freaks. Problem with drugstore muscles, though, was they weren't real, they weren't strong, they weren't powerful. They just looked good. At least that was his theory. Scott Fenney was still 185 pounds of natural muscle and he could still kick Darrell's ass up and down the seventy floors of this skyscraper. He now took a step toward Darrell, so close he could smell Darrell's foul breath. Scott said through clenched teeth: "I wouldn't recommend trying."

Scott wadded up the letter and tossed it in Stewart's

face, then he turned and walked away. They were ten paces down the corridor when he heard Bobby's voice: "Scotty."

Scott stopped and turned back. Bobby was pointing to a portrait on the wall, one of the club's founders: Mack McCall.

If Mack McCall had appeared before him at that moment, Scott Fenney might well have found himself sleeping in a cell like Shawanda Jones that night. He had never before been this mad at another human being, not even on a football field. He knew he couldn't return to the office in that state, so he and Bobby took the skywalk across to the athletic club.

"They got a juice bar," Scott said.

They were met at the front desk not by the trim little blonde Scott normally saw after work but by Han, a hulking bodybuilder who made Darrell look like a runt. Han greeted Scott like a stranger.

"Please wait here, Mr. Fenney."

"Oh, shit," Bobby said. "Déjà vu all over again."

Han returned with a cheap little gym bag the club gave to guests. He held it out to Scott.

"What's this?"

"The contents of your locker."

"Why?"

"Your membership is terminated."

"As of when?"

"This morning."

234

"Why?"

"Orders."

"From whom?"

"The club manager."

"And who gave him orders?"

"I don't know."

Han crossed his arms over his chest, creating a mass of muscle, bulging biceps and triceps and forearms and pectorals. Scott wasn't sure he wanted to test his theory about steroid-induced muscle on Han. Scott had been in his share of bar fights in college, but never in a juice bar and never sober and never with anyone as big as Han. And he had always been backed up by one or two offensive linemen; those guys were crazy enough to fight a grizzly bear hand to hand. So when Bobby grabbed his arm and said, "Let's get out of here," Scott did not resist.

For the first time since he made partner at Ford Stevens, A. Scott Fenney, Esq., ate a hot dog for lunch, purchased from a street vendor, in the company of people whose collective net worth was less than the price of his suit.

After choking down two dogs, which he was beginning to regret, he and Bobby walked down Main Street, something else Scott hadn't done in years. Or ever. And for a good reason.

Five minutes in the July heat and Scott was soaked from head to toe in sweat. His hair and face were wet, and his crisply starched shirt now clung to him like wet tissue. The sweat from his chest and back was rolling down and collecting in his underwear; the sweat from his legs was collecting in his socks. Hoping to at least save the coat of his $2,000 suit, he removed it and draped it over his shoulder. Bobby was saying something, but to Scott it was just background noise. Scott's mind was on Mack McCall.

Bobby said, "Can you believe those civic boosters, actually thinking the Summer Olympics might come to Dallas? Half the athletes wouldn't make it out of this blast furnace alive."

A block later, Bobby said, "Used to be whorehouses and saloons all up and down Main Street. Doc Holliday practiced dentistry and killed his first man right here."

And later: "You know Bonnie and Clyde grew up here? They're both buried here. Clyde's grave is over in West Dallas. I don't know where Bonnie's is at."

They walked like that, Bobby giving Scott a brief history of Dallas and Scott responding with only nods and grunts the same as if he were listening to Rebecca telling him about her day. They arrived at Dealey Plaza on the western edge of downtown, a tiny triangle of green grass wedged between Houston, Commerce, and Elm Streets, the Triple Underpass to the west and the School Book Depository and the grassy knoll to the north. The place remained exactly as it had been on November 22, 1963.

Bobby said, "You ever been up to the Sixth Floor, looked out the window?"

Scott shook his head.

"No way Oswald did it alone," Bobby said. "Had to

be a shooter on the grassy knoll. You want to go over?"

Scott shook his head again.

Bobby pointed down the street. "Right over there, that's where Ruby shot Oswald, down in the basement of the old jail."

Scott grunted. Oswald shot Kennedy, Ruby shot Oswald, Shawanda shot Clark, Scott shot Mack. It was a thought.

Bobby said, "Right here, this is where Dallas got started, a hundred and sixty years ago, at the exact spot Kennedy got shot. Kind of creepy, ain't it? Anyway, guy named John Neely Bryan set up a trading post right on the banks of the Trinity River—you know it used to run right here? Every spring it flooded downtown, so eighty years ago the city leaders moved the whole damn river a mile west, built big levees so it wouldn't flood downtown. Course, ever since it's flooded black people's homes in South Dallas. They didn't build levees down there."

They started back toward Dibrell Tower.

Bobby said, "People that started Dallas, they were running from their creditors back East. 'Gone to Texas,' they said, which is like saying 'chapter seven bankruptcy' today. They figured their creditors might be brave enough to chase them into Indian territory, but they sure as hell weren't stupid enough to follow them into this hellhole."

When they arrived at the six-story Neiman Marcus flagship store at Main and Ervay, Scott stopped and watched an old homeless woman pull her shopping cart full of junk over and admire the window display, designer clothes on skinny white mannequins, while inside the fine ladies of Highland Park were attending the Estée Lauder Focus Week, or so the sign in the window said. The old lady looked up at Scott and gave him a big toothless smile.

They walked on and Scott began to notice the other strange people populating downtown, the people who walked the streets amid the heat and the noise and the nauseating exhaust fumes of buses and cars, so thick in the air he could taste it, the vagrants and the panhandlers, the old women without teeth and the old men with beards, Hispanic girls with little children in tow, black boys looking tough, and the cops walking the beat. There was another world down here on the streets. Driving by in his Ferrari, Scott had noticed these people no more than he did the inanimate objects of downtown, the light poles and parking meters and trash cans. His life was lived 620 feet up, in air-conditioned comfort. Scott was terribly uncomfortable down here on the street. Bobby was passing out business cards.

"What the hell are you doing, Bobby?"

"Trolling for clients, man. Scotty, I'm a street lawyer and this is the street. You look at them and see homeless people, vagrants, dime players, bottom-feeders—I see clients! This is my Downtown Club."

Bobby quickly realized his error.

"Shit, I've been trying my best for an hour to get your mind off that, now I bring it up. Sorry."

But Scott's thoughts had already returned to his perfect life sixty-two stories above them. He now knew that

Mack McCall was not going to beat Scott Fenney sense-less with brass knuckles. He was going to do something much worse. He was going to take Scott's perfect life away.

That feeling of impending doom enveloped Scott Fenney.

If she made this putt, Rebecca Fenney would finish with a 74, her lowest score ever. She stood behind the ball and took two practice strokes, then walked over and assumed her putting stance, carefully placing the putter behind the ball and adjusting her weight until she was comfort-ably balanced. She knew Trey, the young golf pro whom she was paying $500 for today's playing lesson, was watching her closely, but he wasn't eyeing her putting stroke. He was eyeing her butt. He always managed to stand directly behind her when she putted.

Trey had already holed out for a 62. He was twenty-six, gorgeous, and a former All-American golfer. He had just received notice from the PGA that he was eligible to play in the remaining tournaments that year. This was his last week at the club.

She made a smooth stroke, sending the ball on a true line six inches outside the cup, and watched as the ball broke left and rolled into the hole.

"Yes!"

Trey walked over to her. They high-fived on the eighteenth green of the country club. He looked at her like he always did, and she saw the need in his eyes: he needed her more than life itself. They had been having sex for the last seven months.

They turned and walked up the grassy slope to their cart and climbed in for the short drive to the clubhouse. Trey parked the cart, and the black bag boy appeared.

"Your car be the black Mercedes coupe, Miz Fenney?"

"What?"

"Your car, it the black coupe?"

"Yes, what about it?"

"Make sure I take your clubs to the right car."

"Don't take my clubs to my car. Put them in the clubhouse, like always."

"Mr. Porter, he tell me take them to your car."

"Why?"

He shrugged. "Don't know, ma'am."

Rebecca turned to Trey. He shrugged. She walked inside the clubhouse, into the golf shop, and directly to the head pro's office, where Ernie Porter was sitting. Ernie couldn't make it on the pro tour, so he had spent the last twenty years giving golf lessons, running tournaments, and pocketing a percentage of every club, golf ball, and pair of shoes sold in the pro shop.

"Ernie?"

He looked up. "Yes, Mrs. Fenney?"

"The bag boy, you told him to take my clubs to my car?"

"Yes, ma'am."

"Why?"

"If that's inconvenient, Mrs. Fenney, I'll have them delivered to your house."

"I don't want my clubs at my house. I play here every day."

Ernie suddenly appeared sick. "Mrs. Fenney, you don't know?"

"Know what?"

Ernie shuffled some papers, squirmed in his chair, then said, "Your husband, Mr. Fenney . . . Well, he's . . . He's, uh . . . He's no longer a member here."

"*What?* We've been members for four years."

"Well, technically, Mrs. Fenney, your husband is the member. You have playing privileges as his spouse. Since he's no longer a member, you no longer have privileges. It's in the bylaws."

"Since when isn't Scott a member?"

"Since today."

She found her husband sitting at the kitchen table, their daughter cradled in his lap and sobbing into his shoulder as he stroked her braids. Pajamae was sitting across the table, her face glum, her chin resting on her hands on the table.

"Mother, Consuela's gone and she's never coming back!"

Rebecca put her hands on her hips and tried not to scream.

"Didn't Sue pay our club dues this month?"

Scott raised his eyes to her. He nodded blankly.

"Ernie said you're no longer a member."

His hand slowly came up and fell on a piece of paper on the table. She recognized the club's letterhead. He pushed it her way. She picked it up and read:

Dear Mr. Fenney:

The Membership Committee believes that your continued presence at the club will detract from the collegial social atmosphere of the membership. Therefore your membership has been revoked effective this date. Please do not return to the premises. Your personal belongings will be delivered to your residence, along with your final bill.

"It's McCall," he said. "He got me kicked out of the Downtown Club and the athletic club, too. He's trying to pressure me to drop our defense."

"Goddamnit, Scott, I told you!" Her arm dropped and the letter floated to the floor. The Scott Fenney ride was coming to an end. The only question now was whether the end would be a soft landing or a fiery crash.

The girls were sitting up in Boo's bed when Scott picked up the book and sat down in the chair next to the bed. All the strength had drained out of his body. In one day, he had lost his maid and his memberships at the dining club, the athletic club, and the country club. Just the idea of it, that Mack McCall possessed that kind of power, that he could sit in Washington and pull strings in Dallas, make a few phone calls and affect Scott's perfect life, made Scott realize his relative place in the world. Maybe 193 yards against Texas didn't make Scott Fenney so special after all.

"You broke your promise," Boo said, her voice stern, "and now Consuela's gone."

Scott had suffered all manner of physical pain, but none compared to the pain he felt now for letting his daughter down.

Scott removed his glasses. "I'm sorry, Boo."

"Get her back."

"I'm trying to." Scott replaced his glasses and opened the book. "Where were we, the Thirteenth Amendment?"

Boo said, "We want to talk about something else."

Scott shut the book. "Okay. What?"

"What's a will?"

"A will is a legal declaration evidencing a testamentary intent to dispose of one's property upon one's death."

Boo had a blank expression. "In English," she said. Pajamae was nodding.

"A will says who gets your stuff when you die."

The girls glanced at each other and nodded. Boo said, "So who gets your stuff if you die?"

"Your mother."

"Who gets her stuff if she dies?"

"Me."

"Who gets your and Mother's stuff if you both die?"

"You."

"Who gets me?"

"Oh."

"My grandparents are dead, I don't have any uncles or aunts or older brothers or sisters . . . and now I don't even have Consuela."

"Well, first of all, Boo, your mother and I don't plan on dying anytime soon, so this is all hypothetical."

"All what?"

"Hypothetical. You know, what if. But don't worry, your mother and I are going to be here to take care of you."

Pajamae said, "Mama says all my kin are dead or in prison."

"So what if?" Boo said.

"What if what?"

"What if you and Mother die?"

"I don't know, Boo. I guess I haven't thought much about it."

Boo held out a handful of one-dollar bills and assorted coins. "We want to hire you as our lawyer, but we've only got thirteen dollars between us, so you'll have to work really fast."

"And what do you want me to do?"

"Write us a will that says if Pajamae's mother dies, we get her and she gets to live with us, and if you and Mother die, her mother gets me and I get to live with them."

"*In the projects?*" Scott said before he could catch himself.

"*No.* I'll get this house, we'll live here."

Both girls were nodding now. And Scott smiled for the first time that day, at the image of Shawanda Jones as the woman of the house at 4000 Beverly Drive in the heart of Highland Park.

SEVENTEEN

MCCALL'S AN ASSHOLE."

"Tell me something I don't know."

It was nine the next morning, and Scott was slumped on the sofa in Dan Ford's office. His senior partner was sitting behind his desk, his hands folded, like a priest taking a confession.

"But he's rich and powerful, Scott, which makes him a very dangerous asshole."

"He's your friend."

"I didn't say he was my friend. Fact is, I wouldn't turn my back on the bastard. But he's going to be the next president, and we want him to be this firm's friend."

"Dan, you tell him I can live without the Downtown Club and the athletic club and the country club—taking my memberships . . . okay, fine, that's playing hardball. But taking Consuela, hurting a poor Mexican girl who never hurt a soul in her life . . . that ain't hardball, Dan, that's just plain fucking mean. You tell him he's a mean son of a bitch to do that." Scott had awakened that morning itching for a fight. "Matter of

246

fact, why don't you give me McCall's number, I'll tell him myself."

Dan smiled. "I don't think so, Scotty."

"You know, Dan, I was never carried off the field. I took the best shot any team could give me, and I always got up."

Dan nodded. "You were tough."

"I'm still tough." Scott tapped his index finger to the side of his head. "Up here. That's where real toughness is, in your head. Everyone hurts physically, but the guys who are mentally tough get up off the ground and keep playing. McCall gave me his best shot, and I got up. You tell him that. I'm still playing—and I'm gonna play harder now. You tell him that, too."

Scott stood and walked to the door but stopped when Dan said, "Scotty?"

"Yeah?"

"How do you know that's his best shot?"

Five minutes later, Mack McCall was saying to Dan, "The boy don't break easy."

"No, he doesn't," Dan said.

"Well, he will . . . or everyone in Dallas is gonna know his wife is screwing the assistant pro at the club."

"*Trey?* Jesus, that boy's cutting a wide swath through the wives out there. He ought to be paying us. How'd you find out?"

"Delroy's been snooping."

"Damn, Mack, hold off on that, see if Scott gets on

board. His wife cheating on him . . . that's gonna be tough on him."

"You sound like you care about Fenney."

"He's the best young lawyer I've ever met . . . he's like a son to me."

"Dan, a son can be a dangerous thing."

The morning mail was waiting for Scott when he returned to his office. But instead of billing a thousand dollars for reading his mail, today's mail was going to cost him many times that sum: one letter was from the Internal Revenue Service, demanding $75,000 for back nanny taxes, penalties, and interest in the matter of Consuela de la Rosa. And Scott knew Dan's words had been a warning: Mack McCall was not yet through with Scott Fenney.

Scott sat at his desk and assessed his financial condition. He had $100,000 cash, more or less—actually, $25,000 less since he had sent a check over to Rudy Gutierrez yesterday—in his savings account, which was generating almost nothing in interest income, and another $200,000 in his 401(k) account, all in tech stocks, all under water, all worth half what he paid for them.

He owed $2.8 million on the house, $175,000 on the Ferrari, and another $150,000 on the Mercedes and Range Rover, and $25,000 on credit cards. Three million one hundred fifty thousand in debt. The cars were probably at breakeven, debt to value, and the house was worth maybe a million over the debt, although the high-end housing market in Dallas had slowed recently.

His only income was his monthly partnership draw, $62,500 gross, but only $42,000 after taxes, which disappeared faster than a raindrop on the sidewalk in July: $4,000 in monthly payments on the Ferrari, $3,000 on Rebecca's Mercedes and the Rover, $16,000 in monthly interest payments on the house note, $10,000 a month in property taxes and insurance premium escrows, and $4,000 a month in utilities and upkeep. Which left only $5,000 a month for groceries, clothes, eating out, entertainment, and club dues—at least he wouldn't have to pay club dues anymore. He had never worried about saving money; the house was his savings account, retirement account, and rainy-day fund. Of course, he could access those accounts only by selling the place or refinancing the mortgage, which was not a likely option since Dan Ford had called in a personal favor with the bank president to get the $2.8 million loan in the first place.

So Scott wrote a check on his savings account for *Seventy-Five Thousand and no/100 Dollars* to the "Internal Fucking Revenue Service." And then he sat back in his chair and wondered what McCall would take next.

From the sofa in Scott's office, Bobby said, "Seventy-five thousand bucks? Shit, I sell everything I own and pay my debts, I'm still seventy-four thousand shy of that. And you wrote a check?"

Bobby had arrived and Scott had brought him up to date.

"Yeah. But it was all of my cash."

"You know, Scotty, McCall's taken this way further than I thought he would. I mean, being pissed off is one thing, but trying to destroy your life, man, he's into Stephen King territory now."

"He can't destroy my life, Bobby. He can take my maid, my memberships, and my cash, but he can't destroy me. I've still got clients that pay me three million dollars a year."

"Mr. Fenney?"

Sue was standing in the door.

"Yeah?"

"Mr. Dibrell called, said he needs to see you ASAP."

The beautiful blonde Dibrell Property Company receptionist did not inquire about Scott's marital status today, and Marlene did not smile at Scott. Instead she averted her eyes as he walked past her workstation and into Tom Dibrell's inner sanctum. From Tom's pained expression, Scott figured he would have to negotiate sexual harassment settlements with two receptionists this time. And he wondered if he could.

"What's up, Tom?"

Tom motioned to the sofa. "Sit down, Scott."

Scott stepped around the coffee table, a long glass top set on a base of horseshoes laid flat and welded together. He plopped down on the soft leather and spread his arms along the top of the back. Attorney and client regarded each other across twenty feet of expensive finish-out.

"We've been together a long time, Scott."

"Eleven years, Tom. As long as I've been a lawyer."

"You're the best lawyer I've ever had, Scott, and I've had more than a few."

"Well, thanks." He chuckled and smiled. "You know, Tom, back in college when I broke up with a girl, I'd always tell her how beautiful she was first."

Tom nodded and exhaled. But he didn't smile.

"We're breaking up, Scott."

"What?"

"You're no longer my lawyer."

Fear shot Scott up off the sofa and across the void to Tom's desk. He was now looking down at his rich client, at three million in legal fees, his heartbeat increasing with each second as all the ramifications of losing Tom Dibrell as a client raced through his mind like a runaway locomotive.

"Tom . . . *why?*"

"It's best not to go into it, Scott. It's done."

"But . . ."

"Don't, Scott."

Scott felt wobbly and confused, like he'd taken a blow to the head. He turned away from Tom and took several steps toward the door, and he saw something he had never seen before or had never taken the time to see. He blinked hard, his eyes and mind coming into focus simultaneously. On the wall was a framed photograph of Tom Dibrell and Senator Mack McCall at a golf tournament. He turned back to Tom, but pointed at the photo.

"It's him, isn't it? McCall. He made you do this."

Their eyes locked for a long moment, then Tom's face sagged and he nodded his head like it hurt.

"Scott, you want to know the answer to the mystery?"

"What mystery?"

"Did Oswald act alone? . . . What the hell mystery you think I'm talking about? How Tom Dibrell survived the real-estate crash and kept his building when everyone else failed and lost theirs."

Scott nodded.

"McCall. He saved me. The pension fund in New York, the bastards holding the mortgage on this building—which they were trying to foreclose—they wanted legislation passed in Congress, some kind of special tax break on their investments. Mack told them if they foreclosed on me, he'd shit-can their legislation. They dropped the foreclosure. And Mack got me the contracts on the new post office building and the justice center, gave me some cash flow. He saved me, Scott, just because we're neighbors and I send my gardener over to mow his grass. And he's never asked me for a goddamned thing . . . until now. He's like the Godfather, Scott—when he finally asks you for a favor, you don't say no. I owe him."

"What about me? I started working for you when other lawyers dropped you like a load of shit. I've been loyal to you for eleven years. Don't you owe *me?*"

Tom recoiled and his expression changed from pained to bemused.

"I paid you what I owed you, Scott. In full, every month. As a matter of fact, more than in full. You've been overbilling me for years. You think I didn't know that? Billing me for your law students, training new lawyers on my tab, marking up your cost of copies and faxes and phone calls, charging your hourly rate for our lunches, padding hours—why'd you think I hired all those MBAs from Harvard, for my health? I know where every goddamned penny in this company goes! I figure over the years you're probably into me for two, three million in overbillings. But that's what you wanted from me—my fees, not my friendship. So that's how I paid you back, Scott, in cash. Not in loyalty. I'm loyal to my friends, damn loyal. But you weren't my friend. You were my lawyer."

"Yeah, Tom, and as your lawyer I've bent some rules for you. I've pushed the ethical and legal envelope for you, to make your deals happen!"

Tom held his hands up, as if surrendering. "Whoa, I don't know nothing about that, Scott. I'm just a dumb ol' dirt developer. I leave that complicated legal stuff to my real smart lawyer."

He smiled.

"Not a month ago, Tom, I was standing right here, and you needed me to pull your ass out of a crack again . . . what was her name, Nadine? I did. You said you'd never forget."

"I won't. I'll never forget that, Scott. But this is business."

He's Ross Perot's lawyer.
He's Jerry Jones's lawyer.
He's Mark Cuban's lawyer.
He was Tom Dibrell's lawyer.

A lawyer would much prefer his wife run off with another man than his client run off with another lawyer. A wife's betrayal makes him question her. But a client's betrayal makes him question himself; fact is, a client's betrayal is the *only* thing that can make a lawyer question himself, what he is and who he is. Because a lawyer without a wife is still a lawyer, but a lawyer without a client is just a man.

A lawyer's identity is derived from the clients he represents. A lawyer's power, prestige, influence, wealth, reputation, and standing in the community—*what he is and who he is*—are determined by the clients he represents. You're only as good as your clients are rich.

Scott had ridden the elevator up as an important lawyer in Dallas, a lawyer with a rich client; he was *Scott Fenney, Tom Dibrell's lawyer.* Now he rode the elevator down as . . . who? He didn't recognize the man in the elevator's mirrored walls.

His first known identity was as Butch's son. Then, from the time his football skills became apparent, it was as a football player. And for the last eleven years it had been as Tom Dibrell's lawyer. He had always had an identity. But who was Scott Fenney now? Just another lawyer without a rich client, no better than Bobby, whose best client was a Latino waiter?

For the first time in his life, he didn't know who he was.

Scott was still in a state of shock when he returned to his office and found Bobby on the sofa and a certified letter on his desk. The name on the envelope—First Dallas Bank—barely registered in his mind. He used the letter opener to slice the top of the envelope with no more thought than if it were junk mail. He removed the letter, four pages of crisp bond paper, and unfolded and smoothed the pages flat on his desk. And he read. And as he did, a slow realization came over him: he was reading his own obituary.

The bank was calling the notes on the house and the cars. He had ten days to pay off $325,000 on the three automobiles and thirty days to pay off $2.8 million on the house. Failure to make timely payment would result in immediate repossession of the cars and foreclosure of the house. Scott Fenney would lose his mansion and the Ferrari.

His perfect life would be gone.

A sense of defeat tried to take hold in his mind, but Scott Fenney had never been defeated, even when he lost. Because when he lost, he did not accept it. Instead, he got mad. As he did now. His respiration accelerated, his jaws clenched, and anger energized his mind and body.

He picked up the phone and hit the speed dial for the private number of Ted Sidwell, the bank president. Ted answered on the first ring.

"Ted, Scott Fenney. What the hell's going on?"

"Demand notes, Scott. And we just made demand."

"Why?"

"These loans were made to you as a favor, Scott. To get favors, you've got to give favors. That's how the game's played."

"I see. McCall. Fine, I'll refinance with another bank."

Ted laughed. "In today's market? And without Tom Dibrell as your client? I don't think so."

"News travels fast."

"I knew before you did."

"I'll sell the damn place, it's worth a million more than the debt."

"Fire sale in thirty days? You'll be lucky to get what you owe."

"I'll throw it into bankruptcy. I can hold you off for six months, maybe a year."

"Also not likely. The bank holds a note on Judge Schneider's home in Highland Park. He's the bankruptcy judge. And he understands favors."

Scott had run out of lawyerly rebuttals, so he fell back on the universal football retort: "Fuck you, Ted."

He slammed the phone down.

Bobby was sitting up. "What was that about?"

Scott realized his face was damp with sweat. "The bank called my notes, on the cars and the house."

"How can they call your mortgage?"

"Because it's not a mortgage like you think. You don't get a thirty-year five percent Fannie Mae mortgage for two-point-eight million, Bobby. You get a demand note callable on thirty days' notice."

"*Jesus.* Can you refinance?"

"Not likely. I got this note only because Dan used his influence with the bank president, that asshole."

"Guess who's influencing the bank president now?"

Scott nodded.

"You could sell the place."

"Rebecca would die. That house means everything to her."

"Shit, Scotty, you got three million in fees. You can swing something."

Scott could barely give voice to the words: "Dibrell just fired me."

Rebecca said, "If you're not Tom Dibrell's lawyer anymore, who am I?"

All the way home, Scott had bucked himself up for this moment; he hoped his performance was more convincing to his wife.

"I don't need him."

"No, but you need his three million in fees. Look, Scott, most lawyers' wives don't have a clue what their husbands do at the office, but I do. God knows you've educated me over the last eleven years. I know how things work in a law firm. And I know that a partner who just lost a three-million-dollar client won't be a partner for long. And what are we going to do then, Scott? How are we going to pay for this house?"

Scott walked to the windows of the master suite. He could not bear to look at his wife when he said what he had to say.

"Well, that's the other thing, Rebecca. The house. The bank called the note. I've got to pay off two-point-eight million in thirty days or lose it. Unless we sell it first."

He turned and saw the color drain out of Rebecca's face and her legs give way; she sat down hard on the bed and stared blankly at the wall in front of her. After a moment, she spoke as if to herself: "Without this house, I'll never be chairwoman of the Cattle Barons' Ball." Her eyes, vacant and lost, turned to Scott. "How will I ever show my face in this town again?"

Scott Fenney felt the sting of his wife's disappointment. He had let her down, failed her, betrayed her. He had promised her this life, a life in this house, with these things, driving those cars. Now he had broken that promise. For the first time in his life, he felt the pain of failure. And behind the pain, he felt something else, an anger building deep inside him, not the anger of a lawyer at a client who doesn't pay his bill or a judge who rules against him, but the kind of anger he had previously felt only on a football field, a base anger that had been in man since Adam, an anger that clouded your mind and strengthened your body, that made you say things you shouldn't say and do things you shouldn't do, the kind of anger that usually resulted in Scott Fenney being flagged for unsportsmanlike conduct. The kind of anger that meant some son of a bitch was fixing to feel some Scott Fenney payback.

EIGHTEEN

OVER THE COURSE of four seasons of Division I-A college football, playing against teams like Texas, Texas A&M, Nebraska, and Oklahoma, teams with players that outweighed the SMU players by forty or fifty pounds per position, Scott Fenney, number 22, had taken a beating. At 185 pounds, he was strong, fast, and tough; but when a 250-pound linebacker tackled him and drove him into the hard turf, he still hurt. He suffered two knee surgeries, a dislocated shoulder, five broken ribs, four broken fingers (the same one twice), two broken noses, one concussion, numerous abrasions and contusions, and a cumulative total of 117 stitches. But he never missed a single game.

Scott Fenney got up every time they knocked him down. And when he did, he always gave them payback, breaking a long run, returning a kickoff, scoring a touchdown. The payback helped make the hurt go away.

Senator Mack McCall had shown Scott the true meaning of hurt. He had hit Scott like no linebacker had ever hit him. Now it was time for payback.

Scott checked his watch and stood. He glanced out at the night lights of downtown. It was almost nine the next evening and Scott was in his office.

"Scotty," Bobby said from the sofa. "I know this was my idea, but maybe it ain't such a good idea."

"You coming or not?"

Bobby stood. "Oh, yeah, I'm coming. Course, I feel like I'm boarding the *Titanic*."

Mack McCall's eyes roamed over the naked body of Jean McCall, and he recalled the first time they had had sex, fifteen years ago, not a month after she had graduated law school and joined his Senate staff. She was young, she was lean, she was sexy, and she was not his wife. His wife was not sexy or lean or young; she was old, forty-five, same age as he was back then, but he did not feel as old as she looked. Martha looked like her mother—not a woman he was particularly interested in having sex with.

At age forty-five, Mack McCall still felt young and randy, and he needed a woman who was young and randy, like Jean. They had sex nearly every day, anytime and anywhere—his private bathroom, the backseat of the limousine, the Senate cloakroom. She had an incredible body, a body that made him feel twenty-five again and brimming with testosterone. And she possessed a sex drive that could permanently disable a man half his age.

She was also a TV camera's dream, beautiful, articulate, charming, and intelligent. When Mack began dreaming of the White House, he had to make a decision:

Did he want a first lady who looked like a grandmother or a fashion model? The decision took less than a minute to make. He divorced Martha.

She hired an asshole for a lawyer and threatened to confirm what the tabloids had suggested: that Senator Mack McCall was having an affair with a member of his staff. Not that that was any big news on Capitol Hill, a member of Congress screwing around on his wife. But it was a sensitive issue when the particular member ran on a conservative family values platform and had his eye on the White House. Of course, Mack McCall could cut a business deal when the need arose. For $100 million, Martha kept her mouth shut and went home to Texas.

Jean had been worth every penny.

But the years had taken their toll on Mack McCall. Now, at age sixty, he didn't feel twenty-five anymore; he didn't feel forty-five, or even fifty-five; he didn't feel young and virile and brimming with testosterone. So he did what any self-respecting sixty-year-old man with money and a wife twenty years younger than him would do: he went to the doctor. Every morning now, Senator Mack McCall showered, shaved, and slapped on after-shave and a testosterone patch, and every night he popped a Viagra pill, all in an effort to satisfy his sexual fantasies and Jean's sexual desires.

That evening she was stretched out naked on their bed. Her body was still incredibly shapely and inviting; her black hair was draped over her shoulders and fell onto her firm breasts; her belly was flat with no stretch marks from pregnancies; her lean legs didn't look like road maps. She was wearing her Clark Kent glasses and working on her laptop; the TV was on but the sound was muted. He was taking no chances tonight: he had replaced this morning's testosterone patch with a fresh one an hour ago when he had swallowed the Viagra pill. The patch was secreting that elixir of youth into his bloodstream and the little blue pill was expanding the arteries leading to his penis, physiological actions that resulted in an impressive erection. Feeling pretty damned proud and young and virile (albeit chemically and momentarily enhanced), Mack went over to Jean and stood by the bed until her eyes left the laptop and found him. Her eyebrows rose, and she smiled.

"I take it we're not going to watch *Dateline* tonight."

Mack could not know his wife was thinking, *Or at least the first five minutes of* Dateline, as she removed her glasses, set the laptop on the night table, slid down onto the bed, and spread her legs. Mack McCall's version of foreplay had always consisted of checking the oil futures, so he climbed on top of Jean and entered her without so much as a howdy-do. She felt incredible, her legs pulled up and wrapped around his waist, her fingernails biting into his butt, her large breasts suffocating him with pleasure, as he pushed into her again and again and again with the steady rhythm of an oil well pump and he wondered what oil futures had closed at today when—

"Mack! Mack, stop!"

Jean reached for her glasses and the remote control. She put her glasses on with her left hand and pointed the remote with her right. Mack slipped out of her, panting heavily.

"*What?*"

Jean pointed at the television. "Look!"

Mack turned to the TV and saw his dead son's face.

"Tonight, from the federal building in downtown Dallas, an exclusive live interview with Shawanda Jones, the woman accused of murdering Clark McCall, the son of Senator Mack McCall, the leading candidate to be the next president of the United States."

On the screen, Mack saw the black face of Shawanda Jones, prostitute, drug addict, and murderer. Sitting next to her was A. Scott Fenney, Esq.

"He's a hunk," Jean said, which ignited the anger already smoldering within Mack.

On the TV: "With Ms. Jones tonight is her court-appointed lawyer, Scott Fenney. Mr. Fenney, every news show in the country has been trying to get an interview with you or your client ever since she was arrested—why tonight?"

"Because certain information has come to our attention that requires a public appeal. And because certain actions of Senator McCall constitute obstruction of justice."

"That's a serious charge, Mr. Fenney. But let's first go back to the night of Saturday, June fifth. What happened?"

Mack McCall's blood pressure rose steadily as the

264

black bitch told her story: That Clark had picked her up, offered her a thousand dollars for a night of sex, took her to the McCall mansion in Highland Park, engaged in sex acts with her, and then beat her and called her nigger; that she fought him off, kneed him in the groin, and left, taking the money he owed her and his car keys; that the last time she had seen Clark, he was alive, lying on the floor, in pain and cursing her; that the murder weapon was in fact her gun, but that she had not held the gun to Clark's head and pulled the trigger and put a bullet through his brain. When she finally stopped talking, the program went to commercial.

During the break, McCall paced the bedroom, naked and angry. And when Mack McCall got angry, someone got hurt. That someone would be A. Scott Fenney. The only question was how McCall would hurt him this time. He had just about decided when the show returned to the air and the reporter turned to Fenney.

"Mr. Fenney, your client is alleging that Clark McCall was a racist and a brutal rapist. But he's not here to defend himself. How can you expect a jury to believe the word of a drug-addicted prostitute?"

"Because she wasn't the first woman Clark McCall beat and raped."

All the anger Mack McCall had experienced in his sixty years of life combined—anger against business competitors, political opponents, his ex-wife—could not compare to the anger that now controlled his being. He wanted desperately to kill Scott Fenney.

"Clark McCall beat and raped another woman a year

ago. She filed a criminal complaint against him, but dropped it under pressure and a half-million-dollar payment from Senator McCall. She has agreed to testify at Shawanda's trial."

"To corroborate that Clark McCall was a rapist?"

"Yes. And there were other women, six others, who were raped and beaten by Clark McCall. I'm asking those women to come forward and testify so that an innocent victim of Clark McCall will not be sentenced to death for a crime she did not commit."

Another commercial break had Mack pointing to Jean's laptop and asking her if she had Dan Ford's home phone number on it. She did.

When the program resumed, the reporter asked: "Now, Mr. Fenney, let's turn to your allegation that Senator McCall obstructed justice."

Fenney said, "Obviously, the trial of the person accused of murdering Clark McCall will be a media circus. The federal court did not believe that the public defender's office could provide an adequate defense for Shawanda under those circumstances. So the court appointed me to represent her."

"That must have been a shock."

"Sure, at first. I'm a partner in a large Dallas law firm and I'm very busy with our paying clients, but I've always believed that lawyers have a professional duty to represent people who can't pay. So when the judge called, I readily accepted the appointment."

"But as they say, no good deed goes unpunished."

"So I've learned. I expected some adverse publicity,

perhaps a few clients who didn't like what I was doing, but I did not expect Senator McCall to try to destroy me."

"And what has Senator McCall done?"

"First he called my senior partner and asked him to get me to exclude any evidence at trial about Clark's past criminal conduct. He said he did not want his son dragged through the mud. But Clark McCall lived in the mud."

"You refused to drop that evidence?"

"Absolutely. To do so would have been unethical conduct by a lawyer and unfair to Shawanda. She's entitled to the very best defense I can muster. And that's exactly what she will get."

"What did the senator do next?"

"He got the U.S. Attorney in Dallas to offer a plea deal, twenty years for Shawanda if we kept quiet about Clark's past. Of course, we rejected the offer. My client is innocent."

"Then what happened?"

"INS agents showed up at my house and arrested my maid, a Mexican national. Consuela—that's her name—had been with us for three years. She's part of our family."

Fenney's eyes looked wet.

"She didn't have a green card?"

"No."

"She was here in America illegally?"

"Yes."

"And you knew that?"

"Look, we can debate the merits of the immigration

laws, but the point is that Senator McCall used his political power in Washington to have my maid in Dallas arrested."

"To pressure you?"

"Yes."

"Did he succeed?"

"No. I will never be pressured to act to the detriment of my client. Senator McCall only hurt a poor Mexican girl."

"Not a smart political move given the percentage of Hispanic voters in America. What happened next?"

"Senator McCall then got me kicked out of my dining club, my athletic club, and my country club."

The reporter offered a shocked expression.

"The man who wants to be president stooped that low?"

"Yes, he did."

"So is that all?"

"No, unfortunately, that's not all. Since I still refused to accede to his demands, Senator McCall used his power to get the bank to call the notes on my cars and my home. I now have ten days to pay off the car notes and thirty days to pay off the house note, or I'll lose everything."

"My God, you're not serious!"

"I'm afraid I am."

"I hesitate to ask, but is there more?"

"Yes. Since all of that did not succeed, McCall called in some favors with a client of mine, Tom Dibrell, a real-estate developer in Dallas and—"

"What kind of favors?"

"Well, Tom told me that ten, twelve years ago, McCall threatened to hold up legislation desired by the lender holding the mortgage on his downtown office building unless the lender held off foreclosure. And that McCall used his influence to swing several federal construction projects to Tom."

"And now he asked Mr. Dibrell for a favor in return?"

"Yes."

"And what was that favor?"

"To fire me as his lawyer."

"And did he?"

"Yes, he did."

"And how does that hurt you?"

"Tom was my biggest client. He paid my firm three million dollars in fees each year."

"That's a lot of money. So when Mr. Dibrell fired you, your professional career was harmed in a very significant way."

"Yes, it was. But I'm here to tell Senator McCall, on national TV, that despite his efforts to destroy me, I will defend Ms. Jones to the best of my ability. And evidence about his son's racism and rapes will be introduced at trial. Shawanda Jones will have a competent defense. I'll make sure of that."

The phone rang just as the program went to commercial again. Mack picked up the phone and answered. It was Delroy calling from Dallas. "You watching this?" Delroy asked.

"Yeah."

"You still just want to control him?"

"Now I want to hurt him. Leak it about his wife and the golf pro."

"Okay, but we can hurt him worse than that . . . and control him."

"You mean . . ." Mack decided not to complete his thought with Jean present. But he didn't need to with Delroy.

"Yeah, I mean. It worked with a Mexican drug lord. It'll damn sure work with a lawyer."

"I don't know, Delroy, that sort of thing . . ."

Mack turned back to the TV. The reporter was speaking directly into the camera: "What kind of man would try to destroy a lawyer for doing his professional duty? For defending a black woman accused of murdering a white man? Apparently, Senator Mack McCall is that kind of man."

Mack's blood pressure and anger spiked again. He said into the phone to Delroy: "Do it."

He could almost see Delroy grinning when he hung up.

On the TV the reporter turned to Fenney: "Mr. Fenney, thank you for coming on tonight so the American people can know what kind of man Senator McCall is before they decide to elect him president. You're a brave man. But Senator McCall is a rich and powerful man. Aren't you afraid he'll hurt you again?"

Fenney said, "McCall can't hurt me anymore."

Mack McCall walked into the closet, returned with a

Smith & Wesson .357 magnum pistol he kept up on the shelf, pointed it at the image of A. Scott Fenney on the television, and pulled the trigger.

"The hell I can't."

After leaving the federal building, Scott drove the Ferrari through the dark and deserted downtown. It was eerily quiet. And it reminded him of his senior season, after his last game, when he walked from the belly of the stadium onto the dark and deserted field, stood on the 50-yard line, and just looked around, knowing it was over.

Rebecca was in the kitchen, staring at the TV, when he entered the house. The late news was on; a reporter was saying, "A flash poll taken immediately after the Shawanda Jones interview shows Senator McCall's poll numbers plummeting. He's fallen to single digits among likely voters, from first place to last, perhaps spelling the end to his White House ambitions."

Scott said, "I showed that son of a bitch."

Rebecca turned from the television; on her face was an expression of utter devastation.

"You just threw our lives away for a whore."

NINETEEN

T HE NEXT MORNING, Scott Fenney felt like he
had the morning after he had run for 193 yards
against Texas: he hurt less because his opponent hurt
more. Sure, he had lost his rich client, all his cash, his
dining, athletic, and country club memberships, and
his Mexican maid, and he would soon lose his Ferrari and
his mansion. But Mack McCall had lost the White
House. Scott Fenney had beaten a Texas roughneck at his
own game.

How about those brass knuckles, McCall?

How's that for hardball, you mean son of a bitch?

So as he pulled the Ferrari into the parking garage
beneath Dibrell Tower a little after nine, Scott was smiling. And why not? He was still a partner in Ford Stevens
LLP, the most profitable law firm in Dallas. He still
made $750,000 a year (although he would have to recruit
new clients to replace Tom Dibrell's fees). He was still a
local football legend, still able to bring a smile to any
SMU alum's face, still able to turn on the famous charm
and flash that movie-star smile.

Scott Fenney was still a winner.

He stuck the key card into the slot on the entrance gate and waited for the gate to rise. And waited. He stuck the key card in again and waited. Still nothing. He punched the button that rang Osvaldo over in the exit booth twenty feet away. When Osvaldo turned and saw him, Scott waved him over. Osvaldo exited the booth and walked over. Scott held up the key card.

"Card won't work," Scott said. "Raise the gate."

Osvaldo retreated a step and said, "No card."

"No, I've got a card. It's not working. Open the gate."

Osvaldo was now shaking his head. "No gate."

"Open the goddamned gate!"

Osvaldo held his hands up. "No card. No gate."

"Jesus Christ!"

Scott backed out and parked the Ferrari on the street, pumped a few quarters into the parking meter, pissed off until he remembered that the Ferrari would be his for only nine more days. Fuck it. Two-hundred-thousand-dollar car gets scratched, it's the bank's loss. By the time he hit the front door of Dibrell Tower two blocks away, he was whistling.

Rebecca Fenney was crying. She was still in bed, hiding from Highland Park. She had bet her beauty on Scott Fenney and lost. Her house. Her car. Her status. Her life. Everything she had acquired over the last eleven years would soon be gone. And it hadn't been lost to a twenty-two-year-old blonde with big tits and a tight ass—to a girl by the pool—but to a heroin addict, a whore, a . . . Rebecca never said that word because even in Highland Park such words are best said only behind the brick walls at the club, but she thought that word now: *nigger*.

Her husband had sacrificed her life for a nigger's life.

There. She had said it. Or at least thought it. As everyone in Highland Park was thinking at that very moment—the town is so small, so insular, that nothing escapes notice. Not that this could have escaped the notice of anyone in America, her husband on national TV, for God's sake! And today at lunch, her (former) society girlfriends would order Caribbean salad, tortilla soup, sparkling water, and for dessert, Rebecca Fenney. She would be today's scandal soufflé.

Oh, how they would gossip! And how they would laugh!

There's nothing the girls love to sink their sharp teeth into more than a juicy scandal: a lesbian affair; a good Highland Park girl knocked up by a black SMU athlete; botched cosmetic surgery; drinking, drugs, and STDs at the high school; criminal fraud committed by a scion of an old Highland Park family; a Democrat in Highland Park; failure in Highland Park. They lapped it up like the family dog laps up leftovers.

Rebecca Fenney had gossiped so many times about other women's scandals. Now everyone in Highland Park would be gossiping about her—at the Village, at the club, at the gym, at every restaurant and in every dressing room. They would all be gossiping and laughing—at her expense.

How could she ever show her face in this town again?

She was crawling back under the comforter when the phone rang.

Boo quietly pushed open the door to her parents' bedroom and stuck her head in. She saw her mother sitting on the far side of the bed and heard her talking on the phone. Her voice sounded strange.

"*What?* . . . Sleeping with Trey? . . . Where'd you hear that? . . . It's all over town? . . . Everyone knows? . . . *Oh, my God!*"

She hung up the phone and put her hands over her face.

"Mother?"

"Oh, God."

"Mother?"

"Oh, God." Finally she turned to Boo. Her mother looked like a frightened little kitten. "What, Boo?"

"Are you okay?"

"No."

"Can I help?"

"No. What do you want?"

"Is it okay if Pajamae and I go to the Village? We'll be real careful crossing the street."

Mother waved her hand. "Fine, whatever."

"Okay. See you later."

Boo started to shut the door, but her mother said, "Boo, wait. Come in. I need to talk to you."

As soon as Scott stepped inside the lobby of Dibrell Tower, he stopped whistling. A tidal wave of reporters and cameramen came rushing toward him, all shouting questions on top of each other.

"Mr. Fenney, what's her name, the woman Clark raped?"

"What are the names of the other women he raped?"

"You brought down Senator McCall—are you happy?"

"Do you think Senator McCall will be indicted?"

"What about Tom Dibrell—will he be indicted?"

Scott squinted at the bright camera lights and ducked and weaved his way toward the elevator bank. But at the speed at which he was advancing against the mass of reporters defending their ground, he wouldn't get into an elevator before noon. He was about to retreat when two enormous blue blazers stepped in front of him. Two black men, Dibrell Tower security guards, were now running interference for Scott Fenney. The reporters had a choice: get out of the way or get run over.

They got out of the way.

The two guards pushed forward until they arrived at the elevators where a third guard stood blocking the doors of an empty elevator. He stepped aside to allow Scott entrance, then again blocked the way. He was joined by the other two guards, three huge bodies in blue blazers protecting Scott Fenney from the reporters and cameras, black guards whom Scott had never before even acknowledged; they were just inanimate objects in the lobby, like the big bronze Remington sculpture. Scott reached over and punched the FLOOR 62 button, then fell to the back of the elevator. Just before the doors closed, the middle guard turned to him and said, "Thanks, Mr. Fenney."

"For what?"

"Standing up for that girl."

Pajamae followed Boo out the front door and down the walkway to the sidewalk. Boo said, "Boy, my mother was acting really weird this morning. The stuff she was saying."

"Is she sick?"

"I don't think so. Why?"

" 'Cause Mama says weird stuff when she takes her medicine."

They turned left down the sidewalk. Boo was talking, but Pajamae was watching. Mama had taught her to keep her eyes peeled when she went outside in their neighborhood, watching for strange people. Of course, in their neighborhood grown men hung around outside the liquor stores on every corner and drank malt liquor out of brown paper bags and peed right into the street whenever nature called, so strange here in Boo's neighborhood was a different thing altogether. But Pajamae still noticed something strange.

A man in a car.

He was sitting across the street and down one house from Boo's. He stared at them as they came down the sidewalk. He was a big man with a bald head in a black car. When she and Mama were outside and a white man looking like him drove into the projects, everyone would stop what they were doing and shout, "The man!" The police. The bald man in the black car looked like a policeman.

Pajamae noticed the car door open partway and the bald man's black shoe come out. She was about to grab Boo and hightail it back to their house when an old man stepped out the front door of the house they were walking in front of. He came down the path toward them, but he stopped and picked up a newspaper on the grass.

Boo said, "Good morning, Mr. Bailey."

The old man smiled and said, "Why, good morning to you, Miss Boo Fenney."

Pajamae looked over at the black car. The bald man's foot was back in the car and the door was shut, but he was still staring. They continued down the sidewalk and came to a busy road named Preston and turned right. Pajamae glanced back and saw that the black car was gone. She shook her head at herself for being so silly: *You're not in the projects, girl!*

They walked on and Pajamae soon found herself enjoying the stroll through Boo's neighborhood, what she called the Bubble. She always felt nervous and scared if Louis was gone and she and Mama had to walk alone through their neighborhood to the nearest liquor store to buy some bread or eggs, even in the middle of the day. Mama always told her, "If I say 'run,' you run, girl." But she wasn't nervous or scared at all in this neighborhood. The sidewalks were so clean, no beer cans or liquor bottles or syringes or those funny long balloons Mama told her never to touch. And no men hanging around outside liquor stores—in fact, there were no liquor stores. No pimps or pushers trying to recruit her or sell to her, no older boys driving by and yelling out nasty words, no loud rap music from cars and boom boxes, and nobody cussing each other 'cause they just got evicted. It was so quiet!

Boo's Bubble was nice.

They stopped at an intersection and waited for the light to change. When it did, they looked carefully both ways and hurried across four lanes of traffic and a short parking lot and onto the sidewalk of—

"Highland Park Village," Boo said.

They were standing outside a store named Polo/Ralph Lauren in a fairyland place Pajamae had never imagined existed, fancy cars lining the sidewalk shaded by little trees and fancy white women getting out of those cars followed by pretty little white girls looking like princesses and giving her second and third glances like they had never seen a black person their whole lives, and leaving behind a smell so sweet that Pajamae breathed it in several times and was reminded of the old fat ladies at church each Sunday morning—only these ladies weren't fat and they didn't gush over her and pinch her cheek. The white women and white girls just hustled by and into the store, the cool air from inside rushing out, making Pajamae's face feel like it did when she stuck her head in the freezer to cool off, as she often did down home in the projects.

Boo said, "Do y'all have shopping places like this?"

"We don't have any place like this."

When she and Mama went shopping, it was generally at yard sales and the Goodwill store, not someplace where she couldn't begin to pronounce the names, and sometimes one of their neighbors would get a good deal on sneakers or stereos or TVs and sell them right out of his car trunk, at real good prices 'cause the stuff was a little warm, Mama would say, although Pajamae was never exactly sure what she meant. And before school started each year, Mama would work extra and Louis would take them to buy her school clothes at the JCPenney, but it wasn't like this.

"Where-*as*," Pajamae said.

They walked down the sidewalk in the shade of the awning, Pajamae feeling like it was Christmas, checking out every window display, fancy clothes on skinny mannequins wearing makeup, and past a kids' store—

"That's Jacadi Paris," Boo said. "My closet is full of clothes from here."

"Does this stuff cost a lot?"

"Mother bought them, so they must."

When they arrived at a store called Calvin Klein, Boo said, "Britney was here a few months ago."

"Britney who?"

"Britney Spears, the singer. Everybody went crazy."

"White girl?"

"Yeah."

"Oh. We don't listen to white girls down in the projects."

Boo shrugged. "I don't listen to her up here either."

And on they went, past stores named Luca Luca and Escada and Lilly Dodson—"Mrs. Bush bought her red party dress here, when George W. got elected the first time," Boo said—and Banana Republic—only they sold clothes not bananas—and they crossed the parking lot and got ice cream cones at Who's Who Burgers.

They walked outside and Pajamae stopped short. A bad feeling swept over her small body: the bald man in the black car was driving by slowly and giving her a creepy stare. She got really scared, and Pajamae Jones didn't get really scared easily.

"Boo, that man's following us."

"What man?"

"That man who just drove by, in that black car. See him? The bald guy?"

Boo laughed. "This is Highland Park. Nothing bad happens here."

Boo tugged on her arm and Pajamae followed reluctantly. They walked past more stores then went inside a store with the same name as the old wino with no teeth who lived three apartments down. Harold.

"This was my mother's favorite store," Boo said.

A saleslady was on them before they made it five steps, and Pajamae thought at first she was going to run them out. But the lady smiled and said hi like she was really happy to see them. She was very pretty for a white girl, with hair that bounced and smooth skin and lips that were painted red. She looked at Pajamae and leaned down, putting her knees together and her hands on her knees, and said, "My, aren't you the cutest little thing!"

Pajamae was wearing Boo's denim overalls, a white tee shirt, white socks, and white sneakers; her hair was in cornrows; and she was licking her ice cream cone.

She said, "Thank you, ma'am."

"So how do you like living in Highland Park?"

Pajamae glanced at Boo, who shrugged. How did this woman know that she was living with Mr. Fenney?

"I like it just fine, thank you."

"You tell your mother to come see me, my name's Sissy. I'll make sure she's as well dressed as any woman in Highland Park."

"My mama's in jail."

The lady snapped up straight with a confused look on her face. "*Jail?* Aren't you the new black family's little girl?"

"I don't have a family. I only have Mama. And Louis, he's like an uncle only he's not."

Boo said, "What new black family?"

"The black family that just moved into town, the first black homeowners in the history of Highland Park." The saleslady was now staring at Boo when a hint of recognition crossed her painted face. "You're the Fenney girl, aren't you?"

"Yes, ma'am."

"I almost didn't recognize you with that hair.

Where's your mother been lately"—her thin eyebrows raised a notch—"and your handsome father?"

"My mother's being weird and A. Scott's been real busy."

"Helping my mama," Pajamae added, and the lady's head swiveled to her. "They say she killed the McCall boy, but she didn't."

The saleslady slapped her hand over her mouth. *"She's your mother?"*

Pajamae licked her ice cream cone and said, "Unh-huh. Mr. Fenney, he's her lawyer, so everybody's mad at him."

The saleslady's face suddenly looked like that boy's face that day in the projects when he tried to get a free-bie from Mama and when she refused, he called her a "white man's whore." As he turned to run away he ran smack into Louis—and that black boy's face turned white. Just as this lady's face had turned two shades whiter. She must not have known what to say, so she said, "Maybe you girls should leave now."

"Mr. Ford wants to see you," Sue said.

Scott grabbed his message slips and walked to the staircase. He greeted his fellow partners along the way, but all he got in return were odd stares, averted eyes, and shaking heads. No doubt they had seen his network interview last night and didn't care for it. Fuck 'em. He found Dan standing by the window in his office.

"Dan, what's up?"

Dan turned; his face looked like he hadn't slept last night.

"Come in, Scotty. Shut the door."

Scott did as instructed and said, "Dan, can you talk to Ted at the bank? He's being a real asshole. He called the notes on the Ferrari and my house."

"I'm afraid I can't."

"Why not?"

"Because, Scotty, as of right now, you're no longer a partner in the firm."

"You're demoting me?"

"I'm firing you."

Dan's words knocked the air out of Scott as fully as a football helmet in the solar plexus. Scott stumbled back and fell onto the sofa. Dan returned to the window and stared out, his hands clasped behind him. Scott struggled to find words.

"You said I was like a son to you."

Without turning from the window: "You were. But when my son embarrassed me with that homosexual nonsense, I disowned him. Now I'm disowning you."

"Why?"

Dan turned to face Scott; he was now an angry father figure.

"Your little spectacle last night! For Christ's sake, Scott, what the hell were you thinking?"

"McCall tried to destroy me, that's what I was thinking!"

"So you go on national TV and accuse the senior senator from Texas of obstruction of justice? Extortion? Bribery?"

"I was just trying to do the right thing!"

"The hell you were! I know you too well. You were giving McCall a little Scott Fenney payback. You weren't doing it for the hooker; you were doing it for yourself. And even if you were doing the right thing, it's no better. I told you, Scotty, this firm doesn't exist to do the right thing; no law firm does. We don't do the right thing; we do what's right for our clients. And destroying Mack McCall's presidential ambitions isn't right for our clients. But you took care of that, didn't you?"

"What was I supposed to do, let him take everything I have? My club memberships, my car, my house, my best client? McCall did all that."

Dan Ford was now staring at Scott with an expression Scott had seen only once before, five years ago. Scott had stood next to Dan in a state district court as the judge read his ruling, a ruling against their client, against Ford Stevens, against Dan Ford, who had made a substantial contribution to the judge's last campaign. Dan's expression then and now was that of a man betrayed, but a man with the power to do something about it.

"No, Scotty, he didn't do any of that. I did."

"You?"

"Yes, me. When you refused to do what I asked, I wanted you to see what your life would be like without all the things success buys—*It's a Wonderful Life* starring Scott Fenney. But you're stubborn, Scotty, too stubborn for your own damn good. McCall asked me for a small favor, to get you to leave his son's past in the past where it belongs, so he could be president. And I asked you for a small favor, so I could be the president's lawyer. And after all that I've done for you, how did you repay me? You betrayed me."

"*A small favor?* Dan, without that evidence, Shawanda will be sentenced to death!"

"So?"

"What, she's just a nigger?"

Dan laughed. "Oh, yeah, I'm a racist. My son grew up wanting to be Michael Jordan and my daughter's in love with Tiger Woods . . . No, it's the other way around, my daughter wanted to be Jordan and my son's in love with Tiger. Anyway, I'd love to have both of them as clients. Because they're rich. Because they pay their lawyers lots of money. Scotty, the color of law isn't black-and-white, it's green! The rule of law is money—money rules! Money makes the law and the law protects the money! And lawyers protect the people with money!"

Dan's face was red and his neck veins were purple cords. He paused and gathered himself.

"Scotty, this firm is my life. I built it from nothing to the richest firm in town. No one makes what we make. No one! And no one's gonna hurt this firm, not your hooker, not you, not anyone. I'll run over anyone who gets in my way."

"What about me, Dan? You gonna run over me, too?"

Dan sat down in his chair, reached over and buzzed

his secretary, then looked back up at Scott and said, "I think I already have."

Scott stood in the middle of the office, surrounded by Dan's trophy heads. Their sad eyes seemed to look down on him, as if they were saying, *We've saved a place up here for you.* And now Scott knew how John Walker and the others had felt standing right here when Dan had fired them without warning. He had chuckled when another lawyer had shown him John's ad in the TV guide—one day a successful lawyer in a big firm and the next day just another shyster trying to sleaze out a living. Now his mind conjured up his own ad, situated between ones for a psychic and an escort service: CAR ACCIDENT? DIVORCE? BANKRUPTCY? CALL A. SCOTT FENNEY, ATTORNEY-AT-LAW. WE CARE. E-Z TERMS. SE HABLA ESPAÑOL.

This can't be happening, not to me!

The door behind Scott opened and two of the three black Dibrell Tower security guards from downstairs were standing there, puzzled looks on their faces.

It was happening to him.

"Your personal belongings will be delivered to your house, Scott," Dan said. "Firm policy."

The game was over. Scott Fenney had lost. There was nothing more to do but to walk off the field. The guards parted and Scott walked down the corridors that he had so proudly strutted just days before, A. Scott Fenney, Esq., Tom Dibrell's lawyer, wired on success. Yesterday, the other lawyers had greeted him like a star; today they averted their eyes as from a patient dying of AIDS. Dead lawyer walking. Scott Fenney's legal career as he knew it was over.

He and his escorts walked down the staircase to the sixty-second floor and ran into Missy walking up, looking sexy in a tight knit dress. But she did not wink at Scott Fenney today; she did not act like they were on the brink of an affair; she acted like he had a contagious disease. They continued down to the landing, where Sue stood, holding out his briefcase and 9-iron. Before he reached her, Sid Greenberg walked up to Sue with a stack of documents.

"Sue, I'm putting these documents on your desk. Copy them and get them up to Dibrell ASAP. Put the originals in Scott's . . . I mean, in my office."

"Yes, Mr. Greenberg."

"Sid?"

Sid spotted Scott and said, "Oh, hi, Scott. Sorry to hear the news. Good luck."

"You're taking my client, my secretary, my office? I taught you everything you know!"

"Yeah, Scott, you did. You taught me practicing law is just business. Nothing personal."

"I wasn't talking about me!"

Sid shrugged lamely and walked off. Scott turned to Sue, her hands extended toward him. Scott took his brief-case and 9-iron from her.

"Good-bye, Mr. Fenney."

"That's it? Good-bye? Eleven years you've been my secretary. Don't you care?"

Sue got a look on her face he had never seen and she seemed to grow six inches.

"For eleven years I've fetched your dry cleaning and coffee, run your personal errands, paid your personal bills, shopped for gifts for your wife and child and clients, lied to clients for you . . . Did you care about me? About my life? You never once asked about my life. Do you know I have a handicapped child and that's the only reason I've put up with you for all these years? Because I needed the money? You didn't know and you didn't care. Did you care when Mr. Walker got fired? No. Like every other lawyer here, you care only about yourself."

Scott turned from this stranger standing on the marble floor in the lobby, talking to him like that in front of a gathering crowd. Followed by the two guards, he walked to the elevators and pushed the down button. The doors opened and they stepped in. One of the guards said, "What happened, Mr. Fenney?"

"I got fired."

" 'Cause of what you did, standing up for that girl?"

"Yeah."

"I know where Mr. Ford parks his Mercedes down in the garage. You want I should flatten his tires?"

"Yeah." Then Scott shook his head. "No."

The doors started to shut, but at the last second a hand pushed in and the doors receded. Standing there was Sue. She said, "John Walker's wife died last week."

They stepped outside the store and Pajamae froze.

"Boo, there he is again."

"Who?"

"The bald man in the black car."

"Where?"

Pajamae motioned with her head to the parking lot. Boo turned that way, but Pajamae said, "Don't look!"

They turned and faced the store window. In the Village, cars could park in slanted spots right at the sidewalk. Then there was a little one-way road for cars to drive around the center and then two more rows of parking in the middle of the open parking area. The bald man in the black car was parked there, maybe thirty feet away. Boo acted casual and kind of looked around at different things and finally got around to glancing at the bald man in the black car: he was staring straight at them. Boo turned away.

Pajamae was frantic. "Let's run, Boo!"

Boo took Pajamae firmly by the arms. "No. Act normal. He can't grab both of us, not here. He's just trying to scare us."

"Honey, it's working!"

Boo started patting around her pockets.

"What are you doing?" Pajamae asked.

"I'm pretending I'm looking for something." She threw up her hands and pointed inside the store. "Now I'm acting like I left something inside. Come on, we'll go back in and I'll call A. Scott. He'll come for us."

"He better get here fast."

"He drives a Ferrari."

They walked back inside and Boo went directly over

to the same saleslady. "Ma'am, may I use a phone? It's an emergency. I need to call my handsome father."

Scott had always enjoyed the ride home at the end of each day, jumping into a $200,000 automobile, exiting the parking garage, saluting Osvaldo like the president saluting the Air Force One attendants, and pointing the Ferrari north toward Highland Park . . . Driving leisurely through the Uptown area just north of downtown where the singles commingled, young men and gorgeous girls, their heads swiveling his way as he passed by, envy written all over their faces, wondering what it must be like to be living a perfect life like the handsome man in the Ferrari . . . And finally entering the Town of Highland Park, where the kids are smart, their parents are successful, and everyone is safe and secure.

But today was different.

He wasn't enjoying the ride home. Because at the end of the ride, he would have to tell his wife and daughter that he had been fired, that he was no longer a partner at Ford Stevens, that he would no longer be bringing home money each night, that he had lost the family fortune. That Scott Fenney was now a loser.

How could he face his wife as a loser? His daughter? His neighbors in Highland Park? Scott hit the right turn signal and braked to turn onto Beverly Drive . . . but at the last second he changed his mind and accelerated straight through the intersection and continued north past Highland Park Village. He couldn't go home. Not yet. A few blocks later he turned left and pulled over in front of the Highland Park High School football stadium, where life as he knew it had begun the first day of fall football practice his freshman year.

Inside a stadium that shamed many college stadiums, this year's team was practicing on the artificial turf. Scott cut the engine and got out of the Ferrari. He walked over to the fence and watched the boys working out on the field while the cheerleaders went through their routines on the sideline, white boys dreaming of being another Highland Park football legend like Doak Walker or Bobby Layne or Scotty Fenney and white girls dreaming of being another Hollywood starlet from Highland Park like Jayne Mansfield or Angie Harmon, but knowing that if their dreams were not realized they could always fall back on their daddies' money, fortunes that assured them futures as bright and certain as the blue sky above. And he wondered if he had fooled himself all these years, thinking he belonged here, that his football heroics were enough to make him one of them. Maybe the son of a construction worker is always the son of a construction worker. Maybe a renter is always a renter. Maybe the poor kid on the block is always the poor kid on the block, even if he lives in a mansion. Maybe you are what you've always been.

His dream had begun right out there, on that very field, twenty-one years ago when he was fifteen. And that dream had ended today. And he found himself wondering, for the first time since that day so long ago, what he would do with the rest of his life.

He walked back to the Ferrari. Now he would drive home and tell his wife and daughter that he had lost everything, his only consolation being that there was nothing more for Mack McCall and Dan Ford to take, nothing more for Scott Fenney to lose.

When he opened the car door, his cell phone was ringing.

A. Scott said he'd be there in less than a minute. He didn't lie. They were standing on the sidewalk outside the store again when Boo heard the familiar roar of the Ferrari's engine. She turned and saw the bright red vehicle veer sharply into the Village and accelerate through the parking lot. She held her arms above her head and waved wildly and jumped up and down. And then she pointed directly at the bald man in the black car. He sat up quickly when he saw her pointing; then he saw the Ferrari coming toward him. He started his car and drove out of his parking place and turned left, but another car was backing out of one of the slanted spots by the sidewalk.

His car was blocked.

The red Ferrari screeched to a stop behind the bald man's black car. A. Scott jumped out. He didn't even shut his door. He ran up to the black car with a golf club in his hand.

Why did A. Scott have a golf club in the Ferrari?

Boo's lawyer-father, wearing one of his starched white shirts and a silk tie flapping over his shoulder, reared back and swung the club at the driver's window.

WHACK!

The glass cracking sounded like an explosion and froze everyone within earshot. A few old people ducked. Ladies from inside the store rushed outside. Now it was the bald man's turn to be scared. A. Scott yanked on the man's door, but it was locked. So he stepped forward and swung the golf club again and again at the windshield of the car and screamed words Boo had never heard him say:

"You're following my girls, you sonofabitch!"

WHACK!

"McCall sent you, didn't he!"

WHACK!

"You come around my girls again, I swear to God I'll fuckin' kill you!"

WHACK!

The car in front drove off. The bald man gunned the black car and sped away and around the corner. A. Scott stood there in the middle of the Village parking lot, red-faced, breathing hard and sweating, and holding the golf club over his shoulder like an ax. He looked like an action figure. Shoppers were staring, shocked at such a commotion in Highland Park. Boo was grinning: it was great! The same saleslady was standing next to her.

"God, he's handsome," she said.

Boo Fenney had never been so proud of her father. She ran to him, wrapped her arms around his waist, and clutched him tightly. Pajamae joined them.

"You girls okay?"

"We are now. Who was that man?"

"Delroy Lund."

Pajamae said, "Mr. Fenney, you're the man!"

Boo said, "A. Scott, you said the F-word."

"Yeah." His breathing was calming. "I'm sorry."

The adrenaline rush had receded by the time Scott turned the Ferrari into the driveway at 4000 Beverly Drive and drove into the back motor court. The girls were doubled up in the passenger seat.

Pajamae said, "That's why Louis walks with me and Mama. No one messes with him, not even in the projects."

Scott cut the engine, grabbed his cell phone, and hit a number he had recently added to the speed dial. When a familiar voice answered, he said, "Louis, this is Scott Fenney. I need your help."

He hung up and they climbed out of the car. There was still his wife. He still had to tell Rebecca the bad news. They entered the house through the back door. It was quiet.

"Rebecca?"

Boo said, "Oh, I forgot. She's gone."

"Gone? Gone where?"

"On a trip."

"Where?"

"I don't know. She just said she had to leave."

Scott took the stairs two steps at a time and ran down the hall to their bedroom. He found Rebecca's letter on the bed, a handwritten good-bye. He had lost her home, her cars, and her chair of the Cattle Barons' Ball. In short, he had ruined her life, she said, so they were through, just as she had promised. And since she could no longer hold her head high in Highland Park, she was leaving with the assistant golf pro at the country club. He was going on the PGA tour. She would be a golfer's groupie.

"When is she coming back?"

Scott looked up to Boo standing in the door.

"She's not."

Boo was crying facedown in bed. *Every girl she knew had a mother—even Pajamae!* She felt Pajamae's arms around her, hugging her tightly.

"Boo, I don't have a daddy and now you don't have a mama, maybe your daddy and my mama could get married. We'd be sisters."

"Pajamae, A. Scott can't marry your mother, she's . . ."

Pajamae's hug went soft. Boo felt her pull away. Boo wiped her face and sat up. Pajamae had a funny look on her face. Her fists were on her hips, like Mother when she got mad.

"She's *what*?"

Boo shrugged. "She's twenty-four. That's way too young for him. He's really old."

*

Louis arrived an hour after Scott's call. He pulled his old car around back. Scott met him in the motor court. They shook hands this time.

"Thanks for coming, Louis."

"Ain't no problem, Mr. Fenney. I been watching over Pajamae most of her life. Been missing her." He looked around. "Course, you probably don't get as much shootin' up here."

"Come on inside, Louis, I've got a bedroom for you."

"Aw, no, sir, Mr. Fenney, I don't feel right with that."

Scott could tell that Louis was uncomfortable with the idea, so he didn't press him.

"You can stay in the cabana. Consuela, our maid, lives out there, but she's gone for a while. INS."

"No, sir, that her place. I sleep in my car. In the garage. I can keep a better eye out back here."

"It's air-conditioned, there's a full bath. I can fix up a bed for you . . . and I'll bring out a TV and a recliner."

"TV and chair be nice, but not the bed. Backseat of my car work just fine." Louis smiled. "And, Mr. Fenney, don't you worry none. Ain't no one gonna hurt them girls now."

Scott would not be spending the rest of his day in his fancy office on the sixty-second floor doing the things lawyers do and eating lunch at the swanky Downtown Club and working out among gorgeous girls at the athletic club. He did not feel special today, sitting in the den at home and staring out the windows at the pool and the professionally landscaped yard. His career was gone, his wife was gone, and his house and cars would soon be gone. Mack McCall had won. And his prize was Scott Fenney's perfect life.

For the first time in his life, Scott felt defeated. He didn't know if he could get up off the ground this time.

Twice Boo came downstairs and crawled up into his lap and they cried together. The third time Pajamae came with her. The two girls sat on the wide arms of the big leather chair and buried their faces in his broad shoulders and cried until his shirt was wet. They never said a word.

Scott sat there as the sun's rays moved slowly from one side of the den to the other. He heard the girls in the kitchen, and Pajamae brought him a scrambled egg sandwich, but he had no appetite. When the sky turned dark, he pushed himself out of the chair, climbed the stairs, and put a brave face on for the girls. He found them huddled in bed and his chair next to the bed. He sat and they said prayers.

Then Boo said, "I don't want to read tonight. I want to talk."

Pajamae said, "We want to talk."

Scott removed his glasses. "Okay. What about?"

"We saw you on TV last night," Boo said, "with Pajamae's mother. I know I'm not supposed to watch TV at night, but I went downstairs and saw Mother watching you on TV, so I had to, you know that."

Scott nodded. "And?"

"And you have some explaining to do, A. Scott."

"Ask your questions."

298

Scott knew better than to launch into a narrative with Boo. He always made her ask the questions. He figured if she asked, she was ready to know.

"What's sex?"

He hadn't figured on that question. That was a question for a girl to ask her mother, but when her mother runs off with the assistant golf pro, it falls to the father. And now he had two girls facing him, their legs curled under them, hands in their laps, apprehension on their faces, asking about sex.

"That's a boy's thing, right, Mr. Fenney?"

"A boy's thing?"

"You know, a boy's privates. Like, when I go outside in the projects, some boy's always saying, 'C'mon over here, little girl, an' I shows you my sex.' "

"Oh. Well, sex is when a boy and a girl . . . I mean, a man and a woman . . . when they, uh . . ."

"Do the nasty?" Pajamae blurted out. "That's what the big girls call it. I told Mama what they said, and she said I couldn't play with those girls anymore."

"Look, do either of you have any idea what sex is?"

The girls shook their heads.

"Why do you want to know?"

"Because Mama said the dead man gave her money for sex."

"Oh."

"Then he hit her, and boy, that was his first mistake. My mama, she doesn't let any man hit her, not since my daddy. So she kicked his butt good." She smiled. "Like you beat up that man's car, Mr. Fenney."

Boo said, "That was awesome! You were great! Did you ruin your golf club?"

Their attention thus diverted, Scott did not have to explain sex to two nine-year-old girls. After the girls had relived the scene at the Village, Boo said, "Clark wasn't very nice, was he?"

"No, he wasn't."

"And now his father, the senator, he's mad at you because you're trying to help Pajamae's mother?"

"Yes."

"To keep the po-lice from killing Mama?"

"Yes."

"That man today, he works for the senator?"

"Yes."

"Is he going to come after us again?"

"No, baby, he's not."

Pajamae smiled. "He'll have to come through Louis."

Boo said, "Do we have to sell our house?"

"Yes, Boo, we do."

"Why?"

"Because I got fired today."

"You're not a lawyer anymore?"

"No, I'm still a lawyer, just not with the firm."

"And that means what?"

"That means as of right now, I don't have any income."

"No money?"

"We have some money, but not enough to keep this house."

Boo nodded. "When Cindy's dad got fired, they had

to sell their home. You said that would never happen to us."

"I was wrong."

"And you've got to sell the cars?"

"The bank will just take them."

"Are we poor now?"

"No, Boo, we're not poor. Poor people are like—"

"Mama and me," Pajamae said.

"So all these bad things, Consuela, the cars, the house, your job, Mother leaving, it's all because McCall's mad at you?"

"Yeah . . . well, maybe not your mother."

"Mama always says she's bad luck."

"Pajamae, your mother's not to blame. I made a decision. And decisions have consequences. Sometimes bad consequences."

They were quiet for a long moment then Boo said softly, "Mother was crying. She said I'd be better off without her."

TWENTY

JULY EXITED THEIR LIVES and August entered, ushering in the dog days of summer when hot air masses called Mexican Plumes settle in over Dallas like mushroom clouds, fending off cool air from the north and rain from the south and trapping the occupants of the land below in an unmerciful mixture of 110 degree temperature and 80 percent humidity, day after day after sweltering day. The winds subside and the air is so still that even the slightest breeze feels like a blue norther. Pollution watches reach level purple, which means just breathing the air can kill you. Sidewalks are vacant of pedestrians, dogs lie all day in the shade, too weary even to engage their tails to swat the flies buzzing about their hindquarters, and TV reporters inevitably fry eggs on the sidewalk as stunts for the evening news. Time seems to slow to a crawl. Women's hairdos and their prize-winning gardens wilt, car radiators and drivers' tempers boil over, and incidents of road rage rise dramatically, as do domestic violence calls to 911. The reservoirs supplying Dallas's drinking water run precipitously low, the city rations lawn watering, the green grass bakes to a crisp brown, and the pest control business picks up as the entire rat population emerges as one from their nests in search of a drink, usually from the family pool. Poor people without air conditioners die.

The only thing Dallas has going for it in August is knowing it's worse in Houston. Houston's a goddamned swamp. If the heat and humidity don't kill you in Houston, mosquitoes the size of small birds will.

"It's hot," Scott said.

Life in Dallas in August is lived indoors and in pools. Where Scott Fenney now was, sitting on the steps of the backyard pool in the cool water and wearing sunglasses, a sombrero-style straw hat, and a number 50 sunblock to protect his fair skin from the deadly UV rays. He sucked iced tea through a straw from a big plastic mug like he was siphoning gasoline while Bobby sucked on a cigarette. Boo and Pajamae were playing with a Frisbee in the shallow end of the pool, Louis was sitting in the shade of the patio awning, and out front the FOR SALE BY OWNER sign was slowing traffic on Beverly Drive.

Scott had decided to sell the place himself, without a real-estate agent, an unheard-of transaction in Highland Park. Selling your own house was way too similar in job description to mowing your own grass or washing your own car, manual labor that no Highland Park homeowner with pride, money, and a religious upbringing dared engage in, for to do so called into question the whole concept of divine infallibility: "If the good Lord wanted us to mow our own grass and wash our own cars, then why did He make Mexicans?" Or so the prevailing thought went. Bottom line, if you're too damn cheap to pay a real-estate commission, then you're too damn cheap to live in Highland Park. But as he watched his income evaporate before his eyes, Scott had become damn cheap lately.

His asking price was $3.5 million, the market value. But market value didn't mean squat when the seller was desperate and everyone in the market for a Highland Park home knew it. The best offer to date was $3 million, only $200,000 more than he owed. A broker's six percent sales commission would take $180,000 and leave Scott only $20,000 in sales proceeds. Once closing costs were deducted, he'd be lucky to break even. After doing the math, Scott drove to the nearest hardware store, purchased the red-and-white FOR SALE sign, and hammered the son of a bitch into the front lawn.

"How's Boo handling it?" Bobby asked.

Scott slapped a June bug off the water and wondered why June bugs hung around through August. Rebecca had been gone fifteen days today.

"Okay, I guess. Hell, I think Boo misses Consuela more—she was more of a mother to her than Rebecca."

"Rudy gonna get her back?"

In spite of Rudy Gutierrez's best efforts, the INS had deported Consuela de la Rosa to Mexico. She was now living in the four-star Camino Real Hotel in Nuevo Laredo on Scott Fenney's American Express card and waiting for Rudy to secure her green card so she could return to the Fenney family in Dallas. A week ago, Scott had put Esteban Garcia on a bus south to keep her company.

"She cleared the background checks, I'm sponsoring her for citizenship, guaranteeing her employment . . . but the INS is slow-balling her green card." He shook his head. "But I'll get her back. I promised her. And Boo needs her more than ever now, her mother running off with a goddamned golf pro."

"I understand Rebecca leaving you"—Bobby shot Scott a smile—"but how could she leave Boo?"

Scott shrugged. "The humiliation, I guess. This is a tough town if your life is less than perfect. Failure is not an option in Highland Park." Scott paused and looked over at the girls. "Thank God she didn't take Boo."

"Maybe she just changed."

"Maybe. Maybe I never really knew her. Back then, we were exactly the same, that's why I married her. We were young and ambitious, two poor kids on the block trying to make it big in Dallas. When we stood in that church and said 'for better or for worse,' we weren't thinking for worse. Things were good and getting better fast. I never figured on things getting worse."

He shook his head.

"It's just like football. You never really know your teammates until you start losing."

"One problem with that, Scotty."

"What's that?"

"She started up with that guy while you were still winning."

Scott nodded. "So the home, the cars, the clothes,

none of it made her happy." He looked over at Bobby. "What the hell do women want?"

Bobby chuckled. "Like I would know? Shit, Scotty, *two* women have walked out on me."

"The last seven months, she didn't want to have sex."

Bobby caught an errant Frisbee flung by Boo and said, "My wives didn't want to have sex on our wedding night."

"I'll probably never have sex again," Scott said.

Bobby flipped the Frisbee back to Boo and said, "*You?* Shit, Scotty, half the married men in Highland Park are worrying their wives are gonna want a second shot at you. It's me who's never gonna have sex again. Been almost three years." Bobby took a drag on his cigarette. "Course, I can crush an armadillo with my right hand."

"That's going to kill you one day, Bobby."

"Nah, it'll only make you go blind."

"Not that. Smoking."

"Oh. One can only hope."

"Don't start that depressed crap with me, Bobby. I'm the one who's lost everything."

Bobby exhaled smoke and said, "Yeah, but at least you had everything for a while. At least you know what it feels like."

Scott sucked his tea and said, "You loved her back then, didn't you?"

"Yeah, but mostly I loved your life."

"Me, too. Right up until two months ago. If Buford had called anyone but me, my life would still be perfect."

"It wasn't perfect, Scotty. You just didn't know it."

Scott felt the emotion building inside him again and the tears forming and thought he would burst out crying as he had each night in the shower until Bobby said, "You think he'll make it?"

His tone was that of asking whether a patient would survive a life-threatening operation.

"Who make what?"

"Her golf pro—you think he'll make it on the tour? It's pretty tough out there."

Bobby maintained his deadpan expression until Scott jumped on him and dunked him, Bobby holding one arm aloft to keep his cigarette dry. Scott released him when Boo yelled, "Oh, boys—we've got company!"

Over by the entrance to the motor court stood a burly man wearing mirrored sunglasses and a cap turned backward, his greasy hair and black tee shirt stained with sweat, his huge belly lapping over his waist like a lava flow over a cliff. He was looking around at the Fenney estate like a kid at Disneyland.

The repo man.

He was here to take away Scott's beloved $200,000 Ferrari. Two days ago, knowing this moment would come, Scott had cashed out his 401(k) and purchased a replacement vehicle: a $20,000 Volkswagen Jetta.

Scott walked over to the motor court. Two more tow trucks were idling at the curb, here for the Range Rover and Rebecca's Mercedes-Benz. The repo man held out a clipboard and said, "Nice hat." Scott signed the document acknowledging the repossessions on this date and watched as the red Ferrari 360 Modena two-seater with Connolly leather interior and an engine capable of hitting 180 miles per hour was hoisted onto the flatbed by a winch and secured in place. Even though he knew he was losing something he never really had, it still hurt like hell to see his perfect life being dismantled and carted off piece by piece.

An hour later, Scott, still hurting, was stretched out on the chaise lounge by the pool.

"Mr. Fenney," Louis said.

Scott looked over at Louis, who nodded his head in the direction of the motor court. Scott twisted around and saw a young couple standing there. The man was slim, in his early thirties, and dressed in a starched, long-sleeve, button-down blue shirt, khaki slacks, and black loafers. His hair was dark and curly, his skin pale and pasty. He was wearing wire-rimmed glasses. He seemed vaguely familiar.

The man said, "We had an appointment to see the house at three. We rang the doorbell, but no one answered."

Scott checked his watch and climbed out of the chair.

"Sorry, I lost track of time."

Scott walked over in his swim trunks, bare-chested and barefooted, and held out his hand.

"Scott Fenney."

"Jeffrey Birnbaum. And my wife, Penny."

Standing next to him was a pretty young Highland

Park Junior League wife, perfectly made up and wearing a red sundress and red sandals. Her hair was jet black, her legs were bare and tanned, her body trim, and her lips matched her dress. Jeffrey had married up in looks, way up.

Penny said, "You're famous."

"Infamous is more like it."

She smiled, that flirtatious smile so familiar to Scott Fenney, and he immediately knew Penny, because he had dated so many Pennys during high school and college: a nice Highland Park girl who had taken a walk on the wild side and was now ready to settle down with a nice Highland Park boy who could provide a nice Highland Park mansion. Scott motioned around at the motor court, garage, and backyard.

"Four-car garage, heated and air-conditioned, pool and spa, one-bedroom, one-bath cabana, all on one acre in the heart of Highland Park. Come on, I'll show you the place."

Scott led Mr. and Mrs. Birnbaum through his house, starting with the commercial-grade kitchen with the Italian tile floor, the mural of a French bakery scene on one wall, hand-painted on hundreds of six-inch tiles, and the walk-in freezer big enough to hold a side of beef. He proceeded through the butler's pantry, the formal living and dining rooms, the den, and then down to the basement for the wine cellar, the home theater, the game room, and the exercise room with the framed blowup of himself running the ball against Texas, the one that had hung in his office for eleven years, leaning against the far wall.

"You're a legend," Penny said. "Did you really get a hundred ninety-three yards against Texas, like the paper said?"

"Sure did. You a big football fan?"

"Oh, I love football," Penny said.

Jeffrey glanced at the exercise machines with indifference and walked out. Penny lingered behind, and as she squeezed past Scott at the door, she gave him a look and whispered, "But I love football players more."

They found Jeffrey in the game room rolling billiard balls across the pool table, then they proceeded upstairs to each of the six bedrooms and six baths. The tour ended in the master suite with the stone fireplace separating the bedroom and the bathroom, the steam shower suitable for three adults, the Jacuzzi tub, and the sitting area overlooking the pool. Jeffrey was proving himself a royal pain in the ass, complaining about something minor in every room of the house and acting as if he could take it or leave it. But he wasn't fooling Scott; Scott saw it in his eyes. This was the house Jeffrey had dreamed of owning his entire life. Scott knew because he had seen the same look in his own eyes three years ago, in the mirror of this same master bathroom. Jeffrey asked for the third time if the theater in the basement had Dolby Surround sound. Scott assured him it did, but Jeffrey said he was going downstairs to make sure.

Jeffrey departed and Penny said, "He likes to watch action movies," then went into the master bathroom. Shortly, he heard Penny's voice again: "Scott, what's this, in the steam shower?"

Scott walked into the bathroom and over to the shower. The door was open; Penny was inside, sitting on the built-in bench.

"What?"

"This."

Scott stepped inside to look, and without another word, Penny grabbed his swim trunks, yanked them down, and took him in her mouth like she knew what she was doing. She did. He was wrong about Penny: she hadn't finished her walk on the wild side. Scott had not had sex in more than seven months and had been too depressed to masturbate since Rebecca left, so he did not last long.

"Jesus!"

Scott's face was now plastered to the tile wall and he felt like a nap but—

"Penny!"

Jeffrey was back. Scott pulled up his trunks and Penny wiped her red lips with her hanky just as Jeffrey stuck his head in the steam shower and said with a big grin, "Wow, you do have Dolby down there!"

Scott stepped out of the shower, followed closely by Penny, who squeezed his butt as she passed. Fifteen minutes later, they were all standing at the front door.

Jeffrey said, "You don't remember me, do you, Scott?"

Scott said, "No. Should I?"

"We worked a real-estate deal a few years ago. You were representing Dibrell, a garden office project in North Dallas."

311

"Oh, yeah. You're with Dewey Cheatham and Howe."

"Dewey *Chatham* and Howe."

"Oh, right."

"You were pretty tough on us. But I learned a lot about negotiating from watching you in action."

"I'll send you a bill." Jeffrey smiled and Scott said, "Just business. Nothing personal."

"Then you won't take my offer personally."

"What's your offer?"

"Three million one hundred thousand."

"No, I won't take it personally, Jeffrey, because I won't take it."

Jeffrey smirked. "Come on, Scott, your life story's been in the paper. Everyone knows you've got to sell. You can't expect top dollar."

Scott reached over to the entry table and picked up a big brown envelope that contained his final bill from the country club for the last month, during which Rebecca had run up over $4,000 in charges. Scott held the envelope up to Jeffrey.

"I've already got an offer for three-point-three million."

Jeffrey's smirk vanished. "You're kidding?"

Scott put on his most sincere look and said, "Nope."

Jeffrey glanced at Penny. She gave him that pouty face mastered by Highland Park girls by middle school, a face that walked a fine line between obnoxiously whiny and incredibly sexy, between making her man want to slap her into next week or rip her clothes off and ravage

312

her. Penny was very good. And Scott knew Jeffrey would find the extra money to make Penny a happy Highland Park wife.

"Three million three hundred ten thousand."

Scott smiled. "Jeffrey, it's nothing to be ashamed of if you can't afford this place."

Scott had learned years ago, when he was the poor kid on the block, that you could insult a Highland Park boy's mother, his sister, his girlfriend, his athletic ability, and even the size of his dick without getting a rise, but question his financial standing in the community, and the fight was on. Jeffrey's face was getting redder by the second, and not just from Scott's needling; Penny was squeezing his forearm like she was checking his blood pressure.

"Can't afford? I can afford this place! Three million four!"

Jeffrey should've paid closer attention to Scott during those negotiations because the boy obviously hadn't learned much. First rule of negotiating, don't bring your ego to the bargaining table. Second rule, don't bring your wife. Jeffrey had violated both rules; now he would pay dearly. Scott stuck his hand out.

"You just bought yourself a house."

Jeffrey said, "I want the appliances, the window treatments, and the black man."

"*What?*"

"The appliances—"

"You can have the appliances, Jeffrey. What do you mean, you want the black man?"

"Doesn't he come with the house? He's your help, right?"

"No, he's my friend. And he doesn't go with the house. Slavery ended a few years back, maybe you read about it."

Jeffrey frowned, but Penny smiled and said, "I'll have to measure for furniture, maybe Monday morning? Will you be available, Scott? I'd really like to come."

"I can't believe none of Clark's other victims have come forward," Scott said.

It was after dinner. The girls were upstairs, Scott and Bobby were sitting on the kitchen floor drinking a beer, and the trial was only two weeks away.

"They're scared," Bobby said. "They've seen what McCall did to you."

"Our whole case rests on Hannah."

"And my briefs," Bobby said. "You read them yet?"

"Yeah. You're a good writer, Bobby."

"That's the only thing about the law I really like doing."

"Why do you stay in it?"

Bobby shrugged. "Too late to do something else. And debts—I can't afford to quit. And, dumb as it sounds, I care about my clients, probably because no one else does."

"You were always taking in stray dogs."

"I was at that."

"I remember that brown-and-white mutt, you called him Shitface. What ever happened to him?"

"Got run over by a delivery truck."

"Ouch."

"I liked that dog." They sat in silence, and then Bobby said, "When this is over, maybe you should get out of Dallas."

"McCall's not running me out of town. I'm staying."

"Good." Bobby drank his beer, then said, "Let's subpoena Dan Ford, make him give up the names of the six other girls he paid off for McCall."

Scott shook his head. "No way he gives them up. And the judge won't bust through the attorney-client privilege. I've hidden enough damaging evidence about my clients behind the privilege to know."

"Then Hannah's our only witness, other than Shawanda."

"Did you tell Carl to check into Delroy Lund?"

"Oh, yeah. Way into Delroy."

"What about the prosecution witnesses?"

"I got Ray's list, shows how the trial's gonna go."

"And how's that?"

"It's a circumstantial case, most cases are. Ray'll first put on the Dallas cops who found Clark's car and called it in. Then he'll put on the Highland Park cops who went over to the McCall mansion and found Clark. Next, the FBI agents who processed the crime scene and took the photos, which he'll put up on the big screen. Then the Dallas County medical examiner will testify as to cause of death and time of death. And last up will be the crime lab guys who lifted Shawanda's prints from the gun and the car, test-fired the gun, and matched the ballistics, and a forensics expert to give his opinion as to how the crime was committed. Scotty, by the time Ray's through, the jury's gonna believe she did it for sure."

"And then we'll put Shawanda on, a heroin-addicted hooker."

"She has to testify, Scotty. Fifth Amendment sounds great, but juries expect an innocent person to take the oath, look them in the eye, and swear she's innocent."

"She looks like hell."

"You would too, Scotty, if you were injecting Mexican black tar heroin three times a day."

Four miles due south, Shawanda Jones withdrew the needle from her right arm, leaned back on her cot in her cell, and waited for the heroin to enter her bloodstream, travel to her brain, cross the blood-brain barrier, and bind itself to the opioid receptors on her brain's nerve cells. When the heroin hit the receptors, it triggered a euphoric rush that swept over her slim body like an orgasm, only better. Then the rush dissolved and she drifted off into a peaceful little dream world.

She thought of her short life. She had turned her first trick at twelve. Unless you counted her uncle, who fingered her when she was six, then gave her fifty cents for a snow cone. She was using cocaine regularly at fourteen, pregnant at fifteen, and hooked on heroin at sixteen. Twelve years a prostitute, eight years a smack addict.

The only time she felt good about herself was times like this. When she was on the stuff, she felt like a little girl again, all happy and light and clean. She wasn't poor or a white man's whore. She was young again and didn't know anything about drugs or hooking on Harry Hines or white men wanting black girls. She was just a happy little girl like Pajamae.

And thinking of her baby made her cry. She cried because she pictured her Pajamae shooting smack into her arm and lying down for money and never being loved for anything else. She wanted her baby to have better than she'd had. She wanted her to have a good life, marry a good man, and live in a good home. She wanted someone to love her Pajamae as much as she did. The only thing Shawanda Jones loved more in life than heroin was her daughter.

TWENTY-ONE

SCOTT, LOUIS, and the girls arrived at the federal building at noon the next day, Saturday. Louis stayed outside in the car because of his outstanding issues with the Feds. Scott carried the big picnic basket inside, which the weekend security guard manning the metal detector checked thoroughly, as he always did. Now that Scott was no longer eating lunch at the Downtown Club, they had gotten into a regular habit of eating lunch with Shawanda at the federal lockup.

"Another picnic, Mr. Fenney?"

"Yep. How 'bout some fried chicken, Jerry?"

Jerry, an overweight white man about fifty, smiled and took a drumstick. They rode the elevator to the fifth floor and were met by the black guard.

"Ron," Scott said. "Picnic time, buddy."

Ron led them down the hallway to the same small conference room, but he seemed different today, silent and solemn. He had already moved the table and chairs to one corner. Boo and Pajamae spread the blanket on the cement floor and plopped down in their places. Ron left and returned shortly with Shawanda, who hugged Pajamae first and then Boo. She turned to Scott.

"Mr. Fenney, your woman leave you?"

"Yeah."

" 'Cause of me?"

"No, Shawanda, because of me."

"We've got chicken, Mama, from the Colonel!" Pajamae said. "And potato salad and beans and rolls, the kind you like."

Ron scratched his head and said, "Mr. Fenney, I, uh—"

"Ron, how many times I gotta tell you? It's Scott. You can't eat fried chicken with me and call me Mr. Fenney."

"Scott, I've, uh . . . I've got to search everyone."

"What? *Why?*"

"We searched Shawanda's cell and found some, uh"—he glanced down at Pajamae—"some controlled substances."

"You think I'm bringing it to her?"

Ron shook his head. "No, sir, not you."

When the meaning of Ron's statement finally registered with Scott, they both slowly turned to Pajamae. Scott said, "Pajamae, when we stopped by your apartment, did you get something for your mother?"

With Louis riding shotgun, Scott felt no fear returning to the projects. But the Jetta did not attract a crowd. The few residents who did notice them were actually friendly. One young boy asked, "Louis say you run for a hundred ninety-three yards against Texas—that true? A white boy?" When Scott assured him it was true, the boy said, "You the man." He waved when they drove off.

Pajamae shrugged. "Just Mama's medicine."

"And where was it at?"

"In the medicine cabinet in the wall under the sink in the kitchen."

"Please give it to me."

She stuck her hand in her pocket and retrieved a plastic Baggie filled with a black substance. Scott handed it to Ron.

"Mexican black tar," Ron said. He looked at Shawanda. "This stuff is eighty percent pure. It can kill you, girl!"

Shawanda lunged at Ron and snatched for the Baggie.

"Give it here!"

Scott grabbed Shawanda and held her until she gave up and slumped in his arms.

Ron said, "I'm sorry, Mr. Fenney. I'll leave now." He opened the door, but stopped. "Shawanda, why don't you let the judge put you in the prison hospital in Fort Worth? They'll put you on methadone."

Shawanda said nothing, so Ron left, shaking his head. Scott released Shawanda, and she dropped to the floor. He sat in one of the chairs and looked down at this young black woman.

"Why do you do it?"

Shawanda's eyes came up. " 'Cause it make me feel special."

"You don't need that. You are special."

She laughed. "You sound like Louis. He always saying 'Shawanda, you God's special girl.' "

"He's right."

"No, he ain't, Mr. Fenney. Nobody never give a damn 'bout Shawanda, not my daddy, not my mama, not no one."

"Pajamae does." He turned to her. "You love your mother, don't you?"

"Yes, sir, Mr. Fenney, I love her very much."

"So that's me, Louis, Pajamae, Boo, Bobby . . . and Ron. Six people who think you're special."

"That sound real nice, Mr. Fenney, but if I get out, I don't figure me and you gonna see much of each other."

"Sure we are. Our daughters are best friends. They're like sisters."

She turned to Pajamae. "That right? Boo like your sister?"

"Yes, Mama."

She turned to Boo. "Pajamae like your sister?"

"Yes, ma'am."

And she smiled the sweetest smile Scott had ever seen on her face. "That's good." She looked up at Scott. "Mr. Fenney, if I don't get out of here or if they . . . well, you know . . . you promise me something?"

"Sure. What?"

"Take care of my Pajamae."

Five weeks ago, when Scott had taken a little black girl home to Highland Park, his wife had asked him what he was going to do with her when her mother was convicted: Adopt her? Raise her as his daughter? Send her to Highland Park schools? He did not answer his wife that day because he wasn't thinking of Pajamae that day; he was thinking only of himself, his fear of returning to the projects. But this day he answered.

"Yes, Shawanda, I promise."

"It's perfect!" Boo said.

They had looked at six houses, Scott and the girls, each cheaper than the prior one, until they walked into this tiny fifteen-hundred-square-foot, two-bedroom, two-bath cottage over by SMU with a backyard that had a rope swing and a pool the size of the master bathtub at 4000 Beverly Drive. It was priced at only $450,000, within Scott's reduced financial reach, and it was in the Highland Park School District, so Boo wouldn't have to start over at another elementary school.

"One bedroom for us," Boo said, "and one for you. You can have the big bedroom."

Pajamae ran into the backyard, and Scott said to Boo, "Honey, you understand, if her mother gets out of jail, Pajamae's going back to live with her."

Boo turned her green eyes up at him. "Well, we've been thinking."

"I bet you have."

"She doesn't have a father and now I don't have a mother, so we thought maybe you and her mother could get married or something."

"*Married?* But she's—"

"Only twenty-four, I know. But Pajamae said it's

okay for a man to marry a younger woman. She said they do it all the time in Hollywood."

"But, Boo—I'm still married to your mother."

Scott was running at 7.5 miles per hour up a ten-degree incline on a commercial treadmill. But he wasn't at the athletic club in downtown Dallas; his mind was not clear, his spirits were not high, and his eyes were not firmly attached to the backside of a beautiful young woman running in front of him; there was no girl running on a treadmill behind him checking out his butt; he did not feel young and successful and virile—or special. He was running on the treadmill in the exercise room of his Highland Park house, which would be his for only two more weeks.

Their visit to Shawanda that morning had raised the same questions in his mind: Had he done the right thing? Had he made the right choice? Was saving Shawanda's life worth sacrificing his perfect life? Was a heroin addict's life worth his lawyer life? He couldn't save her life, not with the evidence Ray Burns had against her. She would be convicted and sentenced to death or a long prison term. But he had already made the sacrifice; his life was already ruined. There was no quid pro quo, no something for something, to this bargain. He had given up his perfect life and would get nothing in return. And thinking about that brought the darkness back into his mind. So he did the only thing he knew to do when he was down: he exercised. Hard. Twice a day.

Every day. He had begun working out as if he were getting in shape for another football season, running and weight lifting, torturing his body to ease his mind.

But working out made him think about football, and thinking about football made him think about the cheerleaders, and thinking about the cheerleaders made him think about Rebecca. He thought about their life together, the incredible sex, their vacations to Hawaii and San Francisco and London, and, of course, Boo. They had had eleven years together, and now she was gone. Had their marriage been a mistake from the beginning? Had she ever really loved him? Of course, it had never occurred to him that she might not have loved him because everyone—fans, coaches, cheerleaders—had always loved Scott Fenney.

He had so many questions, and no one to ask for answers. His mother would have said, "It's God's plan, and God has a reason, even if we don't understand." Butch would have said, "She's a selfish bitch, running off like that." The truth lay somewhere in between. But one truth he knew: if he hadn't married Rebecca, there would be no Boo. And without Boo, there would be no life for Scott Fenney.

"What the hell was I supposed to do, kill him?"

"Jesus, Delroy, in the Highland Park Village?"

Delroy Lund was standing in the den of the McCall town house in Georgetown. The senator was standing at the window. He wasn't happy to hear Delroy's report about the incident with Fenney at the shopping center.

"I was just trying to send him a message, but Fenney went fuckin' nuts . . . Oh, by the way, you bought a rental car."

The senator dismissed that news with a wave of his hand. Delroy particularly appreciated that aspect of working for a guy worth $800 million: He didn't blink an eye at an unexpected $35,000 expense. He just wanted results and screw the costs. Delroy Lund got results.

"Now he's got a big black dude playing bodyguard. But I'll try again if you want."

"No, leave it alone. You and the black guy get together, someone will get killed. And that's all I need, another murder connected to me. So Fenney's wife left him?"

"Yeah, she ran off with the golf pro."

The senator smiled for the first time that day. "Good."

"Look, Senator, Fenney talked big on TV, but he ain't got nothing to back it up. Those other girls, they're not testifying. All they got is Hannah Steele."

"She's enough, goddamnit!"

The senator turned from the window and paced the room, talking like he was thinking out loud.

"Fifteen months until the election. If the hooker's convicted, everyone will figure what Fenney said on TV was just the lies of a lawyer. It'll all be forgotten a few months from now . . . The public's got the attention span of a two-year-old. I can still get into the White House,

Delroy, if she's convicted. But if Hannah Steele walks into that courtroom and testifies that Clark beat and raped her . . ."

The senator started shaking his head.

"But, Senator, if she don't testify, it's just the word of a whore."

The senator stared at Delroy a long moment.

"Delroy, go see if the fish are biting in Galveston."

Scott Fenney hadn't cried since his mother died. And the only time before that was when his father died. He didn't cry when they drove his body into the ground, he didn't cry when they broke his fingers or his ribs, he didn't cry when they tore his knee ligaments. You don't cry on a football field.

But Scott Fenney wasn't on a football field now; he was in bed and he was crying.

His wife had left him for a golf pro. The final humiliation in a long list of humiliations, every detail of which had been duly reported in the local newspaper. All of Dallas knew about Scott Fenney's fall from grace. A few weeks ago, he had had the perfect Highland Park family: a trophy wife and a smart daughter and an illegal Mexican maid and a fast Ferrari. Today his family consisted of a white girl with cornrows, a street-smart black girl, a jailed prostitute, a lawyer who advertised in the TV guide, and a six foot six, 330-pound black bodyguard who lived in the garage.

"A. Scott, you okay?"

Boo's voice in the dark. Scott wiped his face on the bedsheet and said, "Yeah."

She climbed up onto the bed. "It's okay. I cry, too."

Scott sat up and pulled his daughter close. He felt her little body sag slightly in his arms. He thought she was falling asleep, but she spoke quietly.

"I've always been different. Now I'm really different."

"How so?"

"I'm the only kid I know without a cell phone *or* a mother. Pajamae says none of the kids she knows have dads, but they all have mothers. Rachel and Cary, they don't have dads . . . well, they have dads, but they don't live with them. They're divorced. But they see their dads on weekends." She was quiet again. Then she said, "I don't think we're gonna see Mother on weekends."

Scott held her tightly.

"It's just us now, baby."

And they cried together.

TWENTY-TWO

BOBBY CAME BY at nine on Monday morning. He gave Scott the once-over and said, "You're wearing jeans and a polo shirt to a pretrial conference with the judge?"

"What's Buford gonna do, fire me?"

"Good point."

They walked out the back door just as Louis was walking in. After almost three weeks living in the garage and nonstop pleading by Scott, Louis had finally relented and agreed to come inside the house for his meals. Pajamae was cooking breakfast.

When Scott turned the Volkswagen south on Turtle Creek Boulevard, Bobby asked, "How do you like the Jetta?"

"Well, the Ferrari could do zero to sixty in four-point-five seconds and the Jetta takes half a day, but hey, this little baby gets great gas mileage." Bobby laughed, but turned sober when Scott said, "Why aren't you mad at me?"

"For what?"

"For quitting on you back then."

"Oh." He shrugged. "What good would that do? You were gone. Didn't know what to do, so I married the first girl who said yes. Lasted less than a year, took her that long to figure out she'd married a loser. Second wife, we got married four years after the first divorce. She's the sister of the guy who owns the bar next door to my office, Mexican girl, most beautiful woman I ever saw naked. Problem was, I wasn't the only guy seeing her naked. She was stepping out with most of the guys at the bar. Some of them were my clients. Still are."

Bobby made a face.

"Is that a conflict of interest?"

"They repo your suits, too?"

Ray Burns had that same smart-ass expression on his face. Scott and Bobby had met him outside Judge Buford's chambers, where the pretrial conference would take place.

"Shit, Scott, why didn't you just stick a gun to your head and blow your brains out like your girl did to Clark? Would've been a hell of a lot less painful."

"What are you talking about, Ray?"

"Throwing your career away for her. Jesus, were you really making seven-fifty a year? And driving a Ferrari? What, you got a death wish or something?"

Scott glared at Ray Burns as he stepped past him and entered Judge Buford's chambers, but he heard Bobby say, "Ray, your mouth is writing checks your body can't cash."

"Jury selection on the nineteenth, opening statements on Monday the twenty-third," Judge Buford said. "Anything else, gentlemen?"

"Yes, Your Honor," Scott said. "Mr. Burns is persisting in claiming that the alleged crime is eligible for the death penalty when that is clearly not the case."

Ray Burns shrugged. "Our position is that the victim was an officer of a federal agency, and the defendant killed him in the perpetration of a robbery."

"Give me a break, Ray. Clark McCall was with a prostitute. The statute requires that the officer be engaged in the performance of official duties. And she didn't commit robbery. She only took the thousand dollars Clark owed her. He had another sixteen hundred on him. She didn't take that or anything else in the house."

"She took his car."

"Only to get back to her part of town."

"She had his skin under her fingernails."

"She scratched him when he attacked her. She's not denying she was there."

"But she's denying she pulled the trigger, even in self-defense. See, Scott, if she'd come clean about that, maybe we'd be willing to discuss dropping the death penalty."

"Using the death penalty to coerce a confession—that's prosecutorial misconduct, Ray."

Ray shrugged. "We call it prosecutorial discretion, Scott."

"You're full of shit, Ray," Scott said.

"And you're unemployed."

"Gentlemen," Judge Buford said as Scott fought back the urge to punch the Assistant U.S. Attorney. "The death penalty has been well briefed by Mr. Burns for the government and by Mr. Herrin, I presume"—Judge Buford eyed Scott over his reading glasses—"for the defense. We will address that issue if and when it becomes necessary. Anything else?"

"No, sir," Ray Burns said.

"No, Your Honor," Scott said.

"Fine. We'll reconvene on the nineteenth."

The three lawyers stood to leave, but the judge said, "Scott, may I speak with you alone?" Buford turned to Ray. "If you have no objection, Mr. Burns?"

"No, sir, I have no objection."

Ray and Bobby exited the chambers and shut the door.

"Sit down, Scott."

Scott sat. Judge Buford stared at him like a psychiatrist addressing his patient. "You holding up okay?"

Scott lied: "Yes, sir."

"I've read what's happened. I suppose all of Dallas has. They really deported your maid?"

"Yes, sir. She's down in Nuevo Laredo, waiting on a green card. I've done everything, but the INS says they're backlogged."

"Scott, if I had any idea all this would happen, that

you'd lose your job, I would've never appointed you. I'd expect something like that from McCall, but Dan Ford . . ." His shoulders slumped and he shook his head. "I don't know what's become of the legal profession. When I was practicing, handling a case like this, it meant something. Now it's to be avoided because it might hurt the firm's business."

He looked at Scott with an expression of genuine puzzlement.

"Do lawyers today care about anything except money?"

Scott spoke the truth: "No, sir, not in my experience."

The judge grunted. "Scott, may I ask you a personal question?"

"Sure, Judge."

"Your speech, that day at the bar luncheon . . . did you mean it, what you said about defending the innocent, protecting the poor, fighting for justice?"

Lie or tell the truth? Scott saw in the judge's eyes the desperate hope that he had meant it, so his first inclination was to do what experienced lawyers do often and well: lie. But the judge needed to hear the truth today. So A. Scott Fenney, Esq., went against fourteen years of legal training and told the truth, the whole truth, and nothing but the truth.

"No, sir. Not a word. I said what those lawyers wanted to hear."

The judge nodded solemnly and said, "I appreciate your honesty, Scott. I'm letting you off the case." The judge's eyes dropped to his docket sheet. He began writing. "I'll substitute Mr. Herrin. He seems capable. He's certainly written some good briefs."

Two months ago, Scott would have jumped for joy at the judge's words. But now he sat stunned and suddenly afraid of losing his last client, even a nonpaying client, because a lawyer without a client is just a man.

"Judge, I know I'm not the lawyer you are, or the lawyer my mother wanted me to be . . . hell, I'm not even the lawyer I wanted to be. But I'm not a quitter. I never quit in a game, I've never quit on anything in my life. I'll play it out."

The judge's eyes came back up, and now he glared at Scott.

"This isn't a goddamn football game, Scott!"

Scott recoiled at the judge's harsh voice.

"This case isn't about you, your life, you proving something to yourself or Dan Ford or Mack McCall! This case is about Shawanda Jones, about her life! She's the defendant! It's her right to counsel, goddamnit!"

The judge stood abruptly, stepped to the window, and stared out. After a time, he spoke softly.

"I'm an old judge who needs to retire and tend to his garden. But a case like this comes along, and I know I can still contribute to justice, one human being at a time—and that's how justice is served, Scott, one person at a time. Today we're here to protect Shawanda Jones. That woman is my responsibility as long as she's in the custody of the federal government. Which arrested her, took her from her home and child, and is putting her on trial for her life. Now, maybe she did it, maybe she didn't, I don't know. But until the jury speaks, she's innocent in the eyes of the law—and thus in my eyes. And I will protect her. That's my duty. And her lawyer's duty is to defend her, to make damn sure the government proves she did it, beyond all reasonable doubt. That's what the Constitution requires, a lawyer standing up to the government on behalf of a citizen. That's what it means to be a lawyer, Scott."

The judge returned to his desk and sat.

"When I was practicing, I had half a dozen cases like this, where the defendant's guilt was truly in doubt, and in each case I made damn sure the government had to prove its case. Which the government did not do. They were innocent, and they were acquitted. Six people, Scott, six human beings whose lives I saved. I cared about those people, and I care about Ms. Jones. I'm not gonna die rich, Scott, but those few cases, they're my contribution to justice. They're what made my life worthwhile. Ms. Jones needs a lawyer who cares about her, someone to stand up for her, someone who understands the honor of defending an American citizen facing a death sentence. She needs her hero. You were such a football player, I thought you might be such a lawyer. I was wrong." The judge picked up his pen. "You're off the case. I'll appoint Herrin and postpone the trial."

Scott jumped up and leaned over the judge's desk.

"Judge, you can't postpone the trial! It'll kill her! She's barely hanging in now. I've been telling her it'll be over soon. If you postpone the trial, she'll die in her cell!"

The judge sat back, a curious expression on his face.

"What's this, concern for your client?"

"You're right, Judge, I haven't thought about her. But I'm a damn good lawyer, and she needs me."

Judge Buford removed his reading glasses and wiped them with his white handkerchief. He replaced them and gazed at Scott.

"She's a heroin addict, you know that?"

"Yes, sir."

"Why didn't you file a motion to have her transferred to the prison hospital, for drug treatment?"

"I . . . I never thought about it."

"Well, I did. She refused. She wants to be close to her daughter. You ever see a heroin addict go through withdrawal?"

"No, sir."

"Go downstairs and look. She's going through hell, alone in her cell, so she can see her daughter. What's that tell you about her? Tells me there's something good inside that woman, that maybe we need to look past the prostitution and the heroin and not just assume she's guilty, that maybe we ought to give her the benefit of the doubt. Beyond all reasonable doubt, Scott." He sighed. "So I've got Burns trying to send her to death row on his asinine legal position, which the appeals court will probably uphold, and I've got you. There's no hope for him—he's the worst kind of lawyer, a political animal, using the law to gain power over the people. And you, A. Scott Fenney . . . what's the A stand for, anyway?"

"Nothing."

The judge grunted. "You don't want power; you just want money. So the question I've got to answer is, Is there hope for you? I know you bring her daughter up here to see her, the guards say three, four times a week. That's good. And that you took her in, to live in your Highland Park home. That's very good."

The judge paused; a chuckle escaped.

"You're probably not up for citizen of the year in Highland Park, are you? But that tells me there's something good inside you, too, Scott, that perhaps there's still hope for you, that maybe you won't become another Dan Ford. That one day you might make your mother proud."

The judge fell silent and stared at Scott in the same way all those college coaches who had come to the Fenney rent house to recruit him had stared, seeing him in the flesh, trying to size him up, figure him out, decide if he was the real deal. Then Buford abruptly waved Scott off and said, "Go away."

"Wh . . . *what?*"

"Go think about it. I've got hearings until noon. You come back then—but only if you're ready to be her lawyer. If you don't show, I'll substitute Herrin and postpone the trial."

Outside, Bobby and Ray were waiting.

"What's up?" Bobby said.

Scott shook his head. "Personal." Then he addressed Ray Burns. "You're being a prick, Ray."

"Yeah, Scott, a prick with a career. A death penalty gets me an office in D.C."

"How do you sleep with yourself?"

Ray laughed. "Uh-oh, a born-again lawyer. Eleven years you spend every waking minute billing hours, making boatloads of money, living in a mansion, driving a Ferrari—how much did that cost your clients? Then you get fired and suddenly you see the light like a dying man: *I wanna do good, Lord!* Bullshit, Scott. You don't give a flying fuck about her. She's just a nigger, right? Two months ago, you were trying to bail on her faster than you can spit, now you're gonna be her hero? Tell it to Oprah. Oh, and I don't sleep by myself, Scott, I sleep with a gorgeous redhead from accounting. Who you sleeping with? Not your wife; she's sleeping with her golf pro."

Scott lunged for Ray, but Bobby jumped in between them.

"Hell, Scott," Ray said with a little laugh, "don't worry. The bitch probably won't live through withdrawal."

In one quick movement, Bobby released Scott and punched Ray in the mouth. Ray fell back against the wall.

Bobby said, "I told you, Ray."

"I'm real worried about her, Mr. Fenney," Ron the guard said. "I'm thinking maybe I made a mistake, taking her H."

They were standing outside Shawanda's cell. Inside,

she was lying on her bed facing the far wall, curled up in a ball, her entire body shivering uncontrollably. She was groaning as if she were dying, her skin glistened with sweat, and her legs kicked involuntarily.

"That's why they call it kicking the habit," Bobby said. "Right now, she'd give everything she has in life for one fix."

Bobby was rubbing his right fist. "Hitting someone hurts."

"I'm proud of you, Bobby." Scott pointed the Jetta toward Highland Park and said, "You know what pisses me off the most?"

"The Ferrari?"

"No, about Burns."

"What?"

"The prick's right. About me."

Bobby worked his hand and said, "What did Buford want?"

"He wanted to take me off the case. Said he was going to appoint you."

"You still want out?"

"No. I told Buford that, but he told me to think about it, come back at noon, tell him if I'm ready to be her lawyer."

They were silent until they exited downtown. Then Bobby said softly: "I can't try this case, Scotty. I'm not good enough. She needs you."

*

338

An hour later, Scott left the house by the back door and ran west on Beverly Drive. It was exactly eleven A.M.; he had sixty minutes to make the biggest decision of his life.

Scott turned south on Lakeside Drive and ran past the stately old mansions that had stood for almost as long as Highland Park had existed. The homes sat higher than the street and looked down on a little park and Turtle Creek, where Scott often took Boo to skip rocks across the water.

Scott headed west on Armstrong Parkway a short distance, then turned north on Preston Road and ran up the sidewalk, the road to his left and to his right the massive wall that shielded the grand estates of Trammell Crow and Jerry Jones and Mack McCall and—

Tom Dibrell.

Scott had damn near run right into the long silver Mercedes as Tom exited his estate and stopped to check for traffic, blocking the sidewalk. They stared at each other across a distance of just a few feet, Tom wearing a suit and tie but cool in the air-conditioned luxury of a German sedan, Scott wearing only shorts and running shoes and sweating profusely in the hundred-degree heat. For eleven years they had talked daily; they had traveled the country, negotiating deals, making deals, and closing deals; they had celebrated victories and lamented defeats; they had eaten together and gotten drunk together; but they had never been friends. Successful lawyers, Scott now knew, have rich clients, not loyal friends.

Now, seeing this man who had given him his identity

and had taken it away, Scott saw a sad man. This man had had four wives, but none of them had made him happy. He had six children by three of those wives, children who chose not to live in this fabulous estate with their father, because their father loved his skyscraper more than he loved them. He was a man who had lawyers, but not friends. Who had money and everything that money could buy, but little happiness. Three weeks ago, after Tom had fired him, if they had crossed paths like this, Scott Fenney might have shot him the finger.

Today Scott only nodded and smiled at the sad man in his Mercedes-Benz.

Tom opened his mouth as if to say something, then abruptly broke eye contact and hit the accelerator hard, sending the silver sedan roaring out onto Preston Road. Scott watched Tom drive away in a cloud of exhaust fumes, then started running again. He ran north past the Village and across Mockingbird Lane. A mile later, he turned east on Lovers Lane. He knew now where this run would end.

His journey took him along the boundary of the Highland Park Country Club, its tall brick wall discouraging gawkers. But there was one break in the wall where wrought iron spanned a few feet, and Scott stopped and looked in. A foursome of old white men was putting out on the seventh green, getting a round of golf in before the summer sun sapped their strength.

Growing up in Highland Park, Scott had often looked in through this opening at the old white men playing golf; it was like window-shopping with his mother at Highland Park Village, where she couldn't afford to shop. He'd always said that one day he would be rich enough to own a mansion in Highland Park, play golf at the country club, and buy his mother anything her heart desired at the Village. She had died before he could buy her anything at the Village, but four years ago, when Scott Fenney was admitted to the membership of the country club, he thought how proud his mother would have been of her son. For the last four years, he had played golf with pride inside these walls and looked out at others looking in.

Today the view was different.

From inside the walls, these old white men had seemed so special because they were so rich. But from outside, they just seemed old. And Scott realized that just as he was looking in at them, they were looking out at him. And in their eyes he saw their envy: they would gladly give every dollar they had to be young again, to have a head full of hair and sharp eyes and a clear mind with a memory that did not play tricks on them several times a day; to again live in a strong muscular body instead of the broken-down body they were left with; to run down the street instead of barely making it back to the golf cart; to again have a prostate gland instead of having to wear a diaper because the surgery had left them permanently impotent and incontinent; to again feel the pleasure of sex. They were looking out at a young man with his life in front of him; he was looking in at old men with nothing in front of them except the end of their lives.

The old men were tended to by their caddies, middle-aged black men wearing white canvas overalls, black men who caught the bus each morning before dawn in South Dallas and rode north to Highland Park to work at a club where they could never be a member because they had been born black. They were good men, like Louis, but they weren't good enough for the club, these black men who fixed old white men's divots, found their lost balls, and carried their clubs, all the while performing like actors in *Gone With the Wind*—"Yassuh, Mistuh Smith, that there swing sure 'nough make you look like Arnold Palmer hisself"—because making these old white men feel like Southern plantation owners meant a bigger tip. Scott had always been uncomfortable with the whole black caddie thing, but he had always employed a caddie for every round because it was club policy.

After each round, he would retire to the men's grill for drinks and cards with these old white men, and he had felt so proud to be accepted by them, to be seen in their company, to share their special space and breathe their rarefied air. He would hang on their every word—usually jokes and commentary about "niggers" and "wetbacks" and "kikes" made without regard to the presence of the black waiters hovering about. But Scott's eyes would always meet those of his waiter, and he would feel the heat rise within him. Yet Scott Fenney, who had played football with black guys, showered with black guys, roomed with black guys, and partied with black guys, had never stood up and told those old white men that he would no longer be available for a game of golf with a bunch of racist anti-Semitic sons of bitches in shorts. No, A. Scott Fenney, Esq., had smiled politely at their jokes and nodded approvingly at their commentary so as not to offend them. Because to offend these old white men would have been bad for business.

One day a year or so ago, Scott had asked Dan Ford whether these old white men just hated blacks, Mexicans, and Jews. Dan had laughed and said, "Oh, no, they hate lots of people, not just blacks, Mexicans, and Jews. They hate Democrats, Yankees, Californians, Asians, feminists, Muslims—anyone who's different from them. See, Scotty, the glory days for these old farts were the fifties, back when they were young and white men ruled Dallas and the only black in their world was their oil, and the Texas Railroad Commission controlled the price of oil in the whole goddamn world. Now the best golfer in the world is black, the mayor of Dallas is a woman, and the price of oil is controlled by a bunch of Arab sheikhs. The only part of their world that's still run by white men is this club. Drive through those gates and it's 1950 again. And they aim to keep it that way until the day they die. Like it or not, these bastards own most of Dallas, so if you want to be a rich lawyer in this town you've got to join their club. Scotty, my boy, it's just business."

Dan Ford was wrong: it wasn't just business; it was just bigotry. And A. Scott Fenney was wrong: his mother would not have been proud of her son.

Scott gave the members and their caddies one last

glance—and noticed one of the caddies staring at him. The caddie's face changed; he recognized Scott. He smiled and gave Scott a discrete thumbs-up. Scott thought he recognized the caddie but he couldn't remember his name—he had never asked his caddies their names—but he returned the gesture, then ran on.

A few blocks later his thoughts were still on the club and the caddies and his good mother when he heard a high-pitched voice: "Scott! Scott!" He slowed, turned, and saw an arm waving out the window of a red Beemer: *Shit, Penny Birnbaum!*

"Scott! Wait!"

Penny was heading in the opposite direction down Lovers, so Scott cut through Curtis Park, two backyards, hit an alley, ran a few more blocks, and came out on Hillcrest Avenue. He turned south and ran along the western boundary of the SMU campus. He entered the campus at University Boulevard right in front of the law school.

He stopped.

Three years he had spent in that building, three years studying the law—torts, taxes, contracts, conflicts, procedure, property, and ethics, a subject he studied in school and quickly forgot in practice. The practice of law isn't about ethics; it's about money.

Scott began running again, past the sorority houses placed all in a row, conveniently, he had thought back then, so he wouldn't have far to walk between girls. And he recalled all the pleasures he had experienced in those houses with those girls, and he found himself wondering, as he had never wondered before, if their lives had turned out well.

He ran along University Boulevard into the heart of the manicured campus, then turned south on Hilltop Lane, which became Ownby Drive and led him directly to the new Gerald Ford Stadium, named after the billionaire Dallas banker, not the former president. He found an unlocked gate, entered the stadium, walked to the nearest ramp, and emerged from the concrete underbelly onto the green grass.

He was alone on the field.

The best times of his life had played out in this small arena—120 yards long, 53⅓ yards wide. And the worst times, too, he used to think. Glorious victories and crushing defeats. Moments of immeasurable joy and unspeakable sadness. He could still close his eyes and see the crowd. He could still hear them cheering and smell the freshly cut grass. He could still taste his blood. He could still feel football.

Scott climbed the steps to the spectator stands and abruptly did what he had done so often back then: he ran the stands. His arms pumping, his legs burning with pain, he ran all the way to the top. He turned and looked at the downtown skyline in the distance, the skyscrapers silhouetted against the blue sky. Dibrell Tower stood above them all, and on the sixty-second floor, Sid Greenberg was standing in Scott's office. Sid couldn't see Scott four miles away, but Scott shot him the finger anyway, just on principle.

Back in college, he had often run the stands at night

just so he could sit at the top of the stadium and gaze at the lights of downtown, the Emerald City rising out of the endless Texas plains: Dibrell Tower outlined in blue argon lights; the lighted ball above Reunion Arena looking like a Christmas tree ornament; and Pegasus, the neon red flying horse above the old Magnolia Building. Like so many other young white men, Scott Fenney had been seduced by the lights, by dreams of getting rich in Big D. That's what they call Dallas—"Big D"—because it's a mecca for men with big dreams. Big dreamers come to Dallas like sinners to Jesus: you want to get saved, come to Jesus; you want to get rich, come to Dallas. Sitting right here, Scott Fenney had dreamed big.

"That ain't bad for an old man!"

The booming voice startled Scott out of his thoughts. He searched the stadium until he saw a big black man standing on the sideline below. He looked familiar. Scott walked down the stands toward him. As he came closer, he recognized the man.

"Big Charlie, is that you?"

"Scotty Fenney, how you doing, man?"

Scott arrived and stuck out his hand, but Big Charlie wrapped his huge arms around Scott and bear-hugged him, as if Scotty Fenney had just scored the game-winning touchdown.

Charles Jackson stood six four and weighed 285 pounds—when he was an eighteen-year-old freshman. By the time he was a senior, he weighed 325. He played right guard, which required that he pull and lead running plays around either end, removing any obstacle from Scotty Fenney's path. Scott scored the touchdowns, but Big Charlie led the way.

Big Charlie came from Tyler, an East Texas town known for its red roses and black football players. Earl Campbell was the best known, but Big Charlie was the biggest. He attended SMU instead of Texas because he didn't want to be too far from his mama and his sisters. He drove the two hours home every Sunday morning for church and came back every Sunday night for curfew.

The last Scott had heard, Big Charlie had been drafted by the Rams. Charlie now told him that he had played two seasons and had been a knee injury away from fulfilling his dream. He had returned to SMU, where he had coached the offensive line for the last ten years. Scott had attended most of those games but he'd never noticed Big Charlie. It was a long way down to the sideline from Ford Stevens's private skybox.

"We could always use a good running back coach," Big Charlie said. He had read about Scott's troubles.

"Thanks, but I've still got some lawyering left in me."

"You gonna win?"

"I don't know."

"You think she's innocent?"

"Of murder, but not of killing Clark."

"Which means?"

"Worst case, she gets the death penalty. Best case, they convict her of second-degree murder, give her

347

twenty years in prison. But she won't live that long, without heroin or her daughter."

"Read you took her in."

Scott smiled. "Yeah, her name's Pajamae; she's a great kid. You got kids?"

Big Charlie nodded. "Two girls, seven and ten."

"I bet you're a good dad."

"I love those two kids more than football."

"They're lucky then. Anyway, Pajamae was down in the projects by herself, so I went down there and got her—"

"You went into the projects? By yourself?"

"Yeah, in a Ferrari."

Big Charlie's head rolled back, and he let out a belly laugh. "White boy in a Ferrari down in the projects—that must've been a sight! I'm amazed you got out alive!"

"I had a friend, Louis. He ran interference for me, like you used to. He's living with us now, too. Anyway, first night, Pajamae did my daughter's hair in cornrows. Rebecca damn near fainted."

Big Charlie smiled. "How you doing since she left?"

Scott shook his head. "I only cry at night."

"That's 'cause you got heart, Scotty. You cried when we won and you cried when we lost. You cried 'cause you cared, about winning, about your team, about me. You know, Scotty, I never told you, but you were my hero."

Scott must have appeared shocked, because Charlie said, "No, man, I mean it. A hundred ninety-three yards against Texas—nobody does that! You wouldn't quit and you wouldn't let me quit. Twenty-three end sweeps that day, pulling my big butt around right end, then left end, then right end: I thought I was gonna die right out there on the field. But I'd look at you, getting the crap beat out of you every play but getting up and never quitting . . . man, you were tough."

Scott sighed. "Life is tougher."

"No, it ain't. You're forgetting your heart. Look inside yourself, it's still there. Scotty, God gave you a gift back then, your athletic ability. But what we did out there, that was just a game. That girl's life, that ain't no game." He put his hand on Scott's shoulder. "Scotty, don't you see? God's given you a better gift than being a football star. You've got the ability to save that girl's life."

Scott looked at Big Charlie, who had given everything he had to Scott Fenney on a football field; and now, on a football field again, he had given Scott even more. At that moment, Scott realized that he needed Shawanda Jones as much as she needed him. He needed to be her hero. It was who he was. It was who he wanted to be again. It was what had been missing in his life. Scott was brought out of his thoughts when the bells at the Methodist church on the campus rang out.

"Shit, what time is it?" Scott asked.

"Noon, straight up," Big Charlie said.

"Damn, I'm late!" Scott held his hand out, but Big Charlie bear-hugged him again. Scott said, "Thanks, my friend."

And he ran toward the Emerald City.

*

349

United States District Court Judge Samuel Buford was sitting in his chambers behind his desk checking his watch. Twelve-thirty. No Scott Fenney. He wasn't going to show.

Sam Buford sighed. He had thought there was hope for young A. Scott Fenney, Esq. But he had thought wrong. Fenney had the brains to be a hero, no doubt; and Buford had hoped he still had the heart. But now he saw that he didn't. There was no hope for Scott Fenney . . . or for Shawanda Jones . . . or for the law.

At that very moment, Sam Buford decided to retire.

His time had come. He would retire and tend to his garden. Clear out those weeds, till the soil, plant carrots and squash and cabbage and tomatoes, maybe go organic; get that garden in good shape, something he hadn't had time to do since . . . well, ever. Yep, time to put down the gavel and pick up the hoe.

He buzzed his secretary on the intercom and said he needed to dictate several orders. First order, postpone the trial date in *United States of America versus Shawanda Jones.* Second order, substitute counsel for Scott Fenney. But who? Herrin? The boy was a good writer, no doubt about it; but the defendant needed a hero, not a writer. He wished he were still Samuel Buford, attorney-at-law. He'd take her case. He'd be her hero. But he was Judge Samuel Buford. Soon to be a retired judge. Third order, dictate his resignation letter. As usual, Helen was prompt. In seconds the door swung open and—

Scott Fenney stood in the doorway, wearing only running shorts and drenched in sweat.

"Judge, I'm ready to be her lawyer."

Sam Buford damn near got out of his chair and walked over to embrace the young lawyer, but that would probably violate some rule of judicial ethics, so he reined in his emotions.

"All right, son. Her life is in your hands. I hope you're man enough to handle that responsibility."

"I am. And, Judge, I'll make her proud. My mother."

Scott Fenney turned and walked out the door. Helen stepped into his place, dictation pad in hand.

"Ready, Judge?"

Buford waved her away. "Go back to your desk, Helen. I've got judging to tend to." Helen turned away. "Oh, Helen, wait." She turned back. "Get me Bob Harris on the phone."

"Bob Harris?"

"He's the INS regional director." Buford leaned back and smiled. "My mama always said, one good deed deserves another."

TWENTY-THREE

ON SATURDAY the circus came to town.

Men and women, boys and girls, young and old, the wealthy residents of Highland Park came in droves. They parked on the side of the street, without the benefit of valets. They braved the 110-degree pressure cooker of a day and walked a block or more up the sidewalk to 4000 Beverly Drive. They had come to see something that only happened in other parts of Dallas County, in *those* neighborhoods into which they did not venture.

A yard sale.

But this was not a yard sale offering used toasters, beat-up couches, hand-me-down clothes, and an assortment of toys, baby strollers, car seats, and golf clubs. No, this yard sale boasted a walnut sideboard by Francesco Molon, a mahogany bookcase by Bevan Funnell, a pecan armoire by Guy Chaddock, a leather chair by Ralph Lauren, and a billiard table by Brunswick. It promised an assortment of sofas and tables and lamps and bedroom suites and Oriental rugs, an eclectic mix of furnishings with only two things in common: the former lady of the house once fancied them, and they were terribly expensive. It offered designer clothes, footwear, and accessories for women—dresses by Rickie Freeman and Luca Luca, handbags by Louis Vuitton and Bottega Veneta, shoes by Dior, Donna Karan, Marc Jacobs, and of course Jimmy Choo, shirts by Anne Fontaine, and silk scarves by Hermès. And there were girls' clothes by Jacadi Paris. In all, over $500,000 worth of pricey personal possessions were on sale. And while Highland Parkers might joke about white trash and minorities engaging in curb shopping and Dumpster diving, a bargain purchase is a basic human desire that transcends race, color, creed, national origin, political affiliation, or socioeconomic position.

So they came.

They came up the brick-paved driveway and arrived at the rear motor court and backyard and four-car garage where the Fenney family possessions were on display and for sale. For cash. Pajamae told Scott you don't take checks or credit cards at yard sales.

At dinner a week before, Boo had asked Scott what they were going to do with all of their stuff. They had enough things to fill the little house by SMU five times over. Scott said he didn't know, but Pajamae said she did: "Have a yard sale, Mr. Fenney." Pajamae had volunteered to run it because of her prior experience as a customer at numerous South Dallas yard sales. So the day of the event Scott was sitting at a makeshift checkout counter at the entrance to the motor court and taking cash from buyers while Pajamae and Boo made the sales.

"Two hundred," said the old lady in the sun hat who had introduced herself as Mrs. Jacobs.

"Now, Miz Jacobs," Pajamae said, "Miz Fenney, she paid two thousand dollars for that couch, and you want to buy it for two hundred? We priced it at seven hundred but"—she glanced around and lowered her voice—"long as you don't tell Mr. Fenney, I'll let you have it for six."

"I'll take it."

With her Sharpie, Pajamae wrote "SOLD" and "JACOBS" on the tag and changed the price to $600. She pointed at Mr. Fenney.

"Pay the man."

Mrs. Jacobs walked toward Mr. Fenney.

"Yoo-hoo, little colored girl!"

An old biddy was waving at Pajamae from over by the garage. Pajamae walked over. The woman was pointing at a leather chair.

"Is that a Ralph Lauren?"

"Lady, I'm not colored, I'm black. Well, I'm a quarter black, at the most. See, my mama's daddy was white and so was my daddy. So that'd make me a quarter black and three-quarters white." She smiled at the woman. "Why, I wouldn't be surprised if we were related! And no, ma'am, that's not Ralph Lauren, that's a chair."

"That's a Ralph Lauren."

Pajamae shrugged. "Whatever."

"The price is six hundred fifty, but I only have hundred-dollar bills," the lady said. "Do you have change?"

"No, ma'am, sure don't."

"But I want this chair!"

"So does that man over there."

The woman turned. "What man?"

"Bald dude in the blue shorts, with the big belly, talking to the fat woman in the striped shirt? He said he was bringing his wife over to look at it."

In fact, Pajamae had not spoken to the man.

"Don't you let him have this chair!"

"Ma'am, first rule of yard sales is, cash rules."

The woman again studied the chair, then the bald dude, then the chair. Finally she said, as Pajamae knew she would say, "I'll pay seven hundred."

Pajamae removed her Sharpie from behind her ear and wrote as she spoke: "Sold to Miz . . ."

"Smythe, with a *y* and an *e*. S-M-Y-T-H-E."

"Pay the man."

"I live just down the street. Can you deliver?"

"No, ma'am, but Louis can carry."

Pajamae waved at Louis standing off to the side like he was trying to go unnoticed, as if a six foot six, 330-pound black man in Highland Park could blend in. When he arrived, she said, "Louis, this nice lady needs this chair carried to her house."

Louis leaned down, spread his arms, grabbed the sides of the big chair, and lifted it without effort. He began walking toward Mr. Fenney like he was carrying a sack of groceries.

The lady said, "Do I have to tip him?"

"No, ma'am," Pajamae said, "just don't make him mad."

Mrs. Smythe with a *y* and an *e* looked at Louis's broad back walking away with her chair, frowned, and said, "I'll tip him. Twenty. No, fifty." She followed Louis over to Mr. Fenney.

Pajamae shook her head: *White people wouldn't last a day down in the projects*. When Boo walked up, Pajamae said, "Mama would love this."

"What?"

"Rich white people at a yard sale."

"Do you shop at yard sales often?"

"Yard sales are our shopping malls."

"Do you get good stuff?"

"Nothing like this. Course, we don't look for designer labels. We just make sure the clothes don't have blood stains, and no one's thrown up on the furniture."

Just then a woman wearing big sunglasses walked over holding out a handbag. "Is this a knockoff?" she asked.

Boo gave her a look. "Ma'am, my mother would rather have died than be seen with a knockoff. That's a Louis Vuitton original, retails for seven-fifty. We're offering that bag for two-fifty. My mother never even took it out of the house."

"I'll take it."

"Pay the man."

The woman left and Pajamae said, "Your mama has some fine stuff."

356

Boo nodded. "Mother always said, any girl says money can't buy happiness just doesn't know where to shop. But I guess she was wrong."

Boo pulled a black party dress off a rack. "A thousand dollars. She wore it one time to a party at the club." She replaced the dress and picked up a red spike-heeled shoe. "Three hundred dollars."

"For shoes?"

"Dior."

"Dee who?"

"Christian Dior. Women kill for these shoes."

Pajamae took the shoe and examined it. "My mama could wear these to work."

Scott had moved Rebecca's entire closet down to the backyard, hundreds of dresses and shoes and pants and shirts and garments of every kind and color. He had never once ventured into her huge walk-in closet so he had never realized just how many clothes she owned. He wondered now how much they had cost. Scott smiled as he accepted money from another customer buying his wife's clothes.

Pajamae was holding up a powder blue fringed miniskirt.

Boo said, "That was Mother's Cattle Barons' Ball outfit."

"Wearing this, she'd fit right in with Mama and Kiki working Harry Hines."

Pajamae replaced the skirt and picked up red pajamas.

"Neiman Marcus," Boo said. "One hundred thirty dollars."

"You think Mr. Fenney would sell these to me? I can pay seven dollars."

"You want red silk pajamas?"

"For Mama, so she doesn't have to sleep in that jail uniform."

"Oh." Boo thought for a moment, then said: "A. Scott put us in charge of pricing because he doesn't have a clue how much Mother paid for this stuff—he'd stroke out if he knew—so I'm going to mark these down to seven dollars. Pay the man."

"The little black girl said to pay you."

"Yep."

Scott looked up to see Penny Birnbaum.

"Oh, uh, hi, Penny. Did you find something you like?"

"I found something I liked the first time I was here." She smiled that smile and licked her red lips wet. "You want to go inside and see if I can find it again?"

"Well, uh, Penny, I've, uh, I've got to tend to the cash register, see?"

"You don't need cash. I'm giving it away."

She leaned in and her shirt gaped, revealing the top of her tanned breasts. Scott inhaled her perfume and he remembered that day in the steam shower and he became weak. He thought of feeling Penny's naked body against his and his hands on her and hers on him and her mouth on . . . but he thought of Boo. She wouldn't be very proud of her father if he gave in to his weakness.

Penny said, "I've come by every day and you haven't been home. Don't you want to see what else I can do?"

In fact, Scott had been home, but when he had seen who was standing on his front porch, he had hidden until she left.

"Oh, well, I know you're a very talented girl and—"

"Girl with the cornrows, she said to pay you."

Thank God. An old lady had walked up with a handful of clothes. Penny dropped three hundred-dollar bills on the counter and sashayed down the drive with two of Rebecca's purses, her narrow bottom in the tight shorts moving side to side so temptingly.

Bobby couldn't afford to buy any of the stuff Scotty had for sale—not that any of the furniture would go with the East Dallas flea-market decor of his little house—and he wasn't helping Boo and Pajamae sell the stuff because he'd probably punch out the first rich bitch who tried to negotiate him down on a price. So he was shooting pool in the garage, hoping the GQ dude checking out the pool table wouldn't buy it because he was hoping Scotty might give it to him in lieu of some of his fees. He could put it in his combination living/dining room.

"Your wife shopping outside?" he asked Mr. GQ.

"Yeah." Mr. GQ picked up a cue stick and said, "Wanna play?"

Bobby shrugged. "Why not."

Bobby played pool at the Mexican bar next to his office in the strip center two, three hours a day, sometimes more. Okay, usually more. In fact, his regular clients knew to call there if they had an emergency, which is to say, if they were unexpectedly arrested by the vice squad.

Bobby racked the balls and pulled out a twenty-dollar bill. "For a twenty? Or is that too much?"

Mr. GQ recoiled. "Too much?" He slapped a twenty on top of Bobby's bill and busted the rack. Not a ball fell.

Bobby chalked his cue tip. On his eighth straight stroke, he rolled the eight ball into the side pocket for the win. He reached over for the two bills when Mr. GQ said, "Double or nothing?"

Bobby smiled. The GQ dude didn't make his money playing pool in a Mexican bar. Two games later, when his wife came looking for him, Bobby had netted $140, more than he made lawyering most days.

Boo saw a familiar face and said, "See that woman over there, the blonde?"

Boo pointed and Pajamae followed her finger. "Wearing the short shorts and heels? The real skinny girl?"

"She's a lollipop."

"A lollipop? You mean, like a sucker?"

"Unh-huh. See how her head looks too big for her body?"

Pajamae studied the woman. "She does look like a lollipop. That white girl needs to put some meat on her bones."

"Mother said she eats and then she throws up."

" 'Cause she's sick?"

"No, on purpose! So she doesn't gain weight."

"Boo, you pulling my leg?"

"No! She was Mother's sorority sister. She married money."

Pajamae frowned. "How do you marry money?"

"You look like her and you find an old man with money."

"Oh. Kind of like Mama does, only it lasts longer."

"Mother said she's only thirty-three, but she's had breast implants, a tummy tuck, a butt lift, and liposuction. Mother said the only part of her that's real is her brain, and that's only because they don't do brain implants." Boo shrugged. "That's what Mother said, anyway."

"Is her old man here?"

The lollipop turned and walked over to a white-haired man sitting on the love seat from the formal living room that was selling for $1,000. She sat down and he patted her skinny thigh.

"That's him. Mother said he's a billionaire."

"He looks like her granddaddy. Mama would charge double to entertain a man as old as him. He must've paid a lot of money for his lollipop."

*

Scott was taking cash faster than he could count for clothes he had never seen Rebecca wear, furniture he had never sat on, and rugs he had never stepped on. Rebecca had filled every square foot of the 7,500-square-foot residence with her stuff. Now Scott was selling six thousand square feet of her stuff. And he was enjoying it.

"Your daughter said to pay you."

A middle-aged black woman had walked up to Scott.

"Hi, I'm Scott Fenney."

"I'm Dolores Hudson. We just moved in down the street"—she smiled—"the first black homeowners in Highland Park history?"

"Oh, yeah, I read about you. Welcome to the neighborhood, although I won't be here much longer."

She gave him a sympathetic look. "I've read about you, too."

"Yeah, well, you should believe everything you read."

"I don't think so. When are you moving?"

"I close on the sale of this place Thursday, then on the new place Friday. We'll move right after the trial."

"Well, if the timing doesn't work out and you need a place to stay, you and the children come stay with us. And I bet those girls haven't had any home cooking since your wife—"

She was embarrassed. But Scott smiled and said, "My wife didn't cook."

"Well, I do. I'll bring something over."

"Thank you, Dolores."

"No, thank you, Scott. For what you're doing. You

know, we weren't sure we were doing the right thing buying a home here. I didn't know if I wanted to be the Rosa Parks of Highland Park, whether we'd be accepted here."

"You did the right thing, Dolores. Most of the people here, particularly the younger ones, they'll be fine. Some of the old-timers won't accept you, but take it from me, you don't want to be friends with them anyway."

Dolores paid and said thanks again.

Boo was holding up a flowery sundress for a young woman.

"Luca Luca, you've heard of him, the Italian designer?"

"Of course. Who hasn't?"

She took the dress from Boo and held it against her body. It was a perfect fit.

"Almost as pretty as it looked on my mother."

"You know, I pledged the same sorority as your mother. She was six years before me. But she's still a role model for all the girls—Miss SMU marries a football star who becomes a rich lawyer. It's like Cinderella."

Boo nodded. "I must've missed the part where Cinderella walks out on her family for a golf pro."

Bobby was lining up a shot when someone stepped directly into his line of sight at the opposite end of the pool table. He raised up to tell the idiot to get the hell out of the way—

"Hi, Bobby."

—and damn near hit himself with the pool cue.

"Karen, what are you doing here?"

"I quit."

"What?"

"Ford Stevens."

"You're shi . . . You're kidding me? Why?"

"I didn't like the way they were making me think."

"Like a lawyer?"

"Yeah."

"Smart girl. What are you gonna do?"

"Work with you and Scott on your case."

When the summer sun set on the yard sale at 4000 Beverly Drive in the heart of Highland Park, nothing was left—not a shoe or a dress or a lamp or even the pool table. In less than nine hours, Scott had sold most of the material possessions he had acquired during eleven years of marriage, all the things that evidenced his existence, his ambitions, his career, and his wife.

The girls were at the other end of the kitchen, adding up their profits on the floor. Louis was counting his tip money—"Six hundred dollars for carrying stuff"—and sitting with Scott, Bobby, and Karen Douglas on the floor and eating fried chicken Dolores Hudson had brought over. The table and chairs had sold for $1,500.

"Karen," Scott said, "forget everything I ever told you about being a lawyer. I was wrong."

"You're a great lawyer, Scott, everyone at the firm says so, even since you left."

"I didn't leave. I got fired."

"Well, even after that."

"No, Karen, I was a corrupt lawyer. I cheated my clients, I cheated the law, and I cheated myself. I did whatever it took to win. I practiced law like it was a football game. It isn't."

"Karen wants to help us," Bobby said.

"Why?"

Karen said, "Because you need help. And I like Bobby."

Bobby dropped his drumstick.

Boo yelled over, "Sixty-seven thousand, four hundred fifty dollars."

TWENTY-FOUR

"VOIR DIRE" is a legal phrase meaning "to speak the truth." In the American legal system, "voir dire" refers to the process of picking a jury, perhaps because of all the players in a criminal trial, only the jurors are truly interested in the truth. Everyone else just wants to win.

In federal court, jurors must be citizens; at least eighteen years old; proficient in reading, writing, understanding, and speaking English; not be physically or mentally infirm; not have been convicted of a felony; and not have felony charges currently pending against them. Finding twelve people who meet such qualifications is easy; finding twelve people you would want to sit in judgment of your life is not.

That's where voir dire comes in. The judge and lawyers question the prospective jurors to uncover biases, prejudices, and predispositions that might prevent them from rendering a fair and impartial verdict. At least that's the theory. The reality is that every juror comes to court with his or her personal biases, prejudices, and predispositions that will absolutely prevent that person from rendering a fair and impartial verdict—which is precisely the kind of jurors both sides want. The real goal of voir dire is to find twelve jurors who are biased, prejudiced, and predisposed in your favor.

A trial in a court of law is not about truth, justice, and the American way. It's about winning. Prosecutors want a conviction so that they can build a track record of putting criminals in jail, a prerequisite for election or appointment to higher political office; defense attorneys want an acquittal because acquittals in high-profile criminal cases bring fame and fortune. Thus neither the prosecutor nor the defense attorney is concerned with truth or justice: truth is whatever they can get a jury to believe, and justice is when they win.

As he sat in a federal courtroom in downtown Dallas on a hot day in August, Scott Fenney believed his client had put the barrel of her .22-caliber gun to Clark McCall's head and pulled the trigger. He also believed she had done so in self-defense. Now he had to question the men and women sitting before him in the hope of finding twelve jurors who might agree with him and, if not acquit his client, at least not send her to death row.

Judge Buford had already questioned the prospective jurors concerning their legal qualifications and dismissed only one, a man who, when asked if he had any pending felony charges, answered, "They haven't been able to prove anything yet!"

Ray Burns had then questioned the prospective jurors about their willingness to find the defendant guilty knowing she might be sentenced to death. Seven prospective jurors said they were morally opposed to the death penalty and were excused.

Now twenty-nine prospective jurors were staring at Scott Fenney and Robert Herrin, waiting for the defendant's counsel to question them. In every prior voir dire, sitting next to A. Scott Fenney had been an expensive psychologist trained in the art of jury selection, not a lawyer who practiced street law in a strip center next to a Mexican bar. For fees up to $1,000,000, such jury experts conduct mock trials, focus groups, and pretrial polling to develop a detailed psychological profile of the ideal juror. They investigate the prospective jurors' employment, income, religion, hobbies, and politics. They study their clothes, their body language, and their answers during voir dire. They coach the lawyers on what to drive to the courthouse (leave the Mercedes-Benz at home because jurors might see you in the parking lot), what to wear to trial (no Rolexes or double-breasted Armani suits), and how to act in front of the jurors (try to "humanize" yourself; that is, pretend to be a normal human being in front of the jurors, a more difficult assignment for most lawyers than merely dressing down). They give the lawyer a thumbs-up or a thumbs-down on each prospective juror.

A lawyer learns with his first jury trial that the case is won or lost during jury selection. Today, with enough money, you can legally fix a jury. But since neither Scott nor his client had enough money to hire a jury expert, there was no paid consultant sitting next to Scott, only Bobby.

So Scott said to the men and women before him, "I'm nervous, about this. I've never represented a person accused of murder. Are you nervous, too?"

Heads started nodding.

"Well, rather than me asking you a lot of questions, maybe we'll just visit for a while. Forget what we're here for, forget you might be jurors, forget we're lawyers—as you might have read, my former law firm's been trying to forget I'm a lawyer."

A few chuckles from the jury box, which gave Scott an idea.

"What's the difference between a rattlesnake lying dead in the middle of a highway and a lawyer lying dead in the middle of a highway?"

A female juror: "Skid marks in front of the snake."

The jurors laughed.

"You know why New Jersey got all the toxic waste dumps and California got all the lawyers?"

A male juror: "New Jersey got first choice."

Louder laughter from the jury box.

"What do lawyers and sperm have in common?"

A male juror: "They both have a one-in-a-million chance of turning out human."

Raucous laughter.

The same juror: "How do you know when a lawyer is lying?"

An old lady: "His lips are moving."

Another: "A lawyer is a liar with a permit to practice."

And another: "If an IRS agent and a lawyer were

both drowning and you could save only one, would you read the paper or go to lunch?"

Scott finally interrupted the revelry.

"Hey, I went to law school. I get to tell the jokes."

The jurors' laughter died down, but their smiles remained.

"I take it you people don't care for lawyers?"

All twenty-nine heads shook emphatically.

"You hate lawyers?"

All heads nodded emphatically.

"Why?"

An older man: "Because lawyers don't know the difference between the truth and winning an argument."

An older woman: "Because lawyers think being clever is the same as being smart."

A young woman: "Because a lawyer will tell you the sky is green if that'll help his case."

A young man: "Because lawyers are greedy."

Bobby: "Yeah, and they're—"

"Bobby!"

Scott turned to the jurors. "And he's a lawyer!"

The jurors were chuckling again.

Ray Burns stood. "Your Honor, if Mr. Fenney is through with his stand-up comedy act, perhaps we could—"

"Sit, Mr. Burns," the judge said.

Ray Burns sat. Scott addressed the prospective jurors.

"Okay, I think we've established that all of you hate lawyers. And that's okay. We deserve it. But my client doesn't. You can hate me because I'm a lawyer, but don't hate her because you hate her lawyer. Her life is in your hands. Give her a fair shake. Can you all agree to that?"

The smiles were gone, replaced by sober expressions. Every single juror nodded.

"All right, now I need to ask you a few questions. First, have any of you participated in voir dire before?"

One young man with a nose ring raised his hand and asked, "Is that like when there's four?"

"Four *what*?"

"Four people. You know, like ménage à trois plus one."

From behind, Judge Buford's weary voice: "You're excused."

The man rose, shrugged, and shuffled out of the courtroom.

Scott said, "Any of you *not* heard about this case?"

No one raised a hand.

"All right. My client is a prostitute and a heroin addict. You all know that, right?"

Their heads nodded.

"Again, I ask only one thing of you: Don't prejudge her. Don't assume. You don't know what another person's life is like until you've walked around in her shoes awhile. Ms. Jones is not here today because she's ill. She's suffering withdrawal sickness. How many of you smoke?"

Eight jurors raised their hands.

"Imagine if you had to quit cold turkey."

They nodded.

"Have any of you ever retained a prostitute?"

No hands were raised, but one man glanced around. "Sir?"

"I ain't never retained a hooker, but I had sex with one."

The judge: "You're excused."

Scott thumbed through the jurors' questionnaires and stopped at one completed by a high school football coach. Most football coaches considered themselves smarter than the general population because they understood the definition of pass interference. But one other predisposition of football coaches gave him pause. So he turned to juror number 28 and said, "Coach, who's the greatest running back ever produced by the State of Texas?"

Without blinking, the coach asked, "Negro or white?"

The judge: "You're excused."

After the coach had left, Scott turned to another juror, an older man whose sunburned face told Scott he worked outdoors.

"Sir, in response to question number eleven asking how far did you go in school, you answered twelve miles."

"Yes, sir, we lived in the country, so that's how far we had to go."

"Uh, well, the question means, you know, what was the highest grade level you attained?"

The man seemed genuinely embarrassed. "Oh, hell, I'm sorry. I made a B once."

The judge: "You're excused."

Scott now turned to an older woman clutching a big purse in her lap and wearing a worried expression.

"Ma'am?" She looked up. "Ma'am, is there anything that would interfere with your serving on this jury?"

"Will I be home in time for *Oprah*?"

The judge: "You're excused."

On the drive home, Bobby said, "Will I be home in time for *Oprah*? That was a good one."

Scott had struck seven prospective jurors and Ray Burns nine. The twelve jurors who would determine whether Shawanda Jones would live or die had been selected and seated for the trial that would start on Monday: there were seven men and five women; six were white, four were black, and two were Hispanic; there was a teacher, a nurse, a carpenter, a dental assistant, a car salesman, two housewives, a mechanic, a junior college professor, a contractor, a bartender, and a grocery store clerk.

Scott said to Bobby, "Do you trust Karen?"

"Yeah, why?"

"I'm worried Dan Ford planted her."

"You mean as a spy?"

"Yeah, to learn our strategy."

"What strategy? *Prayer?*" Bobby smiled. "Don't worry, Scotty, she's not a spy."

"How can you be sure?"

"Remember a few weeks ago, in the pool, I said I'd probably never have sex again?"

"Yeah."

"I was wrong."

"You mean . . . ?"

"Yeah. And no girl would have sex with me just for money. Believe me, I know."

Money could not make the rape go away. The physical pain was gone, but the mental pain would never leave Hannah Steele.

It was a beautiful afternoon in Galveston. The sun was warm, but the sea breeze was cool against her skin. Hannah was strolling down the seawall, seventeen feet above the beach. To her left, across the boulevard, were restaurants, bars, gift shops, and beach-front condos and hotels; to her right was the sandy beach and beyond that the Gulf of Mexico, a body of brown water whose swells rolled ashore and broke into small waves that died in the sand around the feet of kids wading at the water's edge. Their parents were sitting in chairs under colorful umbrellas that dotted the beach in both directions as far as Hannah could see. Other kids were building sand castles or hunting for seashells, and a few surfers were trying to find waves strong enough to provide a ride, but without much luck.

Hannah liked to walk the seawall.

Her therapist said it was good for her to take these walks and to realize that all around her life went on and that her life must as well. But Hannah always focused on the kids; her therapist said she would have children one day, but Hannah didn't think she would ever be able to have sex again. Clark McCall had destroyed her life.

And now his life was over.

She had tried not to feel happy when she had heard about Clark's death. But somewhere deep inside her she hoped he had suffered. Now she was the accused woman's only hope, Mr. Fenney had said. Her only hope. So she would fly to Dallas on Sunday. It would be her first trip back since she had left.

Could she do it?

Could she go into that courtroom and sit up there and see Senator McCall and tell the world what Clark did to her? *He kissed me . . . he touched me . . . I said no . . . he said yes . . . he slapped me . . . hit me . . . once, twice, three times, harder each time . . . he was wild-eyed, crazy, strong . . . he pinned me down . . . pulled my panties down . . . pried my legs apart . . . yes, I fought him . . . but he was too strong . . . he pushed into me . . . the pain . . . the pain . . .*

The pain would never go away.

She had gone to SMU on a dance scholarship. She loved to dance. She had not danced since that night. The rape had changed her life. She hadn't been able to get over it, to get on with her life. Her therapist had convinced her that testifying at the trial might be just the closure she needed to move forward. She almost walked into a man.

"Excuse me," she said.

"Hello, Hannah," the man said.

Hannah looked up at the big bald man in front of her and started to cry.

*

The only open chair was next to Penny Birnbaum.

Scott and Bobby had returned home and eaten lunch with Louis and the girls. Scott had then driven the Jetta to the title company that was closing the sale of 4000 Beverly Drive. The receptionist led him to the small conference room where he would sign over his home to Mr. and Mrs. Jeffrey Birnbaum.

Penny was smiling and patting the seat of the empty chair.

Scott introduced himself to Joy, the closing agent sitting on the near side of the table next to Jeffrey, who was poring over the stack of documents like a jeweler over a new batch of uncut diamonds. Scott walked around the table, sat next to Penny, and scooted his chair up under the table. Before he had settled in, her right hand was on his left knee.

"I still need to measure for furniture, Scott," she said.

She was wearing a sundress that accentuated her round breasts and narrow waist. Her hand moved up to Scott's thigh and began closing in on his crotch. He reached down, grabbed her wrist, and placed her hand firmly in her lap. She pushed out her lips in a pouty face. But when he released her wrist, her hand returned to his thigh like a spring-action screen door slamming in place. She smiled.

Joy pushed a pile of papers across the table to Scott and began reciting the numbers shown on the closing statement.

"Three-point-four million sales price due to the seller, less deductions for the loan payoff, two-point-eight million principal plus twenty-four thousand eight hundred ninety accrued interest, the title policy premium, nineteen thousand, miscellaneous title company charges for the escrow fee—"

"Two-fifty?" Jeffrey said.

Joy said, "Standard charge."

"But there's no escrow."

"We still charge the fee."

"But—"

"I'll pay the two-fifty, Jeffrey," Scott said.

He wasn't in the mood to argue over a $250 charge in a $3.4 million deal. Even with that deduction, Scott would net over $500,000 from the sale. After paying taxes and closing on the little starter home by SMU, with the rest of his 401(k) and the $67,000 from the yard sale, he'd have enough to start a new life.

He removed Penny's hand again and whispered, "Stop!"

Across the table, Jeffrey and Joy were huddled over the buyer's closing documents, more voluminous because of the mortgage documents between Jeffrey and his bank. Scott's thoughts drifted back to that day three years ago when he had signed similar mortgage documents to purchase this very home, but before he could get very far he felt a soft whisper in his ear: "I'm not wearing any panties."

Penny pulled back and their eyes met. Her eyes dropped and led his down. She twisted slightly in her chair and spread her legs a little and slowly slid the end of her dress up to reveal her tanned lower thighs, her smooth upper thighs, and finally that lovely intersection of thighs and torso. Scott inhaled sharply. She wasn't lying.

Scott felt the blood rush southward. He began signing the closing papers as fast as his hand could scribble his signature: the closing statement, lien affidavits, non-resident alien certification, tax proration agreement, and the deed conveying his dream house to Jeffrey Birnbaum et ux Penny Birnbaum. Scott's hand trembled when he signed *A. Scott Fenney*. He pushed the deed across the table to Jeffrey. And with that, his dream home was gone. He felt as if he had handed over his manhood.

But he knew he hadn't because Penny had a firm hold on his manhood below the table. Scott's face felt hot, whether from the emotion of signing away his home or the movement of Penny's hand, he couldn't say. All he knew was that he had to get out of this closing fast, so he scratched his name on the final document, the temporary lease by which he would lease the home back from the Birnbaums for ten days, enough time to vacate the premises. He pushed the paper across the table to Jeffrey, who glanced up from his stack of documents and at the lease, then at Scott and Penny and back to Scott, his eyes narrowing with suspicion.

"What the hell's going on?" he said.

Scott froze, as did Penny's hand.

"Uh, what do you mean, Jeffrey?"

Jeffrey picked up the lease. "Ten days? It was supposed to be seven."

Scott exhaled with relief; Penny's hand went back to work.

"Jeffrey, you moved up closing to today."

"Well, can't you get out sooner? We're ready to move in."

"No, Jeffrey, I can't. I've got a murder trial starting Monday—you might've read about it. That's a little more important than you getting into my house a few days earlier."

"It's not your house anymore, Scott."

Jeffrey said it with the arrogance of a man completely unaware that at that very moment his wife was massaging another man's penis.

That night, after prayers, Pajamae asked Scott, "So those twelve people are going to decide what happens to Mama?"

"Yes, baby, they are."

"Do you trust them, Mr. Fenney?"

"Well . . . I don't know them well enough to know whether I trust them or not. I hope they can find a way to be fair."

Pajamae said, "I'm going to pray for them."

"The jurors?"

She nodded. "Mama always says to pray for other people, so they do the right thing. Like she said I should pray for you."

TWENTY-FIVE

WHEN SCOTT WOKE UP on Sunday morning, his mind instantly filled with fear. The trial would begin in twenty-four hours: Was he a good enough lawyer to save Shawanda? For the last eleven years, when he needed help, Scott had always gone to Dan Ford. Now he needed help and his thoughts went to Butch Fenney: Son, when you need help, hit your knees.

Scott rolled out of bed, put on his shorts, and hurried down the hall and up the stairs to the third floor. He found the girls on the bed. Pajamae was fixing Boo's cornrows.

"Get your clothes on, girls, we're going to church."

Boo's mouth fell open.

Louis led the way up the sidewalk to the front entrance of the small church in East Dallas and Pajamae said, "I wondered why y'all never went to church. Mama and me, we go every Sunday. I figured maybe white people just didn't go to church."

"Why didn't you say you wanted to go?" Scott asked.

"Wouldn't have been polite, Mr. Fenney."

Scott Fenney had attended church regularly with his parents, but after Butch died, he'd lost any enthusiasm he had for religion. Why would God take a good man like Butch Fenney? But he still attended church with his mother until she died. The last time he had entered this church was for his mother's funeral.

The preacher had nothing on Big Charlie.

Before they had parted back at the stadium that day two weeks ago, Big Charlie had said, "When God gives you a gift, it doesn't mean you're special. It means you're blessed."

Scott finally understood what his mother had meant when she had said he had a gift and she didn't mean football. He knew that his entire life had led him to this one moment, to this trial, to Shawanda Jones. The judge was right: She needed a hero. She needed him. And he needed her. But it had been a long time since Scott Fenney had been someone's hero. And he honestly didn't know if he had it in him to be a hero now.

He glanced down at the two little girls sitting next to him. Boo and Pajamae turned their eyes up to him, the way he had often turned his eyes up to Butch in this very church. He remembered his father's words again, and he slid forward and knelt.

And he prayed for help.

*

A mile away, Bobby Herrin was sitting in his dingy office drafting a trial brief. The front door was propped open because the landlord didn't turn on the air-conditioning on Sundays. He inhaled and caught the scent of cheap cologne. He looked up. Standing in the door was a white man, bald, burly, and thick-necked. Delroy Lund.

Carl's more thorough background check on Delroy Lund had revealed a DEA career checkered with reprimands for unnecessary use of force. Carl said he was digging deeper, but he hadn't reported back yet.

Bobby tried to maintain his composure, but flinched when Delroy reached into his coat.

"Don't try anything, Delroy! I yell out, Joo-Chan will come over—and he knows karate!"

Delroy chuckled. "That gook knows how to make donuts—but not on Sunday. You're all alone, Herrin."

But Delroy didn't pull out a gun; he pulled out an envelope. Bobby exhaled with relief. Delroy tossed the envelope on the desk. Bobby opened it; inside was a check made payable to Robert Herrin, Esq., for the sum of $100,000. Bobby suddenly felt better about his standing in the legal profession: finally, he was important enough to be bribed. He examined the check.

"Bank check issued by a Cayman Island bank. That's cute, Delroy. Not traceable back to McCall."

"We ain't stupid."

"That's open for debate."

"Here's the deal, Herrin. That little fuckup Clark ain't gonna cheat his dad out of the White House, alive

382

or dead. So you got a choice: take the money and get out of town or get arrested."

"For what?"

"Dealing drugs."

"I don't have any drugs."

"You will when I'm finished. I'll call my buddies at the DEA and they'll bust your ass."

"With your record at the DEA? I don't think so. I'll tell them you planted the drugs, take a polygraph, and they'll arrest you. So, what, McCall thinks Scotty can't defend her without me? Scotty doesn't need me."

"He proved that before, didn't he?" Delroy grinned. "You're the only conscience he's got, according to Burns."

Bobby replaced the check and tossed the envelope to Delroy.

"Get out."

"You're making a big mistake."

"Won't be the first time. See you at the trial, Delroy."

"Sorry, I can't make it."

"Sure you can." Bobby picked up a subpoena, wrote *Delroy Lund* in the witness blank, and tossed it to Delroy. "You're served, asshole."

As soon as the word was out of his mouth, Bobby knew he had pushed Delroy's button—and that he shouldn't have. Delroy bent over and picked up the subpoena from the floor. He glanced at it; his face changed. He came over to Bobby, grabbed Bobby by the shirt, and yanked him halfway out of his chair. Delroy's mouth was about six inches away from Bobby's face when he said, "You little mother—"

"Hey, *hombre*!"

Standing in the door was Carlos Hernandez. Carlos was six feet tall, weighed maybe one-ninety, and was dressed for church: black leather pants, black pointed boots, a black tee shirt tight on his muscular tattooed arms, and two-inch silver bracelets on each wrist. His black hair was slicked back.

"Get your stinkin' hands off my lawyer, gringo!"

The two men glared at each other. Finally, Delroy chuckled, released Bobby, walked a few steps, then turned back.

"Oh, your star witness took her check. She figured a vacation was better than being fish bait in Galveston Bay."

Delroy laughed as he walked out the door past Carlos's mean face. When he was gone, Carlos broke into a big grin and said, "Good thing you got me bail, huh, Mr. Herrin?"

"Yeah. Thanks, Carlos."

Carlos held out a twenty-dollar bill. "From my mother."

"Can we go see Mama?" Pajamae asked.

Scott opened the car door for the girls and said, "Sure."

The drive from the church in East Dallas to the federal building in downtown took only minutes on the vacant Sunday morning streets. Louis stayed outside in the car. Scott and the girls went inside and rode the elevator to the fifth floor. They were escorted to the small bare room and waited for Shawanda. When she entered the room, she hugged Pajamae and Boo. Then Scott hugged her.

When he released her, he held her shoulders and said, "Shawanda, don't be afraid of what might happen at the trial. With Hannah Steele testifying, we've got a fighting chance. And if we lose, we'll appeal all the way to the Supreme Court."

Shawanda smiled softly. "I ain't scared, Mr. Fenney. People like me, we been on the wrong side of life long enough to know what to expect in a courtroom. But most of all, I ain't scared 'cause you my lawyer."

An hour later, they arrived back home to Bobby's car parked in the driveway and Bobby sitting on the back steps smoking a cigarette. Bobby said, "Hannah Steele's disappeared. McCall bought her off or Delroy scared her off; either way she ain't testifying. We're screwed."

TWENTY-SIX

SCOTT PARKED the Jetta in an open lot two blocks down from the federal building. There was no shade to be found, so he lowered the windows an inch hoping the inside temperature wouldn't rise high enough to melt the dashboard, then he climbed out. The girls followed him, both wearing the best outfits Rebecca had purchased for Boo at Neiman Marcus. Pajamae had on a white sundress with black polka dots and a wide-brimmed white hat; Boo wore a light blue sundress with a matching hat. They looked like two little Southern belles—except for the cornrows.

Scott pulled his handkerchief from his back pocket, removed his glasses, and wiped away the sweat already accumulating on his forehead. He then replaced his glasses, put on his coat, locked the car, and picked up his briefcase. He paid the attendant ten dollars for all-day parking, and then they walked up the street. Scott felt like he always did right before a game, his body alive with nervous energy, particularly when the opponents he would soon face were bigger, stronger, and meaner.

He looked down at the two little girls walking in front of him. Boo was the love of his life and Pajamae had become like a second daughter to him. They were excited, as if they were going to the zoo instead of a murder trial, chatting and giggling—until they turned the corner onto Commerce Street.

Then all three of them froze. Hundreds of people were gathered at the front entrance to the federal building: local, network, and cable TV vans lined the street, their satellite dishes and camera crews ready to capture and transmit breaking news; several dozen police were keeping the peace. It was the media circus Buford had promised.

"A. Scott, who are all those people waiting for?" Boo asked.

"Me."

He pulled the girls close and forged ahead. When they were spotted, the cameras and reporters came rushing forward like the kicking team rushing downfield to tackle number 22 returning the opening kickoff. Scott would rather have faced those foaming-at-the-mouth football players than these crazed reporters wanting a sound bite for the evening news. They stuck microphones in his face and shouted from a foot away:

"Is Shawanda claiming self-defense?"

"Will other women testify that Clark raped them?"

"Are you gonna call the senator to testify?"

To all of which Scott answered, "No comment," and pushed ahead. But then they went after Pajamae, sticking microphones in her face and shouting at her:

"Do you think your mother killed Clark?"

"Where will you live if she's convicted?"

"Do you still love your mother?"

Scott got mad. He shoved the microphones and cameras away.

"Leave her alone!"

But Pajamae had stopped dead in her tracks. Her head was tilted up at the last reporter, an odd expression on her face, and she said in the softest voice: "Of course I love my mama."

Her words struck the reporters silent. A little black girl had embarrassed the media circus into submission. The crowd parted and allowed Scott and his two little girls free passage into the courthouse.

They got off the elevator on the fifteenth floor and walked down the hall and around the corner to Judge Buford's courtroom, where Delroy Lund was sitting on a bench, reading the sports pages. They hadn't seen each other since that day at the Village, but Delroy only glanced up at Scott and then back at the newspaper, without comment or expression. Per his subpoena, Delroy was legally obligated to sit outside the courtroom for the duration of the trial, waiting to be called inside to testify.

Scott pulled the big double doors open and escorted the girls into the courtroom, up the center aisle to the front row, and as he was pointing out where they should sit, he glanced back at the second row and found himself staring at United States Senator Mack McCall and his wife. And they stared back. Scott thought he noticed the senator's right arm come up slightly, as if he were going to reach over and shake Scott's hand, a politician's habit, but the senator pulled back. Scott's eyes fell on Jean McCall; she looked straight into his eyes and her eyebrows rose slightly, as if asking a silent question, then she recrossed her legs, left over right. The movement drew Scott's eyes down to her short skirt, and she looked away, but ran her hand down the length of her smooth thigh. Scott was turning his head back to the girls when he noticed Dan Ford. His former senior partner, mentor, and father figure was sitting next to Jean McCall with a grim expression. Dan broke eye contact with Scott and looked down, slowly shaking his head.

Scott got the girls settled in on the jury side of the spectator section. He wanted the jurors to see the defendant's daughter and think, *How could the same person be a loving mother and a cold-blooded murderer?*

"Oh, that's a nice touch."

Ray Burns's smart-ass voice. Scott turned to his adversary, but Ray just shook his head and walked to the prosecution table. Bobby and Karen were already seated at the defendant's table.

"Clark McCall was lying on the floor of his bedroom, writhing in pain after being kneed in the groin, when the defendant, Shawanda Jones, walked over to him, grabbed his hair, yanked him up, stuck the barrel of her .22-caliber pistol to his forehead, and pulled the trigger, killing him instantly. Then she stole his money and his car. Shawanda Jones murdered Clark McCall, a federal official, during the commission of a robbery. That is what the evidence will show. And that is why I will ask you to return a verdict of guilty and a sentence of death."

Assistant United States Attorney Ray Burns turned away from the jury, walked from the podium back to the prosecution table, and winked at Scott, knowing that he had just made a very effective opening statement, telling the jury exactly what he would prove and knowing he could back up his words.

"Mr. Fenney," Judge Buford said.

Scott stood and glanced at the spectator section crowded with gawkers gathered to witness a trial the likes of which Dallas had never seen. At the back of the courtroom were the groupies, old men who came to the courthouse each day like other old men went to the golf course. Next up were several rows of the general public who had lined up outside before daybreak to get a seat. Then came five rows of reporters taking notes and courtroom artists sketching portraits. Then came an assortment of lawyers and state court judges who viewed the trial as continuing legal education. And finally there were Senator McCall and his wife, McCall staring holes in Scott's skull, Jean just staring, and Dan Ford shaking his head. Directly in front of them, Boo and Pajamae sat like two little prim and proper Highland Park girls, knees together, hands in their laps. He looked at Boo and she smiled and gave him an emphatic thumbs-up. He wished he shared her confidence. He walked over to the podium and faced the jury. He would not dispute the government's evidence. He would only dispute the government's conclusions.

"Shawanda Jones is a prostitute and a heroin addict. She's not present this morning because she's sick; she's suffering withdrawal. Judge Buford permitted me to make you aware of her illness so you would not hold her absence against her. If you remember, at jury selection, I asked only one thing from each of you, and that was to give Shawanda a fair shake."

There was a time, not that long ago, when a black defendant could not get a fair shake in a Southern courtroom; when a complete stranger could walk in off the sidewalk and, without knowing anything about a case, instantly pick out the defendant, the only black person in the courtroom; when a jury of a black defendant's "peers" would be white men. But the times had changed and so had the law. Scott now looked into the eyes of the black and brown and white men and women sitting in the jury box—the teacher, the mechanic, the nurse, the bartender, and the others—and wondered if they could be fair.

"You hold her life in your hands. Listen carefully. Think for yourself. Be fair."

Dallas Police Officer Eddie Castille swore to "tell the truth, the whole truth, and nothing but the truth so help me God" and sat in the witness stand. Castille was in his midtwenties, Hispanic, a young cop eager to please, and still under the impression that he could make a difference on the streets of Dallas. He was the prosecution's first witness. Ray Burns addressed him from the podium.

"Officer Castille, what is your position with the Dallas Police Department?"

"Patrol officer."

"Were you patrolling the Harry Hines vicinity of Dallas on the afternoon of Sunday, June sixth?"

"Yes, sir."

"And during that patrol did you come upon an abandoned Mercedes-Benz?"

"Yes, sir."

"Please tell the jury what you did next."

"I saw the vehicle parked on a side street and pulled up to it. We don't generally see cars like that in the Harry Hines area, except at the strip joints. The vehicle was unoccupied, so I ran the plates. Dispatch came back, said it hadn't been reported stolen, said it was registered to a Mack McCall."

"As in Senator Mack McCall?"

"Yes, sir, that's what dispatch said, but I didn't know who that was."

That brought light laughter from the courtroom and a self-deprecating shrug from the senator.

"And then what did you do?"

"The registration address was in Highland Park, so the duty sergeant said he would call Highland Park PD and have them go over to the residence."

"And did that end your involvement with this case?"

"Yes, sir, other than waiting for the car to be towed to impound."

"And what time was this?"

"Approximately one P.M."

"Thank you, Officer Castille. No further questions."

Judge Buford turned to Scott, who said, "No questions, Your Honor."

"Mama, you okay?"

Instead of going out each day for lunch, the defense team had decided to eat lunch with the defendant. So they were now in the small bare conference room, eating the ham and cheese sandwiches the girls had made that morning. Scott pulled his coat off the chair back and wrapped it around Shawanda's shoulders. His client was having chills again.

"Yeah, baby."

"Why can't you have your medicine?"

"Don't know."

"Mama, the jury people keep looking over at me."

"That 'cause you so pretty." She warmed and she said, "How the trial going, Mr. Fenney?"

"Nothing much this morning, Shawanda."

"Mama, that Mr. Burns, he's a little prick. He stood right up there and lied to those jury people. He told them you killed that McCall boy, just like he meant it."

"He did, baby."

*

After the lunch break, Ray Burns, the little prick, called Sergeant Roland James of the Highland Park Police Department as the prosecution's second witness. Sergeant James was one of those middle-aged cops who had long ago made his peace with the fact that he wasn't going to make a difference, so he would just ride out his shift until his pension kicked in. He testified that he had been on duty on the afternoon of Sunday, June 6, and had taken the call from the Dallas PD regarding the McCall Mercedes-Benz. He had arrived at the McCall estate at one-thirty P.M.

"Sergeant James," Ray Burns said, "when you arrived at the McCall residence, did you notice anything out of the ordinary?"

"No, sir—except that the front gates were open."

"What did you do?"

"I drove in, went up to the front door, and rang the doorbell several times. No one answered. I tried the door, but it was locked. So I walked around to the back of the house and found the back door open. I stepped inside the residence and called out, but no one answered."

"What did you do then?"

"I commenced searching the residence, the ground floor first. Nothing was disturbed, and I found no one. I walked up the stairs to the second floor, started on the west wing. I found the body in a bedroom in the east wing."

"What body was that?"

"White male, naked, gunshot wound to the head, lying on white carpet soaked in blood."

"Was the body that of Clark McCall?"

"Yes, sir."

"You knew that from having met Clark McCall on a prior occasion?"

"Yes, sir."

"Did you check the body for vital signs?"

"No, sir."

"Why not?"

"From the appearance of the body, there was no question that the victim was dead and had been for some time. I didn't want to contaminate the evidence."

"And was that in accordance with your police training?"

"Uh, well, no, sir. That was in accordance with O.J.'s trial. They accused those L.A. cops of contaminating the evidence. I wasn't going there."

"So what did you do?"

"I stepped out of the room and called headquarters, talked to the chief. He called in the Feds. The FBI."

"Thank you, Sergeant James. No further questions."

Scott stood and went to the podium.

"Sergeant James, why did your chief call in the FBI?"

"He figured they had jurisdiction."

"Over a murder?"

"The victim was a federal official."

"You knew that at the time, when you were standing in his bedroom door?"

"Well, no, sir, I didn't know that. I guess the chief did."

"But you knew who the victim was?"

"Yes, sir."

"And how did you know Clark McCall?"

"Well, Clark McCall, he, uh, he had a history with us."

"A record?"

"Yes, sir."

"How long have you been with the Highland Park PD?"

"Twenty-three years this December."

"And had you ever personally arrested Clark McCall?"

"Yes, sir."

"On how many occasions?"

"Three that I recall."

"For what?"

"Disturbing the peace."

"What was he doing?"

"Drinking in public, when he was in high school."

"Is that all?"

"Drugs."

"Is that all?"

"One time he was standing naked in the SMU fountain."

"Was he ever arrested for a sexual crime?"

"Not that I'm aware of, sir."

"Was a complaint ever filed against Clark McCall alleging a sexual crime?"

"Not that I'm aware of."

"So, bottom line, your chief called in the Feds because he knew the victim was the son of Senator McCall?"

"Yes, sir. And because we'd never worked a homicide in Highland Park."

The next witness for the prosecution was the FBI agent first on the scene, Agent Paul Owen, fifty, ex-military with a soldier's bearing and haircut.

"Agent Owen," Ray Burns said, "you arrived at the McCall residence at what time?"

"Approximately two-thirty P.M."

"And what did you do?"

"I entered the residence, which Highland Park PD had secured, and went upstairs to the crime scene. I observed the victim's body lying on the floor. I commenced documenting the crime scene, and I called in the Evidence Response Team. They arrived at approximately three P.M."

"You were in charge of the investigation?"

"Yes, sir."

"And did you process the crime scene?"

"Yes, sir, we collected the evidence."

"And what evidence did you collect?"

"We cut out the carpet under and surrounding the body to obtain blood samples. We collected hair next to the body, fingerprints, various pieces of clothing, personal effects, the sheets off the bed, drinking glasses, a .22-caliber bullet imbedded in the floor, a .22-caliber pistol, and the body."

"And what did you do with this evidence?"

"The body went to the Dallas County medical

examiner. The rest of the evidence went to the FBI lab at Quantico, Virginia, for analysis."

"Did you conduct a luminol test to locate blood elsewhere in the room?"

"Yes, sir, we did."

"And did you find blood elsewhere?"

"No, sir."

"So the victim died where he was found?"

"Yes, sir. The body had not been moved."

"Did you immediately run a check on the fingerprints?"

"Yes, sir, we did that in Dallas."

"And did you get a match?"

"Yes, sir. The fingerprints on one of the drinking glasses and the pistol belonged to the defendant."

"Shawanda Jones?"

"Yes, sir."

"What did you do then?"

"We obtained an arrest warrant for Shawanda Jones."

"Did you make the arrest?"

"No, sir. I sent Agent Edwards."

"What did you do next?"

"I called next of kin."

"Senator McCall?"

"Yes, sir. I informed the senator that his son had been murdered in their residence."

"And what did Senator McCall say?"

"He asked how his son had been killed."

"And did you tell him?"

"Yes, sir."

"All right. Back to the crime scene, Agent Owen. Were photographs taken of the crime scene?"

"Yes, sir."

Ray Burns stepped over to Scott and handed him the four photographs he would show the jury. The crime scene photos had been the subject of heated pretrial arguments over their prejudicial effect on the jury. Burns wanted to introduce two dozen photos, but the judge had approved only these four, one of which was particularly graphic. Scott handed the photos to Karen, who was sitting next to him. She inhaled sharply. He forgot she hadn't seen the photos. Which reminded Scott; he twisted in his chair, caught the girls' attention, and gestured that it was time for them to lower their eyes. He knew the photos were coming and had discussed it with them on the drive over that morning. He told them to stare down at their feet until the photo show was over.

"Agent Owen, would you look at your computer screen and identify the photo being displayed to the jury on the overhead screen?"

Agent Owen turned in the witness chair to view the computer screen. Scott kept an eye on the jury box.

"This is the view of the crime scene from the bedroom door, as I first observed the scene. The bed is directly in front of the door, the bathroom over to the right, and the body over to the left. Only the victim's legs are visible in this photo."

"This is an accurate representation of the crime scene?"

"Yes, sir, it is."

The next photo came up on the overhead screen.

"Agent Owen, can you identify this photo?"

"This is a close shot of the bed, evidencing that it had recently been, uh, occupied."

"And is this an accurate representation of what you saw?"

"Yes, sir."

"And this photo?"

"The bathroom, and it is accurate."

"And finally, this photo."

A collective gasp went up in the courtroom. In the jury box, the two housewives averted their eyes, the bartender grimaced, and the car salesman stared. Ray Burns had displayed his climactic photo, a close-up of Clark McCall's body, his eyes open and vacant, a hole in his forehead, his head in a pool of blood.

"This is a close shot of the victim's body. He was naked, no wounds evident except about the head. There is apparent swelling around the right eye, some scratch marks on the face, and the entry wound in the left forehead."

Scott turned to the girls. They were staring down at their feet as instructed, but Pajamae's hat brim rose slightly; she was peeking. Scott snapped his fingers at her; she looked at him. Her expression said it was too late. She had seen the photo.

Ray allowed the gruesome image to sink into the jurors' minds before saying, "No more questions."

For the next thirty minutes, Bobby cross-examined Agent Owen about the toxicology reports, which showed alcohol and cocaine in Clark McCall's blood, so that the jurors would leave the courtroom that day with something on their mind other than the crime scene photos. After he passed the witness, Judge Buford adjourned for the day. Scott, Bobby, Karen, and the girls returned home; Senator McCall held a press conference on the courthouse steps. The senator spoke with the confidence of a man who knew his words would not be contradicted by Hannah Steele: "Clark was the kind of son every man dreams of having."

"Now, Scotty, don't get depressed," Bobby said through a mouthful of Chinese takeout. "The first day of a criminal trial is always bad. At least he didn't surprise us with anything."

"I'm not depressed about the prosecution's case, Bobby. I'm depressed about our defense. We've got nothing!"

They were at their designated places on the kitchen floor and the girls were at theirs.

"Carl's still working the case."

"Where the hell is he?"

"Del Rio."

"What's he doing down on the border?"

Bobby shrugged. "With Carl, you give him full rein and don't ask questions. He always finds something."

"I hope he finds something soon, Bobby, 'cause this isn't looking good."

Bobby stuck a little spare rib in his mouth, worked

it over, pulled it out clean, and said, "Shit, Scotty, don't worry about today. Tomorrow's gonna be a lot worse."

Boo and Pajamae were already in bed when Scott entered their bedroom to say prayers.

After prayers, Pajamae said, "One night, a man got shot outside our apartment. When the po-lice came, Mama and me, we went outside. The dead man, he had a white sheet over him. I always wondered what he looked like, that dead man. Now I know."

"Pajamae, you promised not to look."

"I'm sorry, Mr. Fenney, but I had to. They're saying my mama killed that man. I had to look. But she didn't do it. You believe her, don't you, Mr. Fenney?"

Scott looked into her big brown eyes and lied, "Of course I do."

TWENTY-SEVEN

T HE NEXT MORNING Scott and the girls walked unimpeded into the federal building. The reporters did not shout questions. Instead, from a respectful distance the cameras silently recorded the entrance of Shawanda Jones's lawyer and their daughters, dressed in smart short outfits, color-coordinated from head to toe. Boo, who had steadfastly refused to wear these outfits despite Rebecca's continuing threats, had meticulously selected their wardrobes; she knew it was important to look good for Pajamae's mother.

They again walked past Delroy Lund, looking like he hadn't moved since yesterday, except that he was holding the current day's sports section. They again entered the courtroom to heads turning their way, as if craning to see a bride's entrance into the church. They again walked to the front row, where Scott deposited the girls for the morning session. And Scott again exchanged glances with the McCalls and Dan Ford. Apparently his former senior partner wanted to witness his protégé's final defeat.

Scott soon learned that Bobby was right. The second day of the trial was a lot worse than the first day. The prosecution's first witness was the FBI agent who had made the arrest. Agent Andy Edwards, forty, professional in every way, testified on direct examination by Ray Burns that he had arrested Shawanda Jones at approximately six P.M. on Sunday, June 6, at her apartment in South Dallas; that he had advised her of her Miranda rights; and that his agents had executed a search warrant for her apartment, finding and taking into custody heroin packets, clothing, ten hundred-dollar bills, and a blonde wig.

He further testified that he had taken her to the federal detention center and that she had given a voluntary written statement admitting that she had been with the victim the night of Saturday, June 5, that she had engaged in sex with him at a mansion in Highland Park, that they had fought, that she had hit him, that she had taken the keys to his Mercedes and the thousand dollars he owed her, and that she had abandoned the car on Harry Hines Boulevard.

As Ray Burns left the podium and walked to his table, his eyes met Pajamae's; she made a face and stuck her tongue out at him. Ray just shook his head, but two jurors, the dental assistant and the teacher, smiled. So far the girls were the best thing the defense had going for it.

Scott stood and began his cross-examination.

"Agent Edwards, what was Ms. Jones doing when you arrived at her apartment?"

"Sitting on the front steps playing with her daughter."

Scott pointed to Pajamae in the first row.

"Is that her daughter?"

Agent Edwards looked at her and said, "Yes, sir, I believe she is."

"Did Ms. Jones attempt to run?"

"No, sir."

"Did she resist in any way?"

"No, sir."

"Did she exhibit the demeanor of a murderer?"

Ray Burns jumped out of his chair. "Objection. Calls for speculation."

Scott turned to the judge: "Your Honor, Agent Edwards is an experienced FBI agent who has arrested . . ." He turned back to the witness: "How many murderers have you arrested?"

"Dozens."

Back to the judge: "Who has arrested dozens of murderers. He knows the demeanor of a murderer."

"Overruled."

"Agent Edwards, did Shawanda Jones exhibit the demeanor of a murderer when you arrested her?"

"No, sir."

"Did you tell her she was being arrested for the murder of Clark McCall?"

"Yes, sir."

"And what did she say?"

"Who?"

"Ms. Jones."

"No, sir. That's what she said. 'Who?' I said Clark McCall and she said, 'Who?' "

"She didn't know who Clark McCall was?"

"Apparently not."

"And when Ms. Jones gave her written statement, did she personally write the statement, in her own hand?"

"No, sir. We had a stenographer take it, then type it up. Ms. Jones read it, I read it to her, and she signed it."

"I notice that in her statement she does not admit to killing Clark McCall. Did you ask her?"

"Yes, sir, I did. She denied it."

Ray Burns next called FBI Agent Wendell Lee, the crime lab analyst, to testify as to the results of his analysis of the evidence taken from the crime scene. Agent Lee was methodical, like an accountant giving a quarterly report. Burns took him through the FBI procedures for accepting evidence, logging it in, and maintaining an unbroken chain of evidence to prevent mix-ups. Then he got to the specifics.

"Agent Lee, the blood collected from the carpet removed from the crime scene was Clark McCall's blood?"

"Yes, sir. DNA tests were conclusive."

"The clump of hair, who did that belong to?"

"Clark McCall. Also confirmed by DNA tests."

"And what part of his body did that hair originate from?"

"His scalp." Agent Lee put his hand on his scalp above his right eye. "From this region. It was yanked out by the roots."

"What about the clothing?"

"We examined a blue polo shirt, jeans, and sneakers. Nothing was found on the clothing."

"And the bedsheets?"

"No semen was found on the sheets. We did remove a condom from the body with ejaculate present."

"Did you find anything else on the sheets?"

"Yes, sir, pubic hairs that matched Clark McCall's and synthetic blonde hair fibers."

"And did you match these fibers?"

"Yes, sir, we matched them to the blonde wig seized from the defendant's residence."

Ray Burns removed the blonde wig from a plastic evidence bag and held it up like a dead skunk.

"This wig, labeled government's exhibit fifteen?"

"Yes, sir."

"What about the fingerprints?"

"Fingerprints were lifted from the drinking glasses, bathroom countertop, the pistol, and the vehicle. All prints matched either Clark McCall or Shawanda Jones. The prints on the murder weapon matched only Shawanda Jones."

"Were there any unidentified prints?"

"No, sir."

"All right. Now to the murder weapon. The .22-caliber bullet retrieved from the bedroom floor—you ran ballistics tests on it?"

"Yes, sir. It was fired by the .22-caliber pistol found at the crime scene."

"So the bullet that killed Clark McCall was fired from Shawanda Jones's gun?"

"Yes, sir."

"No further questions."

Scott walked to the podium. "Agent Lee, the defendant's clothes were seized during the search of her residence, correct?"

"Yes, sir."

"Was Clark McCall's blood found on any of the defendant's clothes?"

"No, sir."

"Wouldn't you expect to have found his blood on her clothing if she had shot him at point-blank range?"

"Not if she was naked when she shot him."

After that disaster, Scott did not cross-examine Dr. Victor Urbina, the Dallas County medical examiner, who testified next as to the cause of death—"gunshot wound to the head"—and the time of death—"approximately ten-thirty P.M., Saturday, June fifth"—and the entry and exit wounds and angle of the bullet's path through the brain. He figured that cross-examination would only extend the time the evidence was in front of the jury, which couldn't be favorable to his client.

That day's picnic lunch featured egg salad sandwiches prepared by Pajamae Jones, wrapped in foil and kept cool in a cooler, along with Vanilla Coke, her favorite. After Scott summarized the morning's testimony for Shawanda, Pajamae said, "Mama, I stuck my tongue out at Mr. Burns."

"Pajamae, that ain't nice."

"Neither is he. You should hear the things he's saying about you, Mama. Your ears must be burning!"

"Shawanda," Scott asked, "are you feeling better? Up to testifying?"

"When?"

"Tomorrow."

After lunch, FBI Agent Henry Hu, a forensics expert, took the stand. After agreeing with the testimony of Dr. Urbina as to the angle of the bullet's path through Clark McCall's brain, Agent Hu, in a long, painstaking, and detailed direct examination, proceeded to offer his expert opinion as to how he believed the murder occurred, according to the forensics evidence and with the help of a graphic exhibit on which was depicted a human figure, halfway between lying down and kneeling up, and standing over him another human figure, holding a gun to the victim's head. Measurements were noted around the perimeter of the figures, with lines drawn to show various heights and angles and a dark line showing the path of the bullet from the gun, through the skull, and to its impact point in the floor. Dr. Hu pointed to the exhibit with a metal pointer as he testified.

"The victim was in a semi-kneeling position when he was shot. We believe that because, as you can see here, the bullet's path through the skull must align with the point at which the bullet impacted the floor. The victim was seventy-one inches tall. If he were standing when shot, the twenty-eight-degree downward angle of the bullet's path through the skull would require that the perpetrator hold the gun overhead and then shoot at a downward angle, a physically difficult act"—Agent Hu demonstrated the difficulty for the jury—"or that the perpetrator be unusually tall.

"So, if the victim were kneeling, the point of entry—his forehead—stands only fifty inches above the floor, still a little high. But if he's in a semi-kneeling position, as if he were getting up off the floor, with the point of entry approximately forty inches above the floor, which is the approximate height at which a normal-sized person would hold a gun in front of him, like this, give or take several inches"—Agent Hu again demonstrated for the jury—"then the bullet's path through the skull and the point of impact in the floor align precisely."

The jurors nodded in agreement with his analysis.

"We also know that the victim's hair was ripped out by the roots, which requires great force. This leads us to conclude that the murder occurred as follows: the victim was on the floor of the bedroom. The perpetrator grabbed the victim by the hair on the right side of his scalp and yanked him up to approximately forty inches off the floor. The perpetrator placed the barrel of the gun to the victim's forehead over his left eye and shot the victim. The force of the gun's discharge knocked the victim to the floor—which is consistent with the location in which the body was found—and extracted his hair from his scalp."

Clark McCall was a rapist, but he had died a horrible death. By the time Dr. Hu completed his testimony, the jurors were somber. Their sympathies may have been with the little black girl sitting in the front row, but they had to face facts; and the facts pointed to her mother as the murderer of Clark McCall. Ray Burns could barely suppress a grin when he stood and announced, "Your Honor, the prosecution rests."

Scott noticed that Ray turned and caught Senator McCall's eye; the senator nodded at Ray, obviously pleased with the prosecution of his son's killer. No doubt, he had told Ray Burns he would never forget this, particularly if Ray's name should ever come before the United States Senate for confirmation to a high government office.

Dan Ford caught Scott's eye; his ex-senior partner's expression asked a silent question: *You gave up your career for a murderer?*

Judge Buford adjourned for the day. Shawanda Jones's defense would begin at nine in the morning. Now all Scott had to do was come up with a defense.

Dinner on the kitchen floor was like a funeral reception.

"Everything Hu said is true," Bobby said, "except it doesn't prove Shawanda's guilt. Problem is, she was in that room with him that night, they fought, and her gun was the murder weapon. So any reasonable person would assume she did it. And without Hannah Steele to back up a claim of self-defense—which is unavailable so long as Shawanda refuses to admit to shooting Clark—we can't ask the jury to acquit her on that basis."

"So what's left?"

"We've got to answer one question for the jury, Scotty—what they want to know: Who killed Clark McCall? If Shawanda didn't, who did? Who came into that house right after she left, before Clark could get up off the floor and get dressed, picked up her gun, stuck it to Clark's head, and pulled the trigger?"

Scott shook his head. "Have you heard from Carl?"

"He'll call when he gets something."

"Well, he's got twelve hours to save us. Right now all we've got is Shawanda, her word against the evidence."

Pajamae said, "Mama's going to testify?"

"Yes, honey. She has to."

"What's she gonna wear?"

"I hadn't thought about that."

"We saved some of Mother's things at the yard sale," Boo said, "for Pajamae's mother. For when she gets out."

Scott turned to Karen. "Will you help the girls pick out some clothes?"

"Sure."

"At least she'll be nicely dressed."

They ate the take-out Mexican food in silence now. Scott absentmindedly watched the girls eat, wondering how Pajamae would handle life with her mother on death row and then life without her mother after the execution, when he noticed something: Boo was holding her fork in her left hand.

"Boo, come over here."

She got up off the floor and stepped over to him.

Scott took the aluminum foil wrapping from his entrée and fashioned it into the shape of an *L*. An aluminum foil gun. He placed it on the floor.

"Please pick that up."

Boo frowned. "What's it supposed to be, a gun?"

"Yes."

She shrugged, leaned down, and picked up the foil gun with her left hand.

"Now grab my hair."

She stood directly in front of him and with her right hand grabbed his hair above his left eye.

"Now point the gun at my forehead like you're going to shoot me."

She put the barrel of the foil gun to Scott's forehead, above his right eye.

Bobby said, "Clark was shot above his left eye."

"By a right-handed killer."

Seeing Boo hold her fork with her left hand, Scott had remembered his first meeting with Shawanda, when she had held his pen with her left hand.

"Pajamae, your mother's left-handed, isn't she?"

"Yes, sir, Mr. Fenney, she sure is."

413

TWENTY-EIGHT

T HE DEFENSE CALLS FBI Agent Henry Hu."

Ray Burns was out of his chair.

"Your Honor, Mr. Fenney declined cross-examination of Agent Hu yesterday; now he's calling him as a defense witness?"

The judge looked at Scott: "Mr. Fenney?"

"That's exactly what I'm doing, Your Honor."

"Proceed."

Scott had been so sure that his client had killed Clark McCall that he had failed to ask a basic factual question of the government's forensic expert: Was the murderer right- or left-handed? He had been so sure his client was lying that he had failed to even consider that she might be telling the truth. Now, for the first time since he had been appointed to represent the defendant in *United States of America versus Shawanda Jones*, Scott knew his client was innocent. Shawanda Jones did not kill Clark McCall.

But then, who did?

Agent Hu took the stand, with the judge reminding

him that he was still under oath, and Scott said, "Agent Hu, your testimony yesterday was quite illuminating, and I mean that as a compliment."

"Thank you."

"If you don't mind, I'd like to reenact for the jury the manner in which you believe Clark McCall was murdered."

"Certainly."

"My cocounsel, Mr. Herrin, will assist. Bobby, if you'll kneel on the floor."

Bobby walked over and knelt in front of Scott.

"Now, Agent Hu, your testimony is that Clark was halfway between lying and kneeling on the floor like Mr. Herrin is here when he was shot, correct?"

"Yes."

"And the killer was facing Clark, as I am now, correct?"

"Yes."

"And the killer grabbed Clark's hair on the right side of his scalp, like this?"

Scott grabbed Bobby's hair with his left hand.

"Yes."

"And the killer than stuck the gun to Clark's forehead above his left eye, like this?"

Scott fashioned his right hand like a gun and stuck his index finger to Bobby's forehead.

"And the killer then shot Clark?"

"Yes. That is how I believe the crime occurred."

"Well, I agree with you. But doesn't this demonstration prove something else, something important about the killer?"

Agent Hu frowned. "I'm sorry?"

"The killer was right-handed."

Agent Hu's expression revealed his realization. "Yes, most likely the killer would have been right-handed."

"The killer grabbed Clark's hair with his left hand and held the gun with his right hand, correct?"

"Yes, that would be correct."

"One other thing, Agent Hu. The medical examiner testified that there was a contusion around Clark's right eye, as if he had been hit with a fist."

"Yes, there was."

"As a forensic expert, is it more likely that the person who hit Clark's eye was right- or left-handed?"

"Left-handed."

"So the person who punched Clark McCall was left-handed, but the person who shot him was right-handed?"

"Yes, that would be the most likely scenario."

Scott called FBI Agent Edwards to the stand again.

"Agent Edwards, you testified that you arrested the defendant?"

"Yes, sir."

"And that you took her statement?"

"Yes, sir."

"You typed what she said?"

"Yes, sir."

"And then she read it over and signed it?"

"Yes, sir."

"With which hand did she sign her statement?"

Agent Edwards thought for a moment, then said, "Her left hand."

The jurors had yet to see the defendant in person. They had seen her mug shots and pictures in the newspapers and on television, but they had not seen her. And they needed to see her and hear her, to listen and watch as she denied killing Clark McCall. Scott knew he had to put Shawanda on the stand, the Fifth Amendment to the Constitution notwithstanding, but he wanted to give her the best possible chance of success. So he had done two things: he had persuaded the judge to allow her methadone treatment, and he had kept her out of court until this moment.

Now all eyes—those of the judge and the jurors and the prosecutors and the spectators—were focused on the door at the side of the courtroom, anxiously awaiting the arrival of Shawanda Jones. Boo and Pajamae and Karen had been allowed in her cell—after being searched by a female guard—to help Shawanda get dressed. They had come into the courtroom a few minutes ago. Boo gave Scott another thumbs-up.

The door opened and a murmur ran through the room. Shawanda did not look like the heroin addict Scott had seen earlier that morning; she looked stunning and young. Scott had forgotten she was only twenty-four, the heroin had aged her so. But today she had recaptured her youth. She was wearing Rebecca's navy blue suit,

Rebecca's high heels, and Rebecca's makeup; her hair was fluffed lightly and brushed smooth; her eyes were sharp and alert. She looked at Scott and smiled. Shawanda looked like Halle Berry on a very good day.

The jurors' eyes followed her as Ron escorted her over to the defendant's table and pulled out her chair. She sat daintily and Ron pushed her chair in. She turned and looked at each juror, one by one, and they looked at her. Their first impression was a good one. Scott glanced back at the McCalls: the senator's face revealed his worry, Jean's face her jealousy. Beside them, Dan Ford's face showed renewed interest in the proceeding.

Scott stood and said, "The defense calls Shawanda Jones."

Shawanda stood and walked to the witness stand, took the oath, and sat down. Scott stood at the podium.

"Ms. Jones," he said, "are you left-handed?"

"Yes, sir."

"Did you kill Clark McCall?"

"No, sir, Mr. Fenney. I did not."

"All right, Ms. Jones, let's talk about your life. Where were you born?"

"In the projects."

"The projects in South Dallas, same place you now reside?"

"Yes, sir."

"What was your mother's name?"

"My mama, she was called Dorena."

"What was your father's name?"

"Mr. Fenney, you know I don't know that."

"Your mother and father, they weren't married?"

"No, sir. My daddy, he was a white man my mama worked for. She cleaned his office."

"Okay, so you were born illegitimate?"

"No, sir, I was born in a hospital, Parkland."

"Uh, okay. You never knew your father, correct?"

"No, sir."

"You grew up in the projects?"

"Yes, sir."

"Your mother died when you were thirteen?"

"Something like that."

"What did she die of?"

"No doctor."

"No, I mean, did she die of cancer or what?"

"No, sir, she died 'cause she ain't got no doctor. She fall over and we call for the ambulance and no one come."

"And so you raised yourself."

"Yes, sir."

"And you fell in with a bad crowd."

"Only crowd we got in the projects, Mr. Fenney. People got nothing to do, they get in trouble."

"And you got in trouble."

"Eddie, he my trouble."

"Eddie was your child's father?"

"Yes, sir. White man selling dope in the projects, seen me one day, when I was fourteen. He like what he seen, so he give me some dope and I let him touch me."

"And Eddie gave you heroin?"

"Yes, sir."

"And you became addicted at age sixteen?"

"Yes, sir."

"And by that time you were a prostitute?"

"Yes, sir."

"Why?"

Her eyes dropped. "Mens, they think they gonna find all they been missing in they lives between Shawanda's legs. Ain't so." She looked up. "It the only thing men ever want from me."

"Ms. Jones, do you have a daughter?"

"Why, you know that, Mr. Fenney. She staying with you."

The teacher and the housewives smiled. Scott turned to Pajamae behind him and gestured for her to stand. Pajamae stood, the most innocent expression imaginable on her face.

"Is she your daughter?"

"Yes, sir, that my baby."

Pajamae turned to the jury and curtsied. Now every juror was smiling. The kid was good.

They broke for lunch before beginning Shawanda's testimony about the night Clark McCall was murdered. Shawanda was not sitting on the floor with the girls, but at the table with Scott and Bobby and Karen, being very careful not to spill tuna fish on her Neiman Marcus suit.

"We've got a really pretty outfit for you to wear tomorrow, Mama," Pajamae said from the floor.

"How I do, Mr. Fenney?"

"Fine, Shawanda. But the hard part's this afternoon."

"Think they gonna believe me?"

He thought no but said yes.

"Ms. Jones," Scott said, "let's go back to Saturday, June fifth. Did you take heroin that day?"

"I was alive, so I must have."

"You took it every day?"

"Two, three time."

"So before you went to work that night, you injected heroin?"

"Yes, sir. Make it easier that way."

"Make what easier?"

"Sex."

"All right, then Kiki, another prostitute, came by and the two of you drove over to Harry Hines Boulevard?"

"Yes, sir, our regular location."

"And you waited for men to come by?"

"We never wait too long."

"And did Clark McCall come by?"

"Yes, sir, but I don't know him. He just a white boy in a black Mercedes."

"And he offered you one thousand dollars to spend the night with him?"

"Yes, sir."

"Oh, before Clark, did you, uh, work for another client?"

"No, sir, I don't work for no one. I'm self-employed."

"I mean, did anyone else pay you for a sex act that night?"

"I give a blow to a cop, but he don't pay."

"You engaged in oral sex with a police officer?"

"Yes, sir, Mr. Fenney, that way he don't bother us. Me and Kiki, we take turns with the cops. They freebies."

"Okay, so back to Clark McCall. You got into his car and he drove you to his mansion in Highland Park?"

"Yes, sir."

"And you went inside?"

"Yes, sir."

"And upstairs to his bedroom?"

"Yes, sir."

"Tell the jury what happened then."

Shawanda turned to the jurors and told them the story of that night without shame or guilt, just as a matter of fact. That she and Clark engaged in sex, after, that is, she made him put on a condom—"I can't get that AIDS. I gotta take care of my Pajamae"—that he became rough, started slapping her, calling her nigger, that she scratched and punched him in the eye and kicked him in his balls, that he fell to the floor, and that she took her thousand dollars and his car keys, drove herself back to Harry Hines, and abandoned the car.

"And Clark McCall was alive the last time you saw him?"

"Yes, sir, he sure was, cussing me like a redheaded stepchild."

"What did you and Kiki do then?"

"Go home, go to bed."

"What did you do the next morning, Sunday?"

422

"Got up, fixed breakfast for Pajamae, go to church."

"You went to church?"

She had a bemused expression. "Mr. Fenney, without sinners, no need for churches."

The jurors smiled at that remark.

"And what were you doing when the FBI came to arrest you?"

"Sitting outside on the stoop, watching Pajamae."

"Did you know why they were arresting you?"

"They say for killing some man. I said, I don't kill no one. They don't believe me."

"No further questions, Your Honor."

Ray Burns nearly knocked Scott down, he was in such a hurry to cross-examine Shawanda.

"Ms. Jones, you're a prostitute, correct?"

"Yes, sir."

"And a heroin addict?"

"Yes, sir."

"And you were with Clark McCall the night he was murdered?"

"That what the police say. I don't know when he be killed."

"He picked you up for sex, is that correct?"

"Yes, sir."

"He offered you a thousand dollars for the night?"

"Yes, sir."

"You got into his car, a Mercedes-Benz, correct?"

"Yes, sir."

"He drove you to his home?"

"Yes, sir."

"You went upstairs, he gave you alcohol to drink?"

"Yes, sir."

"He removed his clothes, you removed your clothes, and you and Clark McCall engaged in sexual intercourse, correct?"

"Yes, sir."

"And then you hit him in the eye?"

"Only 'cause he slap me and call me nigger."

"And you kicked him in the groin?"

"No, sir, I didn't kick his growing, I kick his balls."

"Okay, his balls."

" 'Cause he be coming after me again."

"And then you grabbed your gun and you shot him?"

"No, sir, I didn't shoot no one."

"You know your gun was the murder weapon?"

"I don't know no such thing. You say that."

Ray Burns picked up the .22-caliber pistol.

"This is your gun, isn't it?"

"Yes, sir."

"And why do you carry a gun?"

"You live in the projects, you die of old age waiting for the po-lice to come when someone trying to get in your place."

"You shot Clark McCall, didn't you?"

"No, sir. I didn't shoot no one."

"And you stole a thousand dollars from him?"

"No, sir. I earned it."

"And you stole his car?"

"No, sir. I borrowed it, to get back where I belonged."

"To flee the scene of the crime?"

"To get away before he hit me again."

"And you went home to your daughter like nothing happened?"

" 'Cause nothing happened."

"Ms. Jones, do you really expect this jury to believe you?"

Shawanda looked at the jurors and said in a soft voice: "No, sir, I don't expect no one gonna believe me."

On his way upstairs to tuck the girls in for the night, Scott stopped at the small TV on the kitchen counter where the late news was replaying the day's events at the trial. An artist's sketch of Shawanda was on the screen. The reporter said that the defendant was quite beautiful and had comported herself well on the stand. The jurors, he said, were attentive and respectful and, by the end of the day, thoroughly confused by the idea of a killer who was probably right-handed and a defendant who was certainly left-handed. "If Shawanda Jones didn't kill Clark McCall," the reporter asked, "who did?"

Upstairs, Scott was leaning over the bed, tucking the girls in, when Pajamae said softly, "Mr. Fenney, I know what my mama does now, with her tricks."

"You do?"

She nodded. "Mama lets them touch her private

parts, put their private parts in hers. That's what sex is, isn't it, Mr. Fenney?"

"Yes, it is."

"Why, Mr. Fenney? Mama always tells me never ever to let a boy touch my private parts. Why does she let men touch hers?"

"It's like you said, Pajamae: she loves you, but she doesn't love herself."

"Mama, she's had a sad life, hasn't she, Mr. Fenney?"

"Yes, she has."

"Now I know why she's so sad always. She's never had anyone who loved her all over, not just her private parts."

"No, she hasn't."

"But she looked pretty today, didn't she?"

"Very pretty."

"Pretty enough to marry?"

Boo sat up. "A. Scott, we want to live together, with you and her mother. Wouldn't that be a wonderfully happy ending?"

Scott sat on the edge of the bed. So many times he had fudged the truth with Boo, but after three days of a murder trial, she and Pajamae could handle the truth.

"Girls, happy endings happen in fairy tales, not in real life."

TWENTY-NINE

SHAWANDA LOOKED equally stunning the next morning in Rebecca's tan suit. Scott was standing beside her in the courtroom, all eyes on him but his eyes on her. She had told him the truth. But Scott was her lawyer and he knew, as all lawyers know, that the truth seldom prevails in a court of law. Bobby was right. When the jurors retired to decide Shawanda's fate, they would ask each other one question: If Shawanda Jones didn't kill Clark McCall, who did? They needed an answer. But Scott didn't have an answer. He didn't even have a clue.

So he went fishing. When a lawyer takes a deposition in civil litigation and doesn't have a clue, he goes fishing. He asks every imaginable question and then some, hoping the witness will slip up and tell him something he didn't know. It never works. But Scott threw out his fishing net anyway.

"The defense calls Mack McCall."

Ray Burns exploded out of his chair. "Objection. Senator McCall is not on the witness list."

"That's true, Mr. Fenney," the judge said. "Do you

have a good reason for calling a witness who is not on the list?"

"Yes, sir. Mr. Burns is trying to have my client executed. I'd like to keep him from doing that."

Judge Buford's mouth turned up in half a smile. "Very well. Overruled."

Senator McCall slowly rose from his seat in the second row of the spectator section, adjusted his coat and tie, and walked past Scott without so much as a glance. After taking the oath, he sat in the witness chair as if he were having his portrait taken.

"Senator McCall, your son had a history of alcohol and drug abuse, is that correct?"

"Clark had some problems with substance abuse, but he had overcome them."

"Did he also have some problems with rape?"

"I'm sorry, I don't understand the question."

"Do you know a woman named Hannah Steele?"

"No, I don't."

"Have you ever heard that name, Hannah Steele?"

"No, I haven't."

"Have you ever paid money to someone named Hannah Steele?"

"No."

"Are you aware that Hannah Steele filed a criminal complaint against Clark a year ago, alleging that he had beaten and raped her?"

"I'm not aware of any such thing. Do you have a copy of this complaint?"

"Senator McCall, did you pay Hannah Steele five

hundred thousand dollars to drop her rape complaint against Clark and move out of Dallas?"

The senator stared directly at Scott and did what only a politician could do better than a lawyer. He lied.

"Of course not."

"Did you pay six other women to drop their rape complaints against Clark?"

"Do you have any names to go with your allegations, Mr. Fenney? You made these false statements on national TV, but you have no evidence to back up your allegations, do you?"

Scott glanced over at Dan Ford. His former father figure and senior partner sat there without any outward acknowledgment that a U.S. senator was committing perjury. Dan Ford knew the women's names because he had personally paid off all seven. But, as Scott well knew, the attorney-client privilege allowed an attorney to hide his clients' misdeeds, everything from letting lead leach into a river to committing perjury in a federal court; so Dan Ford remained silent. Scott turned back to McCall.

"Answer the question, Senator."

"No, I did not pay other women."

"Did Clark have an apartment in Washington?"

"Yes, he did."

"He lived there when he was in Washington tending to FERC business?"

"Yes."

"Did you expect Clark to attend your campaign kickoff on Monday, June seventh, in Washington?"

"Yes. He said he'd be there."

"Did you know Clark had come to Dallas on Saturday, June fifth?"

"No. Not until the FBI called."

"Were you surprised to learn he was in Dallas?"

"I was surprised to learn he was dead."

"Clark returned to Dallas often?"

"Yes. He didn't like Washington."

"Clark would just fly back to Dallas on a whim, without telling you?"

"Yes. Clark was . . . impulsive."

"And when he was in Dallas, he lived in your Highland Park mansion?"

"Yes."

"Do you know Delroy Lund?"

"Yes, I do."

"Is he an employee of yours?"

"Yes, he is."

"What does he do for you?"

"He's my bodyguard."

"Is that all he does, provide physical protection?"

"Sometimes he carries my luggage. Bad back."

"Does he bribe witnesses for you?"

"No, he does not."

"Did he bribe Hannah Steele for you?"

"No, he did not."

"Did you send him to bribe my cocounsel, Bobby Herrin?"

"No, I did not. I don't even know who Mr. Herrin is. Would you point him out?"

Bobby was not at the defendant's table. He had

gotten a message on his cell phone and had run out of the courtroom at the first opportunity.

Ray Burns stood. "Your Honor, is Mr. Fenney going to spend the morning insulting the senior senator from Texas or is he going to ask questions relevant to this murder case?"

"Do you have an objection, Mr. Burns?"

"Objection, irrelevant."

"Overruled." The judge turned to Scott. "Mr. Fenney, please tie the senator's testimony to this case."

Scott was thinking, *I wish I knew how*, when the courtroom doors opened and Bobby entered. He gave Scott a time-out gesture. Scott asked the judge for a fifteen-minute recess.

Scott walked out of the courtroom with Bobby and down the corridor to where Carl Kincaid was leaning against the wall and holding a large yellow envelope. Carl was long and lanky and wore a plaid sports coat over a golf shirt. When they arrived, Carl handed the envelope to Scott. Scott removed and examined the contents. Then he looked back at Carl.

"You know what this means?" Scott asked.

"I think I do," Carl said. "He's dirty."

"How did you get all this?"

Carl smiled. "I won't tell you how to bribe judges if you don't tell me how to do my job."

*

431

When the court reconvened, Scott knew how Senator McCall was tied to the murder of his son: by his bodyguard.

"Your Honor, the defense calls Delroy Lund."

"You have no further questions for Senator McCall?"

"No, sir."

"Very well."

The judge nodded at the bailiff, who went outside. When the courtroom doors opened, Delroy Lund strode in like the ex-Fed he was. He was a big man and carried an attitude with him; clearly he was a cop who had banged a few heads together in his day. He walked up to the witness stand and took the oath. Then he sat down, leaned back, and crossed his legs, right ankle over left knee, like he owned the damn place. Scott saw his effect on the jurors: before he had said one word, they hated him. Which made at least thirteen people in this courtroom who hated Delroy Lund.

"We meet again, Mr. Lund."

Scott first elicited from Delroy his background: He was fifty-one years old, born and raised in Victoria, Texas, college at Texas A&I, street cop in Houston for three years, then twenty years with the DEA, working in South Texas, fighting the war on drugs. Divorced, no children. Six years ago, he had retired to Senator McCall's payroll.

"Mr. Lund, did you ever frame a suspect?"

"Nope."

"Ever plant dope in a suspect's home or car?"

"Nope."

"Ever beat up a suspect?"

"Nope."

But his eyes said yep. And the Hispanic and black jurors saw the truth in his eyes.

"You ever kill anyone?"

"Yeah."

"How many?"

"Nine I'm sure of."

"Might be more?"

"When you're in a firefight with the Mexican drug cartels, you don't stop to count."

"Did you ever kill anyone up close and personal, face-to-face?"

"Yeah."

"When and where?"

"Laredo, 1994."

"What were the circumstances?"

"I was a DEA agent. He was a drug trafficker. He didn't want to go to jail. He pulled a gun on me, I shot him first."

The jury knew Delroy Lund was capable of killing.

"How did you feel afterward?"

"Happy. He was dead; I was alive."

"Mr. Lund, that wasn't the only time you killed someone up close, was it?"

Delroy's eyes narrowed. "You talking about Del Rio?"

"Yes."

"I was completely exonerated."

"Being no-billed by the grand jury isn't the same as

433

being exonerated, Mr. Lund. It only means there wasn't sufficient evidence to prosecute."

Ray Burns stood. "Objection. Irrelevant. Your Honor, Mr. Lund is not on trial here today."

Scott said, "Maybe he should be."

"Overruled," the judge said.

Scott turned back to the witness. "Mr. Lund, what happened the night of March thirteenth, 1998, in Del Rio, Texas?"

"I shot a suspect during a confrontation with drug dealers."

"You shot a sixteen-year-old boy."

"He looked older."

Scott picked up Carl's envelope, removed the documents, and placed them on the podium. When his background check of Delroy Lund had revealed reprimands for unnecessary use of force, Carl had decided to dig deeper. He found more dirt.

"Mr. Lund, the internal DEA incident report—"

"That's supposed to be confidential. How'd you get that?"

"Sorry, attorney-client privilege, Mr. Lund. As I was saying, the internal DEA report states that on the night in question, you approached a group of Mexican nationals, approximately a dozen boys and girls, outside a bar in downtown Del Rio after observing them selling drugs. At least that was your story. Witnesses said you were drunk and propositioned one of the Mexican girls."

"They lied."

"In any event, an altercation ensued and when it was

over, you had shot and killed an unarmed sixteen-year-old boy."

"He was going for a gun."

"The report says no gun was found at the scene."

"His *amigos* took it when they ran off."

"Did the boy mouth off to you, Mr. Lund, is that how the confrontation started?"

"The suspect refused to obey my orders. He got in my face. Things got out of hand."

"Things got out of hand?"

"Yeah. It happens."

"It seems to happen a lot with you, Mr. Lund. Your record shows nine deadly shootings, numerous other questionable discharges of your firearm, a dozen reprimands for unnecessary use of force, internal affairs investigations for freelancing, running interdiction operations without agency approval—you put together quite a career at the DEA, Mr. Lund."

Delroy shook his head with disdain. "Civilians. Mr. Fenney, the war on drugs ain't gin rummy at the country club. Mexican drug cartels are violent and ruthless narcoterrorists. They've killed over a hundred women in Juárez, many of them young American girls. They've kidnapped and killed dozens of American tourists in Nuevo Laredo and dumped their bodies in the Rio Grande. They've murdered border patrol agents and Catholic priests who spoke out against them. They own the police throughout Mexico and those they don't own they kill. You want people like them running around Dallas? People like me, Mr. Fenney, we keep people like them on their side of the river."

435

"That may be true, Mr. Lund, but the fact is your superiors at the DEA grew tired of your practices, didn't they?"

"Bunch of desk jockeys who couldn't cut it on the border."

"Shortly after that incident in Del Rio, you were forced to retire from the DEA?"

"Yeah. By bureaucrats more concerned about getting promotions than results. I got results."

"You got results with Hannah Steele, too, didn't you?"

"I don't know what you're talking about."

"Mr. Lund, did you bribe Hannah Steele to absent herself from this trial?"

"Nope."

"Did you threaten to make her fish bait?"

"I don't fish."

"Answer the question."

"No, I did not threaten anyone."

"Do you know Hannah Steele?"

"Nope."

"Did you attempt to bribe my cocounsel, Robert Herrin, to drop out of this case?"

"Nope."

"You didn't offer him a hundred thousand dollars?"

"Nope."

"Did you know Clark McCall?"

"Yeah."

"What did you think of him?"

"Honestly?"

"Why not, we're in a court of law."

"He was a little fu . . ." Delroy stopped and glanced past Scott to Senator McCall.

"A little fuckup? Isn't that what you called Clark? Isn't that the term you used to describe him?"

Delroy looked back at Scott and said, "He was a real nice boy."

"A real nice boy who liked to beat and rape girls?"

"I don't know anything about that."

"Where were you on the night of Saturday, June fifth, of this year?"

"D.C."

"Washington, D.C.?"

"Yeah."

"You're sure?"

"Yeah."

Scott picked up another document from Carl's envelope. "Mr. Lund, I have a copy of a first-class plane ticket from Washington to Dallas, flight number 1607 on American at eight-twenty-three A.M. on Saturday, June the fifth, in the name of Clark McCall."

"So?"

Scott picked up the next document. "So I also have a copy of another first-class plane ticket from Washington to Dallas, at eight-thirty A.M. on the same day, flight number 1815 on US Airways. It has your name on it."

Delroy didn't blink an eye. "Must be a mistake."

"You think there's another Delroy Lund running around out there?"

"You never know."

"Clark's flight was booked at four-thirty-seven P.M. on June fourth. Your flight was booked twenty-eight minutes later. You had someone in Clark's office keeping tabs on him, didn't you?"

"Nope."

"May I see your driver's license?"

"What?"

"Your driver's license, would you please produce it?"

The slightest hint of unease invaded Delroy's dark eyes. He leaned slightly to his left and reached around to his right back pant pocket. He pulled out his wallet, removed his license, and somewhat reluctantly held it out to Scott.

"Your Honor, may I approach the witness?"

Judge Buford nodded. Scott walked over, took the license, and walked back to the podium. He compared the license to the next document.

"Mr. Lund, you're sure this isn't your plane ticket?"

"Yeah."

"And you're sure you weren't in Dallas on June fifth?"

"Yeah."

Scott held up the document. "Well, then how do you explain this rental car agreement with Avis at the Dallas airport dated June fifth with your signature and driver's license number on it?"

Delroy uncrossed his legs. His eyes turned down. His expression did not change, but his jaw muscles began flexing rapidly, like he was grinding his teeth into chalk. A thin sheen of sweat glistened on his broad forehead. He was lying and everyone in the courtroom knew it. He knew that they knew it, and that he was on the verge of a perjury charge. But Delroy Lund hadn't gone toe to toe with Mexican drug lords without having brass balls. His faced turned up, he looked Scott straight in the eye, and he said, "You know what, now that you remind me, I was in Dallas that day. I forgot."

"You forgot?"

"Yeah, I forgot."

"Okay, Mr. Lund, we'll go with that. You arrived in Dallas on Saturday, June fifth, at eleven A.M. and you left Sunday afternoon on US Airways flight number 1812 at four-fifty-five P.M.?"

"Sounds about right."

"So why did you come to Dallas for just thirty hours?"

Delroy grinned. "To get laid. To pick up a two-bit hooker"—he gestured at Shawanda—"like Blondie there and get laid."

"Mr. Lund, do you usually carry a handkerchief?"

"Yeah. Allergies."

"May I see it?"

He reached back, pulled a handkerchief out of his pocket, and held it out to Scott.

"Keep it."

Scott walked over to the defendant's table to get a pad and pen. He looked at Shawanda and froze . . . her hair was brown. Not blonde like the . . . Scott glanced over at the prosecution table . . . wig. The wig she had been wearing that night was blonde. Delroy just called

Shawanda "Blondie." Delroy had been there that night.

Delroy Lund murdered Clark McCall.

Scott's adrenaline pump kicked in like an overdrive. His mind started working fast. The murderer was sitting in the witness chair ten feet away, but Scott had nothing to tie this man to that crime. Delroy Lund was an experienced lawman; he had left no incriminating evidence at the crime scene. Scott's only hope was to get Delroy to confess on the stand, to break down and blurt out the truth, to tell the world that he had murdered Clark McCall. A Perry Mason moment. A moment lawyers dream of. A moment that happens only on TV and in the movies.

Scott walked over to the witness stand and placed the pad and pen in front of Delroy.

"Mr. Lund, would you please sign your name?"

Delroy shrugged, picked up the pen with his right hand, and signed his name.

"You're right-handed, Mr. Lund."

"Yeah, so what?"

"So the FBI's forensic expert testified that the person who shot Clark McCall was right-handed. You're right-handed, the murderer was right-handed. The murder occurred in Dallas on June fifth, you were in Dallas on June fifth."

"Ninety percent of the people in this room are right-handed. And more than that were in Dallas on June fifth."

"Yes, but none of them had a reason to kill Clark McCall, did they?"

"You'll have to ask them."

"I'll ask you: Did you kill Clark McCall?"

The judge was studying the witness when Ray Burns stood to object. "Your Honor—"

"Sit, Mr. Burns," the judge said without removing his gaze from Delroy. Ray sat. "Answer the question, Mr. Lund."

Delroy said, "No, I didn't kill Clark. Why would I want him dead? I work for his dad."

"Who wants to be president."

"So?"

"So if it became known that his son used cocaine and engaged prostitutes and maybe even raped a few girls, Senator McCall's chances of getting into the White House would be about as good as the defendant's, isn't that true?"

Delroy snorted. "Give me a fuckin' break."

The judge: "Mr. Lund, watch your language."

Delroy said, "Hell, if having a screwup for a kid was a motive for murder, half the politicians in D.C. would've already killed their kids. I don't know nothing about rapes, but you think Clark was the only politician's kid out drinking and doing drugs and other stuff their daddies want to keep quiet? The town's full of 'em, rich kids who had life handed to them on a silver platter then shit on it."

"Mr. Lund, why did you decide to get laid in Dallas on June fifth?"

Delroy shrugged. "Most beautiful women in the world are in Dallas."

"That may be true, but you work for Senator McCall in Washington. Certainly you could have found an acceptable prostitute in the nation's capital so you could remain in town, especially since two days later, on June seventh, the senator was scheduled to announce his campaign for the presidency. But instead of staying in D.C., you came to Dallas on June fifth to get laid, on the same day Clark came to Dallas? Mr. Lund, did you come specifically to kill Clark?"

Delroy sighed. "I said, I didn't kill Clark."

"Then why did you come to Dallas? Why did you leave Washington two days before Senator McCall's big day? Why did you fly down to Dallas to pick up a prostitute instead of staying in Washington and protecting the senator—"

It hit Scott.

"That's it, isn't it?"

"What?"

"It's just that simple, isn't it?"

"What are you talking about?"

"You didn't come here to kill Clark. You came to Dallas to protect Senator McCall."

"I don't know what the hell you're talking about."

"Mr. Lund, what usually happened when Clark was in Dallas?"

"I give, what?"

"He got in trouble. He always came home to get into trouble. Fact is, Clark was smart enough to get in trouble *only* in Dallas, because here his daddy could buy his way out of anything. The McCall name means something in Dallas. The McCall money can buy anything in Dallas—even seven rape victims."

"Like I said, I don't know anything about that."

"And the last thing Senator McCall needed right before he announced for the presidency was Clark getting arrested, and not just for drinking or drugs—like you said, that's common. But getting charged with rape, that's not so common, is it? Particularly for the son of the next president. The press would go into a feeding frenzy, maybe even dredge up the other girls. The senator had spent millions to keep Clark's past hidden so it wouldn't ruin his political future. And now the presidency was his, he had a commanding lead in the polls, his dream was about to come true . . . and what was the only thing that could lose the White House for him before he had even won it? A rapist for a son. That would do it. That would destroy Senator McCall's dream, wouldn't it?"

Scott pointed back at the senator in the spectator section.

"When Senator McCall learned that Clark was coming to Dallas right before his big announcement, he sent you here to follow Clark, to keep him out of trouble."

Scott held up another document from Carl's envelope.

"Clark had booked a return flight to Washington on June sixth at three-twenty-one P.M. so he would be back for his father's campaign kickoff. The senator knew that if Clark was flying to Dallas just for a Saturday night, that meant only one thing: his demons were calling again and he was answering. He was coming home to get drunk and stoned and pick up a girl. And the senator knew what usually happened when Clark's dark side took over—exactly what he couldn't let happen. He couldn't wake up Sunday morning and read that his son had been arrested for beating and raping another girl in Dallas. So he sent you to Dallas to make sure that didn't happen. Your job was to wet-nurse Clark, to be his guardian angel, to keep him out of trouble and out of the press. You came to Dallas to protect Senator McCall from his own son."

Delroy's eyes again looked past Scott to McCall. Scott turned to McCall as well, and what he saw surprised him. In the senator's eyes and on the senator's face Scott saw that he had it exactly wrong. He turned back to Delroy.

"The senator didn't send you, did he? You freelanced this one. You ran this operation without his approval. Why? Why didn't you tell the senator? Did you think it best to keep him out of the loop? Did you just not want to bother him right before his big day?" Scott shook his head. "Either way, you came here to make sure Clark didn't screw things up for his father. That's why you came to Dallas on Saturday, June the fifth, isn't it, Mr. Lund?"

"No."

"You flew to Dallas, you rented a car, you followed Clark that night, didn't you?"

"No."

"You followed him down to Harry Hines where the prostitutes hang out, didn't you?"

"No."

"And there you watched Clark pull his Mercedes over to two black girls, one wearing a red wig, the other a blonde wig, isn't that right?"

"No."

"The girl in the blonde wig got into Clark's car, didn't she?"

"I don't know."

"That girl was the defendant, wasn't she?"

"I don't know."

"Then why did you just refer to the defendant as 'Blondie'?"

"I . . ."

"Her hair isn't blonde, Mr. Lund, it's brown. She hasn't worn her blonde wig since that night. She's been in jail, Mr. Lund."

Scott stepped to the prosecution table, removed the blonde wig from the evidence bag, and handed it to Shawanda.

"Your Honor, may the defendant put on the wig?"

"Yes."

Shawanda pulled the wig on. Scott returned to the podium and pointed at Shawanda.

"Mr. Lund, you saw the defendant wearing *that* wig *that* night—that's the only way you'd know to call her 'Blondie.' You saw her get into Clark's car. You followed them to the McCall mansion in Highland Park. You parked out of sight on the estate. You figured Clark couldn't get into too much trouble with a black hooker. Oh, he might slap her around, but what's she gonna do, call the cops? She wasn't an SMU coed, she was just a hooker. So you sat outside while Clark had his fun.

"But then you saw the defendant drive off in Clark's Mercedes. You ran inside and upstairs to Clark's bedroom and you found Clark lying naked on the floor and holding his balls. And you . . . you laughed at him. The little rich boy got kneed in the balls by a black hooker, that was pretty damn funny. So you laughed at Clark. You mocked him. Did you call him a little fuckup?"

"I wasn't there."

"Clark didn't like that, did he, someone like you mocking him? You were just an employee, and employees don't mock Clark McCall. So he cursed you. You outweighed him by, what, a hundred pounds? But the alcohol and cocaine made him brave and getting beat up by a hooker made him mad, so he cursed you just like he cursed her. And then he . . . what? What else did he say to you? What could he say that would make you want to kill him?"

Scott snapped his fingers and pointed at Delroy.

"He threatened to get you fired. He was gonna tell Daddy and get you fired. Now, maybe he could, maybe he couldn't, but you couldn't take the chance. Because what would you do if he did get you fired, go back to the DEA? Not with your record. Your job prospects weren't exactly bright, were they, Mr. Lund? Hell, if you got fired, your best hope for a job would be as a security guard at Wal-Mart. Delroy Lund, former big-shot DEA agent chasing Mexican drug lords on the border reduced to chasing shoplifters in a parking lot. That was your future without Senator McCall, wasn't it? And that pissed you off, didn't it, that little rich boy lying naked there on the floor, threatening your future? That little fuckup!

"Things got out of hand again, didn't they, Mr. Lund? Clark got in your face just like that Mexican boy in Del Rio. Rage took over. You wanted desperately to kill Clark McCall. You saw a pistol lying there on the floor. You pulled your handkerchief from your pocket. You wrapped it around the pistol and picked the pistol up with your right hand. You stepped over to Clark. You reached down with your left hand and you grabbed the little fuckup's hair and yanked his head up. Then you put the gun to his forehead above his left eye. And you pulled the trigger. You killed Clark McCall just like you killed that Mexican boy in Del Rio, didn't you, Mr. Lund?"

Delroy's eyes again went to Senator McCall. Scott turned and watched as bodyguard and senator stared at each other for a long moment; then McCall's eyes dropped. His face sagged and he suddenly looked old, either from the realization that his own bodyguard had murdered his son or that his dream of living in the White House was over for good. Scott returned to Delroy.

"You thought the defendant would be blamed. Her gun, her fingerprints, but you didn't know one critical fact. You didn't know she was left-handed. That's what happened that night. Things got out of hand and you killed Clark McCall. Didn't you, Mr. Lund?"

Scott paused. All twelve jurors were leaning forward as

if bracing against a wind. Judge Buford had turned in his chair and was focused intently on the witness. Ray Burns's expression said he knew his coveted Washington assignment had just been lost. Bobby and Karen and Shawanda were practically on top of the defendant's table. Dan Ford's elbows were resting on the back of the pew in front and his hands were folded, as if praying. Boo and Pajamae were holding hands like finalists in a beauty pageant. The entire courtroom was waiting to hear Delroy Lund confess to killing Clark McCall. Scott decided Delroy needed a little push; he decided to get in Delroy's face.

He grabbed the crime scene photo of Clark McCall from the defendant's table and asked the judge for permission to approach the witness. When the judge nodded, Scott walked to the witness stand and dropped the photo in Delroy's lap under his now downcast eyes. Then he got in Delroy's face.

"Come on, Delroy, admit it! I know you killed Clark! This jury knows you killed Clark! Even the senator knows you killed Clark!"

Delroy's face was red and sweaty. His breathing became faster and labored. His blood pressure was rising, causing the veins in his bald head to protrude like blue ropes against his white skin. His meaty hands closed in on the photograph in his lap and crumpled it into a ball, mashing it mightily as if trying to pulverize the memory of Clark McCall into pulp. Scott knew things were about to get out of hand; Delroy's rage would soon take over and he would scream: *Yeah, I killed Clark! Yeah, I killed that little fuckup!*

But when Delroy's big bald head finally turned up, his eyes were defiant. He said, "Then prove it."

"The defense rests, Your Honor."

Ray Burns tried to save his Washington job by calling FBI Agent Henry Hu to the stand again and eliciting somewhat reluctant testimony that a left-handed person could have fired the murder weapon with her right hand. When Ray sat down, Scott stood and picked up the nearest document.

"Your Honor, may I approach the witness?"

"Yes, Mr. Fenney."

Scott walked around the defendant's table and toward the witness stand, and at the last moment, stumbled on an imaginary obstacle, tossing the document to the floor next to the witness stand. As Scott righted himself, Agent Hu, courteous as always, got out of the chair, took two steps, leaned over and picked up the document. Standing no more than two feet from the jury box, Agent Hu held the document out with his right hand.

Scott said, "Agent Hu, are you right-handed?"

Agent Hu realized his silent testimony, that he had picked up the document with his right hand because that was the natural thing to do, what anyone would do, even Clark McCall's killer. He smiled slightly.

"Yes, I am."

"No further questions."

*

Karen and Bobby were cooking pasta in the kitchen, the girls were taking their baths, and Scott was slumped on the floor, mentally and physically exhausted. Bobby opened the refrigerator, pulled out two beers, walked over to Scott, and held one out to him.

"No matter what happens tomorrow, Scotty, you've done right by her."

"Thanks, Bobby. And just so you know, I did this for Shawanda. Not to get back at Mack McCall or Dan Ford. For her."

"Thanks for telling me that, Scotty. I needed to know."

"I know. And thank you, Bobby."

"For what?"

"For doing this, being part of this, working your tail off even though you're not getting paid."

The beer halfway to his mouth, Bobby froze: "I'm not getting paid?"

After prayers, Pajamae opened her eyes and said, "Mr. Fenney, I don't want that McCall man to be the president."

Scott smiled. "Me neither."

"And that Delroy, he's a bad man, isn't he, Mr. Fenney?"

Boo said, "He killed Clark?"

"He is and he did."

"Is he going to jail?"

"I don't know." Scott stood. "You girls go to sleep.

450

We've got another big day tomorrow, closing arguments, maybe a verdict."

"Mama might get out tomorrow?"

"She might. But she might not."

Pajamae thought about that, then said, "Thanks, Mr. Fenney."

"For what, baby?"

"For caring about my mama."

Scott removed his glasses and wiped his eyes. "Pajamae, my life is better now because of your mother. And because of you."

THIRTY

A SCOTT FENNEY, ESQ., stood before the twelve members of the jury and said: "When I was a boy, my mother used to read her favorite book to me at bedtime, *To Kill a Mockingbird*. You might've read it or seen the movie. It's the story of a little girl and her father, a lawyer named Atticus Finch. He was an honorable man and an honorable lawyer, unusual even back then, in the 1930s when the story took place.

"Every night my mother would say to me, Scotty, be like Atticus. Be a lawyer. Do good. She even named me after him, Atticus Scott Fenney. Well, my mother's dead and I'm a lawyer, but I'm no Atticus Finch. I haven't done much good. I made a lot of money, but I didn't make my mother proud.

"But that's another story.

"Or maybe it's the same story. Because this story, our story, the story playing out in this courtroom, is also about making your mother proud.

"See, in the book, Atticus was appointed to represent a black man named Tom Robinson. Tom was accused of beating and raping a white girl. Atticus showed the jury that the girl had been beaten by a left-handed man because the right side of her face was bruised, but that Tom's left hand was disabled due to an accident years before. Atticus proved that Tom didn't do it. And Atticus also showed the jury that the girl's father was left-handed and a mean drunk to boot. Well, everyone in the courtroom knew that Tom didn't commit the crime and that her father did. But the jury, twelve white men, convicted Tom Robinson anyway, just because he was a black man.

"Now, that story took place in Alabama in the thirties—in a different time and a different world, back when the color of law was black-and-white. But our story is taking place seventy years later, in Dallas, Texas. The world's a different place today, things have changed—not everything and not everywhere and not enough, but in our courts of law things have surely changed. Judges have changed. Juries have changed. The color of law has changed. It's no longer black-and-white. My former senior partner told me the color of law is now green. Today, he said, the rule of law is money. Money rules. And he's right. Lawyers use the law to make money, politicians sell the law to special interests for money, people sue each other for money. Everywhere in the law, it's all about money—except one place. Right there where you're sitting, in that jury box. You're not here for money. You're here for the truth.

"And what is the truth of this story? The first truth is, Clark McCall was murdered by a right-handed person, a person strong enough to yank him up off the floor, mean enough to stick a gun to his head and look him in the eye when he pulled the trigger, and experienced enough in the ways of murder investigations to know how not to leave incriminating evidence behind. The truth is, Delroy Lund murdered Clark McCall.

"The second truth is, Delroy Lund followed Clark to Dallas, followed him down to Harry Hines, saw him pick up the defendant wearing her blonde wig, and followed them home to Highland Park. When he saw the defendant driving off in Clark's Mercedes, he went inside. He found Clark alive, naked and holding his privates after being kicked in the groin by the defendant. He laughed at Clark and Clark got mad. Clark cursed Delroy, Delroy got mad, and Clark got killed. Things got out of hand, and Delroy killed Clark.

"And the third truth is, Shawanda Jones is innocent. Clark McCall was killed by a right-handed person. Shawanda Jones is left-handed. She didn't do it.

"That's the truth. That's what the evidence shows. We've proved that the defendant is innocent and we've answered the question this trial presented: Who killed Clark McCall? Now there's only one part of this story left and you've got to write it: the ending. How is this story going to end? Like *To Kill a Mockingbird*, with an innocent defendant convicted just because she's black? Or are you going to write a new ending, where the color of law is not black or white or green, where truth and justice prevail even if the defendant is poor and black?"

Scott paused and glanced over at the judge for a long

moment, then turned back to the jurors. He said: "Ladies and gentlemen, before Judge Buford appointed me to represent the defendant, I thought I was a winner in the game of law—and that's how I viewed the law, as just a game. When I tried a case, I wanted to win. I wanted to beat the other lawyer. It wasn't about truth or justice; it was just about winning . . . and money. But I was wrong. The law isn't a game. It's not about winning or money. It's about truth and justice . . . and life. Today, it's about the defendant's life.

"This case has given me a chance to do something I had never been able to do before as a lawyer: make my mother proud. I hope I did that. I hope my mother is finally proud of me." He paused. "And I hope you'll make your mothers proud of you, too."

The judge instructed the jury at 11:45. The jurors retired to the jury room for lunch and deliberations, Judge Buford to his chambers, Shawanda to her cell, and Scott, Bobby, Karen, and the girls to the house on Beverly Drive.

Scott had waited for jury verdicts many times in his career, all in civil cases where only money was at stake. While waiting for his last jury verdict, he had spent the time back in his office calculating alternate bills for his client, one at a straight hourly billing if they lost, and one with an added bonus if they won. Clients won or lost, but the lawyers always won.

This case was different.

It wasn't about money; it was about Shawanda's life. Twelve people were deciding whether she would live or die, whether she would spend the rest of her life in prison or free, whether Pajamae would have a mother or a memory.

The court clerk called at 1:30. The jury had a verdict.

"Ms. Jones," Judge Buford said, "please rise."

Shawanda Jones and her three lawyers stood and turned to the jury. Several jurors, black and brown and white, had tears in their eyes, as Shawanda did in hers. Scott felt Shawanda's hand next to his, trembling, her entire body shaking. He put his arm around her shoulders and pulled her close.

The foreperson of the jury handed the verdict to the bailiff who handed it to the judge. Judge Buford put on his reading glasses, gazed at the piece of paper, then raised his eyes to the defendant.

"In the matter of *United States of America versus Shawanda Jones*, the jury finds the defendant not guilty."

Shawanda sagged and would have fallen to the floor if Scott had not caught her. She buried her face in his chest and embraced him. He held her tightly, his tears mixing with hers. Boo and Pajamae ran to them as the courtroom erupted in cheers and shouts and applause. The jurors hugged each other, reporters crowded Scott and Shawanda, Ray Burns sat at the prosecution table shaking his head, and Bobby and Karen kissed like newlyweds. Senator McCall pushed his way through the crowd and out of the courtroom. Dan Ford sat shaking his head in wonderment at the turn of events. Shawanda whispered in Scott's ear, "That a righteous name, Atticus."

Scott turned to the bench and his eyes met Judge Buford's. The judge nodded at Scott and Scott nodded back.

Shawanda Jones was free. Half an hour later, they finally made their way through the mob of reporters and cameras and to the sidewalk fronting the federal building. Dan Ford was waiting there. Scott sent Shawanda and the girls ahead and walked over. Dan held out his hand and Scott took it.

"Scotty, my boy, you are one fine lawyer."

"Dan, I'm not your boy anymore."

"Yes, well . . . look, Scotty, Mack won't be in the White House now, so why don't you come back? You can have your old office, I'll fix things with Dibrell and the bank, you can buy another big house, get the Ferrari back . . . you can go back to your old life—with a substantial raise, say a million a year. Not bad for a thirty-six-year-old lawyer. What do you say?"

There was a time. And a place. And a lawyer.

But they were no more.

"Dan, I'm just not the Ford Stevens type."

Scott turned away from Dan Ford only to find his

path blocked by another familiar face: Harry Hankin.

"Harry! How you doing, buddy?"

During his four-year tenure as a member of the country club, Scott had played golf with Harry most Saturday mornings—and usually won a hundred bucks from Harry most Saturday mornings. Harry fought a wicked slice. They shook hands, and Scott threw a thumb back at the courthouse.

"You got a trial?"

Harry Hankin was the premier divorce lawyer in Dallas, admitted to the membership of the country club only after his written promise never to represent a member's wife.

"Uh . . . well . . . no." Harry glanced down at his shiny shoes, then back up. "Here."

Harry held out a thick document, almost as if he were embarrassed. Scott took the document and his trained eyes immediately found the caption: PETITION FOR DIVORCE.

"I wanted to do this personally, Scott, so I could explain."

"She filed for divorce?"

Harry nodded. "Trey, the pro, he hired me—or he's paying me. He's already won a tournament, a million bucks, so he can afford me."

Scott almost laughed. "We played golf how many times, Harry? A hundred? And you're taking money from the guy my wife ran off with?"

"I couldn't say no, Scott—he cured my slice."

Scott laughed now. "Well, sure, Harry, straightening

out your golf swing, that's pretty goddamned important."

"You thought so once." Harry turned his hands up. "Look, I'm sorry, Scott."

"Is she happy?"

Harry shrugged lamely. "I was married to a woman like her. With them, you never really know."

"Does she want Boo?"

"What?"

Scott held up the petition. "Does she want custody of Boo?"

Harry shook his head slowly. "No. She said the PGA tour is no place for a little girl. And she said you need Boo more than Boo needs her."

Scott started to walk away, but stopped when Harry said, "Scott." Scott turned back to the divorce lawyer. "I'll take his money, Scott, but I'd never take your girl."

The two lawyers locked eyes, and Scott recalled that some years back, Harry Hankin had lost his own children in a bitter divorce.

"Thanks, Harry."

Scott caught up with the others a block down the street, where Louis was leaning against his old car and Shawanda was turning in circles, her arms spread, her face to the sky, a young beautiful woman, her tan skin radiant in the sun's reflection. Pajamae and Boo were watching and laughing joyously. Scott smiled at the sight. It was without question the best moment of Atticus Scott Fenney's legal career.

Boo said, "A. Scott, they want to help us move."

"Boo, I don't think Shawanda wants to spend her first free day in three months helping us move."

Shawanda said, "Yes, I do, Mr. Fenney. Me and Pajamae, we come tomorrow. Louis, he bring us over."

Louis walked over to Scott and they shook hands.

"You a good man, Mr. Fenney."

"Thanks, Louis, for watching the girls. For everything." To Shawanda, Scott said, "Look, I want you to go into rehab, okay. I'll pay for it."

"Thought you ain't got no money?"

"I sold my house. And I want you to work for Bobby and me, we're gonna start a firm. I want you and Pajamae out of the projects."

"Thanks, Mr. Fenney, for being my lawyer. And for caring about me."

Shawanda smiled and reached up and touched his cheek and gazed at him in the oddest way, as if memorizing his face. She stretched up and he leaned down and she kissed his cheek.

"I ain't never gonna forget you, Mr. Fenney."

And he would never forget her. And when Scott Fenney returned home, he would be greeted by enchiladas and Consuela de la Rosa, who had just arrived by bus from the border—the INS had granted her green card "out of the blue," Señor Gutierrez had said when he called her that morning. He did not know how and he did not know why and she did not care; she only knew that now she would always live with Señor Fenney and Boo, her *familia*. And later that night when Scott Fenney tucked his daughter into bed and kissed her good night, she would smile up at him and say, "See, A. Scott, there are happy endings in real life."

EPILOGUE

T HE GIRLS SQUEALED with delight.

Four months later, Scott was sitting in his pajamas and robe on the couch in the small house over by SMU and smiling as the girls opened their presents early on Christmas morning.

Their lives had been irrevocably changed.

This Christmas, he didn't have a wife and Boo didn't have a mother. Rebecca had left and never come back. Every few weeks, he still found Boo crying quietly in bed, and he had cried when the divorce became final. But they were both doing better now. He was sure he wouldn't marry again, despite Boo's attempts at matchmaking; she said her teacher had a really big crush on him. Ms. Dawson did seem nice at carpool.

But Boo now had Pajamae and Pajamae had Boo. They attended fourth grade at Highland Park Elementary where Pajamae was the only black girl and Boo the only white girl with cornrows. They were like sisters, and would be when the adoption was final.

Scott had Bobby and Bobby had Karen and Consuela

had Esteban and they were having a baby who would be an American citizen. They had married a month ago in a traditional Mexican wedding in the Cathedral Santuario de Guadalupe Catholic Church in downtown Dallas. Scott gave the bride away and Boo was her maid of honor.

Scott also had Big Charlie back in his life. He often brought his girls over to play with Boo and Pajamae. But they no longer talked about playing football in the old days; they talked about raising kids in these new days. Scott Fenney and Charles Jackson were fathers now and that was good enough.

Scott lost the state bar election to a big firm lawyer in Houston. He now practiced law with Bobby and Karen on the second floor of an old Victorian house renovated into office space and located just south of Highland Park. The Fenney Herrin Douglas law firm represented the thirty homeowners whose residences were being condemned by the city to make room for Tom Dibrell's hotel; and they were preparing a class-action suit on behalf of the residents of the South Dallas projects against the city for violation of federal fair housing laws. Louis had gone door-to-door signing up residents; Scott's suddenly lofty reputation in the federal judicial system had allowed him to resolve all of Louis's outstanding issues with the Feds. Bobby still represented his regulars from the Mexican bar in East Dallas; charges against Carlos Hernandez were dropped due to prosecutorial misconduct. He was training to be a paralegal and acted as translator for their Hispanic clients. Scott wore jeans to the office, ate lunch once a week with the girls in the school cafeteria, and played hoops with Bobby and John Walker at the YMCA.

His office faced due south and offered a nice view of the downtown skyline. He could sit at his desk and see Dibrell Tower out his window. Karen's ex-secretary at Ford Stevens told her that the firm would close out the year with record profits. Dan Ford sat on top of his world, perfect but for the fact that vandals had repeatedly slashed the tires of his Mercedes-Benz in the parking garage, while Sid Greenberg sat in Scott's former office, drove Scott's former Ferrari, and practiced aggressive and creative lawyering for Scott's former client.

Oddly enough, Scott felt no satisfaction when Frank Turner filed a $10 million sexual harassment lawsuit against Tom Dibrell on behalf of the blonde receptionist; or when Harry Hankin filed a divorce petition against Dibrell on behalf of Tom's fourth wife alleging infidelity and seeking over $50 million in community property; or when the Environmental Protection Agency filed suit in federal court against Dibrell Property Company and Thomas J. Dibrell jointly and severally seeking $75 million in costs required for the cleanup of lead contamination on the fifty-acre tract of land located adjacent to the Trinity River.

Scott did feel relieved when Delroy Lund was arrested and charged with the murder of Clark McCall and obstruction of justice in the Shawanda Jones case; Hannah Steele agreed to testify. Mack McCall withdrew from the presidential race but was elected senate majority leader; soon after, he was diagnosed with prostate cancer. Ray Burns was now an Assistant U.S. Attorney in Lubbock. United States District Court Judge Samuel Buford remained on the bench in Dallas.

Right after the trial, Scott had moved Shawanda and Pajamae out of the projects and into a rent house near Highland Park. He paid for Shawanda's drug rehabilitation; she fought hard and gave it all she had, but she couldn't break the hold heroin had on her. Two months after the trial, Shawanda Jones injected heroin into her right arm, drifted off to sleep, and never woke up. Pajamae missed her mama very much, but said she's in a better place now where she doesn't need her medicine to be happy. She prayed for her mother every Sunday morning when Scott took the girls to church.

Scott had begun reading a new bedtime book to the girls: *To Kill a Mockingbird.* They loved Boo Radley.

THE ABDUCTION

4:59 A.M.

BEN BRICE opened his eyes to a dog needing to pee. "Don't worry, Buddy. I'm still alive."

This man's best friend slapped a wet tongue across Ben's face once more just to make sure. Ben wiped the golden retriever's saliva on the sheet and pushed himself to a sitting position. He groaned. Each beat of his pulse through the veins in his head felt like a ball-peen hammer pounding the inside of his skull. He didn't remember finishing off the empty whiskey bottle sitting on the night table. But then, he never did.

He rubbed his bare arms against the chill of an April dawn and stood, but he had to grab the door to stay upright. He leaned against the wall until the world stood still, then he rode a hand-hewn pine log into the main room of the small cabin. He let Buddy out the back door and dropped down to the floor.

Lying face down on the coarse wool rug in his long underwear bottoms, he inhaled the Navajo scent that would forever inhabit the native weave. He closed his eyes and considered trying to sleep again, but he knew it would be in vain: a lifetime of hitting the deck at 0500 wouldn't allow it. Resigned to his fate, he brought his legs together, placed his hands palms down under his chest,

3

inhaled deeply, and exhaled as he pushed. His triceps trembled as his rigid body rose from the rug. *One.* He dropped down hard and felt as if he might pass out. But he inhaled and exhaled and pushed his body up again. *Two.* Down to the rug. Pushed up. *Three.* Down. Up. *Four.* He reached a rhythm at twenty-five and finished at fifty.

He rolled over onto his back. He locked his hands behind his head, lifted his knees to a ninety-degree angle to his spine, contracted his abdominal muscles until his shoulders lifted off the rug, and twisted his torso to touch his left elbow to his right knee then his right elbow to his left knee. Then down. And up again and twist right then left and down. And up. Right. Left. And down. Fifty times.

He stood, steadied himself, and walked over to the kitchen sink. He stuck his head under the gooseneck faucet and turned the cold water on full; he braced himself as the well water traveled four hundred feet from inside the earth's gut and sputtered then gushed out of the pipe. His body shivered; it felt like he had plunged his head into a bucket of ice water. He dried off with a dishtowel then opened the refrigerator and drank orange juice out of the carton. He closed the door and paused to look at her—the blonde hair, the blue eyes, the bright smile. The refrigerator door was covered with photos of her, alone and with her family, the only blonde in the bunch.

Ben walked out the back door of the cabin and without looking dropped the empty whiskey bottle into the recycling bin filled with empty whiskey bottles. His breath fogged in the cold air. He was now wearing jogging shoes, sweats, and a baseball cap pulled down low to shield his blue eyes from the bright morning sun. The endless sky was empty except for a vulture circling breakfast in the distance. He went over to the garden, picked a few weeds, and watered the neat rows with the sprinkler bucket. Buddy was barking, ready to get it on.

"Okay, boy, let's go."

They ran into the rugged terrain surrounding the cabin, Buddy leading the way, Ben lagging behind; his body ached from sixty years of life and thirty years of Jim Beam. He soon lost sight of Buddy in the sagebrush. But Ben knew he'd find his four-legged friend at the rock outcropping two miles out; and when Ben arrived, Buddy was there, sitting and waiting patiently for him to run up, bend over, and throw up, a morning ritual.

Ben spat out the last of the bile and wiped his mouth with a red handkerchief; he took a moment to gather himself. Only his hard breathing broke the silence of the land. All around him stretched the vast solitude that is New Mexico: the Taos Plateau bordered by the snow-capped peaks of the Sangre de Cristo mountain range rising tall into the blue sky, a land so beautiful and harsh that only an artist or a man running from his past would find it hospitable. To the north was Colorado, to the south Albuquerque, to the west Taos, and to the east the solitary cabin situated on a low rise, the metal roof reflecting the sun.

"Beat you back to the cabin, Buddy."

Ben ran toward the rising sun and Buddy gave chase, delighted—this was the fun part.

Half an hour later, Ben had cleaned up and was wearing jeans, boots, and a corduroy shirt, eating a granola bar, and drinking a cup of coffee brewed from the strongest beans available in Taos; they had come with a money-back guarantee to break through the haze of the worst hangover.

He walked outside, past the garden, and to the workshop. Inside, woodworking tools hung on the walls and what rich people in Santa Fe regarded as fine art in the form of furniture crowded the floor. He pulled a low stool next to the rocking chair he had fashioned out of mesquite, ran his hands along the arms, and began sanding the rough spots. Buddy spun around three times, plopped down in the doorway, and settled in for the day. The sound of sandpaper scraping over wood and Buddy's snoring soon joined in a melody of sorts, the only music of Ben Brice's life.

The sun's rays now angled low across the workshop floor, the only evidence that another day of his life had passed. Ben laid his tools down, stood, and stretched his back. He walked outside and around to the west side of the cabin porch and sat in his rocking chair where he would watch the sun melt and the sky over Taos turn orange, where he would listen to the coyotes' lonesome cries and sometimes he would answer them, where he would remain until the distant city lights dimmed and the night chill set in. His thoughts would then return to the past, always to the past that owned his life like a bank holding a mortgage that would never be paid in full. He would think of the life that might have been—a young man's dreams, the great adventure that was not, the death of the brother he never had, a wife who loved him but left him . . . and then he would think of his failures, re-visiting each one until he arrived at the failure that would forever haunt

6

his nights, and he would reach for the bottle. And so his life would go until one morning he would not answer Buddy.

But the day was not yet over and his thoughts not yet there. He whistled, and Buddy appeared and bounded up onto the half-sized rocking chair next to his. Ben reached over and scratched Buddy's neck then ran his fingers over the block letters carved into the seat back: GRACIE.

5:47 P.M.

SEVEN HUNDRED miles away a blonde-haired girl was sprinting down a soccer field in Texas.

"Run, Gracie, run!"

Gracie Ann Brice could run like a boy, faster than most boys her age, ten going on thirty, which made playing soccer against girls her own age seem almost unfair. But she was fun to watch, if your daughter was on her team.

She was driving the ball up the sideline, past the parents cheering in the stands and Coach Wally wearing a Tornadoes jersey and her dad filming her with the camcorder—she made a face for the camera—while shouting into his cell phone: "Cripes, Lou! Tell those New York suits it's my killer app, it's my company, it's my IPO— and the price is gonna be thirty a share and not a freaking penny less!"

Multitasking, he called it.

Without breaking stride, Gracie drove the laces of her white Lotto soccer shoe into the ball, kicking it over the oncoming defenders' heads and right to Brenda on the far side of the field. Then she pulled up and looked back at her skinny thirty-seven-year-old SO (Significant Other) on the sideline. He was now gesturing with the camcorder, swinging it up and down and videotaping the ground, the

8

sky, the ground, the sky, all of his attention on the cell phone. She couldn't help but shake her head and smile, the kind of smile grownups use on small children, but only those related to them by blood.

"God bless him," she said.

Her father was a total geek. He was wearing black penny loafers with white socks, wrinkled khakis, a long-sleeve blue denim shirt with the tail hanging out, a yellow Mickey Mouse tie (the one she had given him last Father's Day), and narrow black-framed glasses; his curly black hair looked like he had styled it by sticking his finger in an electrical socket. (Mom always said he looked like Buddy Holly with a blow dryer, but Gracie didn't know who that was.) All that was missing from this picture was a white pocket protector stuffed with mechanical pencils. John R. Brice was a doofus to the max, but Gracie loved him dearly, as a mother might love a child with special needs. He was now filming the parking lot.

"God bless him," she said again.

"Gracie, gosh darnit, we need a goal to tie! Quit foolin' around and score!"

Jeez, Coach, don't have a cow. Gracie turned away from her dad and focused on the game. Across the field, Brenda was losing the ball to number twenty-four, the Raiders' star player (she was eleven) and a real snot. Brenda was chubby and not much of an athlete. She hadn't scored a goal in the three seasons they had played together. Gracie grimaced as the snot charged Brenda and knocked her to the ground then stole the ball. Bad enough, but then the snot stood over Brenda like the football guys do after a big hit and snarled down at her: "Give it up, Fatty!"

Gracie felt the heat wash over her, the same as right before she had beaten up Ronnie down the street for

9

tripping Sam, a five-year-old alien who had taken up residence in their home. (They swear he's her brother.) Afterward—after running down the street to a safe distance, of course—Ronnie had yelled "lesbo" at her, which had seemed a particularly mean remark given that she was in love with Orlando Bloom like every other girl in fourth grade. She figured Ronnie had called her that because she was a tomboy and kept her blonde hair cut boy short, or because she had bigger leg muscles than him, or because she could bloody his big fat nose—or maybe because she wanted a tattoo for her eleventh birthday. Mom, however, said that her superior athletic ability threatened Ronnie's masculinity, always a fragile component of the male psyche. *Um, whatever.* The next time Gracie saw the little dweeb, she threatened his life and gave him a black eye.

"Gracie, she's on a breakaway! Stop her!"

The snot was now driving the stolen ball down the field toward the Tornadoes' goal, obviously suffering from some kind of—what had Mom called it?—oh, yeah, diminished capacity, thinking she could actually outrun Gracie Ann Brice to the goal. *As if.* Gracie turned on the speed.

"Watch out for number nine!" someone yelled from the Raiders' bench. Gracie wore number nine because Mia Hamm wore number nine. The select team coaches currently competing for her talents said that with proper coaching (by them), she could be as good as Mia one day. Mom said they were just blowing smoke up her skirt, saying anything to get her to play for their teams. Still, the thought of being another Mia Hamm and leading the USA team to World Cup victory, that was, like, way too cool to imagine.

"Gracie, block the shot!"

But maybe she'd better lead her team to victory in the girls' ten-to-eleven-year-old age bracket first.

Up ahead, the snot was slowing down and maneuvering for the best angle on goal; Gracie was sprinting up from behind and thinking, *You know, for an eleven-year-old, she's got a really big butt.* But she also had a really good shot opportunity at low post. The snot planted her left foot, kept her head down, and drove her right foot into the—

Air?

Nothing but air, girlfriend! Gracie thought as she slid feet first under the snot, executing the most totally awesome sliding tackle in the history of girls' youth soccer, clearing the ball from goal, and leaving the snot's foot kicking at nothing but air.

The crowd cheered!

But not the snot. "She fouled me!" she screamed, pitching a red-faced hissy fit right in the middle of soccer field no. 2. "She fouled me!"

But the referee shook his head and said, "All ball."

Gracie jumped to her feet and chased down the loose ball. She had the entire field and eight defenders between her and the Raiders' goal and not much time to get there. She decided on a sideline route—*duh*—but she first had to eliminate some of the defenders. So she dribbled the ball straight up the middle of the field, suckering the defenders in from their sideline positions—*come to mama, girls*—until five of the Raiders had congregated at the center line close enough to hold hands like the kindergartners on a class outing. Then Gracie exploded—*drive hard right at them, stop on a dime, spin left, and go, girl!*—and left them in her dust as she hit the sideline and turned on the speed, an all-out race down the chalk line, past the Tornadoes' stands, parents on their feet and shouting—

"Go, Gracie!"

"Run, Gracie!"

"Score, Gracie!"

—Coach's arms windmilling her on as he ran down the sideline with her, his exposed belly jiggling like pink Jell-O below his jersey—*now that is like, majorly gross*—past her SO filming the other parents in the stands, God bless him, and to the Raiders' goal and—*POW!*—blasting the ball past the diving goalie's outstretched arms and into the net.

Tie game!

Gracie threw her arms into the air. She considered ripping off her jersey and throwing it into the air, too, revealing her stylish black Nike sports bra, but she decided against it because she wasn't wearing a bra. Mom said her breasts might come in next year.

The other girls mobbed her and congratulated her and jumped up and down with her . . . but they all froze when those two words boomed out from the Raiders' sideline, instantly silencing players and spectators alike and making Gracie feel as if someone had punched her in the stomach.

"Not again," Brenda groaned.

They all turned to the Raiders' sideline as the words rang out again—"Pa-a-a-a-nty che-e-e-ck!"—and hung over the field like a foul odor. The man had a megaphone for a mouth, the big creep! He was dressed in a slick suit, grinning like a fool and drinking from an oversized plastic mug—and from his red face he was drinking something stronger than Gatorade.

"Does he really think there's a penis in your panties?" Brenda said.

"He knows you're not a boy," Sally said. "He's just

jealous 'cause you're way better than his daughter, that little snot."

He was the snot's father and a big butthead, a football dad at a girls' soccer game, taunting the players from the sideline. Gracie bit her lower lip and fought back the tears. Coming from Ronnie the dweeb down the street was bad enough, but from a grownup? She wished she were bigger and older; she would run over and beat this guy up, too. She looked over at her dad, wishing he would—*Daddy, do something! Please!*

But he did nothing. He hadn't even heard the jerk. He was in his Helen Keller mode (deaf, dumb, and blind to the real world), facing away from the field, holding the phone to his ear with one hand and waving the camcorder around with the other like he was swatting gnats by the pool. Of course, what could he do anyway? The big butthead was twice his size; he would pound Dad's meat-ware (as he called his brain) into the turf. Gracie instinctively touched the silver star dangling on her necklace.

"Pa-a-a-nty che-e-e-ck!"

Sally said, "If your mother was here, she'd kick his big butt into next week."

Mom was definitely not one to turn the other cheek. She was one to rip your face off. *Don't get mad, get even.* Mom's words of wisdom. Not exactly "sticks and stones will break your bones, but names will never hurt you," but then, her mother *was* a lawyer. She wished Elizabeth Brice, Attorney-at-Large (as Dad called her behind her back), was here.

But most of all, she wished to die.

Over on the Raiders' sideline, the other parents were shaking their heads in disgust at the creep, but he was too big to risk saying anything and getting punched out, always a possibility with a football dad. A mother, obviously the creep's wife, was pulling on his arm, desperately trying to move his big butt away from the field. He was protesting all the way: "What'd I do? I was just kidding, for chrissakes!" From Mrs. Creep's embarrassed expression, she had been there and done that with Mr. Creep before. Brenda shook her head and sighed.

"Another deranged dad at a children's sporting event."

Brenda's words brought the smile back to Gracie's face and another original country song by Gracie Ann Brice to mind. Facing the Creep family, she started singing, loudly, in her best Tammy Wynette twang:

> "D-I-V-O-R-C-E,
> Hey, lady, don't you see?
> Your man ain't no Or-lan-do B.,
> You best dump his fat ass A-S-A-P."

The girls laughed. The referee, a way cute guy about fifteen, smiled at her. The parents in both stands applauded. *Shoot, maybe she had the next hit single for the Dixie Chicks!* Gracie's spirits soared; the creep was now a distant memory, just another painful life experience for her to sing about. Like all the country girls say, you've got to experience pain in order to sing about pain, especially in front of fifty thousand screaming fans chanting *Gra-cie, Gra-cie, Gra-cie . . .*

"Gracie! Gracie!"

That was no screaming fan. That was a screaming coach. Gracie snapped; the whistle had blown to restart the game, and Coach Wally was spazzing out on the sideline, frantically pointing at his watch like he had just discovered time.

"Time's running out! We need another goal to win! Gracie, it's up to you!"

Focus, girlfriend!

Gracie's official position was striker, but Coach had told her to play the entire field. That required extra running, but she could run the whole game. She could run all day. She was running now, to the sideline, to the ball—

—to the ground, face first, breaking her fall with her hands and elbows, hitting hard, sliding across the field, and eating dirt and grass.

"Panty check!"

A snarling voice from above. Gracie rolled over to see the snot glaring down at her. The snot had tripped her from behind, a flagrant foul and a real cheap shot, especially for a girl.

What a total hussy!

The snot ran off. Gracie spat out the gritty dirt and grass and vaulted to her feet; her teeth and fists were clenched and her entire four-foot-six-inch eighty-pound being was filled with an overwhelming urge to chase after the snot and thrash her right there in the middle of soccer field no. 2.

"Gracie, get a goal!"

But the victory was more important than introducing the snot's face to Ms. Fist. So Gracie chased after the ball instead, barely noticing the blood and burning on her elbows.

Sally blocked a shot at goal and cleared the ball. Gracie anticipated Sally's kick and thigh-trapped the ball. One quick fake and she was sprinting up the sideline toward the Raiders' goal; the referee was keeping pace down the middle of the field, and the snot, her face screwed up with anger, was closing down on Gracie. The snot had the angle, which meant Gracie couldn't simply outrun her. So Gracie slowed slightly, allowing the snot to catch up, then she took a big step forward, hoping the snot would think she was going hard up the sideline like she had on the previous goal. The snot went for the fake big time, taking one step that way to protect the sideline route, one step too many—and Gracie punched the ball between the snot's open legs, spun around the snot, and recaptured the ball. The snot tried to stay with her, but she lost her balance and hit the ground hard, right on her big butt, and rolled out of bounds. Gracie glanced down at her and said, "I'm so sorry . . . *Not!*"

Then she raced to the goal—*a breakaway!*—only the goalie standing between her and a last-second victory for the Tornadoes and glory for Gracie Ann Brice, the next Mia Hamm. The referee put his whistle in his mouth and checked the time; only seconds remained in the game. Gracie moved into position for her patented power kick— the goalie ran out to meet her this time, leaving the goal unprotected—aimed just inside the near post, planted her left foot, timed her kick perfectly, and—

—slotted a through ball to Brenda in the goal box behind the goalie instead. Brenda kicked the ball into the open goal just before the cute referee blew his whistle to end the game.

The Tornadoes' stands erupted in cheers!

The Raiders' goalie was now looking at Gracie with a stunned expression on her face, as if to say, *You passed off the game-winning goal?* Gracie shrugged. She figured Brenda needed the glory more than she did. Heck, Mia Hamm was a team player.

The other girls mobbed Brenda. Gracie was about to

join in when she heard a manly voice: "Number nine—you're a player!"

The studly referee was walking past and pointing to her—and winking at her. *Oh, my God, I'm so sorry, Orlando, but I'm like, totally in love!* She stopped dead in her tracks and stared open-mouthed at the referee as he walked off the field; he was dreamy and she was dreaming of him coming to the house after the game on a Friday night like tonight and picking her up to go to a movie—of course, it would have to be rated PG because she was only ten, which might prove a bit of a problem but . . . she was rudely bumped back to reality by Coach Wally barreling past. His big belly was bouncing, his arms were spread wide, and he was blubbering like a baby. He scooped up Brenda and bear-hugged her like he hadn't seen her in years. Coach Wally was Brenda's dad.

The other dads were running onto the field and bear-hugging their daughters. But not her dad. Sometimes, like this time, Gracie wanted him to be more like a dad and less like a big brother who played Nintendo with her and took her and Sam to Krispy Kreme every Saturday morning and giggled until it hurt when Mom caught them throwing water balloons from the balcony off her bedroom at Ronnie and the other boys roller-blading down the sidewalk, and whose worst threat of punishment was to eBay her. Just once, she wanted him to be a real *father*, to scoop her up and bear-hug her like he hadn't seen her in years—to be her grownup manly DAD, for Pete's sake! She looked for him.

"Stupid, stupid rat creatures! Lou, you tell those brain-damaged bagbiters I'll take my IPO and go home!"

A shrill whistle interrupted John R. Brice's rant. He glanced over to see the girls formatting themselves in a linear sequence in the middle of the field while the parents were forming parallel lines and joining hands overhead to configure an arch. *Cripes*, the victory arch, a post-game protocol that required social engineering, interpersonal contact with the other parents. John was thinking, *Maybe I'll give it a miss this week*, when he spotted Gracie giving him the eye and gesturing for him to get out there! *Beam me up, Scotty*. He much preferred interfacing with AI systems over liveware, not that he was antisocial in the extreme; he was just uncomfortable (Elizabeth would say inept) when exchanging content in an offline mode, like most hackers who had spent the vast majority of their lives interacting with a cathode ray tube rather than with human beings. Part of the firmware.

He sighed and said to the phone, "Time out, Lou . . . the arch thing."

John jogged over and joined camcorders and cell phones overhead with a *GQ* dude who was everything John was not: tall, handsome, Hollywood hair, athletic build, wearing a starched white shirt, a stylish tie knotted like he knew how, and a beeper clipped to his belt—a college jock upgraded to real-estate, no doubt. Another football dad.

"Great game, huh?" the dude said through out-stretched arms.

"Yeah, great."

"Who's your girl?"

John sighed again. He never missed Gracie's games, and he couldn't help but enjoy himself, his daughter the star player, particularly since he had never been much of an athlete himself. Fact is, he was so lame at sports that back in grade school the girls were picked for the recess teams before he was. *Little Johnny Brice*. He was ten years old before he realized *Little* wasn't his first name. Fast forward twenty-seven years and now Little Johnny Brice was standing in the middle of a soccer field across a victory arch from one of those guys who was picked first for every recess team and the dude's asking him who his daughter is and his daughter is the best athlete on the field but he doesn't want to tell this room-temperature-IQ lamer that because he knew all too well what was coming next. John braced himself.

"Number nine," he said.

"*Gracie?*"

The dude's thick eyebrows shot up, and he looked John up and down with that familiar bemused smile.

"Gracie's *your* daughter?"

It wasn't the first time John had suffered that bemused smile at one of Gracie's games. Point of fact, it had become an every-game thing ever since the football dads started attending the girls' soccer games. Five years ago, when Gracie had first started playing soccer, John had been the only dad at the games, the football dads no doubt thinking, *What's the point if the girls can't even hit each other?* But now, Elizabeth had informed him, federal law required gender equality in college sports, so girls were getting scholarships to play soccer, softball, volleyball, and just about every sport but football. And that had brought the football dads to their girls' soccer games like sleazeware to cyberspace: Suzie might not be able to play middle linebacker at the University of Texas, but if her soccer skills could save dear old daddy tuition and room and board for four years, he'd dang sure make her games.

Problem was, these high-testosterone dads brought their

football instincts with them to the soccer field, yelling and screaming and getting into fistfights with other dads whose daughters were trying to steal Suzie's scholarship. The quest for college scholarships had turned youth soccer into a ruthless competition among the parents. So John always stayed by himself down the sideline and never commingled with the other dads, except for the post-game victory arch and the inevitable bemused smile. After next week's game, John R. Brice would throw his narrow shoulders back, look the dude straight in the eye, and say, *Dang right, she's my daughter! And I'm a freaking billionaire!*—a response guaranteed to wipe that bemused smile off his smug face. But this week Little Johnny Brice just shrugged.

"Yeah."

The dude shook his head as if pondering one of the great mysteries of the universe. "I played college ball at Penn State, but my girl's not in the same league as Gracie. Guess you never know where it comes from."

"eBay."

"What?"

"I bought her on eBay."

The girls filed past the other team, exchanging low fives like they were afraid of getting cooties, as Gracie would say, then raced through the arch as their parents cheered insanely:

"Great game, girls!"

"Way to go!"

"Yeah, Tornadoes!"

The final girl ran through, the arch broke up, the mothers embraced each other, the dads swapped hard high fives like they had just won the freaking Super Bowl, and John R. Brice stood there in the middle of a dang soccer field holding a camcorder and cell phone and feeling like a lurker in a chat room, as he always felt when male bonding broke out. So he said, "I'm outta here," hit the Esc key, and exited this app.

Gracie got her concession ticket from the team mom then waited for Brenda and Sally. When they arrived, Brenda leaned in close and whispered, "Thanks for giving me the goal."

Gracie gave her a little hug. "I gotta tell my dad we're going to the concession stand."

They walked over to dadrnerd@we_be_geeks.com; he was yelling at the phone and filming his shoes now, God bless him.

"Harvey doesn't have the brainwidth to understand the value of the technology! Lou, this is the next big thing, dude!"

He ran the phone and his hand through his curly black hair—it was now standing on end—and he stood out like a, well, like a geek among grownups. The other fathers wore suits and ties and starched white shirts and looked like the lawyers and doctors they were. Her dad looked like the college kid who lived next door. The other girls choked back giggles. Dad noticed her and smiled and aimed the camcorder directly at her face. Gracie reached up and switched the camcorder off then pointed to the concession stand and whispered, "Snow cones."

"Hi, honey," Dad said. Then, into the phone: "No, not you, Lou, my daughter. Hold on a minute."

John R. Brice squatted, wrapped his arms around his daughter, and embraced her; he inhaled her sweaty scent.

A thin glaze of moisture glistened on her flushed face, her short blonde hair was damp and stuck to the sides of her head, and her blue eyes sparkled like a multimedia LCD monitor. He placed the camcorder on the grass, flicked a drop of sweat from her cheek with his finger, and admired her. She was swell.

Dad was looking at her like she was a brand new eight-hundred-gigabyte hard drive just out of the box.

"Gracie version ten-point-oh," he said. "Best of breed."

Gracie said to the other girls, "I'm the applet of his eye." With her index finger she pushed the glasses up on her father's face. "And he's my favorite propellerhead in the whole W-W-W."

Dad grinned like he was embarrassed. "Your shoe's untied," he said. She held her foot out like Cinderella trying on the glass slipper. He reached down for the white laces but grabbed his blue shirtsleeve instead. It was stained. He looked from his sleeve to her arms.

"Hey, you're bleeding!"

Gracie examined her hands and arms. She *was* bleeding, from both elbows, where she had hit the ground when the snot had tripped her—which reminded her. She looked across the field to the Raiders' sideline and spotted the snot standing next to her father, the big butthead. Their eyes met; the snot raised her hand. Gracie thought she was going to wave, ready to put their hard-fought athletic competition behind them; instead, the snot stuck her tongue out and gave Gracie the finger. Gracie's face flashed hot, as if she had just stuck her head in the convection oven—she wanted the snot alone, like way bad. But it wasn't going to happen here and now. She turned back to her dad.

"No big deal," she said. She glanced over at the parking lot. "Guess Mom's trial didn't end. Oh, well, maybe she'll make the playoffs. You want to get a snow cone with us?"

Dad held the phone up. "I gotta talk to Lou."

"Hi, Lou!" Gracie shouted at the phone.

John R. Brice watched the girls skip off and merge into the stream of colorful bodies flowing toward the distant concession stand set back against the thick woods. He filled his shallow chest with the smell of popcorn riding out on the breeze and smiled. Ph.D.s in the Algorithms Group at MIT's Laboratory for Computer Sciences aren't given to emotion, as a general rule. Emotion had no place in the virtual world, where logical, ruthless intellect prevailed. In fact, the closest hackers came to emotion was emoticons, using ASCII characters to configure facial expressions in online communications. Virtual emotion. Real emotion belonged in that other world, that nonvirtual arena of pain and shame and smart-ass-ex-college-jocks-upgraded-to-real-estate that John Brice visited (like today) but did not inhabit.

But standing alone on a soccer field in an upscale suburb on a brilliant spring afternoon, he had to admit it: he was feeling pretty dang robust! And why shouldn't he? For the first time in his life he was on top of a world that was not accessible via a keyboard. In five days the IPO would hit the street and Little Johnny Brice would have his revenge—*he would have it all!*—everything he had dreamed of having all those lonely days and nights at Fort Bragg: two cool kids, a Range Rover, a big home, a drop-dead gorgeous wife who consented to sex twice a month (an unheard-of frequency during his premarital existence—computer geeks at MIT don't get much sex, as another general rule), fame, fortune, respect, manhood, and maybe even love. After all those years, moving from Army base to Army base, never fitting in with the other Army brats, being bullied by brutish boys who dreamed only of following in their daddies' bootsteps, a nerd in a soldier's world—now, finally, the world belonged to the nerds.

Little Johnny Brice had found his place in this world.

But he had lost Gracie. *Cripes*. He pushed his glasses up and squinted. He spotted her golden head bobbing between the other girls when she suddenly stopped and turned back to him. The last rays of the setting sun spotlighted her perfect face, and father and daughter shared one of those rare moments in life you wouldn't trade for the Windows source code. She smiled and waved to him. He loved her and he envied her. She was everything he had always wanted to be: confident and athletic, blonde and beautiful, social and popular, physically strong and mentally tough. She was entirely unlike him, and she was better. Often, like now, he would behold her and wonder exactly what part of her DNA he had contributed. But no matter: she was his daughter. John felt a catch in his throat and an inexplicable urge to run to her, snatch her up, and hug her again. Instead, he waved back with the phone and the moment evaporated—he had forgotten Lou.

"Shit." He put the phone to his ear. "Sorry, dude, I had a brain fart. Look, Lou, while other kids were outside playing baseball, I was in my room hiding from bullies, hacking code, and dreaming of being a billionaire like Big Bill. Thirty bucks a share makes me a billionaire—and that's the ticket to happiness! A billion dollars buys me everything I ever wanted! . . . Maybe even love . . . Yeah, Lou, geeks need love, too."

One hundred yards away, ensconced in a silver Lexus sedan circling the packed parking lot in search of an empty space, Elizabeth Brice was jabbing a finger into the climate-controlled air: "Truth and justice *demand* you acquit the defendant, a good and decent man who is *not* guilty of looting his bank or hiding a million dollars in an offshore account but only of falling in love with a cheap tramp— Look at her! Those aren't even real! She's nothing but a gold digger willing to destroy his reputation, his family, and his bank—for *his* money! Blame her!"

She paused and smiled at the memory.

"Guilty as sin, and they bought it—lock, stock, and pantyhose. Twelve good citizens with the mental range of a windshield wiper."

She spotted a family of four heading to their car on the third row from the front. She followed them, hit the turn signal to warn off all competitors for this particular piece of pavement, and waited for them to stow the kids and soccer gear.

And waited.

And waited.

"Jesus Christ, get in the goddamn car!"

Another family walked up and stopped to talk with the first family. That did it. She had neither the patience to wait for the Cleavers' conversation to end nor the inclination to hike from the farthest reaches of the concrete parking lot in high heels. Nor the need to. She whipped the Lexus around to the front row and into a handicapped parking space, cut the engine, retrieved a blue handicapped permit from the console, and hooked it onto the rearview mirror.

She was not physically handicapped.

In fact, as every married man passing by couldn't help but notice when she exited the sedan, Elizabeth Brice was physically fit and quite beautiful; her makeup and jet black hair remained perfect even after a long day in court; and her slim figure and shapely legs were showcased by her tailored suit with the short skirt. She always wore short skirts to trial.

Elizabeth Brice had graduated first in her class at Harvard Law, but she had learned the hard way that female lawyers do not win trials on brains and hard work alone. Women needed an edge, something extra to take into court with them, something to level the playing field, especially a female lawyer from New York trying to win in a Texas courtroom: the old joke that Texas had the best football players, politicians, and judges money could buy was no joke. Consequently, bench trials were more financial negotiation than courtroom drama—negotiations the good ol' homeboys inevitably won.

But jury trials were crap shoots. There was simply no way to predict what a jury of twelve bored and biased citizens being paid minimum wage would do. Thus, most lawyers hated jury trials; but Elizabeth A. Brice loved them. Because she had an edge that no bald pudgy down-home Southern-fried good ol' boy lawyer could possibly compete with in front of a jury: short skirts. Really short skirts that for the past two weeks had revealed her long, lean, Stairmastered legs to the all-male all-moron jury that had spent more time examining her than the prosecution's damning evidence.

Defendant Shay was forty-six, married with two children, and a respected banker from an old Dallas banking family; he was also indicted by a federal grand jury on fifty counts of bank and tax fraud, charges founded on the unfortunate fact that he had used federally insured bank funds to maintain his twenty-four-year-old receptionist/mistress in a comfortable lifestyle and had funneled the money through a Cayman Islands bank account to avoid paying taxes. "Keeping that little gal happy is damn expensive enough with pre-tax dollars," Shay had advised Elizabeth during one of their attorney–client privileged conferences. The government had tape recordings, surveillance photographs, offshore bank account records, and the mistress as the star witness under a grant of immunity. Conviction was a foregone conclusion, or so the prosecutors from Washington had thought.

But they didn't know Dallas. *Keep your prick out of the payroll* was a maxim seldom heeded in Big D. To the contrary, humping the help was not considered a crime but instead a perk, something to be praised and pursued, not prosecuted. If the government prosecuted every businessman in Dallas who had used bank money or company money or investor money or city or county or state money to pay for pussy, there wouldn't be enough members left in the chamber of commerce to play gin.

So she had carefully selected a jury of white middle-aged men, men who might once have had a mistress or who hoped to one day have a mistress or who would spend most of the trial imagining her as their mistress. Then she made the bank examiner and IRS agent appear to be pathetically incompetent old men on the stand; she called experts who (for sizeable fees) ripped to shreds every piece of evidence offered by the government; she brutalized the prosecution's star witness on cross-examination (the poor thing cried so diligently her thick mascara ran down her face and into her surgically-created cleavage); and she shortened her skirts six inches.

Elizabeth A. Brice, Attorney-at-Law, had won another not-guilty verdict for another guilty client.

Just as she decided that first thing Monday morning she would raise her hourly billing rate to $500, the merry voices of the kids and parents at the concession stand brought her thoughts back to the moment. She looked that way as the cool evening breeze hit her. She wrapped her arms, but the cold she felt was inside her. A vague sense of unease invaded her mind, as if the wind had whispered in her ear.

Grace.

She beeped the Lexus locked and hurried toward the vacant soccer fields and the solitary spectator sitting in the stands.

Where John was saying into the phone, "Oh, and what do you know about love, dude? Lou, are you aware that the boot sequence required to produce an orgasm in a full-grown American female is more complex than the ignition sequence of a neutron bomb?"

She saw him before he saw her. But he felt her presence, like one felt impending doom.

"Spousal unit alert," John whispered into the phone.

He lowered the phone from his ear—he could still hear Lou yell, "Don't mention my name!"—pushed his glasses up, and saw her eyes locked on him like proton blasters as she approached at a rapid pace from midfield in her Elizabeth Brice, Attorney-at-Large mode. Fear shot through his brain like a bullet—*Cripes, what did I do wrong this time?* His wife appeared very much as she had when they had first met in Washington ten years earlier; she was forty now but still insanely attractive (even when she was in a bad mood, like now) and just as intimidating, looking totally perfect in her best closing argument outfit (black on black on black) and acting in complete control of herself and everything and everyone she touched. Elizabeth Brice was a perfectionist control freak, hard-wired at the factory. Which made them a complete mismatch, like a Wintel program on a Mac. Which made John wonder, as he had often wondered: *Why did she ask me to marry her?*

Her fists punched holes in her hips when she arrived. "Where's Grace?"

"Dangit, Elizabeth, you promised her you'd make at least one game this season."

"I promised my client I'd win his case, and I did. Now where's Grace?"

John opened his mouth to remind his spouse that she had made and broken the same promise to Gracie before every game this season, that Gracie was more important than some bogus criminal even if he did pay her $400 an hour, that . . . but she seemed more agitated than usual tonight, tapping her foot at a furious pace, a sure sign she was seriously fried about something. Elizabeth's personality was a binary system—off and pissed off. He wanted to ask her now, as he had always wanted to ask her, *What are you so mad about?* But, as always, he quickly decided that discretion was the better part of not being blasted with a streaming audio of profanities that would make a complete system crash seem pleasurable. So he kept his mouth shut rather than chance a random explosion of his wife's volatile temper; he thought of it as risk management.

And besides, Elizabeth did not allow him sex during her trials; this weekend would present his first opportunity in more than two weeks. He couldn't afford to blow it with ill-advised flamage. He pointed the cell phone at the concession stand.

"Snow cone," he said.

Coach Wally bit the top off his cherry-flavored snow cone; some of the cool red juice trickled down his double chin. He wiped his mouth on the sleeve of his Tornadoes jersey.

Wally Fagan was walking away from the concession stand and toward the field to retrieve the game ball he had left behind in all the excitement of Brenda's winning goal. He bit into the snow cone again, wiped the juice off his chin, and noticed a woman approaching fast like a distant thunderstorm—dark hair, dark clothes, and a dark expression.

Gracie's mom.

Wally's pulse ratcheted up a notch and not because of her short skirt. He had talked to Gracie's mom only a couple of times in three seasons, but for some reason she had always made him nervous. Fact is, Wally Fagan stood just under six feet and weighed just over two hundred forty pounds, but he was wholly intimidated by the slim woman walking his way. She was maybe ten years older than him, but he always felt like he was talking to his mother—*Oh, shit, her mother!* Which made seeing her tonight seem odd, now that Wally thought about it.

She approached and they made brief eye contact. Wally smiled politely, waiting for a hint of recognition to cross her face. None did. He was a complete stranger to her. Wally debated whether to speak to her, since she was about to walk right past him. Without consciously deciding, he did.

"Gee, Mrs. Brice, I didn't expect to see you here tonight."

She turned on him in a heartbeat: "I had a trial, okay!"

Jesus! Her response so startled Wally he almost squeezed the snow right out of his cone. He immediately regretted not letting her walk on by.

Now that he had interrupted her journey, she took the time to look him over: the high-topped Reeboks, the blue coach's shorts stretched tight around his considerable belly and the gold jersey that didn't completely cover it, the Texas Rangers baseball cap on backward, the heart tattoo on his left arm, and the cherry snow cone juice dripping down his chin.

"Who *are* you?" she demanded.

That hurt. Wally wiped his sticky hand on his jersey before extending it to her. She had a very firm grip.

"Coach Wally . . . I coach Gracie's team."

"Oh."

No apology. She was staring at her hand; the sticky had rubbed off. She was apparently trying to decide whether to wipe her hand on her skirt; she said, "Well, Wally, I had an important case go to the jury today, so I was late for Grace's game."

"No, ma'am, I meant because of, uh . . . you know . . . your mother."

She looked up from her hand and frowned. "My *mother*? What about my mother?"

"Oh, my gosh, don't you know?"

"Know *what*?"

Not even his executive experience as a night manager at the Taco House out on the interstate had prepared

31

Wally Fagan to deliver this kind of news. But he had opened his big mouth too far to shut up now.

"Mrs. Brice, your mother had a stroke."

She recoiled. "*When?*"

"Uh, today, I guess. She's in the hospital."

She appeared confused. She pointed back toward the field. Wally looked that way; a man was sitting alone in the bleachers.

"My husband didn't say my mother had a stroke."

"Gracie's dad was at the game?"

She was now looking at Wally like he was a complete idiot.

"He's sitting right over there in the goddamn stands!"

Now Wally was confused; he removed his cap and scratched his burr-cut head. He kept his hair cut short because that way he didn't sweat as much under the hair net at work.

"You're not looking for Gracie, are you?"

She exhaled loud enough for him to hear. "I didn't come for the snow cones, Wally."

"But . . . but she's . . . she's *gone*."

"Gone where?"

"To the hospital, to see your mother."

"My mother lives in New York!"

"But your brother said your mother had a stroke and he came to take Gracie to the hos—"

The woman lunged at Wally and grabbed his jersey, her eyes and face suddenly wild like an animal; she clawed so close he could feel her hot breath on his face when she screamed.

"I don't have a brother!"

Wally was so scared he felt a drop of pee drip out. He dropped his snow cone. The wild woman released him

32

and ran toward the concession stand screaming her daughter's name.

"Gra-cie!"

Police Chief Paul Ryan's voice mixed with the other voices coming from all around him in the dark, the voices of cops and civilians searching the woods bordering the park for the missing girl, and he thought, *Kids don't get abducted in Post Oak, Texas!*

"Gra-cie!"

When he had gotten the call, Ryan figured a rich Briarwyck Farms soccer mom was throwing another conniption fit, as they often did over their very special children. His wife, a teacher over at the elementary school, called it the Baby Jesus Syndrome, every rich mom thinking her spoiled little brat's the second coming. He had no doubt the mom would get a call on her cell phone and learn the girl had gone home with a friend, and the mom wouldn't say "I'm sorry" or anything, she'd just wave and climb into her SUV and drive off for the post-game pizza party over at Angelo's, figuring the police department was her private security force to call out anytime she wanted. But when he had arrived on scene and talked to the girl's coach, Paul Ryan knew immediately that this was a real abduction: a blond man in a black cap had asked for the girl by name.

"Gra-cie!"

All Ryan could see were the five feet of trees and ground cover in front of him illuminated by his Mag flashlight as he advanced deeper into the dark woods.

11:22 P.M.

HE HEARS THE others around him, but all he sees now is a vague vision of trees and vines and undergrowth, dense and impenetrable—a jungle. He's fighting his way through a jungle on a dark night. He hears a child's distant cry. He picks up his pace, but it's like trying to run through molasses. He's got to hurry, something terrible is about to happen, is happening. He hears more cries. He's drenched in sweat now as he struggles onward through the steamy jungle. Vines strangle him, branches slash his face and arms, undergrowth grabs his boots, the cries grow louder, his breath comes faster, his heart pounds harder against his chest wall—

—and he suddenly stumbles out of the darkness and into the light. Fires light a hamlet, straw huts burn, and flames spit out of rifle muzzles. He hears the BOOM BOOM BOOM of high-powered weapons, people screaming, pigs squealing, and water buffaloes grunting. He smells the stench of burning animal flesh. He sees women and children being dragged out of their hiding places and thrown into the dirt, the blaze of their burning homes illuminating their terrified faces, their Asian features so delicate and desperate. He watches them being herded up and driven forward down a dirt path, carrying babies wailing in the night and begging for mercy—

"NO! NO! NO! NO VC! NO VC!"

A young girl, a fragile china doll stripped of her clothes and innocence, stumbles along, desperate to escape the savagery suffocating her, pushed forward by big hands connected to big arms. Terror seizes her face because she's heard stories about what these men do to pretty young girls like her. She searches for sympathy in the hard faces and she finds it in his. She turns to him, silently pleading for help. He knows he must save her to save himself: her life and his soul hang in the balance as she falls face down in the dirt. A big hand grabs at her, but he shoves it away and gently lifts her delicate arm. He hears her sobbing voice in her native tongue: "Save me. Please save me." The china doll turns her face up to him, in slow-motion she turns into the light, and he sees her face, the face of—

Gracie.

Ben Brice screamed himself awake and sprang to a sitting position in bed, gasping for air. His heart was beating rapidly, his chest and face and hair were matted with sweat, and his ears were ringing. The phone was ringing. He reached for the phone and knocked over the empty whiskey bottle. He put the phone to his ear and spoke.

"What happened to Gracie?"

DAY TWO

5:18 A.M.

DAWN WAS BREAKING when Ben parked the old Jeep, grabbed the duffel bag from the passenger's seat, and double-timed into the Albuquerque airport terminal. His head throbbed with each jarring step. Skiers heading home after the season's last runs already crowded the gates early on that Saturday morning. He located an arrival/departure monitor. The first flight to Dallas departed at 0600 from gate eight.

"I understand it's an emergency, sir," the female gate attendant said, "but the flight is overbooked, and we have twenty stand-bys. In fact, all our flights to Dallas today are overbooked." She glanced at her computer. "Earliest available flight out is Monday."

She gave him a sympathetic expression and a shrug and held her hand out to the next person in line. Ben picked up his duffel bag, stepped away from the counter, and studied the waiting passengers, bleary-eyed college kids returning to school from spring break; none seemed likely to surrender a seat to a stranger.

But he had to get to Dallas.

He spotted three men in uniforms marching down the

main corridor toward the gate: the flight crew. The man in the middle appeared about his age and wore captain's wings.

He stepped over and intercepted them.

Karen, the nineteen-year-old gate attendant, shook her head when the man stopped Captain Porter. Six months on the gate and the story was always the same: *It's an emergency! A crisis!* She always wanted to say, *Well, so is my social life!* But it was against company policy to be rude to customers, so she just smiled and shrugged. The man seemed sincere, though, not the type to lie his way onto an overbooked flight. He had nice eyes. Still, she picked up the phone just in case she needed to call security.

Karen handed a boarding pass to the next customer in line and then glanced back at the man pleading with Captain Porter. She liked Captain Porter; all the girls did. The airline hired only military pilots; the younger ones thought they were such studs, always bragging on themselves and expecting every female employee to drop her skirt on command. The older ones, like Captain Porter, were different. They were respectful of the girls, probably because they had daughters the same age, and they never bragged on themselves or what they had done in the military. The younger pilots thought Captain Porter was some kind of god; they said he had been a real top gun in some war she barely remembered from history class in high school and had been held prisoner for, like, three years. Karen shuddered at the thought: no MTV for three whole years!

The man was now pointing up at the CNN monitor. Karen leaned around the counter to see the monitor. On the screen was the face of a little blonde girl under CHILD ABDUCTED and above RANSOM SUSPECTED. She was cute. Karen looked back at Captain Porter, fully expecting him to send the man packing with a sympathetic expression and a routine shrug—*What can I do, I just work here?*—the universal response to any passenger complaint quickly mastered by all airline employees. But Karen stood slack-jawed and oblivious to the passengers waiting in line when Captain Porter dropped his flight bags and hugged the man like he was his long-lost brother then released him, picked up his duffel bag, and carried it over to Karen.

"Karen, stow the colonel's gear," Captain Porter said. "And bump someone in first class."

Karen could swear Captain Porter had tears in his eyes.

41

8:13 A.M.

OVER HER MOTHER'S objections, Gracie had come to visit him every few months and for a month each summer, for five years now. But for her visits, the morning Ben would not answer Buddy might have already arrived. He needed her and he knew why; she needed him but he did not know why. All he knew was that God had bonded them together in a way he neither understood nor questioned: his life was inextricably tied to hers, and, somehow, hers to his.

Ben was now in the back seat of a yellow cab doing seventy on the Dallas North Tollway, a turbaned Arab behind the wheel, the city noises beyond the windows a ferocious pounding behind his eyes. Outside, a concrete world was racing past; inside, his stomach was stewing over the thought of never seeing Gracie again. He felt as if he might puke the peanuts-and-coffee breakfast he had had on the plane; and if he continued to focus on the four little Dallas Cowboy dolls standing on the cab's dashboard, their oversized helmet heads bobbling around, he surely would. So he leaned his head back and closed his eyes; his thoughts returned to Gracie's last visit. They had sat in their rocking chairs on the porch and watched the sunset; after a period of silence, she had said, "Mom says you're a drunk."

He had said, "She's right."

"But you don't drink from those whiskey bottles when I'm here."

"I don't need to drink when you're here."

"Why not?"

"I don't know. I guess I only think good thoughts when you're here."

"Then that settles it: I need to be here all the time."

He had smiled. "That's real nice of you to offer—"

"No, Ben. I mean it. I want to live here with you."

"Honey, this is no place for a girl."

"Then you come live with us. It's a really big house."

"That's no place for me. Once you've lived in a jungle, you can't live in a subdivision."

Gracie was quiet, then she said, "She still loves you."

When Ben opened his wet eyes, the cab was pulling up to the entrance guardhouse at BRIARWYCK FARMS, AN EXCLUSIVE GATED COMMUNITY, or so the sign embedded in the tall brick wall read. Black iron gates with TRESPASSERS WILL BE PROSECUTED across the bars blocked their way. Ben recalled the front doormat at his childhood home in West Texas that read *Welcome, Y'all*.

After Ben's ID checked out, the guard gave the cabby directions and activated the automatic gates. They passed through the gates and entered an oasis in the concrete desert: tall oak trees shading the wide road, expansive stretches of green grass, sparkling blue man-made ponds encircled by walking paths, and magnificent mansions set deep into large lots, homes that would cause most visitors' jaws to drop; but Ben barely noticed. His thoughts were of Gracie.

The cab driver turned up the radio: "At six-fifteen last

43

night, Post Oak police issued an Amber Alert and provided descriptions of both the victim and the suspect. Gracie Ann Brice is white, ten years old, four feet six inches tall, weighs eighty pounds, and has short blonde hair and blue eyes. The suspect is white, twenty to thirty years old, six feet tall, two hundred pounds, has blond hair, and was last seen wearing a black cap and a plaid shirt. Police are asking anyone who videotaped any of the games at Briarwyck Farms Park yesterday to bring the tapes in."

The Arab cabby made eye contact with Ben in the rearview. "Little girl, she was taken. In my country, we find the man"—he slapped the edge of his open right hand down on the dash—"we cut off his dick. Then we cut off his head."

The cabby's eyes returned to the road—"*Aah!*"—and he slammed on the brakes; Ben was thrown forward. The cab had almost plowed into a police barricade across Magnolia Lane; two uniformed cops stood in front of the cab, their hands on their holsters and shaking their heads. The cabby turned in his seat, shrugged, and said, "Can go no more."

Ben paid the $45 fare with a fifty and un-assed the vehicle. The morning sun punished his eyes; he patted around his clothes for his sunglasses, then remembered he had left them in the Jeep. He rubbed his temples, but it did not relieve the pounding in his head. He needed his morning run to exorcise last night's demons, but that would not happen this morning. So he slung the duffel bag over his shoulder and walked past the barricade, down the sidewalk, and into a media circus.

Satellite uplinks mounted above TV vans lined both sides of the street and had lured the residents out of their homes before breakfast. Kids, parents, cameramen, reporters, and cops crowded the street and sidewalks; their voices competed with the incessant THUMP THUMP THUMP of a news chopper hovering low overhead.

His head ached.

Ben continued down the sidewalk, deep into the circus, and past a reporter talking to a camera: "Gracie was last seen at Briarwyck Farms Park wearing blue soccer shorts and a gold jersey, the team name, Tornadoes, across the front and a number nine on the back."

Kids were riding bikes and rollerblading in the street, media technicians were setting up their equipment, and photographers were snapping pictures of the mansions. Another reporter addressed another camera: "She was abducted at a soccer game last night in this upscale suburb forty miles north of Dallas."

Parents were huddled in small groups and holding their children close, evident on their faces that fear peculiar to parents, the fear that their children might be taken in the night. Ben had seen that fear before.

Making themselves at home on the sidewalks and lawns were grungy (a word Gracie had taught him) cameramen wearing sunglasses and baseball caps on backward. They were lounging in lawn chairs, drinking coffee, complaining about the early morning assignment, and offering expert opinions: "It'll be someone in the family. Always is."

This was their kidnapping now. Gracie Ann Brice was news.

And the world was waiting for news outside her home where a dozen TV cameras sat fixed on tripods and aimed at Six Magnolia Lane, a three-story French chateau-style mansion that looked more like a hotel than a home. Gracie hadn't exaggerated: it was a really big house.

Ben started up the long walkway leading to the front

door but paused to listen to a lone reporter speaking into a camera: "Gracie played in a soccer game here in Post Oak late yesterday, went to the concession stand, and hasn't been seen since. Her parents are praying that Gracie was taken for ransom, that money can save their daughter. Only fourteen hours since her abduction and a massive effort is already underway to find Gracie and the man who took her. The FBI is setting up a command post, local police are organizing search parties, and at the park where Gracie was taken, bloodhounds will soon be combing the woods . . ."

Ben continued to the porch. Written in colored chalk on the gray slate steps, in a child's hand, were the words WE LOVE YOU, GRACIE. The words had the same physical effect on Ben as his morning run: he stepped to the side of the porch and puked behind a low bush. He wiped his mouth with a red handkerchief, and then he rang the doorbell.

Inside the residence the doorbell could not be heard over the ringing phones and blaring TVs and cops hustling about and FBI agents shouting into cell phones and a little boy running around in a Boston Red Sox baseball uniform, pointing a finger-gun at everyone, and yelling, "Stick 'em up!"

Walking calmly amid the chaos down the wide gallery that stretched the width of the mansion was a tall black man. FBI Special Agent Eugene Devereaux was wearing black cowboy boots, blue jeans, a gold badge clipped to a wide black belt, a semiautomatic pistol in a belt holster, a blue nylon jacket with FBI stenciled in gold letters across the back, and an FBI cap. Devereaux was the lead FBI agent on the Gracie Ann Brice abduction. Searching for abducted children had been his life for the past ten years.

The heels of his 14EE boots resounded under his considerable weight with each step on the immaculate hardwood floor as he passed fine art on the wainscoted walls and furniture that looked like it would break if you even leaned on the damn stuff. Walking beside him was Special Agent Floyd, an index finger pointing up like he was gauging the wind.

"Is that the damnedest thing you've ever seen?"

Painted on the high-arched ceiling over the gallery was a mural depicting an old-time French street scene with shops, pedestrians, horses, and carriages; the street continued to the foyer where it merged into a village square. A similar street scene entered from the gallery ceiling over the east wing of the residence. It was in fact the damnedest thing Eugene Devereaux had ever seen.

"You ever work an abduction where the victim lived in a place like this?" Floyd asked.

Devereaux's line of work did not bring him into homes like this. The typical abduction victim's home was on wheels or in a run-down apartment complex or a cheap-rent house; it was not a mansion with fine art on the walls and French murals on the ceiling.

"Nope. Rich girls don't get abducted by strangers."

Devereaux was an abduction specialist with the Bureau based out of the Houston field office; he investigated only abductions of children by strangers. Gracie Ann Brice was his eleventh this year and it was only early April.

He stopped. On the wall hung a formal family portrait illuminated from above by a spotlight; the parents and the boy were dressed in black, the victim in white. Her blonde hair was a stark contrast to the others' black hair. She looked like a sweet kid. On a small table below sat a copy of *Fortune* magazine with the father's face on the cover under *The Next Bill Gates?*. Devereaux picked up the magazine and flipped it open to the feature article about the father. The same family portrait filled an entire page of the magazine—for all the world to see. All the world knew that John Brice was about to be very rich and had a wife named Elizabeth, a son named Sam, and a young daughter named Gracie.

Devereaux replaced the magazine and said, "Maybe this really is a ransom grab."

He hoped it was. A ransom grab was the only real chance the girl was still alive: you don't ransom a dead girl.

"The father," Floyd said, "he's a basket case. I don't think he's up to taking the call, if there is a call. We may need to go with the mother . . . defense lawyer, white-collar perps."

From down the hall, Devereaux heard a voice, female and firm: "Hilda, your only job is Sam."

The victim's mother—forty, slim build, intense expression—appeared at the far end of the gallery, marching toward them with an entourage trying to keep pace: the family nanny, a young Hispanic female; an older white female of Eastern European descent in a maid's uniform; and a local cop, young, flattop, muscular, wearing an expression that said he would rather be in a shootout with a Mexican drug cartel than taking orders from the mother. She was dressed for the office, looking impeccable in a tailored suit and heels. Her hair was done, and her makeup was in place. She was a woman you would notice on the street. Her finger was punching holes in the air.

"Find him, feed him, follow him. Don't let him out of this house or your sight. *Comprende?*"

"*Sí, señora.*" The Hispanic woman exited the entourage.

The mother, to the maid: "Sylvia, call the caterer. They can't find my daughter on empty stomachs."

"Yes, ma'am." She was off before the words had died. To the officer: "Get those people off my front lawn."

"I'll try, Mrs. Brice, but—"

"No buts. Do it. Shoot them if you have to."

"Uh, yes, ma'am." The young officer was no match for the mother; he surrendered, shaking his head.

As the mother came closer, Devereaux noticed her eyes, alert and focused, not the vacant, lost eyes he was accustomed to seeing on mothers of abducted children. Devereaux gave her a sincere nod—"ma'am"—as she passed him in the foyer. The morning after her daughter's abduction and she was dressed for court and in control, barking out orders. Devereaux knew that this was her way of coping, acting as if she were still in control of her life. Of course, she wasn't; her daughter's life—and so her life—was now controlled by the abductor.

"She's one tough broad," Floyd said.

"She'll need to be," Devereaux said, "if the girl wasn't taken for ransom."

8:39 A.M.

G OD, *PLEASE LET it be ransom.*
Alone for the moment, Elizabeth Brice paused, leaned her head against the gallery wall, and closed her eyes. Her adrenaline was pumping at a verdict's-about-to-be-read velocity, but she had no place to go this day, no guilty defendant's case to plead, no prosecution witness to brutally cross-examine, no closing argument about truth and justice to make to a jury of good and gullible citizens. Nothing to do but pace the house and hope and pray. That morning, in the shower, she had said her first prayer in thirty years.

God, please let it be ransom.

She inhaled deeply and exhaled slowly. Her heart was beating like she had just put in an hour on the Stairmaster. Her disciplined body had surrendered to fear, just as her equally disciplined mind had to anarchy, a mob of thoughts running wild through her head: Where was Grace? Was she dead? Was she alive? Who had her? What had he done to her? Did he want money? Why hadn't a ransom call come yet? Did the FBI know what they were doing? Would she ever come home? Why me? Why my child? How could John have let someone take her? *How?*

Damn him!

She felt the rage rise within her, the rage that resided just below her surface, always ready to emerge and take control of any situation, the rage she fought to suppress every day of her life like a patient taking chemotherapy to force the cancer into remission. The battle was proving particularly difficult today because it was completely incomprehensible to Elizabeth Brice how her daughter could have been abducted right from under her husband's goddamn nose at a goddamn public park!

She had cursed her husband last night at the park, after panic had given way to rage. But first she had panicked and lost complete control, screaming, yelling, grabbing kids and parents—"Have you seen Grace? Have you seen Grace?"—running around in circles and shouting Grace's name until her voice was hoarse. Then rage had taken its turn in the driver's seat, and she had lashed out, first at John and then at Grace's coach: "You pointed Grace out to the abductor? What kind of fucking idiot are you?"

Parents and police had searched the park until late in the night. When the FBI had arrived and assessed the chaotic search efforts, they declared the park a crime scene and ordered everyone out. The search had to be organized, they said. Evidence could be trampled. The park and woods were too vast and dense to search thoroughly at night, and if Grace hadn't been found after eight hours of searching she was no longer at the park. So Elizabeth had returned home, prayed in the shower, and dressed; she had been awake now for twenty-seven straight hours, wired on caffeine and adrenaline. She had trained her mind and body to function without sleep; it would catch up with her around the thirty-sixth hour when her mind would give way to her body's physical exhaustion, and she would sleep. But not now. Not yet. Her body was tiring but her mind remained alert and angry: *Damnit, how could John have let someone take her!* She clenched her fist and hit the wall.

"Uh, you okay, Mrs. Brice?"

The doorbell rang again, and Elizabeth opened her eyes to a young cop holding a cup of coffee and a donut; he had white powder around his mouth and an indolent expression on his face, as if this were the start of another routine day of donuts and traffic stops. He was a fine example of small-town law enforcement and the reason she had demanded the FBI be called in immediately.

"Yes. But my daughter's not. Go find her!"

The cop choked on his donut then turned and hurried away. She took several deep breaths to compose herself and then marched down the gallery, resolved thereafter not to act in public like other mothers of abducted children, slobbering pitifully on television and begging for the safe return of her child. Elizabeth Brice, Attorney-at-Law, would go on TV, but not to beg.

She arrived at the formal dining room for the third time that morning. Leaning over the dining table and studying a large map illuminated by the chandelier above were the Post Oak police chief and four uniformed officers. They didn't notice her.

"A line search," Chief Ryan was saying. "Start at the south end, proceed due north. Instruct your searchers to walk at arm's length, slow, this ain't no goddamn race. They see something, tell 'em to hold up their hands, don't touch a fuckin' thing. FBI boys'll tag it and bag it." Chief Ryan was stocky but paunchy, like an aging athlete. When he finally noticed Elizabeth standing in the door, he grimaced. "Pardon my French, Mrs. Brice."

She held up an open palm. "Just find her."

"Yes, ma'am. Oh, Mrs. Brice, we need clothing Gracie wore recently, something that's not been washed. For the bloodhounds." Elizabeth nodded. The chief again addressed his men: "Be in position at nine-thirty sharp. Bobby Joe'll run the dogs in the woods first, while we walk the playing fields. Then we'll search the woods again—maybe we'll have better luck in daylight."

Elizabeth turned to resume her pacing and came face to face with an earnest young woman wearing a blue nylon FBI jacket and holding a pen to a notepad. They had been introduced earlier, but Elizabeth could not recall the agent's name.

"Mrs. Brice, what color, size, and brand of underwear was Gracie wearing?"

The agent asked the question as if asking whether she wanted cream in her coffee. Elizabeth clenched back her emotions.

"I don't know. I left yesterday before she got up. I had a trial. My husband might know, ask him. He let someone take her."

FBI Special Agent (on probation) Jan Jorgenson watched the victim's mother march off down the fancy hallway; they called it a gallery. They don't have galleries in Minnesota farmhouses.

Jan ducked into the kitchen, made sure she was alone, and pulled a protein bar from her waist pack; she hadn't eaten since last night when the call had come and she didn't do donuts. She had survived this long without food only because she had carbo loaded the past week for the marathon she was supposed to be running at that very moment. She took a big bite then jumped—someone had jabbed her hard in the back.

"Reach for the sky!"

A kid's voice trying to sound older. Jan turned and looked down on the Brice boy, the spitting image of the father. He was holding his right hand like it was a gun and grinning.

"I got that from Woody, in *Toy Story*."

He laughed and ran off. She shook her head. His big sister was abducted, and he's playing cowboys and indians or cops and robbers or whatever his game was. The kid didn't have a clue.

Jan ate the protein bar in four quick bites while watching the small TV on the counter; a reporter standing on the front lawn was saying, "Ransom. John Brice is soon to be a very wealthy man . . ."

Old news. Jan exited the kitchen, but she could still hear the reporter on the kitchen TV or on the TV in the next room or on other unseen TVs in rooms she passed, as if someone were deathly afraid of missing breaking news: "His company, BriceWare-dot-com, is going public next week, which is expected to make John Brice worth well over—"

Jan entered the study.

"*A billion dollars?*"

Special Agent Eugene Devereaux, the agent in charge, was interviewing the victim's father. The father nodded blankly. Sitting slumped on the couch, he looked as if he would fall over from exhaustion if not for Agents Floyd and Randall sitting on either side of him like book ends. His curly black hair was a mess, his khakis and blue denim shirt were wrinkled and dirty, the knot of his yellow Mickey Mouse tie was pulled halfway down, and his face

54

was drooped like a balloon after most of the air had leaked out. He appeared even thinner than the last time she had seen him. But what struck her was the incredible sadness in his eyes, brown eyes visible over black glasses sitting low on his nose, the eyes of a man suddenly lost and adrift in a harsh world. His slender fingers were kneading the tie like a rosary.

"She gave this tie to me," he said to no one in particular.

A telephone attached to Bureau hardware sat on the coffee table in front of the father. An agent wearing headphones was testing the equipment that would record, trap, and trace the ransom call. If the call came. If the motive was money.

"A billion dollars," Agent Devereaux repeated.

The father looked up at Devereaux and said in a barely audible voice: "He can have it all if he'll let Gracie go."

Agent Devereaux dropped his eyes and gave a sideways glance at the other agents. "Mr. Brice, is there any reason someone would want to hurt your family?"

Almost a whisper: "No."

"Have any threats been made against you?"

"No."

"Did you fire any employees recently?"

"No."

"Do you suspect anyone?"

"No."

"Did you notice any strangers in the neighborhood?"

"No. Those gates are supposed to keep bad people out."

Agent Devereaux studied the father for a moment, obviously concluding that he was neither the abductor nor a source of information. Devereaux then turned to Jan.

"Yes, Agent Jorgenson?"

"Sir, I'm completing the detailed description of the victim's clothing. The mother said Mr. Brice might have the information I need."

Agent Devereaux nodded. "Proceed."

This was Jan Jorgenson's first child abduction. Engaged to the Bureau for eleven months now, she had always assumed that one day she would marry and have children; but now, seeing the father's pain at the loss of his child, a pain that a billion dollars could not erase, she wasn't so sure. Her question now seemed an awful burden.

"Mr. Brice . . ."

John was staring at the female FBI agent and trying to understand her words. His brain felt fragmented. He couldn't process what he thought he had heard her say. Why was she asking about Gracie's—

"Underwear?"

John turned to the other FBI agents, the ones setting up the recording equipment for when the kidnapper called and demanded ransom—a million, five million, ten million—he didn't freaking care how much. He would pay it and Gracie would come home. *That's the deal!* His eyes darted from agent to agent to agent. They were staring down at their equipment.

"But you said . . . I thought . . . I thought it was about money."

Until that very moment, it had never occurred to John R. Brice that his money might not be the motive for his daughter's abduction. He suddenly felt sick. A searing heat spread over his face. He thought he might faint. His upper body fell forward until his hands caught his head. He pulled his glasses off his face; the world around him was a blur, but the image inside his head was 20/20 sharp: *Gracie . . . and a man . . . and . . .*

"Oh, God."

He started crying. He couldn't stop himself. He didn't even try. He gave up the fight.

The doorbell rang again just as Elizabeth entered the study. Five grim-faced FBI agents simultaneously looked at her then quickly averted their eyes. Her husband was sitting between two agents on the sofa. His face was in his hands; he was crying inconsolably. Her body clenched with her greatest fear.

"Is it Grace?" she asked.

The lead FBI agent shook his head. Fear released its grip on Elizabeth's body. She breathed out a "Thank God." She then turned to her husband. "John, what's wrong?"

His sobbing did not abate. Elizabeth went to him and stood over his pitiful figure, debating whether to console him or to slap him senseless for allowing her daughter to be abducted. The agents sitting on the sofa relocated across the room. Over her husband's slumped head, she asked Agent Devereaux, "What happened?"

Agent Devereaux sighed. "We had to ask, Mrs. Brice. We need a complete description of Gracie's clothing, including her . . ."

"Underwear."

Agent Devereaux nodded. "Yes, ma'am."

Elizabeth's mind was so chaotic with wild thoughts that she had forgotten she had sent the female FBI agent to John with that question. She put her left hand on her husband's shoulder.

"John," she said softly. He looked up at her with red

eyes and tears rolling down his face and snot running out of his nose and a trembling chin. He wiped the snot on his shirtsleeve. Her little boy.

John Brice had married her when she needed a husband. And he had been a good husband: he had never embarrassed her in public or crossed her in private; he had always sent flowers to her office on her birthday and their anniversary, not that she had any inclination for romance; and he was a loving father to both children and a genius at math, the perfect skill in a wired world. John R. Brice was a gentle, brilliant boy . . . and utterly useless in a fight. He had nothing but a Ph.D. to fall back on in times like this, no reserve of intestinal fortitude to draw upon when you had to be hard and mean and ruthless; he was not like her—she could easily stick a gun to the abductor's head and blow his fucking brains out if necessary to save Grace. John Brice was not hard or mean or ruthless. He was just a thirty-seven-year-old little boy, looking up at her like he had just been beaten up by the neighborhood bully and needed mommy to hug him and make it all better. Instead, she slapped him across the face.

"John," she said through clenched teeth, the rage making a move to escape the darkness, "it damn well better be ransom. Because if it's not—"

"Eliza—"

She slapped him again.

"Goddamn you! You let him take her!"

"Mrs. Brice," Agent Devereaux said, "this won't help."

It was helping her. Elizabeth raised her hand again, but a black hand grabbed her wrist. The rage turned on Agent Devereaux.

"Let—me—go."

The phone rang. Agent Devereaux released her and

58

sat next to John. The agent wearing headphones activated the recorder then nodded at Agent Devereaux. The phone rang again.

"Mr. Brice," Agent Devereaux said.

John remained in the same position she had left him: his hands still cupping his face to block her blows and crying and saying softly, "I'm sorry."

The phone rang again.

"Mr. Brice, can you take the call?"

Her husband didn't move. Elizabeth thought, *Utterly useless in a fight*, then she thrust her hand out to Agent Devereaux.

"Give it to me."

Agent Devereaux lifted the phone off the receiver and handed it to her. The tape was running. She put the phone to her ear.

"Elizabeth Brice."

A child's voice came across. "Can Sam play?"

"*What?* No, Sam can't play today!"

The agents exhaled and rolled their eyes in unison. Elizabeth handed the phone to Agent Devereaux and sighed; the child's voice had given her pause. Her anger spent, the rage retreated like a tornado into the dark sky and she now gazed down upon the destruction left behind—her husband still sobbing and his face red and welted—and the slightest twinge of remorse tried to ignite her conscience. But she stomped it out like a discarded cigarette.

It's his damn fault! He let someone take her!

Her respiration spiked. One last glare at her utterly useless husband, then she marched out of the study and down the gallery and was crossing the foyer when the doorbell rang again. She stopped, yanked the front door

59

open, and stared at the man standing on her porch. Anyone who knew his life would have expected a bigger man, a harder-looking man. But there he stood, perhaps an artist who painted the West and dressed the part, wearing rugged Santa Fe-style attire that looked so phony on the models in the Neiman Marcus catalog but seemed born to his lean frame with his chiseled facial features and ruddy skin, the ragged blond hair framing his tanned face and setting off the most brilliant blue eyes imaginable. Remarkably handsome for a sixty-year-old man, he could be a middle-aged movie star. Instead, he was a drunk.

Elizabeth Brice turned and walked away from her father-in-law.

8:59 A.M.

BEN BRICE STEPPED inside his son's home and into the middle of a busy intersection. He quickly retreated as uniformed police and FBI agents and a maid talking into a portable phone and his grandson in a baseball uniform pursued by a young Hispanic woman—"Señor Sam, the oatmeal, it is ready!"—raced past him.

Beneath his feet was a polished hardwood floor; above his head was a lighted dome painted with a mural. A wide gallery extended off the entry into both wings of the residence. A sweeping staircase rose in front of him to a second-floor landing. Beyond the stairs was a living area with a two-story-tall bank of windows looking out onto a brilliant blue pool with a waterfall. Gracie had said her new home had cost $3 million. At the time he thought she had to be mistaken; but now, looking around, Ben could believe this place cost every bit of $3 million, maybe more. Which was good: his son could afford the ransom.

Ben had not spoken to John in five years, when he had last come to Dallas for Sam's birth. He almost didn't recognize the slight young man who had wandered aimlessly into the foyer and who now found himself caught in the middle of a fast-moving stream of bodies like a bug in a whirlpool; he looked defeated and lost, like the senile

61

World War Two vets at the VA hospital, a blank face in a world no longer recognizable. Ben dropped the duffel bag, stepped over to his son, and grabbed him by the shoulders.

"John." A stiff shake. "John."

His son regarded Ben as he would a complete stranger and said, "You think it's ransom?"

"John, it's me . . . Ben."

John pushed his glasses up and blinked hard. "*Ben?* What are you doing . . . How did you . . . Who called you?"

"You should have, son."

A voice from above: "I did."

She had left him right after Gracie was born, determined that her only granddaughter would not be raised by a nanny. Ben had figured it was just an excuse, not that he blamed her; if he could have, he would have left himself a long time ago. She had made regular visits back at first, but the time between visits grew longer and longer. Five years ago her visits had stopped altogether, when she had two grandchildren to raise.

Now, seeing her at the top of the stairs, her red hair and fair complexion glowing in the light of the dome—still the most beautiful woman he had ever seen—the love that Ben Brice had tried to drown in whiskey along with the pain returned with such force he thought his knees might buckle; instead, tears came to his eyes—she was still wearing her wedding ring. A devout Irish Catholic, she would never divorce her husband but could no longer live with a drunk; a devout drunk, he would never love another woman but could not live without a drink.

She descended the stairs, and Ben could tell that she had cried through the night. He knew because he had caused this woman to cry through many nights. Not that he had ever touched her in anger. Ben Brice was not a mean drunk. He was a silent one. The more he drank, the deeper inside himself he burrowed, battling the demons within and leaving his wife to cry herself to sleep. His soul was stained with her tears. Five years since he had seen her, touched her, held her, he ached to hold her now; but he stood paralyzed, like a buck private facing a four-star general.

She knew.

She came to him and buried her face in his chest. Ben pulled her tight and breathed in her scent as if for the first time. And for a brief moment it was thirty-eight years earlier, when the world still made sense. She sighed deeply, almost a cry, and he felt her slim body sag slightly.

"Oh, Ben. What if he hurts her?"

"We'll get her back, Kate. We'll pay the ransom and get her back."

They stood holding each other as strangers and thirty-eight years of their lives rushed past—the good times, the bad times, and more bad times. Ben had always held onto the good times to get through the bad times; she had lost her grip ten years ago. Standing there, they didn't have to say what they both knew: no time would be as bad as this time.

"Grandpa!"

Ben looked down at his grandson clutching his legs. The Hispanic woman arrived in a rush and out of breath.

"Señor Sam, the oatmeal, you must eat."

From below: "I don't want no stinkin' oatmeal!"

Ben Brice embraced his family. Except John. He was gone.

*

63

"What the hell's he doing here?"

Elizabeth ambushed her husband as soon as he set foot in the kitchen; he flinched and his hands flew up to his face then fell once he realized she wasn't going to slap him again.

"I don't want that drunk in my house!"

John did not respond. Instead, he wandered into the butler's pantry, as if hunting for a place to hide. She stared after her husband and shook her head: *utterly useless in a fight.*

"Mrs. Brice."

Agent Devereaux was at the kitchen door.

Ben was standing at the staircase with his family and the young Hispanic woman when a middle-aged FBI agent appeared with Elizabeth. Ben looked at her and she looked away.

"Kate," Elizabeth said, "would you get the photo of Grace from our room, for Agent Devereaux? And something she wore yesterday, something that's not been washed. Maybe her school uniform. Chief Ryan needs it. He's in the dining room." She then said down to Sam, "Have you eaten breakfast yet?"

Sam, from below: "I claim the Fourth Amendment."

"Fifth."

"Fifth what?"

"It's the Fifth Amendment right not to incriminate yourself."

"Whatever."

Elizabeth exhaled and turned to the Hispanic woman. "Hilda?"

Hilda threw her arms up. "Señora, he runs like the wind."

64

Sam, trying to hide between Ben's legs: "Help."

Ben diverted the conversation to save his grandson. He extended his hand to the FBI agent and said, "Ben Brice. I'm Gracie's grandfather."

"Eugene Devereaux, FBI."

He was a big man with big hands and a firm grip. The two men regarded each other.

"Ben Brice," Agent Devereaux said. "That name sounds familiar. Have we met?"

Ben shook his head and diverted the conversation again. "Have you gotten a ransom call?"

"No, sir." Agent Devereaux turned to Elizabeth. "What about Gracie's underwear?"

"Kate," Elizabeth said, "what underwear was Grace wearing?"

"She wears Under Armour to her games."

"Under *what?*"

Agent Devereaux interrupted: "Under Armour. Sports underwear. All the kids wear them now 'cause the pros do. My daughter wears them under her basketball uniform." To Kate: "Did Gracie wear compression shorts?"

"Yes. Blue ones. And a sleeveless tee shirt, blue."

Agent Devereaux glanced down the gallery and called out: "Agent Jorgenson!" He motioned, and a female FBI agent walked up. He addressed her: "We have white Lotto soccer shoes, blue knee socks, shin guards, blue Under Armour shorts and sleeveless tee shirt, blue soccer shorts, a gold soccer jersey with 'Tornadoes' on the front and a number nine on the back." Back to the others: "Anything else?"

"Her necklace," Ben said, triggering a sharp look from Elizabeth.

"What necklace?" Agent Devereaux asked.

"Silver chain with a silver star."

"Are you sure she was wearing it?"

"I'm sure."

Kate confirmed with a knowing nod.

To the female agent, who was writing on a notepad, Agent Devereaux said, "And the necklace. Get the updated description to the media."

"Yes, sir," she said, and then she departed.

Agent Devereaux gave Ben and Kate a polite nod and said, "Mr. Brice, Mrs. Brice," then he and Elizabeth walked away down the gallery. Ben turned to Kate.

"Why are they asking about her"—a glance down at Sam—"clothes? I thought it was about ransom."

She turned her hands up. "Until they get a call . . ."

Sam tugged at Ben's legs. "Grandpa, what happened to Gracie? No one'll tell me the truth." He gestured up at Kate. "Not even Nanna."

Ben squatted and came face-to-face with a miniature version of John—the same mop of curly black hair, the same dark eyes, the same black glasses, although his grandson's glasses had no lenses; Gracie said Sam had taken to wearing the frames so he'd be like his father. Ben had sent his grandson birthday and Christmas gifts each year (hand-carved wooden coyotes and horses and a little rocking chair with SAM carved into the seat back) and had talked to him whenever Gracie had called; and Gracie had sent the photos of Sam that were stuck to the refrigerator in the cabin, so Ben felt like he knew Sam, but he hadn't seen the boy since his birth. Ben had never been welcome in his son's home.

"She's gone," Ben said.

"Can I have her stuff?"

"What?"

"You know, like when she goes to college, I'm gonna get her room and all her stuff."

"No, it's not like that, Sam. She didn't want to go."

"So why did she?"

"A man took her."

An innocent face. "The mailman?"

"No, not a nice man."

"A cretin?"

"A what?"

"A bad man."

"Yes, Sam, a bad man."

"Where did she sleep last night?"

"I don't know."

"Did the cretin feed her dinner?"

"I don't know."

"What's ransom?"

"Money."

"The cretin wants money to let Gracie go?"

"Maybe."

Sam's face brightened. "Well, that's okay."

"Why?"

"Because after the IPO, we'll be a billionaire."

9:17 A.M.

FBI SPECIAL AGENT Eugene Devereaux had no doubt the furnishings in this one room cost more than his entire homestead. He had followed the victim's mother into the elegant formal living room in the east wing of the residence; Devereaux didn't know furnishings from fiddlesticks, but he knew this stuff didn't come cheap. He instinctively pushed his hands into his pockets, like he did when visiting those antique shops the wife loved, so as not to inadvertently break something he couldn't afford.

"Set up in here," the mother said. She dismissed the entire room with a wave of her hand. "Use the furniture, move it to the garage, burn it for firewood. I don't give a damn."

"Mrs. Brice, we normally don't establish the command post in the victim's home, but—"

She pointed a finger his way. "I want it here! I want to know what's being done to find my daughter at all times! I'll call Larry McCoy himself if I have to! He owes me!"

Not that it would affect his decision, but Devereaux couldn't help but wonder if the mother really knew the president personally or was merely a "Friend of Larry," a status earned through a $100,000 contribution to his last campaign.

"—*but*, your home is already wired for twenty phone and fax lines and broadband for computers and it would take us the entire morning to wire another location. So we will set up the command post here. We'll be operational in one hour."

Devereaux hoped he would not regret his decision. Because there was a good reason not to establish a command post in the victim's home: if the victim was not recovered quickly, personnel couldn't be maintained at a remote location indefinitely; the command post would have to be moved to the local FBI field office in downtown Dallas forty miles away. And when it was, the parents would worry that the FBI was quitting on their child. But Eugene Devereaux had never quit on an abducted child.

"Good. Now, what's being done to find my daughter?"

A fair enough question. Devereaux removed his hands from his pockets and ticked the items off on his fingers.

"I've got twenty agents full time on the case, plus ten local police. Chief Ryan issued an Amber Alert immediately upon Gracie's disappearance and broadcast an alert on NLETS, the National Law Enforcement Telecommunications System. Every law enforcement agency in the country knows about Gracie now.

"We've inputted Gracie into the National Crime Information Center Missing Person File. As soon as we get her photo, we'll input her into the National Center for Missing and Exploited Children. They'll put her on their website, and she'll go on the FBI website.

"We'll print up fliers with Gracie's photo and a composite sketch of the suspect for distribution throughout the area and to the media. Chief Ryan is coordinating the search at the park. An FBI Evidence Response Team is also at the crime scene. They'll collect and preserve any evidence and conduct a forensic analysis of the abduction site.

"We've installed communications equipment to record and trap and trace all incoming calls. Our Rapid Start Team will set up the command post, the phone bank, computers, and faxes, and coordinate and track all leads on a computerized system—there'll be thousands. We're interviewing witnesses who were at the park last night, and we're canvassing the neighborhood."

Devereaux decided not to mention that they were compiling a list of known sex offenders residing in the locality.

"Mrs. Brice, we can get a psychologist in here."

"For what purpose?"

"For you, your husband, your son. To help you through this."

"I don't want help. I want my daughter found."

The mother turned away, paced off four steps, and whirled to face him; her arms were crossed, and her eyes were sizing him up.

"And what are your qualifications, Agent Devereaux, to find my daughter?"

Bluntness did not offend Eugene Devereaux.

"Well, ma'am, this ain't my first rodeo." He was met with a blank expression. "One hundred twenty-seven abductions, Mrs. Brice. Those are my qualifications."

Her face deflated as she absorbed his words; her eyes fell.

"One hundred twenty-seven," she whispered. "My God." She lifted her eyes. "Children?"

"Yes, ma'am."

"How many were ransom?"

He hesitated. "None."

"Ben, what if this isn't about money?" Kate asked.

She had taken Ben out to the pool house. She thought it would be better that way, Ben staying out here alone. Just in case he drank. And the nightmares returned. And he screamed, that tortured cry that had punctured her sleep so many nights.

"Take me to the park."

Kate shook her head. "It's a crime scene. No one can go out there until they search it."

Bobby Joe Fannin spat a stream of brown tobacco juice.

"Settle down, boys."

The dogs were straining at their leashes, ready to get it on, the girl's scent fresh in their nostrils. Bobby Joe headed up the county's canine search unit, a team of six bloodhounds he had raised from pups. Good job, good benefits, outside most of the time. Not as good as farming this land thirty years ago when his granddaddy still owned this land, but not bad. Except for finding dead people. Bobby Joe never liked that part of the job. Why did killers from the city always dump the bodies in the country?

On the radio: "Bobby Joe, come in."

Bobby Joe pulled the radio off his belt and pushed the transmit button. "Yeah, Chief?"

He could barely make out Police Chief Ryan at the other end of the park; the search party was stretched out single file across the playing fields. Bobby Joe worked alone, just him and the dogs, which was another thing

71

he liked about the job, not having to work with other people much. In his line of work, other people around just messed things up: the dogs could detect human scent, but they couldn't distinguish between humans. Another human being around would throw them off the girl's scent.

"Bobby Joe, we're fixin' to get going down here," the chief said. "Go ahead and start your dogs. You find something, you call me. Don't touch nothing, you hear me?"

To his radio: "I done this before, Paulie."

Bobby Joe had grown up with Paul Ryan. They had hunted this land together as boys—deer, wild hogs, quail—and these very woods for rabbit, back when these woods covered five hundred acres. His granddaddy said this was one of the last native post oak forests left on the high plains of Texas. But that was then and this was now and only a hundred acres were left. And Bobby Joe was hunting these woods for a little girl.

He spat again.

"Let's go, boys," he said, giving the dogs a little whistle. They set off into the woods, the dogs' leashes in Bobby Joe's right hand and the girl's red-and-blue plaid school uniform in his left.

"Get off the goddamn grass!"

The chief said to make the mother happy, so Police Officer Eddie Yates was chasing the crowd of reporters and cameramen off the Brices' landscaped front lawn. They took one look at him—the angular twenty-three-year-old face, the sharp flattop, the dark sunglasses, the bulging biceps that had the sleeves of his uniform ready to bust at the seams—and moved to the sidewalk, bitching as they did.

One riot, one Ranger.

Except Eddie wasn't a Texas Ranger. He was a patrol cop in a small suburban police department that didn't even have a SWAT team—not that it needed one, seeing as how the biggest crime the town of Post Oak had to offer was kids passing around a beer under the bleachers at the little league field on Saturday nights. Eddie usually spent his shift working the town's speed trap out on the freeway, nabbing speeders while dreaming of being on a big city SWAT team, wearing a black paramilitary uniform, packing military-style assault weapons, busting down doors to drug houses, beating up gangsters, and fighting the war on drugs. He would take the Dallas Police Academy's entrance exam for the fourth time this summer.

Fight back, Johnny-boy!

Be a man!

Go on, run home to Mommy, Little Johnny Brice, you fuckin' crybaby!

All the taunts from all the bullies at all the Army bases came rushing back now. Little Johnny Brice hadn't been man enough to protect his own daughter at a public park. Just like he hadn't been man enough back then to fight back against the bullies. When the colonel returned from deployment, Mom would beg him to stop the beatings and the colonel would order the bullies' fathers to instill discipline in their ranks. But that had only made the beatings worse. He remembered the beatings and his face stung; but from Elizabeth's hand today and the hurt would not go away.

Back then, he had gone inside himself, deep into his inner child while his outer child was getting the crap beat

73

out of it. Afterward, he had run home to his room. Mom would always come in and hold him while he cried, and she would cry too; she would doctor his wounds and tell him it would never happen again. But it always happened again. Other kids had spent their childhood outside, learning to hit a curve ball; John had spent his in his room, hiding from bullies and teaching himself computer code.

Now, he had sought refuge in his home office, secluded on the backside of the house; he was hiding from his spouse and trying to escape the fear and loathing of the real world, as he often did. But there would be no escape this time. Fear and loathing had followed Little Johnny Brice home.

The phone rang. He let the machine take the call. It was Lou in New York, leaving another message: "John, did you get my earlier messages? Jesus Christ, it's on the news up here. I'm stunned! I don't know what to say, buddy. How could something like that happen in a public park? Man, I'm like . . . *shit*. Call me." The machine beeped and went silent.

Because I wasn't man enough to protect her, that's how it happened!

A Cray supercomputer occupied the space inside John's skull; his mind was capable of complex calculations and came with a near photographic memory—but he couldn't remember yesterday.

Was the game just yesterday?

Elbows resting on the desk, hands gripping his head, eyes closed, John tried to reboot his memory: he's sitting in the stands at the soccer field, talking to Lou about the IPO; Elizabeth has gone to the concession stand to find Gracie; then a piercing scream startles him so—*Grace!*

He drops the phone and runs to the concession stand where parents are shouting for their children and panic is racing through the crowd like an e-mail virus until the panic and he reach Elizabeth simultaneously.

Grace is gone!

Gone where?

Taken!

Home?

No, goddamnit! Someone kidnapped her!

He has never before seen Elizabeth panicked and out of control, and it scares him. Then the sound of sirens, the police, the search in the woods. And Gracie was gone. And he might never see her again. And Little Johnny Brice hurt in a place the bullies could never touch.

9:42 A.M.

"You've worked a hundred twenty-seven abductions?" the mother asked.

FBI Special Agent Eugene Devereaux nodded. "Yes, ma'am."

"But no ransoms?"

"I've worked one ransom in thirty years with the Bureau. Not a child."

He knew where this conversation would end. These conversations always ended there.

"Your job is to find abducted children?"

"Yes, ma'am."

"And do you?"

"Do I what?"

"*Find* abducted children?"

He gave her the same answer he always gave the parents, hoping they would not ask the logical follow-up question; most parents didn't because they couldn't bear to know the answer.

"Eventually."

From the mother's expression, he could tell her mind was working through his answer. Her mouth opened slightly and her eyes bore into him. She was a tough broad, tough enough to ask the follow-up question.

"Were any of the children found . . . alive?"

Looking at the mother, Devereaux found himself hoping mightily that her child had been abducted for money, as unlikely as that was. But he had hoped just as mightily one hundred twenty-seven times before for a happy ending to an abduction, each time in vain. One hundred twenty-seven abductions of children by strangers—ninety-three had ended with a dead child; the other thirty-four had never been found and were presumed dead—had taught him that holding out false hope only victimized the family a second time.

"No, ma'am."

The mother's entire body slumped. The tough-broad lawyer façade faded from her face; for a brief moment, Elizabeth Brice was just another desperate, tortured mother, no different from those dirt-poor mothers of victims living in trailer parks, because they now shared something in common—the peculiar pain of knowing your child was in the arms of a stranger. After a silence, she spoke, slowly and softly.

"This isn't going to end well, is it?"

"Mrs. Brice, Gracie was extremely low-risk for a stranger abduction—upper income, non-urban, intact family . . . kids like her just don't get abducted by strangers. And ransom is a long shot. It just doesn't happen in this country. But this wasn't a random grab. He targeted Gracie. He asked for her by name. Why? Of all the little girls at the park, why did he want her?"

Bobby Joe Fannin was breathing hard, fast as he was having to run to keep the dogs in sight. They got

11:13 A.M.

LAST FALL'S LEAVES and twigs crunched and snapped beneath their feet as they ran through the thick woods toward the sound of barking dogs, but Ben's thoughts were of another time and place when he had run through woods to a bad ending.

She's twelve or maybe thirteen. They dragged her into the nearby undergrowth. He heard her muffled cries and came running. "Get off her!" he yells as he drives his boot into the soldier's ribcage, knocking him off her. The other soldier grins and points down at the girl. "Go on, Lieutenant, get yourself some." He glances down at the terrified girl then back at the grinning soldier. He raises his rifle and puts the muzzle against the soldier's forehead; the grin drops off the soldier's face. The urge to pull the trigger is overwhelming. Instead, he pivots and slams the butt of the rifle into the soldier's brow, knocking him unconscious. The two soldiers would have been court-martialed had they not been killed that same afternoon, their legs blown off by VC land mines, their death cries rising above the Plain of Reeds as they bled to death on a hot day in the Mekong Delta.

Ahead, Elizabeth stumbled and fell again; a skirt and heels were not suited to the terrain. Ben stopped to help her up. The heel on one shoe had broken off; she tossed the other one aside, pushed his hands away, and ran on, her face distorted by fear.

The local police chief was now in the lead, followed by Agent Devereaux then John, Elizabeth, and Ben. Chief Ryan had started off walking, carefully pushing limbs aside for Elizabeth's safe passage, but when she had taken off running into the woods, hands flailing at the sharp branches striking at her face and arms and legs, he had realized that walking was not an option. They had overtaken Elizabeth on her first fall.

They were now deep into the woods. From the intermittent sound of cars a road was nearby. Thirty meters ahead, uniformed cops and FBI agents stood silently in a circle, their heads down, as if joined in prayer. Chief Ryan and Agent Devereaux arrived first then turned and stopped John. Ben saw his son slump and fall to his knees; Ben ran faster and his heart beat harder. Agent Devereaux tried to block Elizabeth's view—

"Mrs. Brice, you shouldn't . . ."

—but she shoved him aside and pushed her way inside the circle; she cried out, and her hands snapped up to her mouth like a reflex. Her legs gave way, and she dropped to the ground. Her clothes were ripped and covered in dirt and dried leaves, one shoe was on and one shoe was gone, and her arms and legs and face were striped with fresh scratch marks. Ben stood over her, staring down and breathing hard. He took the pain and buried it deep inside him with all the other pain, clamping his jaws so tight his teeth hurt. The woods were eerily quiet, as if even the creatures understood the violation only they had witnessed.

Elizabeth crawled forward and reached out to the blue soccer shorts and white soccer shoe lying on the ground.

6:11 P.M.

THE TEN-THOUSAND-square-foot residence at Six Magnolia Lane stood silent as night fell. Upstairs, Kate sat in her room saying the rosary through quiet tears. Elizabeth was sleeping in her bed, having succumbed to exhaustion after thirty-seven hours awake; she had managed to remove one leg of her torn pantyhose before falling asleep. Sam was watching *Pirates of the Caribbean: The Curse of the Black Pearl* in his room with Hilda; *Pirates* was rated PG-13, so he wasn't supposed to be watching it, but Hilda didn't know that—heck, she couldn't even read English.

In Gracie's bedroom, Agent Chip Stevens, an FBI computer specialist with the Bureau's Computer Analysis Response Team, aka the "geek squad," was quietly examining the victim's computer; he was reviewing her e-mail history, checking the browser cache to see the websites she had visited and webpages she had downloaded, and trying to determine if she had been contacted over the Internet by a computer-literate sexual predator. Perhaps she had wandered into the wrong chat room and had been lured into disclosing personal information that had led the perpetrator to her soccer game. The Internet had opened a whole new world to sex offenders.

God, he hated child abductions!

Stevens dwelled on the victim's last e-mail. Dated yesterday, from kahuna@BriceWare.com to gracie@ BriceHome.com. On the screen, Stevens saw:

ACK. Hm frm NYC. Nsnly dspr8 2 CU. Gd
wk @ skl? RdE 4 mg gm? Gm tm? Wldnt ms
4 E9$. Rly. Pstgm, srs fdg n qlty fctm,
grilf. CUL8R, alEG8R. X0XO, Kahuna.

He translated the message from Mr. Brice to the victim: *Hi, I'm here. Home from New York City. Insanely desperate to see you. Good week at school? Ready for the big game? What is game time? Wouldn't miss for a billion dollars. Really. Postgame, serious foodage and quality facetime, girlfriend. See you later, alligator. Love and kisses, Kahuna.*

Stevens smiled. The victim and her father obviously had a running joke because no one abbreviated every word of their e-mail like that any more. He found the victim's reply e-mail:

E9$? ROTFL. PANS 2 tl U abt skl. Am I
rdE 4 sccr gm? IMHO, I grok sccr! Gm @
5. BthrRB[]. MB vprmom wl sho . . .
Nt! UR my fv prpllrhd n ntr bg rm.
Ctch U ofln, d00d. OnO. Gracie. :-)

Tears welled up in Stevens' eyes as he read her reply: *A billion dollars? I'm rolling on the floor laughing. Pretty amazing new stuff to tell you about school. Am I ready for the soccer game? In my humble opinion, I am soccer! Game at five. Be there or be square. Maybe vapormom will show . . . Not! You are my favorite propellerhead in the entire big room. Catch you offline, dude. Over and out. Gracie.* Signed off with the online emoticon of a happy face.

The victim and her father must have had a great relationship. Stevens wiped his eyes with his sleeve. Problem was, he got way too emotional working child abductions. Sitting in the victim's room among her personal effects, he couldn't help but wonder about her life and the importance of each object in her life—like this, a framed portrait of a young soldier in full military dress, wearing a green beret, a chestful of medals, and what Stevens knew was the Congressional Medal of Honor around his neck. Who was this soldier and why did he rate a front-row spot on a ten-year-old girl's desk, where she would look at him first thing each morning and last thing each night? Questions like that haunted him for weeks after the child's body was found.

Other than being about five times as big with an adjoining bathroom that was like something out of a fancy hotel, the victim's room looked remarkably similar to his nine-year-old daughter's room: posters on the wall, the same Orlando Bloom one and a life-sized Mia Hamm, trophies, books, TV/DVD, telephone, boom box, electronic keyboard, soccer ball, and a closet stuffed with clothes. Gracie Ann Brice is a real live kid. Or was. She had sat where he sat, done her homework on this computer, watched TV in this room, talked to her friends on that phone, and slept in that bed, where her father now slept, curled up in the same dirty clothes and clutching the girl's teddy bear. He did not appear at all like the genius Stevens had read about in that *Fortune* magazine article. Stevens had felt envious that day: he was a GS-11 geek making $51,115 a year and Brice was a geek about to become a billionaire. But now that Brice's daughter had been abducted and murdered—he had never worked a stranger abduction where the child hadn't been murdered—Stevens was not so envious. He wouldn't trade his daughter for Bill Gates's money.

FBI procedure was to secure the victim's bedroom and seal it off from everyone, even the family. But he didn't have the heart to wake the father, not after what he had been through the last twenty-four hours. So Agent Stevens was working quietly.

The entire house was quiet.

Downstairs, eleven somber FBI agents manned the hotline phones in the command post, logging every lead, no matter how unimportant, and every reported sighting, no matter how inconceivable, into the computer. And waiting. Mostly waiting, as few calls were coming in.

Agent Jan Jorgenson sat at one computer, running database searches on the family per orders; she was still shaken from having witnessed the victim's mother slapping the father, defenseless in his despair. If this was a typical child abduction case, Jan had no desire to become a specialist like Agent Devereaux. She glanced across the room at him.

FBI Special Agent Eugene Devereaux felt tired, so godawful tired. He was holding his personal cell phone to his ear as the call rang through and thinking, *What the hell's wrong with people, a man could do that to a child?* And leaving her soccer shorts behind like a perverted calling card: See what I did? *Yeah, we see—die and go to hell, you sick bastard!* When Devereaux's seventeen-year-old daughter answered, he said, "Hey, baby, I just wanted to tell you I love you." She laughed and said, "What, are you dying or something?" Somewhere deep inside him, he was.

Coach Wally Fagan sat at another computer; he was scrolling down mug shots of the forty-two thousand registered sex offenders on the state's official sex offender website—pictures, names, addresses, and criminal histories—starting with those registered in the county, hoping to ID the blond man in the black cap and plaid shirt who had asked about Gracie after the game and wishing he had never pointed her out to him. The mother was right: he was a fucking idiot.

In the kitchen, Sylvia Milanevic, the Brice family maid, was preparing a fresh pot of coffee for the FBI agents. Sixty-three, an immigrant from Kosovo, she had lost two children in the war. She had concluded long ago that life was about enduring pain: you're born, you suffer, and you die. The small TV on the counter was on: "A child abducted by a stranger has a life expectancy of three hours. Gracie Ann Brice has been missing for twenty-four hours now . . ." Sylvia looked out the window over the sink at the lonely figure by the pool.

Ben was sitting in a patio chair. His face was wet with tears and the pain was eating at his insides like a cancer. He closed his eyes and thought back to 1964 when he was eighteen and boarding the train to West Point. His father had shaken his hand and said, "Do your country proud, son." His mother had hugged him tightly and whispered in his ear, "God has a plan for Ben Brice." Ben opened his eyes now and turned them to the heavens above.

"Do you still have a plan, God?"

DAY THREE

7:08 A.M.

THE MORNING SUN filtered through the shutters of the spacious master suite on the second floor of Six Magnolia Lane. Elizabeth stirred under a thick down comforter in the tall king-sized four-poster bed that was accessible only by wooden steps. A faint smile crossed her lips.

Not guilty on all counts.

She rolled over and groaned. Her body was sore. Her head was groggy, like she had a hangover, but she didn't remember having anything to drink last night. It was probably just the trial; a long trial always left her physically and mentally exhausted, especially after coming down from the adrenaline high of victory.

Twelve good citizens with the mental range of a windshield wiper.

Was today Saturday? Or Sunday? Must be Sunday. John and Kate probably had the children at church. She did not attend church; religion and the law were the opiates of the masses in the twenty-first century, holding the peasants at bay with their firm faith in God and justice. Elizabeth Brice knew better. Her faith in the justice of the law had ended five years out of law school, late for most lawyers, and she had not prayed to God since . . .

Yesterday?

Did she pray yesterday?

Elizabeth tried to shake her head clear of the fog. She took a deep breath and realized she was hungry. Very hungry. When had she last eaten? She couldn't remember. A big breakfast on Sunday morning while the others were at church would be nice, a quiet time to drink coffee, read the paper, and relive her courtroom victory—there might even be an article about the stunning *Shay* verdict! Thus inspired, she stretched, threw off the comforter, and rolled out of bed.

She hit the wood floor hard.

What the hell? Her legs were tangled in her pantyhose . . . The hose was ripped and shredded . . . She pulled dried brown leaves from one leg of the torn hose . . . Why was one leg off? . . . Why was she sleeping in her pantyhose? . . . Why were her legs dirty and streaked with fresh scratch marks? . . . And her arms . . . And her hands . . . Nails broken . . . Clothes dirty and torn . . . Why was she sleeping in her clothes? . . . She touched her face . . . Why had she gone to bed without cleaning her face of makeup? . . . *What the hell was going on?*

A nauseous tide washed over her. She crawled on her hands and knees to the front windows, dragging one leg of her pantyhose behind her like a bridal veil, knelt up, and peeked through the shutters. Down below, out front of her house, were police cars, TV trucks, cameras, and people. The media circus. She slumped against the wall. She remembered now.

Grace was gone.

Downstairs, Ben entered the kitchen from outside. Kate and Sylvia were busy cooking enough breakfast for a battalion, and the smell of pancakes, sausage, eggs, and biscuits was luring a steady stream of cops and FBI agents to the kitchen.

Ben had woken at dawn after only a few hours of fitful sleep. He had heard the back door, Kate leaving for early Mass to do what Irish Catholic women have done for centuries in the face of famine, poverty, pestilence, war, and evil: pray. He had showered and dressed, then he had gone outside and watched the sun rise over the trees, the start of another day without Gracie—and the first day knowing that money would not save her.

Now Ben was trying to pour a cup of coffee, but he was fighting the morning shakes. Kate took the coffee pot from him and poured then walked the cup and saucer over to the breakfast table without a word. Ben sat down, held the cup with both hands, and sipped the coffee. Five years since she had made his morning coffee, but Kate remembered the routine; there was enough caffeine in this coffee to defeat the mother of all hangovers. But Ben Brice had not surrendered to the bottle last night.

Sam sat across the table. He was still wearing the Boston Red Sox uniform, but he now had a blue scarf wrapped around his head. He was alternating between taking syrupy bites of his pancakes and reciting lines as if acting out roles in a play:

"Wait! You have to take me to shore. According to the Code of the Order of the Brethren—"

Sam turned slightly as if facing another character; his voice changed.

"First, your return to shore was not part of our negotiations nor our agreement. So I must do nothing. And secondly, you must be a pirate for the pirates' code to apply and you're not. And thirdly, the code is more what you'd call guidelines than actual rules. Welcome aboard the *Black Pearl*, Miss Turner."

Ben looked at Kate by the stove. She said, "Movie dialogue. He got John's memory. He can recite entire movies verbatim."

Sam continued: "So that's it then. That's the secret grand adventure of the infamous Jack Sparrow. You spent three days lying on a beach drinking rum!"

Sam gestured as if his knife and fork were bottles.

"Welcome to the Caribbean, luv."

Kate said, "Sam, is that from a PG-13 movie?"

Sam froze, his mouth full, his arms still outstretched, and his eyes suddenly wide like he'd been caught red-handed. His eyes darted to Ben. He decided to save his grandson again.

"The Red Sox are your team?"

Kate shook her head and turned back to the stove; Sam turned back to his pancakes and said, "After the IPO."

"What?"

"Dad's gonna buy the Red Sox for me, after he's a billionaire."

"Really?"

"Yep." Sam took a huge bite of pancakes—his cheek was now bulging like a baseball player's with a wad of chewing tobacco—and said, "So how much money does the cretin want?"

"Who?"

"The man that took Gracie."

Ben glanced over at Kate. "Oh. He hasn't said yet."

Sam sighed. "Well, I wish he'd shit or get off the pot."

"Sam!" Kate said.

Sam shrugged. "Yeah, then Dad can write a check and Gracie can come home."

7:23 A.M.

"**O**UR TOWN's a damn safe place to call home!"

Across town, Police Chief Paul Ryan was standing in the mayor's office, looking at the mayor's broad back, and listening to the mayor's whiny voice as His Honor pleaded with a Dallas newspaper reporter not to write a negative story about Post Oak, Texas. But as if his mind was repeatedly pressing the ALT CH button on the remote control, his thoughts kept switching back and forth between dark images of a little girl he didn't know lying dead somewhere and the bald back of the mayor's head, wondering how much hair spray it took to keep his comb-over in place. Paul Ryan never trusted men who combed over.

The mayor never came in on a Sunday and never early on any day of the week. But this Sunday, Ryan had arrived at seven and been immediately summoned to the mayor's office. He knew the mayor would not be pleased, what with the town just getting over the heroin OD at the high school, and now this. Bad for business, heroin in the high school and kidnappings at the park. And the mayor was all about business.

Theirs was a tenuous relationship at best. Ryan was a holdover from the old days, back before the Dallas developers had discovered their sleepy little town forty miles north of the city and had bought up the open land he used to hunt as a kid and carved it up into exclusive gated communities promising peace and prosperity, bait to Boomers fleeing the ills of urban life. And the Boomers had come, arriving in their Beemers and Lexuses and Hummers like fire ants in the backyard—one day they're not even here, the next day they've taken over the goddamn place. Ten years ago this had been a farming community with a land bank and a feed store; today it had a Victoria's Secret and a Starbucks.

Paul Ryan hated the Boomers.

But the mayor had welcomed them with open arms. Because the mayor owned the land, or damn near most of it, inherited from his daddy or acquired at foreclosure for pennies on the dollar during the drought years when the farmers couldn't keep up their payments to the bank, which the mayor and his daddy before him owned. Paul Ryan's father had committed suicide less than a year after the mayor's father foreclosed the farm.

Paul sighed. The mayor was a short, pudgy bastard who couldn't even make the high school football team that Paul Ryan had starred on. But now, just like the mayor's daddy had held the note on the Ryan family farm, the mayor held the note on Paul Ryan's career, a career he could foreclose at any time: the town charter expressly stated that the police chief served at the pleasure of the mayor. And the mayor was not pleased. He hung up the phone and glared at Ryan.

"Paul, why the hell did you bring in the FBI?"

"To find the girl! The Feds got more experience and a helluva lot more resources than we got."

"Yeah, but they don't got jurisdiction!"

"FBI helps local police in all child abductions. They bring a lot to the table, Mayor."

"They bring the media to my town!" The mayor pointed a fat finger at Ryan. "Paul, you either find that girl alive or you find her dead, but I want her found, I want someone arrested, I want this deal closed in forty-eight hours or you'll be a goddamn security guard at the Wal-Mart!"

7:31 A.M.

FBI Special Agent Eugene Devereaux dodged the little Brice boy as he entered the kitchen for a cup of coffee. He knew the caffeine would only inflame his prostate, but a little girl was missing and he needed a shot of caffeine to get sharp. He had gone to the motel at midnight and just returned with an empty gut. He would normally lose ten pounds over the course of an abduction investigation. Hell of a way to diet.

Devereaux was about to walk out when the grandmother shoved a plate of food at him. The smell reminded him of his own grandmother's breakfasts back on the farm in Louisiana. He figured it was better to eat her food than donuts all day. So he sat across the breakfast table from the grandfather; they acknowledged each other with grim nods. The grandfather's hands exhibited the morning tremors of an alcoholic. After Devereaux had eaten half his stack of pancakes in silence, the grandfather said, "Why would he leave her shorts in the woods?"

Devereaux was trying to think of an appropriate answer other than *because he's a sick bastard* when the father rushed through the kitchen looking like he had just rolled out of bed; his black glasses were riding low and lopsided on his face, one side of his curly hair was pressed flat, the

96

other side was standing on end, and he was still wearing the same dirty clothes. He exited through the back door without a word. Minutes later, he returned and walked directly over to Devereaux; he held out a camcorder like the one Devereaux had given the wife for Christmas.

"I forgot," he said.

"Forgot what, Mr. Brice?"

"I taped Gracie's game."

She was Michael Jordan in soccer shorts.

The other girls seemed like typical ten-year-olds, awkward, plodding, stumbling at times, while Gracie seemed . . . well, graceful, elegant even, her gait smooth and rhythmic, gliding down the field in her white shoes, then a sudden burst of speed propelling her past the defenders, all the while making the white ball seem like a puppet on a string, dancing in front of her, now to her side, then abruptly racing ahead on her unspoken command. And she owned her opponents equally, moving them about like pawns on a chessboard, a slight shoulder fake sending the defender charging one way only to watch helplessly as Gracie spun off in the opposite direction, where the ball was somehow waiting. Natural athletes always made it look easy. Gracie Ann Brice was a natural athlete.

Watching the victim running up and down the field on the videotape—her smile, her spirit, her soccer skills—FBI Special Agent Eugene Devereaux wanted to find this girl alive so much it hurt. The victim was not that photograph distributed to the media; she was a real live little girl who only two days before had not a care in the world, smiling and laughing and playing soccer. And play she could. As his daughter would say, Gracie's got game.

She had captivated her audience.

Four FBI agents, the father, and the grandparents stood facing the nine-foot-wide projector screen built into the wall of the media room, hypnotized by the victim's image and all too aware that they were likely watching the last moments of her life. The tape was playing with remarkable clarity—Agent Stevens, who was manning the camcorder connected to the TV, had said something about it being recorded in "high def"—and had captured the sights and sounds of the game: the girls playing, a referee's whistle, background noises, then suddenly a loud cheer and "Run, Gracie, run!" and the father's voice: "Lou, I'm hard core about thirty bucks a share!"

The camera abruptly swung from the field to the crowded parking lot in the distance and just as abruptly back to the field, creating a stream of blurred images. The victim appeared in frame again, up close, making a face at the camera as she ran past. Devereaux couldn't help but smile. She then booted the ball across the field—"Go, Tornadoes!"—and the camera angle dropped precipitously, as if the operator had lost all strength in his arm; a pair of black penny loafers over white socks filled the screen. Devereaux glanced over at the father; he was still wearing the same shoes and socks. He had filmed his own feet. On the tape now, the father's voice again: "Lou, if I had e-mail capacity at this soccer field, I'd beam Harvey a freaking shitogram!"

Back on the screen, another violent camera spasm and a close-up of a big white belly escaping from under a gold jersey and a booming voice that Devereaux recognized as the coach's—"Gracie, stop her!" Abruptly back to the field: Gracie was running full speed then sliding, feet first, and kicking the ball away from an opponent trying to score, an incredible play . . . now the blue sky, then suddenly Gracie again, kicking the ball in front of her, racing down the field past her opponents—"Go, Gracie! Score, Gracie!"—to the goal, about to score, pulling her leg back, and . . . now the father's shoes again. The room audibly deflated; Agent Jorgenson had damn near kicked Devereaux trying to score the goal for Gracie. On the tape, loud cheers erupted in the background . . . now the setting sun . . . and parents standing in the bleachers . . . and back on the soccer game . . . and the tape suddenly went silent.

"Did we lose audio?" Devereaux said to Agent Stevens.

"Don't think so," Stevens said, checking the connection.

"Increase the volume, run the tape back."

Stevens did as Devereaux instructed. The tape replayed the same scene of the girls huddled in the middle of the field. There was a muffled sound in the background.

"Again. Louder."

The same scene again. The same sound in the background.

"What was that? *Pant deck?* Again."

The sound came through clearer this time, a male voice yelling, "Panty check."

"The hell's a panty check?" Devereaux said to the room.

"He was taunting her."

All heads turned to the voice behind them: the mother stood in the doorway. She looked like hell. She hadn't changed her clothes; her hair was wild and untouched; her blouse was hanging out; her skirt was twisted; she was barefooted. She said, "He was saying she's really a boy, because she's so good." The mother turned her glare on the father. "You didn't do anything, John? You didn't go across the field and punch that son of a bitch in the mouth? That's what I would've done."

The father: "I . . . I didn't hear him."

"Because you were working the numbers with Lou," the mother said.

On the video, Gracie stood motionless in the middle of the field; her head was down and the other girls were gathered around her.

"You let a man say that to Grace, you let another man take her from me, because you were making goddamn sure you get your billion dollars. Grace is gone because you were on the fucking phone!"

The father's voice on the tape: "Lou, a billion dollars upgrades this geek to manly out there in the real world!"

The mother was looking at the father, but not like she was going to smack him again; instead, with a look of profound disdain.

"A billion dollars won't make you a man, John Brice. And it won't bring Grace back."

And she was gone.

The room was filled with awkward silence until the father's voice came over the tape: "Lou, only way a geek gets respect in this world is to be a rich geek. Doesn't matter how smart you are, without money you're still just a freaking geek."

The father's head was hanging so low Devereaux thought it might just disconnect from his neck and roll down his body to the floor. The mother's words had hurt him more than her hand had yesterday. He sighed. It was not the first time Special Agent Eugene Devereaux had witnessed a marriage destroyed by an abduction; it would not be the last. But he never passed judgment on parents of abducted children, most of whom fit the legal definition of temporary insanity by this stage of an abduction. They often blamed each other. Working through the parents' emotions was part of the job; the FBI abduction protocol called it "family management." But few families managed.

The grandmother went to the father and stood next to him; she put an arm around him and patted his back.

Devereaux took a deep breath to regain focus. He could not concern himself with the parents' marriage. His only concern was the girl on the videotape. He was again staring at the screen, at jerky images of the ground, the sky, the ground, the sky, the parking lot, the parents, the spectators—*What the hell was the father doing with the goddamn camera?*—when he spotted something.

"Stop! Run it back!"

Stevens reversed the tape.

"There—stop!"

The picture was frozen on the people in and around the bleachers. Devereaux stepped to the screen and pointed to the image of a white male with blond hair and wearing a black cap and a plaid shirt. The view was from the rear but Devereaux knew.

"That's our man."

The man was mostly blocked out by a bigger man standing next to him: white male, tall, stocky, flattop, with a large dark spot on his left arm partially visible under the sleeve of his black tee shirt. A tattoo.

To the father: "You know these people?"

The father shook his head. "No."

To Stevens on the camcorder: "Blow this frame up." Devereaux touched the screen at the big man's arm. "And that tattoo."

To Agent Floyd: "Get the coach in here."

The tape ran again: a shot of the parking lot, more deal talk from the father, more game action, Gracie hitting the ground hard—"Hey, she tripped Gracie!" Agent Jorgenson blurted out—back on the tape, the victim jumping up and running all out again, loud cheers, the camera jumping around again, the father's feet, other feet, now a shot of another camcorder—"Yea, Tornadoes!"— more shots of the sky, the grass, the bleachers, a pair of white soccer shoes, one with the laces untied—

"I didn't tie her shoe," the father said like he was confessing to a crime.

—and the victim appeared close up again. Her flushed face glistened with perspiration; her hand reached up to the camera.

"Is she bleeding?" Devereaux asked.

Stevens ran the tape back.

"She is bleeding, from her elbow."

The father's eyes dropped down to his arm; he grabbed his sleeve and pulled it around to reveal the underside. The light blue material was stained a dark brown in several spots. He looked up at Devereaux.

"This is Gracie's blood," he said.

Was Grace dead?

From that moment in the park Friday night when the coach said her brother had asked for Grace—when the thought *Grace was kidnapped* first took shape—Elizabeth had prayed that it was about ransom—*You don't ransom a dead girl,* she had heard an FBI agent say—and she had waged war with her mind. Her mind wanted desperately to force her into a dark world, to reveal to her all the possibilities, the maybes, the what ifs, to torture her with vile, horrible, gruesome images of her daughter being subjected to the sick desires of a sexual predator; but she had fought it off, beaten it back, blocked it out, refused to watch . . . until now.

Grace wasn't taken for money.

Sitting on the marble floor of the steam shower, she had unconditionally surrendered to her mind's dark side and allowed it to torture her with those images, to display them as graphically as if she were an eyewitness. And Elizabeth Brice wondered, as she had wondered once before: if for all intents and purposes you are already dead, is suicide still a mortal sin?

"Why, God?"

Steam inundated the shower. Elizabeth's legs were curled around the drain; her tears mixed with the hot water. She was alone in her despair and wondering if she could slit her wrists with the safety razor she was holding. Once before evil had entered her life and caused her to entertain suicide, to seriously debate the various ways by which to end her life like she was reading a menu at a restaurant. Once before she had stood on the precipice of death and peered over into the abyss, only to be saved by a child. This child. Grace had saved her life. Now, ten years later, evil had come back for Grace.

"Why did you let evil take her, too?"

She had lived only because of Grace. Without Grace, why live? She imagined her blood flowing out of her veins and swirling down into the drain until all the life had emptied from her. She put the razor to her wrist and pressed the blade into her skin and was about to slide it across her veins and spill her blood when a sudden surge of rage swelled her muscles and brain cells like a narcotic,

NOON

TWO HUNDRED CHILDREN a year die at the hands of sexual predators in the United States. Those few cases always capture the public's undivided attention. FBI Special Agent Eugene Devereaux had investigated one hundred twenty-seven such cases. Consequently, he was accustomed to the media events child abductions inevitably became.

But this case was different. Maybe it was because Gracie was a rich white blonde girl who lived in a mansion with murals on the ceiling; maybe it was because her father's face was on the cover of *Fortune* magazine; or maybe it was just a slow news cycle. But this case was fast moving beyond anything he had previously experienced. There was an energy in the air, building with each passing hour without Gracie's recovery, along with the number of people on the front lawn of the Brice mansion, where Devereaux now stood on this sunny Sunday afternoon. He was flanked by the local mayor and police chief and facing microphones clumped together on a stand, TV cameras, reporters, and beyond them, in the street, the residents of Briarwyck Farms. They had posted missing-child fliers with Gracie's image on every car, printed Gracie tee shirts, tied pink ribbons to car antennae, mailboxes, and trees, and pinned a Gracie button on every shirt and lapel.

There was a time when media briefings made Devereaux feel important, a black agent born in the Louisiana backwoods directing a major FBI case; now these briefings just made him tired. He stepped forward.

"I'm FBI Special Agent Eugene Devereaux. The FBI is involved in this case at the request of Chief Ryan. Unless the victim is transported across state lines, jurisdiction is solely local. But we have offered our resources to assist Chief Ryan and his investigation."

Devereaux always maintained the pretense that the locals were in charge of the case. They were legally, but not actually. Locals like Chief Ryan understood that they didn't stand a snowball's chance in hell of finding an abducted child without the FBI—and they didn't mind sharing the failure with the Feds when the child's body was found.

"The status of our investigation of the abduction of Gracie Ann Brice is as follows: Gracie has been missing for forty-two hours. She was taken from Briarwyck Farms Park here in Post Oak at approximately 6:00 P.M. Friday by a white male, twenty to thirty years old, six foot, two hundred pounds, blond hair, wearing a black cap and a plaid shirt. An artist's sketch of the suspect has been distributed to the media. We are pursuing two parallel investigative tracks: the first is to find Gracie, and that is our primary consideration; the second is to identify and locate possible suspects, starting with registered sex offenders. We urge any citizen who may have seen Gracie or the suspect or who has any information to please contact our hot-line number on the missing child fliers. We need your help. Questions?"

Devereaux pointed to the first reporter.

"Agent Devereaux, do you suspect family involvement?"

"No."

"Have they taken polygraphs?"

"Not yet."

The next reporter: "Can you confirm that Gracie's shorts were found at the park?"

"Blue soccer shorts and a single white soccer shoe were found. We believe them to be Gracie's."

And the next, not waiting to be acknowledged: "Do you have any leads?"

"We're taking calls, reviewing videotapes of the soccer games Friday night, developing a profile of the abductor—"

From the crowd: "Forty-two hours and all you've got is a blond man in a black cap?"

Devereaux sighed and felt tired. "Yes."

Shouted from the back: "Was Gracie sexually assaulted?"

That was the question they always asked. Why? Why did they want to know whether a little ten-year-old girl was raped? *What the hell do they think a sexual predator did with her, take her to dinner and a goddamn movie?* They know damn well what he did to her, but they wanted him to say it, to provide the fear factor sound bite for the evening news teaser—fear causes more viewers to tune in. But he never played their game. Even if he knew, which he didn't, at least it wasn't confirmed, FBI Special Agent Eugene Devereaux would never tell. Not until the body was located. Until he knew for sure the child was dead.

Gracie Ann Brice deserved that much.

*

A mile away, Ben was standing in the middle of soccer field no. 2, a solitary figure in the vast, vacant park. He had come out before the FBI reopened the park for that night's candlelight vigil to retrace Gracie's last known movements Friday afternoon; he had to be where she had been. He had to know.

If not for ransom, why would someone take Gracie? For sex? Ben Brice had seen the evil in man, so that was a possibility. Perhaps even a probability. But not a certainty, as the FBI seemed to have concluded. Sexual predators work alone, Agent Devereaux had said. But the blond man in a black cap hadn't been alone; two men had been here at her game.

Ben first had to learn how Gracie had been taken. He now walked toward the low bleachers. According to John, Gracie's game had ended and she had come to him about here. Ben stopped. The other parents had been in the bleachers and the two men just behind. John had spoken with Gracie, then she and the other girls had gone to the concession stand. John had watched them all the way to the building.

Ben walked that way.

Children abducted by strangers have a life expectancy of three hours, that TV report had said. When Gracie had walked this way Friday night, not forty-eight hours ago, had she only three hours of life left? Something inside Ben said no. Maybe it was the strange way their lives were bonded together: he knew that if Gracie were dead he surely would be as well. Maybe he just couldn't bring himself to accept the idea that he would never see her again. Or maybe, just maybe, she was still alive.

When he was almost at the concession stand, Ben stopped and turned back, just as Gracie had when she had waved to John: an innocent little girl waving to her father, unaware she was walking into an ambush. Ben checked the compass on his watch to get his bearings. He was now facing due south toward the distant soccer and softball fields and the homes that bordered the park beyond the tall brick wall. To the east were tennis courts and the wall bordering that side of the park. To the west was the parking lot a good hundred meters away, too far to drag an abducted child through a crowd of people. The brick walls bordered the south and east sides of the park and the parking lot the west; none were likely escape routes for the abductor. That left only the northern route.

Through the woods.

Ben walked around to the rear of the concession stand. The backside of the building was a solid brick façade with a single service door and no windows. A small clearing separated the building from the woods. Ben got down on his hands and knees and examined the ground. He closed his eyes and ran his fingers through the blades of grass like a blind man reading Braille. And he knew.

The abductor had grabbed her right here.

But how had he gotten her back here alone? And how had he kept her quiet?

Ben stood and walked into the woods. Yesterday, he had been running and his mind had been clouded with fear and thoughts from the past, so he had not focused on his surroundings. Now he stepped slowly; his eyes searched the ground, the underbrush, and the trees for any sign of Gracie. His skills came back to him without conscious recall.

Less than ten meters into the woods, a shiny object highlighted by the sunlight through the canopy caught

Ben's eye. He squatted, moved several leaves, and picked up the object between his thumb and forefinger. He placed it in the palm of his left hand: a silver star attached to a broken silver chain. He recalled the day he had taken Gracie to the silversmith shop in Taos to have this star put on this chain. The proprietor had examined the star and said, "This here's the real thing." Gracie had said she would wear it always.

Ben stood, slipped the star and chain into his shirt pocket, and snapped the flap button. He continued deeper into the woods. He soon arrived at the location where her shorts and shoe had been found; yellow crime-scene tape was wrapped around the trees guarding the little clearing.

The abductor had grabbed Gracie behind the concession stand and taken her through the woods to this position. He had stopped here to . . . Ben fought back his emotions and focused. The abductor had left her shorts and shoe here and had . . . what? Taken her to his vehicle?

Ben walked through the woods to the nearby road, climbed the low embankment, and stood on the rock shoulder. The road was old, and the asphalt surface was potholed; there were only two narrow lanes, barely wide enough for two cars to pass. It was not a major traffic route.

Did the abductor leave his vehicle here while he went to Gracie's game? Or did the other man on the tape drive the vehicle to this position while the abductor grabbed Gracie and carried her through the woods? Were they working together?

Ben started to climb down, but he stopped; the shoulder was standing-room only, too narrow to park a vehicle without blocking the road. He knelt and examined the shoulder where a car might have pulled over and waited for the abductor to arrive with Gracie. He noticed a rock that glistened. He touched his finger to the shiny rock; it was wet. He put his finger to his nose and sniffed.

Oil.

Little Johnny Brice can taste his own blood that is flowing from his nose and mouth. He is curled up in a fetal position on the ground; his arms are wrapped around his head; he is crying. This is the worst beating yet, and it isn't over. Luther Ray is sitting astride him, hitting and taunting, taunting and hitting; his fists feel like iron hammers each time they impact John's body. Little Johnny Brice is praying to God to let him die so the pain will stop.

John opened his eyes. The carpet beneath his face was wet. He was curled up in a fetal position on the floor of his walk-in closet. He had given his shirt to the FBI then come upstairs to clean up. He had showered and come into his closet to dress. But the images of Gracie and the abductor had returned, and he had started crying again. He could not stop thinking of her pain. *Please, God, let her pain stop.*

Kate found John sitting alone in his closet, just as she had found him sitting alone in his room so many times as a boy. Back then, he'd been hurt by the bullies; today, he'd been hurt by his wife. It had been bad back then; it was worse today.

She sat down on the floor next to him. She put her arm around him, and he laid his head in her lap, just as he had so many times. She stroked his hair as she had back then, and she said the same words.

"John, try to have faith. You've got to trust that there's a reason for this, that there's a reason for everything that happens to us in life, even the bad things. God has—"

John's head lifted, and he sat up abruptly. "No, Mom, you're wrong! You were wrong back then and you're wrong now! There was no reason for my getting beat up by those bullies, and there's no reason for Gracie getting kidnapped by some sick pervert. There's no reason, no plan, no purpose, no grand scheme to all this—it wasn't meant to be! It's just random acts of violence. Mean people doing bad things. You go to Mass and you believe all that shit Father Randy says—and that's all it is, Mom. Shit!"

John stood and walked out. Kate Brice covered her face and cried because she could not help her son now, just as she could not help him back then.

1:07 P.M.

FBI Special Agent Eugene Devereaux was back in the command post examining the blow-ups of the two men from the videotape and the big man's tattoo. The large room was quiet—which was exactly wrong. Forty-three hours after an abduction, the phones should be ringing off the hook with hot tips. But the phones were silent.

Where the hell were the calls?

Devereaux removed his reading glasses, closed his eyes, and rubbed his face. When he opened his eyes, Agent Jorgenson was walking his way. She had a muscular build and short brown hair. She was wearing a blue nylon FBI jacket, jeans, and sneakers and carrying brown folders under her arm. He liked Jorgenson. She reminded him of his daughter; she had the same athletic bounce in her step and the same intellectual curiosity. She wanted to learn. She was still in her one-year probationary appointment, but she had already grasped an understanding of the job; it wasn't about the glory of solving a high-profile case or the ego of apprehending a Most Wanted or Washington's public relations obsession. It was about the victim. The job was always and only about the victim.

"Why's it so dead?" Agent Jorgenson said when she arrived; she plopped down in a chair. "Is this normal?"

"No."

"It's like she just disappeared."

"A ten-year-old girl doesn't just disappear."

"What are her chances—that she's still alive?"

"Not good. Statistically, no chance at all."

"Damn."

"Just do your job, Agent Jorgenson. Focus on the evidence."

She nodded. "Yes, sir. You're good in front of cameras."

"Too much experience. So, Jorgenson, what do they grow up there in . . . where in Minnesota are you from?"

"Owatonna. Corn, mostly. For the ethanol."

"Farmer's daughter?"

"Yes, sir."

"My grandfather was a farmer. Cotton. Used to help him pick it when I was a kid. It was an uncomplicated life."

"I wanted excitement."

"Well, Agent, you've found it." He pointed at her brown folders. "What do you have for me?"

"We took blood samples from the family to compare to the blood on the father's shirt. DNA tests are underway."

"Good. What else?"

"Background reports on the family."

"Proceed."

Devereaux did not expect the family backgrounds to reveal anything of importance, but he had learned the hard way never to overlook the routine aspects of the investigation.

"Alrighty," she said, opening the first brown folder. "The father, he's some kind of genius—Ph.D. from MIT in algorithms, whatever that is, one-ninety IQ . . . I didn't know they went that high."

"They don't," Devereaux said. "At least not in the Bureau."

She gave him a little smile then continued. "He founded BriceWare, going public this week, you know all that. He and the mother married ten years ago. He was at MIT, she was at Justice in D.C., Assistant U.S. Attorney. Five years."

"Really?"

"Yes, sir. Maiden name was Austin. Grew up in New York. Her father was murdered when she was only ten."

"Same age as Gracie."

"First in her class at Harvard Law, a rising star at Justice. Then she up and quit, married Brice, moved to Dallas."

"No accounting for love."

"They're an odd couple, aren't they? And the way she slapped him yesterday, and cut him down this morning . . ." Jorgenson shook her head. "And how she talks to the local cops, and to us, so angry and ordering everyone around like we all work for her."

"Her child's been abducted, Agent. Cut her some slack."

"You were very, uh, diplomatic with her."

He nodded. "Two rules, Agent Jorgenson, to keep in mind in abductions. Rule number one: this isn't actually our case. We've got no jurisdiction, not legally anyway. The locals generally defer to us, but technically we're invited guests. So act like a guest. Rule number two: odds are the child's already dead by the time we arrive on scene, so if the mother wants to cuss you out, tell you you're the dumbest cop on the face of the earth, you say, 'Thank you, ma'am.' You respect the fact that she's lost her child . . . and that she's probably halfway to nuts by the time you meet her. You give the parents free rein with their emotions. They need it more than you need to prove you're a tough FBI agent in control of the case. Getting into a pissing contest with the parents won't put you one step closer to finding the victim or apprehending the abductor. And that's your job, Agent Jorgenson. Don't let your ego get in the way of doing your job."

"Yes, sir." She frowned. "But you're still going to make her take a polygraph?"

"Absolutely. If FBI resources are committed to a case, we do it by the book—and the book says to polygraph the parents. But I ask. I don't order. Works just as well." He gestured at Jorgenson's file. "Find out who she worked for at Justice. I know some people over there."

"I did. Her immediate supervisor was named James Kelly."

"Jimmy?"

"You knew him?"

"Yeah, we came up through the Academy together. He went to law school at night then moved over to Justice. He was out in L.A. last I heard . . . What do you mean, *knew* him?"

"He's dead. Hit and run, three years ago."

"Damn. He was a good guy." Devereaux sighed. "The good die young. What else you got?"

Jorgenson opened another brown folder. "The grand-father, he's a retired Army colonel—West Point, Vietnam. Apparently he was some kind of war hero."

"No kidding?" Devereaux waited for her to continue. She didn't. "And . . .?"

She shrugged. "And nothing, sir. He's classified."

Devereaux put on his reading glasses and motioned for the folder. She held it out to him; he took it and flipped open the brown folder labeled BRICE, BEN, and scanned the text.

"Full colonel. Green Beret. Seven tours in Vietnam. Six Silver Stars, four Bronze Stars, eight Purple Hearts, two Soldier's Medals, Distinguished Service Cross, Legion of Merit, the Medal of Honor. Yeah, I'd say he was some kind of hero."

"Why's he classified?"

"Green Beret; he was probably in Cambodia and Laos when Johnson and Nixon were swearing on TV we weren't there."

"The presidents lied about the war?"

He chuckled. "How old are you, Jorgenson?"

"Twenty-six."

He shook his head. "I can't even remember twenty-six. Yeah, Jorgenson, presidents lied about the war, the generals, too. I was ROTC, signed up for the tuition plan. Got a hell of an education in Nam. I went over there just hoping to survive my tour. Guys like Brice, they went over there to free the oppressed, just like the Green Beret motto says. They believed it. All they got for their efforts was spit on when they came home." Devereaux removed his reading glasses and scratched his chin with the earpiece. "Ben Brice . . . that name sticks in my head for some reason. Get what you can from the Army and run a database search on all public records on him."

"You think there might be some connection with Gracie's abduction?"

"You never know what's connected." Jorgenson stood to leave. "I want you at the vigil tonight. Our boy might show."

"Yes, sir. Oh, the coach is here to look at the blow-ups."

"Bring him in, don't call me sir, and have someone find Colonel Brice."

He carries Gracie through the woods to this location. He's in a hurry, worried someone will discover she's missing and come looking, or perhaps has and is. His accomplice is waiting twenty meters away in a vehicle leaking oil. But he stops, removes her clothes, and rapes her right here? With so many people in the park, possibly searchers already in the woods? With Gracie kicking and screaming and putting up one hell of a fight? She's a strong girl and afraid of no one—the only way she wouldn't have fought is if she were unconscious or dead. Did he rape an unconscious or dead victim? Did he kill her here?

No. Gracie Ann Brice did not die here. Ben Brice had been in the killing fields, knee deep in death; death would forever be a part of him—he had seen death, he had heard death, he could touch, taste, smell, and feel death. But not here.

Gracie had left here alive.

But why did the abductor leave her shorts behind? Ben closed his eyes and remembered working in the shop with her. She had been carving her name into her rocking chair when she had paused and said, "Ben, why do you always know when I'm in trouble, when I need you?"

"I don't know, doll. There's something in our lives that binds us together. I don't know what and I don't know why, but there is a reason."

God had bonded them together. Ben Brice knew that as well as he knew how to build a rocking chair or kill a man. And he knew that if she came to him, their bond was unbroken. And she was still alive.

Gracie, show me the way. I will come for you.

"Colonel Brice!"

Ben opened his eyes. He was sitting cross-legged inside the crime-scene tape where Gracie's shorts and shoe had been found. A young FBI agent was jogging through the woods toward him. He arrived out of breath and said, "Colonel Brice, Agent Devereaux needs you back at the command post!"

2:12 P.M.

JAN JORGENSON had been born five years after the Vietnam War ended. Twenty-four years later, she had graduated from the University of Minnesota with a B.S. in Education—the only degree her parents would pay for—and a Masters in Criminal Psychology. She had told her parents that school boards across the country considered crim psych the most relevant degree for a teaching career in America's public schools. They had bought it. Immediately upon graduation, she had applied with the Bureau. Her parents wanted her to be a teacher; she wanted to be Clarice Starling.

So Jan Jorgenson had left the family farm outside Owatonna, Minnesota, driven to Quantico, Virginia, and entered the FBI Academy. She wanted to be a profiler, interviewing and compiling detailed psychological traits of imprisoned serial killers, psychopaths, and sexual predators, and constructing scientific profiles of suspects in pending investigations. But upon graduation from the Academy, she had been assigned to the Dallas field office, where for the last eleven months she had tracked down and interviewed young Arab men who fit the Islamic terrorist profile.

In fact, this was as close as she had ever come to anyone

in the Behavioral Analysis Unit, sitting next to the parents and across the Brice kitchen table from two real live FBI profilers, Agents Baxter and Brumley. They looked like partners in an accounting firm.

"Strangers abduct children for sex."

Agent Brumley had just opened this meeting with the family. He could have worked up to that, Jan thought. The mother obviously thought the same; her eyes were now drilling holes in Brumley's bald head. Oblivious, he forged ahead.

"This perpetrator has a long history of sex offenses, I guarantee it."

The victim's father looked like he was going to throw up; he abruptly stood and almost ran out of the kitchen just as Colonel Brice walked in and leaned against the wall.

"We've constructed a profile," Agent Baxter said, "a personality print, if you will, like a fingerprint." He passed out copies to everyone at the table and then read from his copy. "We believe that the timing of the abduction was relevant to a significant stressor in the perpetrator's life, perhaps the loss of his job or some other personal rejection. And that the abductor is a loner, over thirty and single, immature for his age, has no friends, is unable to maintain a relationship with a female his own age, probably employed in a job involving children, lacks social skills, abuses alcohol or drugs, reacts violently when angered, handles stress poorly, is selfish, paranoid, and impulsive, possesses an inflated self-esteem that cannot handle rejection, and harbors antisocial tendencies." He looked up. "We'll release this profile to the media. Hopefully, a citizen can identify someone they know with these traits."

The mother abruptly stood. "Oh, my God," she said.

"I can." She held up her copy. "Immaturity, no social skills, selfishness, paranoia, inflated self-esteem, can't handle rejection—I can identify every one of those traits to someone I know."

Agent Baxter was almost out of his chair with excitement.

"Who's that, Mrs. Brice?"

"Every partner in my law firm."

Agent Baxter exhaled and sat back down, realizing he'd been had. The mother tossed her copy of the profile on the table.

"Look, Agent Baxter," she said, "cut the psychobabble bullshit. The guy's a pervert who likes to fuck little girls!"

The mother stormed out of the room. Agent Baxter was visibly taken aback. After an awkwardly long silence Colonel Brice spoke in a quiet voice.

"He wasn't alone. There were two men, probably the two men on the videotape."

"Mr. Brice," Agent Brumley said, "sexual predators work alone, that's proven. They're what we call 'loner deviants.' "

"I was at the park," the colonel said, "retracing Gracie's steps. He grabbed her behind the concession stand and took her through the woods to an accomplice waiting for him in a vehicle leaking oil. He didn't work alone."

"Then why did he leave her shorts in the woods?" Agent Baxter asked.

"Because he wanted them found."

Agent Baxter frowned. "*Why?*"

"So you'd do just what you're doing—hunting for a sexual predator."

2:27 P.M.

"ARE YOU OKAY, Mrs. Brice?"

Elizabeth was sitting in her formal living room—now the FBI's command post—and staring across the table at Agent Devereaux.

"No, I'm not okay. My daughter's been abducted."

"Mrs. Brice, I can still get a psychologist in here."

"No."

She had gained control of her emotions again. Her mind was alert and angry again. She had a plan. And it required a banker, not a psychologist.

"Let me know if you change your mind. Now, Mrs. Brice, what kind of kid is Gracie? See, with these guys, it's all about control. They like to intimidate their victims, make the victim feel helpless and cornered so they feel powerful. What would Gracie do if she was cornered?"

"She'd fight."

"Good. That's the key to her survival."

"She will survive."

Agent Devereaux nodded. "Yes, ma'am. So, Mrs. Brice, you used to work our side of the street?"

"Yes."

A little smile. "What made you go over to the dark side?"

123

She paused. "Life took me there."

The agent frowned, then he said, "Well, then you understand why I need polygraphs."

"You said it wasn't random, that she was targeted. Now you think one of us did it?"

"No, ma'am. All I'm saying is, the Bureau is committing extensive resources to finding your daughter and the man who took her. But we've been burned before—you remember the Susan Smith case, said she was carjacked, her kids abducted? Turned out she drowned them herself. We must eliminate any family involvement."

Elizabeth glared at Agent Devereaux, the rage making a move to escape the darkness. "I just left your two brilliant profilers in my kitchen. I listened to them telling me that a predator abducted my little girl for sex." She slammed her fist down on the table. "Goddamnit! And now you're telling me you want polygraphs of me and my husband?"

Agent Devereaux nodded. "Yes, ma'am. And Colonel Brice and his wife, and the household staff. Mrs. Brice, I know it's an intrusion, but from our standpoint it's always a possibility. Fact is, only a couple hundred children each year are abducted by strangers. The rest are family related."

He reached across the table and took her clenched fists in his hands. She refused to allow the tears to come.

"Look, Mrs. Brice, this isn't a family abduction, I know that. But Washington doesn't. And I just got off the phone with my superiors, requesting authorization for additional staffing—ten more agents to help find Gracie. So this ends well. Do this, Mrs. Brice, so the Bureau will give me more people to find your daughter. Do it for Gracie."

"I'll do it."

The voice came from behind them. Elizabeth pulled her hands free of Agent Devereaux's and turned. Her father-in-law was standing in the door. She started to object just because Ben Brice was a drunk and she hated him. But something in his eyes made her hold her tongue. She turned back to Agent Devereaux.

"I want it done here. I don't want us on TV being marched into the police station."

Agent Devereaux said, "We're setting up in the library."

Ben entered the library to a young FBI agent holding his hand out to him. "Mr. Brice, I'm Agent Randall."

Randall was thirty, glasses, an accountant trying hard to be sociable. He was holding a rubber tube.

"If you'll remove your shirt, Mr. Brice, I'll strap the pneumograph tube around your chest." Agent Randall moved around behind Ben, continuing his friendly chatter. "Nothing to be nervous about. A polygraph machine measures your breathing rate, your blood pressure—"

Ben unsnapped the cuffs of his shirt and then the front snaps.

"—your pulse rate, and your skin's reflex to an electrical flow. See, the idea is, when someone's lying they—"

Ben slipped the shirt off his back.

"*Jesus!*"

Ben felt Agent Randall's eyes on his back; his chatter had been cut short. After a moment, Randall reached around Ben from behind to connect the tube; his hands were trembling.

"Is that, uh, is that too tight, Mr. Brice? It doesn't hurt this . . . these . . . your back?"

"No."

Agent Randall returned to Ben's view. "Okay, where was I? Oh, you can sit down, Mr. Brice."

Ben sat in a leather chair next to the polygraph; it looked like a laptop computer. The leather was cool on his bare back. Agent Randall stepped in front of him.

"This is an electrode," Agent Randall said.

He took Ben's hand and slipped a small sleeve onto the tip of his right index finger.

"And this is just an ordinary blood-pressure cuff, like at the doctor's."

The agent wrapped the cuff around Ben's upper right arm and stepped back.

"Okay, I, uh, I guess we're ready." Agent Randall sat in a chair behind the machine and to Ben's right. "Mr. Brice, I'm going to ask you several basic questions, just to get you comfortable so I can establish a baseline. Please breathe steadily, remain calm, and don't take deep breaths. And answer each question truthfully with a yes or no. Okay?"

Ben nodded.

Agent Randall's first question: "Is your real name Ben Brice?"

"Yes."

"Are you Gracie Ann Brice's grandfather?"

"Yes."

"Have you ever taken a polygraph exam, commonly known as a lie-detector test?"

"No."

That was a lie.

Ben closed his eyes and recalled his first lie-detector test: he is naked, his arms and ankles are strapped to a wooden chair, and his eyes are tracking two wires taped to his testicles and running along the concrete floor to a battery-powered field telephone with a hand crank manned by a grinning sadist. The small room reeks with the smell of urine and feces.

The North Vietnamese Army officer administering the test is determined to discover whether Brice, Ben, colonel, 32475011, 5 April 46, is lying about American troop presence in North Vietnam; certainly an American officer of his rank was not operating alone this close to Hanoi. He thought the American colonel would have succumbed to the beatings with the fan belts. Big Ug, as the Yanks called Captain Lu, is an artist with a fan belt; he carved up the colonel's broad back like a woodcarver cutting designs into a block of wood. But, to his great surprise, the colonel revealed only his name, rank, serial number, and date of birth.

However, this test has proved particularly effective at convincing the reluctant Americans to reveal their secrets; the prisoners call it the Bell Telephone Hour. They enjoy their gallows humor, these Yanks. Fortunately, prior to his untimely demise, Uncle Ho had advised his officers that the Geneva Convention did not apply to the American prisoners; since there is no declared war between the United States of America and the Democratic Republic of Vietnam, there are no American prisoners of war, Ho Chi Minh had said. Only American war criminals. Who will never forget their stay at the San Bie prison camp, if Major Pham Hong Duc has anything to say about it.

He nods at Lieutenant Binh, who cackles as he turns the crank, sending an electrical charge racing through the wires and into the colonel's genitals. The American's body snaps taut as the charge surges through him. That's odd, the major thought. Most of the Americans scream like banshees and lose control of their bladder and bowels when the charge hits them—hence the hole in the chair and the bucket beneath—but the colonel only grits his teeth and takes the pain, his arms and legs straining mightily against the leather bindings—

"Mr. Brice! Mr. Brice! Are you okay?"

Ben's eyes snapped open. His teeth were clenched, he was sweating and breathing hard, and his fingers were digging into the leather arms of the chair. Agent Randall was standing over him.

"Your respiration's off the chart!"

5:33 P.M.

"THEY'RE CLEAN," Agent Randall said.

FBI Special Agent Eugene Devereaux was chewing on the earpiece of his reading glasses. He and Agent Randall were standing in the command post next to Devereaux's desk.

"Didn't figure this to be family-related. But headquarters said to follow the protocol."

"The grandfather," Randall said, "his back looks like someone carved him up with a steak knife."

"He was an Army colonel. Must've been a POW."

"In Vietnam?"

"Yeah."

"They tortured American prisoners?"

Devereaux chuckled. "They still teach history in college?"

Randall was looking at him like a kid who didn't know what he had done wrong.

"Yeah, the NVA tortured our guys, and none of that Guantanamo Bay kind of torture, making them listen to Barry Manilow 24/7. NVA beat our guys, electrocuted them, broke their arms and legs . . ."

Randall was now looking past Devereaux to the door. "Here he is," he said, and he walked off.

Devereaux turned. The lean blond man walking toward him was maybe six feet and one-eighty, but he now seemed bigger in Devereaux's eyes.

"Colonel Brice—"

A momentary pause. "You've done some homework."

"Part of the job, sir."

The colonel nodded. "No need to address me as colonel. Or sir."

"You earned it, sir. I was a lieutenant, ROTC, Texas A&M. 'Course, drilling on a practice field didn't exactly prepare me for Vietnam."

"Neither did West Point."

They both smiled, sharing a thought private to combat soldiers who had lived to try to forget it. Devereaux put on his reading glasses, reached across the desk, and picked up the blow-ups.

"The coach couldn't ID the men from these blow-ups," Devereaux said. "And this tattoo . . . I've never seen anything like it in the military, thought maybe you might've. Top half is covered by his shirtsleeve, but what's showing looks like Airborne wings, except for the skull and crossbones." He held the blow-up of the tattoo out to Colonel Brice. "I'm running it through the Bureau's gang database. Could be a biker tattoo. Says 'viper.'"

The colonel abruptly snatched the blow-up from Devereaux's hand then stared at the image like it was the face of Satan. The blood drained from his face. He dropped down hard in a chair. His hand released the blow-up; it floated to the floor. He leaned over and covered his face with his hands.

"Colonel, you okay?" Devereaux retrieved the blow-up. "You seen this tattoo before?"

Colonel Brice ran his fingers through his blond hair,

then he slowly sat up. He inhaled and exhaled like a doctor was checking his heart. He spoke without looking at Devereaux.

"It's not a biker tattoo."

"How do you know?"

The colonel's jaw muscles clenched and unclenched several times. He unsnapped the cuff of his left sleeve and began rolling it up his arm. He was wearing a black military-style watch. His forearm was tanned with sun-bleached blond hair; his upper arm was pale where the sun had not done its damage. The distinctive feature of his upper arm, however, was the Airborne eagle wings etched in black ink in his white skin; but in the center of the wings where the open parachute was supposed to be, signifying a soldier's survival of jump school, was a skull and crossbones instead. Arched above the wings were words in an Asian script, and below that, in English, SOG-CCN; and below the wings, in quotes, VIPER. Devereaux leaned down and held the blow-up against the colonel's arm; the part of the tattoo visible in the blow-up matched up precisely with the bottom portion of the colonel's tattoo.

Devereaux rose, removed his reading glasses, and waited for the colonel to speak. He didn't press him; he couldn't. This man was a real goddamn American hero. When Colonel Brice finally spoke, his eyes remained on his boots.

"SOG team Viper conducted those covert operations presidents lied about. SOG was Studies and Observation Group, CCN was Command and Control North. We conducted cross-border operations in Laos, Cambodia, and North Vietnam. Our mission was to disrupt shipments on the Ho Chi Minh Trail, assassinate NVA officers, recon for air strikes . . . none of which officially happened. We operated off the books."

Devereaux pointed to the Asian script on the colonel's arm.

"These other words, they're Vietnamese?"

The colonel nodded.

"What do they say?"

The colonel hesitated a moment, then he said, "'We kill for peace.' The unofficial Green Beret motto." He now turned his eyes up to Devereaux. "Damn hard thing to get rid of, a tattoo."

Devereaux handed the blow-up of the big man to the colonel.

"This is the man with that tattoo. Do you recognize him? Be kind of hard to forget that scar."

The colonel stared at the photo of the big man; Devereaux thought he saw a hint of recognition cross the colonel's face. But Colonel Brice finally shook his head slowly and said, "No."

"How many men got this tattoo?" Devereaux asked.

"Viper was a twelve-man heavy recon team, operated for four years before I joined up. Casualties were high. Maybe twenty-five men got that tattoo, maybe more. I only knew the eleven men I served with."

"So we'll pull SOG records—"

"You'll never get those records, if they even exist." The colonel stood and rolled his sleeve down. "Agent Devereaux, my wife knows what I did over there, but my son doesn't. I'd like to keep it that way."

"I understand, sir."

Devereaux thought, *Only a Vietnam war hero would feel obliged to keep his heroism from his own son.*

"He's seen the tattoo," the colonel said, "but he doesn't know what it means. And he knows nothing about Viper team."

"What about Mrs. Brice?"

"Elizabeth? No. She knows I served in Vietnam, nothing more. She wouldn't understand. Anyone who wasn't there, they just can't understand."

"Amen to that."

The colonel snapped the buttons on the cuff of his sleeve and said, "Agent Devereaux, I'd consider it a personal favor if you didn't mention the tattoo in front of my family."

Devereaux studied the colonel a moment and said, "All right, Colonel, we'll keep it between us for now. Just as well, I don't want to go public with the tattoo anyway, in case I can get the names of those Green Berets."

The colonel stared at Devereaux but it was as if he were looking straight through him. Eugene Devereaux had been Army infantry in Vietnam. A grunt. Green Berets were the Army's elite, trained in the art of killing. Ben Brice did not have the look of a trained killer. He was not a physically intimidating man, as were the Green Berets Devereaux had seen in the Army. Nor was he the macho commando stereotype. In fact, he seemed almost too gentle a man to have done what Green Berets did in Southeast Asia four decades ago. But there was something in his eyes that told Devereaux otherwise.

His blue eyes betrayed him like a cheating wife.

7:14 P.M.

G RACIE WAS IN pain, scared and crying and praying to be saved. And her father wasn't doing a damn thing to save her. He didn't know how.

Instead, Little Johnny Brice was staring at a life-sized image of his daughter's soccer photo attached to the side of the concession stand under a banner with WE LOVE YOU, GRACIE painted in big letters; stacked below were pink ribbons, cards, fancy balloons, and hundreds of flower arrangements and teddy bears. The concession stand was now a memorial to his daughter.

Gracie was gone because her father wasn't much of a man.

John had not wanted to attend this vigil, but the FBI said it was important to appeal to the abductor's sympathy—if he saw on television the pain he was causing her family, he might let her go. But John could think only of Gracie's pain.

He felt a hand on his shoulder. John turned and looked into the eyes of his father, this man he had called Colonel and now Ben but never Father or Dad, who was once a hero with a family but who was now a drunk with a dog. His mother had told him that his father was a good man destroyed by a bad war; that terrible things had happened to him in Vietnam; that the war had ended but Ben Brice had never found his peace.

John Brice had never allowed himself the slightest sympathy for his father.

"Come on, son," Ben said, gently pulling John away from the makeshift memorial.

His son's eyes remained locked on Gracie's image. He said in a whisper, "I didn't tie her shoe."

Ben turned John away, and they walked past the local mayor giving a TV interview—"A safe place, a wonderful place to build your dream home and raise your children"—and around to the front of the building where a young priest was leading the crowd in prayer. Ben and John stood among hundreds of parents and children wearing *Gracie* buttons and tee shirts with Gracie's picture on the back and holding candles flickering in the night. Mingling with them were FBI agents; several were inconspicuously video-taping the candlelight vigil with palm-sized camcorders. Agent Devereaux said it was not out of the question that the abductor might show.

"Mr. Brice." A young blond man and a pregnant woman had come up to John, who turned and looked at them but did not seem to see them. "Mr. Brice," the young man began again, "I just want to say how sorry I am. We're having a baby and . . . I mean . . ."

He glanced at Ben; he was at a loss for words.

"Thanks for your thoughts," Ben said to the young man. The couple left. Up front, a young girl stood and sang:

"A-ma-zing Grace, how sweet the sound . . ." And the crowd joined in:

"That saved a wretch like me,
I once was lost, but now I'm found,
Was blind, but now I see . . ."

The overhead park lights dimmed slowly until the only light came from the flickering flames of hundreds of candles held high as the people sang.

The stars in the dark Vietnam night seem to flicker in fright, as if flinching at the sound of high-powered weapons firing on full auto and bringing death to this village. But not to this girl. He is determined to save her.

Lieutenant Ben Brice is now carrying the china doll like a football, dodging livestock and running through the burning hamlet toward the jungle where he can hide her. He glances back and trips over a dead pig, sending himself and the china doll sprawling into the dirt. The china doll scrambles up first. Before he can get to his feet, her head explodes like a ripe watermelon; her brains and blood splatter the twenty-two-year-old second lieutenant's face and fatigues. He looks up to see the major standing there, smoke from the barrel of his .45-caliber sidearm hanging in the humid air, clouding the Viper tattoo on his bare left arm.

"She was just a girl!" he screams at his SOG team leader.

"She was just a gook," the major responds calmly, wiping the girl's blood from his weapon. "They're all just gooks, Lieutenant. And your job is to kill gooks."

SOG rules are few but absolute: never leave a live team member behind; never let yourself be captured by the enemy; and never question the team leader in the field. The major turns his back on the naïve and idealistic young lieutenant, who violates a SOG rule on his first mission.

"You violated the law of war! And the rules of engagement!"

The major stops, pivots, and two steps later he is towering over the lieutenant, glaring down at him, his blue eyes burning with anger.

"Out here in the bush, I'm the law! I make the rules! And I say we kill VC! We kill livestock that feeds VC! We burn huts that shelter VC! We kill civilians that aid VC! Those are *my* rules of engagement, Lieutenant!"

The major blows out a breath and calms. He squats in front of his newest disciple, the anger subsided now, and for a moment Ben thinks the major is going to console him, perhaps offer a personal word of encouragement to a young Army soldier unversed in fighting a war in a moral vacuum; instead the major puts the barrel of his .45 to Ben's head and says in a steady voice: "Soldier, you ever question what I do out here again, I'll put a bullet through your head and let the VC make soup out of you, too. I guarangoddamntee it."

The major stands and walks away through smoke and fire and blowing ashes. Ben raises his hand to wipe the blood from his face and sees that his hand is trembling.

Ben felt proud when he had learned the major had selected him to fill a vacancy on SOG team Viper. The major was thirty-seven and a living legend in the Special Forces. Ben Brice was twenty-two and naïve. "You're a goddamn warrior now, Brice," the major said after Ben got his Viper tattoo in Saigon. "One of us." And he was proud when they ambushed that NVA convoy heading south on the Ho Chi Minh Trail through Laos, bearing supplies that would aid the enemy and arms that would kill Americans.

Today, he is not proud.

Lieutenant Ben Brice slowly stands and looks down upon the china doll, her arms and legs splayed grotesquely, her vacant eyes staring back at him, the final moment of her life frozen on her face—a face that will haunt him the rest of his nights. He turns and walks away, leaving the china doll and his soul to rot in the rich black soil of the Quang Tri province of South Vietnam.

God has a plan for Ben Brice, or so his mother had always said and so he had always believed, right up until that dark night in Vietnam. Each evening now, thirty-eight years after the fact, Ben would sit in his rocking chair on the porch of the small cabin he had built with his own hands, watch the sun set over Taos, and wonder what God's plan had been and why it had gone so wrong. Now, staring at the stars above his son's mansion outside Dallas, the vague outline of an answer was taking shape in his mind.

DAY FOUR

6:05 A.M.

FBI SPECIAL AGENT Eugene Devereaux gave a little salute to the uniformed guard wearing a Gracie button as the gates parted in front of his sedan. Briarwyck Farms was the American Dream, an upscale community entered through black iron gates, surrounded by a ten-foot-tall brick wall, and guarded 24/7 by a private security force, a place where all the homes cost at least $1 million, all the parents were successful, and all the children were safe.

But these walls and gates hadn't kept Gracie safe.

It was Monday morning—sixty hours post-abduction—and Devereaux was stumped. He had a command post equipped with phones, faxes, and computers running *RapidStart*, the FBI's sophisticated information management system capable of filing, indexing, comparing, and tracking thousands of leads simultaneously—he just didn't have any leads.

The girl had vanished.

Devereaux stopped at an intersection in front of the elementary school. A crossing guard holding up a stop sign escorted several children across the street; over her long-sleeve shirt the guard was wearing a white tee shirt with Gracie's picture on the back under HAVE YOU SEEN ME? Below her image was CALL 1-800-THE LOST.

The guard waved him on. He drove down the next block and turned right. The uniformed officers stationed at the end of Magnolia Lane recognized Devereaux's car and were already removing the wooden barricades blocking the street as he turned. When he did, he saw that the media circus had gone national. The networks had arrived.

"Shit. She's gonna do it."

6:49 A.M.

"MRS. BRICE, PLEASE don't do this. It'll bring out every kook in the country. It won't help. It's a waiting game."

"I'm through waiting."

Elizabeth left Agent Devereaux standing in the kitchen, obviously frustrated with a victim's mother who refused to play her designated role. Well, too damn bad. The victim had been missing for sixty-one hours now and this mother was through waiting—for a ransom call to come, for the abductor to be arrested, for a dog to track down her daughter's dead body, for God to save her. This mother wanted her daughter alive or the abductor dead. Or both. So this mother was taking matters into her own hands.

She was dressed for court; her hair was done and her makeup concealed the bags under her eyes. She would not be the pitiful grieving mother today, looking like hell, voice quivering, tears running down her face and makeup giving chase, begging a pervert on national TV to spare her child's life. Today she would be a tough-broad lawyer negotiating a deal, just like any other day and any other deal: you have something I want; I have something you want. Let's make a deal, asshole.

She proceeded down the gallery; the familiar adrenaline rush energized her to the coming performance, the same as when she stepped into the courtroom for the start of a trial. All heads turned her way when she entered the library, which now resembled a television studio. The three networks were represented with cameras and behind-the-scenes personnel; the national morning show hosts in New York would conduct the interviews; and the interviews would run live. Those were Elizabeth's terms.

"Five minutes, Mrs. Brice!" a little twerp wearing a headset shouted while holding up five fingers just in case she was deaf.

She sat next to John in a straight chair positioned in front of the bookshelves, a backdrop that gave the impression more of a law office than a home. Elizabeth had planned this event down to the last detail, the same as if she were about to bargain with a prosecutor for her client's freedom; instead, she was about to bargain with a pervert for her daughter's life. And only she would do the bargaining. She had given her husband the same explicit instructions she gave her guilty clients before a plea-bargain negotiation: *Keep your fucking mouth shut!*

John was dressed in black penny loafers, white socks, jeans, a yellow shirt, and a goofy blue tie with cartoon characters, his most solemn tie; at least he had tried to do something with his hair. He was staring off into space. She leaned into him and said, "Lose the tie." While he obediently removed the tie, she plucked the tiny wads of toilet paper stuck to his face where he had cut himself shaving—and she saw the evidence of her attack two days ago. Remorse again tried to sneak into her thoughts; it got a foot in the door this time.

Elizabeth sighed. She always hated herself afterward—

after the rage had romped. After she had lashed out at John. He didn't deserve it. But then, he never deserved it. She had cursed him too many times, but she had never hit him. This time the rage had crossed the line . . . and it scared her. She stared at her husband and wondered if he hated her half as much as she hated herself.

Playing on the color monitor in John's mind was his image of the abductor—coarse, thick, hairy, dirty, mean, and ugly—a man who, coincidentally, looked just like the Army bullies who had terrorized him as a boy.

He thought of the bullies again, Luther Ray in particular, wondering where his redneck life had led to—no doubt a double-wide mobile home in rural Alabama. John had always pictured Luther Ray sitting in his Barcalounger under a Confederate flag on the wall and looking forward to a big day during which he would drive his piece-of-shit pickup into town to collect unemployment (having been laid off from the local chicken-processing plant) and on the way back home he would engage in some curb shopping (checking out rich people's trash for stuff that might fit the double-wide's decor). Luther Ray would be hung over from the previous night's meeting of the local Ku Klux Klan chapter when he opened his morning paper and read that John Brice was a billionaire.

"God-damn, is that our Little Johnny Brice?" Luther Ray would say to the wife over at the stove fixing grits for breakfast. "That wimp's a fuckin' billionaire?" Then he'd laugh and say, "Shit, we used to kick his scrawny little ass just for fun."

And then his wife (fat and missing a front tooth) would fart and say something like, "Well, Luther Ray, maybe you should've been nicer to Little Johnny and he'd've give you a good job and me and the kids wouldn't be livin' in this goddamn trailer park." And from then on, every time they fought about money or his drinking (which is to say, every day), his wife would spew forth that flamage like green vomit from the *Exorcist* girl, reminding Luther Ray for the rest of his cretinous life that Little Johnny Brice had a billion dollars and he had a double-wide.

John had played out varying versions of that scenario at least once a day for the last nineteen years, conjuring it up on his first drive to MIT, when he had set a goal of being a billionaire by age forty, and improving on it each time. He had added the wife a few years back.

And that was why he had been so brain-damaged about becoming a billionaire. With the stock market and real-estate boom, everyone and their mother was a millionaire. But becoming a billionaire in one day like the Google guys—that would still make every newspaper in the country, even in rural Alabama.

But now Luther Ray would be watching him on TV, hearing how his daughter had been kidnapped in a public park with him right there, and he'd say, "No pervert would've snatched our Ellie May with me around and live to tell about it, that's for goddamn sure. Little Johnny Brice got money, but he ain't much of a man. Never was." And the wife would nod in agreement.

And they'd be right.

"Mrs. Brice!"

Elizabeth jerked her eyes off John and focused on the task at hand—and the twerp standing directly in front of her; he was bent over, his hands were on his knees, and his round face was not two feet from hers.

"There'll be a setup piece, three minutes,"—he held up three fingers, then pointed to a TV monitor off to the side—"you can watch it there. Then DeAnn will go live with you." Four fingers. "Four minutes, then commercial break. When I signal break, shut up. Don't go on or we'll cut you off."

When the twerp vacated his position in front of Elizabeth, she found herself looking directly at Agent Devereaux standing back behind the cameras; he was leaning into the doorjamb and staring at her. *Hey, fuck the FBI! You haven't found my daughter!*

"Quiet!" the twerp yelled. He pointed to the TV monitor.

The morning show first up was coming back on the air. The host introduced the reporter on the story, live from Texas, standing on the front lawn, a Gracie button on his lapel, the house looming large behind him.

"DeAnn, Gracie Ann Brice is ten years old"—Grace's soccer picture flashed on the screen—"and she is missing this Monday morning. She was abducted by a blond man wearing a black cap and a plaid shirt after her soccer game Friday night here in Post Oak, Texas, a wealthy enclave forty miles north of Dallas. I am standing outside her family's three-million-dollar mansion in this community of mansions."

Playing on the monitor was a video of Briarwyck Farms, the media circus outside, and their home. The reporter's voice-over continued: "The park where she was abducted now serves as a makeshift memorial to Gracie." Now the monitor showed shots of the park and the concession building, the banner, and the flowers.

"Children have brought flowers and notes of prayer for their friend. A candlelight vigil was held there last night. Hundreds of people turned out to pray for Gracie's safe return. Her abduction has frightened the residents of this community."

The distraught face of a neighbor: "This isn't supposed to happen in a place like this. We're supposed to be safe out here."

The reporter's voice over video of the search efforts: "Searchers have hunted for Gracie for two days without success. Other than her soccer shorts and shoe, which were found by bloodhounds Saturday, there's been no sign of her. The Heidi Search Center has organized a massive volunteer effort to search fields and farmland on the outskirts of town."

The monitor played video of people hugging each other and wiping tears from their faces. "We're here because our child could be next," one searcher said.

"At Gracie's school"—a live shot of kids arriving at Briarwyck Farms Elementary School—"parents clutch their children closer today."

The face of a young woman above the byline, NORA UNDERWOOD, GRACIE'S FOURTH-GRADE TEACHER: "We're not supposed to pray in school, but we're praying today."

And AMY APPLEWHITE, PRINCIPAL: "We've brought in crisis counselors for the children to talk to, to talk out their fears."

Back live to the reporter out front, holding up the flier with Grace's picture: "DeAnn, friends and neighbors have distributed thousands of these missing-child fliers throughout the area and as many pink ribbons to show their support. The National Center for Missing and

Exploited Children has posted Gracie's picture on its website at www-dot-missingkids-dot-org, as has the FBI at www-dot-fbi-dot-gov. Her face will be seen around the world. This is a confirmed stranger abduction—the FBI eliminated any family involvement with polygraph exams. The parents are hoping for the best, but fearing the worst. Most children abducted by strangers are dead within a few hours. Gracie's been missing for over sixty hours. Back to you, DeAnn."

Elizabeth turned from the monitor and spotted Sam sitting on the sofa in the back of the room and staring stone-faced at a TV monitor. She could see the fear in his eyes. *Damnit, where's Hilda?* Elizabeth tried to get Sam's attention to send him out, but the twerp was again gesturing at her and pointing to the monitor. Elizabeth turned away from Sam and looked at the monitor.

Now on the screen was the concerned face of DeAnn, the host in New York, an index finger pressed to her tight lips, a slow sad shake of her well-coifed head. What empathy so early in the morning, Elizabeth thought, and right before she hosts a segment on liposuction. Now she would interview the distressed and tearful parents, who would dutifully slobber and plead for their daughter's return on national TV, a sure ratings hit. That was the script. That was the way things were supposed to go. Well, DeAnn, hold onto your skirt, girlfriend, because today's show is going to be a little bit different.

DeAnn, from New York: "We have with us this morning, from their home outside Dallas, Texas, Gracie's parents, John and Elizabeth Brice."

The twerp pointed at them; the cameras went live.

"John Brice is the founder of BriceWare-dot-com, which is going public in two days, when he will become another overnight high-tech billionaire. Elizabeth Brice is a prominent Dallas criminal defense attorney. Mr. Brice, your daughter's kidnapping is a front-page story in the *Wall Street Journal* today. You were just days from your dream, now your daughter's been abducted. This must be devastating for you. How do you feel?"

Oh, shit, Elizabeth thought, bracing herself for a blast of John's goofy geek-speak on national TV, something like, *DeAnn, my freaking wetware is fried! I'm talking toast! Some brain-damaged meatbot uninstalled my daughter from my network and that is evil and rude in the extreme!*

Instead, John looked into the camera and said softly, "I feel empty."

Elizabeth stared again at her husband and saw a stranger.

DeAnn, from New York: "Why do you think the abductor left Gracie's soccer shorts in the woods? And her shoe?"

She was pulling out all the stops to get the tears flowing. But John's answer momentarily set her back: "I forgot to tie her laces after the game."

"Well, yes, but this is clearly not a ransom abduction. A sexual predator took your daughter—but Gracie had none of the risk factors associated with children abducted by sexual predators. Why do you think he took your daughter?"

John shook his head. "I don't know."

"Were there problems at home? Could she have run away?"

"No. She knows we love her."

DeAnn appeared visibly frustrated now. "Do you think she's still alive?"

"Yes."

Still no tears.

"Mr. Brice, were there problems in your marriage?"

"My *marriage?*"

The rage stirred and stretched and required all of Elizabeth's strength to hold it back; if this nationally televised therapy session continued much longer, the rage would escape her grasp. She interrupted.

"DeAnn," Elizabeth said, and the camera zoomed in on Elizabeth Brice. "We're not here for marriage counseling. We're here because a stranger abducted my daughter. He took her, and we want her back. And we will pay to get her back. For information leading to the safe return of my daughter, we will pay twenty-five million dollars, cash."

Elizabeth imagined viewers across America spitting out their morning coffee; she had just seized control of her audience.

"If you've seen Grace, call us and you're rich."

A slight pause for effect, but not long enough for DeAnn to break in.

"Another offer, this one to the abductor: release my daughter, alive and well, and we will pay you the twenty-five million instead. We will deposit the funds in a Cayman Island bank account under a pin number—it's completely anonymous. The IRS cannot trace the money, the FBI cannot trace you. You can wire the money anywhere in the world. You can get on a plane and fly to Costa Rica, Thailand, the Philippines, where you can have all the little girls you want. You're rich and you're free to pursue your perverted desires—what more could you want? All I want is my daughter back. My offer remains open until midnight Friday, Dallas time. Twenty-five million dollars for my daughter. It's a good deal. You'd better take it."

Now a slight lean forward and her best intimidate-the-witness glare into the camera: "Because if you don't take this deal, if you don't release my daughter by the deadline, if you can't release my daughter because you've already killed her, know this and know it well: you're a dead man. I'm putting a bounty on your head same as the government put on Osama bin Laden's head: commencing one minute after midnight Friday, we will pay the twenty-five million to anyone who hunts you down and kills you like the disgusting perverted animal you are. And know this: you're not going back to prison to serve a few years then get released only to violate another little girl—that is not going to happen! You're either going to release my daughter or you're going to die. It's your choice."

DeAnn, beside herself in New York: "Mrs. Brice, this is national TV! You can't—"

Now, the closer: "Take the deal. Take the money. Give us Grace."

Elizabeth would repeat the same offer on the other network morning shows.

8:08 A.M.

"WELL, AIN'T THAT neat, our own fucking Powerball lotto!" the mayor said. He hurled a paperweight against the far wall of his office in the town hall. He had a pretty fair arm for a fat boy. Chief of Police Paul Ryan stood out of harm's way, watching the mother on TV and enduring another mayoral venting.

"Twenty-five million dollars! That much money, she made goddamn sure her kid stays on national news every goddamn day!"

His Honor let loose with a stapler this time.

"And we're gonna stay on national TV until you find her body or her killer!"

"You mean kidnapper."

"I mean killer. She's dead just like that reporter said and you know it. Goddamnit, Paul, find this pervert!"

"Mayor, we're rounding up every sex offender in the county but—"

A stiff fat finger in Ryan's face: "No buts, Paul! Find him, arrest him, and get us off national TV! Or else!"

Paul Ryan exited the mayor's office, imagining himself driving a golf cart with a flashing yellow light around a parking lot twelve hours a day and wondering what kind of retirement plan Wal-Mart offered its security guards.

153

9:27 A.M.

"DO YOU HAVE twenty-five million dollars in cash?" FBI Special Agent Eugene Devereaux asked the mother.

Without looking at him, she said, "My husband arranged a line of credit. He put up his stock. It'll be worth a billion dollars in two days. We've got it."

Before the mother's image had faded from the TV screen, every fax machine in the command post was spitting out paper, every light on every phone was blinking, and a dozen federal agents were logging leads into the computer as fast as they could type:

"You saw her, in Houston?"

"You're sure it was her? Where in Oklahoma?"

"Arkansas?"

"Louisiana?"

"Mexico? New Mexico the state or Mexico the country?"

Devereaux would personally review the computer's analysis of the leads and determine which leads to follow, hoping in his heart they were legit but knowing in his head they were worthless calls from people after a piece of the reward, calling in to report every blonde girl they saw, hoping theirs might hit, like buying a lottery ticket.

He heard Agent Floyd's voice: "Uh, no, ma'am, you can't get any of the reward for being close. This isn't horseshoes."

And Agent Jorgenson's: "And who is she with? . . . A man and woman? . . . And you're in a grocery store in Abilene with them right now? . . . I hear someone saying 'Mommy.' Is that the girl? . . . Well, ma'am, if the girl is calling the woman 'mommy,' maybe that's her mother."

Devereaux turned to the mother. "Well, Mrs. Brice, we've had almost five hundred sightings in the two hours since you offered the reward." He was standing in the middle of the command post with the mother.

"Excellent."

"No, ma'am, not really. At this rate, I won't have the manpower to clear that many leads."

The mother looked at Devereaux like she had told a joke and he was too dumb to get it.

"I don't expect you to. Grace isn't walking around some shopping mall somewhere—you think he bought her new shorts? If she's alive, she's with him. I offered the reward to pressure him to give her up. That's the only chance we have to get her back alive, and you know it."

Devereaux had to remind himself of his own rule: getting into a pissing contest with the mother wouldn't put him one step closer to finding the girl or apprehending the abductor. And odds are, the child's dead anyway.

11:17 A.M.

"HER BODY, it is cold."

Angelina Rojas stood five feet tall and weighed two hundred pounds. She was wearing a pink sweat suit. She had teased her hair into a nice tall mound atop her round face to which she had applied extra makeup. She wanted to look her best today.

Angelina lived and worked in the Little Mexico area of Dallas. Normally at this time on a Monday morning she would be contacting the spirits of dead relatives of poor Mexicans or reading their futures in their palms or tarot cards. *Angelina Rojas, el medium.* She was a psychic. At least that's what it said on her business card.

But yesterday she had opened the Sunday paper and seen the kidnapped girl's picture on the front page; she had been drawn to the image. She had stared at the picture, then she had touched it. She had felt something and heard something. Something real this time. Something that scared her. "*La madre de Dios,*" she had said. *Mother of God.*

So she had woken this morning, gotten dressed, and made Carlos put on a shirt and drive her out here. When they had arrived at the big gates, she explained the purpose of her visit to the guard, but he refused to let them in.

She begged him to call Señora Brice. When he refused that also, Carlos said he was going to get out of the Chevy and kick his fat Anglo ass. The guard decided that making a phone call was a smarter move than having some Hispanic *hombre* in a low-rider pounding on him with his muscular left arm, the one with the tattoo of the Virgin Mary. So he called, but he got Señor Brice instead. He let them in.

Carlos had stayed in the car at the end of the street outside the police barricade; he was nervous due to the fact that he had immigrated to America via the Rio Grande just outside Laredo. Angelina had then walked down the street and up to the front door of the house— it was as big as the office building she used to clean each night, before she had become a full-time psychic. Normally she insisted her clients pay her in cash up front; Angelina did not accept personal checks or credit cards, not that her clients had bank accounts or credit cards. But today she did not care about money. In fact, she did not want money. She just wanted to give them the girl's message and get back home.

Angelina Rojas was afraid that she might really be psychic.

Now she was sitting in the kitchen across a table from Señor Brice and several other Anglos; her eyes were closed and she was clutching the girl's white school blouse tightly to her face, trying to feel the child. Another cold chill ran through her considerable body, more intense than the first one. But it was not Angelina who was cold.

"Her body, it is very cold."

"My daughter is not dead!"

Angelina opened her eyes to a woman she recognized from TV. The mother. She was very beautiful, even when angry, as now.

1:24 P.M.

"BEN! BEN!"

Kate Brice is straining to see down the jetway at San Francisco International Airport; six-year-old John is standing next to her. It's 1975 and Ben Brice is coming home. That damn war is finally over.

Passengers begin appearing in the jetway. Her eyes search the crowd for a green beret, but her mind is dreading a repeat of five years earlier in this same airport. They were walking down the concourse; Ben was wearing his uniform, pushing John in a stroller, and ignoring the whispered "baby killer" comments. A young man with long hair suddenly stepped in front of Ben and said, "My brother died in Vietnam because of officers like you!" Then he spat in Ben's face. Ben grabbed the young man by the throat and pinned him to the wall, terrifying the young man but Kate more. She had never seen that Ben Brice before; his blue eyes were so dark. He could have easily killed the young man, and for a moment she thought he would. Instead, the darkness dissipated; he wiped the spit from his face, released the frightened young man, and said, "I'm sorry about your brother."

They had married three days after he graduated from the Academy. It was a fairy-tale wedding in the West Point

159

chapel; afterward, still wearing her white wedding dress, she was escorted by Lieutenant Ben Brice in his dress white uniform through the saber arch, an Army tradition. Her fairy-tale marriage lasted exactly three weeks. Twenty-one days a married woman, her husband left her for Fort Bragg and Special Forces school. Ben Brice was going to war. He deployed the day after Thanksgiving 1968. She saw him off at the airport; she never saw that man again.

That damn war destroyed the fairy-tale marriage she had dreamed of as a girl. She is praying for a fresh start today.

There! She sees a green beret above a sea of heads . . . and now his face, tanned and angular, and so handsome. He sees her and smiles.

Ben turned back to her now: the same face, still tanned and angular, and still so handsome. But the smile was gone. He had been walking out to the pool house when she called to him. He came back to her, and they sat on the back porch.

"When will you leave?" she asked.

"When I know where she's at."

Kate studied her husband's face. "Gracie?"

He nodded.

"You believe that psychic?"

He nodded again.

"Ben, that was odd that she knew your name, but—"

"She's alive, Kate."

She calls out for someone named Ben, the psychic said. Why not me? Why not her mother?

But with Grace it had always been Ben. And Elizabeth

160

had always hated Ben Brice because he shared a bond with Grace that she did not. Now, sitting alone in her bedroom, her thoughts were not angry; her thoughts were of her father and the bond they had shared.

Her memories were of their time together.

Arthur Austin had been a lawyer, but he did not sell his life by the billable hour, so he had time for his daughter. During their last year together, when she was ten, he had taken her to at least one Mets game a week, often leaving the office early to make a weekday game. Mother wasn't good in the heat, so it was just the two of them. She had been so proud to sit next to her handsome father in his suit and tie, his sharp features and head of thick black hair attracting the eyes of other women. But he belonged to her. Those were glorious days she thought would never end.

How could a thirty-five-year-old man be murdered?

She could still close her eyes and see him lying in the hospital bed at St. Mary's Catholic Hospital, his eyes shut, the white sheets pulled up to his chin (to conceal his wounds, she realized years later), his skin pale and cold, and Mother saying it was time to say goodbye. But Elizabeth Austin, the good Catholic girl, had said, "No, God will save him." She had knelt next to his bed and held his cold hand; she had prayed to God to save her father. But God had refused. He had ignored her prayers. He had forsaken her. "I will never forgive you," she had said to God that day. And she never had.

She had missed her father terribly. But somehow she had gone on with her life, always thinking of everything they would never do together. That was before evil had come into her life. Afterward, she had been relieved her father hadn't been there; it would have broken his heart

161

to see what his happy ten-year-old daughter had become: a forty-year-old rage-filled lunatic forever haunted by her encounter with evil. Just as it was breaking her heart to imagine what her happy ten-year-old daughter would become—if she survived her encounter with evil.

What if she didn't?

How could this child's life story end this way? After the way her story had begun? She had given this child life, and this child had saved her life. How was she now supposed to go on with her life without this child? Without Grace? How was Elizabeth Brice supposed to get up one day—*when, next week or the week after?*—drive to the office, and again care about guilty clients? How was getting a rich white-collar criminal off supposed to fill the empty space inside her?

Her private phone line rang. It was her mother, offering to help in any way she could—which was in no way. It took only a few minutes of pleading to get her to stay in New York.

Mother had been only twenty-nine when Father had died. She had married him right out of high school, while he was in law school. He was her life. After his death, Mother had retreated into her own world, seldom leaving the house, helpless in a harsh world. For all intents and purposes, her mother had died with her father.

And Elizabeth Austin had grown up alone.

"I don't want to be an only child."

John squeezed Sam's shoulder and fought back tears. He had come into Sam's room to comfort his five-year-old son. Sam had finally begun to grasp the reality that he might never see Gracie again. As had his father.

"I don't want her room or her stuff," Sam said. "I just want her to come back. I miss her." He wiped his nose on his shirtsleeve. "That guy on TV, he said she's probably dead."

"She's not dead," John said, trying to sound convincing. "She'll be back soon, buddy."

"But you don't know that for a fact, do you?"

"Huh? Well, no, Sam, I don't know that for a fact."

"So you're just saying that to make me feel better 'cause I'm just a stupid kid."

John beheld his kindergartner son, indisputable evidence that cloning works.

"Sam, A, you've got a one-sixty IQ, so you're not stupid, and B, I'm saying that because I believe Gracie will come home."

"Why?"

"Why what?"

"Why do you believe she'll come home?"

Cripes, Sam was like Microsoft after a competitor!

"Uh, well, because I have faith."

"In God?"

"Uh, yeah, that's it."

"So you believe in God?"

John hesitated. Fact is, he wasn't sure he did believe in God. As a kid, Little Johnny Brice had often begged God to save him from the bullies' beatings, but God never did. And John R. Brice hadn't spent much adult time thinking about God, what with getting the Ph.D., hacking code for a killer app, and now working the IPO. And he went to church with the kids only because Mom would be disappointed in him if he didn't. A week ago, if Sam had asked such a question, he would have automatically clicked into avoidance mode and responded to Sam like a big brother: "Hey, buddy, God is one of those deep philosophical choices that each humanoid must make for himself or herself, kind of like whether to go Windows or Mac. But look, man, don't worry about that serious stuff now, wait till you're older, you know, after your own IPO. Hey, let's go to the kitchen and get down on some Rocky Road ice cream, dude."

And that was the role he had played all these years for the kids, which was, in fact, the role he preferred: big brother, pal, buddy. Nothing more had been required of him. And besides, with Elizabeth around, the man-of-the-house role had already been taken.

But now, looking into Sam's eyes, he could see that Sam needed something more from him. At the office, John was the Big Kahuna because he always had the answers to the toughest technical queries posed by his employees. But their questions paled next to Sam's: Is there a God? The answer couldn't be found in the online Help menu. John wanted to say, *Shit, dude, I don't have a freaking clue!* But his five-year-old son didn't need the big brother mode; he needed the mature adult fatherly mode. So John lied.

"Of course I believe in God."

"But you don't know if there really is a God, do you? I mean, like, you don't have any evidence that proves He exists beyond a reasonable doubt, right?"

"No."

"But you believe God is real?"

"Yes." The second lie required less consideration.

"So you believe Gracie's coming home because you believe in God and God takes care of kids, right?"

"That's right." No consideration at all.

"See, that's why I decided God is bogus."

"Sam, don't say that. God's not bogus."

"Well, if God is spending so dang much time taking care of Gracie now, why'd he let that cretin take her in the first place?"

John gave up. "I don't know, Sam."

Sam frowned and said, "You think that cretin wants more than twenty-five million bucks to let her go?"

"I . . . I don't know."

Sam stared up at John for a moment, then said, "Your face looks better. From when Mom smacked you."

4:33 P.M.

"PLEASE TAKE the money."

Elizabeth touched the image on the computer screen and gently traced the outline of her daughter's face. She had logged onto the FBI's website, the *Kidnapped and Missing Persons Investigations* page at www.fbi.gov/ mostwant/ kidnap/kidmiss.htm. Two columns of pictures and names of children abducted in Saginaw, Texas; Deltona, Florida; Santa Fe, New Mexico; Oregon City, Oregon; Jackson, Tennessee; Oklahoma City, Oklahoma; Chicago, Illinois; San Luis Obispo, California; Las Vegas, Nevada.

Where in America are children safe?

She clicked on the image of her daughter. She saw the same photo of Grace enlarged on a page that read:

KIDNAPPING
Post Oak, Texas

GRACIE ANN BRICE

DESCRIPTION

Age: 10
Place of Birth: Dallas, Texas

Sex:	Female	Hair:	Short Blonde
Height:	4'6"	Eyes:	Blue
Weight:	80 pounds	Race:	White

THE DETAILS

Gracie Ann Brice was kidnapped after her soccer game at approximately 6:00 P.M. on Friday, April 7, at Briarwyck Farms Park in Post Oak, Texas. She was last seen wearing a soccer uniform, gold jersey with "Tornadoes" on the front and a number 9 on the back, and blue shorts, blue socks, and white Lotto soccer shoes, and a silver necklace with a silver star. Gracie may be in the company of a white male, 20 to 30 years, 200 pounds, blond hair, blue eyes, wearing a black baseball cap and a plaid shirt. He asked for Gracie by name at the park.

REMARKS

Gracie Ann Brice has a muscular build, light complexion, and short hair. Her elbows may have recent abrasions.

REWARD

The parents of Gracie Ann Brice are offering a reward of $25 million for information leading to her recovery. Individuals with information concerning this case should take no action themselves, but instead immediately contact the nearest FBI Office or local law enforcement agency. For any possible sighting outside the United States, contact the nearest United States Embassy or Consulate.

Elizabeth grabbed both sides of the monitor and put her face against her daughter's image.

"Take the money! Let her go! Please!"

11:39 P.M.

A CHILD ABDUCTED by a stranger warrants a featured slot on the network morning shows and a mention on the evening news. But when the victim's mother puts a $25 million bounty on the abductor's head, dead or alive, that's lead story news.

Under orders from headquarters, FBI Special Agent Eugene Devereaux had given live interviews on the network evening news, back to back to back. He had protested that he was too busy trying to find the girl, but he had been informed that his orders came straight from Director White himself. The Bureau brass liked its agents—particularly articulate agents like himself—on national TV. Good for PR. And next year's budget requests.

Devereaux sighed; his investigation had become a goddamn $25 million sideshow.

He was now in the command post, slouched in his chair and alternating between his left and right buttock so as not to put additional pressure on his inflamed prostate while reviewing the latest leads. He had yet to read one that rang true.

"Prostate?"

Devereaux looked up to see Colonel Brice standing there.

"Recognize the butt position," the colonel said.

"You, too?"

The colonel nodded. "Try saw palmetto."

"Saul who?"

"S-A-W P-A-L-M-E-T-T-O. Berry from the palmetto tree. Relieves the pain. You can buy it in any health food store."

"I heard about those places."

The colonel gestured at the stack of leads. "Anything?"

"Yeah, over two thousand sightings," he said. "Couple more days, we'll know where every blonde, blue-eyed girl in the Southwest lives."

"You think they're after the money?"

"I'm afraid so, Colonel." The colonel sat in an adjacent chair; Devereaux adjusted his butt position. "Rewards of a few thousand dollars can be productive, but twenty-five million dollars—that's a whole 'nother ball game. Two thousand sightings, we're wasting too much time chasing too many false leads." He put his hand on the stack. "What if there *is* one good lead in all this?"

"May I?"

"Sure. Here, I've been through these." Devereaux pushed a stack of papers toward Colonel Brice and yawned.

"You need some sleep. Give your prostate a rest."

"I'll sleep after we find Gracie."

The colonel gave him a firm look. "You're a good man."

"And you were a great soldier." The colonel did not respond. The silence was awkward, so Devereaux broke it by confessing to an American hero. "I wasn't. I just wanted to come home. Nineteen days left in my tour and I'm walking point on patrol again and all I'm thinking is, My luck, I'm gonna be the last American soldier to die in Vietnam, when this VC steps out from behind a tree not ten feet in front of me, his weapon on me. I'm a dead man. Except his rifle misfires—it was an old bolt-action piece of shit. I raise my M-16 and shoot him dead. I step over to him, see he's just a kid, maybe fourteen. I threw up." Devereaux was too embarrassed to look directly at the colonel. "I've carried a weapon most of my adult life, but that's the only time I've ever killed another human being." He paused and shook his head. "Looks like we've both done some confessing now. I've never told anyone that story, not even my wife."

The colonel's voice was almost a whisper when he said, "Killing isn't an easy thing to talk about . . . or live with."

The two men were silent with their own thoughts of war and killing until Devereaux said, "How long were you a POW?" The colonel appeared puzzled, so Devereaux answered his unasked question. "Agent Randall, he saw the scars on your back, during your polygraph."

The colonel nodded. "Six months, barely enough time to get settled in."

"Hanoi Hilton?"

He shook his head. "Outlying camp, San Bie. After we escaped, NVA closed all the camps, moved all the Americans to Hanoi."

And then it dawned on Devereaux, why the name Ben Brice sounded familiar.

"You're the one. You're the guy that rescued those pilots." He paused and stared at this man. "You saved a lot of soldiers that day."

Colonel Brice showed no emotion. He broke eye contact and squinted as if trying to see something in the distance. Or in the past. When he spoke, his voice was soft.

"Commander Ron Porter."

"Who?"

His eyes returned to Devereaux. "One of those pilots, he flies out of Albuquerque."

"Colonel, they gave you the Medal of Honor."

The colonel picked up the papers, stood, and said, "So they did." Then he walked away.

Six months before the day he had walked into the San Bie POW camp in North Vietnam, Colonel Ben Brice had been living in the jungles of Vietnam with the Montagnards, the indigenous inhabitants of the country known to GIs as the "Yards," a people much like the American Indian. The men wore loincloths; their bronze-skinned bodies were lean and muscular and their facial features were hard and sharply etched, but they were not without humor or intelligence. The tribal elders spoke French fluently, learned when the French took their ill-fated turn at colonizing Vietnam. Eighteen million people called Vietnam home; the Montagnards numbered one million, scattered among numerous tribes. Ben's tribe was the Sedang.

When first deployed to Vietnam, the Green Berets' primary mission was to organize the Montagnard tribes into Civilian Irregular Defense Groups to stem Communist infiltration into South Vietnam along the western borders with Laos and Cambodia. Ben was supposed to teach the Sedang guerrilla warfare tactics; but it was the Sedang who taught him: how to live off the land, how to hunt wild game and Viet Cong on the mountains that rose eight thousand feet and in the thick jungles that covered the valleys below, and how to move through the night like a shadow. The Sedang were natural hunter-killers. He became one of them. They even presented him with a hand-fashioned brass bracelet, which represented membership in the tribe; it was a great honor for a white man. Ben Brice had "gone native."

They were operating in North Vietnam just inside the Seventeenth Parallel—the DMZ that divided North from South, Communist from free—when they spotted a USAF F-4 Phantom flying low overhead and trailing smoke, hit on a Rolling Thunder raid over Hanoi. The two-man crew ejected just before the jet crashed and exploded in a fireball; both parachutes opened, so Ben and the Montagnards made for the Americans. But they arrived too late; the NVA had captured them.

The NVA marched the pilots north to the San Bie prison camp. On still nights, camped a thousand meters out, Ben heard the blood-curdling screams of the Americans being tortured. The next morning he heard them singing 'God Bless America.' Ben and the Montagnards planned a rescue, which required he be captured. The NVA had standing orders to kill their American prisoners in the event of a rescue attempt. The only successful rescue would come from inside, with help on the outside.

Now, six months a prisoner of war, he will escape and take one hundred American pilots with him, with the help of the Montagnards. Ben Brice had taught them a few things too, including the proper use of C-4 explosive. Together they destroyed enemy arms depots, disrupted supply convoys on the Ho Chi Minh Trail, ambushed VC, assassinated NVA officers, radioed in grid coordinates for B-52 Arc Light bombing raids, and snatched that Marine slick driver back from the NVA in Laos. Today they will rescue American POWs.

He remains sprawled in the same position on the concrete floor of the cell in which he had been deposited five hours earlier, awaiting the morning guard. He soon hears the familiar sound of keys rattling, so familiar that he knows the guard's exact location in the hallway outside as he comes closer and closer to Ben's cell. The guard arrives and bangs on the cell door, then looks in through the small barred opening and sees the American colonel still lying on the floor, the blood on his raw back dried and caked and the rats nibbling at his feet. Ben hears metal grating against metal as the guard slips the key into the rusty lock. The key turns, and the lock releases. The door creaks open. Footsteps, a bit wary, come close; the guard wonders if the highest-ranking American officer in the prison survived the fierce beating inflicted by Big Ug and his fan belt last night. Ben braces himself not to react to the kick that is sure to come and does; he stifles a groan as the guard's boot drives into his side. The prisoner does not respond, so the guard circles around and squats to check his pulse.

It is his last living act.

Ben grabs the guard by the throat with hands made strong in the oil fields of West Texas and the jungles of Vietnam and chokes off all sound and jerks him to the floor. Ben Brice does not kill him out of vengeance; he kills him because he must. The guard's neck sounds like a brittle chicken bone snapping when Ben rotates his head past the breaking point.

Ben stands and surveys his cell for the last time. The thick odor customary to the cell is joined by that of fresh urine and feces as the guard's body accepts its death and surrenders its dignity. More death will follow. He must kill to save these pilots. He takes no satisfaction in the killing, but he is skilled in the art of killing. It is what he knows.

This is his moment in the great human tragedy known as the Vietnam War.

John ducked under the yellow crime-scene tape and walked into Gracie's room. He hit the overhead light switch.

"Hiya, pal," she would always say when he knocked on her bedroom door each day when he got home. He would usually find her on the floor, reading the sports pages or doing her homework or singing a new song. But her room was empty tonight. Her stuff was still there, but without her there was no life in this room. Or in this house. Gracie Ann Brice was the life of the house.

He turned on the nightlight and turned off the overhead. He crawled into her bed. He pulled the comforter up and buried his head in her pillow. He cradled her big cushy teddy bear. He closed his eyes, breathed in his daughter, and remembered.

"One day you'll be singing on the radio," he had said to her once, sitting right here on this bed.

She had frowned and said, "You know how hard it is to get radio stations to play a new artist's songs?"

"No. How hard?"

"Like, totally."

"Then I'll buy a bunch of radio stations and play only yours."

"You can't do that."

"After the IPO I can. I'm gonna buy the Red Sox for Sam."

"No, I mean it doesn't work that way. I've got to struggle

175

a long time trying to break in so I'll have material for my songs."

"Oh, so that's how it works."

"Yeah, see, the Dixie Chicks struggled for like, well, a really long time, and they had to move to Nashville. I guess I'll have to, too."

"And leave me? No way, girlfriend. I'll buy a jet, you can fly to Nashville to record. Or I'll build you a recording studio here, and they can come to you. And they will."

"Yeah, right. You know how many great singers are out there totally begging to break into country music?"

"No. How many?"

"Well . . . a bunch."

He shook his head. "Odds don't apply to statistically unique occurrences."

"Huh?"

"There's only one Gracie Ann Brice."

She had looked at him with a strange expression, one he had never before seen on her sweet face; he immediately thought, *Cripes, I said something wrong! You bogoid, you never could talk to girls!* But she abruptly hugged him and said, "You're the best father a girl could ever want." When she pulled back, her big blue eyes were wet. "Thanks for not making fun of my dreams."

He had cupped her perfect face and said, "Gracie, ill-behaved cretins can thrash your user interface, frag your hardware, unplug your peripherals, uninstall your components—but dreams are proprietary technology."

"Huh?"

"No one can take your dreams away."

But he had been wrong. Someone had taken his dream away.

12:09 A.M.

Ben was now sitting at the kitchen table and flipping through the stack of FBI lead sheets. By this time of night he was usually drunk enough to sleep. He wanted a drink now, just one shot of whiskey. Or two. He could feel its warmth inside him.

But there would not be another drink for him. On the drive from Taos to the Albuquerque airport, alone in the pre-dawn hours, he had made a vow to Gracie, a vow that now required he reach back almost four decades to find the strength to overcome: when they had beaten him at San Bie, he thought of Kate and John and found strength; now, when the cravings came, he thought of Gracie and found the same strength.

He went over to the refrigerator, a commercial-sized one concealed behind wood paneling that matched the cabinetry. Inside he found orange juice. Maybe a glass of juice would relieve his craving. He opened several overhead cabinets searching for the glasses; he found a liquor cabinet instead. He stared at the bottles. He reached in and removed a fifth of Jim Beam. Only his third sober night, but looking at the familiar label brought the cravings back. He was still staring at the bottle when he heard, "Ben."

He turned and saw his wife standing in the door—and the disappointment in her eyes. He replaced the bottle in the cabinet and shut the door.

"I won't let her down, Kate."

Nothing is more disappointing to a lawyer than a client's deal falling apart—all right, next to not getting paid, nothing is more disappointing to a lawyer than a client's deal falling apart. How many times had a lawyer arrived at the bargaining table ready to close a deal only to have the other party shrug lamely and turn his palms up, empty-handed? No money. Nothing to put on the bargaining table. Can't close the deal. Lying in bed, alone, as she had felt most of her life, Elizabeth Brice now wondered: What if the abductor can't close the deal? What if the abductor had nothing to put on the bargaining table? *Three-fourths of all children abducted by strangers are killed within three hours.* Grace had been abducted seventy-eight hours ago.

What if her daughter was dead?

1:18 A.M.

PATROL OFFICER Eddie Yates hated working double shifts, especially evenings and deep nights, 3:00 P.M. to 7:00 A.M., mostly because he couldn't spend four hours pumping iron at the gym. But on the chief's orders every cop on the force was working double shifts, rousting out sex offenders around the clock—there were a hell of a lot of perverts out there, Eddie had discovered. He was hoping the girl's killer was on his list; arresting a child killer would look awful good on the résumé he would give the Dallas PD.

He checked the in-unit computer screen for the next pervert on his list: Jennings, Gary M., white, twenty-seven, blond, blue eyes, five-ten, one-fifty-five (heck, Eddie could take this guy with one hand), charged with stat rape eight years ago, pleaded out to indecency with a child, received probation, not even a speeding ticket since. *Risk level 3: no basis for concern for re-offense.* That's all the entry said, but Eddie could read between the lines. This boy had been nineteen at the time of the offense, probably in college; he and a girl were partying, ended up in bed, turned out she's jail bait. But she had to be damn close to legal or they wouldn't have let him plead out. And now he's branded a sex offender for life.

Eddie sighed. Gary Jennings wasn't a sex offender; he just screwed the wrong girl at the wrong time. What was it Eddie's mom used to say? *There but for the grace of God?* Well, this'll be a monumental waste of time. But still, why didn't Jennings register with the police department when he moved to town like he's supposed to?

Apartment 121, that was Jennings's place. DMV records showed Jennings owned a black '99 Ford F-150 pickup. Eddie drove slowly through the apartment complex parking lot until he spotted a black Ford pickup. The plates checked out.

Eddie parked behind the pickup and exited the cruiser; he slid his nightstick into his holster, not that he expected any trouble from Jennings—but he could dream, couldn't he? He grabbed the big heavy flashlight—actually a sledge-hammer with a light on the end, a more effective tool for subduing a reluctant perp, not that he had ever had to. He shone the light inside the cab then tried the door, gently, so as not to set off the alarm. No need—it was unlocked, like half the cars in town tonight. There hadn't been a car stolen in Post Oak, Texas, since Eddie had been on the force. The place was a regular fucking Mayberry—and he felt like Barney Fife. How can you fight crime when there ain't no crime? Which was why Eddie Yates yearned for a job with the Dallas PD: they had some real crime down there, the most dangerous city in America.

Eddie opened the door and shone the light around the cab. It was clean as a whistle. He looked in the console and found a cell phone. Jennings wasn't even worried someone might steal it.

Aunt Bee, you seen Opey?

Eddie checked under the seat. Nothing. He lifted the

rubber floor mat on the passenger side. Nothing. He lifted the mat on the driver's side and—what's this? A photograph? He picked it up and shone the light on it. It was a photograph all right, like the copy you got when you printed a mug shot off the computer. Except this wasn't a mug shot of a criminal. This was a picture of a naked girl. A young naked girl. Kiddie porn. Eddie shook his head. Damn, he'd been wrong about this Jennings. He really was a pervert.

Of course, having a picture of a naked girl in his truck didn't make Jennings guilty of abducting the Brice girl. And how would he explain to the duty sergeant what he was doing inside Jennings's truck? Eddie thought for a second, then he rubbed the edge of the picture where he had touched it and replaced the picture under the floor mat.

Eddie shut the door quietly then stepped to the bed of the truck. Jennings had a matching fiberglass bed cover, the kind with the little hatch so you could get stuff out without taking the whole damn thing off. Eddie tried the hatch; as he expected, it was unlocked.

Opey's gone fishin' with his pa, Sheriff Andy!

Eddie opened the hatch and stuck the flashlight and his head in. He started at the nearest corner of the bed and moved the light around the bed and was about to pull his head out when—*What the hell is that?* In the far corner of the bed, it looked like a shirt, gold with a number . . . a jersey.

Eddie's adrenaline kicked in big time.

He pulled his head out and tried to stay calm and figure out what to do. If he called this in and it turned out to be Jennings's bowling shirt, the guys would be on his ass for a month. On the other hand, if it was the dead girl's jersey, he might screw up the evidence, conducting a search without a warrant. He vaguely remembered the training class on search and seizure, something about a plain view doctrine, that if the evidence was in plain sight, that was okay. Eddie wondered, *If he had to open the hatch and stick his head in with a flashlight, would that be in plain sight?*

Well, shit, no sense in getting ribbed for a month. He would pull the shirt out; if it was a bowling shirt, no harm done. If it was the girl's jersey, he'd throw it back in and deny ever touching it.

Eddie walked to the patrol unit, opened the trunk, and retrieved a tire tool. He returned to the pickup, stuck his upper body back under the bed cover, and reached for the shirt with the tool. He dragged the shirt along the bed until it was at the hatch opening. He spread the shirt out, holding the light on it, until he could read the blue letters.

Tornadoes.

He flipped the jersey over. A number nine on the back.

Eddie now wondered, *Could an on-duty patrol officer claim the $25 million reward?*

2:02 A.M.

INSIDE APARTMENT 121, Gary Jennings couldn't sleep. He rolled over close to his wife, his chest to her back—she had taken to sleeping on her side with a pillow between her legs—and slid his hand around her round belly. She was seven months' pregnant and bigger than he was now, but he didn't care.

He was going to be a daddy.

Gary wished his own dad could be here to see his grandchild; he had died eight years ago of a heart attack right after that incident in college. His father had died of embarrassment. He had been embarrassed by his son. And Gary couldn't blame him. Jesus, he had been a real fuckup in college, a frat rat, drinking, partying, playing golf, earning eighteen hours of fucking-off credit per semester, and screwing girls—*What the hell was a sixteen-year-old girl doing at a goddamn frat party?*

And he'd still be a fuckup today if he hadn't found Debbie.

Debbie had changed his life. She had said he would forever be a fuckup if he didn't give up his sinful ways—well, she didn't say *fuckup*, she said *lost child*, which he translated into *fuckup*. And, man, he was tired of being a fuckup. And she said he'd never have any money. And, man, he was really tired of being broke. So he had figured, what the hell, it was worth a shot. All he had to do, she had said, was go to church, quit drinking beer and smoking dope, and cancel his subscription to *Playboy*.

And she was right.

Only two years since he had given up sinning, he was married, soon to be a father, and working at a great job. He had hired on six months ago; right now, he was just a code monkey, grinding out computer code twelve hours a day, wired on Snickers and Red Bull.

But the long hours were about to pay off: his stock options vested in six months and they'd be worth a million bucks after the IPO. *One million dollars!* As soon as the lockout period expired, he would cash out. He would tithe 10 percent to the church, Debbie would insist on that (although he might be able to negotiate her down to 7.5 percent), pay 15 percent in taxes, and net about $750,000. He'd put a hundred thousand in an education trust for the baby so she wouldn't be a fuckup, then he'd buy Debbie a real nice house and use the rest to start his own Internet company.

Lying next to Debbie and looking forward to the future, a slight smile crossed his face. He had finally found his place in this world. Gary Jennings counted his blessings as he drifted off to sleep.

Gary jumped up in bed at the sound of his apartment door being battered off its hinges. Debbie woke and screamed. Men were suddenly inside their bedroom, shouting and shining bright lights and pointing guns, men wearing black uniforms with POLICE in white letters.

DAY FIVE

6:17 A.M.

LIEUTENANT BEN BRICE carries a black XM21 sniper rifle fitted with a Starlight Scope and a Sionics suppressor. Twenty ammo magazines, six high-explosive and two white-phosphorous grenades, a .45-caliber handgun, C-4 explosive, a claymore mine, and morphine are packed in his web gear. An Uzi, his backup weapon, is secured to his rucksack. An eleven-inch Bowie knife is strapped to his right calf. He carries the tools of killing because he is a professional killer, an Army Green Beret special operations soldier. *WE KILL FOR PEACE* reads the tattoo on his left arm. Seventeen days in-country and Ben Brice has already seen enough killing for a lifetime. But he knows the killing has only just begun.

And after this night, he will never know peace.

He is walking through smoke and ashes thick like gray confetti and out of the smoldering hamlet in the Quang Tri province of South Vietnam, leaving the china doll and his soul behind.

He stops.

He is standing above an irrigation ditch; down below is a tangled mass of pale bodies. The stench of death hangs in the humid air like a thick fog. The sounds of death rise from below, the last gasps and groans of the dying.

He drops his rifle and jumps down into the ditch. He checks each body for life, frantic now, trying to find life, any sign of life. But there is no life to be found. There is only death. He counts forty-one—old men, women, and children.

His boots are soaked in blood. His hands are dripping with blood. The china doll's blood and brains cling to his fatigues like souvenirs of death.

He is drenched in death.

He extends his bloody hands to the heavens and screams into the still night: "Why, God?"

He feels faint and his body sways. He closes his eyes. He falls forward, down onto that white blanket of death.

But he is not falling.

He is floating.

He opens his eyes. Below him, the pale bodies are now bright white—a blinding white world as far as he can see. Above him his parachute is deployed, but he doesn't remember the violent jerk when the chute caught air.

He's sailing now, skimming the surface, almost able to reach out and touch the white, as pure as the driven . . . snow. Pure white snow. A white world of deep heavenly snow. Sailing faster and faster, higher and higher above the snow.

Dark objects down below come into view. Trees. Tall thick trees of timber country. And among the trees, curled up and shivering and wrapped in a blanket of snow like a present under a Christmas tree, is God's little creature.

He floats down to the creature and lands on both feet. He unbuckles the parachute harness and lets it drop and disappear into the deep snow that he walks through without effort to the cold and shivering creature. He's now wearing his dress uniform and green beret and all the medals pinned to the jacket and the Medal of Honor around his neck. He removes his jacket, squats, and wraps the coat around the creature; he gently lifts it from the snow, takes it into his arms, and holds it close, warming God's little creature. He brushes the snow from the creature's face and through his tears he sees her, his saving Grace.

"Ben, wake up! They got him!"

And then she is gone. Ben opened his eyes to Kate leaning over him.

"Got who?"

"The man that took Gracie."

6:21 A.M.

"MIGHT BE HIM. I'm just not sure."

Coach Wally Fagan was staring through the two-way mirror at the sad young man in the white jail uniform sitting at a metal table in the bare interrogation room; his cuffed hands were spread flat on the table, and he appeared dazed and confused. He had blond hair and blue eyes, but he didn't seem nearly as big as the man who had asked for Gracie after the game. He seemed different.

"Look, Coach," the police chief said, "the guy's a convicted sex offender and we found child pornography and Gracie's jersey in his truck—where do you think he got that from?"

"Well, yeah, then I guess it's him."

Still, there was something about him that didn't fit. Wally just couldn't put his finger on it.

Ben sat on the edge of the bed and rubbed his bare arms and chest, trying to suppress the shakes.

"Gracie wasn't with him, was she?" he said to Kate.

"How'd you know?"

"Angelina was right. Gracie's cold. They've taken her up north."

"They *who?*"

Ben rubbed his face. "The abductors."

Kate punched the power button on the small television. The screen flashed on to a video of a police team using a two-man battering ram to knock down an apartment door early that Tuesday morning. They shouted "Police!" and stormed the place with weapons drawn; minutes later, they led a sleepy young man out of the apartment and into the bright lights of the media. He appeared anything but dangerous in red plaid pajamas with his hands cuffed behind his back and escorted by cops who towered over him. He looked like a skinny kid. Trailing behind him was a distraught young pregnant woman wearing a robe. The early morning arrest had been a made-for-TV event. Kate pointed at the screen.

"But *he's* the abductor!"

6:45 A.M.

He doesn't look like a pervert, John thought as he stared at the suspect through the interrogation room window. He didn't look anything like the Army bullies; he wasn't coarse, thick, hairy, dirty, or ugly. But then, what's a pervert supposed to look like? The mug shots of sex offenders in the paper were always of unshaven miscreants with greasy hair and acne scars and missing teeth. This guy was clean and clean-cut. In fact, his face seemed vaguely familiar, like the kids just out of college who worked at BriceWare.com; but then, his was a face John saw every day in the high-tech world—young, white, male, and pale.

John knew now that he would never see Gracie again. Never hold her again or talk to her again or admire her swell face again. This guy had taken her away. For ever. John wanted to get mad, but he couldn't muster any anger. He could barely muster the strength in his wobbly legs to remain standing. So he leaned forward and rested his weight against the window. Tears came into his eyes. At least her pain had stopped. And he found himself envying her again: his pain would never stop.

*

The abductor had nothing to put on the bargaining table.

He couldn't close the deal.

Her deal was dead.

Elizabeth was also standing at the window staring in at the abductor, so close to him she could have reached out and strangled the son of a bitch if they had not been separated by the glass, and wondering if she could make it inside the interrogation room and choke the life out of him before Chief Ryan and Agent Devereaux could react. She turned to John; he was leaning into the glass, his forehead plastered against the pane, his arms hanging at his side, staring at the abductor like a kid looking in at the gorilla exhibit at the zoo.

Elizabeth turned back to the abductor, imagining him on top of her daughter while she lay motionless, silent tears streaming down her face, wondering why God had forsaken her. Heat spread across Elizabeth's body; her fists clenched. Her entire body ached to strangle the bastard.

She glanced over at Ryan and Devereaux, standing a few steps behind her, engrossed in conversation, paying no attention to the victim's distraught mother over by the interrogation room. She inched toward the door. Her pulse raced with anticipation.

"We got an anonymous tip," Chief Ryan said to FBI Special Agent Eugene Devereaux.

"You should've got a warrant," Devereaux said. "Paul, your man conducted an illegal search—under a floor mat and a bed cover ain't in plain view. That picture and the jersey, they won't ever see the inside of a courtroom. What else you got?"

"The coach ID'd him."

"Positive?"

"Pretty much."

Devereaux raised an eyebrow. "Pretty much ain't much in a courtroom. Any other tangible evidence?"

"Well, nothing at this time."

"Nothing in his apartment?"

"No."

"Nothing else in his truck?"

"No . . . but your people are on it, checking for DNA."

"Well, they damn sure better find some, Paul, 'cause we can't take what we got to a grand jury."

Ryan almost laughed. "The hell we can't. Our county grand jury will indict a goddamn Greyhound bus if we tell 'em to!"

"Chief!"

A police officer came running up the corridor toward them.

"Chief," the officer said when he arrived, "we got his cell phone records. Nine calls last week to the Brice residence."

Elizabeth had worked her way almost to the interrogation room door when the police officer's words jolted her. She turned to him but pointed sharply at the abductor behind the glass.

"He called *my* house?"

"Not any of your numbers, ma'am," the officer said. "He called Gracie's phone number. It's listed in the book."

"*He stalked my daughter?*"

That did it. A sudden surge of rage propelled Elizabeth to the door and inside the interrogation room before the others could react. The abductor recoiled as she lunged across the table at him and landed in his lap. They toppled over backwards in his chair onto the cement floor. He couldn't break the fall with his hands and feet shackled. Elizabeth fell on his chest, knees first, knocking the air out of him. His mouth gaped and he sucked for air as she punched him in the face, again and again, trying to drive her fist through his face, the adrenaline and rage giving her strength she had never known, spit spewing out of her mouth along with her words.

"Where's my daughter, goddamnit?"

She tried her absolute best to break his nose with the knuckles of her fist. He groaned.

"You killed her, didn't you!"

She extended her right leg, as if she were doing her tight buns exercise, then drove her knee into his groin, hoping to drive his balls into his brain. His eyes rolled back and he screamed in pain.

"You're not on top now, you sorry fuck!"

She grabbed his neck and commenced choking the bastard that took her daughter.

"You fucking pervert!"

Thick black arms suddenly wrapped around her midsection from behind, and she was lifted off the abductor until she was dangling in midair—but her strong hands remained locked around the pervert's scrawny neck. She held on for as long as she could, but her grip finally gave way. She got in one last good kick, a Nike cross-trainer right in his ribs, which produced a low groan from the bastard.

"Mrs. Brice, control yourself!"

Devereaux's arms were wrapped around the mother's torso, and he was trying to back out of the interrogation room with her kicking and screaming and spitting at the suspect. *She was no longer just halfway to nuts—she was all the way there!* He got her to the door, but she grabbed hold of both sides of the doorjamb and held on for dear life, still screaming profanities at the suspect, her eyes blazing with feral rage.

"You're gonna die, you sick bastard! You're gonna die and go to hell!"

Christ, she was incredibly strong for her size! Devereaux was trying to pry the mother's fingers loose while holding her with one arm. He could feel her rock-hard midsection expanding and contracting rapidly; her adrenaline was pumping big time.

"I'll inject the poison myself, you fucking pervert! You killed my baby! Fuck you! Fuck you! Fuck you!"

Devereaux outweighed the mother by at least a hundred pounds, but he'd be damned if he could get this woman out of the room! And choke-holding a victim's mother was entirely out of the question. He decided to lean backward slightly to see if she could hang on with his big self pulling against her. She hung on. *Damn!* It must be the adrenaline, giving her this kind of strength. He looked to Chief Ryan for help.

But the chief was trying to get the suspect, who was bleeding profusely from his nose and mouth, bound by leg and wrist irons, and cupping his genitals with both hands, up off the floor and back into his chair. The suspect struggled to his knees; Ryan stood behind him and yanked up on the iron belt shackled to his waist, practically lifting him off his feet. The suspect stood. Then he puked.

The mother screamed: "Choke on it, you sonofabitch!"

Once Ryan had the suspect in place, he hurried over and pried the mother's fingers loose one by one, first her right hand—the mother craned her head around Ryan and got in one final "Fuck you!" at the suspect—and then her left hand. Devereaux almost fell backwards into the corridor with her in his arms. Chief Ryan shut the door to the interrogation room behind them.

"Put me down, goddamnit!" the mother demanded.

Devereaux released her. She pushed his arms away and straightened her clothes. She was wearing a black-and-white nylon sweat suit over a black tee shirt; her face was red and shiny with sweat; her chest was heaving with each gasped breath. She cleared her face of tears, saliva, and snot with one swipe of her sleeve.

"I want to know what he did with her!"

"So do we, Mrs. Brice, but he's in police custody and you can't beat it out of him!"

"Then you beat it out of him!"

"Mrs. Brice!"

FBI Special Agent Eugene Devereaux had never before yelled at a mother of an abducted child. But then, he had never met a mother like Elizabeth Brice. Most mothers fell apart: some started smoking again, some drinking, some didn't get out of bed, some ended up in the psych ward with nervous breakdowns. Elizabeth Brice beat the hell out of the prime suspect. Devereaux was glad she wasn't his wife, but she was an impressive woman nonetheless.

She was now pacing around like a caged animal, allowing her adrenaline to ease and examining the traces of blood on her raw knuckles; she stuck her knuckles in her mouth and sucked the blood clean.

"Now everyone just calm down!" Chief Ryan said. To several uniforms who had come running to see what the commotion was about, he said, "Get someone in there to clean that mess up . . . and a paramedic for the suspect." Then, satisfied that the mother was under control, he turned to the young officer who had brought the news of the phone records. "That it? The phone calls?"

"No, sir. He works for Mr. Brice."

"*What?*"

"Yeah, Chief, the guy works at BriceWare."

The chief turned to the father: "You don't know him?"

Most victims' fathers begged Devereaux for five minutes alone with the abductor. But this victim's father had maintained his position at the window throughout the mother's attack on the suspect. Mr. Brice shook his head.

"No."

"Chief," the officer said, "the phone company can identify the cell tower nearest the call's origination. There's a tower next to the BriceWare building."

Chief Ryan gave Devereaux an I-told-you-so shrug. As the new information slowly sank in, all eyes turned and fixed on the young man bleeding and sobbing at the table in the interrogation room. The mother turned to Devereaux and pointed a finger at him.

"Find out what he did with my daughter."

7:38 A.M.

"YOU HAVE THE right to remain silent. Anything you say can be used against you in a court of law. You have the right to an attorney prior to questioning and to have an attorney present during questioning. If you cannot afford an attorney, you have the right to have one appointed for you prior to any questioning."

Chief of Police Paul Ryan looked up from his Miranda card at the prime suspect. "Gary, do you understand your rights as I have explained them to you?"

The interrogation room reeked of the cleaning solvent used to disinfect the floor and table where Jennings had vomited. Ryan was sitting with his back to the two-way mirror; Agent Devereaux sat at one end of the rectangular metal table, and Jennings sat across the table. His nose was swollen and his lips were fat; the area under his left eye was already turning purple. It looked to be one hell of a shiner. He nodded at Ryan.

"Son, you gotta state your answer for the tape recorder."

A recorder sat in the middle of the table. They had decided to audiotape rather than videotape; Jennings's battered face would give his lawyer ammunition to claim any confession was coerced. A judge was not likely to believe that while in police custody the victim's mother beat up the prime suspect.

"Yes," Jennings said.

"Yes, you understand your constitutional rights?"

"Yes."

"And you're waiving your right to have an attorney present during questioning?"

"Yes."

Once a lawyer enters the room, any hope of a confession exits. Obtaining a quick confession was particularly urgent in this case because the evidence collected from Jennings's truck would likely be inadmissible in court—but mostly because a confession got the story off the evening news and the mayor off Ryan's back. So Paul Ryan put the Miranda card in his shirt pocket, folded his hands on the table, and said in a soft voice, one of disappointment in a teenage son who had taken the family car without permission:

"Gary, why'd you take Gracie?"

"I didn't take her!"

"Mr. Brice said she went to the BriceWare office over the Christmas holidays, nearly every day. Is that when you first became acquainted with Gracie?"

"Yes . . . I mean, no! We weren't *acquainted*."

"What were you?"

"We were . . . *nothing!* I work for Mr. Brice, that's all!"

"But you saw her in the office?"

"Yeah. She delivered mail, on rollerblades."

"And you knew she was Mr. Brice's daughter?"

"Sure, we all did."

"Has Mr. Brice been a good employer to you?"

"Yeah, it's a great place to work."

"Good pay, good benefits?"

"Yeah."

"Stock options?"

"Yeah."

Ryan threw a thumb at the two-way mirror behind him. "Gary, Mr. Brice is standing on the other side of that mirror, looking at you, listening to everything you're saying." Jennings looked up at the mirror. "For God's sake, son, at least tell him where his daughter's body is, so he can bury her properly. Don't just leave her out there in some field, buzzards picking her over."

"I don't know where she's at!" Jennings tried to stand but the leg irons restrained him. To the mirror, he said, "Mr. Brice, I swear to God, I didn't take her!" He looked like he might start crying again.

"But you've done this sort of thing before."

Jennings fell back into the chair. "No, no, no, that was in college, a frat party, we were drunk . . . How was I supposed to know she was only sixteen?"

Agent Devereaux gestured to Ryan for Jennings's file. Ryan slid it down the length of the table to Devereaux, who thumbed through it while Ryan continued his questioning.

"The law doesn't require that you know, only that the victim be under the age of seventeen when you had sex with her."

"The *victim*? She was putting out for a bunch of guys at a frat party the next weekend—I saw her!"

Ryan shrugged. "You're required to register with the police department when you move into town. You didn't do that, Gary."

"Yeah, and have my photo plastered across the newspaper again with 'sex offender' in big print. I'm branded a sex offender for life and she's married to a doctor."

"Why didn't you register?"

"Because I didn't want my wife to find out. I wanted a clean start." Tears welled up in Jennings's eyes. "I just got drunk at a frat party. I was five days too old for her."

An exception to the Texas statutory rape statute states that if the defendant is less than three years older than the victim, there is no crime. Jennings was nineteen years and twenty-seven days old at the time of the sexual act; the girl was sixteen years and twenty-two days old. Five days' difference made him a sex offender for life.

"You're not a child molester?"

"No!"

Ryan reached over to the file and removed the plastic-wrapped picture of the naked adolescent female found in Jennings's truck. He pushed it in front of Jennings.

"Well, son, why do you look at pictures like this?"

Jennings glanced at the picture and recoiled.

"I've never seen that picture before!"

"It was in your truck, under the floor mat."

"In *my* truck?"

"Yes, son, in your truck. Possession of child pornography is a federal crime, Gary—that picture alone can put you in prison for most of your adult life."

"I don't know how it got in my truck."

"Well, what about her jersey? How'd that get in your truck?"

"What jersey?"

"Gracie's soccer jersey. It was in the back of your truck, under the bed cover."

"Her jersey was in my truck?"

"Yes."

"This has gotta be a joke, a big mistake!"

"What about the nine phone calls you made to Gracie last week, are those a big mistake?"

"I never called her!"

"We traced the calls to your cell phone."

"My cell phone? I don't know . . . I leave the phone in my truck. I never lock it."

"Why not?"

"Because there's no crime out here, just like the mayor says! Do you lock your car? Maybe someone used my cell phone while I was at work."

"Oh, okay, someone's framing you?"

"Yes!"

Ryan leaned back in his chair, crossed his arms, and studied Gary Jennings. Twenty-seven years old with a boyish face and frame, he didn't look like your typical sexual predator; in fact, he looked like Ryan's son-in-law, a proctologist in Dallas. And most predators weren't nearly so convincing in their claims of innocence—the boy was good. But he had made a prior trip through the system, so he knew to deny, deny, deny; juries liked that when they listened to the interrogation tape. Ryan decided to ratchet up the pressure, give the boy something to think about.

"Okay, Gary, let's summarize your defense for the jury: a sexual predator premeditates his abduction of Gracie weeks in advance. He searches the state's sex offender database and finds you, a convicted sex offender who just happens to fit his description to a T, who just happens to live three miles from the park, and who just happens to work for Gracie's father. Then, during the week prior to the abduction, he goes to your place of employment, finds your truck unlocked, plants child pornography in it and uses your cell phone to place nine calls to Gracie. Then, after he abducts Gracie and rapes her and kills her in the woods behind the park, he dumps her body and drives over to your apartment and tosses her jersey in your truck to frame you." Ryan turned his hands up. "Gary, you're a smart fella, do you really expect a jury of adults to believe that?"

Jennings was shaking his head slowly, as if in disbelief. "No . . . I mean, yes! I guess he could've done that, I don't know. But I didn't do it!"

"Gary, who's the jury gonna believe when Gracie's coach takes the stand and points his finger at you"—which Ryan was now doing—"and says, 'He's the man that took Gracie'?"

"I didn't take her!"

"Okay, Gary. One last question: what else are we gonna find in your truck? FBI's best people are examining every square inch of that vehicle—are they gonna find Gracie's fingerprints, her hair, her blood?"

"No! She's never been in my truck!"

Ryan stood and walked to the door, then turned back to deliver the clincher that would surely have this boy making a tearful confession later today.

"I hope you're right, son, 'cause if they find her DNA in your truck, that puts her in your vehicle and you on death row."

8:26 A.M.

B EN HAD ARRIVED while Agent Devereaux and Chief Ryan were interrogating the suspect. The boy's face seemed familiar. After a moment, Ben placed him: he was the young man with the pregnant wife who had come up to John at the candlelight vigil Sunday night and offered his sympathy. Ben was standing at the window to the interrogation room when Devereaux and Ryan emerged.

"Drunken sex?" Agent Devereaux said to the chief. "That's his only prior offense? He and a girl get drunk at a frat party, have sex, she regrets it the next morning and files charges? Jennings pleads out because he's nineteen and she's one month from legal and gets probation? That makes him a sexual predator?"

Chief Ryan shrugged. "No defense to stat rape. Besides, he pleaded guilty."

"To indecency with a child, Paul, so he didn't spend the next twenty years in prison! This boy hasn't had a speeding ticket in eight years, all of a sudden he decides to abduct and kill a child?"

Ben stepped forward. "He doesn't fit the profile. He's not a loner deviant. He's married, his wife's pregnant, he's about to make a lot of money. No bad news in this boy's life to trigger the abduction, like your profiler said."

Ben held up the flier with the composite sketch of the suspect that had been distributed to the media immediately after the abduction. "He doesn't look anything like this guy. And the coach put the abductor at six foot, two hundred pounds. What's this boy, five-ten, one-fifty?"

"He probably looked taller in the black cap," Chief Ryan said. "Look, Colonel, we got the bad guy, okay? The coach identified him, he had child porn and Gracie's jersey in his truck, and he called Gracie nine times last week." He threw his hands up. "What more do you want?"

"The truth."

A sharp look. "Sorry. The law only gives you a conviction."

11:00 A.M.

"WE'VE GOT TO follow the book or a federal judge will overturn a death penalty."

Not an hour after the Jennings interrogation, the local mayor and police chief had stood on the front steps of the town hall and proclaimed Gary Jennings guilty of the abduction and murder of Gracie Ann Brice. The locals were always desperate to close a child abduction case—bad for property values; but FBI Special Agent Eugene Devereaux had refused to participate. He was troubled by Jennings's demeanor; it wasn't the demeanor of a sexual predator. Was Jennings that good a liar? Maybe. But Devereaux decided to wait for the Evidence Response Team's report before making any judgments about Gary Jennings; he would wait to see if Gracie's DNA was found in Jennings's truck. DNA never lied.

But the mayor's proclamation had brought the family into the command post; Devereaux was now standing on the other side of his desk from Gracie's parents and grandparents.

"The court's got to appoint a lawyer to represent Jennings, one with experience in death cases, because the appeals courts will order a retrial if the trial lawyer didn't know what he was doing. So then we go through another trial all over again, three years down the road."

"But we've got to find Grace!" the mother said.

This was the part that Devereaux always hated. "Mrs. Brice, if Jennings is the abductor, Gracie wasn't with him. Which means—"

"She's dead," the mother said.

"Yes, ma'am. If Jennings is the guy."

"At least he can tell us where she's at."

"Yes, ma'am. If he knows."

"You're not sure he's the abductor, are you?" Colonel Brice asked. "Things don't fit."

"No, sir, things don't fit."

"Make him take a polygraph," the colonel said.

"If we administer a polygraph before his lawyer is appointed and he fails, we know he's guilty but anything we learn from the polygraph may not be admissible."

"And if he passes?"

"We cut him loose. Polygraphs aren't admissible in court, but they're 95 percent reliable, which is a helluva lot better than a jury."

"What about the other man from the game tape?"

"Colonel, I don't know. Maybe they weren't together. Maybe Jennings didn't know the other man like he says."

"So what's the time frame?" the mother asked.

"Several days. The court will appoint a lawyer today, he'll be arraigned tomorrow. It takes longer to do it right, but if we screw this up, his conviction will be overturned and we'll never execute Gary Jennings for the murder of your daughter."

1:48 P.M.

"WELL, EDDIE, you fucked up the jersey," the chief said. "Plain sight? In the back of a truck under a bed cover? What, you got X-ray vision?"

Patrol Officer Eddie Yates was sweating. Chief Ryan had called him at home and asked him to come in early before shift change and see him in his office. That had never happened before. Eddie had figured the chief wanted to congratulate him on a job well done. He had figured wrong.

"And the porn picture, now that's kind of interesting, Eddie, 'cause the only fingerprints they could find on the damn thing were yours. How you figure that?"

The pores on Eddie's forehead were popping sweat beads like popcorn.

"Chief, I—"

"You entered his truck, searched it, looked under the mat, picked the picture up, and put it back under? How stupid is that?"

"Shit, Chief, I thought I rubbed off my prints."

"Eddie, you ain't supposed to tell your chief that, goddamnit!" The chief shook his head. "Damnit, Eddie, that son of a bitch could walk 'cause of you! You'd better pray the FBI boys find her DNA in his truck."

Barney Fife done screwed up and Sheriff Andy was pissed.

"I'm real sorry, Chief."

"Did you jimmy the hatch?"

"Oh, no, Chief, I swear I didn't! It was unlocked, the door, too."

"Where was the cell phone?"

"In the console. Is that stupid or what? I mean, no one locks their cars in this place, but leaving a cell phone in there? I could've taken it, sat in the parking lot, and run out his air time without him knowing it till he got the bill."

Eddie laughed; the chief didn't. Instead, he waved Eddie out of his office. Eddie walked to the door then thought of something. He wasn't sure this was the best time to ask, but he couldn't wait.

"Uh, Chief . . ."

The chief looked up.

"Any way I get some of that reward money?"

The chief blinked hard and said, "You're shittin' me?"

Eddie walked out just as the chief's secretary stuck her head in and said, "Jennings's wife is here."

She was just a kid, really.

Ryan had left the door to his office open so his secretary could see and hear them, him and Jennings's wife. Debbie Jennings had come in to plead her husband's innocence. He had reminded her that she could not be compelled to testify against her husband; she said they had nothing to hide. She was twenty-five and seven months' pregnant. They had married two years ago. She knew nothing of his college conviction.

"That doesn't mean he's a child molester," she said. "Gary would never do anything like that."

She looked like she hadn't slept since the arrest. She took deep breaths.

"You okay?" She nodded, but Ryan wasn't so sure. "Mrs. Jennings, where was Gary Friday night?"

"With me. He got home a little after five, we took our walk—the doctor wants me to walk every day—we ate dinner, watched TV. And we picked out names for the baby. It's a girl."

"Did you decide?"

"Decide what?"

"Her name."

"Sarah."

"Nice name." Paul Ryan wanted a grandchild, but his son-in-law the proctologist wanted a Porsche. "Gary never left the apartment that night?"

"No."

"And you never left the apartment?"

"No."

"Are there any other witnesses?"

"We usually don't have sleepovers, Chief. Can anyone other than your wife confirm where you were last night?"

She had a point.

"And your cops found nothing when they ransacked our apartment—they went through my underwear drawer, for God's sake!"

"Mrs. Jennings, do you know anything about Gracie's jersey, how it might have gotten into Gary's truck?"

"No. I've told him a hundred times to lock his truck, but he always says that's why we moved out of the city, because there's no crime out here. Anyone could have put it in his truck."

"Not anyone, Mrs. Jennings. Only the abductor. Why would he do that?"

"I don't know."

"What about the phone calls?"

"I don't know."

"Did Gary ever talk about Gracie?"

"No. The only time he's ever spoken to Mr. Brice was at the vigil."

"What about when he hired on?"

She shook her head. "Gary's only been there six months. Mr. Brice has been in New York most of the time, on the IPO."

"Why'd Gary go to the vigil?"

"She was his boss's daughter. The whole town went."

"Has Gary's behavior changed in any way since Friday night?"

"Yes, at two this morning when the police kicked our door down and pointed guns at us. He freaked."

"Did he dispose of any clothing recently?"

"No."

"Did he clean his truck over the weekend?"

"No."

"Has Gary ever displayed an unusual interest in children?"

"No. Kids drive him nuts."

"Has he ever referred to children as 'pure' or 'innocent'?"

"No. He thinks my sister's kids were sent by Satan. Chief, where are you getting these questions? Out of a child-molester manual?"

He was, in fact.

"Does he have any friends you would describe as deviants or weird?"

"Have you been to his workplace? People there got rings in their ears, noses, tongues, navels, nipples, and genitals. That's weird."

He had to agree with her.

"Mrs. Jennings, do you and Gary have a, uh, normal marital relationship?"

"Do we have sex?"

He nodded.

"Yes, Chief, we have sex. Gary likes sex with his wife, not little girls."

Ryan hesitated. He wasn't getting very far with her. Of course, he hadn't told her about the child pornography. He debated whether he should, but he decided that it would come out at trial anyway, probably sooner. So it wasn't as if he would be intentionally upsetting her. And maybe she would then realize that her husband was guilty and she could pressure him into confessing. Paul Ryan needed a confession to keep his job. So he retrieved the picture from the desk drawer and held it in his lap.

"Mrs. Jennings, does your husband practice pornography?"

"Oh, no, he's never asked me to do anything like that . . . well, one time he asked me to put it in my mouth, but I told him that was sinful. He's never asked again."

"No, uh, I mean, does he have pornography around the apartment, you know, magazines or movies?"

"No, he doesn't even get *Playboy* since he accepted God into his life."

"Has he ever possessed child pornography?"

"No!"

"Mrs. Jennings, we found this in Gary's truck."

Ryan placed the picture on the desk and slowly pushed it toward her. Her eyes locked on the image, her mouth came open, as if she were going to speak, but no words came out. She looked up at Ryan then back at the picture. Finally, she spoke.

"This was in Gary's truck?"

"Yes, ma'am, it was."

Her face went pale. She put her palms on the desk and pushed herself up out of the chair. Halfway up, she suddenly groaned and grabbed at her round belly, down low. She bent over and cried out in pain. She collapsed.

Jesus Christ!

Ryan vaulted to her side of the desk. Blood was on her bare legs.

"Call the paramedics!" he yelled to his secretary.

2:12 P.M.

A RISK LEVEL 3 offender is defined as an offender for whom there is no basis for concern that the person poses a serious danger to the community or will continue to engage in criminal sexual conduct.

Gary Jennings was a risk level 3 offender.

Elizabeth had logged onto the Texas Department of Public Safety's online Sex Offender Database. She entered *Jennings, Gary* in the search box and clicked. Jennings's photo came up along with his record.

JENNINGS, GARY MICHAEL

DPS NO.	DOB	RISK LEVEL	SEX	RACE
156870021	3/10/79	3	male	white

HT	WT	EYE COLOR	HAIR COLOR	SHOE SIZE
510	155	blu	bln	085

ALIAS NAMES
Jennings, Gary

CURRENT ADDRESS
1100 Interstate 45
Oakville Apartments
Apt. 121
Post Oak, Texas 78901

OFFENSE DATA

OFFENSE:	Indecency w/child sexual contact
COUNTS:	1
VICTIM'S SEX:	Female
VICTIM'S AGE:	16.11
DISPOSITION DATE:	07/08/1998
TIME:	1Y PROBATED
STATUS:	DISCHARGED

Forty-two thousand registered sex offenders resided in the State of Texas. And one of them had abducted and murdered her daughter.

2:30 P.M.

Briceware.com Incorporated occupied an abandoned grocery store in a nondescript strip shopping center across the interstate from the affluence of Briarwyck Farms. FBI Special Agent Eugene Devereaux followed the father through the automatic sliding-glass doors and into the store along with Agents Stevens and Jorgenson. They had come to check Gary Jennings's workspace and personnel records.

Inside, the cavernous space was, in fact, an empty grocery store. Big neon signs—DAIRY . . . MEATS . . . BAKERY . . . PHARMACY . . . VIDEOS . . . PRODUCE—still lit up the walls. Hanging from the ceiling were grocery store fluorescent lights and grocery store aisle markers with product listings. But where the aisles of groceries used to stand were now aisles of low cubicles; heads were bobbing up and down. Young men and women, boys and girls really, glided by on rollerblades or personal scooters, headphones wrapped around their skulls, their ears and noses adorned with rings, their arms and ankles with tattoos, their hair representing all the colors of the rainbow; some pushed grocery carts filled with mail or boxes; they were dressed like they were at a rock concert instead of a business.

If there was anyone over the age of twenty-five, Devereaux had yet to see him or her. The workplace of this high-tech company looked more like the cafeteria during lunch at his daughter's high school. And the father looked more like a skinny teenager than the CEO of a company worth billions.

At the CUSTOMER SERVICE desk a young receptionist with purple hair and narrow black-framed glasses stood abruptly when she saw the father; her neon-red shirt did not cover her navel, which was pierced with a silver ring. She stepped to the father and put her head in his chest, then she wrapped her arms around him. The father patted her stiffly.

"Oh, Kahuna," she said softly. She released the father and wiped her eyes. "How could he hurt her? He seemed like a righteous dude. I mean, he was here yesterday, like he hadn't done anything." She shook her head. "The real world is too random." She bit her pierced lower lip. "I'll really miss her."

The father nodded and said in almost a whisper, "Terri, tell everyone the IPO will go forward tomorrow. They deserve it."

Terri nodded. "Okay, Boss. But just so you know—the IPO's cool and all, but we're here because of you. You're the man."

The father sighed and stared off into space for a moment. Then he said, "Yeah . . . I'm the man. Where's Jennings's cube?"

The young woman checked her computer screen. "Cookies and Crackers, cube twenty-three."

Devereaux and his agents followed the father toward the PHARMACY sign and past the VIDEO section where a collection of foosball, air hockey tables, and road racing simulators stood, an exercise room, a coffee stand, an open area with a regulation basketball hoop, and a dozen soda and snack machines standing along the wall like suspects in a lineup. A young Hispanic male with platinum-blond hair was banging on the side of a Red Bull vending machine. The father stopped so they stopped.

"The dang thing stole my money again!" He glanced up at the father. "Oh, sorry, Boss. I mean, not about this, but, uh, you know, about . . ."

The father eyed the young man, then he stared down the machine like Devereaux's daughter stared down the goal before attempting a free throw. Then he suddenly swung his right foot up in some kind of karate kick and drove the heel of his shoe into the side of the machine: *BAMM!* The machine rocked back and forth, settled, and spat out two cans of Red Bull.

The Hispanic man grinned broadly, grabbed the two cans, and said, "Cool. A freebie." Then to the father: "You da man."

He held his fist out to the father. They bumped fists like the pro athletes do, then the Hispanic man walked off in one direction and they walked off in the opposite direction. They turned up an aisle marked *Cookies and Crackers*. Chairs in the cubicles swiveled away from computer screens as they walked past; behind them, heads poked out from the cubicles.

They arrived at cubicle twenty-three, a small crowded space, maybe six feet by six feet; two adults could not occupy the cubicle simultaneously because most of the space was taken up by a computer perched on a slim table, a few drawers, and boxes stacked on the floor. The walls of the cubicle were covered with yellow stickums, company memos, and pictures of Jennings and his wife smiling, kissing, and hugging—and one of Jennings patting her swollen belly. He did not appear to be a psychological time bomb. He was wearing a black baseball cap in one photo.

"Stevens," Devereaux said, "you take the cubicle. Find out if Jennings contacted Gracie through his computer or accessed child-porn sites from here, then box up his personal belongings." To the father: "Personnel files."

The father silently led Devereaux and Jorgenson toward the DAIRY section of the company.

5:33 P.M.

Elizabeth pointed the remote at the TV and increased the volume. The reporter was saying, "A convicted sex offender sits in jail this Tuesday night, arrested in the early morning hours for the abduction of Gracie Ann Brice last Friday. Gary Jennings worked for the victim's father, where he apparently became acquainted with Gracie. He made nine calls to Gracie in the week preceding her abduction. Gracie's jersey was found in his truck, along with child pornography. Although not confirmed, sources tell us that traces of blood were also found in his truck. DNA tests are underway to determine if it's Gracie's. Jennings will be charged with kidnapping, murder, and possession of child pornography. While this community holds out hope, authorities concede privately that Gracie Ann Brice is presumed dead."

8:05 P.M.

*S*HE'S ALIVE.

    Their bond was unbroken.

She had come to him. She was showing him the way. She's up north, where it's cold. Where there's snow on the ground. Where the trees stand tall.

But where up north?

Ben had found the weather channel on the pool house TV. The entire northern part of the country was under a blanket of snow from a late spring snowstorm. Was Gracie in Washington or Montana or Minnesota or Michigan or Maine? He didn't have time to cover three thousand miles. He needed to be pointed in the right direction.

Ben was hoping the FBI's computer printout of leads would do just that. After returning from the police station, he had spent the rest of the day reading 3,316 lead sheets for sightings of blonde girls. None sounded promising. All were in Texas, Louisiana, Arkansas, Oklahoma, Arizona, and New and Old Mexico, where there was no snow on the ground in early April and nowhere near timber country. Ben turned the page to sighting number 3,317: Idaho Falls, Idaho.

*

Clayton Lee Tucker had just about gotten the wheel bearings back in when the phone rang. Well, it was just going to have to ring. It did. Ten, fifteen, twenty times—whoever it was, they weren't going away.

He was working late, as usual. Since the wife had died, he didn't have much else to do. The phone kept ringing. Hell, some old lady might be broken down somewhere. Clayton Lee Tucker had never failed to help a little old lady broken down in his part of Idaho.

Clayton slowly pushed his seventy-five-year-old body up off the cold concrete floor, looked around for a rag, gave up, and wiped his greasy hands on the legs of his insulated overalls. He limped the twenty feet from the repair bay to the desk inside the shop; his arthritis was inflamed by the cold. He picked up the phone.

"Gas station."

"Is Clayton Lee Tucker available?"

"You got him."

"Mr. Tucker, I'm calling about the girl."

"Hold on a minute, let me wipe some of this grease off."

Clayton set the phone down on the desk and stepped over to the wash bin. He squirted the industrial-strength cleaner on his cracked hands and washed them under the running water. After fifty years of fixing cars, his hands looked like road maps; the black grease filled every wrinkle line. They would never come clean. He wiped his hands dry and picked up the phone again.

"Sorry about that. You with the FBI?"

"No, sir. I'm the girl's grandfather. Ben Brice."

"Got three grandkids of my own, that's why I called the FBI number."

"You saw the girl Sunday, with two men?"

"Yep, they come dragging in here, maybe eight, eight-thirty, leaking oil like a busted pipeline. I'm the only fool open on Sunday night. Got nothing better to do, I guess."

"Can you describe her?"

"Yellow hair, ratty, short—thought she was a boy at first, but she was too pretty to be a boy. And she was wearing pink."

"Why do you think it was her?"

"Seen her picture, online."

"Did you call because of the reward?"

"I don't want your money, Ben. I called 'cause the girl looked like the picture and 'cause she looked scared and cold."

"What's your weather like?"

"Colder'n a well-digger's ass. Up in the panhandle, they got upwards of three foot of snow."

"What kind of vehicle were they driving?"

"Blazer, '90 model, four-wheel drive, 350 V-8, white, dirty. They were on the road a while, said they was heading north. They were in a big hurry, wanted me to work through the night. I told 'em, you can't hurry a ring job. Finished up last night, Monday, about nine, got it running pretty good. I ain't got no help, so that's the best I could do. Big man, he picked it up first thing this morning. Paid cash. After they left, I was checking my Schwab account and I saw an Amber Alert on my homepage, with her picture. That's when I called."

"Can you describe the two men?"

"Didn't get a good look at the driver. He stayed in the car with the girl."

"The other man, what about him?"

"Looked like that California governor, Arnold Schwarzen-berger, real muscled-up fella. Crew cut, fatigues,

Army boots, short gray hair. We see them types every now and then, militia boys wanna play GI Joe."

"Did you get a license number?"

"No. But they was Idaho plates."

"Anything else?"

"Well, I ain't much at reading lips, but I'd swear she said help me."

"Mr. Tucker, do they grow Christmas trees in northern Idaho?"

"Biggest industry up there."

"Mr. Tucker, I appreciate your ti— . . . How did you know the second man was muscled up?"

Clayton chuckled. "Hell, it's about fifteen degrees outside, and he ain't wearing nothin' but a black tee shirt."

"His arms were bare?"

"Yep . . . and he had the damnedest tattoo I've ever seen."

9:16 P.M.

JOHN WAS EATING dinner with a spoon: a dozen Oreo cookies crushed in milk. It was his favorite meal, but he didn't taste anything.

Because he was no longer living. He was just going through the motions of life, like one of those creations in the MIT Humanoid Robotics Laboratory. All day, he had engaged in what appeared to be human activities—eating, walking, taking the FBI to the office—but it wasn't. There was no conscious human thought behind his actions.

His only thoughts were of Gracie.

He spat a mouthful of the mushy Oreos into the kitchen sink, a black blob of nothing. Like his life.

"You want refried beans with that?"

Coach Wally was working the late Tuesday shift in the drive-through window at the Taco House out on the interstate. He stood in the small booth, taking orders from motorists hungry for a quick burrito, chalupa, or taco, bagging the orders, making change, and asking each customer the same question: *You want refried beans with that?*

Over the intercom: "No!"

Into the intercom: "That'll be seven-twenty-three. Please drive up to the window."

Wally Fagan clicked off the intercom's transmit button, grabbed a bag, and went back to the kitchen.

"Hey, Wally, you da mon, mon!" Juaquin Jaramillo, the night cook, said. "Puttin' that kid fucker in jail, that's real good, mon."

Juaquin gestured at Wally with a large spoon dripping refried beans on the cement floor.

"Mon, some mu'fucka wanna try an' stick his dick in one a my girls . . ."

Juaquin continued his nonstop rant, which came out in a kind of rap rhythm, as he scooped refried beans onto two flour tortillas, dropped a handful of grated cheddar cheese on top of each, folded the bottoms, rolled them into neat burritos, then wrapped them in the Taco House trademark serving paper.

". . . make a fuckin' burrito outta it, pour some chili over it, feed it to my dog, mon."

Juaquin thought that was real funny.

"Ya understan' what I'm sayin', mon?"

Wally nodded at Juaquin, then he filled the bag with the two bean-and-cheese burritos, chips and salsa, and two Dr. Peppers. He returned to the drive-through booth and reached out the window for the customer's money; he handed the change back to the customers, a man at the wheel and a woman passenger leaning over and looking up at him.

"You're Gracie's coach, right?"

Wally nodded. "Yeah."

"Good job, getting that pervert off our streets," she said. The man gave him a thumbs up.

Wally held out their bag of food. They took it, waved, and drove off; they had taped Gracie's missing child flier to the rear window. Wally gave them a weak wave. He felt slightly nauseous and not because he had eaten three of Juaquin's burritos for dinner—because his gut was stewing with doubt. Something wasn't right about Gary Jennings. He just couldn't put his finger on it.

Wally had played and replayed Friday night in his head, trying to figure out why his ID of Jennings didn't feel right: *He's standing with the team at the concession stand after the game, getting down on his cherry snow cone . . . Gracie comes running past, heading around back . . . The man, blond hair, blue eyes, black cap, plaid shirt, walks up and says, "I'm Gracie's uncle. Her mother, my sister, sent me to get her. Her grandma had a stroke. Where's she at?" Wally answers, "Around back." "That way?" the man says, and he points with his right hand, his fingers . . .*

The intercom buzzed with another drive-through customer. Wally extended his right arm and with his right index finger he flicked on the transmit button and said, "You want refried beans with that?"

And he froze.

"That's it!"

9:35 P.M.

V IC NEAL, a sixth-year associate recently relocated to the Dallas office of Crane McWhorter, a prestigious 1,900-lawyer Wall Street firm, gazed upon his newest client curled up in a fetal position on the cot in the jail cell and facing the concrete wall.

"Jennings," the guard said. "Your lawyer's here."

Jennings didn't move. The guard shrugged, opened the cell door, allowed Vic entry, and then closed and locked the door behind him. Vic pulled the metal chair over near the cot, sat down, placed his briefcase in his lap, opened it, and removed a yellow pad and a pen. He closed the briefcase and wrote at the top of the pad: *Gary Jennings/State of Texas v. Gary Jennings/99999.9909*. The client's name, the client matter, and the client billing number, in this case the firm's marketing number. It was a habit ingrained from his first day at the firm; a Crane McWhorter lawyer didn't take a crap without writing down a client billing number first.

Of course, this client would never get a bill. The firm had taken this case *pro bono:* for the good. For the good of Crane McWhorter's marketing program, that is. A high-profile death penalty case guaranteed invaluable publicity for the firm and the lawyer handling the case. As Old

Man McWhorter had said on more than one occasion, "Clients can't hire you unless they know you." And as the number of lawyers trolling for clients from D.C. to L.A. had reached three-million-plus, the need to get known had reached epidemic proportions among the learned members of the bar.

So now you can't turn around and not bump into a lawyer trying to get known. In the name of marketing, lawyers insinuate themselves into and onto every city council, county commission, civic committee, charity, church, club, conflict, crisis, controversy, commotion, corridor of power, or *cause célèbre*. Vic Neal had chosen *causes célèbres*, in particular, death penalty cases; he had recently transferred to the Dallas office because Texas was executing prisoners faster than Saddam Hussein in his heyday. When the call had come tonight, he had jumped at the opportunity to represent a sexual predator facing death by lethal injection.

Crane McWhorter, on the advice of its marketing consultant, had begun accepting death penalty cases a year after Vic had joined the firm. At first, the firm took only appeals, the sanitized version of the crime. Reading the transcript of a gruesome murder trial was considerably less painful than reading a legal thriller, and the firm's Ivy League-educated lawyers didn't have to meet face-to-face with a stone-cold killer. Appeals courts address only legal technicalities, not whether the defendants were actually guilty, which of course they always were. But, to the firm's dismay, appeals cases generated minimal publicity, not all that surprising since the cases were argued a year or two after the verdict, long after the victim had faded from the public's short attention span. The time to reap the full publicity value of a vicious murder was at trial, when emotions and media interest ran the highest. So the firm began taking cases at the trial stage.

Vic had tried his first death-penalty case four years ago and his sixth last summer, a black man accused of raping and murdering a white woman in Marfa, Texas—in godforsaken West Texas. The trial had lasted ten days: ten days of hundred-degree heat, ten days of popping Tums after Tex-Mex and chicken-fried lunches, ten days of media briefings on the Presidio County Courthouse steps after each day's testimony, dozens of reporters and TV cameras—even the BBC—all focused on Vic Neal, defender of the oppressed!

He had especially enjoyed the BBC reports, whose correspondent had always said something like: "Ian Smythe reporting from Marfa, Texas, a desolate spot in a vast desert frontier known as West Texas, a dusty locale whose only claim to fame is that Elizabeth Taylor and Rock Hudson filmed the American movie *Giant* here in 1955. Now, fifty years later, another American drama is being played out here in a Presidio County courtroom, starring a dashing young American lawyer from New York, Vic Neal, fighting to prevent the State of Texas from executing yet another impoverished black man . . ." That case had made Vic Neal a "prominent" trial lawyer! The defendant—*what was his name?*—had been convicted and executed last year. Which was surely the fate of this defendant.

"Gary." No response. "Gary, I'm Vic Neal, your lawyer. The court appointed me."

Jennings slowly rolled over and sat up.

"Shit, what happened to your face? The cops beat you up?"

Jennings shook his head.

"The FBI? That's even better."

Another shake of his head. "The mother," he said.

"The *mother*? Elizabeth Brice kicked your . . . did that to you?"

A nod of the head. "She kneed me in the balls, too."

"Ouch."

Vic knew of Elizabeth Brice—white-collar defense, tough as nails, foul-mouthed, great body. Criminal defense was man's work and she fit right in.

"Well, guess we can't make anything of that." Vic thumbed through his notes. "Did you really have stock options worth a million bucks?"

Jennings nodded.

"And you threw that away to have sex with your boss's ten-year-old daughter? Well, I suppose we could plead insanity."

A little gallows humor to break the ice. Vic chuckled; Jennings didn't.

"Our goal, Gary, is to keep you off death row. To do that you must show remorse. Juries like that. And you can start showing some remorse by telling the police what you did with the girl's body."

"I didn't take the girl!"

Vic leaned back in the chair and sighed. How many times had he heard that? Every death penalty defendant he had represented was utterly and completely innocent— *I was framed!*—right up to the moment they strapped him to the gurney and inserted the IV, then he's begging God to forgive him for brutally killing a family of four because he wanted a new stereo.

"You know, Gary, if you lie to your lawyer, I can't help you. Understand, this case isn't a question of acquittal or conviction, it's a question of life or death. Your life or your death. Life without parole would be a great victory, given the overwhelming evidence against you."

"I want a lie-detector test!"

"Well, yeah, Gary, you could do that. And when you fail and the D.A. tells the world you failed, you will absolutely get the death penalty because every juror will know you're guilty before the trial even starts. We won't have a chance for any sympathy from even one juror to get you a life sentence."

"But I didn't do it! I was framed! Why don't you find who put that picture in my truck, and her jersey, and made those calls? I'm innocent!"

"Her blood in your truck, but you're innocent?"

"Gracie's blood?"

Vic nodded. "FBI confirmed it's hers with DNA tests. Media's already got hold of it, but it'll be officially announced tomorrow morning, right before your arraignment. So don't even think about bail. This is home sweet home, pal."

"But how did Gracie's blood get in my truck?"

What an innocent face this guy could put on! Vic couldn't help but laugh.

"Save the O.J. imitation for trial, Gary. Nobody planted blood in the white Bronco and nobody planted blood in your black truck."

Vic checked his watch and stood.

"Look, I gotta go, I'll see you at the arraignment. I'm gonna be on *Nightline*, railing against the death penalty. Time I'm through, I'll have that McFadden broad crying like a baby wanting a bottle."

10:38 P.M.

Network television that night was like election night, all focused on one subject: Grace Ann Brice. *Strangers abduct children for sex. A child abducted by a stranger has a life expectancy of three hours. Grace's blood in Jennings's truck. Presumed dead.* Every channel, the same words, over and over again. Elizabeth was in bed crying when John walked into the master suite. She muted the TV and quickly wiped her face.

John disappeared into his bathroom without saying a word. She hit the volume and switched channels. She stopped again on *Nightline*. Jennings's court-appointed lawyer wasn't claiming his client was innocent, only that the death penalty was barbaric. How can he represent a guilty pedophile? Her guilty clients had only stolen money, not a child's life.

Fifteen minutes later, John reappeared in plaid pajamas; his hair was wet and combed back. With the black glasses, he looked like a skinny Clark Kent. She again muted the TV. He walked to the bed and paused as if he wanted to say something, then decided against it and continued to the door.

He had slept in Grace's room the first two nights; Elizabeth had thrown him out of their bedroom last night and the remote control at him. The rage. Now she was scared and alone and her child was presumed dead—*God, her blood in his truck!*—and she needed someone to hold her, but she couldn't bring herself to ask her husband, not after what she had done to him. What the rage had done to him.

If she asked, he would come and hold her. He would say he loved her. He would forgive her. He always forgave her. If she could ever let go of the past—*Let go? If she could ever escape the past*—perhaps she could love John as he loved her. He wanted her love, and she often found herself wanting to love him. There was something inside John R. Brice, something beneath the brainy geek façade. Something worth loving. But she could not love him as long as she hated herself. Her past wouldn't allow it.

John stopped at the door, turned back and said, "She was my daughter, too. I loved her just as much as you did." He walked out and shut the door behind him.

11:11 P.M.

Ben stood at the door to the command post. Agent Devereaux was gone, as were most of the agents. The young female FBI agent he had met—Jorgenson, he thought—was at one computer station, telephone headset on, talking and typing. But the intensity level of the command post had noticeably decreased, as if the battle were over.

Ben laid the lead sheet on Devereaux's desk, sighting number 3,317, Idaho Falls, Idaho, and wrote in the margin: *Spoke to this Clayton Lee Tucker. Said he saw a blonde girl with two men, one with a tattoo, muscular, wearing a black tee shirt, at his gas station Sunday evening. If that was Gracie, you've got the wrong man in jail.*

The wrong man was in jail and Gracie was in Idaho, where it was cold and where the trees stood tall and where snow covered the ground—a white blanket of snow. Not that the FBI would release Jennings on the basis of Ben's dream. But once Clayton Tucker positively identified the men or the tattoo or Gracie from the FBI's photos, they would. And if not then, surely after Jennings got a lawyer and passed a polygraph.

Ben Brice had spent six months in a POW camp; he figured one night in the town jail wouldn't kill the boy.

"Jesus, boy, she sure kicked your ass!"

Jim Bob Basham, the night-shift jail guard, was looking in through the steel bars at the sicko pervert. He was slumped on his cot in his cell, his head was buried in his hands, and he was crying. The mother's attack on Jennings had made the rounds at town hall.

"How's your nuts? Don't that make you wanna just puke your guts up, getting kneed in the nuts? Shit, makes me wanna puke just thinking about it."

No response from the pervert. Jim Bob figured, fuck being nice to him.

"Jennings, if I was you, I'd be praying they give me the death penalty, that's a fact."

The pervert raised his head.

"Yeah, see, that way they put you on death row, segregate you from the general population. You get life, you're in with the rest of the inmates—the gangbangers, the Aryans, the Latinos, the brothers. Nothing they'd like more than to wear your ass out, and I don't mean what the mother did to you."

A confused expression from Jennings; the dumb ass didn't understand what Jim Bob was saying. Jim Bob figured he'd put it in plain English, maybe the pervert could understand that.

"Those dudes gonna butt-fuck you five times a day, girlfriend. Time they get through with you, your asshole's gonna be the size of a water main."

Jim Bob cackled as he walked down the empty cell corridor. *Water main, that was a good one.*

"Yep," he shouted back to the pervert, "they just *love* child molesters."

Minutes later, Gary Jennings was alone, standing in the jail cell, in near darkness, only a dim red glow from the emergency exit lights.

It had taken him eight years, his father's death, moving to another city, marrying Debbie, and getting a job to get over that college incident. Or so he had thought. He now knew he would never get over it. And he would never get over this.

In the morning he would be marched into the court-house through a gauntlet of cameras to be formally charged with abducting, raping, and killing Gracie Ann Brice. His face would be on national TV again: Gary Jennings, child molester, sexual predator, murderer. And Debbie—poor, sweet Debbie, she didn't deserve this. But they'd stick the cameras in her face just the same and identify her as the wife of the child molester, sexual predator, and murderer, pregnant with their child who would forever be identified as the daughter of the child molester, sexual predator, and murderer. She'd be like Lee Harvey Oswald's daughter.

He had never told Debbie about his college convic-tion—what was she thinking of her wonderful husband now? And what would his daughter think of her father when she learned all this? There would be no education trust for her. No vested stock options worth a million dollars. No house for Debbie. No company of his own. No future. He would be forever shamed. As Debbie would be. More like devastated. They would have to move to yet another city—*if* Debbie believed him. *If* he was acquitted.

But how would he be? Gracie's blood in his truck. Child

pornography and her jersey. Calls from his cell phone. The coach pointing at him in court. *Overwhelming evidence*, the lawyer had said. Who would believe Gary Jennings, Fuckup?

Gary's only prior experience with the law eight years ago had taught him that the American criminal justice system was about everything but truth and justice. Which was why he had agreed to plead guilty to a lesser charge and receive probation, on his lawyer's recommendation.

"Gary," his lawyer had told him, "if you're willing to put your life in the hands of twelve citizens who ain't even smart enough to get out of jury duty in the first place and who'd rather be catching the Early Bird specials at the Wal-Mart instead of sitting in that jury box deciding your fate in the second place, then we need to change your plea to not guilty by reason of insanity because you're fucking nuts!"

Gary Jennings would surely be convicted. Then what? Death row, waiting a decade to die by lethal injection? Or life without parole, waiting for the next inmate to enter his cell and rape him, eventually contracting AIDS and dying a long, slow, painful death? Debbie would divorce him and his daughter would never know him or want to. His parents were dead, he had no siblings, he soon would have no one. He was destined to die a lonely fuckup.

Darkness enveloped his mind as hot tears ran down his face. He felt so alone, so empty, so without faith, hope, or a future. His life was over. That he was still breathing was just a technicality. He looked up. There was only one thing to do.

Gary Jennings unzipped his white jail pants.

DAY SIX

6:02 A.M.

LYING AWAKE last night, Chief of Police Paul Ryan had begun having doubts about the prime suspect. Had Gary Jennings really abducted and murdered Gracie Ann Brice? All the evidence said yes: the jersey, the porn, the phone calls, the prior offense, the coach's ID, and now her blood, but still . . . it just didn't seem to fit. It was too pat. All the evidence pointed at Jennings when it shouldn't. An educated employee at a computer company stalking the boss's daughter? Calling from his own cell phone at work, no attempt to cover his tracks? Leaving her jersey in his truck? Child porn under the floor mat? Was Jennings really that stupid? And if that dumb-ass Eddie had found Jennings's truck unlocked, who else might have?

A thorough search of his truck by the FBI's finest turned up nothing but a thin blood smear, not another piece of evidence that put Gracie in his truck, not her hair or fingerprints or fibers from her clothes or grass from the soccer field or leaves from the woods. And the coach's ID wasn't all that positive, even though Jennings fit the suspect's general description.

Of course, Jennings's photo and residence address were on the state's sex offender website; anyone who wanted to find a blond, blue-eyed convicted sex offender living in the county could easily do so. But one who worked for the victim's father? What were the odds of that? And why would anyone want to? To frame a sex offender? It made no sense. He weighed in his mind the upside and down-side of looking deeper and quickly decided there was no upside, at least not for Paul Ryan.

Fifty-two years old, there were no other police jobs out there for him. This was the end of the line. Seventy-five thousand a year plus benefits. Eight more years, he would earn his pension. Enough to retire to a little house in Sun City, him and the wife. A good life, or at least good enough. Was he willing to throw it all away for Jennings? For that little frat boy fuckup? Hell, maybe his big-time lawyer can prove the boy is innocent. Not likely in an emotionally charged high-profile child abduction case— death by lethal injection, that was this boy's future. But that wasn't Ryan's fault; that was the law! Why should Paul Ryan risk his financial security for this boy? On the off-chance that Jennings might not be the abductor? Even a step in that direction would cost Ryan his job—the mayor would not be pleased—and where would that leave him? Unemployed and unemployable. No health care. No pension. Working at the Wal-Mart. He could not think of one good reason to look deeper.

Except that it was the right thing to do.

And there was the baby. The baby named Sarah was lying in the neonatal unit in critical condition, born almost two months' premature. Was the baby on Paul Ryan's tab? Damnit, he didn't put the victim's blood and jersey in Jennings's truck! He didn't make nine phone calls to the victim! He didn't haul Jennings's pregnant wife into the station!

But he did show her the porn.

Because he needed a confession to keep his job, a baby might die. So Paul Ryan felt guilty—a guilt that kept him awake through the night and pacing the house until a sense of shame had overwhelmed him: Baby Sarah.

By 4:00 A.M., whether born of a need for personal redemption or simply sleep deprivation, Paul Ryan had made a life-altering decision: he would do the right thing.

By 6:00 A.M., Jennings had done it for him.

Ryan was standing outside Gary Jennings's cell, looking in at his lifeless form hanging there, one leg of his white jail pants tied around his neck, the other tied around the pipes of the new sprinkler system the town had installed last month to meet code.

Innocent suspects don't commit suicide.

6:30 A.M.

IT WAS WEDNESDAY morning and Coach Wally was whistling as he walked up to the entrance to the Post Oak town hall. Unlike most visitors who would arrive today to pay traffic tickets, Wally Fagan was a happy man. Happy and a bit proud of himself—heck, he felt so downright patriotic he wanted to salute his reflection in the glass doors.

He was here to free an innocent man.

At the entrance, Wally paused and checked himself over and adjusted the clip-on tie he had added to his short-sleeve shirt just in case cameras were present. Shoot, he might even make the national news, maybe even get interviewed by Katie Couric. They might even call him a hero.

He pulled open the door and entered the building. Just inside the door was a security checkpoint with metal detectors, like at the airport, manned by a uniformed cop. Wally began emptying his pockets into a small plastic container but looked up when another cop hurried over; he was grinning like he had just won a lifetime supply of donuts.

"Sonofabitch offed himself!"

The other cop's mouth fell open. "No shit?"

"Yep." The grinning cop grabbed his neck, stuck his

246

tongue out the side of his mouth, and made a gagging sound. "Hung himself in his cell last night. Course, he might've been playing some kind of perverted sex game with himself."

The two cops laughed merrily, but a sick feeling crept over Wally. He didn't want to ask, but he had to know.

"Who?"

The grinning cop turned his way and said, "Jennings. Guy that abducted Gracie."

"He's . . . *dead?*"

"As a doornail. Did the world a favor. No trial, no appeals, no execution. Case is closed."

At that moment, the double doors behind Wally flew open and excited reporters and cameramen rushed inside and pushed past Wally.

"Is it true?" they shouted. "Jennings committed suicide?"

"Yep," the first cop said, waving them through the checkpoint without checking. "Give himself the death penalty."

In a split second, Wally Fagan's mind played out two alternate paths in life for him to choose from, as clearly as if he were watching a movie of his life, a choice he knew would determine the future course of his life. The first path was to continue inside, straight to the chief's office, which would be crowded with the media, stand in front of the microphones and bright lights and cameras and tell the world what he knew, what he had remembered last night at work: the blond man in the black cap and plaid shirt who had asked about Gracie after the game was missing his right index finger. Gary Jennings was not. He had all of his fingers. Jennings was not the abductor. He was innocent. But now he was dead. And it was Wally's fault. That's what they would say—the chief, the press, the FBI, Jennings's pregnant wife, the world. Wally Fagan would make the national news all right, but they wouldn't call him a hero. They would blame him for the death of an innocent man.

Someone is always blamed.

Wally chose the second path. He retrieved his personal items from the small plastic container, stuffed them into his pockets, and exited the building, vowing to take his secret to the grave.

7:00 A.M.

A T SEVEN IN the morning Texas time, being eight on the floor of the NASDAQ exchange in New York City, only ninety minutes prior to the opening trade in the BriceWare.com IPO—that is, on the day all of his dreams were supposed to come true—the company founder, president and CEO, chairman of the board, and creative genius, John R. Brice, who boasted a Ph.D. in algorithms from MIT and a 190 IQ, lay crashed on the couch in his home office. He was curled up under a Boston Red Sox souvenir blanket. His boyish face was buried in the thick folds of soft leather where the couch back met the seat. He was wondering why his wife did not love him.

And he was sure she did not love him.

They had had sex exactly two hundred forty-nine times—twice a month for the ten years and four months they had been married plus once before marriage. Which sounded like a lot of sex when you said it out loud, way more than he had ever hoped for at MIT, once every fifteen days. But then, major league pitchers take the mound every fifth day. FYA (For Your Amusement), during the same period, Roger Clemens had pitched three hundred two games!

He didn't think Elizabeth enjoyed sex with him, much less had orgasms. But he was too afraid to ask. Little Johnny Brice had asked his only other sex partner, a sixteen-year-old Army brat who had done every soldier's son before him at Fort Bragg, if she had had an orgasm; she had laughed in his face and said, "It takes me longer than five seconds, stud."

Sex was not plug and play.

For him, sex was plug and pray, female orgasms being so highly nontrivial and all, what with hardware that had to be booted and software that had to be tweaked for optimal performance. No point and click on the female architecture. No Help button. No Progasm Wizard to guide him through the procedure. So he had searched for technical solutions, even buying a user's manual—*The Female Orgasm*—and learned to his dismay that writing twenty-five thousand lines of code was cake compared to bringing a full-grown female to orgasm. But John R. Brice, Ph.D., was nothing if not determined; he had devoted his considerable intelligence to learning the deep magic of orgasms, because he knew, as well as he knew the back of his computer, that if he could take Elizabeth Brice to orgasm just once—*just freaking once!*—her indifferent attitude toward him would instantly morph into extreme love.

Geeks need love, too.

He had studied the manual's recommended trouble-shooting techniques like it was a final exam at MIT, applying a new one every two weeks until he had tried them all; he even did algorithms in his head during sex to prevent premature cache burst. In the hacker world, that was known as the brute-force method, trying every conceivable solution to a problem until you found one that worked. He had employed that method on numerous occasions at work and with great success. But not with Elizabeth. He had no doubt that pilot error was to blame, that he simply wasn't up to the manly task of driving a beautiful and complex woman like Elizabeth to brain-banging orgasms—as they say in the tech support department when the customer doesn't have a clue, PEBKAC (Problem Exists Between Keyboard and Chair). John R. Brice didn't have a clue.

And the few times he had thought the techniques might be enabling her, when he had felt her body responding to his hardware, just at the moment when he thought she might experience a power surge, she seemed to freeze up, as if he had performed an illegal operation and her control panel shut down her program. He had downloaded his content and uninserted his floppy; she had gotten out of bed, gone into the bathroom, and left him alone to wallow in unexplained failure. *Why didn't women come with a freaking Error Message box?*

He had never forgotten her birthday, their anniversary, Valentine's Day, or Mother's Day, always sending flowers and gifts to her office. He had even signed up with the company's personal trainer and worked out daily. But his efforts had had no discernible romantic effect. He should have taken Gracie's advice, upgraded his graphics, dressed in cool clothes, gotten a stylish haircut, and ditched the glasses for laser eye surgery. She had said he'd be totally studly then. Which had sounded like a good thing.

If only being totally studly would have brought him Elizabeth's love.

But he had lived for ten years without her love and without regret, from the moment he had first laid eyes on Gracie in the hospital nursery. It didn't matter if he loved Elizabeth more than she loved him because

Gracie's love more than made up the difference. Now Gracie's love was gone. And for the first time in ten years he felt the difference, an emptiness inside him that no IPO could fill.

Someone sat down on the couch next to him and put a hand on him, over the blanket. He prayed it was Elizabeth, that she had come down to tell him that together they would survive without Gracie, to ask if she could lie next to him and hold him, to whisper that she loved him with all her heart.

Ben sat next to John on the couch, quietly so as not to wake him, and rested his hand on his only son. He recalled the day in 1969 they had brought John home, wrapped in an Army blanket and in desperate need of a father. But all he had gotten was a mother. A month later, Lieutenant Ben Brice had returned to Vietnam to free the oppressed.

He had failed.

By the time Ben had left Vietnam for good, John had already departed on his lifelong journey leading away from Ben Brice, two wounded souls fighting their own demons. Army life had been tough on John; he hadn't fit in with the other Army brats on the bases where they had been stationed over the next decade as the Army tried to hide the most decorated soldier of the Vietnam War—tried to find a way to forget a war and its warriors. Ben would have left the Army, but he couldn't; he needed twenty years of service to qualify for a pension to take care of his family. It wasn't as if Colonel Ben Brice's peculiar skills were in great demand in the private sector.

At least John's life had become his own when he left

Fort Bragg and North Carolina for Boston and MIT, a perfect score on the entrance exams and a full scholarship in his pocket, the same year that Ben had quietly retired. But Ben Brice's life would never be his own; a warrior's life is forever a chattel of war.

John turned over. His eyes expressed undeniable disappointment, as if Ben Brice were the last person on earth he wanted to see at that moment. Father and son regarded each other silently. Then John spoke.

"Why'd you come, Ben? I grew up without you. Only time you came home was to move us to another base, another school, another set of bullies to beat up the geek. And you didn't save those people—you lost your great war. You were an American hero and what'd it get you? You live with a dog." He sat up. "You weren't there when I needed you. I don't need you now."

His son's words hit Ben like a two-by-four across the face. He gritted his teeth to hold back his emotions.

"I know you don't need me, son. I failed you, and for that I am sorry. Maybe one day you'll find a way to forgive me." He stood. "But this isn't about us, John. This is about Gracie. She does need me, and I'm not going to fail her, too. I'm leaving for Idaho in the morning."

"*Idaho?* What's in Idaho?"

"Gracie."

"Ben—"

"She's alive."

"Jennings isn't."

Kate was standing in the door.

7:47 A.M.

THE TIRES ON the Lexus sedan screeched to an abrupt stop in the handicapped parking zone directly in front of the town hall. If any of the police officers standing on the sidewalk and watching in amazement had detained the woman wearing a nylon warm-up suit and sneakers and no makeup, her black hair pushed back behind her ears but otherwise untouched this morning, and asked her if she knew she was parked illegally, she could have said no and passed a polygraph.

The woman ran up the sidewalk and into the building and directly through the metal detectors without slowing, setting off loud alarms. The cop manning the security desk intercepted the woman, but once he recognized her he retreated and followed at a respectful distance. She proceeded through the lobby and into the police chief's office; the chief sat alone behind his desk.

"I want to see him," the woman demanded.

The chief looked the woman up and down—she looked like hell—then he sighed and nodded slowly. He waved off the cop from the security desk. He stood and led the woman down halls and through secure doors and into the small jail; neither spoke a word as town personnel along the way recognized her but quickly averted their eyes from her. From the entrance to the jail corridor, the woman could see several police officers and FBI agents standing outside an open cell door; a photographer was snapping pictures from various angles. As the woman came closer, the photographer's subject gradually came into view until it fully confronted her: Gary Jennings's body, hanging limp from the sprinkler pipes.

The officers looked at the woman then at the chief for instructions. He gestured with his head; the officers parted and allowed the woman entry into the cell.

She stepped close to Jennings hanging there in his white underwear. His eyes were bugged, his face pale, and his bare legs bloated with blood. Staring up at the man who had abducted, raped, and killed her only daughter, the woman felt jealous. His demons were gone now. But hers had just set up shop. Because now she would never know. Elizabeth Brice punched the corpse, setting it to swinging gently.

"Damn you! You took her to the grave with you!"

9:47 A.M.

"THE CRETIN IS dead?" Sam asked Kate through a mouthful of Cheerios.

"Yes."

"Did the cops shoot him?"

"No. He . . . he just died."

"So how's he gonna let Gracie go if he's dead?"

"I don't know."

"Did he hide her somewhere?"

"I don't know."

"Did he tie her up?"

"I don't know."

"When is she coming home?"

Kate went over to Sam at the table. She sat next to him and cupped his little face with her hands. How could she tell him that Gracie would never come home?

"Nanna, why are you crying?"

"Because I just don't know about Gracie."

Now Sam started crying.

"But you know she's not dead or nothing, right? Right, Nanna?"

2:55 P.M.

"I WANT TO BURY my daughter," the mother said quietly.

FBI Special Agent Eugene Devereaux was sitting behind his desk in the command post; he was facing the victim's family. The final family meeting was always difficult, particularly when the victim's body hadn't been found and probably never would be. Families needed the closure that burying their child brought. As a father, he respected their anguish, not having had a chance to say goodbye to their child; but as an FBI agent, he had to move on to the next case. Otherwise, the dead children would drive him mad.

"We searched the fields next to Jennings's apartment. Nothing. I'm sorry."

"So that's it?"

"Mrs. Brice, Chief Ryan closed the case—and it's his case. I don't have independent jurisdiction to continue the investigation. And FBI resources are not unlimited." Her face fell. "Mrs. Brice, we've conducted the most extensive search in all my years with the Bureau. And your reward, the national publicity—if she was out there, someone would've seen her. We usually locate the body with the abductor's help. With Jennings dead, it's not likely we'll ever find her. I'm sorry."

He did not tell Mrs. Brice that her daughter's body might be found one day, maybe a year from now, maybe two, by a hiker or a hunter or a farmer or a road crew; by that time, her body would be decomposed and unrecognizable as Gracie Ann Brice.

"What about all the sightings?" the mother asked.

"Mrs. Brice, before your reward offer, we had zero sightings. In the two days since, we've had over five thousand. We've cleared a thousand. The others just weren't credible."

Colonel Brice said, "What about Clayton Lee Tucker in Idaho? He seemed credible. You're not even going to check him out?"

Devereaux was stung, the colonel thinking he hadn't done everything possible to find Gracie.

"Colonel, I would never fail to clear a lead like that. We e-mailed Gracie's photo and the blow-ups from the game to our office in Boise. I got an agent out of bed at five his time to fly over to Idaho Falls to interview Mr. Tucker this morning." He put his reading glasses on and flipped open a file on the desk. "Agent Dan Curry just faxed in his 302, his report. Mr. Tucker could not ID Gracie or the men or the—" He was about to say "tattoo," but he remembered his promise to the colonel. And the tattoo meant nothing now anyway. "Or anything about them."

A puzzled look came over the colonel's face.

"Colonel, Agent Curry's report also states that Mr. Tucker wanted to discuss the government's monitoring of UFOs in Idaho, said he sees them all the time. And the report states that Mr. Tucker admitted he drinks heavily since his wife's death." He shook his head. "That's the problem with big rewards, they bring out the nutcases."

"Why'd he say something different to me on the phone?"

"Happens all the time. An agent shows up, flashes the badge, all of a sudden they decide to tell the truth instead of some story to get a piece of the reward."

The colonel seemed unconvinced, so Devereaux held Agent Curry's report out to him. He took it; his eyes ran down the page. He shook his head slowly.

"Colonel, sexual predators don't travel halfway across the country to abduct a child. And they don't abduct a child then take her halfway across the country. Child abductions are local crimes by local predators against local children. Gracie's body is within a few miles of the park, I guarantee it."

The colonel tossed Curry's report on the desk.

"I'm sorry, Colonel, but there's no mystery—Jennings did it. That's the only plausible answer for the jersey, the photo, the phone calls, his description, the coach's ID, and most of all, the blood—that DNA puts Gracie in his truck."

"Maybe it's someone else's blood."

"Colonel, the odds that that blood is not Gracie's is— and I've checked this—is one in twenty-five *quadrillion*, and I don't even know what a quadrillion is."

The father: "A million billion."

"Look, sir, I know this is tough to accept, but sexual predators don't plot out their crimes and they don't frame someone else to avoid apprehension . . . and innocent people arrested for a crime they didn't commit don't hang themselves. They hire a lawyer."

"He didn't fit your profile."

"No, sir, he didn't. Not even close." He shrugged. "An aberration. Or those guys in Behavioral don't have a clue. Either way, it doesn't matter."

The mother gestured around the room. The agents were packing up the equipment.

"So you're giving up?"

"Mrs. Brice, we never quit until the body is found. We will always respond immediately to any new evidence or information, I promise you. But we can't operate out of your house indefinitely, I told you that when I agreed to establish the command post here. We're moving the command to the Dallas field office. Agent Jorgenson will be able to reach me in Des Moines—"

"*Des Moines?*"

"A five-year-old boy was abducted—"

"You're *leaving?*"

"Yes, ma'am. We have a known sex offender at large up there, and a child is missing. That's where I'm needed now." *God, this was hard.* "Look, I know this isn't the ending you were praying for. I know every piece of the puzzle doesn't fit together, it never does. Some things just can't be explained. We never get every question answered. That's just the way it is." He stood. "I'm sorry for your loss. Gracie must have been a wonderful child. But it's over."

Devereaux's eyes went from family member to family member, all of whose eyes dropped when they met his, until he came to Colonel Brice. His eyes did not drop.

"No, Agent Devereaux—it's just begun."

3:18 P.M.

After the family had departed the command post, FBI Special Agent Jan Jorgenson got up from her station and went over to her superior. Agent Devereaux's eyes were sad and tired. He slumped down in his chair. He exhaled audibly.

"If I ever get a child back alive," he said, "I'm through. I'm giving up the chase."

She nodded. "I made some contacts, about the mother, at Justice."

"Proceed." Then he added, "Not that it matters any more."

Jan checked her notes. "Her unit chief was an Assistant Attorney General named Raul Garcia—"

Agent Devereaux was rubbing his face.

"And what did Mr. Garcia have to say about Mrs. Brice?"

"Nothing. He's dead, too."

Devereaux stopped rubbing his face.

"*Both* of Mrs. Brice's superiors at Justice are dead?"

"Yes, sir. Garcia died two years ago, in Denver, shot in a carjacking."

"Jesus." Devereaux stood. "High mortality rate over at the Justice Department these days."

"And I called the Army about getting the names of

those SOG soldiers. All SOG records were destroyed in '72."

"Figures." Agent Devereaux picked up his briefcase. "Jorgenson, it's your case now. I'm catching a flight to Des Moines."

Devereaux thought about Gracie Ann Brice all the way to the airport. Another life ended before it had begun. Another family destroyed by a sexual predator. Another failure for FBI Special Agent Eugene Devereaux. What good had he done here?

He was fifty-six years old. He had handled abduction cases exclusively for ten years now. It was getting to him. His wife had begged him to transfer to the public corruption unit: "What could be more fun than investigating crooked politicians?" she had said. Maybe she was right. Maybe it was time to give up the chase, one hundred twenty-eight dead children. *Good God, one hundred twenty-eight dead children!* And he wouldn't have to travel as much; there were plenty of crooked politicians in Texas. He'd have more time with the family. And maybe in time he wouldn't see the faces of one hundred twenty-eight dead children when he lay down in bed each night and closed his eyes.

Jorgenson pulled the sedan over in front of the American terminal and turned to him. "Agent Devereaux . . ."

"You can call me Eugene now."

"Eugene . . . You taught me a lot. Thanks."

He nodded. "You did good, Jan."

"You know, most of the agents I work with in the Dallas office, they're pretty cocky, like carrying the federal badge makes them special. You're not like them. You're different."

"Difference is, Jan, I've seen ninety-three dead children, up close. That'll take the cocky right out of you."

Devereaux exited the vehicle, shut the front door, retrieved his bag and briefcase from the back seat, then leaned in the front window and said to Jan, "Collect the outstanding evidence, write up a final report. I'll review it when I'm through in Des Moines. You've got my cell phone number, call me if you need me."

He was about to turn away when Jan said, "You really think Jennings took Gracie?"

"I don't know . . . but I know she's dead."

"If we had jurisdiction, would you have closed the case?"

FBI Special Agent Eugene Devereaux stood straight, stared into the blue sky a minute, and then leaned back down to the window.

"No."

9:45 P.M.

L IFE IS NOT a fairy tale.

But Katherine McCullough had not known that in 1968. She had married the man of her dreams only to lose him to the nightmare of war. Ben Brice had given his heart and soul to the Army and that damned war, only to have his heart broken, his soul blackened, and the war lost. When he had returned from Vietnam, he tried to find peace in a bottle. And he had never stopped looking.

The Army tried to put the war and its warriors in the past and move on to a peacetime military. The Army brass couldn't very well demote the most decorated soldier of the war, but it didn't have to give him a command. Ben said you don't get a parade when you lose a football game or a war.

After his retirement, Kate had gone with Ben to the cabin he had built. She had hoped retirement would set Ben free; but he took the war with him to Taos. After a few years, she had woken one morning and accepted the truth: the war would never be over for Ben Brice. He would never find his peace, not until the day he died. And the way he was drinking, that day was not far off.

Kate Brice had refused to stay around for that day. She

couldn't save her husband from himself. So she had left him. Now, pacing her room, she felt like a teenage girl getting ready for her first date; she was working up the courage to go to him. She needed to lie next to him and to feel his arms around her, once more before he left her. He had left her many times, but she knew this time was different.

She knew that Ben Brice would not come back this time.

"When are you coming back?"

Sam was looking up at him, his face full of innocence. Ben Brice wasn't about to say something that would change that.

"Soon."

Sam shook his head. "Typical grownup answer—vague."

Ben smiled. It was like talking to John at the same age. He sat on Sam's bed.

"I'm not being vague. I just can't say for sure."

"But you will come back?"

Ben pondered for a moment. Vague was hard to come by now. He said what the boy needed to hear.

"Yes."

Little Johnny Brice was small, weak, timid, and brilliant. He was teased and taunted, bullied and beaten. He was introverted and lonely, with no friends except his mother and an Apple computer. He was a mama's boy because his father was off at war. He hated his life right up until the day he had arrived at the Massachusetts Institute of Technology, where everyone was a Little Johnny Brice. He possessed a

190 intelligence quotient, he earned a Ph.D. in algorithms at the Laboratory for Computer Sciences, and upon graduation, he founded his own company and set about to write a killer app. Ten years later, today, he became a billionaire: at 9:30 A.M. Eastern time, BriceWare.com went public at $30 per share; by close of trading at 4:00 P.M., the price had bounced to $60.

John R. Brice was worth $2 billion.

This was the day he had dreamed about for as long as he could remember, like a teenage boy looking forward to the day he would lose his virginity, the day he would become a man. This was to be that day for John R. Brice. But now, standing in the master bathroom of his $3-million mansion and staring at himself in the mirror, he still saw Little Johnny Brice.

He had not found his manhood on Wall Street; perhaps he would find it in Idaho.

He had tried to imagine life without Gracie. He couldn't. It was not the life he had lived or the life he wanted to live. And it would be a life without Elizabeth. Gracie's birth had brought them together; her death would drive them apart. Elizabeth would leave him, and Sam with her. His family, his tenuous connection to the real world, would be gone; and he would give every dollar of his new fortune to save his family.

But he knew his money could not save his family. He knew his only hope lay with a drunk. Ben Brice offered hope. Hope that somehow, somewhere, Gracie was alive. Hope that one day she might come home. Hope that her father might again cup her perfect face and think how swell she was. He knew it made no sense. He knew there was no logic to it. No reason. No odds. There was just emotion. And hope. John had read about people with terminal cancer going to Mexico for enemas and other quack therapies, hoping for a miracle. He had wondered how desperate a person must be to do such a thing, to travel thousands of miles hoping for a miracle. Now he knew.

So John R. Brice would unplug from his virtual world of cyberspace and computers and code that defined and protected him and venture forth into the real world, untethered to his technology like an astronaut untethered to the mother ship, chasing Ben's dream and his daughter. And hoping.

For the first time in his life, John Brice would follow his father.

The mansion was dark and silent, as if in mourning. The FBI had packed up and moved out. Everyone had retired to their respective rooms to consider life without Grace. Everyone except Elizabeth.

She was in the media room watching the late news. A child abductor was dead. He would be buried tomorrow. Life would go on as before. But not Grace's life. Or her mother's life.

Her daughter was dead.

Evil had won again.

11:07 P.M.

BEN WAS LYING in bed; the only light was coming from outside. His hands were clasped behind his head and his mind was filled with questions: Why couldn't Clayton Lee Tucker identify Gracie or the men or the tattoo? Was he really a nutcase? And why was his phone line busy all day and night? Why had the two men taken Gracie to Idaho? And the most troubling question of all for Ben Brice: had his past come back to haunt Gracie?

The door to the pool house opened, and Kate's head appeared.

"Ben?"

"Yeah."

Kate came over and sat on the edge of the bed; she stared at her hands and fiddled with the belt to her bathrobe. He gave her time to work up to what she wanted to say.

"Ben, has there been another woman?"

"No, Kate, just another drink."

Kate stood, untied her robe, and let it fall to the floor. She pulled back the blanket and lay beside him, resting her head on his chest. Where she would be when he woke the next morning.

DAY SEVEN

4:59 A.M.

Ben Brice opened his eyes not to a dog needing to pee but to his wife sleeping next to him for the first time in five years. The warmth of her skin against his brought a sense of regret to his mind: all the years he had lost with her.

Dawn was near and he needed to leave, but he lay still; he was not yet ready to let go of the moment. When he was young and life hadn't yet had its way with him, he had let go of such moments freely, assured there would be many more to come; now he held onto each moment for as long as possible. He wrapped his arms around his wife one last time.

Ben recalled the first time Katherine McCullough had lain with him, on 6 June 1968, their wedding night. He was twenty-two and a second lieutenant; she was twenty and a virgin. When she came to him that night and let her gown slip off her shoulders and fall to the floor and stood before him, he knew he would never want another woman.

But life soon had its way with Ben Brice.

She had left him and now he must leave her. He released her and rolled out of bed slowly so as not to wake her. He was dressed and packed when she stirred. He went to her, sat on the edge of the bed, and brushed stray strands of red hair from her face. She opened her eyes and stared into his as if trying to read his mind. Finally, she said, "She really is alive."

He nodded.

"Why? Why'd they take her?"

Ben broke eye contact. "I don't know."

"Don't you?"

Kate got out of bed, slipped into her robe, and pulled the belt snug around her waist.

"Does this have something to do with that tattoo?"

"You mean with the war?"

"Yes, with that damn war."

Ben stood and grabbed his duffel bag. "Kate, everything has something to do with that war."

Elizabeth spat the last of the bile into the toilet and flushed again. The taste burned her throat; the lining was raw from her morning vomits. Still kneeling, she grabbed the bottle of green mouthwash that she now kept by the toilet, took a mouthful, swished it around, and spat it into the toilet. She sank to the floor; the marble was cool on her bare legs. She rested her head on the toilet seat.

When she had woken, her mind had immediately taken advantage of the early morning, when she was most vulnerable, and tortured her again with more gruesome images of her daughter: Grace's body, dead and decomposing and dumped in a ditch, ants and maggots crawling out of her silent open mouth and over her pale lips, vultures pecking at her blue eyes and rats gnawing on her beautiful face, fighting over her flesh . . .

She felt her body's regurgitation process gearing up again.

Seven mornings ago, Elizabeth had gotten dressed in this bathroom in her best closing-argument outfit; that day had begun like any other day but had ended with Grace gone from her life. How can that be? How can life turn on us in a split second? How can life be so unfair? Harsh? Cruel? Evil? She had asked herself those same questions ten years ago. She had no answers then; she had no answers now. But back then, she had Grace. Now Grace was gone.

"I'm going."

John was standing in the doorway. She knew he wanted her to go to him and embrace him and say "I love you" to him. He needed her to, and she wanted to. She tried to push herself up from the floor, but she hadn't the strength. He started to walk away.

"John, I . . ."

He turned back. She had never been able to give voice to those words. And she could not now. Evil had taken that kind of love from her life. John walked out of sight.

She leaned over the toilet and vomited again.

Ben and Kate walked out of the pool house to find John standing next to a shiny red Range Rover. He was wearing sneakers, jeans, and an MIT sweatshirt. He appeared not a day older than the day he had left for college.

"I'm going with you, Ben."

Ben reached out and squeezed his son's shoulder. "I understand your wanting to, son, but this isn't your kind of work."

Ben turned away, but John grabbed his arm. "I know

that, Ben. This is man's work, and I'm not much of a man. But Gracie's my daughter. And if she is alive, I want her back."

Ben started to order John to stay home, but he saw in John's eyes the same truth he felt in his heart: finding Gracie was life or death, for her and for him.

"All right, son. We'll do this together."

Ben walked around to the passenger side of the vehicle. Kate went to John and embraced him. "Be careful," she said. Then, in a lower voice she must have thought Ben couldn't hear, she said, "Do exactly what Ben tells you to do, and we might get Gracie back. This is what he knows."

8:23 A.M.

THE LANDSCAPE BELOW was bleak and endless. It was Thursday and they were somewhere over West Texas. The plan was to fly to Albuquerque, drive to Ben's cabin outside Taos, pick up his gear—the kind you can't take on a plane, he had said—and drive nonstop to Idaho Falls to talk to Clayton Lee Tucker, the last person who had seen Gracie alive.

Ben's hands were folded in his lap, his eyes were closed, and his breathing was steady and slow. The flight attendant raised her eyebrows at John when Ben failed to respond to her offer of coffee, tea, or juice.

"Coffee, black, for both of us," John said to her.

He lowered Ben's tray then his. The flight attendant placed cups of coffee on their trays. John drank his coffee, assuming they would fly in silence; but Ben opened his eyes and spoke.

"Thanks for letting Gracie visit me. She told me Elizabeth was against it but you stood up to her."

It was, in fact, the only time John R. Brice had ever stood up to his wife.

"Last time I saw her," Ben said, "we drove down to Santa Fe to deliver a table. When we got there, I took the table into the gallery. She stayed outside to check out the Indians

275

selling their products on the Plaza. When I came back out, she was on the other side standing next to this old Navajo like they're best friends." A slight smile. "She was wearing a tribal headdress. She smiled and waved at me. I'll never forget her face that day." Ben turned to John; his eyes were wet. "Do you remember the last time you saw her face?"

John leaned back in his seat. He did remember.

Gracie yanks Brenda and Sally to an abrupt halt. It's suddenly very important that she turn and look back for Dad. That same bad feeling has come over her again, like a nightmare while she's still awake. The feeling that something really awful is about to happen to her. The same feeling she has experienced for more than a week now, always when she is outside on the playground during recess or at soccer practice or on the way home from school. Like someone is watching her. Waiting for her.

Her entire body is covered with goose bumps.

The sun is in her eyes; she squints. She spots her dad, looking back at her from soccer field no. 2. Usually, when the bad feeling overcame her, she would get close to a grownup and the feeling would leave. But not today. Not now. She wants desperately to run back to her dad.

"Come on, Gracie," Brenda says, tugging at her arm. "There won't be any banana snow cones left if we don't hurry."

She decides she's just being a silly girl, something Mom always said was not allowed in her house. She's in the middle of a big crowd at the park after a soccer game. The bad feeling can't get her here. She is safe. She smiles and waves at Dad. He waves back with the cell phone. The goose bumps are gone.

They arrive at the concession stand. Holding hands, they weave their way through the crowd of kids and grownups. Sally gets her snow cone first then Brenda orders hers.

"Panty check!"

Gracie whirls around to the snot standing five feet away and taunting her with no adult supervision. Way stupid. The snot realizes her mistake. Her eyes drop to Gracie's hands, now Ms. Fist and her twin sister. The sneer leaves her face and is replaced by fear. The snot starts to back away, then she runs, but Gracie has her by the hair before they're behind the concession stand, alone, no big-mouthed butthead jerk football dad to save her now. Ms. Fist, meet the snot's nose. The snot collapses to the ground like a bunch of pixie sticks.

What a wimp! And she's eleven!

The snot cups her nose and starts crying like a baby. She looks up at Gracie; her eyes are wide with fear. But her eyes aren't on Gracie, her fear not of Gracie, but of—

The goose bumps are back. The bad feeling is back. It's all over Gracie now, smothering her like a thick blanket on a hot day. It's behind her. It's breathing on her. She turns to face it.

Something wet covers her face. She tries to fight it off, but she smells something funny. Every nerve in her body starts tingling and now she's dizzy; her arms lose all strength, her legs go limp, her eyes want to close. She's floating now, a gentle bounce. No, she's not floating; she's being carried. She hears crunching below her, like someone stepping on dried leaves.

The bad feeling is taking her through the woods.

Gracie's mind is fading to black; she fights hard to think of something to save herself. She thinks of Ben. She calls out to him, but no words come out of her mouth.

Ben.

With her last ounce of strength and willpower, Gracie reaches up, grabs her necklace, and yanks hard. Her arm drops. Her hand releases the necklace. Ben's Silver Star.

Save me, Ben . . .

. . . A hard bounce startles her awake, but she can barely force her eyes open, just enough to see that, wherever she is, it is dark. She hears the drone of a car engine and feels the rumbling of tires against the road beneath her.

The bad feeling is taking her far, far away.

Her eyelids outweigh her will. She can no longer hold them open. She drifts off into that murky world again . . .

. . . And coming alive now. But she is groggy, like she can't wake up all the way. She hears voices. She smells cigarette smoke and fast food and body odor. Her stomach feels really queasy, like she might barf. Her mouth is dry, but she does not lick her lips. She does not move any part of her body. Instead, she opens her eyes to slits.

It's morning. She's in a car, wrapped in a scratchy green blanket and lying across the back seat. Up front are two men. The driver has blond hair under a black cap; he's wearing a plaid shirt. The other man is bigger with a flattop, like Ms. Blake, the P.E. instructor, except his hair is gray. His left arm is slung over the seat back. It's a very big arm. With something on it she has seen before.

The big man's big head swivels toward the blond man, and he says, "That geek's gonna be a billionaire." A cigarette hangs on his lip. "Maybe we oughta ransom this little cherry. Bet he'd pay a million bucks to get her back."

"I wouldn't take no amount of money for her," the blond man says. "We was meant to be together."

The big man shakes his head and exhales a cloud of smoke. "Just 'cause you wanna be with her don't mean she wants to be with you. You think about that?"

"Yeah, I thought about that," the blond man says. "She'll learn to love me."

"And what gal wouldn't? Funny thing about women, though, sometimes they're real stubborn about learning to love a man what kidnaps 'em."

The blond man gives the big man a look. "It happened before."

The big man nods. "So it has. All I'm saying is you ain't had no experience with women—whores at Rusty's don't count. And I'm telling you, boy, an unhappy woman . . . *damn*. Only two things you can do with an unhappy woman: make her happy or kill her. Take it from me, it's a helluva lot easier to kill her."

That tickles him.

The engine is making strange noises. And it smells awful. She sees the tops of other cars and eighteen-wheelers passing them. They're on the highway. The sun is shining in the right side of the car. Which means they're heading north. Which must be why she now catches a slight chill, particularly when—

Without moving her head, Gracie checks herself over. Her white soccer shoe is on her left foot, but her right shoe is missing; she's still wearing the blue knee socks and shin guards. She feels around inside the blanket and— her uniform is gone! Her jersey, her shorts—all she's wearing is her Under Armour! Why did they take her uniform? And the answer comes to her: *Oh my God, they raped me!* She bites her tongue to silence her feelings and

279

squeezes her eyes tightly to hold back the tears. But one tear escapes and rolls down her cheek, lands on the seat, and disappears into a crease in the cracked vinyl.

Gracie wasn't entirely sure of everything that being raped included, but she knew it meant some male person sticking his penis into a girl down between her legs without permission (although she could not imagine ever giving a boy permission to do *that*). Mother never talked to her about sex or any of that stuff yet; she learned what she knew from Ms. Boyd in health class. Ms. Boyd told the girls that when a boy makes unwelcome physical advances, they should point their finger at him and firmly say, "No! And no means no!" The girls and boys attended separate sex ed classes; the girls giggled at the drawings of penises in the book. The only real live penises she had seen were Sam's, which was really little and couldn't hurt a girl her age, and Dad's, one time when she walked in on him in his bathroom. He got totally embarrassed and covered up real fast, but she got a good look at it. Dad's penis was big enough to hurt a girl her age.

But she doesn't hurt down there. She doesn't feel different at all. Maybe the two men have little penises like Sam's and that's why she doesn't hurt. Or maybe they didn't rape her.

Or maybe . . . she closes her eyes and sleeps again . . .

. . . Until she is awakened by a door slamming.

She cracks her eyelids. The blond man is gone. The big man turns toward her; she quickly shuts her eyes tight. She feels his gross hand over the blanket, shaking her leg not so gently.

"Wake up," he says.

She pretends to be asleep, but she hears his heavy breath as he exhales, and she knows cigarette smoke is coming her way. She holds her breath, but the toxic fumes find their way into her nose. She coughs. She can't pretend to be asleep now. She opens her eyes. The big man is looking at her and not like he wants to be friends.

He is way past ugly.

His nose is broad and flat, like he had run face first into a brick wall. A long scar zigzags down the left side of his face. One eye doesn't look right. His whiskers look like Coach Wally's hair when his burr cut starts to grow back in. The skin on his face is blotchy and leathery and filled with little pockmarks like that guy at BriceWare. (Dad said the guy had bad acne as a child.) A cigarette is clamped between his teeth and smoke comes out with each breath. He's the biggest human being she has ever seen, and he looks really mean. Gracie realizes she is trembling, she is so afraid. But her mother's advice plays in her ears like a song on her iPod: *Men are like dogs. They can smell fear on a woman. Never let them smell your fear. Never let them see you cry. Always act tough even when you don't feel tough.* So Gracie acts tough.

"You wanna put that thing out?" she says. "Passive smoke is dangerous to a child's health."

The big man snorts like a bull and a stream of smoke comes out both nostrils. "Not as dangerous as me, pissed off as I get when I don't smoke."

He has a point, Gracie figures.

He flips a Twinkie back to her; it lands on the green blanket. Yuk, it isn't even individually wrapped! It's probably covered with cooties.

Still, she is hungry.

She pushes herself up, careful to keep the blanket

wrapped around her, even though the Under Armour shorts and tee shirt cover her up. Her head feels heavy. She's in a sports utility vehicle, a real POS: no plush leather seats or cherrywood trim, no Harmon Kardon stereo system or color-coordinated carpet, no TV built into the dash like Dad's new Range Rover, and no CD player. This SUV is old and has bench seats instead of buckets, and crushed beer cans and cigarette butts and wadded-up fast food bags on the bare metal floorboards, the head liner is drooping in several places, and it sure as heck doesn't have a heater that works.

She looks outside. They're in a Wal-Mart parking lot, a long way from home. She recognizes the yellow license plates on the other cars, just like the ones on Ben's Jeep.

They're in New Mexico.

Gracie picks up the Twinkie and realizes she is not tied up. Her arms and legs are free. She scarfs down the Twinkie in three big bites.

"Um, you got another one of those?" she asks the big man before she's swallowed the last bite.

He turns back in his seat and leans over. Gracie jumps to the door and yanks frantically on the handle. Nothing. To the other door. Nothing. The big man turns back and flips another Twinkie at her.

"Don't bother, honey. Doors don't open from inside. We ain't stupid."

Gracie considers debating that point with him, but she decides against it. She checks out the nearby cars. Maybe she can get someone's attention, bang on the window and scream for help. But there is no one . . . except the blond man carrying a brown bag and walking toward his POS SUV with the kidnapped girl in it.

He doesn't look much older than the boys on the high

school football team. Dad took her and Sam to the big homecoming game last season; the blond man is cute enough to be the homecoming king, except he's wearing a plaid shirt that looks like Dad's pajamas. Homecoming kings don't wear plaid.

He walks to the front of the SUV and lifts the hood. Smoke billows out. He steps back and waves his hand at the smoke like Dad when he tries to barbecue, then he ducks back under. After a minute, he slams the hood down and flings a yellow container aside. Wow, he doesn't even recycle.

The blond man wipes his hands on his shirt, gets in the car with the bag, and says, "Ten goddamn quarts and we ain't even halfway home." He tosses a carton of cigarettes to the big man, who immediately tears into them like Dad into a new bag of Oreos. He then hands the bag back to Gracie. One of his fingers is just a nub. She empties the bag: pink sweats.

She sighs. "Well, kidnapping me is bad enough, but now my mom's really going to be PO'd at you."

"Why's that?" the blond man asks.

"Making me wear clothes from Wal-Mart."

The blond man chuckles as he puts the car into gear and drives out of the parking lot and back onto Highway 666 North, so the sign says.

"Which reminds me—did you, like, rape me or something?"

The vehicle suddenly swerves off the road without slowing down, sending the big man's cigarettes flying—"Jesus Christ!" he says—and Gracie to the seat. The blond man slams on the brakes, stops the car, and practically climbs over the back of his seat. His face is red. He points the three fingers of his right hand at her.

"You think I would do that to you? You think I would let anyone do that to you? You're pure and you're gonna stay pure! Anyone tries to dirty you, I'll kill him!"

She sat up. "You took my uniform."

"I didn't look! And you're wearing them funny underwear, can't see nothing anyhow. I put you in that blanket real fast."

"Then why?"

"To throw the Feds off our trail. They ain't never gonna take you back, Patty."

"*Patty?* My name is Gracie. Don't tell me you two morons kidnapped the wrong girl?"

"No, we got the right girl," the blond man says, turning back in his seat. "That's your name now."

And Gracie wonders why . . .

. . . The old man at the gas station is looking at their SUV kind of funny. He has a nice face. He's standing on the other side of the gas pumps, shaking his head, gesturing at their SUV, and saying something to the big man, who's smoking even though the sign says no smoking. The SUV's hood is up. The engine must really be on fire now because an even bigger cloud of black smoke hangs in the air under the bright tube lights above. Gracie is wearing the pink sweats now. She inches her head higher. She wants to scream, *Help me!*

"Stay down," the blond man says.

Gracie lies back down. But the old man saw her. And she saw him.

They're in Idaho . . .

*

. . . And her head is heavy again, murky images and noises all around her, and the thick cigarette smoke suffocates her. A bed in a room but not her bed and not her room. She remembers being carried in the blanket and the same funny wet smell and the same dizziness and unable to resist when they tied her hands and feet again. And sleeping and dreaming and drifting in and out of dark and light for what seems like days, the TV blaring nonstop and mixing with men's voices and the smell of—*tacos?*—and wondering if they will ever go to sleep.

"Me, I wouldn't never win a million bucks, them questions is real hard."

"That's 'cause you ain't never watched TV, boy."

"That big guy right there, they call him Hoss—"

"*Bonanza?*"

"Why they got so many Mexican channels in Idaho?"

"Go to sleep."

Laughter.

"That Elmo, he's a funny sumbitch!"

"Shut up."

"Gilligan's always messing up and—"

"Shut the fuck up!"

"That guy there, he's a doctor and he's married to her, but he's screwing the blonde, and—"

"Soaps? Boy, you like a kid with a new toy."

"Hey, Patty's on the news!"

"This here show, they put them people on a deserted island, see, then they vote one off each week. Last one left wins a buncha money. Was me, I'd tell them motherfuckers they vote me off I kill 'em."

"I always liked that about you."

"Paper says they arrested Jennings last night."

"Good. The truck's fixed, let's hit the road."

Now they're back in the POS SUV and Gracie's lying across the back seat and her eyes droop until . . .

. . . She opens her eyes to a greasy face pressed against the window and grinning in at her with several teeth missing.

"She's a cutie," he says.

"Get the shit loaded, Dirt," the blond man says.

When the man called Dirt moves away, his face leaves a big smudge mark on the window glass. The rear hatch and tailgate open and the men push in green metal boxes with long shiny metal containers inside and letters on the side—USAF—and a word she had never seen before—NAPALM—then cover them with a heavy tarp.

"And the brass wonders why their inventory never comes out right," the man with the missing teeth says.

They all laugh like he's Jay Leno or something . . .

. . . And now she's lying on a small bed in a small room in a small house. The sheets stink of foul body odor. She'll have to bathe for a week to get this smell off. They think she's asleep. She tiptoes to the door and peeks out. The two men are in the big room with another man with red hair who's holding a long black rifle with a telescope on it and caressing it like a girlfriend. They're drinking beer and smoking and laughing.

The big man says, "That red hair, ain't no one gonna believe you're some Muslim raghead."

"Don't matter none," the man with red hair says. "FBI ain't never gonna find me. Hell, they can't find their butts with both hands."

The big man points a thumb at her room and says, "What does the girl say, Junior? 'Like, *duh*.' "

They all laugh again; then they get real quiet and the big man says, "Easter Sunday, Red. Don't fuck it up."

Gracie goes back to the bed and lies down and thinks, *Isn't Easter Sunday this Sunday?* . . .

. . . She sees a sign that says *Cheyenne, Wyoming.*

She's lying on the back seat of the car again; the two men up front seem happy.

The big man says, "You believe that sumbitch give himself a necktie? Goddamn, we are home free, podna."

"So can we go through Yellowstone?" the blond man asks. "That'd be real neat for Patty to see."

"Why sure, Junior. And after that we'll take her down to Disneyland." The big man looks at the blond man he calls Junior like he's nuts; he exhales smoke and says, "This ain't no fucking family vacation!"

Family? Did this Junior guy take her to be his . . .

. . . Gracie is cold. Her body is shivering uncontrollably. She is all alone. And so terribly afraid. She starts crying. She can't hold it back any longer. But just when she's about to lose it big time, she sees him, high up in the sky, floating under a white parachute. And he sees her. Coming closer now, the green beret, the uniform, the medals glistening in the bright sunlight, just like the picture on her desk.

Save me, Ben.

He is coming. And for the first time since she was taken, she is no longer afraid . . .

287

8:51 A.M.

WHEN GRACIE WOKE, she was shivering. She had kicked the scratchy green blanket off. She sat up, reached down, and pulled the blanket up to her neck. They were on the highway again, but the car wasn't making funny noises any more. The blond man was driving; the big man was smoking and reading a newspaper. Outside, the ground was covered with snow. Distant mountains taller than those in Taos rose high into the sky. Her head finally felt clear.

"Where are we?" she asked. "What day is it?"

"Well, good morning to you, sleepyhead," the blond man named Junior said. "We're in Montana, Patty. It's Thursday."

"Okay, just so you know? That Patty thing is really starting to annoy me."

In the rearview mirror she saw a thin smile cross Junior's lips. She coughed. The car was filled with cigarette smoke. (Does the big man ever stop smoking?) She tried to lower her window, but it was stuck. She waved her hand to clear the air around her so she could breathe. She said to the big man, "Those things are cancer sticks. They can kill you."

Without looking back, the big man said, "So can a nagging woman. Shut up!"

She stared at the back of his big head. "Nice attitude." She noticed another smile from Junior in the rearview. They rode in silence until she said, "He's coming."

The big man tossed his newspaper back to her. "Ain't no one coming for you, girlie. Your case is closed."

Gracie picked up the paper and spread it out on her lap like at home when she read the sports pages after school. Her picture was on the front page; next to her was the picture of a blond man. He looked sad.

"I know him. He works for my dad."

"Not no more he don't."

She read about her abduction, the search for her, and Mom's reward offer. "You two Einsteins are passing up twenty-five million dollars to keep *me?* That seems way dumb."

"Way dumb is right," the big man said, and Junior gave him a quick look.

Gracie continued reading about her case, the investigation—*hey, Dad's IPO went through!*—the arrest of the abductor, the abductor's suicide, and her soccer shorts.

"You left my shorts in the woods? So everyone thinks I'm running around in my Under Armour? That is, like, so totally disgusting."

"Everyone thinks you're dead," the big man said.

Gracie read more. "They found my jersey in this guy's truck? And my blood?"

"From your elbows," Junior said. "Pretty smart, huh? I thought of that myself."

"Oh, yeah, real smart. This guy killed himself."

"That was just lucky. We set him up pretty good, but we was only hoping for a couple days' head start. Didn't figure on him hanging hisself. Now we're home free."

The story said this Jennings guy had hung himself in

his jail cell, and the police had closed her case. Gracie Ann Brice was presumed dead. Her body would probably never be found now that the abductor had killed himself. Gracie didn't understand: Why didn't Jennings just tell the police that he didn't take her? Why would he kill himself? It didn't make much sense to her, but it didn't change what she knew.

"No, you're not. He's still coming."

Junior was shaking his head. "That wimp ain't coming to save you just like he didn't save you from that fucking asshole yelling 'panty check' at the game. Was me, I'd've shot the son of a bitch. I about did."

Ms. Fist made an appearance. Gracie wanted to pummel Junior just like she had the snot. "First of all, numb-nut"—she wasn't sure what that word meant, but she had heard a boy call another boy that at school and he didn't like it—"don't call my dad a wimp. He may be a doofus, God bless him, but he's a genius, smarter than you two meat-bots put together."

Junior: "The hell's a meatbot?"

"And second of all, he didn't even hear the big creep. He was multitasking. And third of all, do you really think that's appropriate language to use in front of a child?"

"Aw shit, I'm sorry, honey," Junior said like he really meant it. "I won't say them words no more."

The big man turned in his seat to face Gracie. He wasn't smiling. "I will. Listen up, sweet cheeks. If that boy calls himself your daddy's smart enough to figure out Jennings didn't take you and stupid enough to come looking for you, I'm gonna take my Bowie"—he held up what looked like an oversized steak knife—"and gut his skinny ass from his dick to his neck and use his innards for bear bait, you understand? So sit back, enjoy the trip, and shut the fuck up!"

He was big and ugly and scary and he smelled bad. Gracie's chin began quivering and her eyes watered. Just as she was on the verge of blubbering uncontrollably, she thought of her mother, the toughest, strongest, meanest person she knew. Gracie wasn't like her mother, but it was in her genes—she could be if she needed to be. She recalled more of her mother's advice: curse. Unexpected profanity from a woman, she had advised, intimidates men. Gracie remembered that word her mother often used when she thought Gracie wasn't around and sometimes even when she was. She jutted her jaw out, leaned forward toward the big ugly scary stinking man, and enunciated each letter deliberately, which would have made Ms. Bradley, her English teacher, very proud.

"Fuck you."

The big man gave her a hard look like he wanted to backhand her into next week, but Gracie's chin held its ground; he abruptly broke into loud laughter.

"Where'd you learn to talk like that, girl?"

"My mother. She's a lawyer."

The two men looked at each other and shrugged. "Oh."

"And FYI, A-hole—"

The big man just shook his big head. "You're a piece a work, girlie. Makes me glad I didn't have no brats—except maybe with some whores in Saigon."

He thought that was funny.

"Anyway, FYI, I'm not talking about my dad. I'm talking about Ben."

"And who the hell's Ben?"

"My grandpa."

The big man laughed again, even louder, and slapped Junior on the arm. "Her gramps." He sucked on his cigarette like Sam sucking on a Slurpee, then he started coughing smoke like he was choking and his face got all red. "Damn angina." He bent over and dug around and came back up with a pill bottle. He put a little pill in his mouth.

Junior said, "No one's coming for you, Patty. You're dead."

"Ben knows I'm alive."

"How?"

"He just does."

After a few minutes the red left the big man's face. He threw his left arm over the seat back again and said, "Well, shit, Junior, gramps is coming to kill us all and save her sweet little ass. We might as well give her up right now."

A stern voice, her best imitation of Elizabeth A. Brice, Attorney-at-Large: "Yes, you should. Because he's on his way right now. And if you two idiots had the sense God gave dirt, you'd let me out of this car so he never catches up with you."

"Well, sweet cheeks," the big man said, "I ain't gonna lose no sleep over your gramps coming after me."

"You should. He's got one of those, too."

"One a what?"

He was looking right at her now. His eyes followed her hand as she extended it and pointed her finger at the big man's tattoo, almost touching his gross arm.

"One of those."

The big man's eyebrows crunched down. "Your grandpa's got a tattoo says 'viper'?"

"Yep, he sure does." She gestured behind her with her thumb. "And he's somewhere back there right now, catching up fast."

The big man's eyes shot up; he stared out the back of the car, as if Ben were tailgating them. His face was different now.

Because Ben was coming.

9:28 A.M.

"WE'RE NEVER GONNA get to Idaho in this piece of shit!"

"Try it again!" Ben yelled from under the raised hood of the Jeep. John turned the ignition and pumped the gas pedal, filling the engine well with the smell of gas-oline; the image of a Vietnamese child drenched in napalm flashed through Ben's mind.

The jet had arrived in Albuquerque at 0900 local time. They had retrieved their bags and located the old Jeep in the parking lot. But the damn thing wouldn't start again. Ben was under the hood and tweaking the carburetor, which usually worked. John was sitting in the Jeep, impatient and annoyed and becoming more of both by the minute.

Ben slammed the hood shut and came around to the driver's side. John climbed over to the passenger's seat. Ben got in, determined that the Jeep would start this time. He turned the ignition and pushed the accelerator to the floorboard.

"Come on, you son of a—"

The engine coughed and wheezed like a two-pack-a-day smoker then turned over. Ben quickly shifted into reverse; the Jeep jerked itself back out of the parking space. Then it died.

"Cripes!" from the passenger's seat.

Ben jammed his boot down on the accelerator again; the Jeep fired up again. He rammed the stick shift into first before the Jeep could change its mind. The vehicle lurched out of the airport, belching a cloud of black smoke.

Once they were on the access road leading to the interstate, Ben glanced over at his passenger. John was his mother's son—the same sharply etched facial features, the same curly black hair, the same slender frame, the same brilliant mind. He was so unlike his father. Ben's thoughts turned back again to that night when—

"Stop!" John shouted.

Ben slammed on the brakes. "What?"

John pointed. "Pull in there!" Then he started punching the buttons on his cell phone like he was calling 911 to report an emergency.

"Hi, this is Gracie. I can't answer the phone right now 'cause I'm on a date with Orlando Bloom—*I wish!* Actually, I'm like, at school or soccer practice or Tae Kwon Do class or chasing E.T. around the house. Anyway, I'm not here to answer my phone, *duh*, so leave a message or whatever. Bye." The machine beeped.

Elizabeth was now sitting in Grace's chair at Grace's desk in Grace's room listening to Grace's voice. It was all she had left of her daughter. She reached over and hit the play button and listened again to her dead daughter's voice.

Gracie said, "Ben Brice was a hero."

The big man was shaking his head slowly like Mom did when Sam acted like a little butthead. "Ben Brice," he said in a soft voice, almost like he was talking about someone who had died. "What are the odds, Junior? We drive halfway across the country to snatch this girl, turns out she's Ben Brice's grandkid. Same wave of His hand, God gives you her and me Ben Brice."

Junior was now looking at the big man like he was from another planet. "The hell you babbling about, Jacko?"

The big man named Jacko said, "The major always said it ain't no coincidence that the world's oil is in the Middle East, same place the world's three religions got started. He said, 'God put that oil there, Jacko, 'cause one day it's gonna bring the Jews, Muslims, and Christians back to the Middle East for the final conflict. Armageddon in the desert. God's master plan.' "

"What's all that got to do with her?"

"She's my oil, Junior." Jacko turned to Junior but pointed a gnarly thumb at Gracie. "She's gonna bring Ben Brice back to me for the final conflict."

"Who the hell's Ben Brice?"

Gracie said again, "He was a hero."

Jacko snorted smoke. "He was a fuckin' traitor. The traitor got us court-martialed."

Junior looked at him and frowned. "You mean—"

"Yeah, I mean. He's the one betrayed the major."

Junior's eyes got wide, like Nanna's that time she hit four numbers at Lotto and won $600. He said, "He's a dead man."

"Not yet he ain't," Jacko said. "But he will be soon enough."

"But how're we gonna find him?"

"We ain't. He's gonna find us."

"He ain't never gonna find us on that mountain."

"Yeah, Junior, he will. I don't know how, but he will. 'Cause we took something belongs to him."

"Now this is my kind of work," John said as he and Ben entered the Range Rover showroom. A smiling salesman wearing a short-sleeve shirt and a clip-on tie appeared before the glass doors shut behind them.

"Morning, gentlemen. I'm Bob."

A Range Rover dealership was like a second home to John R. Brice. When he had spotted it from the Jeep, his spirits had soared like a kid on Christmas morning: a new Rover would dang sure get them to Idaho! John walked over to a Land Rover on the showroom floor—Java black exterior—and opened the door—Alpaca beige leather interior. He had seen all he needed to see. He turned back to Bob.

"How much?"

"Fifty-seven," Bob said. "That's a steal for this baby."

Certainly Bob didn't think he was going to hose John R. Brice on the price of a Land Rover. Like most techno-nerds, John did not possess real-world expertise requiring physical dexterity or social skills; he did not know how to lay tile or change the oil or fix a running toilet (don't even think about a major appliance) or interface effectively with his kids' teachers or his spousal unit. But he knew all the important things in life as defined by his generation: he knew how to write computer code; he knew how to buy stuff on the Internet; he knew how to make a billion dollars from intellectual property; he knew how to compare cell phone calling plans; and he knew the specs for a Land Rover.

"Land Rover LR3 series, HSE package. Four-point-four liter V-8 power plant with Bosch Motronic Engine Management System. Four-wheel-drive with electronic traction control, electronic air suspension, and antilock brakes. Terrain Response, Active Roll Mitigation, and Dynamic Stability Control systems. Five-hundred-fifty-watt Harmon Kardon Logic 7 surround sound stereo system with thirteen speakers and amplified subwoofer. Nineteen-inch alloy wheels. Cold climate package, leather seats, sunroof, Bi-Xenon headlights, rack-and-pinion steering, and the Urban Jungle accessory kit, although I'm partial to the Safari kit. Total MSRP, fifty-six-five. Plus transportation and dealer prep fees and add-ons, fifty-seven-five. I can shop this vehicle on the Net and pay forty-nine-five max. Because I'm in a hurry, I'll pay fifty-one, cash and carry."

John's brain dump had Bob's mouth agape. "But at that price I'm giving it away. Look, I'll come down to fifty-six."

"No way, dude! Fifty-two or we're history."

"Fifty-five?"

"Fifty-three, and that's my final offer."

"Fifty-four." John turned away. Before he took two steps: "Okay, okay, fifty-three."

"Done." John put the phone to his ear. "Carol, you still there? Wire fifty-three thousand to—"

"Plus tax, title and license," Bob said.

"How much?"

Bob started tapping on a little calculator. "Title is two-fifty, license is one-fifty, sales tax is six-point-seven-five percent times fifty-three thousand . . ."

To Carol on the phone: "Plus three thousand nine hundred seventy-seven dollars and fifty cents to—"

John held the phone out to Bob, who was still tapping away.

". . . that's three thousand nine hundred seventy-seven . . ."

"Yes, we know," John said. "Tell her your bank account number. I need this vehicle in real time." He pointed outside. "And you gotta take that POS Jeep off our hands."

Bob hurried off with the cell phone. John turned to Ben.

"And *that* is how you upgrade to a new luxury SUV."

Ben was shaking his head in obvious amazement. "What does 'POS' mean?"

10:36 A.M.

"Piece of shit," Jan Jorgenson said. She flung the dried-out marker across her office and into the trash can.

She had come into the office that morning for the first time since the abduction and tried to focus on the long list of young Arab men residing in Texas, but her mind wouldn't let go of the girl on that soccer game tape. The image haunted her. She felt as if she were quitting on Gracie Ann Brice. But she was not a quitter. Marathon running had taught her never to quit. Twenty miles, you're in a brain fog, your body is on autopilot, your feet are numb, you've lost control of your bowels, and you're hitting the wall—but you don't quit; you never quit. If you quit, you never learn the truth about yourself.

FBI Special Agent (on probation) Jan Jorgenson was determined to learn the truth about Gracie Ann Brice.

So rather than running six miles as she normally did during her lunch hour, she was outlining the Brice case on the large greaseboard in her small office in downtown Dallas. She had written GRACIE ANN BRICE at the top of the board above five subheadings: GARY JENNINGS . . . JOHN BRICE . . . ELIZABETH BRICE . . . COL. BEN BRICE . . . DNA.

Under GARY JENNINGS she had written *BriceWare*

and *blood in truck* and *jersey in truck* and *9 phone calls* and *coach's ID* and *child porn*. Damning evidence. But still, the FBI's Evidence Response Team couldn't find a single hair from Gracie's head in Jennings's truck or apartment or on his clothes; or her fingerprints in his truck or his fingerprints on the porn picture; or child porn in his apartment or on his computers. He didn't come close to the sexual-predator profile. Nothing like a child abduction in his background, and a wife and baby and a million dollars in his future, but he chucks it all to rape and murder his boss's ten-year-old daughter?

As the kids say, I don't think so.

She had next completed the entries under JOHN BRICE: *Ph.D., MIT . . . marries Elizabeth Austin . . . moves to Dallas . . . BriceWare . . . IPO*. Other than his billion-dollar wealth after yesterday's IPO, a possible motive for ransom, nothing else in the father's background sparked her interest. Why would someone take John Brice's child?

She had then written under ELIZABETH BRICE: *Born NYC . . . Smith College . . . Harvard Law . . . Justice Department . . . quits Justice, marries John Brice, moves to Dallas . . . white-collar criminal defense*. Why would someone take Elizabeth Brice's child?

She was now filling in the life of COL. BEN BRICE: *West Point . . . Vietnam . . . Green Beret . . . Colonel . . . Medal of Honor . . . classified duty . . . Viper tattoo*. Why would someone take Colonel Brice's grandchild?

Why would someone commit this crime?

What were possible motives?

She sat back down at her desk, which was covered with information Research had gathered about Colonel Brice from public sources, copies of newspaper and magazine articles, arranged in reverse chronological order. Research had highlighted in yellow each place the colonel's name was mentioned in the articles. She thumbed through several. One was dated 30 April 1975, about the fall of Saigon, with a photograph of a U.S. helicopter rising from the roof of the American Embassy; a soldier was standing on the skid like a fireman on a fire truck and cradling a small object in his arm.

Another article was dated 7 August 1972, with a photo of President Nixon placing the Medal of Honor around Colonel Brice's neck in a ceremony in the East Room of the White House, awarded because Brice had single-handedly rescued one hundred American pilots from a POW camp; the colonel's wife stood beside him.

Jan scanned several articles from *Stars & Stripes*, the military newspaper, then came to a front-page article from the *Washington Herald* dated 12 November 1969. The accompanying photograph showed reporters crowding a grim Colonel Brice outside an Army building, only he wasn't a colonel back then, but a young lieutenant. Her eyes ran over the article: something about a court martial over a massacre in Vietnam. Jan Jorgenson was not born until 1980; consequently, the Vietnam War meant no more to her than the Civil War. She was about to move on to the next article when her eyes caught a word in the fifth paragraph of the story: viper.

A shot of adrenaline ricocheted through Jan's veins: Colonel Brice has a Viper tattoo. The unidentified male at the park had a Viper tattoo. The court-martialed soldiers had been in a special operations unit code-named Viper. She read on.

SOG team Viper, led by Major Charles Woodrow Walker, massacred forty-two Vietnamese civilians on 17 December

1968 in a small hamlet in the Quang Tri province of South Vietnam. Lieutenant Ben Brice reported the massacre. Once the media got wind, Quang Tri became a political cause. Members of Congress opposed to the war demanded that Major Walker be court-martialed. The Army resisted: Charles Woodrow Walker was a living legend. But when a group of senators threatened to hold up military funding, the Army surrendered and charged Walker and his soldiers under Article 118 of the Code of Military Justice: murder.

Lieutenant Ben Brice was the sole witness for the prosecution at the court martial; he testified that Walker incited the massacre and murdered a young girl in cold blood. Major Walker had only to take the stand and deny the massacre. Case closed. A living legend trumps a lieutenant every time.

The crowded courtroom was silent with anticipation when the thirty-eight-year-old Army major, a strikingly handsome figure from the photo Jan was looking at, stepped to the witness stand in his uniform, his chest covered with medals, and stood erect as he addressed the members of the military tribunal.

"Dying, gentlemen, is a big part of war. People die in war. Men, women, and children. Soldiers and civilians. Enemies and allies. And Americans. Communist forces have killed forty thousand U.S. soldiers in Vietnam—*forty thousand*, gentlemen! And the Army is court-martialing me over forty-two dead gooks?"

The major sniffs the air like a bloodhound getting a scent.

"I smell the corrupt stench of politics in this courtroom."

His accuser gazes upon the major, the very image of a Green Beret commando: six foot four, two-hundred-twenty-pound body hard as a side of beef, blond flattop, bronze face, and a voice that sounds like thunder. And he has those eyes, eyes like blue crystal that can see straight into your soul; when he locks those eyes on you, it's like you're looking at Jesus Christ himself, his men say. They call themselves his disciples.

The major locks his eyes on the court-martial panel.

"When we bombed Germany into rubble in World War Two, we killed thirty-five thousand German civilians in Dresden alone. When we bombed Hiroshima and Nagasaki, we killed three hundred thousand Japanese civilians. But we did not cry over their deaths. We did not court-martial the pilots who dropped the bombs or the generals who ordered the bombing. We honored them as heroes. We gave them medals and parades. We put a general in the White House.

"But this war, I am told, is different. This war is unpopular with the people. To which I say, so fucking what! Since when did this man's Army give a good goddamn what civilians think? Do you care what that lawless mob of malcontents protesting outside the gates to this Army base, burning the American flag you and I swore to defend, *thinks?* The soldiers fighting and dying at this very moment in Vietnam are not defending *those civilians.* They are defending *this country!* And I'm not about to let a buncha draft-dodging dopers tell me when and where and who I can kill to defend this country!

"And, I'm also told, this war is immoral, ugly, brutal, and evil. To which I say, yes, it is. Just like every other war this country has ever fought. War, gentlemen, is not pretty or neat or nice or humane fare fit for the evening news. War is ugly. Brutal. Inhumane. Evil. And necessary for the survival of the Free World!"

He points at the window.

"That mob wants America to lose in Vietnam. That mob wants to bring down the American military. We—you and I and this Army—cannot let that happen! We must not let that happen! For if we do, if we let that mob destroy this Army, the world will no longer fear America. Now, we can live in a world that does not love America. We can even live in a world that hates America. But, gentlemen, we cannot live in a world that does not fear America. We cannot live in a world that thinks it can fuck with America. Because once every piss-ant dictator, rebel, warlord, and terrorist thinks he can fuck with America, he will! Gentlemen, I am on trial, but it is not the future of Major Charles Woodrow Walker that is at stake today. It is the future of the United States Army. It is the future of America.

"I stand accused of murder by an Army that cowers before politicians, politicians who have never fought a war but who enjoy the freedom war brings—*the freedom we give them!*—politicians trying to win an election by appeasing that mob. I, gentlemen, am trying to win a war! To defeat Communism and preserve peace and prosperity for the United States of America!"

The major removes his coat. He unbuttons his left sleeve. He rolls the sleeve up. He shows the panel the Viper tattoo imprinted on his bicep. And he translates the Vietnamese words for them: " 'We kill for peace.' By God, if this country is going to enjoy peace and prosperity, we damn well better be ready to kill for it!"

The major now points at his accuser.

"Since Truman betrayed MacArthur, every soldier at

West Point knows that politicians will always betray the military. We expect that. But we don't expect betrayal by one of our own, by a fellow member of the Corps. Just as Jesus Christ had Judas Iscariot, so too do I have Lieutenant Ben Brice. He betrayed me. He betrayed you. He betrayed his Army. He betrayed his country.

"Did we kill those gooks? You goddamn right we did! And I will kill every gook in Vietnam if that's what it takes to win that war! To defeat Communism! As God is my witness, I don't regret killing those forty-two gooks! My only regret is that I didn't put a bullet in Lieutenant Brice's head, too!"

Ben's thoughts were jolted back to the present when the Land Rover bounced hard.

"Now there's a motive—revenge."

Agent Jan Jorgenson turned to the last page of the article. Major Walker and the nine other Green Berets were acquitted of murder but found guilty of conduct unbecoming an officer, stripped of their rank, and dishonorably discharged from the Army.

Did Walker abduct Gracie Ann Brice for revenge against Colonel Brice? And who is Major Charles Woodrow Walker? And where is he now?

11:05 A.M.

THE BIG MAN named Jacko was saying, "I remember one time, me and the major, we got these two VC up in the chopper, five hundred feet off the deck. The major's interrogating them—where's your base camp, how many men, and so on. The one gook, he keeps saying, 'Doo Mommie,' which means 'fuck your mama' in Viet. Well, the major finally got his fill, so he grabs the dink and throws his ass right out the door. We hear him screaming all the way down. Then the major grabs the other dink—that sumbitch pisses hisself. And he talks, gives us the coordinates of their base camp. We called in the B-52s the next morning. They wiped that camp and about five hundred gooks off the face of the earth."

Jacko smiled like he was remembering his last birthday party. "You lived for those days."

Junior said, "What'd you do with the other gook?"

"Oh, we threw him out, too. Five-hundred-foot dive into a rice paddy."

Jacko now had a faraway look on his face, like Sylvia when she talked of her old country.

"Best years of my life. Hell, killing, drinking, and fucking—to an Okie from Henryetta, Vietnam wasn't no war, it was a goddamn vacation." He shook his head. "Politicians fucked up a pretty good war."

They were sitting in a McDonald's drive-through waiting for their order. Gracie was listening. Junior was wide-eyed.

"Gosh, I love to hear them stories," he said.

Jacko said, "Course, when McNamara and Johnson sent in the draftees and the war became a goddamn TV show back home, I knew my Oriental vacation was coming to an end. But I didn't know my Army career was coming to an end when Viper team humped into the Quang Tri province that day in '68 or when we humped out that night. I just followed the major in and followed the major out and in between we wasted some gooks. Just another day in paradise. But the Army sacrificed Viper team to the mob." He sucked on his cigarette, blew out smoke, and said, "Because Lieutenant Ben Brice couldn't keep his fuckin' mouth shut."

"Why didn't the major kill Brice after he ratted you out?"

"After the court martial, CIA hired us to greenback in Cambodia—CIA, they don't give a shit about politics." He chuckled. "With SOG, the major reported to the president. With the CIA, he reported to no one. Anyway, Brice, he was a native by then, living in the zoo with the Yards. After the war, he just disappeared."

Junior handed a white bag back to Gracie. She had ordered a Big Mac, fries, and milk. Mother never let her eat fast food.

Jacko said back to her: "Where's your grandpa been living?"

Gracie thought that if she told the truth, maybe they'd turn around and drive to Taos, which would be better

307

than wherever they were going now. And she knew Ben wasn't at the cabin anyway.

"Taos."

"The hell's he doing in Taos?"

"He makes furniture—rocking chairs, tables, desks. They're awesome. Movie stars buy his stuff."

Jacko thought that was funny. "Green Beret making rocking chairs for movie stars."

"Like who?" Junior asked.

Gracie didn't answer him. Instead, she said, "Let's go to Taos. I'll take you to his cabin."

Jacko snorted. "I think I'll wait for him to come to me."

"Scared, huh? You know, you guys ought to pull over and let me out before he catches up with you."

"Shut up, you little whore!"

Gracie wasn't sure what that word meant, but she was pretty sure it wasn't a compliment. Before she could defend herself, Junior did.

"Don't call her that! She ain't no whore!"

Junior was giving Jacko a real mean face, like Ronnie down the street that day she had beaten him up.

"She started it! Tell her to shut up! You want a woman in your life, that's what you get—a fuckin' mouth won't stop!"

Gracie removed her lunch from the bag and began singing: "Mamas, don't let your babies grow up to be morons . . ."

Jacko pointed a French fry back at her and said, "See? See what I mean?"

Gracie pulled the milk out of the bag and saw her picture on the carton under MISSING CHILD.

11:47 A.M.

THE OFF-ROAD tires gripped the dirt-and-rock trail and the V-8 engine muscled the Land Rover up the steep incline while the plush leather seats cushioned the occupants as they bounced about, albeit less than one would expect due to the electronic air suspension system. For your off-roading needs, no other SUV measured up to a Range Rover product. John's Range Rover back home was a sporty red job with four-wheel-drive, a neat feature even though the thought of actually taking a $75,000 vehicle off-road had never entered John Brice's mind. So when they crested the hill, John exhaled with great relief and his white-knuckled hands released their death grip on the steering wheel as he braked the Land Rover to a stop in front of a small cabin. It was almost noon on the seventh day since Gracie had gone missing.

A dog was on Ben before he had de-Rovered. Ben knelt and petted the dog; the beast licked his face like an ice-cream cone. "How ya doin', Buddy?" If a dog can cry, Buddy was. Ben stood and walked inside the cabin. Man's best friend then greeted John, slobbering all over his jeans and Nike cross-trainers.

"Get away from me, you freaking mutt!"

John was not comfortable around dogs; he had had a

dog for a while as a boy, but the dang beast had bit him every chance it could. Fido finally abandoned his attack on John when it spotted some kind of rat creature and gave chase into the brush bordering the cabin. John shook out his jeans and checked out Ben's cabin; it was smaller than the four-car garage at Six Magnolia Lane, but it was a neat log home just the same.

On both sides of the steps leading up to the porch were gardens; little sprigs stuck up out of uniform rows of black dirt. The porch floor was built of wood planks. Cacti in colorful pots, odd-shaped rocks, and painted wood carvings of coyotes and horses lined the porch rail. John followed the porch around the cabin and gazed out on the brown terrain that stretched to the distant mountains whose white tops were a stark contrast against the deep blue sky. As far as he could see, there was not another human being, not another house, not another anything. This was not an exclusive gated community constructed to keep the masses out. This was not a master-planned subdivision with an active homeowners' association. This was not a place you came to for social engineering. This was where you came to leave the rest of the world behind.

On the west side of the porch were two wooden rocking chairs; one was half-sized with GRACIE carved in the seat back. John sat in her chair and imagined Ben and Gracie sitting there and talking, and he wondered what she had said about her father. He sighed. He should have come with her, as she had always begged him to, and sat in a rocker with JOHN carved into the seat back and talked to his father. But he had always been so brain-damaged about the past—a father not there to protect Little Johnny Brice from the bullies—and so focused on the future—an IPO that would make John R. Brice's life perfect—that he had never found the reason or the time to forgive or forget.

He hoped Gracie had forgiven her father.

He stood and walked around back. Behind the cabin were a vegetable garden and a smaller structure accessible via a stone path. The door creaked as John entered Ben's workshop; unfinished furniture and tools occupied the floor and walls. A rocking chair caught John's eye. He ran his hands along the graceful wood armrests and down the curved back. He sat in the chair and leaned his head back. John had assumed the least about his father, that his woodwork would be crude creations, not works of art like this chair. Just as he had assumed a drunk would live like a drunk, sloppy and dirty. But the cabin and grounds and this workshop were meticulously maintained, as if Ben had a Sylvia Milanevic on the payroll.

John Brice didn't know his own father.

"That's for some movie star in Santa Fe."

Ben was standing in the door.

"I'm going into town to pick up supplies," he said. "There's food inside if you get hungry. We'll load up and hit the road as soon as I get back." He held out an open hand. "Since you traded in my POS Jeep, I need to borrow your vehicle."

John tossed the keys to Ben. "It's yours."

12:19 P.M.

AFTER THE LAND ROVER had disappeared down the hill, John went inside the cabin. He was starving; all he had eaten that day was his normal breakfast of a dozen Oreos crushed in a glass of milk and the black coffee on the flight.

He walked over to the kitchen at one end of the main room and got a potent whiff of whiskey. Five empty whiskey bottles were sitting upside down in the sink. Looking at the bottles, John was sure he was following a drunk on a wild goose chase; but there was no running home to Elizabeth now. He took the bottles outside to the recycling bin.

When he returned, he searched the cabinets for something decent to eat, but all he found were organic granola bars, organic oatmeal, organic pasta, organic peanut butter, vitamins, and health supplements. *A drunk who takes care of himself?* He opened the refrigerator: grapefruit juice, orange juice, yogurt, fruit, cheese, and a bag of bean tamales. Nothing worth eating. Which was just as well, because when he shut the door and saw Gracie's photos stuck there with magnets, he lost his appetite.

He wandered around the main room and found a stack of newspaper and magazine clippings about BriceWare.com and its genius founder on a desk in the corner. On a table next to an old leather recliner by the fireplace was the *Fortune* magazine with John's picture on the cover, opened to the Brice family photo and Gracie's bright smile. Ben had kept up with his son all this time. But his son had never returned his calls or come to visit, convinced that at his age he no longer needed a father.

He was wrong.

The cabin had two small bedrooms, each with a tiny bathroom. One was Gracie's bedroom: her clothes in the closet, her stuff around the room, an Indian headdress on the bed, a colorful totem pole in the corner, and a wooden headboard with *Gracie* carved in a neat script. He walked around the room and touched her things.

The other bedroom was spartan, only a bed, a wooden chest in the corner, and a nightstand. The bed was neatly made; the ends of the blanket were tucked in tightly. It was an Army bed just like the bed John had slept in until the day he had left for MIT. He had never made his own bed again.

Hanging in the small closet were jeans, corduroy and flannel shirts, a winter coat, and, in a clear bag, the dress uniform of a full colonel in the United States Army. On the floor were jogging shoes and boots. On the shelf above were several hats and caps and a green beret wrapped in plastic.

On the nightstand were an old rotary dial telephone, a gooseneck lamp, a small framed photo of Mom, and a stack of letters from Gracie. An old phone, snail-mail letters, no computer in the cabin: his father was living in the past in every way possible. John picked up the top envelope; Gracie had drawn little happy faces around the edges. John sat on the bed and stared at the happy faces; he saw Gracie's happy face. Could she really be alive?

So everyone back home thought she was dead.

Gracie wondered if they would have a funeral Mass for her like the one for the little boy two blocks over who had died a year ago from some disease he had been born with. The altar would be decorated with pretty flowers, Father Randy would be wearing his fancy vestments, and the choir would be singing 'Amazing Grace.' Mom would look beautiful in a black dress and Dad would look . . . Did he even own a black suit?

Picturing the two of them together at her funeral, the beauty and the geek, Gracie found herself wondering again how they had ever gotten together . . . and if they loved each other. Dad loved Mom, that was, like, obvious. He was a puppy dog around her, always licking her shoes. But did she love him? Gracie didn't think so. She had asked Nanna one time, but Nanna said, "Of course she does, but sometimes grownups have issues that keep them apart." She asked Nanna what issues were keeping her and Ben apart, but Nanna started crying so she never asked again.

But back to the funeral. Everyone would file into the church, old ladies would be crying, kids would be messing with each other, and their parents would be telling them to hush; Mass would start and Father Randy and the altar girls would walk up the center aisle to where her empty white casket—yeah, she wanted a white casket—would be sitting just in front of the altar and on top would be a picture of her in her soccer uniform because everyone wanted to remember her that way.

Gosh, it would be a great funeral. Everyone in town would be there, Mom and Dad, Nanna and Sam, Sylvia and Hilda, her teammates, Coach Wally, kids from school—they'd probably let school out that day—her teachers, and the principal; everyone would be crying and praying for the little dead girl. It sounded so neat, she almost wished she could be there. But she wouldn't be there, and neither would Ben. Because she wasn't dead, and he was coming to save her.

Colonel, you saved my life. Lying in that cell at San Bie, I knew I would never see my wife or children again, but you gave my wife her husband back and my children their father. I owe you my life. God bless you.

John had found the boxes in the wooden chest; in the first box he had found dozens more letters, but these letters weren't from Gracie. These letters were from military pilots pledging their lives to John's father.

He did not know his own father.

He returned the letters to the first box. Then he opened the second box. He removed Ben's framed West Point diploma, Army certificates, and a display case containing a hero's medals: eight Purple Hearts; five Silver Stars with an empty spot for a sixth one; four Bronze Stars; two Soldier's Medals; a Distinguished Service Cross; the Legion of Merit; and in a special case, the Medal of Honor, a round gold medal with an eagle over the word *valor* and a gold star with a Roman centurion engraved in the center. John touched the medal with a reverence he had never before felt. He had never looked upon Ben as a hero. John R. Brice's heroes were Tim Paterson, who invented DOS, Ray Tomlinson, who invented e-mail, and Tim Berners-Lee, who invented the HTML, HTTP, and URL conventions that powered the World Wide Web, brilliant men who made Internet shopping possible, not men who fought a war forty years ago that nobody cared about.

What was Ben like back then, when he was young and robust? What were his dreams? What life had he and Mom hoped for? Were they ever happy? What made him a drunk?

John found the answers in the third box. Inside were photos: Ben's formal West Point graduation portrait in his high-necked dress uniform above the Academy motto, *Duty, Honor, Country*; Ben and Kate, him in a white uniform and Mom in a wedding dress, outside a church, ducking under an arch of sabers held out by other soldiers in white uniforms; and other wedding photos with a best man and maid of honor whose images struck John. The woman, with her curly black hair and a certain frailty about her, seemed oddly familiar to John. In another photo, the same man was standing next to the same woman in a hospital bed holding a baby; Kate and Ben were leaning in from behind. Everyone was smiling like their IPO had just hit the street.

John dug deeper and found more photos: Ben and the other man just arrived in Vietnam, looking young and eager in crisp uniforms; a team photo, both of them with other soldiers and handwritten along the bottom the words *SOG team Viper, 2 Dec 68*; Ben sitting in a stirrup and dangling from a rope under a helicopter flying above a dense jungle; Ben lying on the ground, his pants ripped open and an Army medic wrapping his bloody leg; Ben in a hospital bed, a pretty nurse in a white uniform on one side, and on the other side a general pinning a Purple

Heart to Ben's pillow; Ben, in the jungle, holding a long black rifle with a scope, his boot on a dead Asian soldier wearing black pajamas, *1000 meters* written along the bottom; Ben, his smile gone now, replaced by a hardness John had never seen on his father's face, camouflage grease-paint, his uniform no longer crisp but instead dirty and worn with the sleeves cut off, revealing his muscular arms and that tattoo. He was standing among Indians.

He was not the same man.

John realized he knew next to nothing about his father. Ben Brice had been a hero, he knew that, but Ben had never talked about the war and John had never asked. His father was a loser. A drunk. That was all he had ever really known about Ben Brice.

John returned the photos to the box, one by one, but his eyes lingered on the hospital photo of the man and woman with the baby. This same man was in the early photos with Ben but in none of the later ones. Looking at this man and this woman, something strange stirred inside John, like one of those *déjà vu* moments. He touched the image of the woman gently. John didn't know how long he had been staring at the photo when he looked up to see Ben standing over him. John held up the photo.

"Who are these people?" he asked.

Ben was quiet for a time. He ran his hands over his face and through his hair. Then he said, "Your mother and father."

1:43 P.M.

"M Y DAD SAYS life is random," Gracie said.

"What?" Jacko said without turning his head back.

"Random. You know, things happen for no particular reason. He says life doesn't make sense and isn't supposed to. My mom says life is fucked up, but she has some issues."

"The hell you talking about?" His words and smoke came out of his mouth at the same time.

She sighed. "What I'm talking about is, you two lame-brains kidnap me not even knowing Ben is my grandpa, and a long time ago during Ben's war you did something bad and Ben told on you and you got in trouble."

"How do you know we did something bad?"

"Because I know Ben didn't. And now Ben's coming after me and he's going to find out you took me, the same guy he told on. I mean, what are the odds of that? Now my dad—he's a math genius—he'd say that's just random, what normal people call coincidence or luck. But I don't think so. I think it's meant to be."

"Destiny?"

"God's plan. See, Nanna—she's my grandmother—she goes to Mass like, almost every day. She's always saying, 'God has a plan for you, Gracie Ann Brice. God has a plan for all of us.' She says there's no such thing as coincidence

318

or luck, that everything that happens in our lives is supposed to happen because it's all part of God's plan. So you kidnapping me and Ben coming to get me, that's not a coincidence. That's part of God's plan."

Jacko exhaled smoke through both nostrils.

"Well, sweet cheeks, I don't know about God's plan, but my plan is to gut your grandpa."

"Roger Dalton was the brother I never had," Ben said. "We went through West Point together, went to Vietnam together." He paused. "Academy instructors, they told us it would be our great adventure. It wasn't."

John's eyes remained on the photo of his mother and father; his mother was holding him and his father looked so strong and manly. There was manly somewhere in John Brice's genes.

"You were born a week before we deployed. On our flight to Saigon, Roger said, 'Anything happens to me, you be my son's father.' He was killed two weeks later."

"How'd he die?"

"A soldier's death."

Ben's voice cracked. John wanted to know more, but he decided that now wasn't the time.

"What happened to my mother?"

"Mary, she was smart just like you. But when Roger died, it's like her mind couldn't handle it. She was just too fragile to fit in this world."

"Like me."

"She died when you were six months old. We adopted you."

"John Roger Brice." Ben nodded. "Where are they buried?"

"Iowa. Where they were from."

"When this is over, I think I'll go to Iowa. Is his name on the Wall in Washington?"

"I suppose. I've never been able to go."

"Maybe I'll go to Iowa and then to the Wall. Maybe you'll come with me."

"Maybe."

John looked at the photo again. "I always thought Gracie got her eyes and hair from you."

Would she look for her daughter in every blonde blue-eyed girl she saw on the street, in the mall, and at restaurants? Would she wonder what her daughter looked like with each passing year, like those age-progression images she had seen of children missing for five or ten or fifteen years on the missingkids.com website? Would she always hold out hope that her daughter was still alive, somewhere? Would she become one of those pitiful mothers of lost children she had seen on TV, keeping Grace's room exactly as it was now, always believing that one day she would return to this room?

The doorbell rang.

Elizabeth was still in her bathrobe and in her daughter's room, so many thoughts running through her mind, trying to imagine life without Grace.

The doorbell rang again.

Her heart froze. Then it began to beat rapidly; her breathing came faster. She stood. She knew.

It's her! It's Grace! She's come home!

Elizabeth bolted out of the bedroom and ran down the long hall and to the stairs and down to the first floor and through the foyer and to the front door and pulled the door open, ready to embrace her daughter and to hold her and to cry with her and to never let her go.

But you're not Grace.

Standing on the porch was a young woman in a black dress; her anguished face seemed vaguely familiar. It took Elizabeth a moment to place it. Gary Jennings's wife.

Elizabeth slumped against the doorjamb. She had been so sure it was Grace. Now, for the first time since the abduction, she thought she might be drifting toward insanity, floating on a raft down a slow-moving river, steadily and inexorably toward rapids where she would crack up on the rocks, finally to be thrown over the edge of a steep fall, driven down deep into the darkness below, never to resurface. The thought was inviting.

"Mrs. Brice, I'm so sorry about Gracie. But my husband didn't take her. Gary would never do something like that."

She started to leave, but she stopped when Elizabeth said, "Your baby."

She turned back and said, "The doctors say she'll be okay."

She walked down to a waiting car, got in, and drove off. The street was silent and vacant; a few pink ribbons tied to mailboxes fluttered in the breeze and several scattered missing-child fliers skipped along the ground like children playing hopscotch. The TV trucks and police cars and cameras and reporters and gawkers were gone, back to their lives as if the world had not been irrevocably altered seven days earlier; fathers and career mothers had gone back to their offices, stay-at-home moms to exercise classes and shopping malls, children to school, reporters to new stories, and the networks to New York. The circus had moved on.

Elizabeth turned and shut the door on her life.

321

2:38 P.M.

JOHN WATCHED AS Ben opened a door to a vault under the floor of the workshop and then knelt down and shone a flashlight into the dark space below.

"I hate rats," he said.

Satisfied, he hopped down into the hole. His head was below floor level. He handed up three long metal containers. Then he hoisted himself out.

Ben dusted off one container with a cloth. He unlatched the locks and lifted the top. Inside, set into a molded form, were a black rifle, boxes of ammunition, two telescopes, one normal size the other oversized, a black tube, what John knew was a silencer, a leather shoulder sling, two ammunition magazines, and a crude brass bracelet.

Ben slipped the bracelet onto his left wrist, then he removed the rifle and mounted the smaller scope and the silencer. He loaded a magazine and snapped it into the underside of the rifle and attached the sling at both ends. He stood and walked outside. John followed.

Facing the vast open space, Ben knelt, raised the rifle to his shoulder, gripped the underside of the stock with his left hand, extended his right elbow from his body, and sighted in with his right eye. The sound of the rifle's discharge was muffled. Ben grunted, adjusted the scope, sighted, and fired again. Another adjustment and another shot.

"What are you shooting at?"

"Cholla cactus, five hundred meters out."

John slanted his glasses to obtain sharper vision but without success. "Dang, I can't even see it."

"Inside, in one of the other boxes—a spotting scope."

John returned to the workshop and opened the other containers. Inside one were a knife with the word *Viper* etched into the shiny blade, two sets of dog tags, one for *Ben Brice* and the other for *Roger Dalton*, a small machine gun with a shoulder strap, and the spotting telescope. John took his father's dog tags and put them around his neck. He then removed the scope and ran back out.

Ben said, "Straight down the barrel, rock formation."

John looked into the scope, adjusted the focus, and spotted the rock formation. "Got it."

"Beyond that, a cactus."

"With the yellow flower?"

"Yeah."

Standing behind Ben, John figured the theoretical probability of hitting that flower from five hundred meters— 1,640 feet—had to be one in a million, even in the perfectly still conditions, and particularly by a sixty-year-old . . . *the thought crept into John's mind* . . . drunk. The rifle discharged; the yellow flower split off whole from the cactus.

"Dang, Ben, that's awesome! You must've been a dead shot!"

From Ben's expression, John knew he had said exactly the wrong thing. Ben stood and walked over to a big rock and sat; he stared at the dirt for a time. Finally he spoke.

"NVA officers didn't wear insignia. You couldn't tell a

grunt from a general, so you'd sit outside their camp, maybe a thousand meters out, watching them through the binoculars until you picked out the ranking officer, sometimes just because he had more cigarettes in his pocket. Then you'd wait until he was sitting down, eating, and you'd put the scope on him. And when you did, you played God. You decided he'll never see his wife or kids again, or even the next day, that because he was born in Hanoi instead of Houston he deserved a bullet in his head. You observed the last moments of his life, the last smile on his face, the last drag on his cigarette, and you squeezed the trigger. And his life was over."

He looked up at John.

"I didn't kill for God or country, or for those medals, or even to defeat Communism. Well, at first I did, but at the end, when I knew the war was lost, I killed so fewer American boys would come home in a body bag. Like your father did. That's why I stayed over there, John. That's why I wasn't here for you."

John looked out on New Mexico and felt his eyes water. "I should've been there for Gracie. I should've hung up on Lou and gone to the concession stand with her. I should have protected her." He shook his head slowly. "Ben, I just let her go."

"No, son, you didn't let her go. They took her." Ben stood and was the colonel in the photos again. "And we're fixing to take her back."

After graduating from high school, boys in Henryetta, Oklahoma, either go to college on football scholarships, take up farming like their fathers before them, or join the Army. Jack Odell Smith was big and strong and played football for Henryetta High, but he got ejected from most games for unsportsmanlike conduct. And he never took to the plow. So, barely a month after graduating at the bottom of his class, Jack O. Smith had joined the United States Army.

Jacko was not your leader of men, but he was a loyal follower and kept his mouth shut, character traits much admired in this man's Army. Those traits, along with his physical strength, temper, and ability to kill without remorse, earned him a spot in the Special Forces Training Group at Fort Bragg. There he had met Major Charles Woodrow Walker.

Jack Odell Smith had found his place in life.

Major Charles Woodrow Walker had always thought his place in life would be the White House. "Jacko," the major had said, "the American people are sheep. In times of peace, they just want to graze off the land and feel fat and happy. But when the wolves are in the pasture, they want to feel safe. 'Make love not war' sounds good when the war is ten thousand miles away. But when war comes home to America, and it will, the American people will turn to a military hero to make them feel safe. They will turn to me."

But then the verdict was read: guilty. War criminals don't get to be president.

Jack Odell Smith would not call himself a thinking man. He had always left his thinking to the major. But now, driving back to their mountain compound with Ben Brice's granddaughter in the back seat, he found himself thinking about how one event could change the course of history: What if Lieutenant Ben Brice had honored the soldiers' code?

Viper team would have continued covert operations in Laos and Cambodia and North Vietnam. The war would have been won by professional warriors. Soldiers would have come home to a hero's welcome. No one would know about Quang Tri because no one walked away from Quang Tri. And Major Charles Woodrow Walker would be in the White House because on 9/11 the war had come home to America.

Now Lieutenant Ben Brice was coming home to Viper team.

Gracie had seen Ben's tattoo many times, and he had even let her touch it, but he would never tell her why he got it or what the strange words meant. He only told her they were Vietnamese. Looking now at the same words on Jacko's tattoo, she saw her chance.

"What do those Vietnamese words mean, on your tattoo?"

Jacko blew out smoke and said, " 'We kill for peace.' "

Gracie had often asked Ben about his war—she wanted to know why he was a drunk—but he refused to talk about it. "Honey," he'd always say, "you'll learn about the bad things in life soon enough. No need for me to hurry that day up."

She sighed. That day had come.

"Did Ben kill people in his war?"

"Damn sure did. He was a sniper." Jacko sucked on his cigarette, exhaled smoke, and said, "Your grandpa was a traitor, but I'll say this for him: he was one helluva shot. He could put a bullet between a gook's eyes from a thousand meters."

Gracie fell quiet. Because now she knew something she wished she didn't know, like when she'd read ahead in a book and find out the ending. She knew what Ben would have to do, and it made her sad to know it. She had figured out that he drank his whiskey to forget his war; now she knew he drank to forget killing people in his war. She didn't want him to drink more of his whiskey because of her.

Jacko said, "Yep, damn shame he betrayed his team and now I gotta kill him."

Gracie's voice sounded odd, even to her own ears, when she said, "No, you're not going to kill Ben. He's going to kill you. And Junior, too."

The two men didn't say anything for a long while.

4:42 P.M.

"I WAS STILL IN ROTC at A&M when the Quang Tri shit hit the fan."

FBI Special Agent Jan Jorgenson had just reported to her superior her latest findings on the Gracie Ann Brice abduction. Agent Devereaux was still in Des Moines. The boy abducted there had been found dead. A manhunt was on for his abductor, a convicted child molester out on parole. For the third time.

"I'm running searches on Major Walker," Jan said.

"Why?"

"Because Colonel Brice served under Walker in Viper unit. Because he has a Viper tattoo and the man in the park had a Viper tattoo. Because those soldiers committed a massacre, Brice testified against them, and Walker said he should've killed Brice. Because you said you wouldn't have closed the case."

"I know, Jan, but you think Walker's been waiting almost forty years to get revenge on Colonel Brice? And somehow finds his granddaughter living in a gated community in Post Oak, Texas, kidnaps her, frames Jennings, and takes her to God knows where?"

Now that she actually heard her theory aloud, it did sound pretty ridiculous.

"And even if Walker wanted revenge on Colonel Brice, how would he connect him to Gracie and how would he find her? And if he wanted revenge, wouldn't he just kill Colonel Brice? Why would he abduct his granddaughter?"

"He wouldn't. I guess you're right, Eugene, but this Viper connection, that's an awfully big coincidence."

10:33 P.M.

JOHN HADN'T INVITED Ben to his MIT graduation because of that damned Viper tattoo. He was worried that someone important to his future business career might see it and learn his father had been in the Army and had fought in Vietnam: the prevailing thought back then among professors at elite Northeastern schools was that only Southern crackers, minorities, and losers had gone to Vietnam. He had feared that because his father was a loser someone might think John Brice was a loser, too. He had never talked about Ben to anyone, not even Elizabeth. He had never told her about that damned tattoo. But she knew Ben Brice was a loser; and that her husband was a loser, too.

Now, looking over at Ben sleeping in the passenger seat as John R. Brice, billionaire, drove a new $53,000 Land Rover loaded with weapons like the freaking U.S. cavalry through the Navajo Indian Reservation in northwest New Mexico, red cliffs looming large in the moonlight, John realized that those professors had been full of shit. As he had been. As his wife was.

Ben Brice was no loser.

*

Thirteen hundred miles due north, Junior stopped the Blazer in front of his cabin on a mountain in Idaho called Red Ridge. He would give anything for the major to walk out that door and see Patty. She was sleeping in the back seat.

"I got her," Junior said.

Jacko grunted and disappeared into the dark, heading to his cabin. Junior opened the rear door and leaned inside. He slid his arms under Patty and lifted her. He stepped out of the vehicle.

"I'll walk," Patty said in a groggy voice, rubbing her eyes.

Junior gently leaned over until her feet touched the ground. He held onto her lightly to make sure she was stable.

"You awake enough?"

"I think so," she said. Then she punched him in the nose and took off running into the darkness. Damn, she was fast for a girl. And hit hard, too.

Junior didn't give chase because she was running straight for Jacko's cabin. Sure enough, Junior shortly heard a scream. After a moment, Patty appeared again, carried by Jacko like a bag of fertilizer. He dropped her at Junior's feet.

Junior sighed. "Patty, you'd've froze to death before morning. Now, if you run again, I'm gonna have to teach you a lesson you ain't gonna like. I don't want to do that, but I will for your own good. This is your home now, Patty, you got to accept that. We're always gonna be together."

Patty looked up at Junior.

"In your dreams, mountain boy," she said.

*

Kate stirred in bed. She felt someone rustling around beside her. Sam.

"Nanna, I got the creeps again."

"Another bad dream?"

"Unh-hunh. About Gracie."

"You got Barney?"

"Yep."

He wedged the Barney toy in between them and snuggled in tightly. After a moment, she thought he had fallen asleep, but his little voice broke the silence.

"Nanna, some man's not gonna take me away too, is he?"

She propped herself up on her elbow and touched his smooth face. "No, Sam. That won't happen. I promise."

"Good."

He closed his little eyes.

DAY EIGHT

7:10 A.M.

GRACIE OPENED her eyes.

She was lying in a warm bed with a blanket pulled up to her chin, and not the scratchy green blanket from the SUV, but a thick soft blanket that felt brand new. The sheets were flannel and smelled clean and fresh. The pillow under her head was firm. The ceiling above her was low, and there was no fan with fancy little lights or sky-blue paint with clouds in white faux finish or fancy crown molding like in her bedroom at home. The walls and ceiling were wood, flat wood planks with white mortar in the cracks like between the logs in Ben's cabin.

The bed was pushed against one wall of the small room. A little window was in the wall above the bed; the sun was shooting a beam of light into the room. A gas heater was glowing blue in the corner. There was no closet, only a hanging rack with some winter clothes. At the foot of the bed was a metal table with a kerosene lamp on it, like the one Dad had bought last summer for the first annual Brice family camping trip. But Mom had gotten a trial and Dad the IPO, so the lamp and the tent and the rest of the camping gear sat piled in the back corner of the garage. Propped up on the table was a new Barbie doll still in the box.

This was really starting to creep her out.

There were two doors; one led into a bathroom. She could see a toilet, but it wasn't like the marble toilet with matching bidet in her bathroom at home. This one sat low to the ground and had a compartment underneath—a camping toilet.

The other door was closed.

Her closet at home was bigger than this bedroom. But it was a cozy little room, like her room at Ben's cabin, where she wished she were now, safe and secure with Ben and looking forward to a day in the workshop or hiking the hills or driving into town for dinner. She wished she were safe with Ben. She wanted to cry, but she refused to let the tears come.

Instead, she pushed the blanket back and almost screamed out loud: she was wearing pink flannel pajamas. *Like, way pink! What's with this guy and pink?* She vaguely remembered changing into the pajamas but not putting on the thick green wool socks. She knelt up, wiped the moisture off the window, and put her face to the glass; it was cold. Outside, snow covered the ground and icicles hung on the limbs of the tall trees, but they were not at all like the trees back home. They were Christmas trees. In the distance, among the trees, she noticed a movement . . . and then a head . . . and a—wow, a deer tiptoeing through the snow! *Bambi!* Oh, golly, it's so cute, maybe later she could feed it and—

Bambi suddenly shuddered, then its legs gave way and it collapsed. *Oh my gosh!* Gracie heard an echo, like a loud *bang*. Bambi just lay there. Then the snow around Bambi turned red; the red spread out and formed a little river cutting through the snow and running downhill. Her eyes followed the red river until a big boot stepped right into it and splashed the red like Sam jumping into a mud puddle. Two men holding long guns walked up to Bambi; a big fat man lifted the deer's head then dropped it. He was grinning. Gracie fell back onto the bed and dove under the blanket. *I've got to escape before they shoot me too!*

"Patty?" There was a knock on the door. "You awake?"

Junior.

She stuck her head out from under the blanket. "No, but Gracie's awake."

"Got hot water for your bath. You decent?"

"As decent as a girl can be in pink PJs."

The door opened and Junior entered; he was carrying two big buckets of steaming water and wearing another plaid shirt.

"Did you hit, like, a going-out-of-business sale on plaid shirts?" she asked.

"What?"

"Never mind."

"We don't got no running water or electricity up here," he said, disappearing into the bathroom, "but I can still fix you a hot bath each week."

She heard the water being poured into a bathtub.

"Each *week?* I take a bath every day."

Junior appeared in the doorway with a big smile. "Just like my mama. I used to fetch hot water for her every morning. Bathtub, that was hers. And all that girl stuff in there." He paused a moment like he was remembering a good time. Then he abruptly snapped out of it. "It's yours now. Breakfast be cooked time you're done. And I got a big surprise for you."

"Bigger than being kidnapped?"

"Now, Patty, you gotta let that go. What's done is done."

He gestured around the room. "You like your room? Got it done right before we come for you. Everything's new—sheets, blankets—hey, you like that Barbie doll? Ordered that special."

"I don't do dolls."

He motioned to the clothes rack. "Got you some winter clothes, too."

"How'd you know my size?"

"I know everything about you, Patty."

"Except my name. It's Gracie Ann Brice."

His first stern look of the day. "No. It's Patty . . . Patty Walker. Same as my mama." Then, abruptly, he was smiling again. "Make a list of any other stuff you need. I'll get it next week when I go into town."

"I've got a surprise for you, too—I started my period. I need tampons."

Junior blushed like Dad that time she had walked in on him naked. "Uh, okay, I'll, uh, I'll get some. How . . . uh . . . how many do you need—one, two?"

"Hel-*lo*! A whole box. And I need them today, like real soon or I'm going to bleed all over the place!"

"Oh, shit, don't do that! Okay, I'll, uh, I'll go into town and get 'em today. Uh, write it down, so I know what to ask for." He walked out, shaking his head and muttering to himself. "Jesus, why didn't I think of that?"

Boy, talk about diminished capacity. Of course, she had not started her period. They had learned about periods and tampons and all that stuff in health class, but according to Ms. Boyd she was probably two years away from her first period. But how would mountain boy know that? With no electricity, he couldn't watch the Discovery Channel. And she wanted him in town today.

Because Ben might be in town today.

7:13 A.M.

FIVE HUNDRED SIXTY miles due south, the black Land Rover was doing seventy on I-15 North.

Ben's hands were shaking. He squeezed the leather-wrapped steering wheel and summoned the inner strength that had seen him through Big Ug's fan-belt beatings at San Bie. He could not fail Gracie.

It was Friday morning; he had taken over the wheel at 0400. John had crawled into the back seat and fallen asleep. That was over three hours ago, enough time to relive a life that had taken Ben Brice from West Texas to West Point, from Duty, Honor, Country to Quang Tri and the china doll. An hour from now they would arrive in Idaho Falls to talk to Clayton Lee Tucker at his gas station. He was the last person who had seen Gracie alive.

John's cell phone rang. After three rings, John woke, dug the phone out of his pocket, and answered. "Yeah . . . Who's this? . . . Lou? . . . Cripes, what time is it? . . . Oh, yeah, it's later in New York . . . What? . . . Utah, I guess . . ."

"Idaho," Ben said.

"Oh, Idaho," John said, pushing himself up and rubbing his face. "I don't know, Lou, however long it takes . . . What? . . . Price is up how much? . . . Dude, you're breaking up, we're in a freaking black hole out here,

339

man . . . What? . . . Three billion? . . . Lou, I can't hear you . . . Lou? . . . Lou? . . ." John frowned at the phone, then he disconnected. "Thing gronked out."

He shoved the phone back into his pocket and put his glasses on. He climbed into the front passenger seat, leaned over, and dug into the bag of snacks he had bought on their last gas stop.

"Lou, my investment banker on the IPO. He says the stock is trading at ninety. I'm a billionaire three times over." He reappeared with an Oreo cookie stuffed halfway in his mouth. "So why don't I feel like a real man?"

The bathtub had feet like the one at Ben's cabin. Gracie stepped in, sat down, and slid down until the water touched her chin. The hot water felt wonderful; her skin tingled. She couldn't remember her last bath. She closed her eyes and went all the way under. When she surfaced, she smoothed her hair back with her fingers. She needed a shampoo.

Next to the tub was a small wood table with fresh towels and washcloths and a silver bucket like the one in Sam's sandbox except this bucket was filled with little soaps and shampoos with *Best Western Inn* and *Motel 6* on the labels. Gracie closed her eyes and tried to remember, but all she could recall were vague scenes from strange rooms.

She emptied one of the shampoos into her hand. The scent reminded her of Mom's bathroom; they had had their only mother–daughter talk while Mom soaked in the big Jacuzzi tub one night after a verdict. Mom had poured a whole bottle of stress relief pellets into the water and soon the entire bathroom smelled of eucalyptus.

Gracie sat on the floor while Mom lay back against a head cushion, closed her eyes, and offered motherly advice: "Grace, men are like dogs. They can smell fear on a woman. Never let them smell your fear. Never let them see you cry. Act tough even when you don't feel tough. Curse. Don't get mad, get even. If a boy doesn't take no for an answer, kick him in the balls." But she didn't give her any advice for when she was kidnapped and taken to a cabin in Idaho by a crazy mountain boy.

Gracie stayed in the bathtub until the water lost its heat. She stepped out and dried off with one of the towels. Laid out neatly on the vanity were a silver comb and brush with a matching hair clip, a toothbrush and paste, and a small baby powder.

Baby powder never felt so good.

She opened the bathroom door and caught a chill. She wrapped her arms and hurried over to the clothes rack and quickly dressed. This was so strange. All the clothes were her size: long underwear, heavy corduroy pants, plaid flannel shirts, wool socks, and hiking boots. She probably looked like a total dork—"Pretty in plaid? I don't think so." The boots were kind of neat, though.

She tied the laces and stood. *Mountain girl.* She stepped to the door, put her fingers around the knob, and turned slowly. It opened. There was no lock on the door. She opened the door slightly and smelled breakfast cooking. She wished she were back at home and Sylvia was cooking in the kitchen. When she stepped out of the bedroom and into a long rectangular room, she knew she wasn't.

Tables and chairs were scattered about the big space, maps and charts hung on the walls, big metal containers with U.S. ARMY stamped on the side were stacked high against one wall, and a ratty old couch sat in the middle of the room. A door at the far end opened and Junior appeared. He shut the door quietly behind him then turned and saw her.

"Why, don't you look pretty?"

"What's in those Army boxes?"

"Ordnance. Why'd you cut your hair so short? You do look like a boy."

"Soccer season. What's that?"

Junior walked over to the kitchen area. "What's what?"

"Ordnance."

"Oh—grenade launchers, explosives, ammo, detonators, napalm, that sort of stuff. Breakfast is ready."

Junior had set two places with paper plates, plastic forks, knives, and cups, and napkins on a small folding table. He was cooking on a little gas stove; there was a brand new one just like it in the back corner of the garage at home. He picked up a black skillet with a rag and slapped scrambled eggs and a slab of meat on her plate. She was really hungry.

"Mama taught me to cook," he said.

She sat down and tried the eggs. He cooked pretty good eggs for a boy. Junior joined her at the table. She had a mouthful of scrambled eggs when Junior bowed his head and folded his hands.

"Dear Lord, thank you for this here food. And thank you for bringing Patty here." His head raised up. "Let's eat."

She swallowed. "God didn't bring me here."

"Sure He did."

"Hel-*lo*, earth to mountain boy—God doesn't kidnap children."

"No, He don't. He just showed us the way." He chewed with his mouth open. "God wants us to be together."

He smiled and reached over and put his hand on hers; she felt something she didn't want to feel. She jerked her hand away.

"Ya think?"

"Yep, I think."

Gracie cut into the meat and put a piece in her mouth.

"So you followed me all last week?"

He grinned. "Yep."

"Watching me at school and recess and practice?"

"Yep."

"And you called me, didn't you?"

"Yep."

"And hung up every time?"

"Yep."

"So you were just waiting for a chance to grab me?"

"Yep."

"Why after the game?"

"'Cause your mama wasn't there." He pointed at the meat with his fork. "Eats good, don't it?"

She assumed "eats good" was mountain-speak for "tastes good." She nodded. "Sausage?"

"Venison."

"What's that?"

"Deer meat."

Gracie spat out the ball of meat.

8:09 A.M.

CLAYTON LEE TUCKER spat a stream of brown juice into a brass spittoon. His cheek bulged with a big wad of chewing tobacco and his face was wrinkled like used aluminum foil. His skin was darkened a shade from the grease; his black glasses sat lopsided on his bulbous nose; his hands were gnarly. Ben knew what a drunk looked like in the morning; Tucker didn't fit the description. And he didn't look like a man given to seeing UFOs in the Idaho sky. He was examining the blow-ups and Gracie's photo.

The Tucker Service Station, located just off Interstate 15 in Idaho Falls, was a beaten-down place that smelled of gasoline and grease, a throwback to the days when you could get your car repaired at a gas station and it didn't cost four bits to air up the tires. A telephone company truck was parked outside.

Tucker looked up and spat again. "Ain't no doubt about it," he said. "That's the girl."

John collapsed into a chair. Ben said, "What about the men?"

"Can't say for sure, not from them pictures," Tucker said. "But that's the tattoo, I'm sure of that."

Ben removed his jacket and rolled the left sleeve of his shirt up to expose his Viper tattoo. "This tattoo?"

Tucker spat then angled his head to sight in the tattoo through his bifocals. "How come you got the same one?"

"Mr. Tucker, why didn't you tell this to the FBI?"

"They never called."

"No, sir, I mean the FBI agent who came here Wednesday morning and showed you these pictures."

"Ain't no FBI been here. First time I seen them pictures."

"An FBI agent didn't ask you about these men and the girl? You didn't talk to him about UFOs? Tell him you drank?"

Tucker was clearly taken aback. He spat. "Only time I talked to anyone about the girl was when you called me. Hell, my phone's been out of order ever since." He picked up the phone and held it out to Ben. There was no dial tone. He gestured outside. "Phone company's fixing it now, said the line was cut clean through. Figured kids."

"Did the men say where they were headed?"

"The north country. Vehicle was burning oil like a refinery, asked me could it make another five hundred miles. No way, I says, rings is burned up, lucky it made it this far. Oil gets in the combustion chamber, bad news. Sent 'em down yonder to the motel." He gestured down the access road. "They drove down there, big fella come back, left the truck. I got in about six the next morning— that'd been Monday—started tearing that engine apart, finished late that night. Big fella picked it up the next morning—that'd been Tuesday. Paid cash."

"Idaho plates?"

"Yep."

"Five hundred miles north of here, but still in Idaho?"

"That'd put 'em right near the border, up in the panhandle."

"Where they grow Christmas trees?"

"Yep."

"Where it's snowing?"

"Yep."

"I've got a map," Ben said.

Ben spread the Idaho map out on the counter. Tucker said, "You know, I seen something on TV about them militias and Ku Klux Klan and Nazis, how they got camps in the mountains up north."

"Any particular place?"

Tucker leaned over and put a finger on Idaho Falls and ran it north, tracking I-15 then 90, all the way to Coeur d'Alene; his finger left a slight trail of fresh grease on the map. Then his finger turned north, on state highway 95, all the way to—

"Bonners Ferry," he said, tapping the map.

8:34 A.M.

"SHE'S ALIVE, Ben!"

Back on the highway, images of his daughter were racing through John's mind like a DVD on fast forward; his heart was trying to punch through the wall of his chest cavity.

"I gotta call Elizabeth!"

He dug the cell phone out of his pocket.

"Son, we don't need to be pulled over by the highway patrol, not with what we've got in this vehicle."

"What?" John's eyes dropped down to the speedometer. "Shit." He had the Rover doing ninety. He pulled his foot off the accelerator. When the Rover and his heartbeat were both down to seventy-five, John glanced over at Ben. "You were right."

Ben just nodded and held his hand out. "Here."

John handed the phone to Ben. "Home number's on the speed dial, push—"

Ben rolled down his window and defenestrated the phone. John watched in the rearview as the phone bounced on the highway and shattered into pieces.

"Cripes, Ben! Why'd you do that?"

"Because from now on we don't call home, we don't call the FBI, we don't call anyone."

"Why not? We need to tell them she's alive!"

"They already know it."

"How? We just talked to Tucker."

"John, I didn't need Tucker to tell me she's alive. I knew that. But he told me something I didn't know." He turned to John. "The FBI lied about coming to see him."

"Which means what?"

"Which means they know she's up here."

"Why would the FBI lie about Gracie being alive in Idaho?"

"Because they don't want us up here, getting in their way. That's why they cut Tucker's phone line. They're after the men that took Gracie, but for some other reason. And they're willing to sacrifice her to get them."

"*Sacrifice* her? You mean . . . *Jesus* . . . What could those men be doing that's so bad the FBI would sacrifice Gracie to get them?"

Four hundred miles due north Junior said, "Lemme clean up this mess, then I'll show you your big surprise. After that I'll show you around my mountain, before I go to town to pick up your, uh, girl stuff." He smiled real big. "I mean, *our* mountain."

Gracie gave him a weak smile then wandered around the room; she was trying to sort things out.

This was way strange. Mountain boy kidnapped her, but he treated her totally nice. Cozy bedroom, hot bath, new clothes, good breakfast—well, except for eating Bambi.

Gracie pointed at the door that Junior had come out of earlier. "What's in there?"

He smiled. "Your big surprise."

Uh-oh, Gracie thought. The bridal suite. She quickly

continued her tour. On the short wall by the kitchen were photographs, pictures of a woman, a girl really, with an older man who looked like Junior and a small boy who was Junior.

"That's my mama," Junior said from the kitchen.

"Wow, she was beautiful."

"Yep. She died real sudden when I was just a kid. She's buried out back."

"You buried your mother in the backyard?"

"No . . . the major did."

She turned the corner and started down the long wall: more photographs, one of the man who looked like Junior with medals on his uniform and a green beret on his head, like the picture of Ben on her desk. His nametag said WALKER. And photos of soldiers in a jungle and in a city with pretty women who looked like Ms. Wang, the math teacher; they were smiling, but their eyes were sad.

And Junior was real considerate for a boy. He actually knocked on her bedroom door before entering! That never happened at home. Mom just barged in whenever she felt like it.

Next on the wall were big knives and a fancy sword and a leather cord strung with shriveled up . . . ears? *That is so totally gross!* She pulled her eyes away from the ears and looked at the map of the United States that was next on the wall. Various places were marked in black, with dates and names: Kelly, Epstein, Goldburg, Garcia, Young, Ellis, McCoy.

And Junior swore he didn't touch her or look at her and said he'd kill anyone who tried to. Which seemed strange for a kidnapper. Like, if he didn't take her for that and he didn't take her for money, what did he take her for?

Next to the U.S. map was an aerial photograph like

the one Dad had shown her of their neighborhood—
Catoctin Mountain Park, the label read—with everything
marked: the entrance, a big lodge named Aspen, smaller
cabins, stables, swimming pool, skeet range, bowling alley,
gym and sauna, horseshoe pit, chapel, heliport, trails, security checkpoints. That would be a really cool place to go
camping. Maybe they could take their postponed first
annual Brice family camping trip there. Black lines were
drawn from each security checkpoint to a smaller photograph tacked on the wall, photos of little buildings and
soldiers with rifles and dogs on leashes. *Wow, they're way
serious about making sure everyone paid their camping fee!*
Another black line was drawn from the entrance location to a photograph of the entrance with a big metal
gate and the name of the place in white letters on a board
hanging between two posts: CAMP DAVID.

*This was all, like, really weird, but she couldn't help thinking
that maybe Junior wasn't such a bad guy after all. Our mountain, he had said.*

She realized he was standing next to her. When he
smiled, he was kind of cute, except he needed some major
dental work. He put his arm around her shoulders and
she didn't move it.

She pointed to the leather cord on the wall. "Are
those—"

"Ears. The major, he cut 'em off dead gooks. Give them
to me for Christmas, back when I was about your age."

"And I was hoping for new soccer shoes." She gestured
at the maps on the wall. "What's all this?"

Junior pointed at a red flag with a half-moon sword
and a hammer and the face of a man with a wispy little
beard and said, "Commie flag from North Vietnam. That's
Ho Chi Minh hisself. And that's an NVA helmet, and

those black pajamas, that's what the VC wore. That's the major's Bowie knife and his Colt .45s."

"What are all these photographs, the Camp David map?" She pointed. "I know that name, McCoy. What's all this for?"

"Oh . . . we're gonna kill the president."

8:57 A.M.

THREE HUNDRED MILES to the south John smacked the steering wheel hard enough to hurt.

"How are we gonna save her, Ben? How are we gonna find her without the FBI's help?"

"They're holed up in the mountains," Ben said.

"How do you know?"

"That's where a good soldier would be."

"A *soldier?*"

Ben nodded. "John, I don't know why the FBI wants those men—maybe they're racists or Nazis or just nuts—but I know why those men want Gracie. I wasn't sure until Tucker ID'd the tattoo." He paused. "It's about the war."

"The *war?*" John almost laughed. "Ben, you gotta let the war go."

"I've tried. It won't let go of me."

John decided to humor Ben: "Okay, so what's Gracie got to do with your war?"

Ben stared blankly for a time. Then he said, "There was a massacre, in sixty-eight, in the Quang Tri province of South Vietnam. American soldiers murdered forty-two civilians."

"So?"

"So I was there."

"You didn't . . ."

"No, I didn't."

"My father?"

"No."

"But our unit did. Viper team. The big man at the park, he had a Viper tattoo—he was there. He killed those people."

"*You knew that guy?*"

"Yeah, I knew him."

"Why didn't you tell the FBI?"

"Because I knew that if he had Gracie, the FBI couldn't stop him. No one can stop a Green Beret . . . except a Green Beret."

"But you didn't tell the FBI, so they closed her case."

"That's a good thing, John."

"*Why?*"

"Because the men who took Gracie won't be expecting me."

John thought that through, not sure whether it was a plan or the delusions of a drunk.

"Okay, so that guy killed a bunch of people in Vietnam a long time ago—what's that got to do with Gracie?"

"I reported it . . . the massacre."

"What happened?"

"The Army court-martialed those soldiers on my testimony."

"And?"

"They're taking their revenge."

John laughed now. "*What?* Forty years later, they're coming back for revenge? That's a long time to hold onto a grudge, Ben."

"How long have you held onto the bullies?"

They drove in silence for several miles, then John said, "Did my father die there?"

"Yes, he did."

"How?"

"John, some things are best left in the past."

"But it's not in the past, is it? Not if it got my daughter kidnapped eight days ago." He waited for Ben's response, but none came. He looked over at Ben. "I'm entitled to know, Ben."

As night falls over Indochina on 17 Dec 68, SOG team Viper, twelve Green Berets fresh off a successful covert incursion into Laos, descends the limestone façade that is the Co Roc Mountain and crosses the Xe Kong River back into South Vietnam; they are five klicks south of the DMZ in the Quang Tri province. Intelligence reports indicate that Communist forces are now entering South Vietnam directly through the fourteen-mile-wide Demilitarized Zone. SOG team Viper's orders are to interdict the enemy at the Seventeenth Parallel. It is Indian territory, a Vietnamese Communist stronghold, where no regular Army forces dare tread. Of course, there is nothing regular about SOG team Viper; so they venture forth into the night. But, as they say in Vietnam, the night belongs to Charlie.

The major is walking point; leading his team silently through the jungle single file when his voice suddenly breaks the silence.

"Am-bush!"

The soldiers hit the deck a split second before all hell breaks loose, enemy fire incoming from every direction. They walked right into an ambush by a far superior force.

They're pinned down in a crossfire with no avenue of escape. If not for the major's keen instincts and sense of smell—his nose picked up the pungent scent of a Cambodian cigarette favored by the VC—the VC would have had twelve more Americans to add to their daily body count report to Hanoi.

Flat on their backs, AK-47 rounds cracking overhead and ripping through the jungle foliage and leaves falling like confetti, the Green Berets take turns emptying their clips at the enemy, just to let the VC know they're still alive and to give the major time to come up with a "go to hell" plan—a new plan when the original plan goes to hell, like now.

Which he does.

"On my lead," the major says to his men, making a sharp hand signal toward the west. "Jacko, Ace—claymore our back trail."

Captain Jack O. Smith, who is never far from the major's side, and Captain Tony "Ace" Gregory crawl off to the northeast and southeast. The major moves closer to his newest disciples, only seventeen days in-country, and says, "Brice, Dalton, when I move out, you boys act like hemorrhoids and stick to my ass." And he smiles. Under fierce and likely fatal attack by the VC in a dark jungle in Southeast Asia, Major Charles Woodrow Walker smiles. His young disciples think, *That's why he's a living legend*.

And they know what it was like to have followed into battle the great generals they studied at West Point—Lee or Grant or Patton or MacArthur or Eisenhower. The major is the first to hit the ground when inserted and the last to leave the ground when extracted; he walks point, the most dangerous position; he would die for his men, and they for him. He has survived over one hundred covert missions into Laos and Cambodia and North Vietnam; most SOG team leaders don't last a dozen. He is a warrior-god.

To Ben he says, "Let this be a lesson, Lieutenant. We should've taken out the old woman before she had a chance to rat us out to the local VC." Back at the river they had spotted a lone figure down on the bank and the figure them. "Take him out," the major said to Lieutenant Brice, the team's sniper. Ben put his scope on the figure and saw that it was just an old woman filling water jugs. He informed the major. "Then take *her* out," the major said. "But, Major, she's a noncombatant. She's so old, she probably can't even see we're Americans." The major looked at him, shook his head, and said, "Move out." Thirty minutes ago, Ben Brice had felt good about saving the old woman's life.

The two captains return. "Charlie's gonna eat some lead," Captain Smith says with a grin. The captains emplaced claymore mines behind their escape route; when the VC give chase, the claymores will stop them in their tracks. A small rectangular cast-iron box, its business side embossed with FRONT TOWARD ENEMY so some doped-up draftee doesn't take out his entire platoon, the M18A1 claymore antipersonnel mine is a particularly effective killing device; upon detonation by remote control or tripwire, the claymore sprays seven hundred steel balls in a sixty-degree pattern, killing anyone within fifty meters. The balls can literally cut the typical hundred-pound Vietnamese Communist in two.

The major loads new clips into his twin .45s. The veterans of the team pull two hand grenades each. As tracer rounds zip through the darkness overhead like a fireworks show, Brice and Dalton look at each other and nod nervously.

"Let's kill some gooks," the major says. From his backside, he hurls two grenades. The others follow his lead. The noise of the grenades exploding is deafening; the surrounding jungle is suddenly shrouded in white smoke. Every other grenade was a Willie Pete, a white phosphorus grenade. They were warned in training against throwing phosphorus grenades where the burning smoke could envelop them, but apparently there is an exception when surrounded by the enemy.

The Green Berets are suddenly up and running all-out to the west, directly at the VC, who can't see them coming; Major Charles Woodrow Walker is leading the charge with a .45 in each hand and Brice and Dalton tight on his ass. As they hit the enemy line, they unload on the startled VC; the major fires both .45s simultaneously. Ben fires his backup weapon, the Uzi. They hear the claymores detonate behind them and the death cries of the Viet Cong.

No one looks back. The Americans run through the dark night, barely able to see the man in front of them, following only the sound of hard breathing and boots pounding the turf. For fifteen minutes they run.

"Halt!"

The major's voice penetrates the dark. His hands grab Ben and yank him out of the path of the incoming. The others arrive and take cover. No one laughs; no one talks. Ben silently thanks God for the major, then his heart skips a beat: where's Roger?

The major's thoughts aren't far behind. "Where's Dalton?" he whispers to Ben.

"He was right behind me."

"Jacko," the major says, "check it out."

Captain Smith nods and disappears into the night. Thirty minutes later, he returns.

"They got him, Major. Heading north."

"Goddamnit!" The major stands. "Saddle up."

They head back to the ambush point, their minds playing out the consequence of violating one of the three absolute rules drilled into every SOG team member from day one: never let yourself be captured by the VC.

They track the VC through the jungle and into a hamlet. Entering the hamlet, it is apparent the VC were here; the fear shows on the peasants' faces. The Americans sweep the hamlet, searching every hut and hiding place for signs of Dalton or the VC. The peasants huddle together; mothers clutch their children. They are co-operative but tense, as one would expect when confronted by eleven big and heavily armed American soldiers in the middle of VC territory.

"No VC! No Yank!"

In the center of the hamlet, an old man stands next to a big pot cooking over an open fire; it is the community pot of *nuoc mam*, a pungent fish sauce the Vietnamese pour over rice. He stirs the sauce with a long wooden utensil. He seems scared to death and is barely moving his utensil. The Americans find neither Dalton nor VC.

Captain Smith's voice rings out. He's picked up the VC's tracks leading out of the hamlet and into the adjacent jungle. The Green Berets give chase, aware they're probably running directly into another ambush or booby traps or—

"Holy shit!"

—Dalton.

Ben Brice brings up the rear and comes upon his teammates standing shoulder to shoulder, their backs to him.

One thought captures his mind: it must be Roger. He prepares himself to face death again, then he pushes his way through to the front. And in that moment, his life is forever changed. His romantic West Point notions of war and warriors are forever dispelled. His childlike vision of good and evil is forever altered. His innocence is lost. And so it is, when one confronts the evil in man.

Lieutenant Roger Dalton, U.S. Army Green Beret, hangs from a tree by his ankles, naked and disemboweled, his intestines hanging down into the small fire the VC built so the Americans could better see their handiwork. His genitals are missing. As is his head. The only sound is that of the fire sizzling with each drop of his bodily fluids. They know it's Dalton by the fresh Viper tattoo on his left arm and the dog tags intertwined in the laces of the boots sitting below the body, a typical precaution in case you stepped on a land mine and had a leg blown off; the dog tags allowed the medics to rejoin man and leg, if not literally at least for the body bag. But it was not a precaution against decapitation by the VC.

The major's face is grim. "This is why we kill gooks."

After a long moment, Warrant Officer Nunn asks in his Southern drawl, "But where's his head, Major?"

The major's expression changes as if he has had a revelation.

"Goddamnit!"

He pivots and runs back toward the hamlet. His men exchange confused glances, then they chase after their leader. Ben Brice looks at what remains of his best friend and throws up.

The major and nine angry, armed, adrenaline-charged Green Berets arrive back at the hamlet and run directly to the old man at the community pot of *nuoc mam*. He

9:18 A.M.

JOHN'S TEARS STAINED the smooth Alpaca beige leather. He had pulled the Land Rover off the highway shortly after Ben had begun retelling the massacre at Quang Tri. Now his forehead rested on the steering wheel.

"The major was the greatest man I've ever known," Ben said. "Brilliant, natural-born leader, completely without personal fear, an absolute belief that America was destined to defeat Communism in the world. He could have been one of the greatest soldiers in history."

A deep sigh.

"Maybe when a man fights evil every day for so many years, he becomes evil. Maybe a man can't be around that much hate without hating. I fought the hate. The major . . . the hate consumed him. He became the evil he was fighting."

"Where is he now, the major?"

"He's dead."

"We were ordered to war but not allowed to win the war. We were ordered to kill but court-martialed for killing. We were ordered to defeat Communism in Southeast Asia only to see Communism win at home.

"Thirty years of Communist rule over America and

what has our once great nation become? An immoral society that is unworthy of its military. Civilians who demand freedom for free. Politicians who promise peace and prosperity at no cost, an all-expense-paid life devoted to the pursuit of happiness. Politicians who refused to do their duty but now call on the military to fight foreign wars when their political ambitions are thereby served. That is America today.

"Each of us—soldiers in the United States Army—took a solemn oath to defend this nation against all enemies, foreign and domestic. And defend it we did—the Cold War is over, the Evil Empire is no more, Communism is defeated. But now the threat to America comes from within. From domestic enemies. From those among us who want an America subordinate to the United Nations, subject to international laws and courts, who want to dismantle the American military—because we are the last defense of America. We cannot allow that to happen. I will not allow that to happen. Not while I can still pull the trigger."

Seven Days in May starring Major Charles Woodrow Walker.

FBI Special Agent Jan Jorgenson was viewing an old grainy videotape of the court-martialed war criminal Major Charles Woodrow Walker. He was handsome, a charismatic speaker, and the leader of a plot to overthrow the United States government. He commanded a personal army of former soldiers. He was operating under the radar, back before 9/11, back when the Bureau's domestic radar screen was filled not with Islamic extremists but with homegrown hate groups—Aryan Nation, National Alliance, the Order, the Klan, skinheads, the right-wing militia movement: a bunch of dumb-ass white boys who so hated blacks and Jews that they had retired to the mountains of Idaho and Montana to live without electricity or running water or blacks or Jews. But while the Bureau concerned itself with weekend warriors who couldn't overthrow their own town councils if their lives depended on it, completely undetected were Walker and his soldiers, real warriors trained by the U.S. government to overthrow other countries' governments. Walker was a clear and present danger to America: a pissed-off Green Beret can be a nation's worst nightmare.

And the Bureau might never have learned of Walker's plot until the military coup began if this videotape had not been sent to the FBI twelve years earlier with an anonymous handwritten note that read: *Patty Walker said if I don't see her for three months, the major done killed her, and I better mail this. So I am.* The package was postmarked Bonners Ferry, Idaho. The Bureau put a team in Bonners Ferry. They alerted local law enforcement and hospitals. They searched for Walker's secret mountain compound but without success. So they waited to get lucky.

Two years later, they did.

Walker strode into the hospital in Bonners Ferry with his dying son in his arms. The hospital treated the boy and called the Feds; the FBI arrested Walker without incident and airlifted him to the maximum-security prison at Leavenworth, Kansas, to await trial for treason.

A trial that never took place.

Walker's men took a high-ranking government employee hostage and threatened to send the hostage back in pieces unless Walker was released. FBI Director Laurence McCoy refused—until he received the first installment. McCoy released Walker, who then disappeared into Mexico. And there his life ended. Three weeks

4:05 P.M.

BONNERS FERRY, IDAHO, population 2,600, sits along the south bank of the Kootenai River twenty-four miles from the Canadian border, 1,800 feet above sea level, and nestled among three mountain ranges with peaks reaching 8,000 feet into the big sky. The original inhabitants of the "Nile of the North," as this fertile river valley became known, were members of the Kootenai Nation, whose local residency dated back to prehistoric times. The white man came to this part of Idaho on his way to Canada during the gold rush of 1863; he stayed to harvest the tall timber that covered 90 percent of the land. A century and a half later, the Kootenai tribe owns the town's only casino, the descendants of the gold rushers grow Christmas trees, and northern Idaho has become a haven for racists, neo-Nazis, and right-wing antigovernment zealots.

Only the latter fact did Ben know when he parked the Land Rover in front of the Boundary County Courthouse. He and John stepped through the icy slush and walked into the three-story white stone structure. They located the sheriff's office; inside, a plump middle-aged woman sat at a desk behind a waist-high wood partition. Behind her desk was a door marked SHERIFF J. D. JOHNSON. On the wall next to the door were framed photographs in each of which appeared a tall rugged man with progressively less and grayer hair—and one photograph when the man had a full head of black hair, in a place Ben knew all too well.

"Here to pay a fine?" the woman asked.

"No, ma'am," Ben said, "we're—"

"File a complaint?"

"No, ma'am—"

"Service of process?"

John planted his hands on the partition and leaned over. "Cripes, lady, we're looking for the freaking Nazis that kidnapped my daughter!"

The woman stared at him over her glasses. "O-kay."

The door behind her opened, and the man in the photographs appeared, wearing a uniform like he had worn one all his life.

"Louann," the man said, "I'm *occupado* tonight. Tell Cody he's in charge."

He noticed Ben and John; he glanced back at the woman.

"Sheriff, these gentlemen are here about some Nazis," she said as if it were a routine request.

The sheriff gave Ben and John a law enforcement once-over—they probably appeared ragged, almost twenty-four hours on the road—then came around the partition. He walked with a slight limp. Ben stuck out his hand.

"Sheriff, Ben Brice. And my son, John."

The sheriff's hair was combed neatly and he smelled of cologne, as if he had just freshened up in his office. He shook their hands.

"J. D. Johnson. What's this about some Nazis?"

Ben held out Gracie's photo. "My granddaughter's been kidnapped."

The sheriff studied the photo. "The girl down in Texas." Then he answered Ben's unasked question. "NLETS, law enforcement Teletype."

"We think she's up here," Ben said.

"Thought the abductor hung himself?"

"He was the wrong man."

"FBI seems to think he was the right man."

"They're wrong."

"Unh-hunh."

The sheriff scratched his square jaw; his fingernails sounded like number-six sandpaper on his day-old beard.

"And you figure some Nazi type brought her up here?"

"We were told a lot of them live in this area."

The sheriff sighed. "That is a fact."

"She was in Idaho Falls on Sunday evening, positive ID, with two men wearing camouflage fatigues, heading north five hundred miles in a white SUV with Idaho plates."

"Well, that'd put them right about here, wouldn't it?"

"Look, Sheriff, if you could give us a few minutes of your time, look at a few photos . . ."

The sheriff shrugged. "All right, Mr. Brice. First thing in the morning."

"Could we do it now, Sheriff? It's an emergency."

"It's also my anniversary. Taking the wife to dinner, and I gotta pick up this little bracelet I got for her . . ." He turned for the door. "Oh-six-hundred, Mr. Brice."

He had his hand on the doorknob when Ben said, "You were a slick driver at Da Krong?"

The sheriff stopped dead in his tracks. His leathery face rotated; he had a quizzical expression.

"On the wall," Ben said.

The sheriff walked over and lifted a framed photo off

367

its wall hook. "Me and my warrant officer. He came home in a body bag." He paused, his eyes still on the photo; his rough fingers gently brushed dust from the glass. He cleared his throat and turned to Ben. "J. D. Johnson, captain, Marine Corps."

"Ben Brice, colonel, Army Green Berets."

12 Feb 71. Captain J. D. Johnson is piloting the UH-1D chopper transporting seven Marines to a battle zone near the Laos border in the Da Krong Valley. He's flying lead slick in a V formation with four other birds. His .45-caliber sidearm hangs between his legs to protect his privates from ground fire. He's running sixty knots at twelve hundred feet. He has done this hundreds of times and come home every time.

He spots the green smoke marking the landing zone. He brings the Huey down in a steep descent and hears the accompanying gunships firing rockets into the surrounding trees; they're prepping the landing zone, running a racetrack loop over the LZ so that cover fire is continuous during troop deployment.

Another hot LZ.

He sees tracer rounds coming at his ship. His door gunner opens fire with the M-60. Thirty seconds to drop the troops and get the hell out. He comes in fast, flares the nose to slow his air speed, and hovers three feet off the ground as the troops un-ass the bird from both sides; there are no doors on these slicks. The all clear and he dips the nose to gain speed to pull out. Just as he clears the trees, the chopper explodes. When he wakes, he hears voices speaking Vietnamese.

Captain J. D. Johnson is a POW.

Night has descended over South Vietnam and he's wondering if his warrant officer made it out alive. He's bound and sitting in the corner of an earthen bunker carved out of the hillside; he took a bullet in his left leg. From his limited knowledge of Vietnamese, he gathers that a platoon will take the captured American to an NVA base camp in Laos tomorrow.

By the next night, he is in Laos; it's the first night of a three-day march to the NVA base camp. He's sitting up against a tree; his hands are bound behind him. His leg is broken and the wound is infected. He's sweating profusely from the fever and his mind is getting clouded. Except for the guard sitting a few feet away, his captors are sleeping in gray hooches and hammocks strung between the trees, completely unconcerned that their American prisoner might attempt an escape.

J. D. Johnson, from Bonners Ferry, Idaho, never figured on dying in some damn jungle in Laos.

The guard suddenly slumps over without a sound; blood streams from his throat. J.D.'s hands fall; his bindings are cut. A face appears before him—*Jesus! A goddamn Indian!* He is lifted like he weighs fifty pounds instead of one-ninety and slung over a bare shoulder. They walk silently between two NVA soldiers snoring in hammocks.

All night they walk, his head bobbing at a smooth rhythm, his eyes seeing only the trail beneath the Indian's bare feet as they travel through the jungle; his mind comes in and out of consciousness, wrapped in a blanket of fever.

When he wakes, dawn is breaking. As is the sky. A patch of blue up above. And an American voice beside him, calling for a Medevac: "I say again, Johnson, J. D., Marine . . ."

His vision is blurred; he shakes his head, but the fever

grips him like a vice. Who are these people? He tries to focus on the American. He's a soldier. He passes out again.

He comes to, the THUMP THUMP THUMP of a chopper coming out of the hole in the clouds, a red cross on a white square on the chopper's nose: a U.S. Army Medevac. Tears come into his eyes. J. D. Johnson was not going to die in some damn jungle in Laos, at least not today.

He is lifted from the ground and the sound of the chopper grows louder. His face is not against the bare brown chest of the Indian but against the American's fatigues. He sees the blades rotating above him and he hears more American voices—

"Goddamn, you're the one they talk about! Green Beret colonel living in the jungle with the Indians! You're a fucking legend!"

—and he's being lifted into the chopper. He grabs the American's fatigues, and with all the strength left in his body, he pulls his face next to the soldier's chest, to his nametag, and he makes out a name he will never forget: BRICE.

4:33 P.M.

"I F YOU'RE WHITE and pissed off at the world, chances are you call Idaho home."

The sheriff was leaning back in a squeaky swivel chair behind his metal desk; he had changed his mind and decided to talk with them now. Ben and John sat in metal chairs on the visitors' side of the desk.

"State's become a damn mecca for those people—white supremacists, skinheads, militias, neo-Nazis—every goddamn kook in the country's moving to Idaho, living on a mountain and hating everyone don't look like them." He shook his head. "People used to come here to fish."

He handed the photos back to Ben.

"We got a bunch of them living around here, Colonel, but I've never seen no one looks like these two. The ones left stay up in the mountains for the most part. They don't bother us, we don't bother them."

Ben gestured at the Boundary County map on the wall behind the sheriff.

"Any idea where their camps are?"

The sheriff stood and stepped to the map.

"Thirteen, fourteen years ago, before they had real terrorists to deal with, FBI was waging war on these guys. They set up a command post here, flew surveillance over the mountains looking for their camps. Thirteen hundred square miles in Boundary County, lots of room to hide. The Feds identified four camps east of town, seven west, all off unpaved roads. This time of year, you need a four-wheel-drive to get up the muddy roads 'cause of the snow melt. And even if you get up there, you won't see much from the road. The camps are up in the mountains, blocked out by the trees. If your girl's in one of those camps, finding her ain't gonna be easy. And getting her down damn near impossible."

The sheriff put a finger on the map.

"FBI tried to bring one of those guys off Ruby Ridge in ninety-two, got a marshal killed. Brought in the Hostage Rescue Team even though there weren't no hostages, put eleven snipers on that mountain, told them to shoot on sight. They did. Killed the guy's wife. Shot her in the head while she was holding her baby. Government ended up paying him three million bucks."

"Any place they hang out when they come to town?"

"Place just south of town, Rusty's Tavern and Grill, but don't eat the food. Beer joint. Some gals. Rough place, but we leave 'em alone long as they don't shoot each other."

Ben stood. "Sheriff, I appreciate your time. My apologies to your wife."

"Thirty-four years, she's used to me being late."

The two middle-aged men, soldiers of a forgotten war, shook hands; they considered embracing but resisted. Ben and John were at the door when the sheriff spoke again.

"Colonel, if you don't mind me asking, what would a couple Nazi-wannabes living in Idaho want with your granddaughter?"

Ben paused a moment, then he said, "To settle an old score."

The sheriff studied Ben; he nodded. "One more thing, Colonel. Most of those fellas are just dumb-ass white boys couldn't spell cat if you spotted them c and t, lucky just to find their way home at night. But there's a few who ain't just playing soldier. You go looking for your girl, you be ready."

"I am."

A slight smile from the sheriff. "I expect you are. And Colonel . . . thanks. For back then."

Ben nodded. And a thought occurred to him. "Sheriff, there wouldn't be a chopper for hire around here, would there?"

"Matter a fact, boy down by Naples got one. Dicky, we use him for search-and-rescues when a tourist gets lost hiking in the woods. I'll give him a call." He turned to his phone but stopped. "Tell you what, meet me here at oh-six-hundred, we'll drive down there together. Little air recon might do me good."

"Oh-six-hundred," Ben said. "We'll be here."

"Check your time, Colonel. We're on Pacific time up here."

The sheriff stood, walked over, and opened the door.

"You know, Colonel, one good thing about you hunting your girl without the Feds."

"What's that?"

"You don't gotta worry about them getting her killed."

4:52 P.M.

"YOU JUST MISSED him," the store owner said, "not half an hour. Boy didn't know a tampon from a Tootsie Roll."

He laughed at his own words. The General Store on Main Street had been in his family for over fifty years. It was a place where you could buy food, fertilizer, clothes, and tampons.

"Like a boy asking for rubbers. Hands me a little piece of paper with the name on it"—the owner leaned down under the counter; Ben could hear him rustling in a trash can—"yep, here it is."

He bumped his head on the underside of the counter, then he reappeared, rubbing his bare scalp with one hand and holding out a scrap of white paper with the other. Two words had been written on the paper—*Tampax tampons*—and under the words a happy face had been drawn.

"That's her handwriting," Ben said.

"And her happy face," John said.

The owner ducked his head slightly and said, "Am I bleeding?"

Ben shook his head. "Can you describe him?"

"Blond hair, blue eyes, about your height but stockier,

374

maybe twenty-five. I see him a half-dozen times a year. Strange bird."

"How so?"

"What he buys—girls' clothes, pink pajamas, Barbie doll . . ."

"Gracie doesn't do dolls," Ben said.

John gritted his teeth: "Bagbiter."

"No, he didn't want a bag. Stuck the box under his coat like it was a girlie magazine and left . . . say, that reminds me. Few months back, he bought a *Fortune* magazine. I remember 'cause he didn't look like an investor. May still have the one." He bent over again and rummaged around below the counter. "Yeah, here it is." He came back up with the *Fortune* magazine. He looked at the cover picture of John and then at John. "Say, that looks just like you." He glanced back at the cover. "That is you." He opened the magazine to the story with the Brice family portrait. "I was standing right here reading your story when he just snatched it out of my hands."

"Notice which way he drove out of town?"

"North. He was parked right there where you are. Pulled out and headed north, sure did."

Ben thanked the owner for his time, and he and John turned to leave.

"Oh, one more thing," the owner said. They turned back. "He's missing a finger, this one." The owner was pointing at the ceiling with the index finger of his right hand.

Ben and John stepped outside. They were canvassing the town, showing the photos to every business owner on Main Street. The General Store was their fourth stop.

Ben said, "He didn't buy tampons for a dead girl."

"Tampons," John said. "I didn't think she was there yet."

"She's not. She just wanted him in town."

"Why?"

"Because she knew I'd . . . we'd come for her. She's a smart girl, John." Ben faced north; the glow of the sunset was dimming now. "And she's out there somewhere."

5:01 P.M.

GRACIE HADN'T HEARD noises from the other room for hours now, since Junior had knocked on her bedroom door and begged her to come out so he could explain why they had to kill the president. She had refused, so he had said he was going into town to get her "girl stuff." She had heard the truck roar off. Junior was gone. Now was her chance to escape. If she could escape, Ben wouldn't have to drink more of his whiskey to forget killing Junior and Jacko.

She moved everything from in front of the door to her bedroom. She cracked the door and peeked out. The big room was empty. She came out slowly.

"Hi, sweetie."

Gracie jumped at the voice behind her. She whirled around. A big fat ugly man was now standing between her and the door to her bedroom: the man that killed Bambi. His breath smelled of alcohol; his body odor could stop traffic.

"You ever touch one of these?" the fat man asked.

Gracie looked down to his hands cupped by his crotch. He was holding his penis. It wasn't all wrinkly and limp like Dad's that day in his bathroom; it was purple and swollen up like it was going to pop. It was plenty big enough to hurt a girl her age. She recalled Ms. Boyd saying something about erections, that a boy's penis becomes hard in order to penetrate a girl's—

"You touch this bod and Junior's gonna kill you!"

"Well, Junior ain't here right now, is he?"

She now recalled Ms. Boyd's advice from sex ed class. She pointed a finger at the man and said, "No! And no means no!"

He just laughed. "Not to me it don't."

She made a mental note to tell Ms. Boyd that "no means no" doesn't work so well with big fat ugly men on a mountain in Idaho. Finally, she recalled her mother's advice: *If a boy doesn't take no for an answer, kick him in the balls.* Gracie assumed that advice applied to big fat ugly men. So she kicked him in his balls, her best Tae Kwon Do kick with the hiking boots—but the fat man only yelped and waved his hand around. From the look he gave her, she had only succeeded in making him really mad. There was only one thing to do now.

Run.

The cold air shocked her as she hit the cabin door. The fat man would never have caught her if she hadn't slipped on the ice. His hot breath hit her neck like a blow dryer. His hands grabbed at her clothes. Her feet were dangling.

"Come on back inside, girlie. Bubba ain't had no virgin since—"

She heard a dull thud and the fat man groan. He released her, and she fell to the ground. She looked up to see Junior swinging a shovel and hitting the fat man in the head again.

"Bubba, you motherfucker!"

Bubba went down to his knees; his eyes were glazed

over and his head was bleeding. Junior's face was wild; he was swinging again when Jacko grabbed the shovel from behind.

"Now don't go and kill our only munitions expert, Junior," Jacko said. "He's just drunk."

"He's out!" Junior yelled. He kicked the fat man named Bubba in the stomach. "Get the fuck off my mountain!" Junior threw a set of keys at Bubba.

Bubba grabbed the keys, crawled away to a safe distance, and then got to his feet and stumbled over to an old pickup truck. He got in and drove fast down the mountain.

5:11 P.M.

"OH, JUNIOR, you saved me!"

Patty hugged him real tight. Tears were in her pretty blue eyes. Ever since Junior had seen her picture in that magazine, he knew they had to be together. And now they were.

"I was so scared! I was like, oh my God, he's gonna rape me, where's Junior? And there you were—you were totally awesome!" She wiped her eyes on his shirt. "Ooh, I love your shirt. Plaid's my favorite."

She looked up at Junior like that Mary Ann girl looking at the professor on that *Gilligan* show he had seen at the motel. Then she said three words that brought tears to Junior's eyes.

"You're my hero."

She hugged him again, burying her face in his chest. Junior's heart was about to bust, he was so damned happy. Her hugging him, that made it worth losing Bubba and his explosives skills. Patty pulled back and squeezed his biceps.

"Wow, you're buff, Junior. Totally studly. Hey, look, I'm real sorry about this morning, getting so upset and all. I mean, it's not like we're Republicans, for crying out loud. I'm sure you have a very good reason to kill the president."

"He ordered the major assassinated."

"The major your daddy?"

"Yep."

"Well, there you go. That's a totally good reason. I mean, who could blame you for being a little PO'd."

"Now we're gonna return the favor."

"Nanna always says, 'What's good for the goose is good for the gander.' I'm not real sure what that means."

He took her hands. "Patty, are you ready for your big surprise?"

He glanced over at the bedroom door by the kitchen; her eyes followed his and then turned back real fast.

"Well, yeah, sure, but, um, why don't you show me later, after dinner maybe. Show me around your mountain first. I mean, *our* mountain. Before it gets dark."

"Well, okay, I guess it can wait."

"Sure it can."

He smiled; she said *our* mountain. "Sure, okay."

Patty got a funny look on her face. "Uh-oh. Did you get my tampons?"

"Oh, yeah."

Junior went to the kitchen table and returned with the box of girl stuff. "Here."

Patty took the box and said, "I'll be right back."

She disappeared into her room. Her talking about that girl stuff so straight out—*period, tampons, bleeding*—made Junior real uncomfortable. He never figured that would be a regular topic of discussion; he hoped it wouldn't. A few minutes later she came back out.

"All better now. And, hey, sorry about calling you a numb-nut, during the road trip."

"Aw, heck, honey, I been called a lot worse."

Junior leaned down and cupped her pretty face. Then he kissed her forehead.

"Patty, I dreamed of this day—"

"Yeah, Ms. Boyd told us about those kind of dreams in health class."

Damn, there she goes again.

"Huh? Oh, no, I didn't mean that."

"Whatever. Let's go see *our* mountain."

She smiled real big at him and he forgot about the tampon talk by the time they got outside.

"Lemme think here," he said, putting his hands on his hips and turning in all directions as he thought of the best place to start the tour of *their* mountain. What would most impress Patty? "Oh, I know, I'll show you the creek first. It's my favorite place in the whole world. Hey, you ever seen real bear tracks?"

He turned back, and she was gone.

See ya! What a loser! Does he really think I'm going to marry him? The bridal suite—that's his big surprise? As if.

Gracie was running down the mountain like she was running down a soccer field on a breakaway; she was holding the tampons like relay batons. She was making good time on the dirt road, even though there were muddy patches she couldn't see until she slipped. But she managed to stay on her feet each time. The sun was down; the road was getting darker and harder to see as it wound through the trees and down the mountain. She caught a glimpse of the main highway below; she was getting close. She saw a car drive by.

"Help me!"

The sound of her breathing was now joined by another sound—a truck. Junior was coming. She had to get down to the highway . . . The truck noise was gaining on her

. . . She turned on the speed, tricky going downhill . . . *What's that in the road?* . . . Some kind of metal plate, like they use when they repair the streets back home . . . The noise behind her was closer now . . . on top of her . . . She took a quick check behind her and her foot caught the edge of something and—

She went tumbling and the tampons went flying; she hit the ground hard and rolled over and over until her head hit something. Then the world was black.

When Gracie opened her eyes, her head ached, she was cold, and she was in a new place. A tight place. A box. She could see trees above. A face appeared over her. Junior.

Then she realized what he was doing to her.

"Please, Junior, I'm really sorry! I won't run again, I promise! Don't do this to me, *please!*"

Junior's face was hard.

"I'm sorry, too, Patty, 'cause you ruined my big surprise. Now I gotta teach you a lesson. Night or two down there, you won't run again. The major, he used to put me down there when I needed to get my head on straight, and it didn't do nothing bad to me."

"Oh, no, nothing bad at all—you're just some kind of freaking psycho!"

Then it was dark.

8:36 P.M.

Downtown Dallas after five was a ghost town, especially on a Friday night. The lawyers and bankers had retreated to the suburbs for the weekend, gone home to mama and the kids. FBI Special Agent Jan Jorgenson had only an empty apartment waiting for her, so she was running the deserted streets of downtown, not an advisable venue for most joggers. But then, most joggers don't carry a .40-caliber Glock semiautomatic in their waist pack—well, this was Texas; maybe they did.

She had missed her lunch-hour runs every day this week. She needed exercise. Running cleared her mind and allowed her to think. So far she had thought her way into a dead end.

The revenge theory just didn't hold water. Yes, Colonel Brice had a Viper tattoo. Yes, the man at the park had a Viper tattoo. Yes, Brice had served on Viper team under the command of Major Walker. Yes, Brice had testified against Walker and the other Viper team soldiers. But that was almost forty years ago. And Major Walker was dead. She had to face facts: there was simply no connection between Major Charles Woodrow Walker and Colonel Ben Brice and Gracie Ann Brice's abduction. There were only coincidences—coincidences the size of a goddamn whale, but coincidences nonetheless.

Four miles and her body felt good again. She had exited the federal building on the western edge of downtown, run east on Main Street, slowing to check out the Neiman Marcus window displays in the day's last light—she always liked shopping with her mom at the Mall of America when she was a kid—and then to the freeway. She turned north to Ross Avenue, then west past the I.M. Pei-designed symphony center and the Museum, then south a few blocks, then west on Elm Street, past a skyscraper shaped like a rocket ship and one with a hole in the middle of the damn thing—*what's the story with that?*—and now into Dealey Plaza, past the School Book Depository and to the grassy knoll, unchanged in forty years, to the exact spot where an American president had been assassinated—

She stopped short.

She turned back and looked up at the sixth-floor window of the School Book Depository. Crouched in that window—a much greater distance than she had realized— Lee Harvey Oswald had aimed a bolt-action rifle at a moving target and fired three shots in six seconds, putting two bullets within a nine-inch diameter, one in Kennedy's neck, the third shot in his head. Standing here now, seeing the shot required—three shots, no less—she shook her head. No way. The Feds took the easy way out. They never looked past the obvious connection—

And it hit her: she had committed the same sin.

Jan was back in the federal building in under five minutes, running past the security desk with a quick nod to Red, the night guard—she felt his eyes on her backside—then up the elevator to the third floor and down the corridor

11:21 P.M.

ELIZABETH WAS SITTING in the nearly dark den of her mansion and drinking hard liquor. She now understood Ben Brice.

Kate had said he drank to escape the past. To forget so he could sleep. How much would she have to drink to escape her past? To sleep. To not think of the past that had brought her to this present. To this day. To this life. A life without Grace.

Ten years ago she had arrived in Dallas armed only with impressive letters of recommendation from the United States Attorney General and the FBI Director attesting to Elizabeth Austin's legal brilliance, incredible determination, and remarkable courage under extreme personal duress. She was thirty years old, just married, two months' pregnant, and running from her past as fast and as far as possible. Dallas, Texas, had seemed far enough.

Five years before that she had just graduated from Harvard Law School; she had turned down the Wall Street firms for a job with the Justice Department. She wanted to be one of the good guys. She wanted to put the bad guys in jail. She wanted to use the rule of law to make people safe, so no other ten-year-old girl would ever suffer her father's murder.

But she hadn't been safe.

Her daughter hadn't been safe.

No one was safe.

Evil does not obey the rule of law. Evil makes its own rules.

DAY NINE

6:15 A.M.

"*N*ÀM YÊN! NÀM YÊN!*"

He's yelling in Vietnamese—Stay down! Stay down!—so the rotating blades don't take their heads off. They're crowded onto the Embassy roof where the Huey is perched and panicked because they hear the NVA tanks at the outskirts of the city and gunfire from the battle between the Communists and the last of the South Vietnamese forces at Tan Son Nhut airport. An NVA rocket whistles overhead and explodes on Thong Nhat Boulevard just outside the Embassy walls and their panic escalates tenfold. Six stories below, thousands more South Vietnamese civilians are massed on the Embassy grounds; hundreds more scramble over the high concrete wall surrounding the Embassy only to be entangled in the barbed wire, joined in their desperation to flee their imploding country and their innocent faith that the Americans will save them. The end is near, and they know it. They do not know that this Huey will be the last U.S. helicopter out of Vietnam. Ever.

Wednesday, 30 April 1975: the fall of Saigon.

Since midnight he has stood on the roof of the American Embassy in downtown Saigon and loaded thousands of refugees onto a steady stream of Navy helicopters for their evacuation to the Seventh Fleet ships waiting offshore in the South China Sea—Operation Frequent Wind, his final mission in Vietnam. It's now morning and time has run out. This chopper flew in from the USS *Midway* to retrieve the few remaining American soldiers and the American flag flying over the Embassy—"No civilians! Those are my orders!" the pilot said; but he had pulled rank and his sidearm on the pilot. So the troop compartment now holds a huddled mass of refugees from Communism leaving everything they possess behind because possessions mean nothing without freedom; the engine is powering up, kids are crying, women are wailing, sirens are screaming, and outside the Embassy a river of refugees are exiting Saigon on trucks, buses, motor scooters, and bicycles; the looting is already beginning. Another rocket explodes even closer and the Navy pilot is yelling to the last American soldier in Vietnam to get his butt in the aircraft, sir!

Instead, he gives the last place inside the chopper to a teenage girl traveling alone, no doubt orphaned by the war; he will stand on the skid for the flight out to the *Midway*. He hoists her up, her bare feet joining four others hanging out the open hatch, and he recalls kids riding on the tailgates of pickup trucks back in West Texas and wonders if they still do.

He turns and yells, *"Thôi! Dù rồi!"*—No more! That's all!—to those next in line, a young woman and her baby girl, from her features an Amerasian child abandoned by her American father. The woman is the type of Viet the American soldiers favored, slim and smooth-skinned with soft brown eyes and full lips, now a fallen angel; a silver crucifix hangs around her neck. Their eyes meet, and the woman sees the truth in his: the Americans will not return to save her family. Their freedom ends today. As the Huey's engines rev louder and the blades rotate faster and the machine strains mightily to hoist its human cargo, the woman kisses her baby and holds the child out to him.

He hesitates then takes the child. With his free hand, he rips off the nametag stitched onto his fatigues and the silver eagle insignia of a full colonel in the United States Army and presses both into the woman's delicate hand so she can find her child if she survives or die knowing that her child will live free in America. He steps onto the skid and reaches into the cabin with his free hand for a hold; the baby is curled up in his other arm, her tiny fingers clutching his uniform, her brown eyes wide and gazing up at him, her head pressed against his chest.

As the chopper rises from the roof, his eyes never leave the woman; tears run down her face, one face among thousands left behind in the Embassy grounds, their arms outstretched to the Americans, to God Himself, praying to be saved, knowing what their fate will be at the hands of the Communists, their fate for trusting the Americans, for being Catholic, for believing in God. As he knows. Looking down at these desperate people that America and God now abandon, tears fill his eyes. Ben Brice came to their country to free the oppressed. He failed. He closes his eyes, ashamed—of himself, his country, and his God.

"Colonel!"

Ben's eyes snapped open. He was not looking down upon the Viet mother, but upon Misty, Dicky's buxom girlfriend wearing a tight sweatshirt and a smile and waving at them as the chopper lifted off the ground. The sheriff had been good to his word. They had met him at 0600 and driven to an open field south of town where they found Dicky in mirrored sunglasses and a Caterpillar cap on backward and Misty in her sweatshirt standing next to an old helicopter. Ben's billionaire son had hired Dicky and his flying machine for the morning.

"Brings back memories, don't it, Colonel!"

The sheriff turned to Ben from the front seat of the chopper; he had to yell to be heard over the chopper's engine. Ben nodded from the back seat; John was sitting next to him.

The sheriff laughed. " 'Cept you ain't sitting on your pot to keep your dick from being shot off!"

The Viet Cong's AK-47 rounds had easily pierced a Huey's aluminum fuselage; they made sport of shooting at U.S. choppers flying by overhead. Thus, the prudent practice during an airmobile assault in Vietnam was to sit on your helmet in the chopper so as to arrive at the landing zone with your private parts intact. *Butt armor,* they called it.

The sheriff handed a map back to Ben: "Numbered the camps!"

Dicky dipped the chopper's nose to gain speed. They were soon flying over the magnificent landscape of northern Idaho. Ben looked at John; John looked queasy. He said, "I think I'm gonna throw up."

FBI Special Agent Jan Jorgenson was sick to her stomach.

She had come in early this Saturday morning to run database searches on everyone involved with the Walker prosecution ten years before—the judge, prosecutors, and FBI agents—only to learn that most were dead. Federal District Court Judge Bernard Epstein, seventy-two, had drowned three years ago while out alone in his fishing boat on a small lake at his retirement home in northern Michigan when the boat capsized.

Senior Assistant U.S. Attorney James Kelly, fifty-seven, the lead prosecutor on the Walker case, had been killed the same year in a hit-and-run while taking an early morning jog in his L.A. neighborhood. The car was stolen. No suspect was ever arrested.

Assistant U.S. Attorney General Raul Garcia, forty-eight, number two on the prosecution team, had been shot and killed two years ago in an apparent carjacking outside Denver. No witnesses. No suspects.

Assistant U.S. Attorney William Goldburg, forty, had committed suicide four years ago in Cleveland, Ohio. Gunshot wound to the head. He had just taken a new job with a law firm. His wife was pregnant with their first child.

Former Assistant FBI Director Todd Young, sixty-one, head of the Domestic Terrorism Unit, had died in a skiing accident five years ago. A skilled skier on a familiar slope, Suicide Six Ski Area in Vermont, Young had lost his way down in a heavy snowfall. He was found two days later; his skull was crushed, apparently from impact with a tree.

FBI Special Agent Theodore Ellis, fifty-five, had died three years ago in a hunting accident in Macon, Georgia. He had been in charge of the Walker manhunt.

FBI agents, federal prosecutors, and a judge, six in all—all were dead. Different locations, different causes of death, only one common thread connecting these people: Major Charles Woodrow Walker. Who himself was dead. Ten years after Walker's death, every major government player in his case was dead—except FBI Director Laurence McCoy, now President Laurence McCoy, and Assistant U.S. Attorney Elizabeth Austin, now Elizabeth Brice.

*

His hand eases around from behind her and cups her breast over her nightshirt. Elizabeth's first thought is, *Has it already been two weeks?*

Yes, she realizes, it has been two weeks since she last allowed him sex; he must keep the dates on his BlackBerry. She is not interested, but he is a good father to the children and she does not want him seeking sex from some geek-girl at work who might (a) give him something more than a good time, or (b) decide that getting pregnant with a soon-to-be-billionaire's love-child might be more financially rewarding than the company's 401(k) plan, or (c) lure him away from the children.

So she tosses the pretrial brief onto the night table, removes her panties, and pushes her bare butt against him. He likes it from behind, pushing against her firm bottom. He will not last long this way; he never does. She closes her eyes, figuring she'll be back to her brief in five minutes tops, if history was any indication.

But he doesn't enter her immediately this time. Instead, he slides his other arm under her and his leg between hers. They are entwined between silk sheets. One hand slides down her side, over her hips and along her thighs; his hand is soft like a woman's. His other hand is gentle on her breast. Usually he twists her nipples like he's trying to tune the Range Rover's stereo; tonight he's caressing her like he knows what he's doing. Has someone been teaching her puppy dog new tricks on the side?

The hand on her thigh slides around to the inside and moves up, ever so slowly. Her genitals instinctively clench, anticipating his customary all-out assault: rubbing her clitoris like he's trying to start a fire with two sticks then ramming a finger up her with all the romance of a mechanic checking the car's oil. She is surprised when a quiet moan escapes her lips. He did not attack her clitoris tonight. Instead, his fingers swept across it like a gentle breeze. They're circling around now on her lower abdomen and coming in for another pass. When they do, without conscious thought or intent, she pushes herself against his hand. Heat rolls up her body, through her loins, over her abdomen and breasts, up her neck, and into her brain. She licks her lips.

His tongue is light on the back of her neck, not his usual imitation of a Labrador retriever slobbering all over her, but delicate and teasing. She wants to ask him, *Who the hell taught you that?* But she doesn't want him to stop. Her hand reaches behind her and cups his buttock, firmer than she remembered. His entire body is firm, a better body than one would imagine; has her little nerd been working out in the company gym?

Her hand slides down his torso and finds him. He is so ready. To her great surprise, she is ready, too. She guides him into her; a deep moan slides between her lips this time. She rolls over on her stomach then brings her legs up under her. He kneels behind her and pushes into her, retracts, then pushes again, his thrusts building up momentum, until he is driving himself into her with all his strength, deep inside her, and she feels the pressure massing within her and the heat building and the nerve endings firing and it's about to happen, oh, my God, she's on the brink of falling into the glorious depths of orgasm for the first time since—

And her past returns, chasing off the present, seizing control of her mind, and shutting down her body. It's over for her. There will be no orgasm tonight, no orgasm ever.

She is possessed by her past.

Elizabeth woke with tears running down her face. She

began crying uncontrollably. Grace was gone, and she had blamed John. Now John was gone. John who had loved Grace enough to follow a drunk to Idaho, hoping against all reason that she might still be alive. He had left a billion dollars behind to find his daughter. He had put it all on the line for her. He had done what a man would do. She had never given John Brice enough credit as a man or enough love as her husband.

He deserved more.

They had run into each other ten years earlier at the Justice Department. Literally. He had come around the corner with his head down and barreled into her, knocking her to the floor and sending her files flying. She had taken one look at him and assumed he was a gofer, college kids the department hired to run errands. No, he had said, I'm a Ph.D. candidate at MIT, algorithms, Laboratory for Computer Sciences. He was down in D.C. working on a government consulting project, something to do with the department's computer system. He seemed weird but harmless.

Then he began stalking her. With e-mails. The next day and every day thereafter when she arrived at the office, there had been a new e-mail waiting for her. For some reason, she didn't demand he cease and desist. For some reason, she even started to look forward to them. There was something in his words.

Then evil came for her.

Afterward, she had been mired in despair and thoughts of suicide and homicide. Her Catholicism—even twenty years dormant—would not allow her either avenue of escape: for a Catholic, the former would lead only to eternity in damnation, the latter to a lifetime of guilt. Just when she thought there was no hope, there he stood in her office door. She took John Brice to dinner, she got him drunk, and she used him. And she was pregnant when she asked him to marry her.

He had loved the child more than life itself.

Elizabeth Brice wiped her face and made a decision: she would love her husband. But she could not love him as long as her past possessed her. She sat up. There is only one place to go when you are possessed by evil.

7:10 A.M.

"I DAHO!" THE SHERIFF YELLED. "All these fuckers coming to Idaho!"

They were now circling over the next camp. The first three camps west of town had been long abandoned. Ben was again using the binoculars, leaning out the open hatch and surveying the camp: a half-dozen cabins; beaten-up vehicles and a dilapidated bus jacked up on cement blocks; a woodpile; a ratty sofa out front of one cabin and a recliner out front of another; wisps of smoke lifting from a deer roasting over an open pit; and three men, five women, and four children, all straight out of *Deliverance*.

But no white SUV.

Ben wanted a closer look, so he retrieved the ART scope he had removed from the rifle and put into the backpack. Through the high-powered optic he could tell whether a man had shaved with a blade or an electric razor that morning; the men at this camp had shaved with neither. They had beards and scraggly hair, no flattops or blond hair, and wore jeans and flannels, not fatigues. No weapons or military gear of any kind were evident. They were not ex-soldiers, much less ex-Green Berets.

The residents below noticed the chopper. The children pointed skyward, and everyone gathered around and gazed up with gaping mouths like they were witnessing a solar eclipse. Through the optic, Ben observed dirty children, weary women, and missing teeth. They appeared dirt poor. A Confederate flag flapped lazily on the tall pole rising above the camp. One of the men unbuttoned his jacket then his shirt; his enormous belly was covered with tattoos and on his breastplate where Superman wore his S were three large letters in fancy script: KKK. He was probably the grand wizard of this little klan.

Dicky yelled back, "Them people remind me of a joke I heard in town: if a husband and wife move from Alabama to Idaho, are they still legally brother and sister?"

"How long you gonna leave her down there?"

Jacko had found Junior sitting at the table, looking like his dog got run over.

"Long enough to break her."

"She ain't no horse." He took a long drag on his cigarette, exhaled, and shook his head. "The hell you expect, she was gonna love you and live here happily ever after?"

Jacko sighed. The son ain't near the man the daddy was. Maybe Junior would have turned out different if he had had a mama to raise him; she had died suddenly when Junior was only a boy. Jacko had always felt sort of responsible. On the major's orders, he had put a bullet in her brain and buried her out back because she had become a security risk. Of course, Jacko's mama had left them when he was only five because of his daddy always getting drunk and beating her up, and he had turned out okay.

"Look, boy, that's twenty-five million down in that box. You gonna let her die down there, least get the money!"

Junior just glared back at him. Fuck this, Jacko thought. The money would be nice, but the important thing was that the girl, dead or alive, was going to bring Ben Brice to him. Man Jacko's age, settling old scores was a hell of a lot more satisfying than money. He grabbed the keys to the Blazer off a nail by the door.

"I'm going up to Creston."

Jacko went back outside and checked the Blazer to make sure no ordnance was still in the back. Last thing he needed was some Canadian Mountie at the border searching the vehicle and finding a nape canister: *Shit, officer, that ain't my napalm!*

He got in and fired up the vehicle and headed down the mountain. Once a month he drove the twenty-four miles into Canada. He had angina; too much booze and red meat and tobacco, the doctor said. Not that he was going to stop any of those habits. So he took nitroglycerin tablets whenever the angina flared up, which was most every day. Hundred bucks a month for his prescription but only half that in Canada. So he bought his nitro over the border. It ain't like a terrorist group plotting to kill the president had some kind of fucking health plan.

"Dr. Vernon?"

"Yes, Agent Jorgenson, I have the file now."

There was a connection between Major Charles Woodrow Walker and Elizabeth Brice and Gracie Ann Brice's abduction, FBI Special Agent Jan Jorgenson was sure of that. But Walker was dead. And only two persons involved with Walker's case at Justice were still alive: Elizabeth Brice—Jan would talk to her later, face to face—and President McCoy. She didn't figure on talking to him.

So she had called the Idaho hospital where Walker had taken his son ten years before. Dr. Henry Vernon was still the ER chief and the only other person she knew who had seen Major Charles Woodrow Walker alive.

"That's not a day I'll ever forget," the doctor said, "FBI arresting the most wanted man in America in my ER."

"Can you describe Walker?"

"Big man, blond hair, blue eyes—I'll never forget his eyes, the way he looked at me. Sent chills up my spine. Said he'd been out of the country, returned home and found his son like that, rushed him in."

"His son was dying?"

"Arthropod envenomation. Spider bite. Hobo spider. People always confuse it with the brown recluse because the bite effects are so similar, but recluses are rare up here." She heard papers being shuffled. "Let's see, here it is: Charles Woodrow Walker, Jr., white male, fourteen, presented as severe headache, high fever, chills, nausea, joint pain, and a necrotic skin lesion consuming one entire finger, eaten down into the bone. Never seen one this advanced. We admitted the boy, put him on an IV, antibiotics, steroids, and dapsone, but the finger had to be amputated to stop the necrosis from spreading. Right index finger. Boy had gone so long untreated, I didn't think he'd make it. After the FBI took his dad away, I went in to check on him. He was gone. I figured he'd die on a mountain. No record of him being treated here again."

Major Walker was dead and probably his son, too.

"Doctor, thanks for your help, I . . . Doctor, what did the boy look like?"

"Big, like his daddy. Same blond hair, same blue eyes."

7:37 A.M.

DICKY WAS POINTING down and yelling back to his out-of-town passengers over the engine noise: "Elk Mountain Farms. They grow hops for Budweiser!"

Down below Ben could see farmland dotted with patches of snow lying next to a river snaking through the valley. They had flown over all seven of the known camps west of town and were now flying east.

"Best damn fishing in the country!" Dicky yelled. "Cutthroat trout, rainbow, bass, whitefish! Up in the mountains, big game hunting—elk, moose, deer, even bear!"

Minutes later: "Kootenai National Wildlife Refuge! Three thousand acres, couple hundred different species! Summertime, you can see bald eagles!"

The sheriff had been silently shaking his head. Now he turned to Dicky and said, "Dicky, shut the fuck up and fly! You sound like the goddamn Chamber of Commerce! They ain't tourists come to look at birds! They're looking for their girl!"

The phone rang. And rang. And rang.

Elizabeth Austin had been the junior AUSA on the Walker prosecution. An up-and-comer at Justice and slated for a top spot in the department, she had abruptly resigned only two weeks after Major Walker had died in Mexico. Two weeks later, she had married John Brice and moved to Dallas. It was as if she had been running away—but from what? Or whom?

An answer was brewing in the back of FBI Special Agent Jan Jorgenson's head, but she couldn't give it words yet.

She needed to know more about Elizabeth Brice, so Jan had searched through the file for names of co-workers and found the phone number for Margie Robbins in the federal employee database; she was currently employed as a legal secretary at the Department of Agriculture and had been previously employed at the Justice Department. It was Saturday morning, so Jan was trying Robbins's residence number. After a dozen rings, a soft voice answered.

"Hello?"

"Margie Robbins?"

"Yes."

"Ms. Robbins, my name is Jan Jorgenson, I'm an agent with the FBI. I'm investigating the Gracie Ann Brice abduction."

"Oh, yes, Elizabeth's daughter. It's terrible."

Bingo. "You know Elizabeth Brice?"

"Her name was Austin when I worked for her. I didn't even realize it was her child until I saw Elizabeth on TV."

"You worked for her at Justice?"

"For five years. I was her secretary. Did they find her daughter's body?"

"No, ma'am."

"I thought the case was closed."

"I'm tying up some loose ends. Tell me about Mrs. Brice."

"Oh, Elizabeth was a wonderful person, a bit serious

and a bit sad, actually, like something was missing in her life. She never talked about it, except once she mentioned her father had been murdered when she was only a child, said she had never gone to church again. I remember that. But she was brilliant, and so articulate. We all said she'd be the Attorney General one day. But that was before that case."

"Major Walker?"

"Yes, the Walker case."

"Ms. Robbins, are you aware that other than President McCoy and Elizabeth Brice, every member of the Walker prosecution team is dead?" The line was silent. "Ms. Robbins?"

"No, I didn't know that. I read something about the judge, some kind of boating accident? And Mr. Garcia out in Denver. Who else?"

"James Kelly, William Goldburg—"

"Bill? Last I knew, he went home to Ohio."

"Todd Young, Ted Ellis, with the FBI."

"They're all dead?"

"Yes, ma'am."

"It's Walker."

"He's dead, Ms. Robbins."

"His kind of evil never dies." An audible sigh. "That case destroyed everyone it touched, especially Elizabeth. She was never the same."

"Is that why she left Justice so abruptly?"

"Wouldn't you? What woman could just go back to work like nothing happened? When they got her back—"

"*Back?* Back from where?"

"From Major Walker—she was the hostage."

8:16 A.M.

"FOUR-HUNDRED-FIFTY-FOOT drop!" Dicky yelled. "People come from all over for white-water rafting on the Moyie!"

They had flown over three of the four camps east of town. They were heading to the fourth, up north. Dicky was circling over a deep gorge spanned by a two-lane suspension bridge; white water was visible below where the river crashed through the narrow canyon. Ben located the gorge on the map: the Moyie River Bridge. Dicky pointed the chopper east.

They were soon over the next camp. Dicky brought the chopper down, a hundred meters above the trees, and hovered. This camp was not as large as some of the others; there were only seven cabins, several vehicles, and no white SUV. But there was an order to this camp that immediately caught Ben's eye. The cabins were arranged like barracks, fronting a gravel area where the vehicles were parked. From the air, a security perimeter was noticeable among the trees, embankments spaced fifty meters apart and forming a semi-circle a hundred meters down-hill from the cabins; the embankments would not be visible to a force attacking up the mountain. And at intervals along the dirt road leading up the mountain to the camp, metal plates were laid across wide man-made ditches; when the plates were removed, all vehicular traffic would be stymied by the ditches, except perhaps a Patton tank. Ditched roads were stand-ard Viet Cong tactics.

This camp was battle-ready.

Ben viewed the camp close up with the scope, then he circled the location identified as "Red Ridge" on the map. He knew this was the camp they were searching for because of the camp's order, the security perimeter, the ditched roads, and a branding iron.

FBI Special Agent Jan Jorgenson jogged out of the federal building in downtown Dallas and across the street to her car in the parking lot. She would spend the rest of her Saturday in Post Oak, Texas.

Major Charles Woodrow Walker was dead. His son was presumed dead. A son who would be twenty-four now, the approximate age of the abductor. A son who had blond hair and blue eyes, just like the abductor. A son who was the size of the abductor as initially reported by the coach.

But there was still a missing finger.

8:52 A.M.

BEN UNBUCKLED HIS seat belt and jumped out of the chopper before the skids hit the deck. He hunched over to avoid the rotating blades and jogged to the sheriff's cruiser. He spread the map out on the hood, using the binoculars and the scope to anchor the ends against the prop blast.

The sheriff arrived and said, "I seen a scope like that, on a sniper's rifle in Vietnam."

Ben did not respond; instead he pointed to the camp located on Red Ridge and asked, "What's the drive time to this camp?"

"I'd say an hour maybe, depending on how muddy the road is. You see something?"

Ben nodded. "A branding iron on the door of one cabin."

"A *branding iron?*"

"Green Beret team carried that same branding iron, V for Viper."

"And?"

"VC were Buddhists and Confucians, ancestor-worshippers. They believed they would spend eternity with their ancestors, but only if they had a proper burial. If they weren't buried or their bodies were mutilated, no family reunion. So Special Forces teams cut off their ears, removed body parts, marked them in some way. Viper team branded their foreheads. Psychological warfare."

The sheriff grunted and said, "I be damned." And then, "How'd they get the branding iron hot in the middle of the jungle?"

"Lit up a block of C-4 explosive. Won't explode without a detonator."

The sheriff leaned against the vehicle, removed his hat, and ran his hand over his head. "I heard rumors about that kind of shit, but I figured it was just that."

"It was true." Ben turned back to the map. "I was on Viper team."

The sheriff stood silently for a time. Ben felt the sheriff's eyes on him. Then the sheriff said, "Still, Colonel, I gotta have more than a branding iron to get a warrant."

Ben looked up at the sheriff.

"I don't need a warrant."

NOON

COACH WALLY WAS eating lunch with his wife and daughter at the kitchen table before leaving for his shift at the Taco House. From his place at the table he looked out on the front driveway through the bay window. He saw the black sedan pull into the driveway. He saw the young woman get out of the car. He saw her put on a nylon jacket to conceal the gun holstered on her hip. Wally Fagan put his fork down and pushed his plate away. He had suddenly lost his appetite.

"I'm Agent Jorgenson, with the FBI," the young woman standing on his porch said, and Wally Fagan knew instantly that he had chosen the wrong path. She had come for the truth, and he would tell her the truth. And his life would be forever changed.

4:05 P.M.

"BEN, IF YOU'RE sure she's there, let's go get her now!" John was sitting across from Ben at a window table in the local snarf-and-barf on Main Street. Ben was shaking his head.

"John, we're not going to drive up that mountain, knock on the door, and drive away with her. They're not going to just give her to us. We're going to take her. And that's a night op."

"Then as soon as it's dark. Let's don't waste time at Rusty's!"

"Son, we're going to Rusty's on the off-chance we might get lucky on a Saturday night, get a little intel on those men. We'll go up the mountain after midnight, recon the camp, plan our attack, and move in at first light. We need the element of surprise—and we can't take a chance on a stray shot with Gracie in there."

John leaned back and sighed. Ben was right; this wasn't his kind of work. He was such a debbie at man's work. He remembered his mother's words: *Do exactly what Ben tells you to do, and we might get Gracie back. This is what he knows.*

John gulped the foul coffee—*haven't these people heard of Starbucks?* Outside, the good citizens of Bonners Ferry

412

were strolling by, oblivious to the fact that at that very moment his daughter was being held hostage in the mountains north of town.

"Ben, do you think Gracie's okay?"

"She's alive, John."

"Do you think those men . . . you know . . . do you think they . . . with Gracie . . ."

Ben's eyes turned harsh. "Don't say it, John. Don't even think it."

"I can't help thinking it, Ben . . . or wondering if she'll ever be the same again."

"John, listen to me. Whatever they did to Gracie, we'll get her through it. She's strong, in her mind. We'll fix her. I'll take her to Taos. She'll live with me until she's ready to be with people again."

Ben's jaw muscles clenched; he turned to stare out the window.

"Ben, I want to kill those men."

"If there's killing to be done, I'll do it. It's what I know."

Ben abruptly stood and was out the door before John could open his mouth. He jumped up and dropped a $10 bill on the table. Outside, he looked up and down the sidewalk and spotted Ben, already a half-block away. John ran to catch up.

"What's up?" he asked.

"Man up ahead—blond hair, camouflage pants, six foot, two hundred pounds."

The blond man entered a tobacco shop. John and Ben sat on a bench outside, just two dudes enjoying a fine spring day, not a father and his father searching for the men who had kidnapped his daughter. Ten minutes later the man emerged with a cigar in his mouth and continued his walk up the sidewalk. They followed.

Two blocks later they stopped in their tracks. Two little girls ran up to the man; he bent over and picked up the smaller child. A woman walked to the man and kissed him.

A family man.

"Mama, I got me a family now."

Junior stood before his mama's grave out back of the cabin in a little clearing that he kept real nice. He came out and talked to his mama almost every day. Some days she talked back.

"Well, course I'm gonna let her out, Mama. Tomorrow morning. Two nights in the box ought to break her of running. She's awful cute, ain't she, Mama?"

Junior had grown up a mama's boy wanting to be like his daddy. But the major had left them months at a time—business, he had said. Junior had never gone to school in town; the major wouldn't allow it. So his mama had taught him almost everything he knew, except what the major taught him about shooting and hunting and hating Jews. Funny, but mama seemed happiest when the major was off on a business trip. Only then could she go into town and see her old friends; she took Junior with her and she laughed and she sang when she was cooking and they sat under a tree and she read poems out loud. Junior and his mama did everything together. She was beautiful.

And then she was gone.

And Junior never read another poem.

"You take this one. I'll take the one across the street."

John watched as Ben waited for a car to pass then jogged

across the street. John plopped down on the nearest bench. They were staking out every white SUV on Main Street. The three they had seen so far were owned by an old woman, a teenage girl wearing the tightest jeans John had ever seen on a female, and an old coot chewing tobacco.

It was almost five. The sun would soon drop below the mountains, and the fine spring day would turn back to winter for the night. Gracie would be cold.

6:47 P.M.

G ARY JENNINGS had had all ten fingers when he had tied one leg of his jail pants around the sprinkler pipe in his cell and the other leg around his neck and stepped off the jail cot.

An innocent man was dead.

Which meant Gracie Ann Brice might be alive.

FBI Special Agent Jan Jorgenson knew now that Gracie's abduction had nothing to do with Colonel Brice or revenge over the Vietnam War. It had everything to do with Elizabeth Brice and a son seeking to avenge his father's death. Maybe Charles Woodrow Walker, Jr., figured the federal government killed his father, so he'd just kill everyone responsible. But why didn't he kill Elizabeth Brice, too? Why did he take her daughter instead? And did he have plans for the president?

Jan Jorgenson was in over her head. She needed experience. She needed Agent Devereaux. But his cell phone put her to the answering service for the fifth time that day.

"Eugene, this is Jan again. It's Saturday, almost seven Dallas time. Please call me as soon as possible. Jennings was innocent. And Gracie may be alive."

She ended the call.

Jan was sitting on the sofa in the Brice study waiting

for Mrs. Brice. More questions filled her mind: If the major's son was the abductor, where is he now? If Gracie is alive, where is she now? The major and the son had lived in Idaho back then; maybe the son still did. And Colonel Brice thought Gracie was in Idaho because of a call-in sighting in Idaho Falls. But Agent Curry had personally interviewed the Idaho source and reported that the source could not ID Gracie or the men or the tattoo. Odd.

Jan needed to speak to the Idaho source. That required the computer printout of leads which was sitting on her desk in downtown Dallas forty miles south of her present location. There wasn't much chance of anyone being at the office at this time on a Saturday night—except the security guard.

She got Red on the first try. No doubt he was sitting behind the security desk in the building lobby watching TV, where he had been every night the past week when she had signed out after hours. Red was fifty and lonely. He made sweet with her each night.

"Red, this is Agent Jorgenson."

"Well, hidi there! I saw from the log sheet you'd left."

"I have an emergency. Can you help me?"

"You want me to come to your place?"

"Uh, no. I want you to go to my office."

"Oh. Well, I guess I can get up there in a bit."

Yep, as soon as Wheel of Fortune *is over.*

Jan Jorgenson possessed the round face, big eyes, and solid stature befitting a Minnesota farm girl. If she were a horse, they'd call her sturdy. Most guys called her cute. She wore her hair short, stood five-seven, and weighed a rock-hard one-thirty. (Muscle weighs more than fat.) Men often took one look at her and assumed she was lesbian—her muscular legs caused her to walk a bit too manly—but she was hetero through and through. She just hadn't found a man worth letting between her legs. And Red, the security guard, wasn't him; but he wanted to be. Jan wasn't the type to lead men on, but she needed that printout.

She whimpered into the phone. "You know, Red, when this case is over, I'm going to have more free time, and maybe we could—"

"I'll go up there right now!"

"Alrighty, then. On my desk is a thick computer printout with a bunch of yellow stickums on pages. Look through those for a listing from Idaho Falls, start at the back. When you find it, use my office phone and call me at this number."

She gave Red her cell phone number, and he was off, probably packing more than a ring of keys in his pants. She made a mental note to change her cell phone number when this was over.

Red called back in under ten minutes. Clayton Lee Tucker, Idaho Falls, Idaho. With a number. Red said, "Bye, honey."

Gag me.

Jan checked out the Brice's phone system; ten incoming phone lines. That many lines, they could afford a long-distance call to Idaho. She punched a button and dialed direct, hoping Tucker worked late. A man answered on the thirteenth ring.

"Hello? Hello? This phone working?"

"Clayton Lee Tucker?"

"Yep. Didn't know my phone was working again." Then to someone else: "Be right there!" Back in the phone: "Got a customer."

"Mr. Tucker, I'm Agent Jan Jorgenson, with the FBI.

I'm investigating the Gracie Ann Brice abduction."

"They come by yesterday."

"Colonel Brice and the father?"

"Yep."

"What time?"

"Right after I got in, about eight."

"Do you think the girl you saw was Gracie?"

"Oh, I'm sure of it now, after looking at her pictures."

"What made you change your mind?"

"From when?"

"From when the FBI agent showed you those pictures?"

"Like I told them, ain't no FBI agent been here."

What? Jan tried to think that through, but Tucker interrupted her.

"Got me a customer."

"Mr. Tucker, where were Colonel Brice and Mr. Brice heading after they left your place?"

"Bonners Ferry. Up in Boundary County."

"Deputy Sheriff Cody Cox," a voice answered.

"Deputy, this is Agent Jan Jorgenson, with the FBI, calling from Dallas. I need to speak with the sheriff."

"Sheriff Johnson? He's out with the missus, it's their anniversary. Well, actually, yesterday was their anniversary, but the sheriff got tied up and—"

"Did a Colonel Ben Brice and a John Brice meet with the sheriff?"

"Sure did. They went flying around this morning with Dicky in his helicopter. Sheriff said he owed his life to the colonel."

"Deputy, I need to speak to the sheriff. This is an emergency."

419

"Give me your number—I'll track him down, have him call you."

Elizabeth closed the door to the study behind her. Agent Jorgenson was sitting on her sofa.

"What's the emergency, Agent Jorgenson? I'm on my way to church."

The young woman took a deep breath and said, "Tell me about Major Charles Woodrow Walker."

"He's dead."

"Did you know he had a son?"

7:30 P.M.

"BLESS ME, FATHER, for I have sinned. It has been thirty years since my last confession."

The Saturday evening before Easter Sunday was always a busy confession night. So far, Father Randy had listened to four dozen confessions from anonymous confessors kneeling on the other side of the confessional in St. Anne's Catholic Church, all routine sins for which he had dispensed routine penances: ten Our Fathers and ten Hail Marys. But he perked up upon hearing this confessor's voice, for two reasons: thirty years was a long time between confessions and might require a non-routine penance; and the woman's voice sounded oddly familiar. Her next words confirmed his suspicions.

"Father, I am possessed by evil. And now evil possesses my daughter." Her voice was breaking up. "Father, Grace might be alive!"

Elizabeth Brice was in his confessional. Father Randy knew Gracie, the poor girl, and the rest of her family. He saw them every Sunday morning. But Elizabeth Brice had never set foot in his church.

"Gracie might be alive?"

"Yes!"

"What do you mean, she's possessed by evil?"

421

"He's taken her to Idaho!"

"Idaho? *Who?*"

"The devil's son."

Father Randy's shoulders slumped. *The devil's son?* The poor mother was likely having a nervous breakdown. He decided to treat her gently.

"Why thirty years since your last confession?"

"My father was murdered when I was only ten. I blamed God."

"For thirty years?"

"Yes."

"You've not been to Mass for thirty years?"

"No."

"Communion?"

"No."

"You've lived without faith for thirty years?"

"Yes."

"Why now?"

"I want to come home. I want my daughter to come home. I want God to give us a second chance."

It was not easy being a Catholic priest these days. With so many priests being convicted of sexual assault on children and the Catholic Church becoming the favorite whipping boy of plaintiffs' lawyers, he had often thought of quitting. What good was he doing? He was spending more time testifying in depositions than spreading the word of God via Masses and his website and the CDs and audiotapes and tee shirts. And did anyone really believe in God any more? In Satan? That there truly was a daily battle between good and evil waged within our souls and for our souls? Had he saved even one soul in fifteen years? Now an odd sensation came over him and he knew: God was giving him his chance.

"Evil took me ten years ago," Mrs. Brice said. "It won't let go of my life."

"Because you don't possess the power to fight evil. Faith is our only defense to evil—we fight evil with faith."

"But why my daughter?"

Father Randy now said words he did not understand: "Because there is a bond you and Gracie share, a bond with evil that must be broken."

"Yes, there is. Father, how do I break this bond?"

"You don't. Someone must die for the bond to be broken."

"No! Don't take her!"

The woman jumped up and barged out the door and opened the door to his side of the confessional. She lunged at him and grabbed the big silver crucifix hanging down the front of his vestment. Her eyes were wild.

"God, take me instead!"

"Patty, can you hear me?"

No answer.

Junior's mouth was at the opening of the air vent and his hands were cupped around both, so she could damn well hear him. She was just being stubborn.

"You learn your lesson?"

Still no answer.

"Giving me the silent treatment, huh? I used to try that on the major when he put me down there, but he didn't buy it then and I ain't buying it now. You hear me?"

Silence from below.

"Okay, we'll see how stubborn you are after another night down there."

Junior stood and walked back to the cabin.

8:29 P.M.

F BI Special Agent Jan Jorgenson walked into her apartment to a ringing phone. She answered; it was Sheriff J. D. Johnson from Boundary County, Idaho. He confirmed that the colonel and John Brice were in Bonners Ferry.

"They think the girl's up on a mountain. Place called Red Ridge."

"I think she's up there, too."

"Thought the FBI closed the case when the abductor hung himself?"

"We were wrong. Sheriff, you ever heard of Major Charles Woodrow Walker?"

"Hell, yes, I heard of him. You people arrested him over at the hospital what, ten years back? Don't know what happened to him after that."

"He died in Mexico. Do you know about his court martial?"

"Vaguely, something about a massacre in Vietnam?"

"Yes. Place called Quang Tri. Colonel Brice testified against him."

"Don't tell me this major was part of a team code-named Viper?"

"He commanded it."

"Damn. Colonel Brice found their camp all right. Said this was about an old score. Guess that's what he meant."

"Major Walker's son abducted the girl, but not because of Colonel Brice. Because the mother was one of his father's prosecutors. The others are all dead, except Mrs. Brice and the president."

"*The* president?"

"Yes, President McCoy. He was the FBI Director back then."

"Well, Colonel Brice done found your boy and that's probably a good thing."

"Why's that?"

"Because he don't have to play by our rules."

"In Indian territory, Lieutenant, we make our own rules. First rule, we don't follow command's bullshit rules, particularly the rules of engagement that say we can't fire on the enemy unless we're fired upon first. No one gets a free shot at Viper team. We kill them before they kill us.

"Second rule, they all look the same, the enemy we're supposed to kill and the civilians we're supposed to save. NVA regulars, they'll be in uniform. But not VC. They're guerrillas, fathers and sons of the peasant class. Out in the bush, you won't know whether a peasant is going to welcome you or shoot you until he does. When in doubt, shoot the gook.

"Third rule, a conscience is a dangerous thing in a shooting war. Your conscience can get you killed—that's your business. But your conscience can get your team members killed—that's my business. Leave your conscience right here in Saigon. Don't take it out in the bush. Out there, ain't no right or wrong. There's killing the enemy or going home in a body bag."

The major finishes his meal and pushes his plate aside.

"Fourth rule, and the most important rule to remember: you're not fighting this war for the American people. They don't give a fuck about you or this war or these people or the Communist threat to the world. They're back home smoking dope and making love not war and enjoying the peace and prosperity we provide them. Don't ever expect support from civilians.

"You're fighting this war for your Army. The West Point Army. Because your Army does give a fuck about fighting this war and stopping Communism at the Seventeenth Parallel. Your Army understands the threat of Communism. Your Army knows that American civilians won't get behind the fight against Communism in the world until Russian atomic bombs detonate over New York. Then they'll come crying to us to save them and preserve their peace and prosperity and fight for their freedom. And we will—we are now, they just don't know it. But your Army does. Your Army will stand in the door for you, your Army won't abandon you when the going gets tough, your Army will never betray you."

The major's crystal-blue eyes are boring into Ben's.

"And you, Lieutenant Ben Brice, must never betray your Army."

"Yes, sir."

1 Dec 68. The American Bar on Tu Do Street in Saigon, South Vietnam, is noisy with the sounds of rock-and-roll music and giggling Asian dolls and drunken American officers. Lieutenant Ben Brice is in awe of the man sitting across the table. Charles Woodrow Walker graduated from the Academy fifteen years before Ben, but Ben knows all

about him, as does every cadet who attended West Point after the major. Charles Woodrow Walker, they say, is the next MacArthur.

"I wanted you on my team," the major says, "because your commanding officer at Fort Bragg says you're the best damn sniper he's ever seen. You got your Viper tattoo, now you get this." The major pushes a long flat package across the table to Ben. "Welcome to SOG team Viper."

Ben opens the package. Inside is a shiny Bowie knife with VIPER etched into the wide eleven-inch-long blade.

"Every man on Viper team carries a Bowie. Stick that in a gook's gut, guaranteed to ruin his whole fucking day."

"Yes, sir."

The major hands Ben a small ID card with Ben's photo, name, rank, blood type, and serial number—and words in bold type:

**MILITARY ASSISTANCE COMMAND VIETNAM
STUDIES AND OBSERVATION GROUP
THE PERSON WHO IS IDENTIFIED BY
THIS DOCUMENT IS ACTING UNDER THE
DIRECT ORDERS OF THE PRESIDENT OF
THE UNITED STATES! DO NOT DETAIN
OR QUESTION HIM!**

"Your 'Get Out of Jail Free' card," the major says. "We report directly to the president. No one fucks with SOG."

"Yes, sir."

The major drinks his beer then says, "The Academy, Brice, is a great school. But forget every damn thing you learned there. The wars they taught you about, World War One, Two, Korea, they're not this war. Everything you learned over there don't mean dick over here. In this war, napalm is your best friend."

A middle-aged American officer with a Viet bargirl under each arm stops at their table. Ben sees three silver stars and jumps up and salutes the lieutenant general. The major barely lifts his eyes then returns to his beer.

"The great Major Charles Woodrow Walker," the general says with slurred speech. "A legend in his own mind."

The major drinks his beer then says to Ben, "Last time a Saigon commando interrupted my dinner, I slapped his butt into the next lunar new year."

The girls giggle and the general's face turns red: "You stand and salute me, goddamnit! I outrank you!"

The major turns his full attention on the general, who recoils slightly.

"First of all, General, I don't salute rear-echelon officers who ain't gonna get any closer to a Communist in this war than fucking these Viet Minh girls. And second, as long as I'm in-country, only the president outranks me. You got a problem, call him."

The general appears as if he's about to explode, but he says nothing as he storms off.

"American soldiers are dying this very minute fighting the Communists. The general, he sits here in Saigon, lying about body counts to the press, more worried about Walter Cronkite than Ho Chi Minh."

He shakes his head with disdain.

"We move out at dawn, hop a slick to Dak To, meet the team. Then up to Lang Vei, get our gear together, hike into Laos the next day. Tchepone, thirty klicks into Indian territory. Intelligence says there's a major convoy moving down the trail. We're gonna stop it."

Ben is too excited to eat. The major has over one hundred missions into enemy territory under his belt. One hundred! And Ben Brice will be on the next one. The great adventure begins.

"That's the war you've come ten thousand miles to fight." He smiles, as if he's made a joke. "What do you say, Lieutenant—last chance to change your mind, stay here in Saigon and enjoy the amenities?"

The major reaches out and grabs a beautiful young Viet girl as she walks by their table and pulls her onto his lap.

"Like Ling here. Most beautiful women in the world, Viets. You want one? I'm buying."

The bar's proprietress, Madame Le, elegantly dressed and beautiful and preceded by perfume more intoxicating than the bourbon, arrives at their table for the second time that evening, rests her dainty hand with its manicured red fingernails on Ben's shoulder, and says in the English she learned at the finest finishing schools in France:

"Ain't never seen you cowboys in here before."

Ben blinked hard several times to clear his head of the major and the American Bar and Asian dolls and Saigon; when his eyes focused again he was looking at a woman's hand on his shoulder, anything but dainty with fingernails that had been chewed down to the nub. He turned his eyes up to the woman's face; she had an alcoholic's complexion with a wrinkle for every year of her life. She reeked of tobacco and cheap whiskey. She was no Madame Le.

"You boys want some company?" She jutted a hefty hip their way—"I got a Saturday night two-fer special"—and smiled as demurely as one could without a front tooth.

"No thanks," Ben said. The woman seemed offended. So he forced a smile and added, "Nothing personal."

Her eyes narrowed and moved from Ben to John and back.

"We're gay," John blurted out. "Yeah, we're, uh, we're in the movie business."

"Oh," the woman said. She seemed satisfied and left.

Ben turned to John. "We're *gay*?"

John shrugged. "Hey, it got rid of her."

They had been sitting on bar stools in Rusty's for more than an hour. The place was a dive. Country music played on the juke box. The floors were wood and sprinkled with sawdust. Neon lights glowed above the bar and a small TV played silently behind the bar. Pool tables crowded one corner. A few hard-looking men and harder looking women populated the place.

Ben saw in the mirror behind the bar that the woman had tried her luck with a table of four brutes. She gestured back at Ben and John and said something to the men. They laughed. His eyes moved to the front door. A burly man, white, maybe a few years younger than Ben, wearing fatigues, boots, and an old green military jacket, entered, stumbled over to the bar, and sat down hard two stools away from Ben. His face was battered.

"The hell happened to you, Bubba?" the bartender asked him.

"Junior hit me with a fuckin' shovel."

Bubba spoke in a Southern accent. He removed his jacket. He was wearing a short-sleeve tee shirt, exposing part of a tattoo you could only get in Saigon. The bartender placed a beer and three shots of tequila in front of Bubba without being asked.

Bubba downed the first shot, shuddered as the tequila

hit his system, and said, "Al, Junior done kicked me outta camp."

Al the bartender laughed. "What'd you do this time?"

Bubba swiped the back of his hand across his mouth. "The Viet dolls wasn't no older, don't see why he's so pissed off. She's on the rag, she's old enough to fuck."

Ben grabbed John's knee to keep him from reacting. Bubba swallowed the second shot.

"The fuck I'm supposed to sleep tonight?"

"Go on back out there," Al said.

The third shot and a shake of his head. "Can't. Mountain is booby trapped."

"Okay, Bubba," Al the bartender said, "you can sleep here, but not on the goddamn pool table like last time." Al turned and walked away, shaking his head. "Booby traps." As he passed Ben and John he said, "Those boys don't know the war's been over thirty years."

Ben was plotting out a strategy with Bubba when he heard a drunken voice: "Hey, girlfriend, how about a blowjob?"

Ben turned. One of the drunks, the biggest of the bunch, was standing there; his hand was resting on John's shoulder. John's face was frozen.

Little Johnny Brice had gotten the crap beat out of him at least once a week, sometimes twice. But the closest John R. Brice had ever come to a fistfight was a couple of years ago after a brain-damaged bagbiter driving a black Beemer had rear-ended him on the tollway, trashing John's new Corvette, then offloaded his big self and called John a moron! Without considering the possible consequences, John had retorted: "I'm a moron? I've got a 190 IQ, a

431

Ph.D. from MIT, and my own Internet company I'm gonna take public! What advanced degrees do you have, dude?" That had shut the dude up.

But it occurred to John now that informing this over-sized meatbot standing over him of his IQ, advanced degrees, and highly successful IPO might not have the same effect in rural Idaho as it did in suburban Dallas. As a result, he was suddenly paralyzed by the familiar feeling of masculine inferiority. Little Johnny Brice looked to Ben.

"Walk away," Ben said to the man.

John saw none of his fear in Ben's eyes. But the cretin was too drunk to notice. He took a single step toward Ben; John knew that was a mistake. The man's eyes suddenly bugged and he let out a guttural groan. John looked down. Ben's boot was embedded in the man's groin. The man crouched over, like an old man with a bad back, his hands cupped his genitals, and his face contorted with that particularly excruciating pain associated with having your balls busted. Ben stood, grabbed him by the shoulders, turned him around, and gently pushed him toward his table. The man stumbled over; his giggling buddies helped him sit down.

Little Johnny Brice wanted to be a man like Ben.

Ben sat down and nodded at Bubba. "Can't abide a rude drunk," he said.

Bubba drained his beer, belched, and said, "Me either."

"Your tattoo," Ben said. "Highlands or Delta?"

"Delta. You?"

"Highlands," Ben said.

"Green Beret?"

432

"Yeah."

"Well, kiss my ass. How long was you in-country?"

"Seven years."

Bubba shook his head. "Damn. I only got two tours. Would've stayed the whole fucking war, but I got into a little trouble."

"What kind of trouble?"

"Killing the wrong people kind of trouble." Bubba paused. "Seventy-one, night op south of Cao Lanh, free-fire zone. We fuckin' rocked 'n' rolled."

Free-fire zone meant anything that moved was fair game, man, woman, or beast. Rock 'n' roll meant putting your weapon on full auto and firing indiscriminately.

"Sun come up, we see we didn't kill no VC, only women and kids." He shrugged. "Shit happens, man, it was a fuckin' shooting war. Army discharged my ass 'cause of all the bad publicity over Quang Tri and My Lai." Bubba sighed heavily and said, "Best years of my fuckin' life."

"What'd you do after the Army?" Ben asked.

"Went back home to Mississippi, but it weren't the same, all that fuckin' civil rights bullshit, niggers acting like they owned the goddamn place, Feds fuckin' with us. So I come out west, hooked up with these boys, been here ever since. We got us a camp out on Red Ridge. Full squad. All Green Beret except Junior."

Twelve men. "That the Junior kicked you out the camp?"

Bubba frowned and nodded. "Asshole. He ain't never even been in the Army. But it's his mountain."

"So what are you boys doing bunkered up in the mountains?"

Bubba leaned in close; his breath was hot with the tequila.

433

"We're fixin' to change the world, podna. Big time." Bubba looked past Ben and said, "Your friend wants more."

Ben glanced at the mirror behind the bar and saw the big drunk approaching almost at a sprint; he was wielding a beer bottle like a club. When he raised the bottle above his head, Ben spun to his right. The bottle smashed on the bar instead of Ben's head. Ben drove the heel of his boot into the outside of the man's right knee; a sharp *pop* signaled the snapping of ligaments. The man collapsed, hit the floor hard, and writhed in pain.

Ben sat back down next to Bubba, who snorted at the drunk on the floor. "He won't be running track no more." He held out a meaty hand. "I'm Bubba."

Ben shook Bubba's hand. "I'm Buddy."

Bubba's face brightened. "My daddy's name was Buddy, how 'bout that? What brings you to Idaho, Buddy?"

"Hunting."

"Well, Buddy, we got some damn good huntin'—deer, mountain lion, bear. Killed me a fine buck yesterday. Junior, he'll let me come back in a day or two, once he calms down about his little bitch. You wanna come out, do some huntin', meet the boys?"

Ben gave Bubba the biggest smile he could muster.

"Bubba, nothing more I'd rather do than meet your boys. How about another shot there, podna?"

11:03 P.M.

JOHN WAS DRIVING the Land Rover. Ben was in the back seat with the big dude from Rusty's; his given name was Archie, but he went by Bubba. He was puking out the window.

Bubba had been totally shit-faced when they had finally left Rusty's. Ben had poured a bottle of tequila down Bubba but had never so much as licked his fingers himself. Bubba had no place to sleep other than the bar, so Ben had suggested he stay with them. Bubba had accepted and climbed into the Rover.

Bubba pulled his head back inside and said, "Fuck me," then his head fell back, his mouth gaped open, and he started snoring.

An hour later, they arrived at the Moyie River Bridge spanning the deep gorge they had seen that morning from the helicopter, where Dicky had flown in circles for five minutes, bringing John dang close to barfing his guts up.

"Pull over," Ben said.

John stopped the Rover and cut the engine. No other traffic was on the road at that time of night. Ben got out and walked around to Bubba's side and opened the door. He slapped Bubba semi-conscious and yanked him out.

"We there?" Bubba asked.

"Gotta hit the head," Ben said. "How about you?"

Bubba grunted. John went around to their side of the car while Ben helped Bubba over to the bridge rail. Bubba leaned against the low railing, found himself, and starting peeing on his foot. He let out a groan of relief. Down below, white water crashing over rocks was visible in the moonlight.

"What doin' . . . out here?"

The cold air was reviving what was left of Bubba's brain.

"Bubba, what kind of weapons you boys got at the camp?" Ben asked.

"Stingers . . . grenade launchers . . . napalm . . ."

Bubba's words came out slurred and slow, and he was swaying slightly as he spoke.

"How's the perimeter booby trapped?"

Bubba's head rolled around, and he laughed. "Explosives . . . trip wire . . ."

"Girl at your camp, does she have blonde hair?"

"Unh-hunh . . . pretty little thing."

"Why does Junior want her?"

"Says she . . . belongs with him . . . Says she's his . . ." Bubba was finishing his business. "But she's . . . just pussy." He let out a drunken laugh. "Tried to get me some, too . . . li'l bitch kicked me right in the . . . goddamn balls." He turned around, his eyes only slits in his fat face but his mouth grinning and his penis in his hands. "Junior, he wants her for himself, but ol' Bubba's gonna get some of her, sure enough."

"I don't think so, Bubba."

In a sudden, sharp movement, Ben drove his fist into Bubba's Adam's apple and knocked him back into the rail. Bubba gagged and his hands flew up to his throat. Ben grabbed Bubba's legs and lifted hard, flipping Bubba over the rail. John's mouth fell open as he watched Bubba's big body drop four hundred fifty feet and disappear into the gorge below. He couldn't believe what he had just witnessed.

"Cripes, Ben! You freaking killed him!"

Ben was looking down; he nodded. "Unless he bounces real good."

"We gotta call the FBI!"

"We get the law involved, John, and those men will kill her. Or the FBI will kill her trying to kill them." Ben looked up from the gorge and at John. "Son, the law's not gonna save Gracie. We are."

John tried to steady himself: *This is what Ben knows.*

12:31 A.M.

THIRTY MINUTES LATER they were stopped on the side of the highway again; they were searching the area around a dirt road leading up the mountain. John didn't have a dang clue what they were looking for. Ben was up the road, far enough that John could only see the light of his flashlight. Ben's light suddenly came bouncing toward him at a fast pace. Then Ben came into view.

"This is it," Ben said.

"How do you know?"

Ben held his hand out. John shone his flashlight on Ben's palm, on a small white object, tubular, a single word printed on the wrapping: *Tampax*.

"I told you. She's a smart girl."

1:18 A.M.

THE MOONLIGHT REFLECTING off the snow provided sufficient visibility for Ben and John to work their way up the steep mountain; they were crisscrossing at angles to the slope through a thick forest of tall pine trees, large boulders, and deep ravines.

They were wearing black knit caps, black greasepaint on their faces, black gloves, and black thermal overalls; they could stand still and blend in with the trees. The sniper's rifle was slung over Ben's shoulder; a .45-caliber pistol was strapped to one leg and the Bowie knife to the other. His backpack was loaded with ammo, the Starlight Scope, and a power pack, an enclosed car battery used as a portable jump-starter that he had transferred from the Jeep to the new Land Rover in Albuquerque. John was carrying a sleeping bag.

Ben's eyes searched the ground, but his thoughts were of an American soldier, nineteen years old, drafted right out of high school, walking patrol in a Vietnam jungle and thinking about his sweetheart back home instead of the ground in front of him. He swings his foot forward as he steps and just as he realizes that he has tripped a wire hidden in the undergrowth, he learns his fate: a bamboo mace swinging down into him with great force; a crossbow directly in front of him discharging an arrow aimed at his chest; boards studded with fecal-infected nails springing up and slamming into his face; or a huge spiked log rigged up high in the trees hurtling down on him.

Ben spotted the trip wire fifty meters outside the security perimeter. Normally, the wire would have been all but impossible to see in the woods; but it stood out against the white snow.

"Sit," Ben whispered to John, who immediately dropped to the ground. "Don't move. I've got some work to do."

Ben left his son and followed the trip wire through the trees.

2:17 A.M.

THE SEVEN DEAD Vietnamese Communists are laid out in a neat row like sardines in a can; a clean black V has been burned into their foreheads with the red-hot branding iron. Lieutenant Ben Brice will never forget the smell of burning human flesh.

Ben now had the same branding iron in the cross hairs of the Starlight Scope: employing ambient night light, a battery-powered intensifier produced an image seventy-five thousand times brighter than the human eye. A sniper could detect enemy movement up to six hundred meters away. Once Starlight Scopes were deployed in Vietnam, the night no longer belonged to Charlie.

John had buried himself in the sleeping bag; he was exhausted after the two-hour hike and freezing in the zero-degree temperature. Ben was standing behind a tree, using the scope to scan the camp and to locate the best shooting position. A white SUV was parked outside the main cabin. The branding iron hung on the door of the next cabin over. Two old pickup trucks sat in front of the other cabins, blocking his line of fire to the cabin doors from his present position. Tree cover was available on the east, west, and north sides of the camp.

Satisfied with the layout of the camp, Ben swept the

scope up and searched the area above the camp on both sides. A ridge about five hundred meters west of the camp would be the ideal sniping position if sniping were his only mission; but this was a rescue mission. He needed to be closer to the camp. He was about to put the scope down when he noticed something on that ridge: a movement. Not noticeable to the naked eye, but noticeable through a Starlight Scope. Maybe an animal. He focused in on the location again.

That was no animal.

Pete O'Brien was pissed off.

Low man on this totem pole meant Saturday nights on the mountain. Shit rolls downhill in the Bureau and nowhere faster than in HRT. He put the night-vision binoculars to his eyes.

Pete O'Brien, a five-year man with the FBI but the rookie operator on this seven-man sniper team, had caught the overnight shift again. The team leader and the senior operators had taken the Humvee down to Coeur d'Alene for the night; at that moment, they were sleeping in warm beds next to strange women, while Pete was up here on this fucking mountain freezing his ass off. At least the wind had died down. The night was so still and quiet he could hear his heart beating. If anything moved on this mountain, he would know it.

Pete thought of the girl.

And he thought of HRT's motto: *Servare vitas*. To save lives. And of HRT's mission: to rescue U.S. persons held by hostile forces. If he had a daughter and some hostile asshole abducted her, he'd damn sure expect the FBI's elite Hostage Rescue Team to save her life or die trying, not to take pictures while she was being raped or killed. But Pete O'Brien was under strict orders to conduct visual surveillance of the "crisis site," i.e., the cluster of cabins, and shoot 35-millimeter black-and-whites instead of .308-caliber slugs at the bad guys holding the girl.

She's a fucking hostage!

And we're the fucking Hostage *Rescue* Team! Not the Hostage Photography Team! Not the Hostage Hope You Get Out Team! Not the Hostage is Probably Being Raped but We Got More Important Shit to Worry About Team!

This is fucking bullshit!

What could be more important than that little girl's life? We ought to blow the fucking door to that cabin and save her life! Or die trying.

Pete was pissed!

Pete O'Brien had signed on to save lives. But after killing a mother at Ruby Ridge and letting those children die at Mount Carmel in Waco, HRT had been cut off at the knees. They couldn't take a shot or a shit without an okay from a suit at Headquarters. And then the World Trade Towers dealt a body blow to the Hostage Rescue Team: HRT had been created for the specific purpose of rescuing airplane passengers held hostage by terrorist hijackers. But if the terrorist hijackers were willing to fly the plane, themselves, and their hostages right into office buildings, what the hell good was HRT? That realization had sent morale to such depths that highly trained and hightestosterone snipers were chasing pussy instead of shooting bad guys on a Saturday night.

And that was what graveled Pete's butt. HRT was better trained, better equipped, and better funded than any other civilian law enforcement unit in America—*we fly around the country in our own C-130 transport, for God's sake!*—

but we never shoot anyone! We never rescue anyone! We never do anything!

Pete O'Brien was really pissed!

We wear our cammies and face paint and body armor and pack MP-5s and M-16s and 9-millimeter semis but we don't do a goddamn thing! We got Bradley armored vehicles and helicopters, we got night-vision goggles and binoculars and scopes, we got flash-bang grenades and explosives to blow doors, we got black paramilitary outfits and polypropylene panties, we got .50-caliber rifles with bullets that'll blow your head clean off—but we got no balls.

We're a bunch of goddamn career bureaucrats scared shitless of fucking up and facing an administrative review or a criminal investigation or a Congressional hearing and losing our jobs and our pensions instead of doing the right thing: taking a chance and saving lives.

This is wrong!

Pete O'Brien touched the rifle beside him. He was a trained FBI sniper, qualified at the Marine Sniper School, although he had yet to pull the trigger with the cross hairs on a human being. Sniper School had taught him to stalk a target without detection, to lie in wait for days if necessary for a shot opportunity, to camouflage himself so that to the world he was the mud, the swamp, the trees, the bush, anything but an FBI sniper, to wait for that one moment when the target presented himself, to take the shot, to kill the bad guy, and to save lives. All Pete O'Brien wanted was a chance to do what he was trained to do better than anyone else in the world.

He felt something cold against his cheek, cold like steel. Like the barrel of a gun.

3:30 A.M.

"THAT'S HER," the FBI agent said.

Agent O'Brien was looking at the photo of Gracie illuminated by Ben's flashlight. Ben turned the light on the agent's map of the camp. The agent pointed at the main cabin with both hands, which Ben had bound with duct tape. He never left home without duct tape.

"She's in that cabin, last we saw her."

"When was that?"

"Seventeen hundred hours, day before yesterday. She tried to escape. She didn't make it."

"You people didn't help her?"

The agent sighed. "No, sir."

"Why not?"

"Orders from the top. The very top."

"How many men?"

"Eleven, all tucked in for the night. Couple of the men got into a fight yesterday, one left, never came back. We don't know what happened to him."

"We do. Agent, why does the FBI want these men bad enough to sacrifice a ten-year-old girl?"

The young agent shook his head. "Honest to God, I don't know. Need-to-know basis, and I guess I don't need to know. But they've stockpiled enough weapons in the

445

main cabin to start a war. And they look like real soldiers."
He shook his head. "Whatever they're up to, it must be something real important."

Ben doused the flashlight.

"Son, there's nothing more important in the world than getting my granddaughter out alive."

5:30 A.M.

"Eugene, she's alive!"

"Who?"

"Gracie! I called eight times yesterday to your cell phone."

FBI Special Agent Jan Jorgenson had finally reached Agent Devereaux at his Des Moines hotel on a land line.

"Just a second," Eugene said. Then: "Shit, the battery on the cell's dead. We worked late, got our man up here. All right, now what's this about Gracie?"

"She's alive."

"Start at the beginning."

"Okay. After Major Walker was discharged from the Army—"

"Stop. You went ahead with the search on Walker?"

"Eugene, I had a bad feeling."

"All right, Jan. I've had those feelings, too."

"Anyway, he holed up on a mountain in Idaho, got married, had a son. He was plotting a military coup. We received an anonymous videotape twelve years ago. We got lucky, apprehended him in Idaho ten years ago. Top secret."

"Must be why I never heard about it."

"Must be. Anyway, before he could be tried—oh,

447

Elizabeth Brice was one of the Justice Department prosecutors on his case—his followers took a hostage and threatened to return her in pieces unless Walker was released."

"Let me guess—Elizabeth Brice was the hostage."

"Yep. So McCoy released Walker, and Walker released her."

"And what happened to Walker?"

"Died in Mexico. Heart attack. Probably precipitated by a few CIA bullets."

"Probably. Point is, he's history."

"Except he had a son, fourteen at the time, makes him twenty-four today. Blond hair, blue eyes. We captured Walker when he took the boy to a hospital. They had to amputate his right index finger, spider bite. After Walker was arrested, the boy disappeared. Doctor assumed he died up in the mountains."

"From a spider bite?"

"Hobo spider, like the brown recluse. It can be fatal if untreated."

"Did you run a search on him?"

"Nothing. But there's more. Every person involved with Walker's prosecution—the judge, three Justice lawyers, including your friend, James Kelly, and two agents—is dead. Everyone, Eugene, except—"

"Elizabeth Brice and Larry McCoy."

"Yep."

"Jesus."

"There's more."

"I was afraid of that."

"Our ID on the abductor, Gracie's soccer coach, remembered something about the abductor that he didn't disclose after Jennings hung himself."

"What's that?"

"The abductor was missing his right index finger."

"Damn."

"There's more. The call-in from Idaho Falls positively ID'd Gracie in a white SUV with two men, one with a Viper tattoo."

"Stop. I had an agent in Boise—"

"Dan Curry."

"Yeah, Curry. He went to that source and showed him the blowups. His 302 said the guy could *not* ID Gracie or the men or the tattoo."

"That's what his 302 says, Eugene. But I called the source. Curry never visited him."

Eugene was silent for a moment. "I smell a rat."

"You got a bad feeling?"

"Yeah, I got a bad feeling. We're officially reopening the Gracie Ann Brice investigation—and if they took her across state lines, that gives us federal jurisdiction. It's my case now. I'll notify Washington, right after I call Stan."

"The director?"

"The one and only. What else?"

"Colonel Brice and the father have tracked these men to northern Idaho, a mountain called Red Ridge outside Bonners Ferry. Place is a national campground for these Aryan Nations types and militias and other assorted wackos. That's real close to Ruby Ridge."

"Oh, that's great. Two things, Jan: first, if Walker's son is killing everyone he figures is responsible for his father's death, is he after the president?"

"Agent Curry didn't suppress evidence in a kidnapping case on his own."

"Yeah."

"Eugene, if they're after McCoy and we know it, we'd

449

have that mountain under round-the-clock surveillance, right?"

"Absolutely."

"With HRT?"

"Yeah."

"What's the second thing?" Jan asked.

"Why'd they take Gracie?"

DAY TEN

6:00 A.M.

FOUR YEARS BEFORE he will become President of the United States of America, FBI Director Laurence McCoy is having breakfast in the Senate Dining Room with the Majority Leader, trying to convince the senator that the Bureau's budget should be increased despite the FBI sniper killing that woman at Ruby Ridge. An aide hurries over and whispers in his ear. McCoy excuses himself. A situation has arisen.

Director McCoy is briefed on his way out of the Capitol. Elizabeth Austin, an Assistant U.S. Attorney on the Major Charles Woodrow Walker prosecution team, was kidnapped when she returned home last night. A handwritten note states that she will be returned in pieces unless the major is released from the maximum-security prison in Leavenworth, Kansas. They gave him twenty-four hours. The Hostage Rescue Team has been mobilized.

Abductions of federal judges and prosecutors by drug lords and terrorists are daily occurrences in Colombia and Mexico and other third-world countries. But not in the United States of America. That cannot be allowed to happen here; for if it does and if the government gives in to the abductors' demands, the rule of law in America will die. And if it happens on the current FBI Director's watch, his dream of living in the White House will surely die as well.

"I won't do it!"

Director McCoy is back in his office at FBI Headquarters, surrounded by the assistant director, the Special Agent in Charge of the Critical Incident Response Group, and the leader of the Hostage Rescue Team.

"Release Walker," HRT leader Tom Buchanan says. "We'll plant a transponder in his shoe, we'll track him until he releases the hostage, and then my snipers will kill him."

"Like they killed that mother at Ruby Ridge? Shit, Tom, I've got two Congressional investigations and a fucking federal lawsuit over your goddamn snipers! And the Majority Leader said to forget a budget increase!"

Larry McCoy turns and stares out the window. He can see the White House in the distance, just city blocks away geographically but close enough to touch politically. And the decision he makes at this moment will determine if Laurence McCoy ever inhabits that building. He turns back.

"Walker stays put."

Larry McCoy drops the small zip-lock evidence bag.

He didn't think they'd really do it. If the press gets wind that a federal prosecutor—a young woman, no less—is being held hostage by former black ops soldiers and is being dismantled and sent to Washington in plastic baggies, his political career is over. On the other hand, if he releases Walker and Walker kills other innocent citizens, his political career is over. The classic Washington lose-lose situation.

"They pulled them out with pliers," the assistant director says.

McCoy looks down at the evidence bag holding Elizabeth Austin's molars.

Hostage Rescue Team operator Frank Kane is sitting in his idling sedan outside the maximum-security federal prison at Leavenworth, Kansas. For the first time in his ten-year FBI career he is unarmed. He will drive the prisoner to the release point. Transponders have been placed in Kane's shoe, in the vehicle, and in the prisoner's shoe. At that very moment, HRT's C-130 transport loaded with a dozen operators and enough weapons to overthrow a small country is flying overhead at twenty thousand feet; they will track the prisoner with the transponders, they will land on a goddamn highway if they have to, and they will kill Major Charles Woodrow Walker and his co-conspirators.

After, that is, Elizabeth Austin is released.

"Pull over," the major says.

They have driven twenty-seven miles west of Leavenworth on various farm-to-market roads per the major's directions. Kane turns into an abandoned roadside vegetable stand. A late-model black Suburban is parked out front; a young Hispanic male is perched on the hood. They're switching vehicles.

Kane exits the sedan, unconcerned about abandoning the vehicle and its transponders. They have anticipated the major's move; the transponders in their shoes will still lead the HRT team above.

They walk over to the Suburban.

"Keys," the major says, holding his hand out.

Kane tosses the sedan's keys to the major. The major says something in Spanish to the young man and hands him the keys. The young man jumps down, walks over to the sedan, gets in, and drives back toward Leavenworth.

"Drive," the major says. Kane nods, opens the driver's door, and steps up onto the running board. "Naked."

Kane freezes. *"What?"*

The major rips his shirt off and tosses it to the ground. "Remove your clothes."

"You want me to drive naked?"

"I'm pretty sure you didn't stick a transponder up my ass. Beyond that, I can't be sure where you planted them. Don't worry—this vehicle's got a good heater."

Kane's face betrays his thoughts. The major chuckles. "How do you think we tracked downed pilots in North Vietnam?"

They did not anticipate this move. Kane tries to think of a way out but nothing comes to him. He unzips his jacket.

Frank Kane laughs. Not at the fact of two grown men driving naked through Kansas farm country on a Sunday morning in February but at the major's sex and war stories from Vietnam.

"Three Viet women at a time?"

The major shrugs. "If you were man enough."

An hour later and Frank Kane finds himself admiring Major Charles Woodrow Walker more with each mile.

The major is a hell of a man. What would make this man turn against his own country? The major reads his mind.

"Betrayal. You know something about that, don't you, Frank?"

"What are you talking about?"

"Ruby Ridge. You were there, doing your duty for your country, defending your country against all enemies, foreign and domestic. But things went wrong and your country blames you."

"How do you know this? Our names haven't been released."

The major smiles. "Frank, I've got men in every branch of the military, active-duty officers waiting for my order, ready to restore order to America. And I've got men in law enforcement—how many ex-military are on your Hostage Rescue Team?"

"Most."

The major nods. "I knew you'd be my escort before you did."

"You're plotting a coup?"

"I prefer to call it a regime change. You're a good man, Frank, taking on this mission to save the hostage. Took guts. There's room for a good man like you in my administration."

The thought strikes Frank Kane. He is being blamed for Ruby Ridge. Heads will roll. And his might be one of them. Why not jump teams before he's cut, like a pro football player who makes a better deal with another team. Why give a damn about loyalty to his country when his country has no loyalty to him?

Frank Kane sighs. He does. He gives a damn. His answer will likely cost him his life, but he says, "No thanks, Major."

*

They are now a hundred eighty-seven miles into the heart of Kansas, in the middle of nowhere.

"Pull over," the major says.

Kane steers to the shoulder of the road and cuts the engine. They are at an intersection of two farm-to-market roads. He can see for miles in each direction and all he can see are snow-covered fields. The major reaches over and removes the keys.

"Un-ass the vehicle," he says.

Kane opens the door and steps out into the cold. He walks around the vehicle and joins the major, two naked men in Kansas.

"What now?" Kane asks.

"Here comes my slick."

He's looking off in the distance, skyward. Kane squints into the blue sky and sees a black dot growing bigger fast. In less than a minute, Kane identifies an Apache helicopter gunship flying low to the ground.

"Flying contour," the major says. "Under the radar."

The gunship arrives in a flurry of dust and snow blown up by the rotor blast. Kane notices that the pilot is wearing a military uniform. And that the gunship's rockets are aimed at the Suburban.

"You might want to step away from the vehicle," the major says.

"Where's Austin?" Kane asks.

"We'll release her."

"When?"

"Soon."

"How do I know?"

"You have my word, Frank."

The major steps onto the skid of the gunship. He reaches inside and tosses a green blanket to Kane. Then he salutes him, like the president saluting his crew on the South Lawn as he boards Chopper One. He rises off the ground like a god.

As Frank Kane tries to comprehend the sight of a naked Major Charles Woodrow Walker being lifted skyward by an Apache helicopter gunship in the middle of Kansas, a rocket fires from the gunship and blows the Suburban to smithereens.

Elizabeth Austin is locked in a small room in what appears to be a small cabin. Through the tiny window she can see the sand and cacti of a desert. She's somewhere in the southwest, near Mexico or maybe in Mexico.

The last thing she remembers is stepping into her town house. When she woke, she was lying on the bed in this room and in pain. Two of her teeth have been removed. She spits blood and is working her jaw to relieve the throbbing pain when the door opens and Major Charles Woodrow Walker enters. He shuts and locks the door behind him. She thinks, *He's not locking me in; he's locking them out.*

"Sorry about the teeth," the major says. "McCoy wouldn't listen to reason." He shakes his head. "A politician."

Standing there in a long-sleeve black work shirt, jeans, and boots, his blond hair shaggy, his face clean-shaven, with the erect posture of a soldier, Walker seems the embodiment of the man he once was, the chosen one at West Point, the charismatic leader of men, the Green Beret legend; but not the man he is now, the most dangerous man in America.

He stares at her, and she can see the evil come into his eyes. He examines her—she's still wearing the same blouse and skirt from her suit—as if trying to come to a decision. He decides.

"Take your clothes off."

"Go to hell."

He steps to her, grabs her blouse, and rips it off. She swings her fist at his face; he doesn't bother to block her punch. It has no effect on him.

"Make it easy on yourself," he says. "But you will do what I want."

Her bra comes off next and she is standing before him. She does not cower or cry. She will not. He looks at her beauty and his respiration increases; his blue eyes turn dark. He comes close; she knees him in his groin. He backhands her across the face and knocks her onto the bed. Her face and jaw burn with pain; tears fill her eyes. He grabs her skirt and yanks it off with her underwear. His eyes are wide and he's breathing like a wild animal. He unbuckles his belt; his pants fall to the floor. She does not look at him; she doesn't have to. He grabs her hips and flips her over and then pulls her hips up. She closes her eyes and clenches her teeth and groans when he pushes into her with sudden force. She is relieved when he does not last long.

But it will not be the last time.

Each time is rough. He always takes her from behind, as if he does not want to see her face when he rapes her or her to see his. He never undresses; he only drops his trousers. He never tries to hold her or caress her or feel her. He just fucks her. Like an animal, a wild beast. When he finishes with her, he leaves quickly and without a word, almost as if he's ashamed of what he has done. But he does it again. And again. And again. She fights him each time but without effect. She cannot beat him with force. He is a force of nature. Her will is weakening. The major controls her life now. His evil is overwhelming.

After the tenth time, she says, "I love you."

Two weeks later, the major and his men take her across the border into Mexico. They travel to San Jose del Cabo. He says they will live there together and for ever.

"He must die! He must die fast and hard or we'll become another goddamn Colombia!"

FBI Director Laurence McCoy released Walker only to have Walker renege on releasing Elizabeth Austin. Two weeks and no Austin. Major Charles Woodrow Walker must die. McCoy's dream of the White House is riding on it.

But McCoy doesn't know where Walker is or whom he can trust. Walker said he had men in the FBI. So McCoy is going outside the Bureau for this job. He says to the Director of the Central Intelligence Agency of the United States of America: "Find him and kill that son of a bitch!"

The young American woman is sitting at the outdoor coffee shop, sipping her coffee, so serene and beautiful in her wispy white dress and white sun hat and dark sunglasses. Perhaps she is a movie star. Yes, Juan decides, she is a movie star. Many a movie star has sipped coffee in his shop in Baja California, but surely she is the most beautiful of them all.

Juan takes her a fresh cup of his best coffee. She is radiant. He can only dream of having a beautiful woman

461

like her. He sighs. Just having her in his coffee shop these last few weeks will have to suffice. She is alone today; the big blond American man is nowhere in sight. Nor are their bodyguards. Juan wants desperately to talk with her, but he cannot bring himself to do so. He places the cup of coffee on the table in front of her.

"*Gracias*," she says, and then she faints.

Jorge Hernandez, M.D., earned his medical degree at the University of Guadalajara in 1965, back when abortion was illegal in the States. From 1965 until 1973, Jorge specialized in abortions for Americans. He opened abortion clinics in border towns from Matamoras to Tijuana. *Roe v. Wade* ended his abortion career.

He closed his clinics and moved to San Jose del Cabo for the fishing. His last abortion procedure for an American was over thirty years ago. Certainly that is why this American woman is here. Jorge sees no wedding ring. He is patting her hand when she opens her eyes.

"Where am I?"

"Hospital," Jorge says. "You are here for an abortion?"

"What? No!"

"But you are pregnant; you know this?"

From her face, Jorge sees that she does not know this. She says, "I need a phone."

Major Charles Woodrow Walker stops the Jeep at the secluded beach house outside San Jose del Cabo. He enters the house. He has been gone two days; he traveled to the border, only to learn that his face was still on the front page of every newspaper in the U.S. So he sent the men north. He will remain in Mexico for another month, then he will reunite with his men in Idaho. And they will wage war on America.

Until then he will enjoy sex with Elizabeth.

Charles Woodrow Walker was born for war and sex. He possessed the mental toughness to kill and the physical tools for sex, a combination that afforded him a great power over both sexes. Men would die for him and women would lie down for him. He has never tired of sex or killing. And there would be more of both for Charles Woodrow Walker.

Before he leaves, he will kill Elizabeth. She loves him, just as all his women eventually loved him, but she is a security risk. Women are always security risks. Charles Woodrow Walker loved war and sex but never a woman.

"Elizabeth!"

No answer. He walks through the house to the back deck. He scans the beach from north to south. It's vacant, except for one woman at the water's edge. He walks to the beach.

Elizabeth feels his presence and turns.

The major is walking toward her. From his face, she knows what he will do to her. He is smiling, but he suddenly stops and cocks his head, as if catching a distant sound. And they are here. Three black helicopters rise over the trees and surround the major, hovering just off the beach; three snipers' rifles are pointed at Major Charles Woodrow Walker. He glances at each helicopter then back at Elizabeth.

"You betrayed me."

"You raped me."

She had called FBI Director McCoy from her hospital bed and set a trap for Major Charles Woodrow Walker. She told McCoy where she was and where the major would be. "I owe you, Elizabeth," McCoy had said. "You just made me president."

"You said you loved me," the major says.

"I lied."

"No, you didn't lie. I own you, Elizabeth. I will always own you—your mind, your soul, your life. You will never be free of me. And one day I'll come for you. But I won't kill you. I'll hurt you more. I'll take what you love most. I guarangoddamntee it."

He glances up at the helicopters again and shrugs with disdain. "They can arrest me again, but they can't hold me. I'll still come for you, Elizabeth. One day I will come."

He grins and it is Satan's grin. But the grin falls off his face when she says, "They're not here to arrest you."

She turns away and three shots ring out.

Elizabeth Austin walks off without looking back but knowing her life is forever changed. Evil took her for its own. Evil embraced her and violated her and planted its seed in her. That evil is now dead. But should the child she carries also die?

She has considered killing the life within her each day since Dr. Hernandez told her she was pregnant. She has also considered killing herself—but she had to kill Walker first. Now he is dead and she is free to kill herself and the child with her. She wants desperately to die.

But she cannot take the life within her. She cannot kill the child. The child deserves to live, and so Elizabeth must live to give the child life. The child is all that stands between her and suicide. The child saves her life. The child is her saving grace. Her Grace.

She now hears the child's cries. They become whimpers. Then they stop altogether. The child is in the dark again, just as when she was inside Elizabeth. But she cannot save the child's life now and the child cannot save Elizabeth's life. Only one man can save them both.

She hears a voice, that familiar voice of evil: "I have taken what you love most, as I promised I would. Now I will own her as I have owned you."

Elizabeth woke, sat up in bed, and screamed, "No!"

Ben's eyes snapped open. He looked around. He thought he had heard a scream.

He checked his watch: 0400. He stood and went over to John, still snug in his sleeping bag, and squatted next to his son. He recalled those late nights after the war when he had sat on the edge of his son's bed and watched him sleeping and listened to his breathing and thought how much he loved him but knowing he was failing him as a father. John's life had taken him on a different path, a path Ben had thought would never again intersect with his. But their paths were one now.

Ben put his hand over his son's mouth to prevent him from screaming. John jerked awake, startled; he realized it was Ben and relaxed.

"It's time," Ben whispered.

FBI Agent O'Brien lay duct-taped and asleep.

6:15 A.M. CENTRAL TIME, DES MOINES

"THE HELL YOU mean you know all this?" FBI Special Agent Eugene Devereaux shouted into the phone.

FBI agents, even veteran ones like himself, were not supposed to cuss at the Director of the Federal Bureau of Investigation, even a political asshole like Stanley White—the director always had one finger in the air gauging the political winds and another finger up his ass. But Devereaux had no patience for protocol, not after having spent the better part of an hour tracking the director down—he was at Chicago Midway Airport aboard the Bureau jet, about to fly back to D.C.—to tell him everything Agent Jorgenson knew and now having the director tell him he already knew everything.

"We know the girl's there," the director said. "HRT's had that place under surveillance for three months. We've got men on the mountain around the clock."

"They're after McCoy."

"Yes. We believe they're plotting to assassinate the president. Larry ordered Major Walker killed."

"Then go in and arrest them! And get Gracie out!"

"We can't! All we've got them on now are weapons charges. We need more evidence."

"What about Gracie? They kidnapped her and trans-

466

ported her across state lines—that's a federal crime! She's evidence! Stan, she's Elizabeth Austin's daughter."

"Austin? The girl's name is Brice."

"The mother's maiden name was Austin when she was at Justice. She was one of the prosecutors on the Walker case. She was the hostage back then."

"Jesus, I didn't know."

"Yeah."

"Look, Eugene, we've got to get everyone involved with this plot identified and located before we move in. They could have operatives on the outside. I'm not gonna have a president killed on my watch!"

"So you're sacrificing her?"

"The president's life is more important than the girl's."

"You can secure the president!"

"Not from these people, Eugene. They're trained assassins, the very best. Those fuckers went into North Vietnam to assassinate generals—they can kill anyone!"

"So can Colonel Brice."

"Who?"

"Colonel Ben Brice, Gracie's grandfather. Green Beret. He's the guy that walked into San Bie prison camp and rescued those pilots."

"I remember that. He got the Medal of Honor."

"He was one of them, Stan. He was in Walker's unit. He testified against Walker at his court martial."

"No shit?"

"Yeah, and he went after Gracie, to Idaho, on some bullshit call-in tip we got from Idaho Falls. At least I thought it was bullshit because Agent Curry reported that the source could not ID the men or Gracie. Stan, you had an FBI agent submit a false 302 about a positive ID on a child-abduction case? That's obstruction of justice!"

"Not in a case involving national security. Eugene, we couldn't compromise the operation."

"Well, Stan, I figure the operation's not only about to be compromised, it's fixin' to be blown to fuckin' kingdom come!"

"What do you mean?"

"I mean, Colonel Brice is sitting on your boy right now."

Stan laughed. "The hell he is. He'll never find their camp. Took us the better part of four years."

"Bonners Ferry. On a mountain called Red Ridge."

He wasn't laughing now. "Wh . . . how did you know?"

"I didn't. Colonel Brice did. That's where he's at."

"Jesus Christ, if he goes in now he'll fuck up the entire operation—and get himself killed in the process!"

"Stan, I wouldn't bet against Colonel Brice."

4:37 A.M. PACIFIC TIME, BONNERS FERRY

B EN HAD DEFUSED the perimeter explosives then rigged his own remote triggering device using the power pack; he had run the wire to their location behind a rock outcropping, where John would be safe. He could have run the wire to his shooting position and detonated the explosives himself, but this way John had something to do that would keep him out of the line of fire. When John punched the trigger, an electrical charge would race down the line and detonate the explosives. As much explosives as these soldiers had rigged up, half the mountain would be history.

But that was Plan B.

FBI Special Agent Jan Jorgenson wanted to fly to Idaho, but Agent Devereaux had told her to sit tight in Dallas until he and Director White arrived in Bonners Ferry. He wanted her to get to Mrs. Brice with any news before the press did. So she sat in her office, wondering: Why did they take Gracie? Her eyes paused on each heading on the greaseboard: GARY JENNINGS . . . JOHN BRICE . . . ELIZABETH BRICE . . . COL. BEN BRICE . . . DNA. She realized that she had never reviewed the DNA results on the blood in the truck or on John Brice's shirt or from the family. She opened the file to the DNA results and scanned down the page. And she froze.

"Oh, my God. That's why they took her."

She checked her watch: seven Dallas time, five in Bonners Ferry. Jan picked up her phone and began punching numbers.

The FBI Academy is located on a Marine base in Quantico, Virginia, a four-hundred-eighty-acre site shared with other FBI units, including the Hostage Rescue Team. Being in close proximity, Academy trainees got to know the HRT operators. Most were macho assholes who liked to talk tough. But not Pete O'Brien.

Pete was a good guy. He cared. Jan and Pete had gone on three dates during her thirteen weeks of New Agent Training at the Academy. Pete had been in his own training as an HRT sniper, so his free time had been as limited as hers. Then she had graduated and been shipped off to Dallas; Pete had flown to Spain on an HRT mission to arrest an international fugitive—to kidnap him, actually, since an FBI agent had about as much legal authority in Spain as the guy who cleaned up after a bullfight.

They had last talked three months ago, just before Pete deployed on an extended mission; it was so secret he couldn't tell her where he was going. Jan had called everyone she knew at HRT, finally waking up Ray, an HRT operator and Pete's buddy. Their first date had been a double date with Ray and another female trainee. Jan's heart had skipped a beat when Ray finally said Pete was in Idaho. After pleading that it was an emergency, Ray had given her Pete's satellite phone number.

FBI Special Agent Jan Jorgenson wasn't going to let anyone sacrifice Gracie.

5:09 A.M. PACIFIC TIME, BONNERS FERRY

A LOW INTERMITTENT buzz interrupted Ben's thoughts. "My satellite phone," Agent O'Brien said. "In my bag. It's my team leader. If I don't answer it, they'll send in the cavalry."

Ben nodded. He pulled the phone out of O'Brien's bag and handed it to him. O'Brien used both hands to put the phone to his ear and answered: "O'Brien."

"Pete?" Jan Jorgenson said.

"Who's this?"

"Jan."

"Jan, how'd you get this number?"

"From Ray."

"Why?"

"Are you in Bonners Ferry?"

"Yeah."

"On a mountain called Red Ridge?"

"Yeah."

"Pete, this is important. An ex-Army colonel named Ben Brice and his son are—"

"Right here."

"They are?"

"Yeah. I'm sort of, uh, taking orders from the colonel now, if you know what I mean."

"I think I do. Let me speak to Colonel Brice."

There was a momentary silence. Then: "Brice."

"Colonel, this is Agent Jorgenson, FBI."

"I remember you."

"Gracie's alive."

"I know."

"She's on that mountain."

"I know that, too."

"The abductor is Charles Woodrow Walker—*Junior*—the major's son."

The colonel was silent.

"Colonel?"

"I didn't know that. So the son is taking his father's revenge?"

"Yes, sir, but it's not about the war. They're plotting to assassinate President McCoy. When McCoy was FBI director ten years ago, Walker was apprehended. His men took a federal prosecutor hostage. McCoy released Walker in exchange for her."

"Elizabeth."

"Yes, sir. Then McCoy ordered Walker killed. We got him in Mexico. Now the son wants the president dead."

"But why'd they take Gracie?"

Static on the line.

"Colonel, we're losing the satellite connection, so listen, this is important. The director is flying in as we speak. That mountain will be crawling with FBI agents in a few hours. He'll sacrifice Gracie to get those men."

"He won't have the chance."

More static.

"Colonel?"

"I'm here."

"O'Brien is a good man and a good shot. Let him help you."

"Why'd they take Gracie?"

"Colonel, one more thing: don't take prisoners. Kill those men, all of them, and burn everything to the ground."

"Why?"

"Just do it. For Gracie."

The satellite connection terminated.

Ben tossed the phone into Agent O'Brien's bag.

"You were an Army colonel?" O'Brien asked.

Ben nodded.

"What'd Jan say?"

"They're plotting to kill the president."

"I knew it was something big."

"And that your director would sacrifice Gracie to get them."

"Son of a bitch." O'Brien shook his head. "Colonel, let me help. I can shoot."

"So I hear." Ben studied Agent O'Brien's eyes and saw something, the same something people once saw in Ben Brice's eyes. "You'd be disobeying orders."

"Colonel, I joined the FBI to save people like Gracie."

Ben unsheathed his knife and cut the duct tape binding O'Brien's hands.

"Take up a position west of the camp and stay there." He turned to his son and handed him the .45. "John, you stay here. Detonate when you see my flare then hunker down. When this blows, it's gonna rain rocks." He looked his son in the eye. "No matter what happens, John, don't leave this position, understood?"

John nodded.

7:25 A.M. CENTRAL TIME, DALLAS

ELIZABETH BRICE stepped inside the sanctuary of the Catholic church. She walked up the center aisle with Sam and Kate, past wooden pews filled with the faithful for the 7:30 Mass. Her eyes were drawn to the crucifix draped in a white shroud high above the altar. Palm branches and white Easter lilies decorated the altar. Stained-glass windows on the walls depicted the stations of the cross.

Heads turned to her; children pointed; parents offered silent pity. They arrived at a half-occupied pew near the front; Sam and Kate entered the pew first. Elizabeth sat by the aisle. She had come back for Easter Sunday Mass. She had come to pray to God and for Ben Brice.

Only God and Ben Brice could save her daughter now.

5:30 A.M. PACIFIC TIME, BONNERS FERRY

BEN MUST KILL these men to save Gracie.

He had never enjoyed the killing. But killing was what he knew.

He had taken his sniping position, perched behind a fallen tree, on which he had steadied his rifle. He was no more than three hundred meters out; he had a clear line of sight to each cabin. Plan A was simple: put a bullet in the head of each man as he exited his cabin. With the suppressor and a little luck, he could take out the entire camp before they had their morning coffee.

Ben put his eye to the scope and surveyed the camp.

7:32 A.M. CENTRAL TIME, DALLAS

THE PROCESSIONAL MUSIC commenced. An altar girl carrying the Easter candle walked up the center aisle past Elizabeth. Behind her followed two more altar girls with their candles mounted on long holders then an altar boy carrying the crucifix on a standard, a deacon carrying a bible overhead, and finally Father Randy. Their eyes met as he passed.

5:35 A.M. PACIFIC TIME, BONNERS FERRY

A LIGHT CAME ON in one cabin. Ben put the scope on that cabin. A figure silhouetted by the light appeared in the optic. Three hundred meters out and no wind, it would be an easy shot. The cabin door opened and a man stepped into the doorway; he yawned and stretched and presented a perfect shot opportunity, conveniently backlit. Ben adjusted the ballistic cam on the ART until the horizontal stadia lines framed the target's torso and head; he centered the cross hairs on the target's head. He had not put the scope on a human being in over thirty years. Killing another human being was something you lived with the rest of your life. He had lived with his killing back then, and he would live with his killing today.

Ben took a deep breath, exhaled, and squeezed the trigger.

The man fell.

A good sniper always maintains surveillance on the downed target because his comrades will often check the body or remove weapons. That is a mistake. A mistake another man in the cabin was making. But he quickly pulled back out of sight, stuck a sidearm out the door, and fired two rounds into the air—the discharge echoed around the mountains like a pinball. *Damn!* Ben kept the scope on the spot where the second man's head would appear when he peeked out the door, as Ben knew he would.

When he did, Ben squeezed the trigger again.

Two down, nine to go.

Jacko didn't jump when heard the two gunshots. He smiled. Ben Brice had come to him. He was on this mountain, and he would die on this mountain. Jack Odell Smith would take the major's revenge. His destiny was at hand.

He sat up in bed and lit a cigarette.

Proceed to Plan B. Ben fired the flare gun into the air with his left hand then quickly returned to his shooting position. A man appeared at the door of another cabin. The bullet hit him in the forehead.

Three down, eight to go.

John saw the flare and punched the detonator.

Sheriff J. D. Johnson always rose at the crack of dawn. Twenty years living on military time ensured that. Today, he needed to get up early. He was going up into the mountains northeast of town, the mountains he loved to gaze upon as he drank his first cup of coffee of the day, as he was now, to find Colonel Brice and his son. Or to find what Colonel Brice had left behind. Just as he was about to turn away from the window, Red Ridge exploded like a Roman candle.

The mountain shook.

Ben was under the log now, protected from the falling rocks and tree limbs. After allowing a few seconds for the serious debris to fall, he returned to his shooting position and sighted in the camp through the haze of dirt and snow blown into the air by the explosion.

The explosion had the intended effect: chaos had captured the camp. Men in long johns fell out of the cabins; their heads jerked about as they tried to locate their attackers. They fired their weapons wildly and took cover behind the vehicles. Ben put two more down before they had made cover. Five down, six to go.

He was sighting in another man, a big man ducked down behind the white SUV outside the main building, when the man popped back into sight with a shoulder-mounted missile aimed directly at Ben's position. Captain Jack O. Smith was a skilled soldier: the suppressor prevented muzzle flash, so he didn't know Ben's actual position; he was simply aiming the rocket at the shooting position he would have taken if attacking the camp.

An adrenaline rush catapulted Ben up and running before the captain fired. He ran east for the count of five then dove under the nearest cover just as the ground rocked with an explosion behind him.

"Ben!"

Little Johnny Brice was crouched down and his ears were ringing from the first explosion. The second explosion had been right at Ben's location. Ben had told him not to move from this position, no matter what happened. And Mom had told him to do exactly what Ben said and maybe they'd get Gracie back alive.

But neither of them had told him what to do if Ben got himself blown up!

John looked down at his right hand, the one holding the .45-caliber pistol Ben had given him and trembling like a leaf in the breeze. He had fired the weapon a dozen times out back of Ben's cabin; he had hit nothing he had aimed at. He hadn't even come close. This wasn't his kind of work.

Scared shitless in Idaho!

John R. Brice, alpha geek, Ph.D. in algorithms, 190 IQ, billionaire three times over, pushed his glasses up on his nose, took a deep breath, and ran toward Ben's location.

If Ben Brice were defending the camp, he would do what any good soldier would do: he would outflank the enemy. The western route was too steep; an assault would come from the east. So as soon as the sky cleared of falling debris, Ben jumped up and ran toward the east, running the woods just like he had run the woods in Vietnam. The instincts would always be a part of him, the instincts that—

—made him duck behind a thick tree. His ears had picked up a sound, and his mind and body had reacted automatically. He shut out the sound of his own breathing and listened. He heard heavy footsteps crunching in the icy remains of the snow; the enemy was coming closer now. Ben reached down and grabbed a large flat stone, several pounds of rock. The footsteps were almost on him now, closer, closer, closer—*now!*

Ben stepped out and slammed the rock into the unprotected face of a large man carrying an M-16. He was out before he hit the deck. Ben straddled the man. He could not take a chance on the man regaining consciousness and returning to the fight. He thought only of saving Gracie as he broke the man's neck. He patted the man's jacket down and found two fragmentation grenades. Ben put them in the pocket of his coat.

Six down, five to go.

John inhaled smoke then coughed it out. The trees were charred and smoldering along a line where the explosives had detonated. At Ben's location, there was a small crater. Ben had survived the explosion. Or he had been blown to megabytes.

John ran on.

The suspect was ducked behind an old truck and loading a goddamned grenade launcher! On the ground beside him was an MP-5 fully fucking automatic machine gun! And FBI Special Agent Pete O'Brien was betting that truck didn't have an up-to-date vehicle registration on file with the Idaho DMV!

Pete was standing twenty meters behind the suspect. His adrenaline was pumping double-time; his rifle was aimed at the suspect's back. Just as he was about to squeeze the trigger, the voices of his Academy instructors came screaming back to him:

"An FBI agent may *not* shoot a citizen in the back!"

"FBI rules of engagement require that the suspect be given the opportunity to surrender!"

"You must shout, 'FBI! Drop your weapon! Yes, I mean that grenade launcher!'"

"Suspects have constitutional rights!"

Of course, ordering this suspect to drop his weapon would give him an opportunity to shoot Pete first. But that's what the "arresting agent" had done in every training exercise at the Academy; and every "suspect" had surrendered. But this wasn't some bullshit hypothetical training exercise staged in Hogan's Alley at the Academy with fake bad guys and fake bullets, where no one actually died when someone fucked up. This was the real fucking thing, a fucking shoot-out on a fucking mountain in fucking Idaho with a bunch of armed-to-the-fucking-teeth terrorists holding a little girl hostage and plotting to assassinate the President of the United States of America! At the Academy they said 99 percent of all FBI agents would retire without ever having discharged their duty weapon at a suspect, much less ever having killed a suspect. Pete O'Brien sighed; he wasn't going to be one of those agents.

He shot the suspect in the back. Twice, to make sure he didn't file a civil rights complaint.

Ben heard two gunshots from west of the camp. Agent O'Brien's position.

He had to get around behind the camp. He ran north, deeper into the woods, then he turned west. He came upon the first cabin. He worked his way from tree to tree until he was at the east side of the cabin. He put his back to the exterior wall of the cabin then moved around to the backside and to a small window. Ben could see a man huddled inside in the rear corner; he was wearing yellowed long johns and pointing a sawed-off shotgun at the door.

Ben stepped back, pulled the pins on the two frag grenades, and threw them through the window. He heard a shotgun blast as he ran for cover and hit the deck. After the explosion, he looked back.

"*Cripes!*"

John had almost stepped on the man laid out in the snow. His arms and legs were splayed, like he was trying to make a snow angel and stopped in mid-angel; his head was cocked in a grotesque manner, as if he were trying to look behind him. *This is what Ben knows.* Ben was still alive.

John carefully stepped around the body and ran deeper into the woods, toward the cabins.

Ben figured four men remained to be killed, maybe three if O'Brien had killed one on the west side. One was Captain Jack O. Smith. Another was the blond man hiding behind the woodpile out back of the main cabin fifty meters from Ben's location and holding a large-caliber handgun. Ben needed him alive, at least until they found Gracie.

Ben dropped the cross hairs from the man's head to his hand, the one holding the gun, and squeezed the trigger.

Junior had never been in a real firefight before. He naturally figured he'd be a fearless son of a bitch because the major was. He figured wrong. He was shaking all over, and he was worried he might piss his pants.

Charles Woodrow Walker, Jr., was a coward.

As soon as the shooting started, he had run out back and hidden behind the woodpile, hoping Jacko and the others would take out the Feds. He was holding his .357-Magnum a foot from his face when it disappeared, along with his middle finger.

"Get up, you ain't hurt," Ben said, kicking the blond man curled up in a fetal position on the ground; the man was holding his bloody right hand and groaning like a draftee after the first day of boot camp.

"Where is she?"

Before the man's response—"Fuck you"—was out of his mouth, Ben's boot was in it. When the man looked back up, his mouth was bleeding.

He spat blood and said, "You ain't FBI."

"And you ain't your daddy, Junior."

"Ben Brice. You betrayed the major."

"He betrayed himself. Where's Gracie?"

"You ain't never gonna find her."

Ben grabbed Junior by the collar and yanked him to his feet, then pushed him to the back door of the cabin.

"Open it," Ben said, pushing Junior in front of the door.

Junior slowly opened the door. Holding Junior in front of him with his left hand and his rifle in his right, Ben entered the cabin. The main room was vacant. Two doors were at one end.

"Gracie!"

"She ain't here."

Dragging Junior in tow, Ben checked the two small bedrooms at one end of the cabin. No sign of Gracie. Ben looked around the main room. Army ordnance containers were stacked high against one long wall: machine guns, mortars, grenade launchers, LAWS rockets, C-4 explosive, detonators, and napalm. Maps and charts and an aerial photograph of Camp David were on one wall.

"What's Gracie got to do with the president?"

"Nothing."

"Then why'd you take her?"

"Because she's my sister."

Ben jerked around at Junior's words. If he had not moved his head those few inches, the high-caliber bullet would have split his skull like a machete through a watermelon. As it was, the bullet creased the side of his head and it felt as if someone had hit him with a two by four. He went to the ground. He felt warm blood streaming down his face. A big boot kicked Ben's rifle away; a big hand yanked the Bowie knife from the sheath strapped to his thigh and snatched the knit cap off his head.

"I should've killed you thirty-eight years ago."

Captain Jack O. Smith was standing over Ben. He struggled to his feet.

"How?" Ben said to Junior.

Junior nodded to the captain. "Show him."

Captain Smith pushed Ben toward a closed door by the kitchen. "Open it."

Ben turned the knob and pushed on the door. It swung open, into a dark room. Junior moved by him and lit a kerosene lamp. He was standing next to a bed; he held the lamp up over the bed. And Ben saw him.

Major Charles Woodrow Walker.

His form under the blanket was frail, his face gaunt, and his blond hair thin. His eyes were closed. His body made no movement, as if he were—

"Paralyzed," Junior said. "What McCoy did to him."

487

"I thought he was dead."

"After we took the woman and got the major released," the captain said, "we went down to Mexico. The major sent us back up here, said he'd be here in a month. Two months later, he ain't back, so me and Junior drive down to Mexico. Locals was still talking about the black helicopters and finding the big blond man on the beach. Said he was taken to the hospital. That's where we found him, like this. They put three bullets in him, one in the neck, cut his spinal cord. Been in that bed for ten years."

The major's eyes flickered open, found their focus, and looked at each of his visitors, finally coming to rest on Ben. After the recognition came into his eyes, Ben thought the major's mouth moved. Junior leaned over the bed.

"He wants to say something to you."

Ben stepped to the bed. The skin on the major's face sagged now and the fullness was gone. But his blue eyes could still look into a man's soul. He tried to say something. Ben leaned over and put his ear by the major's mouth. The major's words came out in a whisper and with great effort.

"Junior showed me . . . picture . . . magazine . . . Elizabeth . . . the girl . . . blonde . . . mine . . . she belongs . . . to me . . . I will own . . . her life . . . as I've . . . owned yours . . . and her . . . mother's."

"You raped Elizabeth."

A thin smile. "Same as . . . those Viet gals . . . Difference is . . . I didn't put a bullet . . . in her brain after . . ."

And now Ben understood. The major was his connection to Gracie and hers to him. He couldn't save the china doll. Thirty-eight years later, God was giving him a second chance.

488

Ben stood tall.

"You've owned my life, Major, that's a fact, and maybe Elizabeth's, too. But you won't own Gracie's. I guaran-goddamntee it."

The major's blue eyes flashed dark. They moved off Ben and onto the captain. Ben turned to face him. The captain advanced on Ben with the Bowie knife.

John moved around behind the big cabin, hugging the exterior wall, looking both ways anxiously, his heart pounding hard enough to hear. He came to a window. He peeked in.

He pulled back quickly.

Inside, Ben was standing next to a bed; an old pale man was lying in it. Next to Ben was a young blond man holding a gun; across the room from Ben was a big man with a tattoo. The two men from the soccer game. The men who took Gracie. The big man was holding a big knife.

Little Johnny Brice's hands were shaking. The urge to turn tail and run was building when he heard the big man say: "I'm gonna gut you just like the VC gutted your buddy Dalton."

John touched his father's dog tags hanging around his neck, and it was at that moment, he would realize later, that Little Johnny Brice finally found his manhood on a mountain in Idaho. His mind and body calmed. All fear left him. He was no longer afraid: not of failing, not of the bullies, not of dying. There was manly in his genes, and he had found it, or it had found him.

John raised his arms, holding the gun with both hands like Ben had showed him, then stepped in front of the window and fired. The glass shattered. John pulled the trigger as fast as he could until everything went dark.

Jacko felt a bullet impact his shoulder. Next thing he knew, Brice leg-whipped him at the ankles, knocking his feet out from under him. Jacko hit the wood floor hard. Before he could react, Brice kicked him in the mouth, bringing blood. But Jacko always liked the taste of his own blood.

Still, he didn't remember Brice being this good.

But he wasn't good enough. Jacko rolled with the kick and came up quickly, the Bowie in his hand.

Damn, this brought back some good memories!

He moved toward Brice, excited at the thought of disemboweling the unarmed traitor he had cornered. He glanced over at the major. His eyes were alive and he was smiling.

This is my destiny!

When he looked back at Brice, he saw the major's bedpan flying through the air at his face. And Jacko thought, *Fuck, hope to hell Junior emptied it!* He hadn't. Jacko blocked the bedpan with his arms—urine and shit splattered on the floor and on him—only to realize too late that it was a fake, that Brice's boot was coming at him hard and he couldn't block it. The heel of the boot caught Jacko right in the center of his chest and drove his two-hundred-sixty-five pounds back hard against the opposite cabin wall. *Shit!* Jacko was surprised at the severity of the pain that suddenly grabbed at his chest. He had been kicked and punched in the chest many times and had never experienced such pain. *Shit!* He figured it would go away, but it didn't. Instead it got worse and shot down his left arm; his right hand released the knife and grabbed at his chest. *Shit!* And at that moment he understood: he was having a goddamn heart attack! *What a time to have a fucking heart attack!* And he realized the truth: Ben Brice wasn't his destiny; he was Ben Brice's destiny.

He dropped to his knees, sucking hard for air. He looked up at Brice and wanted to say *fuck you*, but he didn't have the breath to get the words out. He took one last glance at the major; his eyes were wide, not believing what he was seeing. Jacko's head felt light and he was suddenly dizzy. The light dimmed. For the first time in his life, Jacko didn't have any strength, not even enough to hold himself up. He fell face down onto the wood floor. His eyes made out a boot just inches away. And he heard Ben Brice's voice.

"Who says old soldiers never die?"

And his last thought before all life drained out of him on the floor in a cabin in northern Idaho and Captain Jack Odell Smith from Henryetta, Oklahoma, met his Maker was:

Oh, that's real fucking funny.

Outside, John struggled to get up. He winced. He felt like someone had hit him in the head with a frying pan. He rolled over to get to his feet and—*Cripes!*—came face to face with another man lying beside him, his vacant eyes wide open. John was struck by the pure ugliness of the man's face—and the ax embedded in his head.

"You okay?"

John looked up to see Agent O'Brien.

"Yeah. Thanks."

"Where's the colonel?"

"Inside . . . *shit!*"

John pushed himself up and stumbled inside the cabin and into the bedroom; Agent O'Brien was right behind him. The big man was lying face down on the floor. Ben was bent over him, hands on his knees.

"Ben, you okay?"

Ben straightened up slowly, like it hurt.

"Yeah. You boys hurt?"

"No," John said. He gestured at the bed. "Who's that?"

"Major Charles Woodrow Walker," Ben said.

"I thought he was dead."

"He will be."

Ben turned to Agent O'Brien: "How many did you get?"

"Two."

Ben nodded. "It's just Junior now."

"Blond guy?"

"Yeah."

"He took off in a white truck," Agent O'Brien said. "I put four rounds in it, guess I missed him."

"He said we'll never find her."

"You go after him," O'Brien said. "I'll look for your girl."

B EN PUT THE OLD pickup in neutral and he and John rode it down the mountain to the Land Rover parked on the side of the road to town. Ben knew where they would find Junior. A white truck, minus the back window—Agent O'Brien hadn't missed by much—was parked in front of the Boundary County Courthouse between the sheriff's cruiser and a black Lexus SUV with new paper plates.

They ran up the front steps into the courthouse and down the corridor to the sheriff's office. The receptionist took one look at them—the black overalls, the face paint, and the blood—and picked up the phone. Sheriff Johnson appeared before she had hung up.

"Colonel, you okay?"

Ben nodded and wiped blood from his face. "Where's Junior?"

"In a cell. He confessed."

"Did he say what he did with Gracie?"

The sheriff shook his head. "He's done lawyered up. Wants immunity."

The sheriff motioned for them to follow and led them through a door. Behind the door were four cells. Three were empty. In the fourth, Junior sat on a bunk; his right hand was bandaged. A fat man in a sweat suit who looked as if he had just gotten out of bed sat in a chair next to Junior, a briefcase in his lap. He looked up at Ben and said, "Who the hell are you, Rambo?"

The sheriff unlocked the cell door. The fat man said, "My client will disclose the girl's location for complete immunity."

"Norman, only the D.A. can grant immunity from prosecution, you know that. And he won't be back till tomorrow."

"Then we'll deal tomorrow," Norman the lawyer said, slamming his briefcase shut. He stood. To Junior: "Keep your mouth shut and you'll walk out a free man tomorrow."

Norman turned to leave, but Ben blocked the cell door.

"My granddaughter's on that mountain. She'll die before tomorrow."

Norman shrugged. "Just doing my job."

"Not much of a job."

"Pays good." Norman smiled. "Sorry about your girl, but she's not my concern."

"She is mine," Ben said. Then he punched Norman the lawyer in his mouth. Norman went down like a sack of potatoes.

From the floor: "I'll sue! Sheriff, I want to press assault charges! You witnessed it!"

"You fell and hit your face on the floor."

"*What?*"

"You heard me, Norman. Now get your butt outta my jail."

Norman scrambled up and stormed out. "You haven't heard the last of this!"

After the door shut behind Norman, the sheriff turned

to Ben. "I hate lawyers. Had a cousin once, become a lawyer. Whole family disowned him."

"Let him go," Ben said.

The sheriff recoiled. "*What?* Colonel, why the hell would I let him go, he's done confessed and—"

It hit him. The sheriff eyed Ben curiously; he smiled slightly. He nodded slowly.

"All right, Colonel. Sometimes the rules just don't work."

Junior glanced from the sheriff to Ben and back, his eyes suddenly wide. "The hell you mean, you can't let me go! I confessed! I'm guilty! I kidnapped her!"

The sheriff turned his hands up. "Junior, there's no girl so I got no evidence to hold you. Son, you got constitutional rights. This is America."

The sheriff grabbed Junior and yanked him out of the cell. He then pushed Junior through the office and out the front door. They stood on the steps of the courthouse.

"Good luck, Colonel. But you better move fast, FBI's coming. Fella over at the airstrip called, said the director himself is flying in."

7:12 A.M. PACIFIC TIME, BONNERS FERRY

JUNIOR WAS SILENT on the trip back up the mountain. When they arrived, Agent O'Brien ran up to the vehicle.

"I couldn't find her. She's not in any of the cabins or the vehicles. I searched a fifty-meter perimeter—nothing."

Ben pulled Junior from the vehicle. "Where's she at?"

"Fuck you," Junior said.

Ben punched Junior in the face. He fell to the ground. Ben yanked Junior up and felt a sharp pain in his gut.

"Junior, I don't have time to play games. If you want to live, tell me where she's at."

"You kill me, you ain't never gonna find her."

"Listen to me, son, you ain't tough enough to handle what I'm gonna do to you. Where's she at?"

Ben grabbed Junior's right arm and twisted it back until Junior fell face down on the ground. Ben put a knee in his back, then ripped the bandage from Junior's right hand and held the hand out flat on the ground, thumb and two fingers spread.

"John, hand me that hatchet."

John walked over to a small woodpile and picked up the hatchet. He returned and handed it to Ben. Junior's eyes were wide, looking at the hatchet and then at his hand.

"You can't do this! I got rights! This is America!"

"Junior, you lost your rights when you took Gracie."

Ben swung the hatchet down hard. John turned away. Junior screamed.

When Junior opened his eyes, the hatchet was buried in the ground barely an inch from his right hand. He still had a thumb and two fingers. The first thought that entered his mind was he couldn't afford to lose another finger because then he'd have to masturbate with his left hand.

"I won't miss next time, Junior."

Way Junior figured, he'd probably do two to five in a federal penitentiary for weapons violations. No way they could tie him to the murders of that judge or those prosecutors or FBI agents. Or even McCoy. *Shit, if they did, he could blame it all on the major!* Of course, a kidnapping conviction might get him another two to five, but he never touched her and he saved her from Bubba, that should count for something. Sure, sleazy Norman the lawyer can do something with that: brother reunites with long-lost sister, show the jury pictures of her room, she'll testify that he fixed her hot baths and breakfasts, and, best of all, Elizabeth Austin will have to testify. Sleazy Norman the lawyer will crucify the bitch, ruin her career, her family, her life. And besides, time the trial's over, Junior might have himself a movie deal. Maybe Tom Cruise would play him.

"She's out back."

*

John followed Junior and Ben around to the back of the cabin. Junior abruptly stopped at a woodpile.

"There," he said.

Junior was pointing at the woodpile. John didn't understand, but Ben put his shoulder to the wood and pushed the pile over. He dropped to the ground and frantically threw the remaining logs aside. A small air vent was sticking up out of the ground.

Ben looked up. "You *buried* her?"

Junior shrugged. "She needed some discipline."

John's entire body began trembling but not with fear. A lifetime of bullies and beatings, of not fighting back, of shame and sorrow, of not being much of a man—all the humiliation and pain came rushing back and washed over John like a tidal wave. His face felt hot. Junior was looking at him with that bemused smile so familiar to John Brice.

"Hell, you ain't even her daddy," he said.

John's eyes fell. He had always thought Gracie had gotten her blonde hair and blue eyes from Ben. But she couldn't have; John had been adopted. So she had gotten her hair and eyes from . . . and John suddenly understood everything. It all came together: Elizabeth, her disappearance ten years ago, her sudden change of heart toward him when she returned, the quick marriage, the move to Dallas, Gracie's birth eight months later. He knew the truth now. But it didn't matter. The only truth that mattered was Gracie down there. He raised his eyes to Junior.

"I've loved her since the day she was born and I'll love her till the day I die. That makes me her daddy."

"Yeah? We'll see about that when she learns the truth at my trial."

But John's 190-IQ mind was way ahead of poor Junior. "There's not gonna be a trial, Junior."

John put the .45 to Junior's head and shot him dead.

"I didn't see that," Agent O'Brien said.

John wiped Junior's blood from his face, then dropped the gun, fell to his knees, and joined Ben, digging with his hands. They hit metal in minutes.

Gracie was buried in a U.S. Army munitions container. A hole had been cut in the top and the air vent inserted. They brushed the remaining dirt off the top. They released the latches and opened the lid. Gracie lay still and straight inside; her eyes were closed and her arms lay across her chest. Her face was dirty. John reached down and touched her face gently. A tear rolled off his cheek and fell onto her face.

"Oh, Gracie, baby."

"Let's get her out," Ben said.

They grabbed her coat and pants and gently lifted her out of the box then laid her on the ground. Ben checked her pulse.

"She's alive. Let's get her into town!"

Ben picked Gracie up and groaned; he carried her to the Land Rover. Her arms and legs hung limp. Agent O'Brien ran ahead, opened the back door, and got in. John jumped into the driver's seat. Ben handed Gracie to O'Brien and they laid her across the back seat. Ben shut the door.

"Turn this thing around and be ready to roll."

Ben ran into the main cabin. Minutes later, he emerged, ran to the Rover, and jumped in. "Go!"

John punched the accelerator. "Ben, where's your rifle?"

Ben said softly, "I don't need it any more."

7:27 A.M. PACIFIC TIME, BONNERS FERRY

FBI DIRECTOR Stanley White loved flying about the country at five hundred miles per hour in the Bureau's Gulfstream IIB Executive jet—*nothing but the best for the United States government!*—the leather seats, the burled elmwood trim, the state-of-the-art avionics, the 3,500-mile range, the six-foot-one-inch cabin height, more than enough for his five-seven height. This morning, instead of flying back to D.C. from Chicago, he was en route to Bonners Ferry, a 1,500-mile flight, three hours' flight time, including a quick stop in Des Moines to pick up Agent Devereaux, who was now sitting in the seat behind Stan. His attitude hadn't improved since their earlier conversation.

"Prepare to land, Chief," the pilot said over the intercom.

Stan gazed out the window to the east. They were descending into a valley surrounded by mountain ridges, down to the Boundary County Airport just north of Bonners Ferry, Idaho. At that moment, one of the mountains erupted like a volcano.

"Jesus!"

The entire mountaintop was engulfed in a huge fireball of red-orange flames of a kind White had seen only once before when the Army had demonstrated for the FBI Terrorism Task Force the destructive capacity of napalm.

Agent Devereaux's voice came from behind: "Kingdom come, Stan."

7:39 A.M. PACIFIC TIME, BONNERS FERRY

They were driving across the Moyie River Bridge; Gracie's head was in Ben's lap. He was stroking her face. He reached inside his overalls, unbuttoned his shirt pocket, and pulled out the Silver Star and chain. He pressed it into the palm of her hand. Her hand closed around it, almost like a reflex.

Gracie is standing on the threshold of double doors as they slowly open to a bright world beyond, a beautiful world beckoning to her. She steps forward—but something shiny on the ground catches her eye. She bends over and picks it up, a Silver Star on a silver chain—and the doors close.

She opened her eyes. The light was too bright; she squinted. Something shielded her eyes. After a moment, her vision cleared and she saw Ben's face. She smiled.

"I knew you'd come," she said.

9:40 A.M. CENTRAL TIME, DALLAS

FBI SPECIAL AGENT Jan Jorgenson pulled open the double doors leading into the sanctuary of the Catholic church. The pews were packed. She searched the congregation, but she could not spot Mrs. Brice from her location.

She walked up the center aisle.

Her legs were trembling and tears were welling up in her eyes. Heads turned her way; she realized she was still wearing her raid jacket with *FBI* in big gold letters. She neared the front and spotted Mrs. Brice, second pew from the front, on the aisle. The Brice boy and the grandmother sat next to her. Jan came to Mrs. Brice and stood there, tears running down her face.

Elizabeth's gaze was locked on the big crucifix above the altar when she realized the priest had stopped short the Mass. Her eyes moved to him. He was looking directly at her. The altar girls were looking at her. Everyone was looking at her. She turned to Kate; her hands were over her mouth, her eyes were wide, and she was looking in Elizabeth's direction, but not at her—at someone behind her.

Elizabeth spun around and saw Agent Jorgenson, tears rolling down her face. Elizabeth's heart froze with fear. She stood and stepped out of the pew. Jorgenson wiped her face. And she smiled.

"Gracie's safe."

All strength left her legs, and Elizabeth dropped to her knees. Tears flooded her eyes. She again looked up at the crucifix. Their bond with evil had been broken.

8:15 A.M. PACIFIC TIME, BONNERS FERRY

"T HERE'LL BE A full investigation, Mr. Brice!"

FBI Director White and his entourage had arrived within minutes after Gracie had been brought into the hospital. Now the short bald man was pointing a finger at Ben.

"That's *Colonel* Brice," Agent Devereaux said.

"You obstructed an ongoing federal investigation!"

They were standing outside Gracie's room—Ben, the director, the sheriff, and Agents Devereaux and O'Brien. John and the doctor were in with Gracie.

The director turned on Agent O'Brien.

"O'Brien, you had the camp staked out. What the hell happened?"

FBI Agent Pete O'Brien did not blink in the face of the director's lethal glare. Pete had learned that morning the difference between right and wrong. He had learned that even the Federal Bureau of Investigation could be wrong and had been wrong. Now he had an important choice to make: tell the truth, which would normally be the right thing to do, in which case Colonel Brice and John

Brice would likely be arrested and charged with murder and those terrorists would live on in the media, which would be a bad thing; or lie, which would normally be the wrong thing to do, in which case the Brices would take Gracie home and live happily ever after and the terrorists' barbecued bodies would rot on that stinking mountain, which would be a good thing. His decision came easily.

"Shit, Chief, all I know is I'm sitting up there and suddenly there's this huge explosion. I mean, I thought it was a fucking volcano! I hightailed it down the mountain. These men gave me a ride to town. They must've gotten wind we were on to them, so they blew themselves up, committed suicide." He shrugged innocently. "Another Waco, Chief."

The director blinked. "Unh-hunh."

Ben turned as the doctor came out of Gracie's room.

"Are you the FBI Director?" the doctor asked White.

"Yes," the director said.

"You may want to hear what she has to say."

They followed the doctor into Gracie's room.

"What is it, Gracie?" Ben said.

Her voice was quiet. "What day is today?"

Ben said, "Easter Sunday."

"They're going to kill the president."

The director nodded. "They were plotting to kill McCoy. We wanted to ensure that we had all the players, but your grandfather took care of that."

"There's another man," Gracie said. "Red hair, with a black rifle. He's going to shoot President McCoy at Camp David on Easter Sunday. Today."

The director's head swiveled around to Agent O'Brien.

"No one with red hair was in that camp," O'Brien said.

The director looked funny at Gracie. "How do you know this?"

"I saw him," Gracie said. "In Wyoming. They said something about making it look like Muslims did it."

The director checked his watch.

"Mister?"

"Yes?"

"Hurry."

The director ran out the door, followed by the other agents.

Sheriff J. D. Johnson was standing just inside the door to the girl's room. Doc Sanders and the colonel and the father were over by the bed. Doc turned and came to the door. He was smiling.

"She'll be fine," he said as he opened the door and left.

The colonel leaned over the bed and kissed the girl, and then he came over to the sheriff. He seemed a bit pale; he was probably just tired.

"Trick to life, Colonel, is living long enough for life to work out."

The colonel collapsed to the floor. J.D. yelled for Doc Sanders. He knelt and unzipped the colonel's overalls and saw his bloody shirt. He heard the girl's shrill scream.

"*Ben!*"

DAY FIFTEEN

5:35 P.M.

"Run, Gracie, run!"

FBI Special Agent (no longer on probation) Jan Jorgenson was standing off to the side of the goal at one end of the field, the goal toward which Gracie Ann Brice was now running. She was kicking the ball out in front of her, chased by the other team. The parents were cheering in the stands.

"Take it to the goal, Gracie!"

"Go, Gracie! Score!"

Gracie suddenly cut across the field and ran directly toward Jan; she kicked the ball past the diving goalie and into the net. The crowd cheered. Jan clapped.

Gracie's momentum carried her to within twenty feet of Jan. She stopped and was about to turn back to the field when her eyes met Jan's. Gracie stared at her, a quizzical expression on her face, as if wondering whether they had met. The other girls surrounded Gracie and pulled her away. Halfway across the field, Gracie turned back. Jan gave her a thumbs up.

I didn't quit on you, Gracie Ann Brice.

She had not wanted this assignment to the Dallas field office, but now she understood. She was meant to be here for Gracie. She was meant to find her place in life. She was not Clarice Starling. She was Jan Jorgenson and she was catching a flight to St. Louis to join Agent Devereaux.

A six-year-old girl had been abducted by a stranger.

The parents in the low bleachers were cheering for his daughter. But no one cheered louder than John Brice.

"Go, Gracie! You're the girl! Be the girl, baby!"

John R. Brice was now worth $3.5 billion, but he had decided not to buy the Boston Red Sox for Sam or a bunch of radio stations for Gracie. Or even a jet. But he had written a $10 million check to Gary Jennings's wife. She said she and her baby were going back to Nebraska to live with her parents on their farm. She said she would be all right, in time. She said she had prayed for Gracie's return. And Gracie had come home. She was back, the bullies were gone, and, with them, Little Johnny Brice.

John R. Brice was a man now.

A different man. The mountain had changed him. He had learned about himself on that mountain. And he had learned about life. He had always held firmly to the theory that life was just an endless succession of coincidences, random events completely without meaning or connection; he had always believed that human beings were like molecules bouncing randomly off each other in the atmosphere. Whom we hit was nothing more than pure coincidence.

It was just a coincidence that Ben Brice and John's real father had been assigned the same dorm room at West Point, which led them both to Vietnam and SOG team Viper and Major Charles Woodrow Walker.

It was just a coincidence that Ben had balked at shooting the old Vietnamese woman by the river, which led to an ambush and to John's real father being killed and to a massacre, which led to a court martial where Ben's testimony convicted Major Walker.

It was just a coincidence that Ben and Kate had adopted John, which led to Army bases and Army brats who bullied him, which led him to his room and his Apple computer and to learn computer code, which led him to MIT and to the Justice Department and to Elizabeth.

It was just a coincidence that a hobo spider had bitten Junior, which led to Major Walker's capture and to Elizabeth's abduction and to Gracie, which led Elizabeth to John and to the son of Walker's accuser marrying the mother of his child.

It was just a coincidence that *Fortune* had run a feature on John R. Brice with the family portrait, which led Junior and Jacko to Gracie's soccer game and to the Viper tattoo on the game tape.

It was just a coincidence that John had been on the phone with Lou and the trial had delayed Elizabeth's arrival at the park, which led Gracie to the concession stand without her parents and into Junior's trap.

It was just a coincidence that Junior's POS SUV had needed repairs, which led them to Clayton Lee Tucker's gas station and to his recognizing Gracie's Amber Alert photo and calling the FBI hotline, which led Ben and John to Tucker and to Bonners Ferry.

It was just a coincidence that Bubba had walked into Rusty's Tavern, which led them past the booby traps and up the mountain called Red Ridge and to Agent O'Brien, who saved John's life so John could save Ben's life so Ben could save Gracie's life so Gracie could save the president's life.

It was all just an endless succession of coincidences.

That had always been his theory of life.

He had always been completely wrong.

Life is not random. There are no coincidences. Human beings are more than mere molecules bouncing around life without reason. We bounce around life with a purpose. We are meant to bounce off specific other human beings during our lives, other human beings who will change the content and course of our lives. We are meant to be exactly who we are. John R. Brice was meant to be husband to Elizabeth, father to Gracie and Sam, and son to Roger and Mary and now Ben and Kate. He was meant to be exactly who he was today: a man standing on a soccer field on a fine spring day with his family.

And he felt pretty dang robust about that.

John started yelling again: "Yeah, Gracie! You go, girl! Hoo-yah! Be the girl, baby! You're the girl! Unh-hunh!"

Elizabeth leaned into her husband and kissed him. She whispered in his ear, "I love you."

When he had returned from Idaho, she saw in his eyes that he had learned the truth about her and about Grace. But he had not spoken of it. Last night, lying in bed with him, she started to bring it up, but he put his fingers to her lips. "I don't care how Gracie came into my life," he said. "I care only that she's in my life and that we have her back. The past—mine, yours, Gracie's—it died on that mountain."

He said they would never speak about what had happened to her ten years ago or what had happened on that mountain in Idaho. That was all in the past now, and Elizabeth Brice was finally able to leave the past behind her. The violation she had suffered ten years ago had owned her life ever since. But no longer. Because that violation had given her a better life—a child's life.

Grace was worth it.

Gracie was driving the ball down the field, but she couldn't focus, not with her SO acting the fool on the sideline, shouting and cheering and doing some kind of funny little dance now. God bless him, he had the rhythm of a rock. Maybe it was better when Dad multitasked during her games . . . No, this was better. Like, totally. She smiled at him as she ran past.

Everything was different now. Everything was better. Her parents seemed to actually like each other—she had never seen Mom kiss Dad before—and in public! PDA! Dad was a new man, a real grownup, a manly father more than a big brother (although he still promised to take them to Krispy Kreme every Saturday morning.) He had bear-hugged her a dozen times since she had come home.

And Mom—wow, Mom was a complete stranger. She had held Gracie and cried and cried when they got off the plane. She hadn't even stopped to talk to the reporters waiting for them. She had even come up to school and had lunch with Gracie yesterday. That had never happened before. And she wasn't mad at the world. She was happy. She wasn't going to be a lawyer any more.

But she still would not allow Gracie to get a tattoo for her eleventh birthday.

Gracie had changed, too. She was a different girl since the last time she had played on this field. She had been abducted, buried, and saved. She had seen things no fourth-grader should ever see and met people no fourth-grader should ever meet and learned things no fourth-grader should ever learn. And she had talked to the President of the United States of America. They had captured the man with the red hair and long rifle, and the president had called just to say thanks. She made sure he knew she was a Democrat. He laughed and said that was okay with him.

She was even happy to see Sam, even though one look at her room and she knew he had gone through all her personal stuff. She decided not to kill him, at least not now.

Her family was finally together.

"Gracie, take it to the goal!"

Coach Wally was having a cow. So Gracie turned on the speed, faked out two defenders, drove to the goal, and blasted the ball just inside high left post. It was Gracie's third goal, and they were still in the first half. The other girls mobbed her.

The team had made it into the playoffs. Luck would have it, their first-round opponents were the Raiders. The snot's team. Her butthead father, Mr. Creep himself, was again standing on the sidelines, wearing a slick suit, and drinking from a big plastic mug. Mrs. Creep was standing next to him like a prison warden. You'd think the big jerk would know when to leave well enough alone. Well, you'd be wrong.

"Pa-a-a-a-nty che-e-e-ck!"

The players and spectators instantly fell silent. Brenda groaned. "Not again."

This time, though, was different for Gracie. She didn't feel as if someone had punched her in the stomach. She didn't bite her lower lip and fight back the tears. She didn't wish to die or that she were bigger and older so she could beat the guy up or that Dad would do something or that Elizabeth Brice, Attorney-at-Large, would—

"Oh shit, Gracie!" Brenda said. "Your mother!"

Gracie turned away from the big jerk and saw her mother marching straight across the soccer field and past the players and directly toward Mr. Creep; her fists were clenched. Gracie heard Sam's high-pitched voice from the sideline: "All right, a fight!" Gracie looked over and saw Dad running after Mom, but she would be punching out Mr. Creep before he could stop her. Gracie heard Sally's gleeful voice behind her: "Your mother's gonna kick his big butt into next week!"

Fifteen days ago, Gracie would have paid to watch this fight. But she was different now. She ran over and cut off her mother.

Elizabeth Brice was no longer a forty-year-old rage-filled lunatic. She was no longer a tough-broad white-collar criminal defense lawyer willing to wear short skirts to win trials. She was no longer hard and mean and ruthless.

But she was still a mother.

And the most dangerous creature on earth is a mother whose child has been threatened, insulted, harassed, or bullied.

Elizabeth Brice was going to punch that big son of a bitch in the mouth.

"Mom, stop!"

Grace suddenly appeared; she grabbed Elizabeth's arm and pulled her to a stop just as John ran up.

"Mom," Grace pleaded, "I can handle this."

"No, Grace, I'm your mother. I'll handle it!"

"No," John said, "I'm your father, I'll handle it!"

"No! Both of you—listen! I'm a big girl now. I can handle it myself!"

517

Elizabeth stared into her daughter's blue eyes. Her anger dissipated as if blown away by the soft breeze. Grace was different, too.

"You are a big girl, aren't you?"

"Yes, Mother, I am."

"You're sure you don't want me to beat this guy up?"

"I'm sure."

John said, "Can I beat him up?"

"No! I've got it covered."

Elizabeth smiled. And then Grace smiled. And Elizabeth Brice saw in her daughter's eyes that Grace did indeed have it covered. She leaned close to her daughter and whispered, "Make it good."

Mom and Dad walked off the field, and the cute referee blew his whistle to restart the game. Gracie quickly stole the ball from a Raider and then kicked the ball on a high arch over the defenders to Brenda, who was open along the Raiders' sideline. Brenda controlled the ball and drove it up the sideline. Gracie's mind quickly plotted out her angle of attack. Precise timing was required to pull this off. She cut across the field and ran toward the Raiders' sideline, to a point that would intersect the ball and . . .

Brenda kicked the ball up the sideline just as Gracie arrived at the exact point, her concentration focused like a laser beam on the ball, now driving the laces of her white Lotto soccer shoe into the ball, with all her might, sending the ball forcefully—

—right at Mr. Creep's head.

He bailed. The plastic mug went flying, ice and liquid splattered all over his expensive suit, and he hit the ground hard on his big butt. The other parents laughed out loud. Mrs. Creep was grinning down at him.

Gracie walked over to the big jerk.

"I'm a girl." She put her thumbs inside the waistband, like she was going to pull her shorts down. "You wanna check?"

Mr. Creep shook his head.

"I didn't think so."

Gracie rejoined the game.

Sam was standing on the Tornadoes' sideline; he was terribly disappointed. Dangit, he wanted to see a real fight.

He had cried when Gracie came home because she wasn't dead or nothing. It was good to have a big sister again. Just the same, he hoped she didn't find out that he had gone through all her personal stuff in her room while she was gone.

Kate Brice was standing next to Sam. Thirty-eight years late, but she finally had her fairy-tale marriage. She looked down at her husband. She had been wrong: Ben Brice had come back.

The war was finally over for Ben Brice.

He sat in the wheelchair, Kate's hand resting on his shoulder and Buddy resting on the ground beside him. The doctors had said he could come to the game but only if he stayed in the chair. He had started to argue but decided against it; he would've come even if they had to roll the hospital bed out here. Gracie was safe. And he had found his peace.

He looked up to John and Elizabeth. They had survived this and were stronger for it. They were one now.

"Thanks, Dad," John said. "Sorry about shooting you."

"You weren't the first."

Elizabeth leaned down, kissed Ben on the cheek, and whispered in his ear: "Thank you, Colonel Ben Brice, for saving Grace."

Ben looked out at Gracie racing down the field. His past had in fact come back—West Point; Special Forces school; Commander Ron Porter; Captain Jack O. Smith; Sheriff J. D. Johnson; Lieutenant Roger Dalton; Major Charles Woodrow Walker; Quang Tri and the china doll—but not to haunt Gracie, as he had feared. His past had come back to save her. The pieces of his life that had never seemed to fit together had fallen into place like a complex puzzle to form a whole life that he only now understood. He thought of that life and he thought of his mother. She had been right all along.

God did have a plan for Ben Brice.